Heart of War

Heart of War

a novel by

John Masters

McGRAW-HILL BOOK COMPANY

New York   St. Louis   San Francisco
Düsseldorf   Mexico   Toronto

This book is the second volume of a trilogy
entitled

LOSS OF EDEN

It is complete in itself, as was the first, and as
will be the third.

Each volume is, or will be, wholly a work of
fiction, in which no reference is intended to
any person living or dead, except that many
historical characters are mentioned, and some
occasionally appear on the scene.

J.M.

Excerpts on pages 270, 271, 362, and 363 are reproduced from
The World Crisis, Vol. III, by Winston Churchill. Copyright 1923,
1927 by Charles Scribner's Sons; renewal copyright 1951, 1955
by Winston S. Churchill. Reprinted by permission of the
publishers.

1 2 3 4 5 6 7 8 9   DODO   8 7 6 5 4 3 2 1 0

LIBRARY OF CONGRESS CATALOGING IN PUBLICATION DATA

Masters, John, 1914–
Heart of War.
(*His* Loss of Eden)
1. European War, 1914–1918—Fiction. I.   Title.
II.   Series.
PZ3.M39384He [PS3525.A8314]   813'.54   80-12491
ISBN 0-07-040782-7

To the victims of the Great War,
among whom were
the survivors

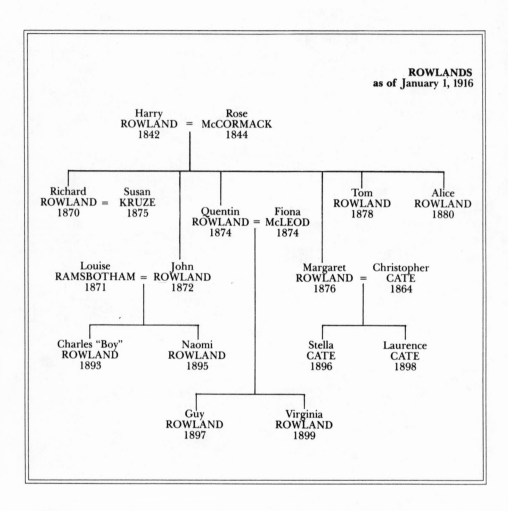

ROWLANDS
as of January 1, 1916

Harry ROWLAND 1842 = Rose McCORMACK 1844

Richard ROWLAND 1870 = Susan KRUZE 1875

Quentin ROWLAND 1874 = Fiona McLEOD 1874

Tom ROWLAND 1878

Alice ROWLAND 1880

Louise RAMSBOTHAM 1871 = John ROWLAND 1872

Margaret ROWLAND 1876 = Christopher CATE 1864

Charles "Boy" ROWLAND 1893

Naomi ROWLAND 1895

Stella CATE 1896

Laurence CATE 1898

Guy ROWLAND 1897

Virginia ROWLAND 1899

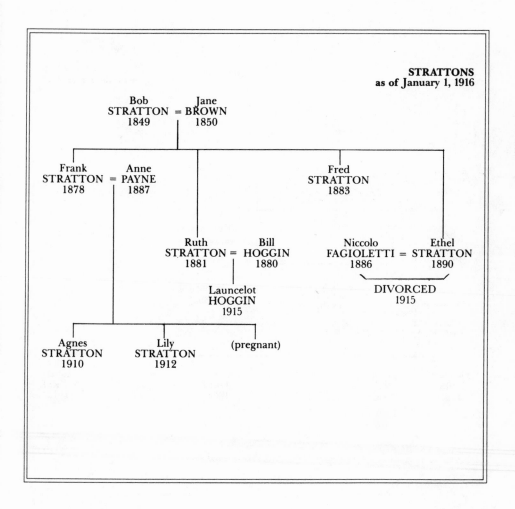

STRATTONS
as of January 1, 1916

Bob   Jane
STRATTON = BROWN
1849   1850

Frank   Anne
STRATTON = PAYNE
1878   1887

Fred
STRATTON
1883

Ruth   Bill
STRATTON = HOGGIN
1881   1880

Niccolo   Ethel
FAGIOLETTI = STRATTON
1886   1890

Launcelot
HOGGIN
1915

DIVORCED
1915

Agnes
STRATTON
1910

Lily
STRATTON
1912

(pregnant)

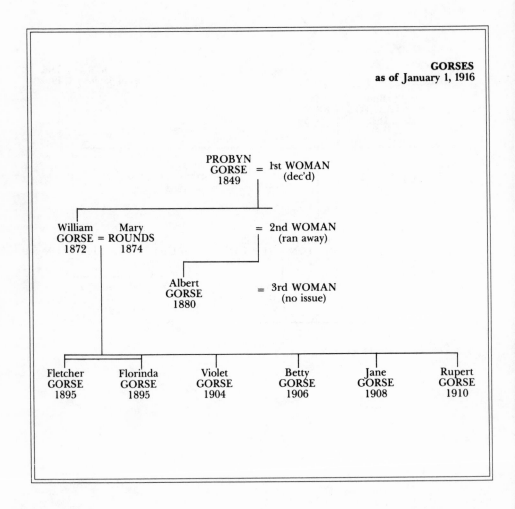

GORSES
as of January 1, 1916

PROBYN GORSE 1849 = 1st WOMAN (dec'd)

William GORSE 1872 = Mary ROUNDS 1874   = 2nd WOMAN (ran away)

Albert GORSE 1880   = 3rd WOMAN (no issue)

Fletcher GORSE 1895   Florinda GORSE 1895   Violet GORSE 1904   Betty GORSE 1906   Jane GORSE 1908   Rupert GORSE 1910

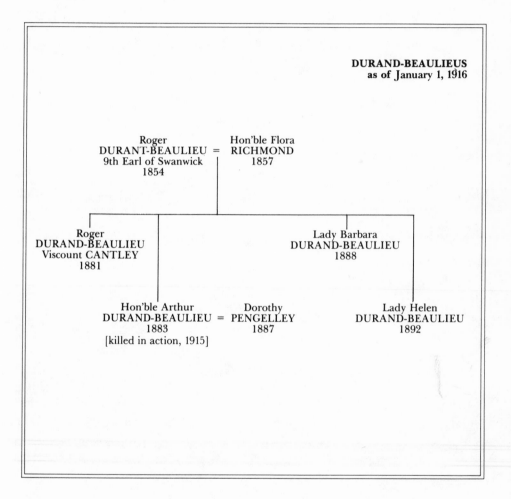

DURAND-BEAULIEUS
as of January 1, 1916

Roger
DURANT-BEAULIEU = Hon'ble Flora
9th Earl of Swanwick   RICHMOND
1854   1857

Roger
DURAND-BEAULIEU   Lady Barbara
Viscount CANTLEY   DURAND-BEAULIEU
1881   1888

Hon'ble Arthur   Dorothy   Lady Helen
DURAND-BEAULIEU = PENGELLEY   DURAND-BEAULIEU
1883   1887   1892
[killed in action, 1915]

Heart of War

January 1, 1916

1 As the arc of noon passes over the Urals its high sun pours down on a continent aflame from end to end with a war that has been raging out of control for seventeen months. It begins, officially, over the murder of an Austrian Archduke by a Serbian schoolboy, but that event, and the increasingly violent emotional reactions of the powers of Europe, are no more than the opportunities given to wills eager to strike. The rich, long-settled world of Europe is bleeding to death, dying in the ruins of its own châteaux, suffocating in the churned mud of its own vineyards. A narrow belt of yellow slime—the trenches—snakes from the English Channel to Switzerland, and beyond the Alps, begins again and crawls across northern Italy. The corpses are rotting in the Polish marshes, on the Rumanian plains, the beaches of Gallipoli, the burning banks of Nile and Euphrates, in the rain forests of Africa. At sea, especially off the coasts of Europe, no ship is safe from the German submarines, for Germany, faced with the overpowering surface fleets of England and its allies, is waging war from under the water.

Only one country in the world has had experience of war on so vast a scale and, as it is turning out, of so long duration; and that country is not a combatant—the United States, fifty-one years after its Civil War. The Americans are a troubled people. Though their commerce is being harassed by the British blockade, they are becoming rich producing war goods for the British side, which, alone, can transport them across the Atlantic. President Wilson, with one year in office remaining of his first term, strives to keep that nation out of the war, which is manifestly becoming more bloody than any in history.

1

England has taken part in no European War since the Crimean War of the 1850s; and before that, the Napoleonic Wars. The nation is mentally quite unprepared for the casualties: 80,174 killed and died of wounds in the first seventeen months—331,719 missing, prisoners, and wounded; all this on the Western Front alone (31,097 British died in the Crimean War, which lasted more than two years: of these, over half died of disease). For England 1915 has been a disappointing year. So much is expected of the offensives at Loos and Gallipoli, so little is achieved. A change of mood cuts deep into the hearts of the people. No one now recites Rupert Brooke's passionate lines:

> *Now God be thanked, Who has matched us with His hour,*
> *And caught our youth, and wakened us from sleeping. . .*

No more cries are heard of *On to Berlin! Berlin or Bust! Home by Christmas!* The war is not fun, but it has to be won. The Regular Army dies at First Ypres, late in 1914; the volunteer army built on its cadres dies at Loos, late in 1915. For the first time in a thousand years military conscription looms over Britain. The war will continue, a presence in every act of living—shopping, fishing, selling goods, electioneering, even reading the newspaper, or celebrating a wedding . . .

Walstone, Kent: Friday, February 4, 1916

THE DATE OF COMPULSION
MARCH 2nd
KING'S PROCLAMATION

At a meeting of the Privy Council yesterday, his Majesty the King signed a Proclamation fixing February 10 as the date upon which the Military Service Act shall come into operation. In a supplement to the London *Gazette* last night, the . . .

Christopher Cate, gentleman, titular squire of Walstone in the County of Kent, read the piece again with a puzzled frown. The Act was to come into operation on February 10th, but the headline stated that March 2nd was the date of compulsion? Ah, of course, the Act had allowed for a three-week period before anyone was actually conscripted, and that would bring it to March 2nd.

He looked out of the window. Low clouds hid the setting sun, and a cold wind, threatening sleet or snow, stirred the bare trees and rustled the hedge beyond the lawn . . . not a good prospect for his daughter Stella's wedding tomorrow. She was upstairs now, with her aunt Fiona, and Garrod the maid. Fiona, his sister-in-law, was acting as hostess and 'mother of the bride,' since Stella's own mother, his wife, had deserted them all for Ireland and the cause of Irish Independence, a year ago. It would be a happy occasion nonetheless, with his tenants and their wives present in the old Saxon church, and all the other villagers; and the staff of the Manor here; and Laurence—his only son, as Stella was his only daughter; and Stephen and Betty Merritt, the father and sister of Stella's groom, from America; his own father and mother-in-law . . . It would be wonderful to see the marriage of such a good-looking young couple, his Stella and Johnny Merritt, with so happy and prosperous a life ahead of them, if . . .

He flung the paper down.

. . . if the war did not devour them and that happiness, as it had so many others'. There would be gaiety and laughter at the wedding, all right, but he for one would not be able to erase from his mind, in the midst of his happiness for his daughter, the faces of those who were not present . . . Fiona's husband, his brother-in-law Quentin Rowland; and his nephew Boy Rowland—both somewhere in France with the Weald Light Infantry; his own brother Oswald, died of wounds received with the Rifle Brigade at Neuve Chapelle last March; another brother-in-law, Tom Rowland, at sea in all weathers, enforcing the blockade of Germany; young Sam Mayhew, one of his tenants' sons, died of wounds the same day as Oswald; and Lord Swanwick's younger son, Arthur Durand-Beaulieu, killed with the Guards at Loos in September . . . Oh, there'd be a wedding tomorrow, for life would go on, and love could not be killed. But there would be few in the old church who would not see writ clear before them, not the words of the service, but that stark headline:

THE DATE OF COMPULSION

*   *   *   *

Saturday:

Dearly beloved, we are gathered together here in the sight of God, and in the face of this congregation, to join together this Man and this Woman in holy Matrimony; which is an honourable estate, instituted of God in the time of man's innocency, signifying unto us the mystical union that is betwixt Christ and his Church; which holy estate Christ adorned and beautified with his presence, and first miracle that he wrought, in Cana of Galilee; and is commended of Saint Paul to be honourable among all men; and therefore is not to be enterprised, nor taken in hand, unadvisedly, lightly, or wantonly, to satisfy men's carnal lusts and appetites, like brute beasts that have no understanding; but reverently, discreetly, advisedly, soberly . . .

"Soberly," Johnny Merritt repeated silently to himself. He was not quite sober, but he had seen bridegrooms in much worse state after the farewell bachelor party of the night before. It might have been worse if Guy Rowland had been at home, but he was at Upavon, flying, and could not get leave; so the party had been relatively small and subdued—just his father, Overfeld, Morgan, Ginger Keble-Palmer, David Toledano, and himself. Overfeld the production expert and Morgan the plant foreman at the Jupiter Motor Company were not the sort of people who would normally have been invited to such an occasion, but they were good company and fellow Americans. He had never met David Toledano before, but he had been a school friend of Guy's, and it was his family's bank that had provided the English capital to match the American capital provided by his own father to found both the Jupiter Motor Company and the new Hedlington Aircraft Company. Besides, there was no one else. The other young Englishmen he had met in his year here, and who might have helped him bid farewell to bachelordom, were in the trenches across the Channel . . . or under that earth. He gritted his teeth. The sense of shame could not be exorcised, however hard he worked, however often Overfeld or his father told him he was more use to the war effort here than over there. How much longer could he stand it, face himself every morning in the mirror?

Secondly, it was ordained for a remedy against sin, and to avoid fornication; that such persons as have not the gift of continency might marry, and keep themselves undefiled members of Christ's body . . .

"Fornication," Stella Cate thought, head bowed and eyes downcast behind the thin veil. She had committed fornication, and knew that she would have done it again, if she had remained unmarried. No one knew it, except Probyn's Woman, somewhere in the back of the church with Probyn, Fletcher, Florinda, and Willum. All of them, except Willum, knew, for the Woman and Florinda had got rid of the fruit of that fornication. Betty Merritt, her groom's sister, suspected, Stella thought; not the specific fact of her night with Captain Irwin a year ago; but that she had somewhere, somehow, eaten of the fruit. Betty was not unfriendly—the opposite, in fact—but there was a look in her eye that said, "You know what I do not know."

She lifted her head instinctively, for she had heard a strange

4

sound, a rhythmic thudding, a subdued creaking, the deep hum or murmur of men's voices. It was outside the church, in the village street. But what was it? Unwillingly, she bowed her head again. She'd have liked to run out and see what it was.

I require and charge you both, as ye will answer at the dreadful day of judgment when the secrets of all hearts shall be disclosed, that if either of you know any impediment, why ye may not be lawfully joined together in Matrimony, ye do now confess it.

Stella's uncle, John Rowland, standing a little stooped in the second row of pews on the right, wished his wife Louise could have been here, as she had dearly wanted to be; but she was attending a course in Wiltshire, being run under the auspices of the British Friesian Society, on ways of keeping Friesian cattle healthy, increasing milk production and improving the breed while importing only a minimum of champion bulls from Holland. Those bulls cost money—foreign exchange, which the country needed to buy shells and steel and beef and wheat and . . . if it needed to go on fighting the ghastly war at all. Whatever the original rights and wrongs, it was surely time that the slaughter, and the plague of hatred, were stemmed . . . when Louise came back he must talk with her about buying some more heifers . . . Stella looked almost ethereally lovely, in spite of the simple daytime dress and short veil she was wearing—perhaps because of them. Christopher Cate had wanted to avoid waste and ostentation when he had decreed a simple wedding, and simple clothes for his daughter; but the effect had been to enhance Stella's classic English rose-petal colouring and complexion. Louise would have been weeping happily long since, of course . . . Johnny Merritt was a fine-looking young man, and his father a tall and distinguished figure beside him, as best man. These Americans crossed the Atlantic, even in wartime, with no more thought than he'd give a trip to London. A son's wedding would be ample justification for anyone, of course; and in Stephen Merritt's case there were also the affairs of the motor and aircraft companies to be looked into. Mr Merritt's fellow directors in the bank in New York would expect him to give those very careful study; after all they must have a great deal of money invested in them . . . The daughter, Johnny's sister, was a good-looking girl, too, just over medium height, lithe and athletic in her movements . . . He cocked his head. He heard a steady tramp tramp tramp outside . . . singing, or rather humming, what was that tune? Ah, the one with bawdy words, *Mademoiselle from Armentières* . . . a soldiers' song. There must be troops marching through Walstone on maneuvers. A barked com-

5

mand confirmed it. He frowned and sighed: even here, he thought, even now . . .

Wilt thou have this Woman to thy wedded wife, to love together after God's ordinance in the holy estate of Matrimony? Wilt thou love her, comfort her, honour, and keep her in sickness and health . . . ?

Naomi Rowland, standing beside her father, John, nodded her head in approval as Johnny Merritt's voice rang out firm and clear—"I will." She had not seen much of him, but she liked what she had; and perhaps he was the right man for Stella, if anyone was. That girl needed a strong hand, and though Johnny was very polite—more polite than Englishmen of his class would have been—she sensed a firmness underneath. The trouble was, or might be, that Stella was flighty. She put the thought away firmly. It would work out well. She smoothed down her khaki barathea tunic and, glancing round, caught the eye of her cousin Virginia Rowland, also dressed in khaki, but in the uniform of the Women's Legion, while Naomi's was that of the Women's Volunteer Motor Drivers. There was much khaki and navy blue in the church, come to see the squire's only daughter wed to the young American. And Uncle Christopher had been so right to forbid long trains, scores of bridesmaids, expensive gowns, and all that tosh—always insulting to women, as though they were heifers to be decked out for the bull—dangerous tosh in times like these. She wished her friend from Girton, Rachel Cowan, had come. A year ago, she would always have found time to be with Naomi, whatever the difficulties. They were growing apart, that was the truth . . . sad; but it couldn't be helped.

Wilt thou have this Man to thy wedded husband, to live together after God's ordinance . . . ?

Betty Merritt listened carefully as the rector, old Mr Kirby, intoned the words. He looked strange in a surplice. The last time she had seen him, just after she and her father had arrived from New York, he'd been sitting low on a fat cob, galloping across a ploughed field, his lined old face purple in the cold, mouth open as he swore at the horse, eyes bolting with excitement, the Master's horn shrilling behind the hill . . . *"Obey him"* . . . Stella would have no difficulty in keeping that part of the oath, she thought. She liked to be told what to do. Whether she would obey Johnny's unspoken but obvious wishes, keep to his standards, Betty could not say. She did not know Stella well enough yet to make that judgment about her. She looked across at Ginger

Keble-Palmer's long profile: a nice, shy man; and, though he did not know it yet, she intended that he should be more than that to her. She had learned already that he was a good aircraft designer, and worked for Richard Rowland and her brother at the Hedlington Aircraft Company. He did not know anything important about her; specifically, he did not know that at Smith she had taken solid geometry, algebra, plane and spherical trigonometry, analytic geometry and calculus, both integral and differential. He was going to learn, soon. And her father was going to be reminded.

She heard the tramp of marching men from outside the church, even through the doors closed against the February cold. She heard the clink of steel on steel. She heard, pervading the candled twilight, the buzz of an aeroplane circling somewhere overhead, a searching, intrusive wasp.

Who giveth this Woman to be married to this Man?

Richard Rowland watched approvingly as his brother-in-law, Christopher Cate, took a step forward, his daughter's hand in his, and, leaving her at Johnny's side, stepped back. Christopher looked sadder than the occasion warranted. His only daughter being married to a rich and personable young American was hardly cause for tears . . . but Christopher had never been one to laugh lightly; and now he was probably thinking of Margaret, his wife, and wishing she was at his side . . . but Margaret had hidden herself in the back streets of Dublin, or in some cottage in the bogs, a gun always by her; and Sinn Fein, not her husband or children, was her only care now. Perhaps she did not even know that Stella was being married, though the announcement had been made in the Dublin papers as well as the *Times, Telegraph* and *Morning Post.* Turning his head, he caught sight of Willum Gorse, beaming in simple pleasure . . . but then Willum *was* simple. He was glad to see that Willum's half-brother Bert Gorse hadn't got a half-day off to attend. That swine had been agitating the men in the J.M.C. again—but now he'd got him. The conscription bill had been passed, making all unmarried men under forty liable to military service. Bert was thirty-five or thirty-six; and he was unmarried; and he, Richard Rowland, would make it his business to see that the responsible authorities were made aware of those two facts. He glanced at his wife, Susan, beside him. Tomorrow the chauffeur was going to drive her up to the orphanage in Camberwell to pick up the two children she was going to adopt . . . that *they* were going to adopt, he should say; but he found it hard to associate himself with the business. In seventeen years of marriage they had not produced any children of their own, and then, late last year, she had suddenly announced that as he had his factories for "children," she intended to adopt not one but two real ones. He should have gone with her on her two previous trips, to visit orphanages, and talk to governors—and children—but he had had no time. The affairs of the J.M.C. and the H.A.C.—both of which he managed, and both of which were ultimately owned by Johnny Merritt's father's bank in New York—kept him more than busy. He should have made time. The children were going to be his, too, whether he liked it or not.

He could hardly hear what old Kirby was saying, for now the distinctive sound of guns on the move was filling the church—the jingle and clink of the harness, the rumble of the gun and limber wheels on the gravelled road. A horse neighed, then someone shouted a series of unintelligible orders, and the hoofbeats quickened to a gallop, the rumbling and clanking grew louder, faster.

I John take thee Stella to my wedded wife, to have and to hold from this day forward, for better for worse, for richer or poorer, in sickness and in health, to love and cherish . . .

Florinda Gorse listened idly. She had heard the words many times, for all her life she had been in demand as a bridesmaid at the village people's weddings. Not of the gentry, of course . . . especially not now that everyone knew she was living with the old Marquess of Jarrow, as his mistress. But if Jarrow wasn't having her on, and if the booze didn't kill him first, she'd soon hear those words spoken about her . . . probably not in a church, though. The Marquess wasn't much of a churchgoer, and she imagined that their marriage would be in a registry office, if it came off at all. She wouldn't mind. There was a nice man inside that shriveled and sodden little shell, somewhere . . . or had been; but the brandy and whisky had long ago all but drowned him . . . Miss Stella had won a fine man, she could tell. Keeping the man and the marriage would be up to her; and Florinda doubted her strength of will. Oh, she had the good intentions, and the training, all right . . . but they weren't much use when your husband had become boring, or neglectful, and another nice man was looking deep into your eyes, or when the bottle in the cupboard seemed to be offering help . . . excitement. That was what Miss Stella wanted most, that was the danger. She looked nice in her light brown wool dress. She would have looked better still in her V.A.D. uniform, but she'd left them a fortnight ago, in readiness for her marriage. So what did she think she was going to do all day, with the husband at the Aircraft Company till all hours? She'd done well to stay in the V.A.D. A woman needed something to keep her hands, and mind, busy these times . . . until she had a baby, of course.

I, Stella take thee, John, to my wedded husband, to have and to hold from this day forward, for better for worse . . .

Laurence Cate, home for the weekend from Charterhouse on special exeat for the wedding of his sister, wondered why his Aunt Alice was called Dormouse by her brothers, his Uncles Richard, John, Quentin, and Tom . . . by her sister, his mother, too. Perhaps she—Aunt Alice—had been very quiet and shy when she was a little girl. She wasn't now. She'd been asking him whether he'd seen any rare birds since Christmas . . . she was nice to talk to . . . always seemed to be interested in what you were doing, or wanted to do . . . Mummy wasn't, often. He thought she loved him, but wasn't sure. She loved Ireland more; or Ireland mattered more, or something. He imagined his mother hiding in a bog—Ireland was full of bogs—listening to strange Irish birds singing . . . and the war went on, and on, and on, and now here they were, all round the church, rifles popping off blanks, and an aeroplane snarling round and round above, and he'd turned seventeen last November. He shivered and closed his eyes and tried to close his ears, but could not.

. . . for richer for poorer, in sickness and in health, to love, cherish, and to obey, till death us do part, according to God's holy ordinance; and thereto I give thee my troth.

Fiona Rowland, the bride's aunt by marriage, hardly heard the long-familiar words, or the warlike sounds of the soldiers outside. Did Archie Campbell, her lover, secretly fear her so much, then, that he could vanish without a word, knowing that she was at last leaving her husband and children and coming to him . . . leaving her to find out from the landlady that he had gone, the studio locked up? It had been like a blow in the face—first the fact of the locked door, then the shame of the humble inquiries, the disdainful old harridan—"No, Mr Campbell left no address"; but of course the woman knew, really, for she must be forwarding letters, receiving the rent. In one sense Fiona knew where Archie had gone: he had joined up—she was certain of that. But in what regiment, or corps? Why no word, and six weeks passed? The slow appreciation of what stood behind his actions was even worse than what the immediate impact had been: that he would rather face death in the trenches than accept her love, and have her live with him, with or without marriage . . . She had been on the point of demanding from Quentin that he divorce her; she had told her son and daughter, Guy and Virginia, what she was going to do; and then . . . she had come back from London, her heart a cold stone . . . *till death do us part* . . . She had prayed for death to cut the bonds that held her to Quentin; but Fate had laughed in her face. Quentin was somewhere in France, still alive; and he had been at the front since August 1914—nearly a year and a half!

She thought, this is ridiculous: here is young Stella embarking on a new life while all I can seem to do is mope and moan. The first thing to do was find Archie. As he was a Campbell, he would have wanted to join the Argyll & Sutherland Highlanders: Campbells were often not welcome in other regiments, whose clan sympathies had decidedly been with the Macdonalds in the affair at Glencoe. The Argylls' depot was in Stirling Castle. She'd ring the adjutant this very night, and find out. And if he jibbed at giving her what she wanted to know, she'd remind him that she was a McLeod of Skye . . . but what if Archie had enlisted under an assumed name? She groaned involuntarily, but it was loud enough to make her daughter Virginia, lumpy with puppy fat in her Woman's Legion uniform, look round at her . . . accusingly?

With this Ring I thee wed, with my body I thee worship, and with all my worldly goods I thee endow: In the Name of the Father, and of the Son, and of the Holy Ghost.

"Amen," Probyn Gorse said loudly. Now 'twas done, and Miss Stella wed. About time, too. Next, squire ought to think of himself. A man needed a woman, for one thing and another, all his life. His Mrs was as good as dead. Probyn didn't know what the law said about it, but as far as a man was concerned, who wanted and needed a woman, as squire did in that big Manor House, she was dead. Perhaps she really was. A good thing, too, as long as it was done in the open, and they found the body, and could say, "This was Margaret Cate"; then squire could marry another woman.

He jumped, and swore under his breath. Good God A'mighty, they were firing off those danged guns right outside the churchyard, cracking the tombstones, jerking the dead out of their coffins. Miss Stella was looking round, her face alive, staring back, fidgeting . . . *bang!* . . . *bang!* . . . *bang!* —the 18-pounders barked.

Those whom God hath joined together let no man put asunder.

Rose Rowland felt the tears fill her eyes. Stella was the first of her grandchildren to be married, as she had always expected. Girls married younger than boys, in their class, and though Naomi was older, Rose had never thought she would marry before Stella. Naomi wasn't pretty and round-figured, like Stella. Naomi was tall and proud and brave; her heart and her future lay where few women had gone before . . . and few had wanted to, till these insane, sad days. She cried soundlessly, because she knew she would not see any great-grandchild. Her husband's hand was on hers, patting in comfort; but Harry could not assuage her grief, though she loved him and he her.

Forasmuch as John de Lisle Merritt and Stella Cate have consented together in holy wedlock, and have witnessed the same before God and this company, and thereto have given and pledged their troth either to other, and have declared the same by giving and receiving of a Ring, and by joining of hands; I pronounce that they be Man and Wife together, In the Name of the Father, and of the Son, and of the Holy Ghost.

And "Amen," the congregation intoned, heaving a long collective sigh, that could be felt in the bowels as well as heard in the ear.

They waited then, while the bridal party followed the rector to the vestry for the signing of the marriage register. Up in the organ loft Miss Morton sonorously embarked on her favourite composition, Bach's *Toccata and Fugue in D Minor*. The guns banged, the west window, which was of stained glass, shook and shivered, men shouted, horses' hooves clattered, motor lorry engines roared, the aeroplane buzzed and whined. At last they came out of the vestry, Miss Morton slipped from Bach to Mendelssohn, and they started slowly down the aisle, the big bouquet of lilies in the crook of Stella's left arm, her right in her husband's. She's walking fast, Probyn thought, she's almost dragging him along . . . faster, faster . . . she doesn't want to miss what's going on outside. They passed and Probyn waited till a dozen or so of the gentry had gone by, following, then slipped in among them and out of the church.

The green was full of hundreds of soldiers with rifles and full packs, some leaning against house walls, some sitting in the gutter or on the grass. Eight guns were lined up in the field beyond the church-yard, clouds of whitish smoke jetting from the muzzles as they fired the blank ammunition. Five lorries ground up the street, and a car was coming fast from the opposite direction. Them dratted soldiers'll have drunk all the beer in the Arms and the Goat & Compasses, too, Probyn thought—who asked them to come here? Even as he turned away, he heard a screech of brakes, and saw that the staff car had come too fast round the corner, and would not be able to avoid the lorries. As he watched, right outside the church gate, the car skidded sideways into the leading lorry and lurched over onto its side with a

11

fearful crash and rending of metal. At once the engine caught fire.
Everyone stood frozen, for everyone, soldiers and villagers and the
wedding party, had had their minds on other things. Then, just as
Probyn told his muscles to move, just as other men close by stirred
toward action, a brown figure burst from the crowd at the gate, and ran
forward. It was Stella, her bouquet hurled away, her wool dress held
up. She was beside the car, dragging out one of the three uniformed
men in it. Before she could get him free a dozen men were there
helping, others covering the flaming engine with coats and blankets.
In ten seconds all three occupants were rescued, scorched, bruised,
bleeding, one unconscious, but all alive; in another minute the flames
were out. Stella walked slowly back to her husband's side. He was
looking at her in awe, Probyn thought. Her dress was scarred and
blackened where she had leaned into the car, her gloves red with
blood, smudges of dirt on her face; but she was happy, radiant. Probyn
shook his head, wondering, a little fearful. The young American
didn't know what he had caught.

*   *   *   *

Afterwards, at the reception in the manor, Ginger Keble-Palmer
stood, glass of champagne cup in hand, stooped over a little, listening
to Betty Merritt. She said, "Ginger, you're a director of Hedlington
Aircraft, aren't you?"

He cracked the big knuckles of his free hand nervously. Betty
Merritt was good-looking without being exactly beautiful to his eyes;
and she was terrifyingly direct—almost as bad as Guy's cousin Naomi,
across the room there. "Yes," he said at last, "your father was good
enough to offer me a directorship."

"Instead of a higher rate of salary, I expect," Betty said. Ginger
made to say something and she raised a hand—"What's your chief
problem?"

"Problem?" Ginger said. "In the factory, you mean? It isn't built yet
. . . We've got the use of one hangar up there, but it's nowhere near
big enough to take the bomber I've designed. We're working as fast as
we can, three shifts a day, to build the proper sheds, and use the
hangar as a sort of temporary office . . . very draughty, it is, too. And
lonely. I feel that I'm working in King's Cross station, or something."

"So you work alone?"

"Almost. I have one man to help me, who's a competent
draughtsman, but . . ."

"But . . . what?"

Ginger looked round for help, and said, "I have to do all the
calculations—stresses, thrust, everything—myself."

"Would you like an assistant designer? Don't you *need* an assistant designer?"

"Yes, we do, but . . . "

"I have three years of advanced mathematics of every kind, and I want to specialize in aircraft design."

Keble-Palmer drank copiously, coughed, and spluttered—"But . . . "

"But I'm a woman, eh? What difference does that make? I can do it, Ginger. I really can. You'll have to teach me the formulas, and give me some practical tips, but in a couple of weeks I'll really be able to help. If *you're* willing to accept me, I'll speak to Johnny and my father."

Ginger felt as if he had been sandbagged. She must be joking. But she wasn't. To gain time he said, "I thought you were going to join the Women's Land Army."

"Not really. Since we came over from America I've been waiting, looking for something that would suit me . . . excite me."

Ginger drank again. It was mad. She was mad. But he *did* need an assistant, badly; and she had drive; and intelligence . . . and more mathematics than he himself had, having gone direct from Wellington to Handley Page. And she was Mr Merritt's daughter. Why couldn't she have been his son, and then it would all be easy? But why *couldn't* a girl do the work, if she had the maths?

"All right," he said.

She leaned forward quickly and kissed him on the cheek, "Thank you, Ginger. You won't regret it. Now I'll speak to my father."

She moved easily through the crowded room, passing close to Stella and Johnny, who were densely surrounded. Both had champagne glasses in hand, Stella flushed, wearing a light tweed suit, tears of happiness and excitement gleaming in her eyes, Johnny standing straight beside her, one arm round her waist.

Betty found her father talking to his widowed sister, Isabel Kramer, and Mr Cate. They turned to face her as she came up, and her father raised a hand. "You have something of great import to tell me, Betty. I can see it in your face. Are you sure it shouldn't wait till we are alone?"

"We won't have much time, will we, Daddy, as you're sailing on Monday . . . Ginger—Mr Keble-Palmer—wants to hire me as assistant designer at Hedlington Aircraft."

"Wha-a-at?" her father exclaimed.

Her aunt, who was petite and dark haired, with snapping blue eyes, said, "Are you sure you didn't *tell* him he wanted to hire you, dear?"

"Well, I suggested it, but he liked the idea. He *needs* an assistant, and there's no one available with better qualifications . . . or *any* qualifications, really. The men who might be are at the war. And there's *no* reason why a woman shouldn't do it. Now, is there?"

Her father surveyed her with a measuring look in his eye. Mr Cate's face was calm in repose, his eyes steady on her. At length her father said, "You really think you've found your mission in England?" In an aside to his sister he said, "Betty's been determined to stay in England, but has not—until this moment—had the least idea of what she was going to do."

"I do," Betty said, answering his question.

"You always were a headstrong girl . . . good luck to you," Stephen Merritt said. "You can live with Johnny and Stella."

"Oh no, Stephen!" Isabel cried. "The groom's sister living with the honeymoon couple? It's out of the question. She must have a little apartment in Hedlington."

Stephen was frowning and Betty cut in: "Daddy, times are changing. Lots of girls live alone—they have to."

"I'll help you find a suitable place," Aunt Isabel said.

Mr Cate broke his silence. "I will put you in touch with estate agents who might be able to help, Mrs Kramer."

"Thank you . . . "

Betty put her arms round her father's neck and kissed him. "Thank you, Daddy . . . I'll be starting work on Monday. And Ginger can fix my salary with Mr Rowland."

She waved her hand, and drifted off, heading by a circuitous route towards the little group of Gorses near the tall windows. The electric lights glowed in Florinda's auburn hair, and the softer wave of her brother's curls. Old Probyn was wearing a yellow four-in-hand tie, and had newly dyed his sparse grey hair to a rich henna quite comparable to his granddaughter's auburn. Willum, Probyn's eldest, the father of Florinda and Fletcher, stood a little apart in worn serge hand-me-downs, beaming aimlessly. Probyn's Woman stood upright and severe at Probyn's side.

They all turned to face her, just as her father's group had done. Florinda smiled at her, Probyn's face remained neutral, as did the Woman's. Fletcher, the gorgeous Fletcher, examined her with his lips slightly curled, the eyes hooded under the heavy lids wandering down her dress, over her breasts, down to her feet, up again, pausing at her loins, up. He smiled at last: "Nice day, Miss Merritt—I don't think."

"What else can we expect in February? I only pray it isn't like this for the poor men in the trenches."

"It is," Fletcher said.

Probyn spoke up suddenly, "Who be that lady with squire and your dad?"

His Woman answered before Betty could speak, "Mrs Kramer. Mr Merritt's sister. Widowed. Younger sister, by the look of her."

"She's nine years younger than my father," Betty said. "She has a son about my age at Yale University. That's in Connecticut."

"What's she doing here?" Probyn said.

Betty said, "Her late husband's brother is Secretary of our Embassy in London. She's been living with him—and his wife—for nearly six months. She likes England."

Probyn grunted, and kept his eyes on her Aunt Isabel Kramer, as though suspicious that she might steal the silver ladle out of the huge silver champagne cup bowl.

Betty turned to Fletcher, "I suppose you'll be going into the Army soon, now that conscription's been voted."

"Maybe," Fletcher said. "Where will you be staying, now that your dad's going back to America, and Mr Johnny's wed to Miss Stella?"

"I'm going to get an apartment—flat—in Hedlington," she said, "and work at Hedlington Aircraft. I may have to take a room at the South-Eastern until I can get one."

Fletcher nodded, and after a while said, "You'll have a motor car?"

She said, "Oh, I'll have to, to get to and from work."

"On Sunday, some time, you could drive down here and we could go to the sea. I've never seen the sea."

"Oh, that would be lovely," Betty cried. She pulled herself together, and added, "It'll have to wait till I get the car, of course . . . and for better weather."

Fletcher nodded as though what she had said was so self-evident that she had wasted her breath in saying it. Betty thought, I must be careful. He is so handsome, so magnificent a male animal, that he makes my hand shake, almost: but what would Mr Cate say or think of her going out with him, alone? He was, after all, not exactly upper class . . . Florinda was smiling quizzically at her; Florinda knew what was in her mind. And what did it matter? She was American, not English. She said firmly, "As soon as I get the car, and we have a nice day, we'll go to the sea. It's only just beyond Hedlington."

"Not that way," Fletcher said. He pointed through the windows, toward the south—"The sea."

"Ah, the English Channel. In Sussex, I think it is there."

"T'other's dirty, and full of muck and oil from London. I seen that, by Chatham," Fletcher said. "I'm going to kiss the bride. There's some room round them now."

"Better hurry," the Woman said, "they'll be going upstairs soon."

15

When the others had left him, skirmishing their way toward the bride and groom, Probyn sidled in the direction of Mrs Kramer, who was now talking to Mr Harry Rowland, the bride's grandfather. Mr Harry, recently elected Member of Parliament for the Mid-Scarrow Division of Kent, was in full cry on the subject of conscription—"It was the only fair way, Mrs Kramer. Our best men were sacrificing their lives while others skulked at home."

"It's a big decision for England to make—the first compulsory military service bill in history, my brother-in-law tells me."

"That is correct. Mr Asquith was very reluctant to take the step, *most* reluctant, but events and circumstances left him, and us, no alternative."

Probyn listened; they had acknowledged his presence by moving a little apart, leaving room for him to join them, but that was all. Mrs Kramer said, "Will the conscription law apply to Ireland?"

"I think it must. Ireland is, after all, part of the United Kingdom . . . but my wife tells me that there will be far greater troubles than we have yet experienced, if we in fact enforce conscription there. She is from an old Irish family."

"My brother-in-law says that it will take 200,000 British soldiers to enforce it there . . . which is just about the number of Irish men who would be conscripted. And it will create even greater bitterness than now exists."

Probyn cut in, "Do you think they'll take Willum for a sojer, Mr Harry?"

"Your Willum, Probyn? I'm sure they won't. He's . . . well, a little simple, isn't he?"

"Aye, but he's got two legs and ten toes. The way they're killing the men off out there, they'll be taking them out of cradles and hospitals and lunatic asylums soon, and sending them to France." He turned to Mrs Kramer—"I'm Probyn Gorse."

She smiled at him, "I'm Mrs Kramer, Mr Gorse. I've heard of you. You're the best . . . ah, game shooter, in Kent, my brother says. And he was told that by Mr Cate."

Probyn said, "Will you be staying down here now?"

"I'm afraid not. I'm going back to London with my brother tonight, and then on Monday he takes the train for Liverpool, and I . . . well, I suppose I'll settle down to my work in London—for the wounded, organizing food parcels from America . . . "

"You like hunting? Fox hunting? Shooting? Fishing?"

"I like riding, and I'm sure I would love to hunt, if I could. I have done a great deal of bird shooting. My husband owned a meat packing plant in Chicago and we used to go out after pheasant and partridge in Wisconsin and the Dakotas. I've also done some elk and deer hunting in Wyoming. And I fish for salmon in New Brunswick, which is close to Maine, where my home is."

"Did he leave you rich?"

She paused a moment, but then answered evenly, without embarrassment, "Very, Mr Gorse."

Probyn nodded and moved away, looking for Squire Cate. He'd got to talk to him, man to man.

When the crowd had swallowed him, Mrs Kramer began to laugh silently. Harry Rowland said, "You must excuse him, Mrs Kramer. He is a sort of child of nature, a relic of the past, and lives by different rules from the rest of us."

Isabel Kramer said, "I think I know what he was up to, the old dear . . . Johnny and Stella have gone upstairs."

Harry said, "Where are they going for the honeymoon, do you know?"

"Yes. Claridge's. I believe Johnny would have preferred to go to the Lake District. Your grandson Guy had been talking to him about it, but Stella wanted the theatres, the restaurants, the great shops . . . the bright lights of Broadway, we say."

Harry shook his head, "Can't think why anyone would prefer London to the Lake District—smoke, crowds, pickpockets . . . "

"But we are not twenty years old," Mrs Kramer said, "nor so beautiful as to exact homage wherever we go. And for that there have to be people to pay the homage . . . But they'll be back in a week, in the cottage you helped them buy in Beighton. It will seem very lonely for them, after this . . . "

Especially for Stella, she thought. Johnny had his work—work that seemed to absorb his whole attention every waking hour. Would Stella expect crashed cars, marching armies, passionate love, every day, every night? She ought to find part-time work—back to the V.A.D. perhaps, or drive an ambulance: but such an idea would not cross Johnny's mind; nor Stella's, probably. She was a wife now, the world at her feet.

Alice Rowland, Harry's thirty-five-year-old spinster daughter, came up to them, smiling. Isabel said, "I've been meaning all day to tell you what an attractive dress that is."

"Thank you," Alice said, "my brother designed it."

Harry started—"What brother? Richard? Quentin? John? Tom? None of them have ever designed a woman's dress in their lives, that I know of."

Alice said, "Tom, father. When I was fourteen and had just, ah, grown a bust, and he was a midshipman on a battleship, home on leave, he drew a dress on a piece of paper that he said would look good on me. He made several sketches, and was as pleased as punch when I said I would make it up myself . . . but then he made me swear never to tell anyone he'd designed it. He'd be ragged to death, he said. And I haven't, till now. But this is a new copy, made a week ago, to the same design, modified to suit me as I am now . . . rather fatter all round than when I was fourteen."

Harry said, "I can't believe it. Tom's never been interested in girls, still less in what they wear."

Isabel said, "It's a *very* clever design, Miss Rowland. It is so simple, and clean, yet it's not severe . . . How old did you say he was when he designed it?"

"If I was fourteen, he must have been sixteen."

"Well, he had an extraordinary talent," Mrs Kramer said, "which I suppose he must still have. You don't lose something like that . . . "

*   *   *   *

Across the room the Countess of Swanwick watched Probyn Gorse maneuver Christopher Cate out of a conversation with two of his tenants, and slowly cross the room. At the same time Florinda had joined Harry Rowland, Alice Rowland and Mrs Kramer, and, a few moments later, somehow removed Harry and Alice, a few seconds before Probyn arrived shepherding Christopher Cate. For a minute or two the four of them stood close, talking, smiling—Probyn and his granddaughter, Cate, and Mrs Kramer, the American widow; then suddenly, the two Gorses had vanished into the crowd, leaving Christopher and Mrs Kramer alone, tête-à-tête in the crowd. The earl said, "There's that blighter, Gorse. I'm surprised that Cate invites him . . . a convicted poacher, and gaolbird . . . and Cate a magistrate."

"He couldn't *not* invite him, even if he'd wanted to which I'm sure he didn't."

"And Florinda, look at her—talking to Naomi Rowland, quite at her ease, and she no better than a whore, really."

The countess sighed, "Florinda's not a whore, Roger, she's a kept woman, a career on which our own eldest son started her . . . and, in a week or two, if the Society gossip columns are correct, she'll probably be a marchioness—when she will take precedence over us."

"It's ridiculous! It's . . . " the earl spluttered for words, but could not find them. His wife said, "Florinda did not invent the system, Roger. We and our ancestors did, and now we have to stick by it."

All the time she had kept her eyes on Cate and Mrs Kramer. They were drifting out of the mainstream, inch by inch, themselves forming a cocoon of intimacy, their faces alight with interest in each other. It

18

looked as though Probyn's maneuvers were going to work. But then, they always did.

And there, talking now to Naomi Rowland, was David Toledano, burly, kindly, darkly handsome, in spite of his oft-broken nose, in the uniform of a lieutenant of the Royal Field Artillery. His battery had been posted to Egypt or Palestine, someone had told her, and he was on short leave before sailing with it. Now *there* was a suitable object for some machinations of her own. David was an Oxford rugby Blue, tried for England, and he'd inherit heaven knew how many millions one day; what better husband could there be for Barbara or Helen? She sighed. Her husband would have a fit: he didn't like Jews, and blamed the late King Edward VII for bringing them into Society. The countess sighed again. David Toledano would make some woman a very, very good husband, one day; but it wouldn't be any daughter of Roger Durand-Beaulieu, 9th Earl of Swanwick.

*   *   *   *

The Daily Telegraph, Friday February 4, 1916

STIRRING STORIES OF MONDAY'S RAID
VERDICT AGAINST KAISER
A JURY'S FINDING

At an inquest held yesterday on thirteen Staffordshire victims the jury declined to accept a suggestion from the coroner as to the form the verdict should take, and agreed upon the following:
That the thirteen persons whose bodies we have viewed were killed by explosive bombs dropped from enemy aircraft, and that a verdict of "wilful murder" be recorded against the Kaiser and the Crown Prince as being accessories to and after the fact.

Cate looked again at the date of the paper. This was Friday's, the same he had been reading yesterday evening. And now the wedding was over, Stella and her Johnny safely in Claridge's, and everyone else back in their own homes. That sister of Stephen Merritt's was a nice woman, thoroughly well bred, vivacious, intelligent: attractive, too, and her accent very pleasant—a Maine accent, Stephen had told him . . .

A knock on the door made him look up, and call "Come in."

The old butler, Blyth, entered and stood respectfully by the door. "I am about to lock up the house, sir, if that is all right."

"Yes, lock up," Cate said. "And thank you for all you've done today

. . . all of you. Please pass on my thanks to the rest of the staff. It was a long, tiring day for them."

"I will, sir."

Cate said, "And . . . good heavens, you're leaving us the next day. The wedding has taken my mind off everything else. Come and see me here tomorrow, after lunch. I will have a little present for you which I hope will enable you to buy a few comforts for yourself that perhaps your sister can not provide."

"Thank you, sir. I do trust that Garrod will be able to look after you in every respect . . . Who'd have thought that a woman would ever be head of the staff at the Manor! I feel that I am deserting you, especially as Madam has . . ." he coughed, not finishing the sentence.

Cate said, "You've looked after us long enough. Since my father inherited, eh? Now it's time someone looked after you. Come and visit, whenever you want to. And write."

"I shall, sir. I have been very happy here, sir . . . so many, many years . . . so much has happened . . . I pray that all may be well for you and yours, sir, through these most, ah, insecure times. Good night, sir."

"Good night, Blyth."

Alone again, Cate pulled down Plato's *Republic* from the shelf where he kept the leather bound philosophers, opened it at random and read aloud.

Οὐκ ᾔσθησαι, ἦν δ' ἐγώ, ὅτι ἀθάνατος ἡμῶν ἡ ψυχὴ καὶ οὐδέποτε ἀπόλλυται;

"Don't you know that the soul of man is immortal and never dies?" he repeated; answering, after a time, "I hope I do." Then he closed the book, and went up to bed.

Flanders: Saturday, February 5, 1916

2 Lieutenant Colonel Quentin Rowland, Commanding Officer of the 1st Battalion the Weald Light Infantry, leaned against the frozen mud of the parapet, elbows clamped against the unyielding ground, and peered into the eyepiece of the trench periscope. The sun was only just risen, casting long shadows over the torn earth, tangled wire, and frosted, jumbled debris of No Man's Land. The German wire was just over seventy yards away—too far for hand grenades, but in comfortable range of grenades fired from the rifle launchers and, of course, of mortars of all sizes, and of the artillery. Plugstreet Wood was a harsh caricature of a forest, done by a cynical artist, few trees and those bare, far apart, and as stiff in the cold as though they had been made of rusty iron. As one of them might be, he thought. The Germans had been known, in another part of the line, to make a tree out of steel or concrete, painted, with loopholes for an observer inside to peer through, and hidden telephone lines leading back to a trench or artillery gun positions.

He swept the front carefully. The battalion had been in the front line in this area for nearly two weeks now, and were due for a move back to reserve, and rest, this evening. The men would be careless, thinking of the sleep to come; and unwilling to risk their lives doing those small dangerous jobs that had to be done, and done well, if they were not to fall victims of a raid, or a surprise local attack. There was no need to worry about a major offensive: that would telegraph itself days or weeks ahead, through intelligence sources, identification of prisoners, and the watchful eyes of the Royal Flying Corps.

He focussed his attention back from the German wire to No Man's Land. He counted seventeen bodies in varying stages of decay and contortion—five German and twelve British, all killed by machine guns in the open, in the middle of the night, when making trench raids to capture prisoners for identification. He spoke down without moving his eyes from the eyepiece, "How many bodies are out there, Stratton?"

"Seventeen, sir," Lieutenant Fred Stratton answered, "five Germans, eleven Black Watch, and one sapper."

Quentin did not answer. Stratton was turning into a good officer, though he'd never be a gentleman; and never as reliable as his brother Frank. All platoon commanders had to keep an accurate count of the dead on their front: the Germans—and the British for that matter— would sometimes slip in three or four live men, by night, close enough to throw grenades into the enemy front line trench, or stage a small raid, from much closer than the sentries would expect.

The view through the periscope suddenly vanished, and the instrument itself was jerked from his hands, as a bullet smacked overhead. Glass tinkled. Regimental Sergeant Major Nelson muttered an expletive. The adjutant, Quentin's nephew Charles "Boy" Rowland, said, "He hit the lens, sir."

Quentin slipped down into the trench. "Who did?"

"The Boche sniper Stratton was telling us about, sir."

"Oh, yes," Quentin said. He looked at the shattered glass and splintered wood of the periscope, and turned to Stratton. "How often does he do that?"

"He fires at periscopes whenever he sees them, but not often at men. He waits till someone gets careless. I lost a man yesterday—clean through the head."

"I know. Private Gates. He was with us in India . . . should have known better . . . Any news of your brother?"

"I had a letter yesterday, sir. Frank's out of bed and doing exercises . . . says he misses the old battalion and wishes he was back with us."

"No hope of that, I'm afraid, with his wounds . . . best Pioneer Sergeant we ever had. Still in hospital, I suppose?"

"Yes, sir, Lady Blackwell's, in Hedlington."

Quentin nodded. "Your sector is in good order, except for six yards of wire missing from the inside of the second double apron. Replace it this evening."

"Yes, sir, but . . . "

"*Early* tonight, Stratton, at dusk—before we are relieved. I'm not going to hand over my trenches to a New Army battalion in this state."

"No, sir. Yes, sir."

Quentin turned to the company commander, Captain McDonald—"I'll be posting two replacement officers to you as soon as we get into our reserve billets. When they arrive, send Stratton back to B, where he belongs."

"Yes, sir."

Quentin led on along the bottom of the trench, followed by Boy; Captain Ian Sholto the Regimental Medical Officer or R.M.O.; Mr Nelson the R.S.M., or Regimental, as all the soldiers called him; Father Caffin, the battalion's padre; and, in each company's sector, that company's commander—at the moment still Captain McDonald. Behind him Quentin heard Boy muttering to the R.S.M. about indents for wire; and, farther back, the soft brogue of Father Caffin telling a story, probably mildly dirty—and now Sholto's chuckle. He frowned, stopped in the bay between one platoon and the next, and turned on his adjutant—"How's Goodman doing as Pioneer Sergeant, Boy?"

"All right, sir," Boy said. "He'll never be a patch on Frank Stratton, though."

Quentin said, "Sergeant Stratton could make a dugout look and feel like a palace . . . and make anything mechanical work . . ." He moved on. Khaki wool gloves, knitted by devoted women back in England, covered all their hands. The officers wore the short greatcoats called British Warms—short, so that there were no skirts to be soiled and weighed down with the mud of the trenches. All four wore khaki wool scarves round their necks, half covering their ears. The cold was the damp, raw cold, a degree or two below freezing, of the ice-sodden flatlands of Flanders. In a month or two spring would come, and release the ground from the iron grip of frost, turning all this, now hard and dry, to heavy clinging mud, and wetter mud would slosh over everyone's boots and into the dugouts where they sought shelter from the sniper's bullet, the stray shell, the sudden grenade.

The little procession passed from A Company to B. Captain McDonald fell back, Captain Kellaway stood forward, a tall thin figure with worried eyes, a little stoop, and waving, long-fingered feathery hands. Quentin acknowledged Kellaway's salute with a glare. Why did he glare? Kellaway was a millionaire dilettante, about thirty-six; he was quiet, almost shy, but a good, brave officer. So why did he always make Quentin feel uncomfortable? He wished he knew, and to hide his own embarrassment, snapped, "Everything all right, Kellaway?"

"Y-yes, sir," Kellaway stammered. "I think we got a German sniper a few moments ago."

"Are you sure?"

"No, sir. But the pile of rubbish where we think he was has altered shape a little—as though something slipped or fell in it."

Quentin nodded and peered down into a cave dug into the front wall of the trench. From behind him the Regimental bellowed "Room—'shun!"

The six figures crowded into the dugout stiffened like marionettes and Boy, peering over his uncle's shoulder, thought as he often had before that the scene was like some weird painting, or an image that comes livid before you in a nightmare.

"Breughel," Kellaway muttered from behind him, and Quentin turned—"What? What's that? Broogle? None of these men is called Broogle. We don't have a Broogle in the battalion."

"I was clearing my throat, sir," Kellaway said, blushing. Boy thought he was right not to try to explain. The only art his uncle liked was fox hunting prints. And he himself would never have heard of the Breughels if Kellaway had not talked of them, in long evenings they'd spent together in billets. Before the war, he'd have been debagged in Mess, at the least, for talking about anything except horse racing or fox hunting.

The five officers and the Regimental stared at the six motionless soldiers. In one corner three candles guttered on the lid of a wooden box full of hand grenades, casting men's shadows on the corrugated iron roof of the dugout. Two dirty planks, stretched across more ammunition boxes, these for .303 small arms, were covered with khaki tunics, shirts, and vests. The men were all naked from the waist up, and beginning to shiver in the raw air. Their bodies were covered with the pink spots and stains of louse bites and louse defecations. Two of the men, totally naked, held lighted candles rigidly in one hand, like reform school altar boys, as they stared straight ahead at the hard mud walls; in their other hand they held their khaki serge uniform trousers, turned inside out.

"They were chatting, sir," Kellaway said.

"I can see that," Quentin snapped. "Is your whole company doing it?"

"No, sir, only six men per platoon at a time . . . They didn't want to waste any time in the rest area delousing, so they're doing it now."

"Carry on," Quentin said, and the frieze broke up. The men holding candles lowered them and ran them slowly along the seam of the trousers, thus killing not only the lice but also their eggs.

Quentin and the others stepped back up into the trench. "I'll have an equipment check at the next dugout," he said.

"Very g-good, sir," Kellaway stammered. "Here, sir." He stood aside at the entrance to another dugout. "Room—'shun!" the Regimental bellowed again.

Quentin looked round in the gloom. "Private Sandilands, show your equipment." Boy took a notebook from a pocket of his British Warm and began to read aloud. At each item the soldier showed the piece of equipment, either hung on pegs stuck into the wall, or in his pack, or on his person—"Greatcoat . . . mess-tin . . . steel helmet . . . forage cap . . . shirt . . . spare shirt . . . socks . . . spare socks, two pairs . . . soap . . . comb . . . knife, fork, and spoon . . . toothbrush . . . housewife . . . holdall . . . razor and case . . . shaving brush . . . cardigan . . . cap comforter . . . paybook . . . ammunition, one hundred and fifty rounds . . . rifle cover . . . oil bottle . . ."

"Check that it's full, Kellaway."

"It is, sir."

"Water bottle, full . . . first field dressing . . . tin of boot grease . . . bootbrush . . . gas mask . . ."

"Put it on, Sandilands. Shut off the tube, Boy . . . . All right."

"Spine protector . . . equipment, complete with frog, belt, and pouches . . . spare bootlaces . . . rifle . . . bayonet . . . pull through . . . entrenching tool."

"Let's have a look at that rifle barrel," Quentin said.

"For inspection . . . port, arms!" the Regimental snapped. "Examine—arms!"

Quentin peered down the barrel of the presented rifle, where the soldier's thumb was reflecting the sparse light up the barrel toward his eye.

"Corroded," Quentin said, "two patches. And cordworn muzzle."

"They've been reported, sir, and another rifle indented for."

Quentin grunted and stepped back up into the trench. The soldier's equipment he had just been inspecting weighed about sixty pounds dry. In mud or rain that would go up to near eighty. The greatcoat weighed seven pounds dry, but he himself had weighed one after hours of continuous cold rain, and it was then nineteen pounds. The average weight of his men at recruitment was 132 pounds . . . nine stone six. It was a damned shame, but what could be done about it?

In the next bay he stopped where a private soldier was greasing his boots on the firestep, his back to the enemy, the feet of a Lewis gun sentry close to his buttocks.

"Everything all right?" Quentin said. "It's Brace, isn't it?"

"Yes, sir. I was houseman at Laburnum Lodge, sir, under Mr Parrish."

"I remember . . . Well?"

Brace was on his feet, the tin of grease in his left hand and brush in his right, just as they had been when he leaped to his feet on seeing the C.O. come round the traverse; he did not salute, for as he was bareheaded that would have been a fearful military crime. He now said, "The jam doesn't taste of anything, sir . . . and the meat's bad."

"All of it?"

"No, sir. But nearly all Hoggin's is. The meat smells rotten, sir, when you open the tin, and . . ."

"I know," Quentin said. "We get it, too."

Brace put down his brush and tin and held out a folded newspaper, on which he had been sitting. He said, "It's the same everywhere, sir. Here's a letter to 'Tommy & Jack,' in *John Bull,* about the rotten food. He specially mentions Hoggin's."

"You didn't write that letter, did you?" Quentin asked suspiciously. Horatio Bottomley was a charlatan and probably a criminal; but his newspaper, *John Bull*, was widely read by the men in France, and the 'Tommy & Jack' section, where soldiers and sailors could air their grievances, wielded more influence than all the efforts of the commanding officers in the field. Writing letters to 'Tommy & Jack' was against regulations, but the soldiers did it, and the authorities at home who could have stopped it by arresting Bottomley, did nothing. Quentin was outraged that a man like Bottomley could get more done for his men than he could, but now, as many times before, he would have to swallow his anger; it was the results that mattered.

"Oh, no, sir!" Brace said; and Quentin said, "Let's hope *John Bull* can get some improvement. But I'll make a complaint, too."

"Thank you, sir."

Quentin nodded and moved on. Over his shoulder he said to Kellaway—"Next time you get some really bad smelling meat, or plum and apple that's all fibres—send it to me at once . . . at once, understand? . . . so that I can take it to brigade."

"Yes, sir."

"And see that your men shave again before the Royal Scots Fusiliers relieve us tonight. Some of them look like out-of-work dago waiters."

"Yes, sir."

Quentin led off down a communication trench towards the rear. Following him, Boy thought, the Fusiliers weren't going to be able to notice much stubble on the men's cheeks in the middle of a dark night, but that wouldn't make any difference to his uncle. In the Weald Light Infantry you shaved properly, whatever the circumstances, and that was that; as also, you died with your boots clean—unless they were under a foot of mud. His uncle really resented the mud, not because it made the going difficult, but because it dirtied the men's boots.

*　　*　　*　　*

The Regimental appeared in the opening of A Company Headquarters dugout, where Quentin waited with Boy and Captain McDonald, the company commander. "Scots Fusilier party approaching, sir," the Regimental said in a conspiratorial hiss. The three officers stood up, put on their steel helmets—their gas masks were already hung on their chests—climbed up the two small steps to the trench level, and stepped over the plank sill.

They waited, not looking at each other. A lisping voice floated to them over the traverse from the next bay, "But then this war's a very dangerous business, I told him," the voice lisped, "so perhaps the cavalry should be excused from it."

Someone gave a servile chuckle, then the speaker appeared, saying, "And here we are, facing Plugstreet Wood . . . *and* Lieutenant Colonel Quentin Rowland, if I do not mistake. It is an honour, sir." He saluted slowly, with a civilian half bow thrown in. Quentin saluted back. Boy, his hand at the rim of his steel helmet, searched his mind . . . the colonel of the 6th Battalion the Royal Scots Fusiliers was quite plump, and not very tall . . . his nose was turned up, his eyes snapping blue. He really looked quite like his Uncle Quentin, except that his uncle was taller and more heavily built, and his eyes popped more out of his head. The newcomer was wearing a French Army greatcoat, the skirts buttoned back as the poilus wore them; and on his head a flanged French Army steel helmet. In his left hand he carried a lighted cigar.

Boy and his uncle recognized him at the same moment, though only Quentin spoke the name aloud, "Winston Churchill!" he gasped.

"The same," Churchill said, "and I trust you will permit me to smoke in your trenches. It is a vice I cannot tame."

Winston Churchill, Boy thought. One didn't often see ex-Cabinet Ministers in the front line, especially not in uniform.

"You look astounded, Rowland," Churchill said, pulling out a cigar case and offering Quentin one. "Perhaps you think I have been conscripted?"

"No, no!" Quentin exclaimed, "only I didn't know . . . No, thanks."

"The air is cleaner here than it is in the Palace of Westminster," Churchill said. "I can think of a good many gentlemen in England now abed who would much benefit from being caught in the net of conscription . . . but those who would benefit the most are also the most adept at slipping through the meshes. It is a law of nature. Preservation of the slipperiest."

Quentin laughed suddenly, and his constraint melted. "Come into the dugout and I'll show you the trench map of our sector, and then

27

we'll go round . . . and later fix details of the relief. My Adjutant and R.S.M. are here . . . "

"Mine, too. I would not dream of venturing into the zone of battle without such competent dragomen . . . What time is it?"

Quentin looked at his watch. "Ten past ten."

"Ah. Time to toast our acquaintanceship." He produced a silver flask from the back pocket of his greatcoat. "In the dugout? And perhaps you can supply us with a modicum of water . . . a very small modicum, sir."

He preceded them down the steps into the dugout, drawing comfortably on his cigar.

*　　*　　*　　*

The five private soldiers sat in the back room of the *estaminet*, singing softly, bottles of *vin blanc* on the bare table beside them, glasses in hand. The top brass buttons of all their tunics were undone, and they were not carrying gas masks, and their heads were bare; but the bowl-like steel helmets were slung over the backs of the chairs, or hung on the coat rack with their greatcoats.

> *She was poor but she was honest,*
> *Victim of a rich man's whim:*
> *For he wooed and he seduced her,*
> *And she had a child by him.*

Private Stan Quick sang the verse in a pleasant tenor, exaggerating the cockney accent, as was customary whenever this song was sung. All five joined in the chorus:

> *It's the syme the whole world over,*
> *It's the poor what gets the blyme,*
> *While the rich gets all the pleasure,*
> *Ain't it all a bleeding shyme!*

Quick began the second verse, while the others drank, hummed or sang, *sotto voce*:

> *Then she cyme to London city*
> *To recover her fair nyme,*
> *But another man seduced her*
> *And she lost her nyme agyne!*
>
> *Oh, it's the syme the whole world over,*
> *It's the poor what gets the blyme,*

While the rich gets all the pleasure,
Ain't it all a bleeding shyme!

One of the soldiers pushed back his chair with a loud scrape and yelled, "Madame Frog, more van blong!" He tried to get up, staggered, and nearly fell. Quick broke off his singing to say amiably, "You've had enough, Harry!"

The owner of the *estaminet* came through from the front room, a slight woman dressed in black, about forty-five, hard of eye.

England yelled again, "More van blong!"

"*Tais-toi*," she snapped. "Ze militaire police will come."

"Fuck the M.P.s, I want some more van blong!"

Madame went out, returning a few seconds later with a bottle. She cradled it in one hand and held out the other, palm up—"Four francs."

"Four francs!" the soldiers cried in unison. "We only paid three for the first two bottles, and that was a bloody rook!"

"Differ'n wine," she said shrugging. "Bettair. No more of othair."

Grumbling, England smacked four silver francs into her hand. She gave him the bottle, and went out.

Quick began to sing again, but no one joined in, and he let a phrase die on his lips.

"Fuck the French," Harry England said sullenly. "Fucking robbers, that's what they are. The whole bloody lot of them."

"Robbers or whores . . . or both," Bob Jevons said, whose father was the baker in Walstone: as Harry England's was the blacksmith, and Charlie "Dusty" Miller's the stationmaster; and Stan Quick's the postman; the fifth man, an old regular with nineteen years service, mostly in India, was called Lucas, an unemployed laborer before taking the King's shilling to avoid starvation in the slums of Birmingham.

"Don't take it so hard," Lucas said now. "Afore we go back up the line, we'll have a few chickens and ducks out of these bleeding Frogs. Are we in France or Belgium?"

" 'Oo the 'ell cares? Wot's the difference?"

"It is in France, just. Like Armenteers," Quick said, breaking once more into song.

Two German officers crossed the Rhine, parly voo,
Two German officers crossed the Rhine, parly voo,
Two German officers crossed the Rhine,
To fuck the women and drink the wine, inky pinky parly voo!

Madame appeared, her sour mouth more tightly pursed than ever. "*Taisez-vous!*" she snarled. "Be more quiet, or I call militaire police!"

The old soldier got up. He had drunk near a bottle of wine to himself but his leathery face showed no sign of it. He said over his shoulder, "Got to treat these Frog cunts nice . . . " He reached the madame—"We very 'appy 'ere, madame . . . Good food, good van blong . . ."

Her stony face softened a little—"Am glad . . . " The rumble of shelling from up the line, ten miles to the east, continually shook the little brick building. Harry England's hand trembled round the wine bottle.

Old Soldier Lucas said, "*Bote thik hai . . . pukka memsahib* you are . . . We all *kushy avec* you, eh?" He put an arm half-way round her waist. She swung a small iron hard fist in a fierce sweep, landing on Lucas's nose. Blood spouted as she turned and strutted out, hurling "*Cochons!*" behind her.

Quick doubled up with laughter. "That's right, Snaky! Treat 'em nice, and they'll eat out of your hand!" He slapped Miller joyously on the back. England drank. Lucas dabbed his nose with a handkerchief soaked in wine, and mumbled, "Now wot the 'ell got into her? All I said was, we was 'appy 'ere . . . *Kushy*. That's 'Industani for 'appy."

"She doesn't speak Hindustani," Jevons said. "She wasn't with the old 2nd Battalion in the Shiny."

"Fuck the war!" Miller said. His best friend in Walstone when they were boys had been Sam Mayhew; and he'd seen Sam's life seeping out of his lungs in red froth, soaking his tunic . . . near Neuve Chapelle that was. Took two days to die. They'd both been eighteen. He still was by the calendar. The calendar didn't tell the truth any more.

"The war ain't so bad," Quick said, "it's the people you meet."

England said, "Why the 'ell did we join up, when we could ha' waited, and they'd have to come and get us?"

"Patriotism," Miller said. "Our King and Country needed us . . . "

"But they don't need half the fellows back there now, going out with our girls, earning five times what we do . . . then going on strike for more . . . eating off the fat of the land while we get Hoggin's fucking pig swill . . . "

"Aren't many left in Walstone, who could go," Bob Jevons said. "The gentry's sons have all gone, too. I can't imagine Walstone without us . . . Why, it's today Miss Stella's being married, and none of us there to drink her dad's champagne!"

"What'll it be like when it's all over?"

"We'll all be napoo . . . This war's going on for bloody ever, if you ask me."

"We didn't. 'Ave some more van blong . . . You'll 'ave to go out into the parlor and get some, Bob. Madame's not going to come back and let Snaky try it on with her again."

"I didn't," Lucas said aggrievedly. "She doesn't understand good English, that's what." Lucas's real Christian name was Rupert, but like all men in the British Army with that surname he was called Snaky, as all Millers and Rhodes were called Dusty.

There was a long silence, while the five soldiers stared into their wine glasses, drank, and stared again. The booming of artillery continued without cease, but they were too far away to hear small arms fire. Closer above in the night an aeroplane flew low, its engine thrumming in the dark. To drown out—useless hope—the shaking of the artillery, England said, "What do you reckon we'll be doing next?"

"Chatting," Lucas said shortly, "what the 'ell do you think we'll be doing?"

England drank—he was already three parts gone, his hand shaking worse than ever. Lucas noticed the trembling hand and said, "Your hand's shaking, man. Shell shock, that's what you've got. The Regimental will have you on a charge tomorrow. Only officers is allowed to get shell shock. Twenty-eight days Field Punishment Number One for you."

England ignored the badinage, or did not hear it. "It's time the fucking Frogs did something. After all, it's their fucking country, innit? But it's us what's dying for it."

Four French civilians came in by the back door, leaving their clogs just inside, on the scrubbed brick floor, and shuffling silently to a table the other side of the room in their bedroom slippers. They were all men in their fifties and sixties, wearing the black velvet coats and the blue trousers of small farmers or farm laborers. As they entered they acknowledged the presence of the British soldiers with a brief— "M'sieurs"; but did not glance in the soldiers' direction.

Madame had learned by some telepathic means that the farmers had come into her back room, and appeared from the parlor, smiling as much as the natural chicken's-arse formation of her mouth would allow. The soldiers heard the muttered French, then she went out again.

"Why aren't those bastards fighting?" England asked belligerently.

" 'Cos they're too old. Is *your* dad in uniform?"

Madame reappeared with two bottles and set them down on the table with glasses. One of the French farmers gave her money; it slipped out of her wet hand to the floor, and all five soldiers saw the two silver francs.

"Look at that!" England gasped, "two bottles of van blong, two francs. One franc a bottle . . . and what's the old bitch charging us?

31

Four francs!" He pushed his chair back hard, so that it flew backward across the room, crashing into the wall. He roared, "Madame, five more bottle van blong, one franc each, *un fronk*, see?" He staggered toward her waving an empty bottle from the table. Two of the farmers stood up, gesticulating; the others poured the wine, not looking up. Madame slipped out to the parlor, slamming the door behind her. England stared after her, followed, wrenched the door open, and found himself in the front room, crowded with British soldiers, some farm girls, and one or two older local men.

"This is bloody robbery!" he yelled. "She's jewing us four francs a bottle but giving it to her own blokes for one franc!"

He hurled the empty bottle at the plate glass mirror, engraved with a slogan for Byrrh, that hung on one wall.

All the British soldiers present jumped to their feet. "One franc? The old bitch!" They started throwing chairs through the windows, hurling bottles and glasses against the wall. The night air whistled fresh and cold through the room, blowing out the thick cloud of tobacco smoke from *caporals* and *bleus*. "Fucking Frogs!" England shouted.

Resignedly, his four friends from the back room joined in the riot of destruction. The *estaminet* had rapidly emptied of all civilians, except Madame, who stood with folded arms and rattrap mouth, watching the carnage. The noise rose to a fortissimo. With the windows open the massed artillery a few miles to the east joined in with heavy rumbling bass under the treble exclamations of shattering glass and the tenor thumps and crashes of chairs hitting against the walls.

The Military Police burst in, led by a corporal about six feet high, and as wide, with a broken nose, two cauliflower ears, and a brass knuckle duster on each fist.

For a few moments the noise increased to an even higher level as the soldiers, who had been destroying in earnest silence, broke into oaths and shouts at the redcaps; and, whereas before they had had no one to fight, now they faced the police with flailing fists and clubbed bottles. Harry England caught one redcap a fair blow in the nose and then he found himself wheeling, whirling, falling. Had he been hit? He did not know. He was on his knees, dragging himself to his feet . . . his unfocussed eyes caught blurred sight of a tunic, a tunic with the big pleated pockets of an officer . . . breeches . . . puttees to below the knee . . . an officer . . . He staggered to his feet and swung his fist, the blow landing fair and square in the middle of the long face above the collar and tie . . . three stars on the shoulder . . . a captain, good, good! "Take tha'," he yelled, the frustrations and fears of months boiling over. The officer fell back against the wall, his hand to his mouth.

He lowered his hand, spitting out a tooth, blood seeping from a corner of his mouth. It was Captain Kellaway.

England stood a moment appalled. He had hit the captain, his company commander. He tried to straighten up to attention, but the wine would not let him. The Military Police stood all round, breathing hard. Three men lay on the floor, unconscious. Everyone else stood rigidly at attention, staring straight ahead.

England staggered forward crying, "I'm sorry, sir . . . I didn't mean . . . Oh Jesus, sir, I didn't . . . " He fell into Kellaway's arms, weeping.

"We'll take him away, sir," the M.P. corporal said, grabbing England by the collar and dragging him off the officer's chest.

Kellaway dabbed his mouth with a khaki silk handkerchief. He looked round the room and said, "Who here's not in B Company?"

A few hands were raised. Kellaway turned to the corporal, "These are all my men, corporal. I'll see that they are punished . . . and that the damage is paid for."

The corporal said, "They was resisting arrest, sir . . . drunk an' disorderly . . . hobstructing the police in the hexecution of their duty . . . striking a hofficer . . ."

Kellaway said quietly, "And you are wearing knuckle dusters, corporal . . . Look, none of us want a fuss."

He turned to the Madame and, pulling a wallet from his pocket, handed her five five-pound notes. Her eyes gleamed and she said, "More. *Dix.* Ten!"

Lucas said, "She was charging us four francs a bottle of van blong, sir, and the Frogs one franc."

Kellaway spoke briefly to the Madame in fluent, virulent French. She almost blushed as he turned to Lucas—"You're the senior soldier? Fall everyone in and march them back to their billets. Give me names and companies of men not in B. Company commanders' orders for all of you at nine a.m." He went out, touching the peak of his cap.

The room full of soldiers looked at each other. The M.P. corporal said, "Lucky for you 'e came in. You lot deserve a good bashing in the Glass House." He went out, followed by his men.

Stan Quick said, "Wot was the captain doing 'ere? 'E knows this isn't an officers' *estaminet.*"

"Looking for handsome young soldiers—like you," Lucas said.

England groaned. "I'll knock your block off, Snaky. The captain's a . . . gentleman . . . good officer . . . I hit him . . . "

"He's a good officer . . . and a millionaire . . . and a pouf. You serve in the Shiny as long as I 'ave and you'll learn that a man can be anything . . . and still a good officer . . . or a bad one. All right. Get fell in." He picked up a bottle off a table near him and emptied it in a

33

single long glugging draught. He put it down, and said, "Never leave a full bottle or an empty cunt . . . By the right, quick—march!"

*   *   *   *

"Post's in, sir," the R.S.M.'s voice was loud in the doorway of the billet. "Two letters for you."

"Come in, Mr Nelson," Quentin said, holding out his hand for the letters. Neither was from Fiona. He hid his disappointment as he looked up at the warrant officer. "Anything to report, before I go to Brigade?"

"Nothing, sir. The men are grousing a bit, because of the route marches ordered for next week, but there'd be something wrong if they didn't grouse."

Quentin grunted. The men had to be kept fit, whether they liked it or not. The funny thing about spells out of the line was that the sick rate always went up. Up the line, living in cold or waterlogged trenches, sleeping in mud and filth, constantly harassed by shell fire, mortar bombs, and snipers, eating nothing but bully beef and army biscuits, averaging three hours sleep a night—the sick rate was so low that when it rose, you automatically suspected malingering. He said, "Tell the Adjutant I'll be leaving for Brigade in twenty minutes, and to have my horse ready. That's all."

The R.S.M. saluted and went out with a crash of nailed ammunition boots. Quentin opened the first letter, from his son: Guy now had a hundred hours in his logbook; a week ago he had almost crashed his aeroplane landing in a sudden snowstorm; he had bought a motor bike and was using it to drive round Salisbury Plain and Pewsey Vale; had his father ever seen Stonehenge?

Quentin smiled a little grimly, to himself. Where did the boy think the Regular Army used to train? He knew that part of the Plain between Tidworth and the Henge like the back of his hand. He continued reading. They were a ripping good crowd of fellows at Upavon; one had unfortunately already been killed; they'd all been sent up immediately afterward so that they wouldn't lose their nerve; Guy thought it would have been more sensible to spend some time telling them exactly what the poor chap had done wrong, so that they could avoid doing the same; he was really not very good at flying, but had so far come out first in all the machine-gun practices, both those on the ground and those fired from the air; it might be different with Boelcke or von Rackow firing back at him . . . Mummy wrote sometimes, and seemed well. Lots of love . . .

Mummy wrote sometimes. Well, he was glad Fiona wrote to someone, but she certainly did not write to him, her husband. His only news of her came through Guy. It was Guy who had told him, in a letter, that she had apparently changed her intention to leave them all. She'd told him—Guy—at Christmas, that she had long been in love with another man and was going away to live with him as soon as Guy joined the Royal Flying Corps; and in the New Year she'd gone to London . . . but had come back, saying nothing. Guy had suggested that she must have changed her mind about the other man, but Quentin found that hard to believe. He didn't know what to believe. Meanwhile, he felt unhappy, and had to be careful not to take it out on the eight hundred men whose lives were his responsibility.

He opened the other letter. His brother Tom's ship had been transferred from blockade duty to the Grand Fleet, and was with the main Battle Squadrons in Scapa Flow. It would be the best assignment in the Navy if the German High Seas Fleet ever came out to fight. In the meantime, it was the most boring imaginable: training, rehearsal, retraining, re-rehearsal, practice alerts, exercises, and always the grey skies, icy winds, and driving rain of the Orkneys. He wished Quentin luck, and advised him to take care of himself.

Quentin smiled again, again grimly. Take care of himself, as Commanding Officer of an infantry battalion on the Western Front? It could be done. Regrettably, it was being done, even by regular officers; but he, Quentin Rowland, could not do it. For twenty years and more he had had only one ambition in life—to command the 1st Battalion of the Weald Light Infantry, in action; and here he was, commanding it in the greatest war in history. He could not cheapen the fulfillment of his dream, however frightened he became and, good heavens, up there, only a madman would not be frightened, at times.

His nephew, Boy Rowland, came in, saluting, followed by a lieutenant of Royal Engineers, who announced that Corps Headquarters were sending him round all battalions in rest areas to run a short course in the care and management of Bangalore torpedoes. "Good, good!" Quentin said, standing up. He felt unaccountably jovial, and said, "Fix it up with my adjutant here . . . Are you mad, married, or Methodist, eh?" He always liked to put visiting sappers and gunners at ease, just as much as he disliked to see red-tabbed staff officers. But the engineer drew himself up and said, "I'm a Wesleyan, sir, and married, but I don't see . . . "

"Sorry," Quentin mumbled, "just a joke we used to make about regular sapper officers."

The lieutenant said coldly, "I am not a regular, sir. Before the war I was assistant chief sewage engineer of Cardiff."

Outside, over the insistent moaning of the wind, they all heard the rapid thud of hoof beats. Boy turned as a soldier burst in through the door, pulled himself together, and saluted—"Message from Brigade, sir. Most Immediate."

Quentin took it and read, while Boy scribbled his signature on the receipt form. The messenger saluted again and ran out. A moment later they heard the galloping hoof beats again, receding.

Quentin looked up—"G.H.Q. believe a heavy German attack against the French is imminent, probably round Verdun. They intend to mass troops in the Arras area, to take advantage of any weakening of the German positions there. The division is to move at once. Our leading companies to entrain at Armentières at twelve noon."

Boy looked at his watch. "It's nine now, sir . . . and Armentières is six miles away." He hurried out, and a moment later the Quarter-guard bugler blew the battalion call, followed by Stand To, then Officers.

The Daily Telegraph, Saturday, February 5, 1916

OVERALLS FOR WORKERS
NEW SHOP FEATURE

Observant people begin to notice little changes that are both interesting and significant in regard to the arrangement of shop windows. A year ago the overall would probably not have been displayed in them, or if it had been it would have found a place along with aprons, round towels, and similar useful but not very attractive wares. Within the last few weeks, however, it has leaped into all the prominence that can be accorded to the dress or the hat. In one great sale at least it has figured among the bargains likely to prove especially alluring, and Oxford-street, Kensington, and other popular centres of shopping have shown it with such labels as "For munition workers," or "Correct pattern for office wear."

. . . The cotton overall has been adopted by the young women who are now serving behind the grocers' counters . . . It is worn, too, by the girl attendants in lifts at large shops or in blocks of offices . . . Further it is taking a more glorified form, in wool or silk, as a "slip on" dress that the girl can assume at her desk, in order to save the more expensive tailored suit in which she arrives at and leaves her office. With the reduced demands for costumes, either of the coat and skirt or one-piece order, the making of the overall, which is a comparatively simple matter, is helping to adjust any displacement of labour that might have arisen in regard to the older and less adaptable of the dress makers.

The writer meant skirted overalls, Christopher Cate said to himself; though some women were wearing the trousered sort. Shocking, at first, but the jobs they were doing really demanded them. They'd be indecent if they were climbing ladders, and painting high walls and cleaning windows, in skirts . . .

Weddings were exhausting. He yawned. Sunday morning, and in an hour he'd have to get ready for church. There was the Sunday paper on the desk . . . he'd never catch up at this rate . . . have to make a determined attack on it after lunch, instead of having a snooze . . . also make notes for tomorrow's meeting of the Mid-Scarrow War Problems Committee . . .

His son came in—"Daddy, I have to go back to school after lunch."

"I know, Laurence," Cate said cheerfully, "I've warned Norton."

"Cyril the stable boy's joined up, hasn't he?"

Cate nodded. "Yes, and barely sixteen . . . gave a false age, of course. Plenty of spirit, that boy has, even if he did insist on wearing those garish ties. Well, I suppose that showed his spirit, too."

Laurence said, "Wish I could go, too." Cate looked up—"You wait till the end of the summer term, Laurence. Officers must have a little more maturity."

Laurence changed the subject. "Can you give me five bob, Daddy? I saw a book called *Raptors of the World*, in the bookshop window in Godalming. I'd love to buy it."

Cate fished in his pocket and gave his son two half crowns. "Here you are." He found another half crown—"And while you're there, buy Ian Hay's new book, *The First Hundred Thousand*. It'll tell you a lot about the sort of men you'll be commanding. It's a citizen Army now."

"All right, Daddy," Laurence said, pocketing the coins. Outside the door he heaved a deep, silent sigh and went to find Jack and Jill, the cocker spaniels, to take them for a short walk before it came time to go to church.

Hedlington, Kent: February 14, 1916

3 Bob Stratton sat in the kitchen, where he always had his high tea, enjoying the sausage and mash that had been served with it today. He was sixty-seven, works foreman at the Rowland Motor Car Company factory. It was bright in there, the gas mantle hissing low over the table with its blue-and-white-checkered cloth. Steam rose from the kettle, and the aroma from the tea filled his nostrils. The two women, Jane, his wife, and Nellie, the servant girl, stood attentively behind him, watching to see what he wanted, Jane now and then murmuring an order to the girl in a low voice.

Without looking up Bob said, "Where's Ethel?"

"Helping Anne with the children. She'll be back by seven . . . Mr Willibanks asked her to marry him again. Came round here special, at dinner time. She said no."

"Still hoping Fagioletti will come back to her?"

"She is . . . but he won't." There was a triumphant note in his wife's voice, and Bob looked up, "How do you know?"

" 'Cos he's going to get his call up notice!"

"But they're not taking married men."

"That's just it! He divorced our Ethel so he could live with that dirty Italian woman he had . . . making Ethel sign that paper she'd gone with other men when she hadn't looked at one, the very idea! But he's not married! So I wrote to the Army people who ought to know that . . . Frank found out who I should write to, and I did, I gave them his name and address and told them he's British by naturalization, as he says, though he'll never be an Englishman if he lives to be a hundred, just a dago . . ."

Bob swallowed a piece of sausage. She was a peaceable enough woman most of the time, but threaten any of her children and she became a tigress . . . out for blood. But this time she was cutting off her nose to spite her face, if their daughter, Ethel, really still loved Fagioletti. A live waiter might, some day, come back and make her happy: a dead soldier never could. They'd had two sons at the war, but now it was only one—Fred, the officer, with the Wealds somewhere out there. The other, Frank, was a sergeant with the Wealds when he'd been badly wounded just before Christmas last year; he was in Lady Blackwell's Hospital here in Hedlington . . . and now one of the two sons-in-law was likely going out there . . .

He finished his cup of tea, nodded to the two women, went out of the room, down the passage, and out of the back door. He always went to his shed at the bottom of the garden after his high tea; there was no need to say anything.

Once inside the shed he lit the gas mantle, closed and bolted the door behind him, placed a certain picture, an advertisement for a motor car, in the window, facing outwards, drew the curtains, stood back, and stared hungrily, like a man gloating over a beautiful, waiting woman: only what he was looking at was a beauty of steel and chrome, the racing motor cycle he was building here for an attack on the world's speed record—Victoria. The handlebars were curved out and down, so that the rider would lie almost flat along the petrol tank, offering little resistance to the wind. The tires were thin and hard, offering little resistance to the road. The engine had two big cylinders. There was no headlamp, nor place for one—no carrier, no mudguards . . . a naked, gleaming beauty, existing for only one purpose.

Bob ran his hand slowly over her, then sat down and stared . . . the vee-twin cylinder engine was a Blumfield . . . he had himself changed the valves from side to overhead, with the help of some high tensile steel that Guy Rowland had got for him from an aircraft company . . . lightweight wheels . . . frame of steel tubing built by Bob himself following Cotton's theories . . . Sturmey Archer gearbox and chain drive for both primary and final drive. He'd started with chain primary and rubber vee-belt final drive, but the vee-belt just wasn't capable of transmitting the power output he was attaining . . . He'd got her up to 92 but he desperately wanted to be the first man to take a motor cycle over 100 miles an hour. What more could he do to Victoria to reach that goal?

Most of the new work was being done over in America. They were building engines with hemispherical combustion chambers, and valve cutaways in the piston tops. And they were using alcohol fuel. He could try that. The engine ran cooler, he'd read—so he could cut off some of the cooling fins on the cylinders, reducing weight. Another way to reduce weight would be to plane down the fly wheel . . . another, to use still narrower tires on the front wheel, and that, according to the technical papers, improved steering as well . . .

The tap at the window made him start violently, for he had forgotten he had put the picture there. He lowered the light and opened the door. The girl who slipped in was about four feet eleven inches tall, pale skinned, lank haired. She was wearing a dress a little below her knees, torn but carefully patched in half a dozen places. On her feet she wore a pair of men's boots, several sizes too large for her, with no stockings. As Bob closed and locked the door behind her, he felt a powerful stirring in his loins . . . there were breasts budding under the thin material of the dress, but they were not yet big enough to put him off. It was still a girl. He was fully erect and straining inside his trousers. It would be there, the slit, dark, mysterious, hairless, pouting from the bulge of flesh that curved down between the thin thighs. He reached out and lifted the dress. She was wearing no drawers, and as the dress rose, the girl saying nothing, her loins came into view. Bob stared, trembling, uncontrollable ecstasy flowing out from him as though from a gaping wound. Oh God, the slit was half hidden by hair, and there was a little patch of it on the mound above. His erection drooped and faded as he let the dress drop. "You've grown," he said accusingly. He turned away in disgust and disappointment. This was a woman, not a girl.

His back to her, he heard her say, "I'm going to 'ave a baby."

He held onto the bench for support, listening, her voice a mile away.

" . . . I 'ad the bleeding twice, before I 'ad any 'air . . . then I come 'ere . . . and I didn't bleed no more . . . three months . . . I'm in the family way."

"How do you know?" he said, the words wrung from him.

"Garn!" she said. "Fink I don't know all about it? Wiv all the kids muvver's 'ad?"

He felt that the shed was swinging slowly round him, and clung more firmly to the work bench. How old was she? Eleven, twelve, just, perhaps? He groaned aloud as the girl said, "Well, wot are you going to do?"

"Who have you told . . . talked to?"

"No one, 'course. But me muvver'll guess soon."

He turned and stared at her. It had had to come and now it was here. One anonymous letter to Jane, warning her that her husband had young girls, he had intercepted before she had seen; and for a while after that he had fought off the compulsion to do it. Also, he had all along told himself that since God had laid the curse on him, it was up to God to decide his fate . . . gaol, or a miraculous release from the compulsion, or more years of shuddering relief in their thin, formless bodies.

He said, "Don't tell anyone. I've got to think. Find someone . . ."

The girl said, "Me granddad's Woman gets rid of babies."

"Who's that?"

"Probyn Gorse's Woman, down to Walstone."

Bob said, "I've heard of him . . . poacher, he is . . ."

"That's right."

"I'll go and see her. With you. Next Sunday, we'll go down, eh? Look, here's two bob. Take the first train down, Sunday. Tell your mum you got the money running errands for the men at the factory, and you want to see your granddad . . . I'll be on the same train. But we don't talk or anything, see? I'll ask my way and when I turn up, you go out and play . . . Your granddad's Woman could do with some money, eh?"

" 'Ow much?" she said.

"Ten quid."

"You can give 'er five . . . and five to me," she said, holding out her thin hand.

"On Sunday," he muttered. His head was splitting and he had an overpowering need to vomit. The girl watched him indifferently.

*   *   *   *

Richard Rowland, Harry Rowland's eldest son, sat in his office at the Rowland Motor Car Company, waiting. It was nearly four o'clock and Bob Stratton would be along any moment from his office down the corridor, just past the point where the linoleum ended and the bare concrete began. Richard leaned back in the swivel chair which his father had installed—what, twenty years ago?—eyeing the pictures on the wall . . . a sepia photograph, much enlarged, of the first motor car turned out after Rowland's had changed from motor bicycles; the visit by the Duke of Connaught in '88; a 1912 impression of the plant as a whole, with smoke belching from chimneys and a line of barges loaded with motor cars sliding away down the Scarrow . . . a lot of artist's license in that one; and a good photo of himself, when young, with his father and Bob Stratton . . . they were both clean shaven in those days, and now both bearded. It was all old fashioned, faintly grimy, redolent of the age of coal and mud and clogs; but modern factories ought to be clean, dust free, run by electricity. You ought to be able to eat a meal off the floor, or off the block of one of your own engines. Instead of old photographs there ought to be diagrams on

41

the walls here, production graphs, output and manpower charts; but he hadn't the heart to change anything when his father handed over control of the firm to him after the election last November. And now perhaps it was too late.

He sat straighter and swung the chair round slowly as he heard the knock on the door. Bob Stratton entered without more ado, as was the custom at Rowland's. He stopped the other side of the desk, his bowler hat set firm on his head, his strong craftsman's hands folded across his belly, over his Albert, the gold watch chain with half sovereign seals that looped from one waistcoat pocket to the other. His square-cut beard and thinning hair were both pepper and salt, and he wore rimless glasses. A snub nose sat in the middle of his lined, square face.

He said, "If they haven't telephoned, we'll have to do something, Mr Richard. The men are on their last jobs . . . and half of them aren't needed on those now. They're sitting around, at the benches, talking, waiting."

Richard said, "I've heard nothing." They both knew that in fact he had heard something—last Tuesday: that the War Office was not interested in ordering the mobile machine-gun platform on a Rowland chassis, which Richard had designed for use in defence of airfields and large headquarters against saboteurs or enemy raiders. Nor was the Admiralty.

Stratton said, "I suppose Mr Harry couldn't do anything."

Richard took off his thick glasses and shook his head. His father had been an M.P. since last November; and had done what he could to get the War Office to order the mobile machine-gun vehicle; but there was a limit to what he could, or ought, to do, as an interested party.

" 'Tis a good idea," Bob said. "They should have taken it."

Richard said, "They should. But there aren't many people with imagination in Whitehall, I'm afraid. And everyone's so busy staring at the trees—the problems under their noses—that they can't look up and see the wood . . . new ideas, new ways to overcome them—get through the trees if you like . . . We'll convert to munitions, Bob. I've seen this coming for some time, and have been making inquiries in the proper quarters. We have a definite government offer of financing to convert, and of course, a guarantee that all the shells we make or fill will be bought. We'll be privately owned, but otherwise we'll be just the same as a National Shell Filling Factory. There's an Assistant Superintendent at Woolwich Arsenal who's an expert on conversion. They'll send him down as soon as we ask for him."

Bob sat down heavily. He did not normally sit down in this office unless asked to, but he was feeling tired, and old, and worried. Perhaps he should have retired when Mr Harry did, after all. That damned girl, turned out to be really a woman when she was still looking like a girl. He pushed the bowler hat to the back of his head—"We'll have to lay off most of the men, Mr Richard."

"We'll need some to make the conversion."

Bob nodded. "That's true, but when we've done that, and we're ready to fill shells, a lot of men will not be coming back at all. We won't need their trades. I've seen a Filling Factory, and it's mostly manual labour, unskilled, too."

"It'll be mostly women," Richard said. "That's why I've been trying to get more women into the plant since I took over . . . and my father had started before that, as you know."

Bob said, "I didn't like it, but he was right. If we hadn't taken women we'd 'a' had to close the gates long since."

"Do you have a list of everyone who works here now?"

"Miss Harcourt has in her office, for the payrolls. But I know them all, and their trades."

"We'll have to make some sort of announcement this afternoon before they leave."

"Miss Harcourt has the lay-off slips all typed out. It's only a question of who we give 'em to. An' that won't be easy till the man from Woolwich comes down and shows us what changes we have to make."

"Right. Look, we'll give them all an extra day's wage by not handing out the slips until tomorrow. Then, I'll get everyone together in the main machine room and tell them what's happening. We'll hand out lay-off slips to everyone, except Miss Harcourt, Beckett the night watchman and two others to caretake in the daytime. You choose those—take Willum Gorse for one . . . Then you and I will go through the roll, and decide first, whom we will probably need to make the conversions . . . and finally, whom we can recommend to Hedlington Aircraft, or the J.M.C."

"The Aircraft'll only be wanting the fabric men and women. J.M.C. might take some others," Bob said gloomily. What if the girl died? They did, from abortions, he knew.

Richard said, "Before I do anything else, I'll call the Ministry of Munitions. They've got some good men there—Lloyd George put them in. They act, not just write memoranda." He reached out for the telephone, and, while Bob Stratton waited, sucking his teeth and looking sightlessly at the Duke of Connaught visiting the plant in '88, half listening to his employer, Richard spoke: "Ministry of Munitions . . . Mr Smiley, please . . . Smiley, Richard Rowland, of the Rowland Motor Car Company in Hedlington here . . . No, the War Office didn't manage to persuade the Navy to take the vehicle, so it'll have to be shells . . . Thanks, so am I. . . . Yes . . . Yes . . . As soon as

43

possible. I have several hundred men and women who will be laid off tomorrow . . . He can come down tomorrow? That's wonderful! . . . Three weeks, if we can install a new big boiler and lagged piping in the time, and build the boiler house. All right. Thanks. Come down yourself to see how we're doing. Any time. We can still give you a good lunch at the South-Eastern . . . and we have to fix the financing. Come soon."

He put down the telephone and turned to Bob—"Well, that's that. So round about April 7th we'll be reborn as Rowland's Shell Filling Factory. It'll be an occasion for a celebration, I suppose."

"Or a wake," Bob said gloomily. The plant would be changed out of recognition—pipes all over the place, wet floors, hand washing all the time, and everywhere—women. He opened his mouth to say what was on his mind when there was a knock at the door and three women entered, their hair hidden under blue factory caps, like mob caps, shirt sleeves carefully buttoned down, long skirts stopping six inches short of the ground to show high buttoned boots of black leather.

Bob stood up instinctively; then, silently, cursing himself sat down again. He *could* not get used to women in the factory. They had no business here, especially ladies, the sort the other women called Miaows: and two of these were Miaows. One of the two spoke, "Mr Rowland, we've come to complain about the treatment the men are giving us in this factory. We've tried to grin and bear it. We've hoped the supervisory staff would notice, and take action. We've hoped that the men would tire of this stupid prep school persecution. But now our patience is exhausted."

Richard said, "What's the matter, Miss Delauncey?"

"Ever since we have been employed here some men—not all, I will say that—have made systematic efforts to hinder us in the efficient execution of our work."

"Why should they . . . ? " Richard began; then stopped. Everyone knew why men would do such a thing: to make the women seem helpless and inefficient, and so get them fired; and so preserve the jobs for themselves; and so avoid conscription and the trenches of Flanders. He said, "What do they do?"

"They don't pass us tools when we need them, the sort of tools that are meant to be handed round any particular bench. If one of our lathes breaks down, they pretend to help us mend it, but actually make it worse. They send us to Coventry, for no reason except that we are women. They pour oil into our drawers, and then nail them up. They . . . "

Richard had a hard time suppressing a smile at the picture *that* conjured up; but this was a serious matter. He turned to Bob, "I know there's been friction. I suppose it's inevitable, in the circumstances, but I didn't know it was as bad as this."

He himself had given only part time supervision to Rowland's since the Hedlington Aircraft Company had been founded; as he was also Managing Director of the Jupiter Motor Company. In fact he was Fairfax, Gottlieb's chief executive for all their English investments: Fairfax, Gottlieb was the New York investment bank of which Stephen Merritt was Chairman of the Board. Bob Stratton had been acting as manager of Rowland's, rather than as works foreman; and obviously he had not been paying much attention to the plight of the women. Perhaps he didn't want to.

Bob said, "The women aren't as good, man for man. How could they be? They never seen a lathe before. Stands to reason . . . "

The working class woman, standing between the two Miaows, said emphatically, "You just look the other way, Mr Stratton, that's wot . . . 'cos you don't want us 'ere, ain't that the truth? Well, we're 'ere to stay, an' 'elp win the war, so you know wot you can do wiv it. Stuff it up your bleeding arse, that's wot!"

"Really, Miss Corbett—" Richard began.

"Mrs Corbett, Mr Rowland. Me 'usban's in the 1st Battalion of the Wealds . . . Lance Corporal. *An'* I'm working to put shoes on my kids' feet. You try to raise three little 'uns on a Lance Corporal's allotment."

Richard turned to Bob, "I think you'll have to speak to the floor and shop foremen about this, Bob. And tomorrow, I'll make the point that Mrs Corbett made just now—that the women are here to win the war, and it's up to us men to help them, not out of mere chivalry, but out of patriotism."

Miss Delauncey said, "I hope your talk takes effect, or we'll have no alternative but to go on strike. And I should warn you that we—all the women who work here—have decided that it is time we had an increase in pay. None of us is getting more than twenty-two shillings a week now, for an eight-hour six-day week, on the pretence that we are untrained and unskilled beginners . . . but in many cases we have long since passed that point."

"I know," Richard said. "We plan to increase all wages soon."

What did they want? Didn't they realize that a soldier in the trenches was getting about ten shillings for a twenty-four-hour seven-day week?

"Thank you," he said, standing up. The women hesitated, then turned and filed out, the two Miaows marching firmly out ahead of the Khaki Girl, Mrs Corbett.

"Pheew!" Richard exclaimed as the door closed behind them.

Then, "Well, back to business. Where are we going to build the boiler house? Let's go and . . . "

The door flew open, without the customary knock, and a large man with a pleasant, vaguely vacant expression behind the wide eyes, hurried in, "Mr Richard . . . Bert's in there, telling them to break everything!"

Richard and Bob stood up simultaneously. The big man was Willum Gorse, eldest son of the old poacher of Walstone, Probyn Gorse, and father of the twins Florinda and Fletcher Gorse, and of four other children. Bert Gorse was Willum's fiery half-brother, son of Probyn by his second Woman, whom he had taken after Willum's mother died; he never married either of those, or his current Woman.

Willum gabbled, "He's in the main machine shop now, Mr Richard. He's speaking to the men, and shouting and saying bad things, but he can't help it, Mr Richard. His mum always beat him and me when we was nippers, and . . . "

Richard listened no more, but hurried out, and, with Bob Stratton at his heels and Willum Gorse shambling fast behind, ran down the passage, across the yard and into the main machine shop.

The silence struck him at once. Only the lineshafting up in the roof turned; the driving belts hung motionless on their pulleys. The electric lights shone harshly down on rows of abandoned machines and tools. At the far end four black-painted Rowland Rubys—the last that would ever be made, probably—stood near the great exit doors, all but finished. Between him and the four cars half the total work force of the factory—two hundred men and women—were crowded round a bench in the middle of the huge room. Bert Gorse was standing on the bench, and now, as they walked forward at a slower pace they could hear his voice, echoing in the cavernous shop. In a moment they made out some of his words: "Rowland's is going to close . . . tomorrow or the next day, no one knows, except the bosses . . . but it's closing . . . "

By now Richard and Bob were close at the backs of the crowd. Willum had fallen aside, his powerful hands wringing as he gazed up at his small, angry half-brother.

Bert continued, "So we'll all get lay-off slips . . . and some of us will get what I already have." He pulled a paper out of his coat pocket and waved it in the air. "A call-up notice! Work today, out of a job tomorrow, blown to bits the day after!"

Richard noticed that the crowd close round Bert was all men. The one-third of the work force that was female was standing in groups round the walls, arms folded, holding themselves aloof from the men.

Bert shouted, "You'll get the call-ups as soon as you're out of here, unless you're married . . . and that won't save you for long, mark my words! Well, I'm going to stay at home! They're not going to get Bert Gorse out of the way and shot to bits that easy, not on your life, they ain't!"

"They'll come and get us, if we're called up," a voice cried. "Wot's the use?"

"There's ways," Bert shouted. "Don't go! None of you. Tell 'em to fuck 'emselves! Stand together!"

" 'Ow do you know about us being laid off?" another voice called, anxiety clear in the pitch.

Richard was about to cut in, but Bert, who had just noticed him, forestalled him, yelling, "I *know*. The War Office don't want to buy Mr Richard's mobile machine-gun vehicle, and Rowland's is going to close until they can refit to fill shells. And all us men will be out of work, and then in the Army, because they'll use only women with the shells!" He seized a huge ball-peen hammer off the bench and waved it over his head. "Show 'em what we think of them!" He leaped down and smashed the hammer into the head of a turret lathe. A piece flew out of its cast-iron driving pulley and Bert swung again. A confused roar arose from the crowd of men, at first formless, but gathering shape and anger as it grew. Other loose equipment was seized and wielded. The vast room echoed to shouts, the clang of steel on steel, the crunch of glass. Tool bins toppled, their contents rolling across the floor, driving belts sagged as they were cut.

Richard shouted in Bob's ear—"Call the police!" Bob pushed away through the mob as Richard jumped onto the bench. His voice cracked in his effort to make the angry and frightened men hear— "Stop!" he screamed. "Think! . . . What choice do we have? No one can buy or use our cars because of the war . . . what else can we do? . . . Some of you will have jobs here . . . but how can we employ master mechanics pouring lyddite into shell cases, turning screw caps? We'll try to find other, suitable work for anyone displaced. For God's sake, stop!"

But the destruction went on and slowly Richard lowered his arms. They were animals. They deserved the Western Front, and by God he'd see that as many as possible were sent there. He walked out, and back to his office, looking neither to right nor left, his ears mentally stopped against the sounds of destruction behind him.

*   *   *   *

"He's coming down the road now," Probyn Gorse said. "You skip out and play by the river, Violet."

Violet and all Willum's younger children lived in Hedlington with their mother and father; only the elder twins, Florinda and Fletcher, lived here with their grandfather, and now Florinda was in London with the Marquess of Jarrow . . . and Violet had come down by train and hurried up from the station to tell her grandfather that she was pregnant, and that Mr Stratton was coming. Now she went out of the front door—the only door—and wriggled through the bushes to the bank of the Scarrow, where brambles and bracken hid her from the cottage. Inside, Probyn waited, sitting by the plain table. His Woman fed a few more chips of wood into the stove; his grandson Fletcher sat in another chair, this one backless, by the window, reading. Outside, the Duke of Clarence barked once, and they heard a man's voice— "Down, there!"—then the knock on the upper half of the door, which was in two parts, like a stable door.

"Come in," Probyn growled. The door opened, and Bob Stratton stood framed in his Sunday best, wearing gloves and a tweed overcoat with a cape attached, and of course his bowler hat and a stick with an ivory knob. He looked ill-at-ease in spite of his obvious prosperity and substance compared with the stark austerity of the cottage and everything in it.

"Mr Gorse?" he said.

Probyn nodded.

"I think we met once, some years ago, when Mr John had a lot of us from Rowland's for the day . . ."

"Maybe."

Bob looked at the Woman, then at Fletcher. Neither glanced in his direction. He cleared his throat—"I wish to speak to you privately, Mr Gorse."

Probyn said, "We don't have no secrets here."

Bob cleared his throat again. There was no help for it. He said heavily, "I have reason to believe that some boy has got your granddaughter Violet in the family way, Mr Gorse. She's run errands for Mrs Stratton and myself, and I thought you ought to know. She's too young to have a baby and care for it, so . . ." He pulled a five pound note from the wallet, "If your, ah, lady will do the necessary so Violet doesn't have it, I'll be happy to pay."

The note lay on the table by Probyn's elbow. Fletcher's lips moved as he read Shelley's *Mont Blanc* to himself, but he heard what was being said, too. Silly old bugger, he thought, as if we were going to believe that.

Probyn spoke over his shoulder, "Would you do it?"

The Woman said, "No."

Bob fumbled in the wallet for another fiver. The Woman said, "She's going to have a dozen afore she's finished, and none of 'em by a husband, so she'd best learn about it now."

48

Bob felt the sweat break out on his forehead, under the band of the bowler. "Please!" he pleaded, "her mother will go to the police . . ."

"No," the Woman said.

Bob took off his hat and wiped his forehead. He looked pleadingly at Probyn, "Can't you help me . . . as man to man . . . you understand."

"Yes," Probyn said shortly.

Bob waited. In a minute he would cry. He must not so demean himself in front of these people. The notes lay on the table. At last he picked them up, and put them back in his wallet.

He turned to leave, and Probyn said, "You'd best tell your wife."

Bob nodded. Tomorrow . . . the day after . . . tonight. There was nothing else for it. God had turned his back.

* * * *

Bob Stratton reached Lady Blackwell's Hospital at four the same afternoon, after returning to Hedlington before lunch, eating his normal large Sunday dinner, and having a nap: in fact only lying down, and hoping that sleep would come, which it did not. At last he got up, restless, and after a while Jane said, "Why don't you go and see Frank? You haven't seen him for a week."

His eldest son was walking carefully round the ward in blue convalescent uniform when Bob arrived. On recognizing his father he said, "Hullo, Dad . . . Sit down . . . tell me about the riot at Rowland's. I've heard all sorts of stories."

Bob sat down in the chair by the bed, and Frank lowered himself onto the edge of the bed. Bob said, "Bert Gorse egged the men on to break up the place because we were going to have to give them all their notices, and then, he said, they'd all be called up."

Frank said, "Do most of 'em a lot of good, if they were. And the R.E.s could use them."

"They broke up some of the machinery. We had to send for the police. We thought there'd be trouble again next day, when they were to come and hear Mr Richard speak and get their slips . . . There wasn't. Mr Richard never said anything about the trouble, just about the shell-filling factory, and they clapped him when he'd finished . . ."

"They were all exhausted and frightened, like, by what they'd done," Frank said reflectively. "Did they do much damage?"

Bob said, "Thousands of pounds, but the insurance will cover some of it, and we'd have had to get all of it off the floor anyway, so it didn't turn out so bad as it seemed at first . . . You're looking well, Frank, considering."

"You look a mite peaked, Dad," Frank said. "That trouble at Rowland's must have worried you."

Bob nodded. Could he tell Frank about his real trouble?

Frank said, "They're going to give me a physical exam tomorrow, and then let me out for a month's convalescence."

"Even before they know the result of the examination?"

"Ah, that's just to decide whether I'll ever be fit for active service again."

"You'll never be . . . not with only one kidney, and a hole in your lung and two or three in your tripes."

Frank was pale and thin, but otherwise looked well. He was still wearing the beard that he had grown when he was appointed Pioneer Sergeant of the 1st Battalion the Weald Light Infantry—for Pioneer Sergeants were the only men in the Army allowed to wear a beard. As Bob had learned, his son, a superb mechanic and craftsman, had been greatly influenced by his seventeen months in the Army, particularly his year in France.

He said, "They'll want you as foreman at Hedlington Aircraft, as soon as you're fit. Mr Richard told me. You'll never go back to France."

"I will Dad, if I'm able. I'm Pioneer Sergeant . . . but I'd like to have a little time with Anne and the nippers first, that I would."

"You'll have the rest of your life," Bob said. He got up to go. "Anything you want?"

"No, Dad. Just give my love to Mum and tell her I'll be seeing her the day after tomorrow, when they let me out . . . Heard anything from Fred? *Mister* Fred, now." He laughed cheerfully.

Bob said, "He was all right in his last letter. They were out of the line, he said. No shelling, but trouble with the French civilians and the military police."

"Same as it always was, and always will be, I suppose," Frank said. "Well, thanks for visiting, Dad."

He accompanied his father to the door of the ward, and watched him until he turned a corner of the corridor, and was lost to sight. The old man's shoulders are stooped, he thought, and his head sagging. Getting old, like all of us.

*   *   *   *

The two elderly women sat alone in the big drawing room of Laburnum Lodge. Jane Stratton kept a handkerchief to her eyes, and cried and sobbed intermittently throughout; but Rose Rowland, sitting bolt upright, almost motionless, was the sicker of the two, the skin of her face yellowish and taut across the bones, the thinning hair hidden under a lace cap, her hands—one on the arm of her chair, the other holding one of Jane's—were those of a living skeleton.

"I don't understand," Jane sobbed, "girls . . . only ten, nine years old even, he said . . . just as long as they weren't women, grown up, like."

"I understand," Rose Rowland said gently, her voice weak.

"But why? . . . We've been married forty years this year, and I never said no . . . though he never was a great one for that . . ."

Rose waited a moment for the sobbing to subside, then said, "We must think about the girl first. I'll try to persuade Mary not to have Bob prosecuted. Prosecuting won't help Violet. Bob will have to pay Mary something, say five shillings a week, until the baby's grown up. You can afford that?"

"Oh yes, m'm, since Bob's been made manager."

"And he'll have to pay all the expenses of having the baby. If Mary agrees to this, she and Violet must promise not to say anything to anyone about who the father of the child is, because the police would have to prosecute on their own, if they heard . . . Neither Mr Harry nor Willum need to know anything about all this."

"Oh, no!" Jane muttered. "Mr Harry wouldn't believe that Bob could do such a thing, them knowing each other so long."

"I'm afraid at our age one learns that men can do anything . . . So, if Mary Gorse agrees, that will take care of Violet and the baby."

"Yes, m'm."

"Now we must think of Bob. Since I have been ill I have had a great deal of time to read. I have learned that there are things which seem like crimes . . . and are regarded as crimes by the law . . . which are in fact diseases . . . or compulsions . . . inevitable results of upbringing, of events that took place when the people concerned were very young. The study and treatment of all this is a new science, called alienism. There aren't many alienists in England yet, but there are some. One is a Dr Deerfield, who lives and practises here in Hedlington. He's an Austrian by birth, a Jew, from Vienna. He came to England about sixteen or seventeen years ago, changed his name from Hirschfeld to Deerfield, and was naturalized in, I think, 1908. He has a medical degree, of course—from Vienna. I have known him well for many years. I think Bob must see him, for treatment."

Jane looked doubtful, "What will he do? Look into Bob's head, like? He won't cut into him, will he?"

Rose shook her head, "No, there's no operation, though Dr Deerfield may give Bob some medicine . . . he's a real doctor, too, as I said, so if the trouble is physical—he'll find that out, before going on to the special treatment."

Jane said, "But . . . what does he *do*?"

"Gets the patient to talk," Rose said. "Tell all that they remember about their lives from the very beginning. He's looking for clues in the past that could explain what the person does in the present. Once the patient sees the connection he himself sees the origin of the compulsion, and can break free from it."

"Bob won't like that," Jane said doubtfully. "He's never talked about when he was a boy, let alone a child . . ."

"That's just the point," Rose said. "He's suppressing something."

"But . . ."

Rose said gently, "It's that or the police, Jane. Bob has to be stopped from ruining other little girls. Society will want to do it by sending him to gaol for a long time. This is better, isn't it?"

Jane began to sob again, mumbling, "Yes, m'm. He'll do it. I'll see that he does."

*   *   *   *

The Daily Telegraph, Thursday, February 24, 1916

WAR
FIERCE BATTLE TO THE NORTH OF VERDUN
ENEMY ATTACKS WITH SEVEN ARMY CORPS

Last night's communiqué said:

Paris, Wednesday (Midnight). **In the region north of Verdun the German attack has developed, as had been foreseen, into a very important action, for which powerful preparation had been made. The battle continued today with growing intensity, and was vigourously maintained by our troops, who inflicted extremely high losses on the enemy. The ceaseless bombardment with heavy shells, to which our artillery replied with equal violence, extended over a front of nearly 40 kilometres (25 miles) from Malancourt to the region in front of Etain.**

Attacks by German infantry in very large numbers, and comprising troops from seven different army corps, followed each other in succession during the day between Brabant-sur-Meuse and Ornes. At the entrance to the village of Haumont the enemy, despite all his efforts, was unable to dislodge us from our positions.

In the Caures Wood, the greater part of which we hold, our counter-attacks crushed the enemy offensive.

East of the Caures Wood the Germans succeeded in penetrating the Wavrille Wood after a series of sanguinary attacks . . .

2nd Year of the War—29th Week, 2nd Day

It is evident from the French and German official communiqués of Tuesday and yesterday that a very severe conflict, which may eventually assume the dimensions of a really great battle, has begun in the region a few miles to the north of the great fortress of Verdun . . .

So, another huge offensive had begun, Cate thought, another war within the framework of the whole gigantic conflict. He admitted that he was glad the blow had fallen on the French; then at once told himself that he was a fool to allow his thoughts to go in that direction. The Allies were in the war together, and if one fell, they all fell; and if the Germans planned to break the French at Verdun, England would obviously have to throw all her forces into the battle, one way or another, or let the Germans take on their enemies one at a time.

He got up, folding the paper. He was already dressed in breeches and Newmarket boots, for he had thought he would be riding . . . and now he knew where—to the cottage; to see his daughter, the bride; and tell her that Johnny's Aunt Isabel Kramer was coming down to spend the weekend at the Manor, in two days' time.

Walstone, Kent: Saturday, February 26, 1916

4 A cold wind from the north blew down the furrows, and there was a hint of snow in the air, the low sun half obscured by a denseness of the atmosphere close to the ground. Probyn Gorse and his grandson, Fletcher, sat under a hedge at the corner of Howard Ashcraft's thirty-acre field of winter wheat, their backs to the hedge, facing the sun. The lame lurcher, Duke of Clarence, lay silent at Probyn's feet. The men had been poaching partridges.

"Are they going to take Bert to court?" Fletcher asked.

Probyn sucked on his teeth and watched the edge of the wood opposite. Without turning his head he said, "Can't do anything to a man for blowing off his own big toe. It's his, not theirs."

"But they can say he did it so they couldn't take him for the Army, can't they?"

"Don't know, boy . . . but they won't. Too many men doing it already, in France. They'll want to keep it quiet."

"I'll go and see him in hospital tomorrow . . . They'll be sending for me, soon."

"You won't like the Army, boy."

"That's what I think. But I'll give it a while . . . a month or two. Perhaps it won't be worse than picking hops, and I do that every year."

"Only for a week or two. Well, one thing, Fletcher, don't you go blowing off your toe or finger. Bert doesn't want his—all he uses is his mouth . . . but you need all your toes and fingers, and always will. So listen to me, eh?"

"I will, Granddad. I won't do anything like that . . . Think Florinda's married yet?"

"Maybe, maybe not. That fellow's drunk enough to change his mind a dozen times, from what Florinda told us . . . Time we went home."

The two men rose to their feet, dropped into a sunken lane, and headed for Walstone. Round a bend a minute later Christopher Cate came walking toward them, wearing a thick tweed suit and cap, with a Norfolk jacket, a stout blackthorn stick in hand. On one side of him walked Betty Merritt, and on the other the older, rich American woman Probyn had talked to at the wedding, Betty's aunt, Mrs Kramer.

He stopped, touching his forelock, as the three came close. Cate acknowledged the salute with a smile and a touch of his finger to the peak of his cap. "Morning Probyn, morning Fletcher . . . You know Mrs Kramer and Miss Merritt, don't you?"

Fletcher nodded. The girl was good-looking, light brown hair, tall, the breasts small but high and firm, a freckle or two on her face—moved well, as though she lived in the country and walked a lot . . . her eyes were the best thing about her, dark blue, large, deep—looking at him now.

Cate said, "A fox got into our chicken run last night, Probyn."

Probyn said, "There's too many foxes around, since the hunt sold the dog pack . . . only meets twice a week, too."

"They didn't sell the dogs," Cate said sadly. "No one would buy them. They had to put them down."

"Oh, what a shame!" Mrs Kramer cried.

Probyn said, "Some of the farmers be shooting the foxes, now."

"Can't say I blame them," Cate said. "Fletcher, I was going to walk down to the cottage later to give you a book, but we're close to the Manor now. Come along with me, and I'll give it to you now."

"Thanks," Fletcher said.

"I'll go on home," Probyn said, touching his forelock again. Fletcher watched him go, then fell in beside Betty Merritt, behind Cate and Mrs Kramer, cheerfully aware of the weight and bulge of the three partridges in the deep pockets at the back of his coat. In front of him Mrs Kramer, too, walked well, in her fashionably cut tweed coat and skirt. She looked as though she could handle a gun or a horse, for all she was much shorter than the girl beside him . . . but handle a man? The squire?

Betty said, "I haven't forgotten our trip to the sea, Mr Gorse—but we'll have to wait till the weather improves, won't we?"

"Suppose so," he said. He liked her accent, sort of flat; and calling him Mr Gorse! Wait till he told granddad about that! He added, "Maybe I'll be in the Army by then."

She turned and faced him full as they walked—"Are you looking forward to going into the Army?"

He looked at her then, gazing into her eyes. Inquisitive, she was, like most women. "No," he said, "but I don't want to go to gaol either. Or blow my toe off, like my Uncle Bert."

"I should think you'd be a good soldier. You can shoot very well, Mr Cate says . . . and move about in the dark without being seen." She was definitely smiling at him now, teasing, flirting.

He said, "I can do those . . . but I don't know about standing still while fat sergeants shout at me . . . be told when to eat, when to sleep, what clothes to wear . . ." If she was asking him questions, he'd ask her some. He said, "Visiting the squire, miss?"

"My aunt was coming down for the weekend, so I came down too—from Hedlington. Between you and me, I'm chaperoning them—Aunt Isabel and Mr Cate." She winked at him.

He smiled lazily at her. She was interested. He could tell. He said, "Ever seen any ferreting, miss?"

"Never. What is it?"

"Killing rabbits with ferrets. They're like weasels, only bigger, and tame, sort of."

"Is it . . . very bloody?"

He shrugged. "You kill the rabbits with your hand, less the ferret gets one underground."

"I'd love to see it once," Betty said. "I can't tell whether I'll like it till I have, can I? When can I come?"

"This evening?" he said. He raised his voice—"Mr Cate, mind if I take a couple of rabbits from that big warren by Cawthon's copse? Miss Merritt here would like to see the ferreting. I'll take her this afternoon . . . about four."

"A good idea," Cate answered over his shoulder. "Do you want to go too, Mrs Kramer?"

"I've seen it," she answered, "and it's cold, and may be snowing. Let the young enjoy the sport, I'll enjoy your fire."

Cate said, "Good. I'll warn Cawthon after lunch."

Then they were coming up to the Manor, walking across the cold lawn, the wind blowing harder, steel-grey snow clouds hurrying overhead, not yet ready to drop their burden.

Inside the house the women excused themselves to go upstairs, and Fletcher followed Cate into his library and music room. Cate wandered up and down the shelves while Fletcher waited, the partridges weighing down the skirts of his coat, his back to the window.

Cate muttered, "The collected works of John Milton . . . not quite right, uplifting, but . . . no. Shelley . . . Keats . . . both guaranteed to bring on acute attacks of homesickness . . . the Restoration poets . . . no. *The Canterbury Tales* . . . Homer, in translation . . . perhaps, but a translation is only as good as the translator, and the fifteenth Earl of Derby, though a worthy nobleman and statesman, was not a great poet . . . Tennyson . . . Swinburne . . . Kipling, even . . . no. Well, as I said, I am thinking, really, that you will have this book by you when you go out on this adventure so vital for England, and for yourself. It will be the greatest event in your life, Fletcher, so it deserves the greatest . . . William Shakespeare." He pulled down a leather-bound gilt-tooled volume and handed it over—*The Collected Works.*

Fletcher looked with a keen sense of pleasure, as though at a flying cock pheasant in the sun, at the artifact in his hand. Cate sensed his feeling and said, "It's even better inside."

"Thank you," Fletcher said. And then, after a pause, "I'd best be going. I'll be back by four."

"Better make it half-past three, Fletcher. You need more time before it gets dark."

Fletcher nodded and walked out into the passage. Betty Merritt was coming down the stairs and paused, one hand on the banister, as he passed. He looked up, and for a moment their eyes locked. As he went out of the front door Fletcher thought, I've got her . . . or maybe she's got me! It was a strange sensation for him, and he didn't know whether he liked it or not. No woman had ever put the tether of even a single silken strand of her hair on him before.

*   *   *   *

Probyn Gorse sat in the chair by the scrubbed deal table, thinking. He'd have to go out when it was well dark, and retrieve the gun and kite, and it was likely to snow: cold work for a cold night. Well, the constable would be in his cottage rather than walking the village, and the keepers, the sort they had now, would be sitting over their fires. He said gloomily, "It's getting too easy . . . taking a brace of pheasants these days. Or snaring a hare, like I did day before yesterday . . . keepers gone to war, or taken work in towns, for more money . . . old fellows hired, instead, or sick men who don't know nothing . . . no chance of a thump on the back of the head some windy night, these days . . . might as well be buying it at the butcher's."

The Woman said, "With berries for coins, like?"

Probyn said irritably, " 'Tisn't the money. It's boring, that's what it is . . . not like when I was a lad. I mind when Fishlock—he was head keeper at the Park before Skagg, and this was when he was young—I mind when him and me stalked each other five hours one night, all up and down the Scarrow. He knew I was there, with a brace of pheasants, and I knew he was there, with a gun, and I knew he meant to put a charge of shot so close to my head I wouldn't have to cut my hair for a month after. I never saw him, and he never saw me . . . but we knew, we knew. These keepers now . . . bah!" He cleared his throat and spat accurately into the fire.

The door opened and his grandson, Fletcher, came in carrying a leather-bound book. "Squire gave it to me," he said, laying it down on the table, and then, fishing in the skirts of his coat, he brought out three partridges and laid them beside the book. "One's for Garner," Probyn said. "I'll take it up, when I go out to get the gun and kite."

Fletcher said, "I'm going out, too, to show the young American lady ferreting . . . in Cawthon's copse, the big warren there. 'Tis squire's game."

"You ain't going to take my ferrets. Mrs Keppel's coming in heat and won't be no good. Queen Alexandra has the colic."

Fletcher said, "I promised to show the lady ferreting. What can I do?"

Probyn scratched his ginger-dyed hair with a dirty nail—"Can't use the long net . . . need another man for that. Running a noose for a hare won't show her nothing . . . Might sneak into the Park and get a brace or two of pheasants out of the trees, with the flashlight and the gun."

"That's poaching," Fletcher said. "Mr Cate don't want us to teach her how to poach . . . I know what! I'll take her to Winsford Pool and tickle a couple of trout!"

"If you can find 'em, should be all right," Probyn said grudgingly. "The water's low enough, but they lie tight at this time of year. Don't let anyone see you though, or they'll have you shut up in the Hedlington Asylum, tickling for trout on a night like this's going to be, in February. And take the toasting fork, in case you can't get one out of the water tickling."

"Right," Fletcher said. He cocked an ear. Probyn had heard it too—the sound of a large, expensive motor car engine, coming to a halt in the road outside the cottage . . . now light footfalls along the path through the nettles to the door. The door opened and a glorious apparition stood in the entrance, arms outspread—a full-breasted young woman with flaming auburn hair piled high on top of her head, held in place under a little hat with two emerald-headed pins. Her dress was of dark green silk, down to an inch above the ankles. She wore two diamond and emerald necklaces, and a diamond brooch. A black sable fur was tossed lightly over one shoulder. Her shoes were green patent leather, the buckles embellished with emeralds, the heels three inches high.

She flung out a hand, encrusted with rings, notably a huge ruby on the third finger of her left hand, outside a plain, heavy gold band.

"Stand up, my good people," she cried in a theatrical contralto. "You are in the presence of the Most Noble the Marchioness of Jarrow."

Fletcher jumped up and hugged her, "So the old bugger did it, after all? When?"

"This morning, at Caxton Hall. Two of his friends held him up and another guided his hand for the signature. Then they took him home and put him to bed . . . and I came down to see you. What's for lunch?"

"Mutton stew."

"Why not roast partridge, Granddad?"

"Those birds have got to hang a while. What about the chauffeur, or did you drive yourself down?"

"I drove some of the way, I've learned how . . . but the chauffeur came, too."

"Send him to the Beaulieu Arms. We've enough for you, but not for him," the Woman said.

The Marchioness of Jarrow, née Florinda Gorse, went to the door, opened it and shouted out, "Woodward! Go into the village and have your lunch at the Beaulieu Arms. Be back in an hour and a half."

Fletcher, watching through the door, saw the chauffeur, an oldish man in livery and peaked cap, standing beside the coronetted door of a huge shiny car, take off his cap, bow slightly, and answer, "Very good, m'lady."

Florinda closed the door, flung herself on the other hard chair and spread out her hands so that they could admire the glittering rings. "Beautiful, aren't they?" she said. "And wait till you see what Cantley gave me, before he passed me on to Jarrow . . . it's a painting of women with funny faces, and Cantley said it would one day be worth more than anything Jarrow might give me. It's by a Spaniard called Picasso, and it's the first version of something called 'Les Demoiselles d'Avignon,' whatever that means." She spoke with the upper class accent quite naturally now. Fletcher listened, and knew she would never go back to the way she used to speak, for she would never go back to the way she used to live.

She said, "Wait till you see the family tree they invented for me, in tomorrow's paper."

"Who's they?"

"Oh, an old pouf . . . another drunk, friend of Templeton's—my husband, Alexander William Templeton Eastman Foudray, 4th Marquess of Jarrow . . . I like him—Gerald, the pouf. He told the papers that I am from an extinct line of Gorses who were barons in the peerage of Ireland till the male line died out . . ."

"So, what are you going to *do*?" Fletcher asked. "Spend money? Sit about sipping sherry, like Miss Stella?"

"Does she, already?" Florinda said. "That's sad. Marriage can be boring, for some women . . . Yes, I'll spend money. I won't be able to help it. You don't know what money is, or rather isn't, until you've seen someone like Jarrow. He gets half a million a year from his mines and lands . . . that's about thirteen hundred quid a day, I worked out. I used to think the Swanwicks were rich, but they aren't."

"Will you still be living in London?"

"Yes. In the town house—27 Berkeley Square. Or sometimes at Blaydon House, about two hundred rooms, up north, near Newcastle. He spends more time there than in London . . . But what I'm going to *do* is go on the stage!"

The Woman said, "Dancing or singing?"

"Both," Florinda said. "I'm going to start singing lessons next Monday, and dancing lessons a week later. The manager of the Gaiety says he'll take me on as soon as I've had some teaching."

"But you may sound like a corncrake," Fletcher said.

"I won't. And I can dance. I've always been a good dancer."

"That you were," Fletcher said. "And now you'll show them your legs up to . . . here." He touched the inside of his thighs, an inch or two below the crotch—"And you'll have all the old battle axes looking down their noses, or sniffing at their smelling salts, even more than you have already."

"Going on the stage will make it better for them, easier to understand," Florinda said. "Actresses can do things labourer's daughters can't."

Probyn said, "It's the title the Gaiety man wants. He knows he'll get all the skivvies in to see the Marchioness of Jarrow, even if she just stood there."

Florinda felt inside the handbag that had been hanging from one wrist, and took out a tight bundle of notes. She held it out to her grandfather—"Here, Granddad, this is for you, to buy something to celebrate my wedding."

Probyn looked at the bundle and shook his head, with a curt, "We're all right . . . Is the food ready, Woman?"

"Just near," she said. "Florinda, wash those bowls and spoons and set them down. And put some more wood on the fire."

*   *   *   *

Fletcher walked down Scarrow bank, on the edge of Cate's land, Betty Merritt at his heels. She was wearing the same tweed suit she had worn this morning, but her hair was encased in a bright red knitted woollen cap—American, Fletcher supposed; he had never seen anything like it before.

"Hope it's not too cold for you," he threw over his shoulder.

"Cold?" she answered. "It's only 36. We have it 20 below zero sometimes, where we live, but it's a dry cold, compared to this . . . Mr Cate told us you are a poet, Mr Gorse. What kind of poetry do you write?"

"What I can," he said shortly.

"I'd love to hear some, some time."

Fletcher grunted non-committally. The village girls never wanted him to read his poems to them—only that he should stroke their hair. They walked on under the leaden sky. The sun was invisible, and the bare trees cast no shadows. The ground was tussocky and hard under-foot, dead leaves making a thin carpet over the coarse grass. Lights gleamed in the windows of the houses across the field, and behind them the clock in the flint tower of Walstone church struck four in damp, muffled tones.

Fletcher stopped. "Here's the Pool, miss. This half belongs to Mr Cate, the other half to Lord Swanwick."

"The fish are protected, like the birds?"

" 'Course," Fletcher said, "they belong to the landlord . . . unless someone else gets 'em first." He grinned at her and she smiled back. "An' you heard Mr Cate—we'd best not be seen, 'cos though they're his fish, no one's allowed to take them out of season. Season don't begin for another month, six weeks . . . but he wants you to see the tickling."

"I didn't believe it, when you told me. Are you sure you're not pulling my leg, because I'm American? You really mean to tell me that the trout lets you tickle it, then it goes silly?"

"Yes, like some girls do," Fletcher said. "The trout doesn't know what your hand is, I reckon."

"I'll believe it when I see it."

"You will," Fletcher said. "We'll stop here, behind the hazel and blackthorn . . . but if a motor car passes, on the road out there, it'll throw light through the bushes, so when one comes, lie down and don't move, see?"

"I see . . . It sounds as though you've been here before, in the twilight."

"Never in winter," Fletcher said. "In summer there's leaves on the bushes, and the trees. And it's warm. And the water bailiffs are about . . . Here, look, see the bank over there?" He pointed across the river, where the grass verge overhung six inches, making a hollow below, like a shallow-backed cave—"That's the sort of place trout like to stay . . . or under the roots, there." He pointed again, at where the roots of an oak made a tangled knot above the water. "Or there—" She saw a rock, pressed up to the bank, water lipping over it. "There's an eddy behind that rock, where the fish don't have to swim, 'cos the back eddy'll keep him in the same place. Now, there's places just like those on this bank . . . here . . . there . . . there."

He knelt on the grass, then lay down. Betty knelt beside him, eager to see what would happen next, still unwilling to believe what Fletcher had told her, even though Mr Cate had confirmed it. Fletcher eased himself forward, his right sleeve pulled up as far as it would go, baring his arm to above the elbow. He slid the hand into the water, and moved it gently, firmly, back, a few inches away from the hidden bank, under water. Almost at once the edge of his hand touched something that moved . . . but moved so sluggishly that for a moment he thought he had hit a twig or small bough, which was pressing back against him; then he knew it was a trout, and whispered, "There's one here." The trout moved an inch or two back. He moved his hand after it, slightly cupped . . . back, back . . . slowly he raised it, and at once felt the barrel of the trout's body inside the cup. The fish moved forward, torpid from the winter cold, but beginning to be nervous . . . Fletcher moved his hand after it, found the barrel again, tickled gently along its belly, moving forward . . . when the front edge of his hand was under the gills he raised it, tickling the trout's flanks now, until he felt the edge of the gills, fluttering with the trout's breathing. Just as he made ready to jam his hand into the gills and jerk the fish out of the water, it moved forward. Slowly, carefully, he found it again . . . again soothed it, again made ready . . . again the trout slid away.

At length he muttered, "Can't get him out . . . Better use the toasting fork."

"Oh no, let me try!"

He muttered, "Lie down beside me, then."

Betty slipped out of her tweed jacket and rolled up the sleeve of the white flannel blouse she was wearing under it. Then she lay down beside Fletcher, and cautiously lowered her arm into the water.

"Forward," Fletcher said, "that way . . . there, can you feel him?"

"No . . . nothing . . . oh, oh, I do!" She was breathless with excitement—"Where do I grab?"

"Not grab—firm, careful, in the gills."

"Oh! . . . Oh! He keeps moving."

The river was becoming flecked with white spots, that disappeared at once; more on the ground, that did not disappear. " 'Tis snowing hard," Fletcher whispered. "Is he still there?"

"No," she muttered, "he must have gone farther out."

She hitched her body forward to reach farther out into the river, and with a sudden panic realized she was going. "Ahhh!" she cried, "I'm . . ." but never finished the sentence, as she slid head first into the Scarrow, there three feet deep. The current caught her and swirled her round. As she struggled to right herself she felt strong hands seize her arms, hold them, pull her upright. She stood at last, gasping and coughing in Fletcher Gorse's arms, locked, body to body, he holding her against the force of the current, their faces close. At length he spoke softly, "Can you stand now?"

"Yes," she muttered. He stood clear, but still held her hand in one of his, and slowly led her to the bank. He climbed out first and then, reaching down, pulled her out and up in one motion. The snow and the darkness almost hid him from her, though he was less than two feet away. Her heart was pounding, and now the cold began to penetrate through her soaked clothes to her skin, and deeper, to her heart and the marrow of her bones.

Fletcher said, "You'll get a trout, another day . . . We'd best take you home now, miss. Running. 'Twill help keep off a cold."

They walked through the wood to the road and there broke into a run, running easily side by side, and ten minutes later came to the front door of Walstone Manor, breathing deeply, glowing with exercise and inner excitement, snow half an inch deep on all their skin and garments. Betty knew already that she was in love; Fletcher thought he might be.

The Daily Telegraph, Monday, March 27, 1916

SUSSEX OUTRAGE
FATE OF AMERICANS

From Our Own Correspondent. *Paris,* **Sunday.**

Captain Mouffet, skipper of the *Sussex,* saw the track of the torpedo at exactly five minutes to three on the port bow, and by quick seamanship escaped being struck amidships, whither the torpedo was aimed. The torpedo threw a column of water and wreckage to an enormous height . . .

Miss Edna Hale, of Tuxedo, New York, who is in a hotel here,

> suffering from severe bruises, tells the *New York Herald* today:
> "Professor Baldwin and his daughter, named, I think, Elizabeth, of
> Bryn Mawr, were both killed outright and lay side by side; she
> received a terrible blow. An American, badly wounded, was a
> young man from Massachusetts, now in Boulogne Hospital. An-
> other American badly wounded was a young physician on his way
> to France to take up hospital work . . . My belief is that over fifty
> persons were killed or drowned . . . I only wish there had been a
> few pro-German Senators and Congressmen on the *Sussex* . . ."
>
> Mr Samuel Bemis, a Harvard University man, was saved and is
> in Paris. He says "I solemnly declare that the torpedo was fired
> without the slightest warning."
>
> The Paris *New York Herald* aptly reprints to-day its cartoon of
> February 24, in which the Kaiser is nailing to the mast a black flag
> with the death's head and cross-bones. This cartoon caused the
> suppression of the *New York Herald* in Switzerland. The paper asks
> to-day whether the Berne censors will again suppress the cartoon.

Cate thought, we are obviously hoping that stressing these outrages
will force America into the war on our side. But Mr Wilson was not a
warmonger or sabre rattler, and every day that passed gave a sensible
man more cause to take very serious thought before committing his
country to the war. He wasn't going to be cajoled or led in; he was
going to be *forced* in, by sheer German stupidity, or overriding American necessity, if it was to happen at all.

He glanced at the opened letter from his son, that lay beside his
plate. Laurence was ecstatic because Guy Rowland had flown an
aeroplane up from Shoreham, and landed it on the Charterhouse
football pitch a week ago. Guy said the plane was an Armstrong
Whitworth F.K.3, and was easy to fly and good for instruction, but
didn't have enough power. Guy had given the school a brief demonstration of simple aerobatics over Godalming, and then flown back to
Shoreham. He was in a bad temper, Laurence reported, because he
was being kept on at the Shoreham Flying School as an instructor,
instead of being sent to an operational squadron of the Royal Flying
Corps in France. A pair of robins were nesting in a hollow tree at the
edge of the town, and . . .

Garrod came in and lifted the domed silver lid over the serving
table. "Anything more, sir?"

"No, thank you . . . well, some more coffee."

The parlour maid poured the coffee for him. Cate said, "Mr Rowland's going to Ireland in April, with a parliamentary committee, you
know. I mean Mr Harry, of course."

Garrod waited, standing beside his chair; a strand of grey hair
escaped from under her starched black cap and ribbon.

Cate said, "The Prime Minister wants them to find out what the Irish really think, about Home Rule . . . about conscription . . . what can be done to work out a compromise acceptable to all but the most rabid Catholics and Orangemen."

"Quite so, sir," Garrod said. She waited, the silver coffee pot in hand.

Cate said, "Mr Rowland is going to try to establish contact with Mrs Cate. I don't know whether he'll have any success."

"I hope so, sir," Garrod answered. "Mr Rowland would want to tell Madam about the wedding, wouldn't he? And Madam would want to hear it. And have news of Master Laurence."

"I'm sure," Cate said, "but she's wanted for murder. I expect that the most Mr Rowland will be able to get from her is some message that she is well, or of affection for the children."

Garrod said, "Quite so, sir. Thank you, sir," and went out. Cate knew she was thanking him for telling her about the new attempt to contact his wife. It was none of her business, of course; but she had served them a long time; she had a right to know. Now, as head of the staff, she had other rights in this family and house; and she would never abuse them.

Dublin: Easter Sunday, 1916 (April 23)

5 Harry Rowland M.P. stood by the fire in the huge main drawing room of Dublin Castle, port glass in hand. Beside him stood Morgan ap Morgan M.P., holding a glass of water. Morgan represented a non-Conformist constituency in the Welsh mountains, where teetotalism and observance of the Sabbath ranked far above faith or works as the road to salvation. Facing them, his back to the fire, port glass in hand, stood Brigadier General Lowe, commanding the cavalry brigade at the Curragh.

Morgan said, "Is it true that the man captured on Friday near Tralee is Sir Roger Casement, then?"

Lowe nodded—"It is. And the steamer that scuttled itself while the Navy was escorting it into Queenstown was the *Aud,* carrying arms from Germany for the Citizen Army and the Volunteers."

"So what will they do now?" Harry asked.

"Do what they've been doing all along—what they're best at doing," Lowe said contemptuously, "make speeches. March up and down in their uniforms and swords."

"You think they'll not take any action, then?" Morgan's voice rose in the classical Welsh singsong.

Lowe shook his head, "They'd be mad to do so—that's what I meant, just now. They had a big day of maneuvers and parades arranged for today, and some of us thought that might have been cover for a real rising . . . but Eon MacNeill canceled it and forbade any of his people to attend any parade or maneuvers. And as you have seen—nothing happened. If we hadn't got Casement and the *Aud,* they might have acted differently, and that *would* have been unpleas-

66

ant . . . not dangerous . . . just that a great many Irishmen—and Irishwomen—would have been killed—which would have done us no good in the eyes of the world—particularly to the west." He waved a free hand in the general direction of America.

Harry said, "The Viceroy's private secretary told me at dinner that Pearse and Connolly and Plunkett are meeting now. They're all extremists, aren't they?"

Lowe nodded again—"Yes—and they have to decide what to do. What can they do, in the face of MacNeill's cancellation? They'll do nothing."

Morgan said tartly, "They're good for nothing, these Irish. Except begging. Begging's the only industry that they work hard at."

Lowe said, "Oh, don't be quite so hard on the Irish, Mr Morgan. Since the beginning of the year the disaffected of every hue have been conducting vigorous recruiting campaigns for their private armies here. They've increased their strength by about ten percent. In the same period we've had a thirty percent increase in Irish enlistment in our army, in the face of everything the Sinn Feiners have done to stop men enlisting . . . The great majority of the country's loyal, sir."

Harry wandered away by himself, glass in hand, his face troubled. He and Morgan and the third member of the commission had been in Dublin a week now; and they'd learned only that there was no possible common ground between Carson the Ulsterman and Redmond the moderate Irish leader. One absolutely refused to be part of any Ireland governed by a Popish majority; the other insisted on a single Ireland, free of Britain in all respects, and ruled by the majority, which would be Catholic. The Home Rule Bill, giving the Catholics something of what they wanted, had been passed just before the war began; but, in the face of violent and organized protests, amounting to rebellion, from Carson and his followers in the North, implementation of it had been postponed till the end of the war. That was only putting off the evil day, Harry thought unhappily.

He had received one message from his daughter, Margaret Cate. Written in another hand, it had arrived yesterday in the post at his hotel, the Metropole on Sackville Street. It read, without greeting:

I am well. Tell Christopher to give Stella the diamond tiara that is in the bank safe, as a wedding present. And Laurence the portrait of Grandfather McCormack, that is hanging in the hall—or was. As to your mission, about which we have read in the papers, follow Mother's advice, which I heard her give many times: persuade the British Government to act generously toward Ireland, that is, grant total independence, now; and get out. They will be repaid. The alternative is

67

civil war. We do not serve king or kaiser, only Ireland, whatever you hear to the contrary.

It was unsigned.

*   *   *   *

Near noon next day, Easter Monday, Margaret Cate waited on Sackville Street, nearly opposite the massive General Post Office. Her father, packing his bags to leave the Metropole Hotel, a few yards down the street, to return to London, would not have recognized her even by close examination, for she had been transformed into a typical Dublin shawlie, only more ragged and dirtier than most. She was sitting on the step of a clothing shop, her head down, watching; an observer, such as the police who passed now and then on their beat, would have thought she was suffering from a bad hangover.

The ragged column came up the street, forty or so men followed by two small lorries, a van, two motor bicycles and a touring car. A few of the men were in grey-green uniform, but most in their Sunday best, all weighed down with rifles, shotguns, pikes, shovels, crowbars, grenades, ropes and various indeterminate packages. All wore bandoliers of ammunition crisscrossed on their chests, and yellow armbands on their left arms.

Harry Rowland, coming out of the hotel with a porter carrying his bag behind, stood and stared. A young lieutenant of Connaught Rangers, standing beside him, said in a marked Irish accent, "Will the ijjuts never tire of marching up and down the street?" The head porter waved majestically; a taxi cab appeared, Harry got in, and drove away.

The column came on. The man in front was short, bandy-legged, square-faced, with a shaggy mustache—James Connolly, Commandant General of the Dublin forces of the Army of the Irish Republic, which latter did not exist. With him were two other Commandants General of the same nebulous force—Joseph Mary Plunkett and Patrick Pearse. They were both poets—Plunkett, no more than skin and bones, dying of consumption before their eyes; Pearse, of medium height with a serious, almost lugubrious manner and a cast in his right eye, a good lawyer, and a good leader—Commander-in-Chief of the whole Army of the Republic, and its first President. Margaret watched with tense excitement, mixed with disdain. She had thought they were mad to continue their plans for the Rising, merely postponing it by twenty-four hours, when MacNeill's cancellation would cut the forces available from nine thousand to a few hundred, in all Ireland. But they had insisted—and insisted on keeping MacNeill, their nominal leader, in ignorance; and they had insisted that she, Margaret McCormack, known to all of them as The Lady (to distinguish her from Constance Gore-Booth, Countess Markievicz, always called The Madame) should keep out of the fight until they had seized their first and main objective, the Post Office—just because she was a woman. But, right or wrong, heroic or idiotic—or both—they were coming on now, acting, at last, instead of talking.

"Halt!" Connolly's command rang out clear in the street. It was emptier than usual at this time, Margaret thought—Easter Monday, and racing at Fairyhouse, including the Irish Grand National. The British would find it easier to get a battalion together at the race course than in the barracks, today.

Connolly, standing almost in front of her, in the middle of the wide street, bellowed, "Left turn! The G.P.O.—charge!"

"Take the Post Office!" another voice yelled from inside the column. Slowly, the men gathered their wits, ran up the steps under the great Ionic columns, shouting, and burst through the doors. Shots rang out at once and Margaret, abandoning her post on the step, jumped up and ran across the street. She arrived inside the Post Office just as Pearse was untangling the mass of men jammed beyond the doors, bayonets interlocking, bandoliers caught in someone else's rifle muzzle, grenades rolling out of haversacks and across the floor. Two young Volunteers were gazing crestfallen at the ceiling, where flaking plaster showed that they had let off their rifles by mistake.

Gradually the Post Office clerks struggled out of their places behind the counter, and ran out of the building. People who had been buying stamps and posting parcels followed, one by one, looking more annoyed than alarmed. Pearse shouted an order and the Volunteers began to smash out the ornate windows with their rifle butts. Plunkett leaned on the counter, recovering his strength. Soon Margaret heard him call "Whitmore!" and his assistant brought him maps. Together they spread the maps on a big table at the back of the main room.

Pearse, passing by, stared at Margaret, stopped, and snapped, "You were supposed to come when we sent for the Auxiliaries, Lady . . . Well, go and help Joseph Mary."

Margaret moved through the crowd to Plunkett's side at the big table. He was looking sicker and gaunter than ever, but his eyes were flashing as he expounded the position to his assistant. He was wearing two large ancient Irish turquoise and silver rings, one on each hand, and a silver filigree bangle on his left wrist.

Plunkett was saying, "We have the Post Office. We'll assume that the other detachments have taken their objectives, too. It was easy enough here, heaven knows . . . De Valera at Boland's Mill . . . St Stephen's Green here." He put a finger on the map, "Jacob's Biscuit Factory, to the south-east here . . . The Four Courts, the Mendicity Institution . . . the South Dublin Union, Gilbey's Distillery . . ."

69

A Volunteer, festooned with ammunition, ran up, "General Plunkett, sir, there's women at the doors . . ."

Plunkett waved the beringed hand irritably, "Go and tell General Pearse or Connolly. I'm making plans."

The man looked baffled and Margaret said, "What is it?"

The man looked even more doubtful, told to give his message to this lank, grey-haired shawlie; but Margaret's voice had an edge of command to it and he said, "There's twenty women outside, screaming at the guards that they've come for separation money. They get it every Monday. It's Monday."

Separation money was an allowance paid by the British Government to the dependents of Irishmen serving in the British forces, who drew it through local post offices. Margaret walked toward the doors, and faced the yelling, fist-shaking women, mostly shawlies. Volunteers with rifles raised and bayonets fixed barred their entrance.

Margaret lifted a hand—"You've come for separation money?"

"Yes . . . yes . . . 'tis our right . . . at the Post Office."

Margaret said curtly, "There is no longer any British Government here. You are citizens of the Republic of Ireland. There will be no more separation money."

She turned her back, hearing the gasps behind her, then the angry cries, the hurled insults. A woman screamed, "Wait till my man comes home! He's a corpril in the Irish Guards and he'll show yez what a real soldier . . ." Gradually the noise died away.

The O'Rahilly came to the table with Connolly, and gave orders to clear the upper floors. Men went out to hoist the new flags of Ireland on poles on the roof and in the street: one flag bore an uncrowned harp of gold on a field of green, with Gaelic lettering; the other was a tricolour—green, white and orange.

Pearse gathered all the Volunteers who were not guarding the entrances and read out the proclamation already printed at Liberty Hall, whence the revolutionaries had started on their march this morning:

POBLACHT NA H EIREANN
THE PROVISIONAL GOVERNMENT
OF THE
IRISH REPUBLIC
TO THE PEOPLE OF IRELAND

IRISHMEN AND IRISHWOMEN: **In the name of God and of the dead generations from which she receives her old tradition of nationhood, Ireland, through us, summons her children to her flag and strikes for her freedom . . .**

Men went out and posted the proclamation in the street.

"When are the British going to do something?" Plunkett muttered.

*   *   *   *

Margaret, writing out a message from Plunkett to be sent to de Valera at Boland's Mill, raised her head. They were shouting something through the upper windows, but she could not make out what they were saying. A man came tearing down the wide steps and into the main room, shouting, "General Connolly . . . Lancers!"

Margaret ran to a window, sandbagged since she had last been there, and peered up the street. The top end of Sackville Street, near the Parnell Monument, was blocked by a column of khaki-clad horsemen, carrying long lances. Red and white pennants fluttered gently from the shafts just below the steel points.

Connolly was close to her, staring, muttering under his breath. He turned back into the room and shouted, "Don't fire till they pass Nelson's Pillar . . . then fire on my command."

Margaret stared up the wide street. The troop was advancing now at a trot, an officer in front. The lances were still held upright, the rifles still in their buckets. What on earth did they intend to do? Ride the horses up the steps and into the Post Office?

She heard now, in the hushed room, the clatter of the hooves, the clink and thump of the harness. They passed the Nelson Pillar and Connolly yelled, "Wait . . . wait!"

But at once a shot rang out, fired by a Volunteer at a window farther along; it was followed by a ragged volley from the higher floors, and the roof. Four Lancers fell from their saddles, to land with jingling crashes in the street. More men were firing from the Post Office, another horse fell, and another . . . The Lancer officer was shouting orders, the troop milling around, aimless, disoriented. The revolutionaries fired with greater intensity, but they did not hit another man, or horse. Under the storm of bullets the Lancers retreated the way they had come, but at a gallop. Inside the Post Office a cheer swelled, rose, and soared to a triumphant paean. Connolly, pointing up Sackville Street at the fast disappearing Lancers, called, "Look! The Fairyhouse races! If that's how the British plan to take a fortified place, we've little to fear here, lads!"

Margaret opened her mouth to speak to him; but changed her mind and said nothing. It was at least possible, she thought, and on the face of it much more probable, that the British troops had merely been passing down Sackville Street on their way from one place to another in the city. But they had been fired on; and men and horses killed; the Rising was a reality now.

The cheering died away. Plunkett called out, "Lady, will you come

back here, please? There's reports coming in from all over and they
have to be marked up . . ."

An hour later reports were still coming in fast and furiously, and
so far things were going amazingly well. Apart from the incident of
the Lancers, British troops did not seem to have come into action
anywhere.

Plunkett, who had been lying down in another room, reappeared.
Patrick Pearse came to the table, his face long, his hand resting on the
hilt of his sword. He said, "That is the sort of thing that makes me
wonder if they're worth it . . . our sacrifice."

"What sort of thing?" Plunkett said, without looking up from the
map.

"Take a look outside . . . Connolly's saying it's just the result of
the capitalist system, but I say it's a damned disgrace to Ireland."

Margaret walked to a window. Two Volunteers standing there were
looking out with rifles rested, their mouths downturned in disgust.
She pushed between them and looked out. The lower end of Sackville
Street was filled with a mob of people. Clothes and food were being
dragged out of shops on both sides of the street, and carried away, or
fought over. Women screamed and pulled each other's hair.

One of the Volunteers said, "Wish I'd as much poteen in my belly
as those whoors have in theirs."

Margaret stared, at first in disbelief, then in anger. It was the
people of the Dublin slums. Word of the rising had reached them,
with news that the police had left their beats; and they'd come running, not to help the rebels, but to loot. Pearse was beside her, reciting
scornfully—"*Only the Irish working class remain as the incorruptible in-
heritors of the fight for freedom in Ireland* . . . That's from Connolly's
book *Labour in Irish History*. Those women down there can't have read
it. He's sending some men down to chase them off the street. He can't
bear to see it."

Margaret watched the little band of would-be police go out of the
front doors, walk into the street, argue, plead, and wave hands. She
heard the women shouting, "Bloody Sinn Feiners, leave us alone! . . .
What's it to do with you what I take home for seven starving children,
I'd like to know? . . . Bloody bowsies! Fuck off!"

She saw the lieutenant in command raise his hand and shout an
order. She saw the dozen men raise their rifles. She heard the shots.
No one fell. Pearse muttered, "They're firing over their heads . . .
Thank God. I couldn't bear to see Irishmen kill Irishmen today."

Connolly was there, surly, angry, determined. He growled, "Unless a few of them get shot, you'll never stop them."

But no one sent orders to fire at the looters, and Margaret returned to the map table. The women of the Volunteers' Auxiliary, Cumann na mBan, started to arrive, in green uniforms with white and orange sashes, Sam Browne belts, knives and pistols. An outlying rebel detachment sent to the Post Office copies of a proclamation issued by the Viceroy of Ireland, which they'd found nailed to house, church, and shop doors. Margaret took one, and began to read; daylight would fail soon, and the British would certainly turn off the power:

Whereas an attempt, instigated and designed by the Foreign enemies of our king and country to incite rebellion in Ireland, and thus endanger the safety of the United Kingdom, has been made by a reckless, though small, body of men, who have been guilty of insurrectionary acts in the city of Dublin:

Now we, Ivor Churchill, Baron Wimborne, Lord-Lieutenant-General and Governor General of Ireland, do hereby warn all His Majesty's subjects that the sternest measures are being, and will be taken for the prompt suppression of the existing disturbances and the restoration of order: And we do hereby enjoin . . .

Margaret read on to the end. Nothing would persuade the English that the Irish rebels were not in the pay of Germany. But it wasn't as simple as that. As Connolly had written: ". . . the instinct of the slave to take sides with whoever is the enemy of his own particular slave driver is a healthy instinct, and makes for freedom"; and that was why Pearse, in his proclamation, had referred to the Germans as Ireland's "gallant allies in Europe." But in fact they'd bought the arms from Germany and paid for them, just as they might have bought them from America; and if Germany won the war and tried to take the place of the English here, as an occupying power, she'd meet the same troubles. The fact was that any war involving England was an opportunity to the Irish cause; every educated rebel could quote the famous passage from John Mitchel's *Jail Journal,* referring to the outbreak of the Crimean War: *"Czar, I bless thee. Give us war in our time, O Lord."* Margaret wondered whether her father would believe the words she had tried to impress on him in her brief note: *"We serve neither king nor kaiser, only Ireland."*

She let the Viceroy's proclamation flutter from her hand to the floor, and returned to Plunkett's side. The first night of the Rising fell slowly with the looters reeling in drunken orgy up and down Sackville Street, the night full of raucous song, and Pearse watching tragically by the light of the street lamps. The English had not turned off the power.

*   *   *   *

73

She was awake early on Wednesday, the third day, feeling like everyone else, tired, frustrated, angry, and let down. She had expected death all night, since a midnight false alarm; and it had not come—not even the catharsis of firing her revolver through the windows at the advancing khaki uniforms in the irregular violet glare from Lawrence's store. She had eaten breakfast, served by girls of the Auxiliary upstairs, and was now at Plunkett's desk, working.

The building shook to the same combination of sound and silent reverberation that had shaken it yesterday: artillery fire. Now the guns were much closer, and they were firing more insistently. Plunkett looked up once, then made a show of continuing his calm study of the map of the city; but Margaret saw that his hand was shaking. Poor devil, she thought, with him it's a race between the British and the consumption, as to which gets him first.

Margaret went to the windows. The Volunteers there greeted her like an old friend, one saying, "Now might that be artillery we're hearing, Lady?"

She nodded. "It's a gunboat at Butt Bridge."

The man said, "But General Connolly told us only yesterday that the British would never use artillery against us, now did he not?"

The other rebel said, "He did, an' I heard him . . . Wonder when we'll next be in the Twangman, on the wharf down there, pints of Guinness in our hands?" His voice became dreamy—"We'll be minding each other about how the British attacked the Post Office and we beat them off . . . and the general marched up with a white flag . . ."

"Ah, hold your gab, ye shitehead!" the other snapped. "Sorry, Lady."

Margaret returned to the table. Connolly was not there, but soon came down the stairs, and joined them. "When the British start using artillery in the centre of Dublin," he said, "it shows what a hurry they're in to finish the job." Margaret made no effort to show that she was accepting the Commandant General's insinuation: that the British were becoming desperate. Connolly said, "There are probably hundreds more of our boys on their way to help us at this very minute."

Margaret took a message from a runner, and bent over the map. No more of the boys would come to the Post Office, except those being driven in from the outposts, such as those who came in from Westmoreland Street yesterday.

When she had recorded the information she looked up at Connolly—"They're just going to advance house by house, destroying them—and us—from a distance, by shell fire."

"It looks like it," Connolly said.

"*We* ought to be out in the streets," she said, "attacking everything

74

in uniform. They'd have to scatter men all over Dublin—all over Ireland, it should have been."

Connolly walked away, his face set. When he had gone, Plunkett said, "I don't know, Lady . . . you may be right. But this is Connolly's plan. We're holding the centre of Dublin—the capital . . . we may hold it for a week. That'll create a new feeling in Irishmen, Irish patriots." His rings flashed as he gesticulated.

Margaret said, "You've seen that report from de Valera?"

Plunkett shook his head, and Margaret said, "He says that a battalion of Sherwood Foresters, just landed at Kingstown, has been attacking him all day. He's inflicting heavy casualties on them."

"There, that's what you want, isn't it?"

She shook her head emphatically—"No, because they're being attacked, at the English's time and place. It should be the other way round. De Valera should have been sent to Kingstown, to attack the troops, as they were getting off the ships, not to wait for them at Boland's Mill. Think what chaos he could have caused!"

Plunkett sighed and shook his head—"We're committed to this . . . and I think it's right. The Republic has a capital—this Post Office."

Margaret hitched up her revolver belt and said, "I'm going up onto the roof to have a look round."

As soon as she appeared on the roof the nearest Volunteer made a violent gesture and shouted, "Down, woman!" The smack of two bullets close by made her drop to her knees, and thus hidden behind the parapet, crawl to the edge. The man who had shouted said, "It's coming from Trinity . . . must be a hundred of the shiteheads hidden up there!"

Margaret stuck her head over and looked down, then quickly drew back as more bullets cracked into the stone close by. "The looting's stopped, at least," she said.

The Volunteer shouted, "Only on Sackville Street. There's plenty of them still at it in Sackville Place and Princes Street."

A twelve-year-old boy farther along the roof attracted Margaret's attention. He seemed to have profited by the looting to acquire a set of new clothes—though he was barefooted—at least a size too large for him, but of a cloth and cut that his parents could never have afforded to buy for him. He was firing a rifle toward Trinity, over the Liffey, with a jar that jerked his whole body at every shot, each time shouting obscenities at the British—"Take that, ye bloody shiteheads . . . limey bastards! . . . I'll blow your fuckin' heads in . . ."

A priest appeared, looking round in amazement as though he had not expected to see any such sights. He was old with flowing white hair and a gentle, baffled mien. He dropped to one knee beside the boy, and Margaret heard his frail, reproving voice—"You should be at home with your mother, my boy. Run along now, while you can."

The boy turned and stared, and after a moment shouted in the old man's face—"Walk away from a foight loike this? Bejasus, you must be daft!"

Margaret suppressed a smile. The adults on the roof were watching in amazed awe. None of them would have addressed a Catholic priest in such a way . . . indeed it was obvious that the old man had just walked in from the street, unchallenged by the guards, with the passport of his Roman collar. That was another area where she disagreed with the other leaders of the Irish rebel movements; she thought that Roman Catholicism was part of Ireland's problem, not part of its solution. Look at the way the Church had hounded Parnell, Ireland's greatest man, simply because of his adultery.

The old priest raised his voice, "The British will be here soon. I came here to give you all unconditional absolution. Do you hear me? Each of you, speak up! Are you sorry for your sins?"

The men crouching and lying behind the parapet all shouted then, "Yes, father. I am sorry for my sins!" And the priest, crouching on one knee, raised his hand and began—*"Dominus noster Iesus Christus te absolvat; et ego auctoritate ipsius te absolvo ab omni vinculo . . ."*

Put your hand down, Margaret wanted to shout; for, whether they had seen the rite or not, the British fire had increased sharply. The priest finished the prayer, made the sign of the cross, and still crouched, left the roof.

*   *   *   *

Next morning Margaret awoke to a new sensation. She had not slept well, troubled by a haunting dream of her son, Laurence, who in the dream had been a little boy, floating away from her on some wide silent stream, his hands outstretched to her. And then, lying awake, she had thought about de Valera at Boland's Mill, and the casualties he had inflicted on the Sherwood Foresters . . . but Pearse had told her that the troops attacking the rebels all over Dublin were from the 3rd Royal Irish Rifles and the 10th Royal Dublin Fusiliers . . . Irishmen all: a bitter taste in the mouth.

There was a terrible smell, all-pervasive, creeping. She got up and, rubbing her eyes, went to a window.

The Volunteer there was holding a handkerchief to his nose. He gestured outside with his free hand—"The Lancers' horses, Lady. They dragged the soldiers away, but they couldn't move the horses."

Margaret looked at the dead horses with distaste. She remembered her pang of sorrow for them when they had been shot, at the Volunteers' second volley. Now they were visibly swollen, their legs sticking straight out from bloated bellies. The soft breeze blew the stench into every corner of the Post Office building.

Margaret could not decide whether the fouling of the atmosphere was the main or only a supporting cause, but she soon saw that today the morale of the men and women in the Post Office was beginning to crack.

The O'Rahilly came up and spoke a few words to Plunkett, then returned to Margaret. "The lads are getting down in the dumps, Lady. Let's sing them a song!" He raised his voice—"Come on, boys! Sing with us, the Lady and me . . . all join in! Let Lord Wimborne hear us in the Castle! Let the soldiers hear us in Kingstown, yet!"

He began in his lusty baritone, bellowing out a song that he himself had written:

> *Though knaves may scheme and slaves may crawl*
> *To win the master's smile;*
> *And though thy best and bravest fall,*
> *Undone by Saxon guile;*
> *Yet some there be, still true to thee.*
> *Who never shall forget*
> *That though in chains and slavery*
> *Thou art not conquered yet!*

A few men joined in the singing, but not many, and those not with much enthusiasm, Margaret thought.

When the O'Rahilly had finished that one she muttered to him, "Sing one they know better . . . *Rory of the Gael* . . . *The Wearing of the Green.*"

"That's it!" the O'Rahilly exclaimed and raised his voice again:

> *O Paddy dear, and did you hear the news*
> *   that's going 'round?*
> *The shamrock is forbid by law to grow on Irish ground;*
> *I met with Napper Tandy and he tuk me by the hand,*
> *And he said, "How's poor ould Ireland,*
> *   and how does she stand?"*
> *She's the most distressful country*
> *   that ever you have seen;*
> *They're hanging men and women there*
> *   for wearing of the green!*

The volume of the singing had hardly changed; but those who did sing sang with more enthusiasm. *The Wearing of the Green* was well known, and very popular; but Margaret thought that the concluding words were unfortunate in the present circumstances.

They're hanging men and women there for wearing of the green.

Many of these young men seemed to be realizing for the first time that hanging by the neck until they were dead was indeed now a likely fate for them.

* * * *

A roaring conflagration occupied the whole block of Lower Abbey Street, and was threatening to cross Sackville Place. British soldiers were running up Sackville Street, shouting at the houses opposite the Post Office, "Come out, come out!" trying to get people out, for the houses were doomed. No one on either side fired until the sad little stream of men, women and children, loaded down with a few belongings, had trickled out and away, and the soldiers had disappeared behind their barricades; then the artillery opened fire again, and again the Volunteers fired at anything that moved.

The Republic flags on the roof of the Post Office were being scorched brown by the heat from across Sackville Street—which was a hundred and fifty feet wide. Inside, smoke filled the building, men coughed and choked and covered their faces with their handkerchiefs.

At three o'clock Patrick Pearse, President of the Republic of Ireland, appeared on the main floor of the Post Office to read another statement:

The forces of the Irish Republic which was proclaimed in Dublin on Easter Monday have been in possession of the central part of the capital since 12 noon on that day . . . I desire now, lest I may not have an opportunity later, to pay homage to the gallantry of the soldiers of Irish freedom . . . They have redeemed Dublin from many shames . . . They have established Ireland's right to be called a Republic, and they have established this government's right to sit at the peace table at the end of the European war.

Margaret listened. Pearse always spoke well. Clearly, he had been trying to raise morale. A little, he had succeeded; but there was only one real way to do that—attack. No words, however noble, could obscure the fact that they were waiting like rats, to be taken, and executed.

Pearse stalked away. James Connolly shouted, "I want thirty men who are not afraid to go out on the street. I'm going to take the *Irish Independent* building."

Men shuffled forward, leaving the windows or the places where they had been sitting in dejection on the stone floor. Margaret joined them. Connolly said, "McLoughlin, you command the troops, I will be with you. You can't come, Lady."

"I'm coming," Margaret said shortly.

Connolly hesitated; then shrugged and called, "Follow me!"

Margaret, in the middle of the thirty men, her revolver now drawn and in her right hand, followed through the back door, across the courtyard behind, to the gate into Prince's Street. McLoughlin swung the gate open and they all ran out, bent low.

Connolly stopped, shouting, "First, we'll build a barricade, here, in Prince's Street!"

Men ran back across the courtyard into the Post Office, returning laden with all kinds of machinery, junk, tables, wardrobes, filing cabinets. Connolly walked up and down, shouting encouragement. Margaret worked with the men, her revolver back in its holster to free her hands.

Connolly stopped in the middle of a sentence and Margaret looked round. He muttered to her, "I'm hit—scratched—in the arm . . . not a word." He walked through the gate and disappeared into the building.

Twenty minutes later he was back, and muttered briefly to Margaret, "Got Jim Ryan to bandage it, in secret . . . Now, lads, the barricade's done. Follow me. We'll get the *Independent* now."

They ran round the corner into Middle Abbey. Bullets smacked and whined all round, but no machine guns were firing, only British snipers from the Liffey and farther west on Abbey Street. "McLoughlin," Connolly shouted, "you take twenty to the *Independent*, there! Charge now . . . The rest of you, follow me." He ran toward the Lucas lamp and bicycle shop opposite the newspaper building, Margaret close on his heels.

The bicycle shop was empty, but bullets were hitting the brick walls and smashing through the door. A man ran over from McLoughlin's group and reported breathlessly, "We have the *Independent* building, general!"

"Good, good!" Connolly seemed transformed and Margaret, following him out of the Lucas shop, said, "We ought to have done this before, general."

They were standing on the kerb, she close to him, crouched, gesticulating energetically. Connolly said, "Lady . . ." then suddenly gasped, and fell.

"What . . . ?" Margaret began, stooping over him, when she felt a tremendous blow in the left shoulder, as though she had been hit full force with a sledge hammer. She pitched forward on her face onto the pavement a yard beyond Connolly. She felt numb on the left side. It must have been a bullet . . . there was blood on her chest now, not flowing hard, but beginning to soak her blouse. But Connolly . . . he was on his knees beside her, his left ankle a mass of bone splinters, and pouring blood. He whispered, "Prince's Street . . ."

He began to crawl along the pavement, a foot at a time, dragging the wounded leg behind him. Bullets smacked and clacked all round. None of the Volunteers in the recently captured building seemed to have noticed. Margaret struggled to her feet, pushing against the wall with her one good arm until she was upright. She swayed, gritting her teeth. If she were to move, it must be now. She followed Connolly, clinging to the wall, until they reached the end of the alley, then turned into Prince's Street. Here Connolly collapsed into the gutter. Margaret slid inch by inch down the wall, until she was sitting at the foot of it, her head hanging. Gradually, darkness approached. Just before it engulfed her she heard men's voices. "Lift them up . . . the general under the arms—have to get a blanket for The Lady . . . Run, man!"

*　　*　　*　　*

She awoke to pain, but with full consciousness, lying on a cot in the "hospital." Connolly was stretched out on a table nearby, being worked on by Mahoney, the rebels' captured doctor.

Mahoney said, "Get me morphine, somebody. Wherever you can. There'll be some in the chemists'."

Connolly groaned in continuous pain, and his face was wet with sweat. Mahoney came over to her and said, "You've been bandaged, Lady—" that was the only name he had for her. "It's a clean bullet wound through the scapula from behind, and out above the left clavicle. You must have been bending forward. All I had to do was irrigate it, take out some bits of cloth. I'm going to put it in a sling now . . . It'll hurt for some time, I'm afraid, but it should heal cleanly. I'll give you some morphine in a minute or two."

She closed her eyes, and clenched her teeth against the pounding ache in her shoulder.

It seemed a moment later, but was actually over an hour, when she heard a voice calling—"Lady! Lady!" She opened her eyes carefully. Patrick Pearse was by her cot. He said, "Can you hear me? Good . . . I'm sending you out of the Post Office tonight, with two girls from the Cumann na mBan. You'll have to walk a quarter of a mile, to a house where you'll be safe, until you can be got out of Dublin."

80

"I'll stay here," she said.

He lowered his voice —"We'll be going tomorrow or the next day. Besides, I want you to live—you and the Madame—to show the men how Irish women can fight. And to guide the leaders when they make plans for the next rising. Who's Laurence?"

"My son. Why?"

"You kept muttering his name, when you were coming out from the morphine. You must miss him."

She said nothing. She thought she had suffocated everything in her that could interfere with her dedication to Ireland; but in what they were calling the subconscious nowadays, she obviously had not succeeded.

Mahoney said, "That's enough, general. If you want her to be able to walk even a hundred yards at midnight, she must sleep now."

Margaret sank back, almost but not quite below consciousness, aware still of the stench of the rotting horses, the sounds of artillery shells, the smoke, the lurid light from the fire across Sackville Street . . . she had had a message from her father . . . it had hurt to receive it, to answer . . . took her mind, her thoughts away from Ireland . . . to Stella . . . Laurence . . . he would be home for the holidays now . . . his favourite holidays, for it was the time he could find birds' nests in every tree and hedgerow, and he'd count the eggs, and watch the nestlings grow, with as much love as though they had been his own children . . . almost his last holidays, these would be, before he left school and joined the Army, that army, out there, coming closer through the streets of Dublin.

*　　*　　*　　*

The house was a big one, outside Drumshambo, in Leitrim, on the bank of the Shannon a mile below Lough Allen. The owners were Anglo-Irish landed gentry, like Constance Gore-Booth, Countess Markiewicz; and, like her, passionate members of the Irish independence movement, but secretly.

It was May 15, and Margaret was sitting in an armchair by the bed in a second-floor guest room. She was wearing no disguise, and anyone who knew her, or had a good picture of her, would have recognized her; but her hosts were above suspicion, and no one came, except, this day, Colleen Fitzgerald, one of the girls who had helped her escape from the Post Office. The girl was sitting in a chair opposite, her hands twining and wringing, tears in her eyes.

"They've done it," she said, "Pearse and his brother Willie, Connolly, Plunkett . . . he was married to Grace Gifford, four hours before, in his cell . . . Tom Clarke, MacDonagh, Edward Daly, O'Hanrahan, John MacBride, Eamonn Ceannt, Michael Mallin,

Heuston, Colbert, Caffin, MacDermott . . . all shot. Connolly in a chair, because he couldn't stand . . . Not all together. Spread out over days."

"Not de Valera?" Margaret asked quickly.

"No. He told them he was an American citizen . . . and they don't want to upset the Americans, do they?"

Margaret's arm and shoulder hurt, though not as badly as they had the first week; but she had been barely conscious for much of that time. A doctor with republican sympathies had been brought to see her the second day and told her there was nothing to do but wait; she was healing well by first intention, but it would take time. He would come again in a month to make sure the healing process had continued as it should.

She said, "It's what was to be expected . . . even to the British doing for us what we could not do for ourselves. These executions will turn the people to us . . . . Things would have been different if Sir Roger Casement had not been caught . . . if we'd had men to unload the *Aud* when it arrived in Tralee, as we were supposed to . . . if MacNeill hadn't cancelled the Sunday rising . . . if they'd done what I wanted them to do—attack everywhere, in small groups, instead of barricading themselves into buildings, in large groups."

"They're saying there were only two thousand British soldiers in Dublin over Easter."

"It's probably true . . . The executions are sad, but what we three saw, you and I and Bridget, in that house, was worse."

The girl said nothing, hanging her head. The house they had taken Margaret to, after working through the British cordon, stood on the route by which the prisoners had been taken to gaol after the formal surrender of Saturday morning, the 29th of April. Half hidden by curtains, from a little room on the upper floor of the brick house, one in a poor row, they had watched the Volunteers being marched down the street, Plunkett dragging one foot after another, while the crowd gathered ever thicker, and the filth flew ever faster—tomatoes, eggs, potatoes, dirty water, mud from the gutter, spit spewed in their faces—the air full of furious screams, "Filthy, murthering shiteheads! Scum, now ye'll get what ye deserve! . . . Ye'll all be hanged! . . . hanged! . . . hanged!" Only the escort of British soldiers prevented the Volunteers from being lynched.

The girls beside her, without her sad experience of age, had broken down completely, wailing and crying uncontrollable tears, turning away, covering their ears with their hands. But Margaret, in grim agony, had watched and listened until the last of the procession had passed.

Now, looking out over the gleaming Shannon, she said quietly, "So in the end, only one of all those men in the Post Office was killed in action—the O'Rahilly—and he not there, but outside trying to fight up the street."

The girl said, "But, Lady, would you be wanting *more* of the poor boys dead?"

Margaret said with force, "Next time, it won't be an affair of a week, with flags flying, but of two, three years, with secret signs, private signals, hidden weapons, burning cottages, men found dead at cross roads and no one knowing how . . . War, not defiance."

The Daily Telegraph, Wednesday, May 10, 1916

FINAL SCENES AT THE FALL OF KUT

From Edmund Candler. *Mesopotamia*, May 3. The last communications from General Townshend were received on the morning of April 20, at 11.40 a.m. He sent them by wireless:

I

Have destroyed my guns, and most of my munitions are being destroyed, and officers have gone to Khalil, who is at Madug, to say am ready to surrender. I must have some food here, and can not hold on any longer . . .

II

I have hoisted the white flag over Kut fort and town, and the guards will be taken over by a Turkish regiment which is approaching. I shall shortly destroy wireless. The troops go at two p.m. to camp near Shamran.

A prearranged signal from the wireless indicated at one p.m. that General Townshend's last message had gone through. On the same day the Turkish General, Khalil Bey Pasha, received our parlementaires. He was anxious, he said, that the garrisons should be well rationed, and that General Townshend, especially, for whom he expressed the most profound admiration, should receive every possible comfort after the privations he had so gallantly endured. He welcomed the proposal to send them stores, and regretted that the supplies at his command were not more plentiful.

Cate read on gloomily. A British force had suffered a stunning setback in a part of the world where "face" was so important—and at the hands of the Turks, whom everyone had so heartily sneered at, when they came into the war on Germany's side. There would be repercussions in Egypt, Afghanistan, Persia perhaps—even in India, where a large Muslim population had been unhappy from the start that the Commander of the Faithful, the Turkish Khalifa, was on the other side. Such Muslim leaders as the Grand Sherif of Mecca and the Aga Khan had done their best to support the Allies by belittling the position of the Khalifa as the spiritual leader of all Muslims, in modern times; but the danger was always there.

This disaster in Mesopotamia, coming on top of the failure at the Dardanelles—also at the hands of the despised Turks—made one appreciate more fully that the war was not confined to France and Russia. The main battlegrounds were indeed along the Russo-German border, where Poland used to exist, and the Franco-German border; and it *seemed* obvious that that must be so. Such huge forces were engaged there, such furious conflicts being fought there—look at the struggle for Verdun, which was bidding fair to become the most important battle of the war so far! Yet, was it really so, that the war had to be won on these two borders? Was it inevitable? Did some law of nature demand that the combatants must grapple there, two crazed elephants facing each other in a narrow pit? Was there no way round? What did sea power mean, in the end—beyond the ability to import food and munitions for survival—if it did not give the Allies the power to choose their point of attack . . . and vary it, at will?

He put down the paper, longing unreasonably for movement . . . the war would seem different if one could read of, and imagine, brigades of cavalry sweeping across great plains . . . dusty columns of infantry marching day and night to strike the enemy in flank . . . horsed artillery galloping down long green valleys. It had been like that, for a few weeks in 1914, and he, like everyone else, had felt the excitement of war . . . the maps, the flags, the pictures of the guns rolling through shattered villages. Not now. Now, only the casualty lists.

Hedlington & Walstone, Kent: Monday, May 1, 1916

6 Betty Merritt gazed unseeing through the window at the scattered huts. Their corrugated-iron roofs, camouflage-painted, half blocked her view of the big hangars by the control shed and its little raised platform. Scents of spring flowers wafted in through the window, which was open, and the distant roar of an aircraft engine running at half throttle on a test bench was almost drowned by the nearer chortling of two blackbirds; but Betty was not aware of any of this. She had been working as Ginger Keble-Palmer's assistant in the design office of Hedlington Aircraft for nearly three months now. At first she had found the work very difficult, and the formulae she had to use, all new to her, almost impossible to understand; yet she had felt that she was standing here not only as herself, but as a representative of all educated women; and, with Ginger's patient guidance, gradually, it had become less difficult.

Her left hand rested on the squared drawing paper, pinned down on the sloping draughtsman's table. Her slide rule lay on the edge of the paper . . . the wings could be longer, narrower, giving a higher aspect ratio and better range and handling, while keeping the same wing loading. But that would give wing stress problems, and nobody really knew enough about the design of wing main spars . . . supposing she put the aspect ratio up by 15 percent, that would increase the span by . . . she picked up the slide rule and began calculating, jotting the figures down on the edge of the paper. Now a new spar length of 16 feet 7 inches from root to tip would produce new stresses and bending moments, requiring a newly calculated cross-section throughout its length. It was going to be a long job; all design was compromise . . . she decided to work it out roughly, and check the stresses with Ginger later.

Across the room, behind her, she heard Ginger exclaim, "Vinton's cut off one engine . . . or it's died on him." He raised his voice and called, "Betty, listen! . . . Come on!" They ran out of the hut together. The aircraft, one of the first two test models of the Hedlington Leopard, was making a sweeping turn beyond the downwind, east end of the field. It was about a mile away and five or six hundred feet up. It came on, lurching as the idle port propeller imparted unexpected yaw at the slower landing speed . . . landed heavily on three points, bounced ten feet in the air, landed again, and rolled to a stop nearly opposite them.

Ground crews ran out with ladders to help the pilot and his passenger down. Vinton, the company's test pilot, threw back his goggles, and said, "That's what they call a series of landings, I believe . . . Port engine was overheating, Ginger. Needle off the clock."

The passenger was Johnny Merritt, now taking off his helmet and goggles. "She was doing fine until that engine went," he said, "but a bit sluggish on the controls."

Betty said, "I'm working on something that should improve that . . . increase the aspect ratio, lengthen the wings a bit. I think she'd be much handier."

Ginger said, "I didn't know you were on that. I've been looking for light materials for the airframe, and asking Rolls Royce either to give the Eagle II an extra thirty or forty horsepower . . . for the same weight, by higher compression perhaps . . . or hurry up with the Eagle III."

A Rowland Sapphire drove up to them and Richard Rowland stepped out, preceded by his chauffeur, a young woman in immaculate green uniform, with breeches, gaiters, jacket and a man's peaked cap with a patent leather brim. "Thank you, Kathleen," Richard said, "I won't be long."

Johnny said, "I'll see if Frank has the deputation ready."

"He'd better," Richard said grimly, "I have to go to Farnborough right after the meeting, to talk to them about planning for the Lion . . . Is Frank Stratton all right?"

Johnny hesitated, "He's fit enough, Richard . . . better than I would have believed possible, knowing how badly he was wounded . . . and he's a wonderful floor man—knows everything, and what he doesn't, he picks up. But he's, well, listless, as though his heart isn't in it. But he does his job."

Richard nodded, noting with approval that Johnny had at last taken to calling him Richard instead of Mr Rowland. He led into the main hangar, where the wings of a Leopard, nearly complete, spread from wall to wall; another, its wings on, but the fuselage only half completed, the engines not mounted, stood behind it, staggered diagonally, and a third, no more than a skeleton, behind that. In one corner, by the table and chair which were the factory foreman's floor office, three men waited, while Frank Stratton sat in the chair.

He got up as Richard and Johnny approached, and Richard took his place. He looked up, "Who's the leader of the deputation?"

"I am," a man in a cloth cap said. "Griffin, frame shop . . . We got to have more money, Mr Richard. We told Mr Johnny two months ago."

"And he told me. The company couldn't afford it."

"Prices is going up," the man said. "Why, bread costs . . ."

"I know," Richard cut in—"Our company . . . which as you know owns the J.M.C. as well as this, already pays more than any other employer in Hedlington. And our production is slow. We can't pay more money until we get increased production."

Griffin said, "That ain't all our fault, Mr Richard. 'Course, you can't expect the sort of men you get now, and women, to work as well and as fast as men that's been on machines twenty years . . . but the machines ain't what they ought to be, either. For one thing, in my work, the steam rooms for shaping the wood ain't hot enough."

"*We* keep running out of lacquer, when the wings are ready for doping," another man said.

Frank said, "It doesn't come on time from the manufacturer, Mr Richard."

Richard frowned, then turned to Frank—"We've got to increase production, if we hope to win the war . . . and if you men hope to get a raise . . . Frank, look into these complaints, and any others the men bring up—any man. Bring Mr Johnny here a list of them. Then get together with the shop foremen and see what can be done to make the work go faster. When you're ready, tell us, and we'll have another meeting with you men—and I want a representative of the women here, too. Then, if you'll accept a plan to increase production we'll agree to raise wages. Not before. Now, I have to go . . . to try to keep the jobs you have now."

He got up and, nodding to the others, walked swiftly out.

*   *   *   *

Rachel Cowan looked at the huge pile of laundry stacked on Mary Gorse's kitchen floor, and at Mary herself, bent over a zinc tub set on the table, up to her elbows in soapsuds. This was what "we" must rescue women from, she thought, remembering the exact tone of Naomi Rowland's indignant voice as they had walked on the lawns of Girton in the spring sunshine, the scent of flowers about them, the distant bells of Cambridge chiming for church: women must be free to realize their potential, women must be educated much as men, women must, women shall, women are . . . And here was Mary Gorse, half-witted Willum's wife, taking in washing to feed the too-many kids . . . particularly the eldest, pregnant but barely twelve . . . and herself, living with Willum's half-brother Bert—why? Because she loved him? Because they were both Socialists? Or because, she, as a woman, couldn't face living without a man? And Naomi was in uniform, doing her bit for this bloody capitalists' war . . . but they had not seen each other for months and then only briefly. The bells of Cambridge seemed as far away as her childhood, the ugly, brilliant, little daughter of Jacob Cohen, peddler, of Whitechapel.

Sweat filled the creases on Mary's worn, calm face. Sheets and pillow cases occupied every inch of the line strung crisscross over the tiny back yard. How could she look so placid, Rachel thought angrily, when she's being so exploited? She said, "I've moved in with Bert, Mary."

Mary did not raise her head from her work. "So I heard."

"We're not married."

"I know." She raised her head, dashed some sweat out of her eyes with the back of a soapy hand, and bent again. A shaft of sunlight glowed in her grey-streaked fair hair. Rachel said, "It saves money . . . we think alike . . . we have a lot in common."

"I'm surprised," Mary said, "you having been at Cambridge, and all."

"I wish I'd never taken that scholarship. I should have stayed with my own people and joined the working class struggle—*our* struggle."

Mary said nothing for a time, then—"If you get on so well with Bert, why don't you marry him? Is it that you don't hold with marriage and the church then, like Willum's dad, Probyn?"

Rachel hesitated, "Not exactly . . . I'm a Jewess, and I can't become a Christian any more than Bert can become a Jew. Who'd marry us? And we don't need it. Why should we do what the capitalist church tells us we must?"

Mary changed the subject, "Bert's walking well, considering."

Rachel said, "Yes, but his toe hurts, and he only gets odd jobs now. The bosses won't employ him after what he did."

"Well, that was to be expected, wasn't it?" Mary lifted a load of washing out of the tub, transferred it to the sink, and ran cold water over it from the tap.

Rachel, stung by the last remark, said, "Bert doesn't understand why you don't have the law on Bob Stratton. There's Violet six months gone, and she only twelve last month."

Mary said, "I don't want to have the law on Mr Stratton."

Rachel said heatedly, "You should! He's going scot free because he's what he is, because Mrs Harry stood behind him and you didn't want to offend her."

Mary said, "I'm sure Mr Stratton has enough troubles of his own without you or me making it more difficult for him. Now, if you'll help me wring out these sheets . . ."

*   *   *   *

They sat close in the saloon bar of the White Horse in North Hedlington, tankards of old and mild at their sides, heads close. Milner, a government food inspector, was speaking in a low voice—"The superintendent heard it first. He didn't say anything to anyone till he'd found out more about it . . . then he warned three of us, on the Q.T., to keep our noses clean."

"Why?" Bill Hoggin, food merchant, husband of Bob Stratton's daughter Ruth, demanded.

"He said, the high-ups are asking questions . . . and the sort of questions they ask point to our department—food inspection."

"No idea of who's behind it, or at the top of it?" Hoggin said. Six months of elocution lessons had done wonders for him; his accent was still clearly of East End London, but much modified. He seldom dropped his aitches, though occasionally putting them in where they had no business to be; his intonation was plummier, and had less of the cockney bite, except when he was much excited or interested.

Milner said, "There's only two possibilities. A departmental inquiry, inside the Ministry . . ."

"Wouldn't worry too much about that," Hoggin growled.

". . . or a parliamentary inquiry . . . Complaints have been made to M.P.s and they've been asking the Minister to look into it. The superintendent says there'll probably be a Joint Select Committee of both Houses of Parliament . . . especially since Bottomley's been on about it in *John Bull* since last year."

Hoggin quaffed his beer, wiped his mouth and sat a while sucking his teeth. His red face shone with color and his neck bulged out over his stiff white collar. Beer spots and food stains marked his expensive worsted suit. "Comes at a bad time for me," he said. "We don't have much to do with the food people any more—*you* know that . . . and we haven't used any unfit consignments for two, three months. So they won't pin anything on us now, unless they search all the grocers' shelves. Another month and it would have been off them, too, and out of the warehouses . . . but I need capital, because—know what I'm going to do?—I'm going to start a chain of retail shops, groceries like, but selling bread, too, and fruit and veg, and meat, and everything cheaper than the little grocers and bakers and butchers can . . . Grocers and butchers and all them are trying to provide *good* stuff everywhere, which is fine for the gentry and rich blokes, but there aren't many of them, and what the rest of the people wants is *cheap* stuff . . . so's they'll have more money in their pockets for motor cars, holidays, send their kids to better schools . . . An' we'll get the women in 'cos everything they want'll be in the one shop—mine. . . . Well, that's what I'm going to do, but I can't buy and build and all the rest all by myself, so I'm going to have to raise a lot of money . . . go to the banks, a few millionaires . . . and I need a big name in front . . . An' I won't get the money nor the big name if there's a stink going on . . . so, listen, Milner, me boy . . ." he bent closer yet, ". . . there's three things to be done, to save our skins. First is to get rid of any evidence. Second, at the same time, is to shut up the ones making the row, like Bumley. Third, if this Committee is appointed in spite of all that, nobble it!"

Milner whistled lugubriously through his stained teeth, "Tall orders, Hoggin."

"They are," Hoggin said. "And your part is the easiest. Make it so that *if* there's an inquiry, no one's going to find the copy of the license you sold me to buy condemned food as a pig farmer. Or the receipts for what I did buy . . . but only for the condemned stuff, see? The rest, what I bought off the docks, was all above board . . . and that was more than three quarters, eh?"

Milner said, "Yes . . . It's a dangerous business, destroying records."

"More dangerous not to," Hoggin said shortly. "Now, what do you know about these Joint Select Committees? Who appoints the members?"

Milner drank deep of his beer, set his tankard down and wiped his lips with his sleeve—"The superintendent said they could be any number up to fifteen members . . . equal numbers from both Houses . . ."

"The fewer members the better for us," Hoggin said. "Can't nobble all of them buggers. 'Ave—*have*—they actually started horganizing this committee yet?"

"The superintendent said not."

Hoggin said energetically, "Then we'd better shove our oar in now. Better our friends organize it than blokes what don't like us, eh? An' I have pals, specially in the Commons—made it my business to. Meantime, I'll deal with Mr Horatio Fucking Bottomley, and find a big name. Which I think I already 'ave, in my bleeding pocket."

*   *   *   *

Bob Stratton, lying on the couch in Dr Deerfield's office, wished he was not wearing his thick porridge-colored woollen vest and long underdrawers; but Jane had insisted—"Ne'er cast a clout till May be out." And here it was only the first of May . . . but he'd heard that the jingle didn't mean May the month, but may, the hawthorn blossom . . . They used to have maypoles in Hedlington when he was a lad, and boys and girls danced round them, entwining each other in the colored ribbons springing from the top of the pole.

"Go on," the doctor's voice, with its funny little accent, was somewhere behind his ear.

"I saw lots of little girls' . . . things," he said grudgingly. "In those days, girls and women didn't wear drawers, so when they bent over, you'd sometimes see . . . the thing. Some of 'em bent over 'a purpose, if you ask me," he said. "I remember . . . "; he stopped, avoiding the memory.

The doctor said, "Go on, Mr Stratton."

"I can't remember now . . . " He'd taken Victoria out a dozen times since—since Violet told him—and he'd never got her above eighty-five, when she'd done over ninety before. It seemed like not doing what he used to do in the shed, with the girls, had changed him, so that he couldn't do the right things for Victoria any more. She was sluggish, and so was he.

"Are you sure you can't remember? Think please."

The thought that he had cut off returned. He saw a girl . . . what was her name . . . Helen Tubbs? . . . about nine, and him the same . . . bending over to tie her bootlaces, she saw him behind her, between her legs, and bent farther . . . all the way down, the dress hoisted up by the motion . . . he'd been four, five feet away, no more, and no one else by . . . It had felt good, amazing, near paralyzed him, and his finger smelled funny for a long time afterward, so that he didn't want to wash it.

"Can't remember," he said.

Dr Deerfield sighed almost imperceptibly, and said, "Well, let's go back to the beginning again. Tell me just what you can remember about your very early years—when you first saw your big sister, naked, for instance . . ."

Dirty nonsense, Bob thought, what has that got to do with it? Why should he answer these impertinent questions from a dratted Ger-

91

man? But he'd promised Mrs Harry, and Jane . . . What a price! Better if he'd gone to prison and be done with it. Then he'd always be himself, at least.

*   *   *   *

Stella Merritt looked across the table at Dr Deerfield from under her eyelashes. It was nice being a married woman and not having to worry about chaperones; better still to be married to a darling like Johnny, who had said, when an unexpected crisis arose at the Aircraft Company, that of course she must go to the lunch with Dr Deerfield without him.

The doctor was of medium height, a little pudgy, in his late forties, with an olive skin, a high-bridged nose, huge liquid brown eyes, and long hands and fingers. She had met him first at the Hedlington Hospital when she was staying with her grandmother at the time of Granny's cancer operation. Stella had met him once or twice since at Granny's house; and then there had come this invitation to Johnny and herself to have lunch with him. In spite of Johnny's words, Stella felt pleasantly excited to be lunching alone with the doctor, while still wishing Johnny could be there . . . poor Johnny, he worked so hard.

They had ordered and were waiting for the food, glasses of dry sherry beside them—Stella's second. The doctor said, "How did the shopping go, Mrs Merritt?"

"Oh, badly," Stella said. "The shops are so empty . . . and what they do have is usually of poor quality, and so expensive . . . but I did find a pretty afternoon dress for myself, and I bought two ties for Johnny."

Deerfield smiled, "You are lucky to have an American husband. English husbands hate their wives' buying clothes for them—especially ties."

She pouted at him—"I know what Johnny likes!" The doctor's smile was understanding. He was not married . . . or perhaps he had married badly when young, and left his wife in Austria. Anyway, he must know what it was like for a girl, the first few months of marriage. She found herself blushing, thinking of the nights of lovemaking, Johnny's strong body and male hardness in her, her own eager responses.

"You look happy," Deerfield said softly.

"Oh I am, I am!" she cried.

His hand crept across the table and covered hers—"I am so glad for you," he said. "But I am older than you, my dear Mrs Merritt . . . a thousand years older, I feel, when I see your radiant young beauty—so English, so perfect . . . and I know that marriages are not made in heaven, but on earth . . . and sometimes young people though very much in love, begin to feel estranged, and cannot understand why. Marriage creates its own problems, as well as its own rewards. It is my profession to solve such problems. I will always be available to you, as a friend."

She responded to the pressure of his hand, her eyes damp. He was so kind! She said, "Thank you so much, Dr Deerfield."

"Please call me Charles," he said. "Charles—an ear to listen to whatever you want to say . . . a safety valve, if you ever need to blow off steam . . . even a shoulder to weep on, though I hope it never comes to that."

Stella found her sherry glass empty. Dr Deerfield signalled a waiter to refill it. "I feel I've known you so long," she sighed. She felt warm inside and out. Dr Deerfield—Charles—was so different from Johnny, but he, too, was a man, a man who understood women, especially her. His hand pressed down, briefly enfolding hers, and briefly, oh so briefly, his finger stroked the inside of her palm, sending a sudden unexpected frisson through all her secret parts. Then the waiter came with the soup.

*   *   *   *

Volunteer Naomi Rowland, sitting high on the driver's seat of the big Humber, thought gloomily that her parents were drifting apart because of the war. Her father had lost faith in it, and now thought it must be stopped, at whatever cost; while her mother was as grimly determined as ever that Germany must be defeated, at whatever cost.

Enough of that. She was on duty, and must not let her mind wander. No one was going to call *her* just a scatterbrained woman dressed up in a uniform. She was a soldier.

A thinking soldier . . . and this was a waste of petrol. She seldom had more than one passenger, usually some senior officer of the War Office: a smaller car would have done the job, saved fuel, and been more handy in traffic. True, a small car might bog down in the mud of remote lanes while she was trying to find some camp or installation or country house—but that would be very rare. If officers had to visit units or installations more than fifty miles from Whitehall, they usually went by train; and the Home Counties were well equipped with roads, compared with, say, the farther reaches of Cumberland or Inverness-shire.

She changed gear, accelerated to pass a pair of lumbering horsevans, and changed back up again. The Woman's Volunteer Motor Drivers needed a uniform that would include trousers or breeches for everything except mess dress. They wore trousered overalls now, for maintenance work on the cars in barracks, but when they went out on duty they had to wear this No. 2 dress, with the khaki tunic, skirt down to two inches above the ankle, high buttoned boots and khaki spats, which was all very well when actually driving, but what if you had to change a tyre? Change a sparking plug? Look for an oil leak? She wondered briefly where and when skirts were invented, or allotted to women, as their "official" garb. She knew that women wore trousers in India, and other Muslim countries . . . in the harem, too, so men obviously admitted them to be feminine there. Why not on . . . ?

The officer sitting beside her said, "You are an excellent driver, Miss Rowland. I can tell that your mind is miles away, yet you are also fully aware of the road and all that is happening on it."

"Thank you, sir," she said shortly. She had driven Colonel Venable two or three times before. He was a full colonel on the Intelligence staff, in his fifties. His red-banded hat lay on the seat between them, with his short leatherbound cavalry swagger cane and a bulging briefcase. She had learned that his Christian name was Rodney and that his regiment had been the 17th Lancers, the Death or Glory Boys. He was tall, with bushy grey eyebrows, smoothed-back iron-grey hair, and a suave, slightly weary manner. The little finger was missing from his left hand.

He said, "Do you know this part of Oxfordshire at all?"

"No, sir," she said, "I went to Cambridge . . . Girton."

"How interesting! Well, Phyllis Court at Henley keeps an extraordinarily good cellar, and I am a member."

"Oh, I know Phyllis Court and Henley," she blurted out. "We used to go there every year. My father was a Blue."

"Ah! Well, is there any reason you shouldn't join me for a little supper at Phyllis Court before we go back to London?"

"Oh, I couldn't do that, sir," she said automatically. It was just as she had thought: Venable treating her as a lady, not a soldier-chauffeur. How dared he . . . ?

"Why not? Surely your Deputy Superintendent—that is the right title, isn't it?—does not insist that you eat bread and cheese in the car, when away from London, does she?"

"No, sir, but . . . "

"But me no buts, uncle me no uncles," he said cheerfully. "I have given you an order. I'll put it in writing, if you like. We shall both be in uniform. It will all be highly official and military . . . but we shall enjoy a Romanée Conti which is as strong, as healthy, as thoroughly sound and beautiful a wine . . . as you are a young Englishwoman."

She felt herself colouring at the compliment; but was about to protest once more when he opened his briefcase, put on a pair of tortoiseshell-rimmed glasses, and said, "Now I must do a few minutes final preparation before I meet this professor, so please excuse me."

She relapsed into silence. He was good looking, for his age, in a rather cynical way. He was more sophisticated than any man she'd met yet . . . probably kept mistresses when he was young. And that missing finger . . . perhaps he'd taken part in the charge at Omdurman . . . or fought Afridis on the North West Frontier, and heard the bullet down the mountain pass, that whistles low, all flesh is grass . . .

*   *   *   *

Susan Rowland sat at the breakfast table in Hill House with the two recently adopted children, one on each side of her. If she'd been English, she'd have hired a nanny for them long since—as soon as she got them—but she was American; and she believed it was her duty to raise them herself, and give them the love and security they had never known in their short lives.

"Tim," she said, "take your elbows off the table . . . eat your porridge in smaller spoonfuls . . . Sally, sit up straight, there's a dear."

Sally sat up, with a wide smile and a murmured "Yes'm," that was halfway between the "Yes, madame" she had learned to use at the orphanage, and the "Yes, Mummy" that was expected of her now. Susan watched them both with love tempered by anxiety. Tim was about seven and a half, Sally nine: no one knew their real birthdays, so she had given them birth dates, March 1, 1907 for Sally, and September 1, 1908 for Tim. Their mother, a well-known prostitute in south-east London, had been killed during the German air raid on Woolwich of October 13 last year. Their fathers had obviously been different men—for Sally was blonde and sturdy and blue-eyed, while Tim was small and sallow and brown-eyed; but they shared a cautious, wary look in those young, innocent-seeming eyes.

Joan the maid came in, a dedicated spinster in her fifties, and Tim snapped, " 'Ere, you . . . sugar!"

Joan stopped and stared, disbelieving her ears. Susan said sharply, "Don't speak like that to *anyone*, Tim! Say 'Please pass me the sugar, Joan.' Go on."

Tim said, "Please pass me the sugar, Joan." His voice was now winsome and ingratiating. Susan saw in his sharp, little face that he did not understand why he could not tell the servants what to do in any way he chose. No one had ever hesitated to tell *him*, at home or at the orphanage, where he was at everyone's beck and call, to be shouted at, ordered about, slapped, whipped, shut up . . . Now, by some miracle, he was on the other side, one of the people who gave the orders.

Joan said, "There you are, Ma . . . " She bit the word short. She had been about to say "Master Tim," which was the proper way for her to address her mistress's small son, but Susan, née Susan Kruze of California, had forbidden the staff to treat the adopted children in the old way. They were to be addressed simply by their Christian names—Tim and Sally—until they were old enough to be treated with respect; then perhaps it would be time to call them Miss Sally and Master Tim.

Sally slipped off the cushions on which she was sitting on her chair, and went to the sideboard to help herself to fried egg and bacon. Joan looked on approvingly and said, "Would you like some more milk, Sally?"

"Yes, please," the girl said. "Thank you, Joan."

She was learning manners, Susan thought; or learning what pleased those who could punish her. It was love they had to learn, really, and that would not be easy. They were, underneath, little animals of the human jungle. Where they would really be at home, if it were allowed, would be on the Western Front, living like the rats they had been, in the trenches of the urban war front.

*   *   *   *

The colonel commanding the depot of the Argyll & Sutherland Highlanders, in Stirling Castle, was tall and gaunt with a sweeping grey mustache and a silver plate in his skull, replacing a piece blown out by a German bullet at Mons. Two of the 2nd Lieutenants of the regiment lined up in front of him were barely nineteen. The third was Archie Campbell, a shortish man of near forty, with dark hair, narrow-set deep-sunken eyes, a broken nose and powerful sloping shoulders. They all gazed at the colonel, backs straight, trying to guess what they had done wrong.

Archie wondered if Fiona had telephoned again, asking whether there was an Archie Campbell at the depot. Last time the adjutant had told her there were five, among the three hundred Campbells; and later had asked Archie whether the lady was a friend of his, and what was he to do if she called again; and Archie had answered, "Tell her there's no Archie Campbell here who knows her." But surely the C.O. wouldn't have him up with the two youngsters about that, even though one of them was also a Campbell?

The colonel said, "The battalions of the regiment have been doing well in France and elsewhere, but they have not been suffering the expected casualties. So they do not need the officers we have ready to send out . . . I have been ordered to find three officers to send to other regiments. Out of many, I have chosen you."

Campbell hardened his expression. What had they found wrong with him? He'd done his best—the two young 'uns, too, as far as he knew.

The colonel recognized their emotion and said, "We're not trying to get rid of you. I had the adjutant pick the names to go out of a hat. You're the unlucky ones . . . You can choose what other regiment you want to go to. A few are in the same boat as we are—don't need any more officers now—but precious few. You'll probably get whatever you ask for. So, what are your choices?"

No one spoke for a time. Archie Campbell's mind was racing. What about the Cameronians, or the Highland Light Infantry, then? He was a Glasgow man and they were Glasgow regiments. One of the Lowland pushes, then—the Royal Scots Fusiliers, King's Own Scottish Borderers . . . ?

One of the young men said, "If I can't stay here, sir, I'd like to go to the Black Watch."

"Very well," the colonel said, making a note on a pad.

Archie thought desperately . . . a Welsh regiment? An Irish one? Rifles? Too damned snooty. They wouldn't mind him having been a painter—but his dad a coal miner? No, thanks! He didn't know any other regiment . . . except one: the Weald Light Infantry.

The second subaltern said, "I'd like to go to the Gordons, sir."

The Wealds . . . Fiona's regiment. Fiona's husband's regiment, to be exact. Quentin's. The man whose bed he'd been dishonoring for the past ten years. The man who'd come between himself and Fiona, in image, ever since this bloody war started—because he was out there, fighting, while he, Archie, was back here, fucking.

He said, "I'd like to go to the Weald Light Infantry, sir."

Like? he thought. That's not true. I *must,* that's the truth. There'll be no peace of mind for me until I'm fighting at his side.

The colonel made another note, and asked, "Any particular reason?"

Archie said, "Family connections, sir."

*　　*　　*　　*

The young man and the young woman walked barefoot on the pebbled beach, under a bright afternoon sun. The little waves crawled up the slope and washed their feet. The turreted baroque mass of Eastbourne pier stretched out to sea half a mile ahead. Beyond the pier towered the white loom of Beachy Head. The fishing and trip boats were drawn up high on the beach, their prows at the edge of the tiled footwalk, the boatmen working on them. Smells of pitch and twine and petrol fumes wafted down the beach into the walkers' faces. Out to sea smudges of smoke trailed behind a crawling tramp, a hurrying destroyer. A few other couples walked or sat in the May sun, a few children played in the pebbles. The summer season had not begun.

"Are you glad you've been called up at last?" Betty Merritt asked.

Fletcher Gorse said, "Don't know, really . . . You get tired of waiting, for anything."

"Do you want to go?"

He said, "I want to see the war, 'cos I'll have to write poetry about it. Wish I didn't have to wear uniform, though." He stopped and stared seaward, his hands on his hips. Betty waited, then asked, "What are you looking at?"

He jerked his chin, "That . . . all that water. That's something else to write poetry about, I reckon. I'd like to see it when the wind's blowing and there's waves, and water flying about."

"A storm at sea!" she said. "You are a romantic, Fletcher." She was laughing at him, and he smiled back at her.

He said, "I'm a poet, ain't I?"

They walked on. She said, "You'll be training in Hedlington for some time, won't you, after you've joined up?"

He nodded. "At the Barracks. Square bashing. Crawling over the Downs at night playing at soldiers."

After a while she said, "What time will you have off, free?"

"Dunno. Some of Sundays, likely. Some of Saturdays."

"We could come down here again."

"Lots of driving, sitting in the car. Better we go to Walstone, and I show you how to run ferrets, and tickle a trout . . . without falling in the river."

She threw her head back and laughed, then looked back at him. "You'll write? To tell me when you can come out. We could dance, too. They have dances for soldiers sometimes, I know."

He said, "I'll write." He looked at the sun, the houses, the sea, the sweeping beach, and last at her. Her eyes were soft, her skin like silk, her hair stirring in the little breeze. She was nearly ready. Not quite though; and nor was he . . . damned strange feeling, that was.

"We'd better go back now, Betty," he said.

*　　*　　*　　*

The drone of aircraft engines filled the air. The wind, heavily charged with salt, blew in off the sea and tugged at the marsh grass along the eastern edge of the field, where the River Adur meandered into

Shoreham and the Channel. Acting Lieutenant Guy Rowland, nineteen years of age a week ago on Shakespeare's birthday, the day before the Easter Rising in Dublin, sat at the little table in the little hut just off the airfield, reading a letter. It was from his uncle Tom:

So we sit here, or do exercises, day after day, waiting for Scheer to come out and fight. We can't pass the minefields and unmarked channels, and get into the enemy harbors these days, as Nelson did at the Nile and Copenhagen. We have to pray that something will make the High Seas fleet go to sea. Sheer boredom, perhaps, or what they think is a chance of cutting off an isolated smaller force of ours, destroying it and returning safe to their bases before we can catch them. We are a real fleet now, a huge one, rather than a collection of ships thrown together and called the Grand Fleet, which we were until recently, I feel. But all we can do is pray that the Germans will come out, a prayer that everyone, from Admiral Jellicoe to the youngest Boy, hopes will become a reality . . .

He put the letter down with a frown. Uncle Tom was waiting in Scapa Flow, in the Orkneys, off the north coast of Scotland. It was easy to understand why *he* had to wait: the initiative was with the Germans. But that was not true of himself. He stood up, put on his R.F.C. tunic, the double-breasted so-called maternity jacket, buttoned it up carefully, and checked the polish on his shoes. Major Capling, the school commandant, had been an officer of the Queen's before he transferred to the R.F.C. and kept all the punctilious polish of that regiment, nicknamed Kirk's Lambs, or the Guildford Guards.

In the outer office the school adjutant said, "What can I do for you, Rowland?"

"I want to see the C.O., please."

"What about?"

"I want to be sent to a squadron in France."

The adjutant said, "The C.O. is well aware of your position, you know."

"I'm sure he is," Guy said obstinately, "but I'd like to see him, all the same."

The adjutant, who was an older man with a limp and no wings on his breast, got up, and went into the inner office. A moment later he came out, and beckoned. Guy marched forward, came to a halt, and saluted, his forage cap at just the right angle, the embroidered R.F.C. wings still bright and new on his left breast.

Major Capling said, "The adjutant tells me you want to be posted to France, Rowland."

"Yes, sir. It's two months since . . ."

Capling raised a hand, "I know. Don't think I have not studied your record of service—frequently . . . You're not really a good pilot, Rowland, but you are an excellent instructor. I don't know why, but it's true. Your own technique and knowledge are improving as you teach others, and soon I hope to post you to France. The date will depend on when I get another instructor posted to me."

And the cricket season, Guy thought to himself: Major Capling was a keen cricketer and liked the Shoreham Flying School to field a side capable of giving a good game to anything short of a first-class county side; and of course he was aware that Guy had bowled for Kent while still a schoolboy.

Capling said, "You should be out of here in six weeks. That's all."

Guy saluted, turned about and marched out, the adjutant on his heels. The door to the C.O.'s office closed. The adjutant said, "That's not long. You'll have enough time in France, believe me. So enjoy the fleshpots while you may."

"Fleshpots? Shoreham?" Guy snorted. He went out, glancing at the roster on the green baize-covered board outside the office. He had a student in fifteen minutes. Just time for a cup of tea in the mess, and then . . . up in an Armstrong-Whitworth F.K.3, up into the windy sky, and over the grey, tossing sea, where, on a clearer day than this, you could see France.

The Daily Telegraph, Wednesday, May 17, 1916

MILITARY SERVICE BILL
THIRD READING CARRIED

Further consideration was given to the Military Service Bill on the report stage.

Mr WHITEHOUSE (R. Lanark, Mid) moved that the lowest age for military service should be nineteen years instead of eighteen as the Bill provided. He was sure that, like himself, all members had received many letters protesting against the Government proposal. (Cries of "No, no," and "Not one.")

Mr LONG, while regretting the national necessity of calling on these lads to take their place in the defense of their country, insisted that never previously had training and discipline been so essential for success in war, and by calling up youths of 18 the physical and mental improvement effected in them by even a few months' military training was extraordinary . . . He was prepared to put into the bill a provision that these young men should not be called on to serve abroad . . .

Mr PRINGLE (R. Lanarkshire, N.W.) moved an amendment to leave out Sub-section 2, which provides that men who have been medically rejected since August 14, 1915, should become liable after August 1, 1916, to be called upon to offer themselves for re-examination, . . .

THE FINAL DIVISION

Having passed the report stage, the House divided on the third reading, when there voted:

For the bill 250
Against 35
Majority 215

The House rose at twenty minutes past eleven o'clock.

The attempt to save married men from conscription hadn't lasted long, Cate thought. The first conscription law, embodying that principle, had been passed only in January, and here it was barely five months later, and every man from eighteen to forty-one now made liable, married or not. Swanwick had been right when he said, about the first bill—"It won't work, you'll see. The best men will go, as they would have done anyway, and the others will get married and thumb their noses at the tribunals."

He glanced through the rest of the paper: the Germans had admitted that it was one of their U-boats that had sunk the *Sussex,* and promised to punish the captain . . . by making him stand in the corner for an hour, probably. The Americans were going to accept the apology, though . . . At the trial of Casement it had been brought out that Germany had sent Russian rifles and ammunition to the Irish rebels. He wondered whether Margaret had been using one during the siege of the Dublin Post Office. At the courts martial of the rebel leaders it had been established that she was present, but had escaped after being wounded. He wondered where she was now, and whether her wound had healed.

A beautiful day, and the guns from France had been quiet during the night. He'd better spend the morning with Frank Cawthon, one of his tenant farmers, and tell Mrs Abell to serve lunch early because in the afternoon he had to attend a meeting of the Mid-Scarrow War Problems Committee, when the Mayor of Hedlington and representatives of the surrounding villages met to discuss and, if possible, solve problems common to all of them, and in some degree or other, caused by the war . . . shortage of labour of all kinds; village girls emigrating to what was, to them, the big city, often to end up as homeless vagrants

101

and prostitutes; military deserters keeping themselves alive by robbery; maintenance and support of illegitimate babies, whose fathers
were often now dead; falsification of medical certificates to avoid conscription. All these problems, and many more, would become acute
once this new bill came into full effect, probably in a month or six
weeks' time.

Tuesday, May 30, 1916:
Scapa Flow, Orkney Islands

7 Tom Rowland pushed aside the pile of sailors' service records on his table and looked at his watch. Seventwenty in the evening, still broad daylight in these high latitudes. The Commander-in-Chief's signal, "All ships prepare for sea," had been hoisted at 5.40, nearly two hours ago. Steam should be up in another half hour, and then the Engineer Commander, Warner, would make sure that the boilers were maintained at constant pressure, and wait. They'd all wait . . . wait for another sweep of the North Sea, or another signal ordering all ships to return to normal harbour readiness.

He sat back looking through the open scuttle without really seeing what he was seeing . . . the battleships of the 4th Battle Squadron anchored in line in the centre of the Flow—*Iron Duke*, wearing Admiral Jellicoe's flag as fleet flagship; *Benbow, Superb, Canada; Bellerophon, Temeraire, Vanguard.* If he turned his head and looked through the open door of his cabin on the quarterdeck he would see the other five ships of the 4th Light Cruiser Squadron, to which *Penrith* belonged . . . And if he got up and went out on deck, he would see the whole Flow full of the dark shapes, in ordered lines, the slate-coloured water lapping the steel walls of the Grand Fleet . . . *King George V, Ajax, Centurion, Erin; Orion, Monarch, Conqueror, Thunderer; Colossus, Collingwood, Neptune, St Vincent; Marlborough, Revenge, Hercules, Agincourt*—all battle ships; *Invincible, Inflexible, Indomitable*—battle cruisers, faster but less heavily armed and armoured . . . *Minotaur, Hampshire, Cochrane, Shannon*—armoured cruisers . . . and there were four more battleships, six battle cruisers, four armoured cruisers, and

103

twelve light cruisers with the Battle Cruiser Force down at Rosyth and Cromarty, ready to take their places with the Fleet at sea when ordered out; and all this took no account of eighty destroyers. Here was the greatest force of sea power ever assembled, the heart and soul of England's ability to wage war, to survive . . . but still a deadly bore to be part of, when the Germans would not come out. You sat . . . waited for signals . . . practised deployments into varying battle formations to suit varying circumstances . . . steamed back to Scapa . . . and looked at the barren rocks, the seagulls, the cormorants, watched the rain slash down on the decks, listened to the hands singing in the mess decks, music hall ditties, sentimental ballads . . .

He picked up the newspaper, a week old, that lay on the back of his table. It was folded at the page for women, and showed drawings of new summer fashions. He had been studying them before he turned to the sailors' service records, and now looked again, pencil in hand. It was amazing how messy this design was—he drew a new line, and another, trying to imagine that the actual lines printed on the paper had been erased: now it was cleaner and more feminine. Women were fussy, heaven knew, but they shouldn't be allowed to wear fussy clothes. The designer of this had probably been a woman. The material should be . . . what? He knew nothing about materials. He tore out the section of paper which he had been working on, tore it into tiny strips and dropped them into his waste paper basket.

The hands were singing *Ah belong to Glescie,* Glasgow's unofficial anthem:

Ah belong to Glescie, dear auld Glescie town,
Wha's the matter wi' Glescie, for it's gannin' roon and roon?
Ah'm only a puir little working chap, as anyone here can see,
But when I get a drap on a Saturday night, why then Glescie belongs to me!

But the singing was not from below decks. He slid out of the chair—it was screwed to the deck so it could not be pushed back—put on his cap with the single line of gold braid denoting his rank of Commander, and went out on the quarterdeck. At once he saw a motor launch approaching from the direction of the Stromness jetty. The daily steamer that linked the Flow with Thurso on the mainland was at the jetty, black smoke drifting away on the light wind. The launch was one of the fleet's liberty boats, and it was the men in the liberty boat who were singing. Four of them would be for *Penrith,* Tom thought—remembering who was due back from seven days leave today. They'd made it just in time for the sweep, exercise, rehearsal, whatever it turned out to be. He glanced at the Officer of the Watch and saw that it was Sub-Lieutenant Lydiard, his telescope under his arm. He had only joined a month ago from *Lion,* where he'd been a midshipman. A petty officer and a couple of quartermasters were waiting at the head of the gangway. There might be some trouble when the returning liberty men, who sounded quite drunk, reached that point; but they could handle it. He returned to his cabin.

Liberty . . . he had just had a week, and would be due again in October if nothing interfered. He had thought of arranging matters so that he could spend this last leave with Ordinary Seaman Charlie Bennett, but it had come up unexpectedly and there had not been time. Between now and October, surely it could be fixed. The mental picture of Bennett came before his eyes—curly blond hair, rounded jawline, soft skin, grey eyes, deep dimple in his chin, the long pale eyelashes. His voice was clear and soft, too, though he spoke in the guttural Northumbrian accent called Geordie. Charlie was due for liberty at about the same time. It could be done . . . it must be done. He closed his eyes and gritted his teeth. He sometimes thought he would go insane, under the strain of wanting this man, as a lover, and having to treat him as nothing more than a cog in the running of H.M.S. *Penrith.* Four more months . . .

The singing was loud and clear now. The liberty men must be at the head of the gangway. The senior quartermaster would be checking their names against the liberty roll. The singing disintegrated into shouting, angry, drunken yelling. He heard Lydiard's high, clear upper-class voice, "Stop that nonsense!" So the men were thinking of taking a swing at the sideboys or the quartermasters . . . and Lydiard must have been close. Tom leaped up and out of the cabin in one motion, and saw what he had feared—Lydiard was there, between a quartermaster and a sideboy, a foot or two from the four reeling sailors.

"Mr Lydiard!" Tom shouted.

Lydiard turned, saluting—"Sir?"

"I wish to speak to you, *at once!*"

"Aye, aye, sir!" The sub-lieutenant, tall, twenty years old with dark brown hair and a thin intense face, doubled across the quarterdeck and stood to attention. Tom spoke in a fierce undertone—"Mr Lydiard, do you realize that those liberty men are drunk?"

"Yes, sir, that's why I thought I'd better help the . . ."

Tom cut in, "Didn't they teach you anything in *Lion?* What will happen if one of them hits a quartermaster?"

"Four or five days in the cells, sir."

"Right. And what will happen if he hits *you?*"

The young officer was silent, the telescope rigid under his arm.

Tom said, "Court martial . . . dismissed the service . . . four or five *years* in gaol . . . When there is any chance of trouble with men who've had too much to drink, officers WILL keep clear. The Master at Arms and Regulating Petty Officers are quite capable of handling any trouble of that sort . . . much more capable than you are. Is that clear?"

"Yes, sir."

"Get back to duty . . . there!" He pointed at the stern, under the gently fluttering White Ensign; and watched till Lydiard had marched himself there, and begun an easy stroll back and forth across the quarterdeck, telescope under one arm, seemingly oblivious of the commotion at the head of the gangway, where the liberty men, now silent, were being hustled forward along the deck.

Tom returned to his cabin, sat down once more, and pulled the pile of service records towards him.

Hardly any time seemed to have passed before he heard the voice at his open cabin door—"Sir . . . signal hoisted by the Commander-in-Chief: Fleet will leave harbour at nine-thirty p.m. by the DT 3 method. The signal was hoisted at eight-seven." Tom glanced at his watch; it was now eight-eight. Lydiard and the duty signalman had wasted no time.

He said, "Has the Captain been told?"

"Yes, sir. I called him on the quarterdeck Navy phone. He's coming up."

Tom went out, and found his Captain already there, together with Lieutenant Commander the Honourable William Mainprice-King, the First Lieutenant; and Lieutenant de Saumarez, the navigating officer.

"DT 3," Captain Leach said, "that's south of the Skerries—twelve knots till the fleet's all clear—then east-south-east, seventeen knots."

"Yes, sir. Formation LS 1—10."

The Captain looked round at the three of them—"Anyone feeling like taking a small bet, say ten bob, that we'll see a Hun ship this time?"

"Not I, sir," de Saumarez said, smiling. "I'm beginning to wonder if the German Fleet exists."

The Captain said, "Well, I have a presentiment that this time we will, so I'll give you three to one—ten bob of yours, one pound ten of mine."

"Done, sir," de Saumarez said. "If you'll excuse me, sir, I'd like to re-read the Standing Orders before we sail . . ."

*   *   *   *

Two-forty a.m.: the misty air, dense with salt, hung low over the sea. The armoured cruisers were shaking out into screening formation. On the bridge of *Penrith* Lieutenant Buchanan had the watch. The

Captain, the Commander, and the Navigating Officer were all there, too—the Captain and the Pilot had been there since sailing; Tom Rowland was up for a brief visit after an hour's nap; as Commander he was the ship's general manager, and, in action, Damage Control Officer; he tried to stay away from the Captain when action was possible in order to lessen the risk of both of them being killed by the same shell. A signal lamp winked ahead: the yeoman of signals read— "From *Calliope,* sir . . . assume screening formation." De Saumarez hurried into the charthouse, where he could turn on the light behind the blackened out scuttles. He came out again in a moment with a course, which he gave to Buchanan. Then he bent over the voice pipe and said—"Engine room . . . bridge. We'll need power for sixteen knots any minute." The Captain did not move. The yeoman called, "Executive, sir!"

Looking back, Tom could just make out the battle fleet now, six divisions of them, each division consisting of four battleships—the divisions disposed in line abreast, the ships of each division in line ahead. The black smoke lay heavy across the sea, so that Tom could see only the leading ship or two of each line in their entirety; behind those only the masts showed, and the fluttering ensigns, flags, and pendants.

The yeoman called, "Signal from Commander-in-Chief to all flag and commanding officers . . . Fleet speed seventeen knots."

Leach nodded without speaking. Tom saluted, left the bridge, and returned to his Damage Control Centre in the heart of the ship. The light strengthened. The masked northern sun rose, but the only sign of its presence in the sky was a thickening of the haze to the east, now dense with sea particles lit by the sun. The surface of the sea was calm and oily and beginning to reflect a glare from the overcast sky. The ghostly fleet slid through it, silently, flags tugging at the halyards. Leach said, "We ought to be hearing something soon . . . if we're going to hear anything today."

De Saumarez thought, we won't hear anything until we hear the sound of guns—if we do—for strict wireless silence had been imposed by the Commander-in-Chief since the beginning, only to be broken to report enemy in sight.

Two-twenty p.m. De Saumarez was still on the bridge, but dozing on his feet. His eyes smarted from the daylong glare on the sea. He had eaten a little lunch in the stripped wardroom an hour ago, and felt heavy, and wished he had not had that glass of sherry before the lunch. All he wanted was to go to his cabin, lie down, and let the gentle motion of the ship and the hum of the turbines waft him to sleep. Below, Tom waited, reading a book; he was ready.

A signal messenger came running up onto the bridge. "*Galatea* has broken silence, sir. She has signalled to the Commander-in-Chief and to the Senior Officer Battle Cruiser Fleet—Enemy in sight two cruisers bearing south-south-east. Course unknown. Time of origin 1420."

De Saumarez jerked wide awake and looked toward Leach. Leach said, "Where's *Galatea*? She ought to be south-south-east of here."

He walked up and down the bridge. He stopped, facing de Saumarez—"My presentiment may come true after all, Pilot." He picked up the Navy phone—"Tom? *Galatea*'s sighted enemy cruisers. Take a look round the ship. I may be calling for action stations in a hurry. Tell Onstott to take preliminary action in the wardroom, so that he's ready to receive casualties there . . . Pilot, see what wavelength our W/T is monitoring. I want to be able to listen to *Galatea*'s net, if they're the ones which have the enemy in sight."

The same messenger returned, his face pale with excitement, his young eyes popping. He handed Leach a message, saying, "From Commander-in-Chief, sir, to all units of the battle fleet—Raise steam for full speed. Time of origin—2.35 p.m."

The messages came in, one by one as the minutes dragged by, all from *Galatea*, invisible over the southern horizon, to her own immediate commander, Vice Admiral Beatty of the Battle Cruiser Fleet, and to the overall Commander-in-Chief, Admiral Sir John Jellicoe.

Have sighted large amount of smoke as though from a fleet bearing east-north-east—1435

Smoke seems to be of seven vessels besides cruisers and destroyers. They have turned northward—1445

"That's Hipper's five battle cruisers and some escorting light craft," Leach said. "Can't be anything else. I'm going to win that ten bob off you, Pilot . . . *and* we're going to have a real battle. Action Stations." The buzzers sounded through the ship.

The two battle fleets advanced towards each other, like huge blindfolded prize fighters, each accompanied by little boys whose task was to find the enemy and lead his master to him . . . but the little boys were blindfolded, too. Admiral Beatty launched a seaplane to try to penetrate the enemy cruiser screen and locate the exact position of the German battle cruisers, but visibility was so poor that the seaplane's crew could not detect anything behind the German cruisers, which were already visible. Ships met, engaged each other with sudden brief violence, and passed on. Jellicoe waited, using his wireless as little as possible, for he commanded the more powerful fleet, and it was his task to lure Scheer, the German Commander-in-Chief, to battle on his own terms, and, if possible, without allowing the German fleet to escape back to its bases.

Three hours after clearing for action, the men now dozing and yawning at their stations, the cruiser next to *Penrith* in the 4th Light Cruiser Squadron's line abreast formation, H.M.S.*Comus,* started signalling to Commodore le Mesurier in *Calliope. Comus* was on the other side of *Calliope,* at the centre of the squadron's line, and the yeoman on *Penrith's* bridge could easily read the signal, as it was being sent by searchlight. He read aloud—"Gunfire and gun flashes three points off my starboard bow."

"It's increasing," Leach muttered to himself. They waited on the bridge, as the cruiser slid onward through the quiet sea, the mighty fleet behind still deployed in cruising disposition—for until the Commander-in-Chief learned the exact position and formation of the main German fleet, he could not deploy for battle.

"From Commander-in-Chief, sir, relayed from *Calliope.* Alter course by divisions, to south . . . executive!"

The cruisers made the turn, sidling off to starboard for four minutes before the Commander-in-Chief signalled resumption of the previous course.

"We're close now," Leach said, "must be."

The yeoman said, "From Commander-in-Chief, sir, relayed from *Calliope* . . . take up Disposition Number 1."

Leach raised his binoculars and watched the destroyer flotillas, smoke belching from the funnels, lean into the sea and race out onto the exposed flanks of the battle fleet. The sound of gunfire increased, shaking the ships and shuddering in the sea so that it trembled though still, showing motion only in the smooth arcs of the bow waves and the churning foam of the wakes.

The yeoman said, "I can see the flagship clearly now, sir." His telescope was to his eye, and he was propped in the port corner of the bridge, looking astern at the six rows of battleships, *Iron Duke* leading the third row from the left as he looked.

The yeoman said, "Equal Speed—CL, sir."

"Deploy south-east by east, preserving the speed of the Fleet," de Saumarez said.

The yeoman said, "Commander-in-Chief . . . General deployment . . . executive!"

De Saumarez cried, "*Calliope* has signalled for full speed, sir, . . . executive!"

Leach hung onto the forward bridge railing, his binoculars to his eyes. "Here they come!" he cried. The funnels and masts of Admiral Scheer's battle fleet appeared out of the sea, coming up from the south-south-west. Jellicoe's deployment would pass the whole British battle line across their front, crossing Scheer's T.

Tom Rowland, feeling the shudder of the ship as she lurched forward at full speed, ran up on deck to see what was happening. From the port side, amidships, he stared out on the most exciting scene of his life, and in a lurid way, the most picturesque. He saw the sudden unveiling of a vision, long known, but never before seen—a fleet action at sea. While *Penrith* had been steaming with the main battle squadrons of the Grand Fleet, Beatty and the battle cruisers, starting from Rosyth, had fought battles of their own, to the south and a hundred miles and more ahead. No one in the Grand Fleet, from Jellicoe downward, knew of these engagements in the drifting fog and sun patches, until *Galatea*'s signal of 2.20 p.m. In the nearly four hours since then the British battle cruisers had tangled with their German counterparts, and two had blown up, from turret flash-back caused by German shells—*Queen Mary* and *Indefatigable*. Cruisers had engaged each other, and finally Beatty had come in contact with Scheer and the German heavyweights. True to his orders, he had withdrawn northward, luring the Germans toward *his* heavyweights, Jellicoe and those twenty-four battleships . . . of whose presence no German was yet aware. Now, all this, hidden by time and distance, suddenly became clear before Tom's eyes and the battle was made whole.

Shells were bursting by hundreds in the sea off the bow of H.M.S. *Marlborough,* the battleship at the rear end of the deployment. A British cruiser, limping into shelter from an engagement with the German battle cruisers, blew up; a British battleship—*Warspite*—her steering gear damaged by a shell, was turning in massive circles, out of control, the target of three German battleships. Over all drifted the smoke of battle, the bellow of the great guns—now hiding, now loud, now displaying, now hushed.

Tom made ready, reluctantly, to go below again. No one seemed to be actually firing at *Penrith,* but there were so many shells in the air that anything could happen.

At that moment an appalling explosion made him pause, a hollowness in the pit of his stomach. Dead ahead one of the battle cruisers racing across the Battle Fleet's front to take station had been hit. It was *Invincible,* Rear Admiral the Honourable Sir Horace Hood's flagship of the 3rd Battle Cruiser Squadron. She lurched out of the line to starboard, seemed to settle, and then, as Tom watched, blew up in explosion after explosion, each a blinding flash of yellow and red. Soon, under a tall column of smoke, *Invincible* vanished. Tom hurried down to his post, and waited.

On the bridge Captain Leach cried, "The Germans have disappeared! They've just . . . gone!"

"Turned round in the mist, probably, sir, a Blue turn—the battle-turn-away Intelligence has been telling us about," de Saumarez said.

Leach said, "Well, if they *have* turned 16 points, they're heading south-west, so we're still between them and their bases."

6.40 p.m., de Saumarez noted. The Commander-in-Chief, apparently as puzzled as his captains as to what had happened to the Germans, was altering course successively more to starboard, closing the last known position of the enemy. Sporadic firing still echoed and drummed in the air, but it was nothing like the universal thunder of the last few minutes when the two battle fleets had been in action against each other.

De Saumarez said, "The C-in-C doesn't seem to be afraid that they're drawing us over a submarine or mine trap."

Leach shook his head, "We've made this contact by accident, that's obvious. Scheer hasn't had time to lay on a submarine trap, and mines aren't likely—too many ships have been ploughing the water here, with no reports."

On the bridge, they waited, peering into the mists, listening to the rush of water along the steel flanks, watching the trails of black smoke from the other ships of the squadron spread out to port and starboard. Below, Tom waited. Where was the German battle fleet?

The wireless room messenger bounced up the ladder—"Intercept from *Southampton* to Senior Officer Battle Cruiser Force, sir. Urgent. Priority. Enemy battle fleet steering east-south-east. Enemy bears south-south-west, number unknown."

7.04 p.m. and still broad daylight. Plenty of time to finish them off yet, Leach thought. But by God!—He pushed the message form under de Saumarez's nose—"Enemy battle fleet steering east-south-east . . . Half an hour ago they turned to south-west. Now they're heading for home, probably hoping to pass astern of us . . . Our squadron ought to be moving across to the starboard side."

He raised his binoculars and peered, first into the south-west, then at *Calliope*. "The Commodore hasn't made any signal," he muttered. He turned to the yeoman and snapped, "Make a signal! To Flag. Suggest enemy battle fleet close submit present maneuver should be at maximum speed."

He waited, watching *Calliope*'s flag bridge.

Two flags whipped up to the commodore's yardarm—*Penrith's* distinguishing letter; and Negative.

Leach turned away, his brows bent, scowling.

Almost at once de Saumarez cried, "Here they come, sir!" He pointed to the west. There, rising out of the mist were the tripod masts of battle cruisers, and behind them, taking ominous form, the tall

111

stacks and mighty deckhouses of battleships; and, ahead, cruisers streaking low through the water.

"By God!" Leach shouted, "the C-in-C's crossed their T again . . . Scheer's blundered right into the centre of the line!" He grabbed the engine room Navy phone and shouted down, "Give her everything you've got, Warner! . . . Tom, they're coming again!"

Calliope was flying the signal: Engage enemy destroyers; and Leach shouted into the increased wind of their passage—"Port twenty! Guns—open fire on the destroyers!" The air was full of a heavy roaring sound as the 15-inch guns of the battleships, firing over their own protective screen of cruisers and destroyers, engaged the German fleet. German shells screamed in from the opposite direction.

"We've got 'em!" Leach exulted. "Got 'em cold!" He watched a German destroyer racing toward them suddenly stop dead in the water, hit by a salvo of 6-inch shells. Flames poured from amidships, and the destroyer settled by the bow.

"Prepare to fire torpedoes," Leach said. "Port twenty . . . Torps, target is enemy battle cruiser . . . fire when ready!"

A shell struck *Penrith* somewhere aft, and Tom tensed at his post below. A moment later he heard the First Lieutenant's voice on the Navy phone—"A hit on B gun, sir. Two killed. Gun destroyed. No fire. All closed up."

Mainprice-King's voice sounded strange, and Tom said, "Are you all right?"

"Shell splinter scratched my head, sir. Blood in my eyes and mouth. It's being bandaged now."

"Well done!"

Penrith reeled from side to side as she jinked and dodged at Captain Leach's barked orders to avoid the German heavy ships' secondary armaments—the big guns had their hands full with the British battle fleet.

De Saumarez said, "The Germans are turning, sir . . . It's only the battleships, turning to starboard. The battle cruisers are coming on."

"Signal to Fleet flagship," Leach said. "Enemy battle fleet turning to south-west, enemy bears west. . . . Did I see our torpedo wakes, Torps?"

A tinny voice answered, "Yes, sir. Fired two at *Derfflinger*—missed . . . two at *Lützow*, which is burning. One hit."

"Good! You may fire when you see a target . . . Starboard thirty! Guns, leave that destroyer and engage enemy cruisers, supporting their battle cruisers—green four five!"

"Aye, aye, sir!"

Once again the sea was full of ships, but now the smoke was

heavier and thicker, for some of the German ships, particularly the destroyers, were deliberately laying a smoke screen.

Huge spouts of water towered up to port and starboard. De Saumarez said, "One of their battle cruisers has straddled us, sir. I think it's *Von der Tann.*"

"Starboard thirty!" Leach called, racing the ship toward the nearest splash. A few seconds later a mighty whistling and roaring passed close overhead, and almost simultaneously the whole 4,800-ton cruiser seemed to leap in the air, then sag down, a foot lower in the water than she had been. "We've been hit by a big one," Leach said quietly.

Tom sprang up and out of the little room below decks. This was serious. The ship had stopped.

*   *   *   *

There was no moon. *Penrith* lay dead in the slow oily swell, her engine room flooded and a gaping hole twenty feet across in her flank. Thirty-seven of her crew had already been committed to the sea, Tom Rowland reading the simple words over their blanket shrouded bodies, as, one by one, they were pushed out from under a Union Jack on the quarterdeck. Captain Leach remained on the bridge. There was nothing to be done except try to keep afloat. The wireless had been put out of action by a 5.9-inch shell from a German battle cruiser soon after the disastrous hit from *Von der Tann.* All battle ensigns were still flying, though hanging limp from masthead and yardarm. Full lookouts were at their posts, all serviceable guns and torpedoes manned. *Penrith* stood ready to give a final account of herself.

Every half hour Tom went round the ship, talking to the strained men, peering into the darkness at the guns; to the bandaged, pale First Lieutenant, watching the watertight bulkheads which, by containing the water in the engine room, alone kept the cruiser from sinking; to the Sick Berth Attendants in the wardroom, where Surgeon Lieutenant Onstott dozed on a sofa, the smell of disinfectant and charred flesh still heavy in the night sea air; to the twenty wounded laid out 'tween decks, covered by blankets, they alone of anyone on board permitted to smoke.

Every time Tom made his circuit, his messenger, Ordinary Seaman Charlie Bennett went with him. Near two-thirty in the morning, the light beginning to spread faint and steely green in the north-east, at the stern of the ship, by the limply hanging fog-damp White Ensign, under the gilt crown topping the ensign staff, Tom turned to Bennett and said in a low voice, "You're due for leave in October."

"Yes, sir."

"So am I. We'll meet in London. Don't make any other plans." He spoke more loudly, "That's all for now, Bennett. Get some kip."

"Aye, aye, sir." The sailor saluted, and in a moment disappeared below decks.

Tom walked slowly to the bridge. As he climbed the ladder he heard the captain's voice, low but urgent, "Stand to! Unidentified ship approaching from red nine oh. Guns, Torps, be ready to fire on my order."

"Ready, sir . . . ready!"

Tom stared into the palpable substance, half-darkness half-light mist, that covered the surface of the sea.

He saw it now . . . three funnels, twin searchlights silhouetted at funnel top height above the bridge . . . God, she looked like a *Stettin*-class cruiser. If she was, she should have another searchlight platform on the mainmast.

Leach said, "She must have seen us. Yeoman, give her the recognition signal. It's June first, remember."

"BK, sir, answered by DZ."

Tom couldn't see a third searchlight. What British cruiser looked like that?

The yeoman switched on the searchlight. The beam sprang out into the mist, making a huge silvery halo. The shutter clacked, long-short-short-short—long-short-long . . . The light bathed, with a ghostly radiance, a warship, her guns trained round, unrecognizable flags hanging limp at masthead and stern. A glaring light shone from her bridge, stuttering long-short-short—Long-long-short-short.

"Correct, sir," the yeoman said.

Leach and Tom and everyone else on the bridge breathed out a huge collective sigh. Leach said, "Yeoman, tell her who we are, and that we need help . . . Well, that's that. Now we'll find out what happened in the battle, perhaps. . . . I've been thinking, Tom. To meet the enemy where we did yesterday, we must have sailed from Scapa about three hours *before* he sailed from the Jade. It looks to me as though we have some means of reading German signals."

Tom said, "I don't really know what happened during the battle. You don't see much from the Damage Control Centre, though I did come up for a look-see two or three times. Could you tell me?"

Leach said slowly, "Weeell . . . we apparently learned that Scheer was coming out, sailed before he did, and put ourselves across his line of retreat. Twice he came at us—blundered into us, it seemed more like—and twice, realizing he was outgunned and outmaneuvered, he did the battle-turn-away they've been practising, and disappeared into the mist. The third time he apparently did get by, either ahead or astern of us. There certainly hasn't been any major engagement since we were hit, or we'd have heard the firing. I don't suppose we'll know the whole story till we get back to Scapa . . . perhaps not until we're old, old men. The fog yesterday wasn't only on the sea, in my opinion."

The Daily Telegraph, Wednesday, June 7, 1916

DEATH OF LORD KITCHENER
DROWNED AT SEA WITH HIS STAFF

At 1.40 yesterday afternoon the Secretary of the Admiralty announced that the following telegram has been received from the Commander-in-Chief of the Grand Fleet at 10.30 (B.S.T) yesterday morning:

I have to report with deep regret that his Majesty's ship *Hampshire* (Captain Herbert J. Savill, R.N.), with Lord Kitchener and his staff on board, was sunk last night about 8 p.m. to the west of the Orkneys, either by a mine or torpedo.

Four boats were seen by observers on shore to leave the ship. The wind was N.N.W., and heavy seas were running . . . As the whole shore has been searched from seaward, I greatly fear that there is little hope of there being any survivors. H.M.S. *Hampshire* was on her way to Russia.

As Johnny Merritt read, he was mentally making notes for his monthly letter to his father. He was alone at the breakfast table in the Manor. Stella liked to lie abed, and his father-in-law, Christopher Cate, had breakfasted early and was riding over to the Park to talk with Lord Swanwick about some problems between Swanwick's agent and one of Cate's tenant farmers, whose land bordered Lord Swanwick's. He felt strange when he and Stella spent a weekend here, as they did once a month or so. Their own cottage was so close, in Beighton, that it seemed silly to pack a bag and toothbrush and sponge and a suit and riding clothes. It would be much simpler if they stayed at home, and drove over for a meal or a talk. Well, they did that too, sometimes, but Stella felt that it wasn't enough. Johnny thought, she wants to feel that this is still her home.

He helped himself to a fried egg, eyed with distaste the fried tomatoes, and took two rashers of greenback bacon . . . that was strange stuff, too, until you got used to it; hardly any fat, and it stayed pinkish and tender when you cooked it, not crisp or crunchy. The British looked down on what he had regarded as bacon, calling it *streaky,* only to be eaten by those who couldn't afford anything better.

Most of the details of the North Sea battle were out now, and though it wasn't a British defeat, as the Germans had been proclaiming from the housetops since the day after it occurred, it was no Trafalgar either. According to the figures, the British had lost more ships and more men than the Germans; but that still left them with a sizeable superiority, so if the Germans came out again in the next few days or weeks, and another battle was fought, it would be on substantially the same terms. And this time, perhaps, the Germans would not somehow, inexplicably to the layman, be allowed to slip away.

The British were taking it hard, and he'd have to tell his father that. But Verdun was more important than this naval battle off Jutland, though the British would not recognize it—yet. Soon they would, for it was common knowledge that a great assault was to be made by the British armies in France, to take pressure off the French. It was even known, apparently, where it was to take place—on the Somme, where the French and British Armies linked. That, his War Office colonel told him, had been insisted on by the French, so that they could more strongly influence the British high command—though Haig wanted to make the assault in the Ypres area.

The only information that everyone didn't seem to know was the exact date for the assault. Surely there ought to be more secrecy? And surely it could be achieved, even for such a huge operation as this promised to be? He must tell his father that if the great assault failed, at least part of the blame must lie on lack of security and secrecy; and if the casualties were very heavy, which in that case they would surely be, the British would suffer a revulsion as great, or even greater, than their frustrated anger at the draw off Jutland. The higher the hope, the greater the disappointment.

Hedlington, Kent: Friday, June 16, 1916

8 The Depot of the Weald Light Infantry was hosting a variety concert for the benefit of all the Depot soldiers, but particularly of the large drafts that were going out to the battalions in France within the week. Several professional actors had given their services for the evening; and a large donation had been exacted from the notables as the price of their dinner, drinks, and admission to the event.

*   *   *   *

The great bare Old Manege was packed. Smoke rose from a thousand cigarettes and pipes as the audience sat back on the folding chairs and watched. The oeuil-de-boeuf windows high along the walls were all open to the summer night, but the scent of flowers, so strong in the Officers' Mess, did not reach into this, the oldest building in the Depot, built because the barracks were originally planned to house a regiment of dragoons; but used, when the dragoons were replaced by the Weald Light Infantry (then marines), as a place for meetings, ceremonial parades, and company close-order drill in bad weather. The tanbark of the dragoons had long been replaced by a floor originally wood, later tiles, now cement—ice cold and damp in winter. The lights, few and scattered, could not pierce the smoke to reach up to the mansard roof.

Harry Lauder was on the makeshift stage, singing, and though the audience had already been in its seats an hour and a half, no one coughed, or cleared his throat, or moved. The little man with the tam o'shanter askew on his head, a great crooked stick in one hand, his kilt

117

baring his knobbly old knees, the tartan plaid flung over his shoulder, held them in the palm of his hand.

> *I've seen lots of bonnie lassies trav'llin' far and wide*
> *But my heart is centred noo' on bonnie Kate McBride.*
> *And altho' I'm no' a chap that throws a word away*
> *I'm surprised mysel' sometimes at a' I've got to say.*

The men in khaki seated on the edge of their chairs were going to the Western Front within the week; but that no longer mattered, for they were now in some misty island off the Scottish coast . . . the heather purple around, the distance a hazy blue.

There was a glisten in Lauder's eyes, too, Florinda saw, watching from the wings; and that was the secret. That was why he was a great artist, and she never would be, for she would never have that ability to give all of herself—to abolish what she actually was, and be only the person, the singer, alone on the Scottish hillside: and she knew it.

Lauder's expression changed; the near-recitative changed to a cheerful rhythmic tune. The audience moved, smiled, began to laugh, chuckle . . . Lauder waved the great stick in the air, banged it down:

> *Roamin' in the gloamin' on the bonnie banks of Clyde*
> *Roamin' in the gloamin' wae my lassie by my side,*
> *When the sun has gone to rest, that's the time that we love best,*
> *O it's lovely roamin' in the gloamin'!*

He stumped off, banging down the stick. The audience rose, clapping, shouting. He came back, waved the stick, and clumped off again. Once more . . . he stopped in the centre of the stage and said, "Let's have *Little Redwing*. And all of ye, sing wi' me. Ready?"

> *The sun shines bright on little Redwing, on little Redwing . . .*

Just right for this moment, Florinda thought; though Lauder had said that he'd sing *A wee deoch an' doris* as an encore. But he had sensed that the people out there—the soldiers and sailors on leave—didn't want cheerful songs. There was no way of cheering them up that wasn't inherently a farce, considering where they were going. They wanted sentiment, tears in the eyes, songs of mother, betrayed love, loneliness.

The performance continued. The professionals were what Florinda wanted to be, and they gave their money's worth—what would have been their money's worth, if they were being paid. Jenny Jenkins had had too much champagne, but that did not prevent her singing half a dozen songs, three of them sentimental ballads, which had the soldiers sitting with heads bent, tears dropping slowly onto the floor. The lords and ladies in front sat quiet, controlled, but moved . . . Russell Wharton relieved the mounting tension with a gay dance with Jenny, and then a monologue that was full of double entendre and on the edge of indecency, but never quite stepped over; it was also very funny. The soldiers let themselves go, releasing in bellows of laughter repressed feelings that were, in truth, at the other end of the emotional spectrum. The jokes and innuendoes took a longer time to reach the pickled brain of the Marquess of Jarrow, who three times burst out laughing a good minute after the joke had been made. The third time he laughed so hard he fell forward off his chair face down on the floor.

Florinda was ready. She had had two soldiers standing by for this since the performance began. One of them was Recruit Fletcher Gorse, her brother . . . but few here knew that, and those that did held their counsel. She said, "Take him to the car—the red Rolls Royce outside the Mess. Woodward will look after him till I can come—he's the chauffeur." The soldiers half-supported, half-carried him out, while Russell Wharton continued his monologue without a break.

Then it was Florinda's turn and she found her pulse quickening and her mouth dry as she smoothed down the milkmaid's dress, just below knee length, with milk pail and bonnet, that was her costume. Ever since the Swanwicks' eldest son, Lord Cantley, had made her his mistress, she'd faced down every kind of public and private disapproval without any emotion other than a fierce joy and pride in living her own life; it had been the same when Cantley joined the Guards and she went to live with Lord Jarrow; but this, facing an audience, was different. She was trembling, her palms wet. "Stage fright," she muttered, "and I've sung a score of times in public now."

Wharton said, "You'll never get over it . . . if you're any good."

She walked out and Wharton, who was Master of Ceremonies as well as his other duties, introduced her. "My lord, ladies and gentlemen . . . Florinda!"

She did her best, singing, dancing, twirling, showing her white stockinged legs to the edge of her frilly underwear, amid swirling petticoats. She sang and danced a duet about the wickedness of men, with Jenny Jenkins; and another, about young love, with Russell Wharton, and found herself able to put her soul into it more than with most other actors she had sung with. Russell was, of course, a nancy, and so she could really throw herself into the fiction that she loved him—nothing would come of it: the singer and the man were not the same.

119

Two or three more turns followed—a conjurer, a pair of acrobatic clowns . . . and then the finale, with the whole cast on stage, Lauder in the centre front, Florinda on one side, Jenny Jenkins and Russell Wharton on the other, all singing "Ta-ra-ra-boom-de-ay!" At last the lights went out—there was no way of dimming them—except for a pair of spotlights over the stage. Lauder walked out of the darkness, stood under the lights, and said quietly, *"Keep the home fires burning . . . I'll sing the verses."* He raised one hand, leaning on the stick.

They were summoned from the hillside, they were called in from the glen,
And the Country found them ready, At the stirring call for men.
Let no tears add to their hardships, As the soldiers pass along,
And although your heart is breaking, Make it sing this cheery song—

He beckoned to the massed soldiers, bringing them to their feet. The deep throb of their voices filled the hall:

Keep the home fires burning; While your hearts are yearning,
Though your lads are far away They dream of Home;
There's a silver lining Through the dark cloud shining,
Turn the dark cloud inside out, Till the boys come Home.

Oh, damn, Florinda muttered, wiping her eyes with her sleeve: Ivor deserves the millions he must be making from that song. It was just right; and it meant something. She couldn't go to the war, but she could keep the home fires burning for those who did, for the nameless, hungry soldiers, by her singing and dancing.

After a pause the lights came up and the performers stood, bowing, as the audience clapped. Several minutes later, while Florinda again felt the tears coming to her eyes, Lauder raised his arms, and in the sudden quiet, said, "Tha's all . . . Gude nicht!" He turned and shepherded the actors off the stage toward the makeshift dressing rooms behind. There he put out his hand to Florinda, "It was gude of you to tak' the time, Lady Jarrow."

Florinda said, "Oh, you know I have nothing else to do . . . Do you think I'll ever be any good, Mr Lauder?"

The little man's shrewd eyes fastened on her with new attention. He hitched the plaid up on his shoulder and took a firmer grip of the crooked stick, "Ye have a gude voice, and gude legs. Ye'll just have to work, lassie . . . work, and lairrn from ithers. Gude nicht, again."

He turned away. Florinda found Russell Wharton at her side. "I heard," he said. "He's right . . . but don't be discouraged. I've seen women with less natural talent than you have, reach the top of the tree, or near it."

120

They were all about their business—at the mirrors, wiping off make-up, taking off dresses, and trousers in full view of performers of the opposite sex across the passage. Professionals.

Florinda's brother Fletcher came in and saluted—"His Lordship is sleeping comfortably, m'lady."

She said, "Come on," and walked out of the side door of the hall with him. "Poor little bugger!" she said; then, "How are you getting on in the Army?"

"All right . . . wasting my time, mostly."

"Have you got a girl?"

"None of your business."

"Well, who is it? I know you have one. I can tell by your voice."

"Is there anything more you'll be wanting of me, m'lady?"

"Oh, fuck you, Fletcher." She kissed him quickly and hurried across the square to the waiting Rolls. She'd better get the poor old drunk home.

*   *   *   *

In the anteroom of the Officers' Mess, its normal furniture now back in place, and the chimney bench again round the hearth, but a faint scent of women's perfume still lingering, the clock over the mantel struck half past one in the morning. Three men sat in a close group in the middle of the room—Captain George Clifford, Captain Charles Kellaway, and 2nd Lieutenant Archie Campbell. Clifford was a Regular, pre-war adjutant of the 2nd Battalion in India, but now wore a black eyepatch over the empty socket of his left eye, which he had lost near Arras with one of the New Army battalions early in the year. On recovery he had been appointed as Depot adjutant, a job which had hardened the lines of his face and considerably shortened his temper. Kellaway had come to the Depot on this, the last day but one of his leave from the 1st Battalion, in order to take a draft of men to the active battalions on the Western Front. Archie Campbell, the eldest of the three, was humming Harry Lauder's *A Portobello Lassie* under his breath and half listening to the others.

"It depends on the French," Clifford said. "If they can hold out at Verdun, we'll end the war this year."

Kellaway said, "They won't be able to hold out unless we help. We're going to make a big push. We must."

Clifford said sharply, "Why do you say 'must'? What do . . .?" He cut himself short. He despised amateur soldiers, Campbell knew, and Kellaway was an amateur . . . and a rich dilettante of the arts, perhaps a pouf into the bargain; but Kellaway commanded a company of the 1st Battalion, while Clifford was staying here . . .

121

Kellaway said placatingly, "Everyone was talking about it when I left. I've even heard it's to be on the Somme."

Clifford nodded, "I suppose you're right . . . Let's hope we don't make a balls of it, like Loos, again."

"It won't be like Loos," Kellaway said, "but there'll be a big butcher's bill. To be of any help to the French, our offensive will have to be far more than a token push."

The room was swaying slightly round Archie, and he knew that if he tried to get up he would sit down again. This talk of war was boring, and . . . what, improper? No shop in the mess, they'd told him in the Argylls, and they had the same rule here; every mess in the Army had it. Perhaps in the old Regular Army war wasn't shop. He giggled at the thought, then said, "That Florinda lassie has a gude pair of legs on her, does she no'? *An'* she can sing better than a corncrake."

Clifford said, "We do not discuss women in mess, Campbell. You've been told that."

"Yes, sir," Archie said. He felt rebellious.

Clifford stood up. "I'm off to bed . . . Sarn't!"

"Sir?" The mess sergeant appeared in the door from the pantry.

"How many waiters are still on duty?"

"Three, and myself, sir."

"Send them to bed, except one. You can go, yourself. The waiter on duty can lock up."

"Very good, sir." The sergeant stiffened in salute, and left the room.

"Good night," Clifford said. He walked out.

Archie peered dimly at Kellaway. "How about a wee drap, Captain Kellaway?"

Kellaway said, "I'll have a small one . . . Waiter!"

The waiter appeared, a stocky black-avised man in khaki uniform trousers, white jacket and white cotton gloves, by now none too clean. "Two small whisky and sodas," Kellaway ordered.

"A large one for me," Archie said. He swayed forward, "You're going out to the 1st Battalion on Sunday, sir?"

"For heaven's sake don't call me 'sir.' Yes, I am. Looking forward to it."

"How can that be?"

Kellaway looked round the room, at the paintings of past battles, dead colonels, and packs of foxhounds; at the leather covered furniture and the mahogany table with its neatly arranged piles of *Tatlers, Sporting Times, Illustrated London News, Spheres, Times, Morning Posts, Daily Telegraphs;* at the tattered French colour taken at Madras, the Napoleonic eagle taken at Waterloo and on a side table the silver pisspot, now filled with flowers, once the property of a marshal of the French Empire . . .

At length he said, "You'll find out . . . You're the painter, aren't you?"

"*The* painter? Goad, ye mean ye've hairrd of me? But of course, ye're not a Regular!"

"I have two paintings of yours," Kellaway said. "A seascape and a Clydeside shipbuilding yard."

"I remember them," Archie cried eagerly. "What do you think of Picasso? Braque? The cubists? Can you make head or tail of them?"

Kellaway nodded, murmuring "Thanks" as the waiter glided in, handed them their drinks, and glided out again. He said, "I don't understand them yet, but then one doesn't really understand an El Greco, for a time, at least." He drank, and glanced at the clock. "I'm going to bed soon. I'm due in the C.O.'s office at eight to check the draft lists."

Archie drank deep and again and leaned forward confidentially. His Scots accent was gone, as he said, "You really think there's a big push coming soon?"

"I'm sure of it," Kellaway said. "The French are insisting."

"Maybe I'll be out by then. Though they seem to think I'm too old . . . The adjutant was talking of keeping me here to do office work."

"Why don't you apply to be an official war artist?" Kellaway said. "You're wasted as a platoon commander. We can find plenty of them, especially with conscription "

Archie said, "The same reason you want to get back to the battalion. I wouldn't be *in* the war if I was only painting it."

Kellaway emptied his glass and stood up—"Well, I'm off. I hope you do get out soon, and to the 1st Battalion. We could talk about art and artists to our hearts' content. There's not much else to talk about."

"Quentin Rowland's your C.O., is he not?" Archie said.

"Yes. He's . . ." Kellaway stopped short: "Well, good night."

"Hold a minute, Kellaway. Quentin's wife is . . ." He had to tell Kellaway the truth; Kellaway would understand, give him advice.

"Fiona," Kellaway said. "Mrs Rowland's name is Fiona. She lives here in Hedlington. I brought her some French perfume from the colonel when I came over. Good night." He nodded and walked out.

The walls continued their stately circling, very slow, steady, with Archie as the hub. He watched the bubbles fizz endlessly up in his glass . . . drinking soda with whisky, God! Sassenach barbarians! Well, this wasn't a malt, it didn't deserve better. He needed to piss . . . damn good mind to piss in the marshal's pot, that was what it was made for, for God's sake . . .

He stood up, sat down again, stood up . . . sat down . . . tried once more, failed.

"Waiter!" he called.

The blue-jowled waiter appeared beside his chair—"Sir?"

"Help me get up . . . There . . . Hold me . . . I have to piss . . . Help me to the W.C."

The waiter's arm was firm round his waist, as Archie staggered across the anteroom, found the door of the W.C., found the door knob, found the urinal, and thankfully leaned against the wall above it.

He began to relieve himself. The waiter cried, "Sir! . . . Your fly buttons!"

"Too late, laddie, too late!" Archie mumbled, feeling the warm flood down his legs.

"Wha's yer name?" Archie said. "Ye're a handy man, a gude man aboot the hoose. Seen you about, but wha's yer name?"

"Fagioletti, sir."

Archie's whipcord trousers were wet down the front, but he was not totally soaked. He staggered back to the anteroom, and flopped down in the same chair. "Get me a drink, Fagioletti . . . Wha's your Christian name?"

"Niccolo, sir . . . I was a waiter at the Savoy."

"I knew you were a pro . . . Get me a drink, Niccolo, an' have one yersel'."

He closed his eyes. Fagioletti came back with two drinks. Archie said, "Sit down, Niccolo. Nick, they call you, I suppose."

"Yes, sir."

"I'm Arch, Archib, Archie, you call me Archie."

"Very well, sir . . . Archie." Archie tried to focus on the waiter. He'd been drinking, too, must have been . . . not a great deal, but enough to relax him, and put a reddish colour in his face . . . the fellow needed to shave twice a day, three times, perhaps. He said, "How do you like the Army, Niccolo?"

"Oh, it's all right, Archie." Fagioletti waved his glass of red wine expansively, "For me, it's no different from before. They find out I'm a waiter, and they put me here . . . I never go to France. The wages are not good, and no tips, but better than going out there."

"Quite right, Niccolo, better than having your balls shot off . . . You got a wife? Lady friend?"

"Lady friends, plenty," Niccolo said. He drank some wine . . . "Plenty of ladies will to fuck with a soldier these days . . ."

"Good for you. I can't get a piece of cunt for love or money . . . to tell the truth, I don't try. I'm terrified of women since . . . well, I'm terrified of getting hooked."

"Don't worry, Archie," Fagioletti said. "Fuck them and leave them. Another one will be around in no time, that's a truth."

"Fuck 'em and leave 'em," Archie echoed. He raised his glass and the two shouted in chorus—"Fuck 'em and leave 'em!" They clinked glasses and drank.

A voice from the doorway lashed them with icy fury. "Mr Campbell! Private Fagioletti! Stand up!"

The adjutant stood in the anteroom door, his face white, his knuckles gleaming, both hands clenched at his sides, his one eye burning. Archie stood up, and, by clutching the back of another armchair, managed to stay upright, Fagioletti beside him, rigid at attention but swaying gently, like an oak in a strong wind.

Clifford glared at Fagioletti—"Lock up the mess. Then go to your quarter. You will be leaving for France with the draft on Sunday. Get out!"

Fagioletti almost ran out into the pantry. Clifford turned on Archie—"I don't think I've ever seen a more disgraceful exhibition. Being filthy drunk is bad enough—Christ, you've pissed in your trousers, you unspeakable cad . . . but lolling drunk and using filthy language with an Other Rank . . . You, an officer and a gentleman! You're not fit to wear our uniform!"

Archie said plaintively, "I never asked to be a gentleman, sir."

"You'll go to France with the draft on Sunday. And I hope you get killed before you disgrace the Regiment in public. Get to bed now."

He turned on his heel. Archie called after him, "Sir, can I go to the 1st Battalion? Ye see, I've family connections there, and . . ."

"You'll go where you're sent," Clifford said viciously, closing the door behind him.

He didn't slam it, Archie thought; there's a *real* gentleman, and certainly an officer. He carefully lowered himself to all fours and crawled out into the night, and to his room, and into his bed.

The Western Front: Saturday, June 17, 1916

The brigade runner had just delivered the bulky manila envelope and Boy Rowland, Adjutant of the 1st Battalion of the Weald Light Infantry, had just signed for it. Now Boy broke the red wax seals, drew out the contents, and swore under his breath. His clerk, writing out a long signal on an Army message form, with three carbons under it, looked up—"Trouble, sir?"

Boy said, "Brigade Instructions for the Forthcoming Operations . . . twenty-seven typed pages . . ." he leafed slowly through the pages—"Intention . . . the Divisional Plan . . . the attack of the flank brigade . . . our objectives . . . artillery support . . . instructions as to rebombardment—preliminary moves—ha, we're going to be withdrawn from the trenches during the first part of the bombardment, which will last for five days . . . cutting of our own wire . . . composition of assaulting columns . . . method of assault . . . that's the usual "steadily behind the artillery barrage"—those blasted brass hats should try to keep a steady straight line across country which a few thousand guns have been shelling for five days . . . mopping up . . . boundaries . . . action of reserve battalions—which is *not* us . . . Machine gun company . . . trench mortars . . . consolidation of positions captured . . . the subsidiary operation . . . concluding operation . . . smoke attack . . . Gas . . . Reports . . . Phew. I suppose I'd better take it right along to the C.O., though there's nothing in it that I can see as to when Z Day will actually be."

"July the first, sir," the clerk said. "The R.Q.M.S. has a pool on it. I bought June the twenty-eighth, but the gup is that it's to be the first."

Boy leafed back over the heavy bundle in his hand, and said, "If this ton of bumf is just a brigade order, what on earth must Division, Corps, and Army orders be like?"

A voice behind him said, "The Corps Instruction is sixty-seven pages. The gunner major showed me a copy he'd got from somewhere this morning. And don't think of it all as just bumf. Those are our orders! By following them, we'll break through this time."

"Yes, sir."

Lieutenant Colonel Quentin Rowland stepped down into the dugout and said, "Give me that order . . . and make ready to receive a draft of five officers and a hundred men."

The Daily Telegraph, Thursday, June 22, 1916

ARABS IN REVOLT
CAPTURE OF MECCA
INDEPENDENCE DECLARED

Cairo, Wednesday evening. Authentic news has been received that his Highness the Grand Shereef of Mecca, supported by the Arab tribes of West and Central Arabia, has proclaimed Arab independence of Turkey and of Ottoman rule, under whose maladministration and inaction the country has so long suffered.

Operations commenced about June 9, and have resulted in the signal success of the Shereef's forces. Mecca, Jeddah, and Taif have been captured, and the garrisons have surrendered, with the exception of two small forts at Taif, which are said to be still holding out.

The numbers of the troops who surrendered at Mecca and Taif

are not yet known; but at Jeddah forty-five officers, 1,400 men, and six guns were captured.

Medina, according to the latest news, is closely besieged and all communications to the Hedjaz are in the hands of the Shereef . . . trade to the Hedjaz ports can now be resumed. It is therefore confidently expected that the difficulties which have attended the annual pilgrimages to the Holy Places during the past two years will now be removed. REUTERS

So, Cate thought, perhaps the disaster at Kut will not have such serious and lasting effects as he had then feared. The war could hardly end now without the disbandment of the ramshackle Turkish Empire, and Kut would be forgotten. In a way it already had been, or the Arabs of the desert would not so readily have thrown in their lot with Britain . . . with the Allies, officially, of course, but in that part of the world only one Ally—England—could give the Arab cause any practical aid. In a year or two there would again be Arab rulers from the Yemen to the borders of Anatolia, from the Mediterranean to the Persian mountain barrier, as there had been before the Ottoman Turks welded those lands into their empire.

He laid the paper down. He had eaten a small breakfast, but had not felt hungry. The guns from France were speaking more insistently, a mutter by day, a rumble in the still summer nights. They must be making ready for the great assault that everyone seemed to be expecting—even demanding. Last night a nightingale had sung in the trees beyond the lawn for half an hour, as beautifully as another he remembered from his boyhood, when he had leaned out, listening under the full moon, breathing in the heavy perfume of night-scented stock and new-mown grass. But this night the bird's paean had soared and swooped over a continuous bass diapason from the distant guns . . . a tragic diapason, preventing him from sleeping, for he had to listen, and in listening, think of the men who heard it close, and would soon hear it no more.

The Somme: July 1, 1916

9 Boy Rowland waited, determined at all costs not to let the queasiness in his stomach and the creeping of his skin become a visible tremble. Last night the Post Corporal had brought him a letter from David Toledano, whose Field Battery was now in Palestine. David had described an idyllic life of warm sun, palm trees, orange groves, and swimming in the Mediterranean. Why the hell couldn't the Battalion be sent to Palestine—or Egypt, Mespot, East Africa—anywhere, rather than here? He might be back at the Depot, where Hedlington would be busy with preparations for the Sheep Fair . . . only the Sheep Fair was not going to be held this year, or until the war ended . . . if ever. If ever the war ended.

Beside him his uncle, Lieutenant Colonel Quentin Rowland, puffed on a pipe, the blue smoke drifting along the trench in a thin trail, past Regimental Sergeant Major Nelson standing properly "at ease," his hands behind his back, as though on a drill parade, his steel helmet set squarely and centrally on his head, not a muscle moving in the hard face or shaven bull neck . . . among the packed soldiers beyond, all waiting, bowed under full packs, extra bandoliers of ammunition slung over shoulders and around their necks, sand-blasted bayonets fixed on the rifles. High above, streaky wind-clouds hurried from west to east across the sky.

The chalk of the trench side was dirty white, soggy from the rain of three days earlier which had caused a postponement of the assault. A look through any of the periscopes positioned at sixty-foot intervals along the trench would have shown, first, the rows of British barbed wire, cut at regular intervals, the gaps blocked by wired knife rests, which would be pulled aside to let the assaulting infantry pass through. Beyond the wire, the torn earth rolled in uneven rise and fall for three hundred yards to more wire—the German trenches. Fricourt Wood and village blocked the view to the north, and the stripped skeletons of Mametz Wood marched along the skyline to the north-east.

No one spoke. If one had, he would not have been heard unless he placed his mouth close to the other's ear, and shouted at the top of his voice. Head bent, appalled even after his nineteen months in the trenches, Boy strove with a sort of desperation to isolate something he could recognize—the burst of a shell, the whine of shell splinters, the rattle of shrapnel. He could not hear them: he could not *hear* anything, only be aware of a solid ceiling of sound arching over the battlefield from far west in the British gun positions to as far east, among the German batteries. The air above the battlefield had been welded into an enormous agony. The ground beneath, the walls of the trench, the pools and rivulets of water, shook, danced to the savagery all round. No part of that arc of fury moved: it *was,* and had been for five days.

The C.O. looked at his watch and Boy looked at his: seven twenty-four . . . six minutes to zero hour. A swarthy soldier in the nearest platoon had turned to retch against the parados of the trench; he was one of the draft which had arrived a couple of weeks ago, Boy remembered—posted to B Company, a foreign name; shit scared now, and showing it . . . so was he himself. Was he showing it?

The platoon commander was Bob Beldring, who splashed along the trench, easing among the tight-packed men, to pat the retching soldier on the back and yell something in his ear. The man straightened. Beldring held out a flask and the man took a swig and handed it back. Beldring took a big swallow himself. His eye caught Boy's and he held out the flask. Boy shook his head. Soundlessly the earth leaped and shivered in terror, the solid air pressed down on them, battering at their steel helmets.

His uncle shook the dottle from his pipe, banged the bowl against a wooden revetting beam and put the pipe away in his pocket. Seven twenty-eight. The men along the trench were stirring, moving back and forth. Beldring produced his whistle from the pocket of his tunic, still on its lanyard, and looked at his watch. The ladders were in place against the front wall. Men waited at the foot of each, one boot on the bottom rung.

Whistles blew all along the trench. The men at the ladders climbed up, ran out and pulled aside the knife rests. Man after man followed, bowed, leaden footed, hands shaking, wet, ice cold with fear, going on, up, out, easing to right and left. "Good luck, good luck!" Quentin shouted, his hands cupped, as he stood near the foot of a ladder. "We'll be right behind you!"

The British artillery lifted off the German front line, and in that moment the German gunners opened up. Heavy shells trundled in like moving wagons, or blocks of concrete, that burst with tremendous explosions among the khaki rows. Machine guns came to life as the lyddite smoke drifted off No Man's Land. Watching through a periscope, Boy saw the lines of the two leading companies, B left and C right, silhouetted against the smoke, begin to thin. Great gaps were torn in them by huge invisible hands, but the lines moved steadily on.

"Ready, Boy?" his uncle yelled.

He nodded, and followed up the ladder. Up on top the churning in his stomach ceased. He felt suddenly hot, and raging. The chalky upland was strewn with dead, blood drained in a hundred streams from smashed bodies and torn bowels, rifles and bayonets lay like cut reeds, packs torn open by shell bursts, their contents scattered—socks, housewife, photo of a woman and a child . . . Machine guns were traversing . . . left to right . . . three, at least, mowing down A Company to his left. Five days of shelling and they were still there, still manned, still firing . . . He saw his uncle, a few paces to his right and just ahead, start, and grab his left arm below the elbow with his right. Soon the sleeve was dark with blood. German artillery shells were falling so thick among the advancing lines that Boy could not see more than a few yards except intermittently, when a gust of wind, or the bursting of another shell, for a moment dispersed the smoke . . . Such a moment came and he stared . . . one man crawling on hands and knees near the edge of Mametz Wood . . . another walking forward far to the left . . . for the rest, humps, and lumps, and grotesque shapes.

He shouted, "They're *gone,* sir!"

"Most of 'em knocked over, poor devils." Quentin shouted back. "The rest, gone to ground . . . Who's due to follow us?"

"14th York and Lancs, sir," Boy looked back over his shoulder, still trudging forward, and dimly saw fresh lines of khaki men coming out of the British front line trenches. "They're coming now."

"Wait for them," Quentin said. "We'll gather our fellows together . . . close them up, here . . . You go that way, I'll go left."

He walked off, his ash plant swinging, shouting to the few men crouched or lying on the ground, "Go to the R.S.M. . . . line up near him . . . Sergeant, line them up over there . . . Get a move on, Corporal!"

Boy broke into a stumbling run. "Move!" he said, leaning down to jerk a lying man to his feet. The man was lying in the correct prone position, rifle outthrust, legs spread, heels pressed flat to the earth. His head flopped over, revealing a round blue hole in the middle of his forehead . . . But others heard and jumped up and ran to the R.S.M. who was kneeling, a rifle taken from a dead soldier in his hands, firing carefully aimed shots at the German trench, now barely a hundred yards away.

The leading men of the York and Lancs arrived and Boy and Quentin and the R.S.M. shouted together, "Up, lads! Up, Wealds, up!"

The R.S.M. doubled over, falling, the rifle hurling away in the convulsion of his death, machine-gun bullets tattooing his falling body. The York and Lancs trudged up, past . . . but, as though a wand had been waved, a cloth wiped across a dirty spot, they were not there. The machine guns traversed on, but there was no one standing, only dead lying piled on top of each other in the mud and water, and a few living and wounded crouched in the new, smoking shell holes.

Boy found himself close to his uncle, both lying against the forward slope of a huge hole left by a large calibre German shell, probably one of their 17-inch guns. Half a dozen soldiers lay to right and left, some of them Wealds, some of them York and Lancs, together with Father Caffin, the battalion's R.C. padre.

An unreal quiet fell on the field. Boy muttered to his uncle, "Do you think it's been like this everywhere, sir?"

Quentin said energetically, "Of course not, Boy! We'll be able to advance again as soon as the other brigades get past the flanks of these fellows in front of us. Here, put my first field dressing on this, will you? . . . There, thanks. Where's the R.S.M.?"

"Dead, sir. Just back there."

"Poor chap. His wife's having another baby next month. Have to think about appointing someone else . . ."

"Dalley's the senior C.S.M., sir. A Company."

"Is he fit for it?"

"I think so . . . He may be dead. The German artillery nearly wiped them out as they left our trenches . . ."

Quentin hauled himself up to the lip of the crater, and put his binoculars to his eyes. "Swine!" he muttered under his breath. "They're waiting . . . machine guns on the parapet . . . wire uncut."

Boy said, "Our patrols reported it was cut two days ago."

"Not ours, Boy. Patrols of the battalion that was holding the front then, and supposed to make all preparations for our attack . . ." He slid back into the bottom of the crater. "Organize these men, Boy. I'm going to see how many others we have, then I'll come back here. Get ready to resume the attack . . . ."

He pushed himself up out of the crater and then, walking fast but not running, went to another shell hole nearby. A solitary German fired one shot, apparently at him, but missed, and Quentin disappeared into the shell hole.

Boy turned on a York and Lancs corporal—"What's your name?"

"Hatfield, sir."

"Put half the men here and half there. Check ammunition, grenades, gas masks. Fill up pouches from the dead. Get those two Lewis guns off the dead out there and use them here." His voice failed him. The corporal, pale and strained, waited. Boy finished, "Get on with it!"

He sat down on the sloping side, his legs turned to water. A voice nearby said quietly, " 'Tis a mess, an' all, Boy."

He looked up. Father Caffin's tunic was covered with blood, as were his hands. He muttered, "You're wounded."

The priest shook his head, " 'Twas one of the boys I was holding in my arms just now."

"You weren't supposed to come forward with us," Boy said.

"Ach, I know, but how would any good Irishman be missing a fight like this?"

Boy looked round to see that none of the men could hear him, then said, "All these poor fellows . . . gone . . . and we're nowhere . . . ."

The priest laid a hand on his shoulder, " 'Twas not your fault, anyway. Or the colonel's. They all know that."

Colonel Rowland came tumbling into the crater behind them. He shouted, "B Company's in the German trench! Up, everyone! Follow me!"

*　　*　　*　　*

Private Niccolo Fagioletti stood frozen in the bottom of the German trench, his rifle gripped convulsively in his right hand. Men passed, hurrying, stumbling, bent on their own errands. Five dead Germans, all apparently destroyed by a single shell, were plastered in pieces against the walls and floor of the trench a little farther along, near the first traverse. From a great distance he heard voices, and recognized the sharp cockney twang of Sergeant Thompson, his platoon sergeant. Opposite him, sprawled back on a sort of seat cut out of what had been the front wall of the German trench and was now the back wall, Lieutenant Beldring stared at the sky, his skin chalky white, spittle dribbling from the corner of his half open mouth, both hands clasped over his belly, hiding the entry wounds of the three machine gun bullets that had hit him just before they reached and fell into the German trench.

Fagioletti realized that he himself was still alive. He could not believe it, and moved his left hand up in front of his face and stared at it. A violent trembling broke out all over his body, and he became aware of the sodden weight in his trousers, and the vile smell surrounding him.

"Wot the bleedin' 'ell do you think you're doing, Dago?" Sergeant Thompson was in front of him, screaming. "Gawd, you stink, man!"

"I . . . I shitted myself," Fagioletti stammered.

"There's plenty done that. Clean yourself up and put on Jones '65's trousers—there. He won't need 'em any more and 'e's about your size. Then get up on the firestep. Jerry'll come back at us, and 'e won't wait till you're ready."

Fagioletti unbuckled his equipment with trembling, clumsy fingers, took off his puttees and trousers, and wiped himself with water standing in the trench. After a long struggle he managed to get the trousers off the corpse of Private Jones '65, and put them on. Now that he was dressed again, fear returned. Machine guns were opening up again. The trench was in bad shape, severely damaged by the long preliminary bombardment, but the deep dugouts were mostly untouched. He sneaked into the doorway of one, and started down the steps.

A roar behind him made him stop. "You, there! Come out . . . So it's you, is it, Dago?" Sergeant Thompson's sharp face contorted as he grabbed Fagioletti by the ear, nearly wrenching it off as he dragged him back up the dugout steps. "There!" he screamed, "there's the firestep, that ammunition box, stand on it, face that way . . . Freeman, shoot this dago if he tries to sneak off." He bustled on, shouting oaths.

Gradually the line of men on the makeshift firestep—the real firestep faced the wrong way—lengthened and strengthened. Two captured German machine guns were in position, facing the Germans. It was nine o'clock, the sun climbing fast in the summer sky, aeroplanes—all British—buzzing and circling far and near.

Beldring began to moan. Fagioletti stole a glance behind him, and saw that the officer's eyes were closed. Sergeant Thompson was on one knee beside him, speaking close—"You'll be all right, sir . . . We'll 'ave you out of 'ere in no time . . ."

Fagioletti turned again to face out over the shell-torn earth, the barbed wire, some cut, some undamaged, that protected the German reserve trenches, and the sunken concrete pillboxes, which did not seem to have been damaged much, if at all.

He heard a strong voice behind him speak sharply, "Who's in command here?" and Sergeant Thompson's reply, "I am, sir."

Fagioletti glanced round again and saw that the speaker was the C.O. of the battalion, Lieutenant Colonel Rowland. He had only seen him once, when he had addressed a few words to the draft, but Fagioletti had a good memory for names and faces. In his business, it meant a lot in tips to call a customer by his right name, especially if he hadn't come in for some time. With the C.O. was the adjutant, whom he had seen two or three times, and knew was the C.O.'s nephew.

"How's Mr Beldring?" the C.O. asked. Sergeant Thompson dropped his voice to reply, as though the wounded officer could hear—"Bad, sir."

"Have you given him morphine?"

"Yes, sir. All I 'ad. 'E caught three or four in the stomach."

"Don't give him any water then. It's bad for stomach wounds. We'll try to get him back when we can . . . Ah, Stratton, what's the situation in your sector?"

"Bad, sir," another voice answered. "My platoon was all but wiped out in the attack. I had three men when we got here . . . I've picked up a dozen more from other platoons, a dozen Yorks and Lancs, and a few Devons."

"I'll come and take a look. Boy, how many have we got together so far?"

"About a hundred and sixty, sir . . . seven officers."

The soldier on Fagioletti's right shouted, "Here they come!"

A hurricane of German shells hit the trench. Fagioletti found Colonel Rowland standing on another ammunition box beside him, a rifle in his hand, glaring out into the flying earth, mud, and smoke. German soldiers were coming out of their reserve trenches a hundred yards on, in groups and bunches, darting forward, disappearing, reappearing. The captured machine guns were in action, with all available rifles and Lewis guns. The colonel began to shoot, aiming and firing methodically.

The colonel turned his head and snarled, "You're not aiming, man! Aim! Kill a Hun each shot or by God they'll kill you!"

Fagioletti tried to concentrate on the flitting grey figures out there . . . picked one out . . . steadied his sights . . . fired. The man fell, bounced, half rose, fell again.

"I kill a man," he cried. "Oh God, I kill a man!"

The colonel did not respond. He must think I am mad, Fagioletti thought, and fired again, and again, increasing his rate of fire as the attacking Germans worked closer.

Now they were forty yards away . . . twenty . . . He never missed now, the wooden stock was hot to his left hand, the cordite acrid in his nostrils. The captured machine guns were eating great bites out of the German groups . . . not lines, Fagioletti noticed, but independently moving bunches, some sprawled or hidden, firing, others coming on at a run. Potato masher bombs whirled through the air, to burst in the trench or on the earth in front of him, hurling mud into his face.

The colonel leaped to his feet, "Up, Wealds! Give 'em the bayonet!"

He scrambled up and into the open. Fagioletti felt a hand shoving him from behind, and he was up, out. There was another officer beside him, the one he'd got drunk with in the Mess—Mr Campbell, now with rifle and bayonet in hand . . . They were on the Germans, face to face, hand to hand. He lunged at a big German at the moment that the man paused to fire at Mr Campbell. The bayonet slid into the German's neck, grated on bone. Fagioletti pulled the trigger. The blast freed the bayonet from the German's spine and he fell, crashing across Fagioletti's feet. To the side, Mr Campbell was darting under the guard of another German, his bayonet sliding into the man's belly just above the belt buckle.

The adjutant was out there, too, and seventy men of three battalions, milling together with the twenty Germans who had reached this far. Suddenly the Germans turned and fled, disappearing into the smoke. For a moment the British stood in the open, braying after them like triumphant cavemen, waving rifles in the air, blood dripping from the bayonets. Colonel Rowland grabbed Fagioletti's arm and yelled, "We showed them!"

A wild exhilaration filled Fagioletti. He'd bayonetted two Germans . . . he'd shot half a dozen . . . he was alive . . . He screamed in his native Venetian, *"Li gàvemo fermai—gàvemo copà quei porsei!"*

Colonel Rowland shouted, "Back to the trench . . . hurry!"

They jumped back and down, just in time, as the German artillery observers, having seen the defeat of the counter-attack, reopened fire on the captured trench.

Fagioletti was back on his ammunition box, facing out over the new No Man's Land. A group of officers was just below and behind him, and he listened to them with a professional competence, just as he used to listen to diners' conversation at two or three tables at once, separating out the voices from his post several yards away.

"Another wave should have passed here long since," Colonel Rowland said. "If one doesn't come soon, we ought to attack. Maintain the momentum of the attack, at all costs . . . that's what the training memoranda all stressed."

Boy Rowland said, "The pillboxes in their second and third lines don't seem to have been damaged by our bombardment, sir. Nor the wire . . ."

"They're disorganized . . . just had their counter-attack beaten back," the colonel said. "But we'll have to wait till dark . . . Meanwhile, we've got to let Brigade know what's happening up here. No one's seen any brigade runners or staff, have they?"

"Not likely, sir." That was Lieutenant Fred Stratton, Fagioletti knew, his brother-in-law . . . or had been, until he divorced Ethel. He was glad he had not been put in Fred's platoon. The Strattons were all angry with him.

The colonel said, "Then we'll have to send someone . . . to make them understand we must have reinforcements here if we are to hold what we have, let alone continue the attack tonight . . . Mr Campbell, you'll go."

After a pause the officer answered, "Yes, sir."

"Get back to Brigade any way you can. Take one man as escort. Tell them that I have about a hundred and fifty men and seven officers . . ."

"Six, sir," the adjutant cut in. "Major Dodson was killed in that last German attack."

"Take over his company, Boy. And when you come back, you'll act as adjutant, Campbell. . . . Tell them we're holding the old German front line trench from the edge of Mametz Wood to a point about three hundred yards east of it. The German wire is uncut in front of us, and their concrete pillboxes are undamaged. I need information about the position on our flanks . . . and reinforcements—quickly."

"Yes, sir."

Fagioletti felt a tap on his legs. "You, Private Fagioletti . . . come with me."

Fagioletti slid down into the trench. The colonel said, "Go with Mr Campbell. You've done well today. What's your name?"

"Fagioletti, sir."

"I'll remember you. Mr Stratton, take command of the sector from here to Mametz Wood. Make sure that the Germans can't infiltrate past you through the wood."

"There's not many trees left standing now, sir."

"Boy, go and take over the right sector . . . and, of course, what's left of D, wherever you can find them. And send me C.S.M. Dalley, if he's alive . . . I want him as R.S.M."

"Come along, Fagioletti," Mr Campbell said. "We'll have a tot of rum at Brigade . . . if we get there in one piece."

"Very good, sir," Fagioletti said. He unfixed his bayonet, made sure his magazine was full, and followed Mr Campbell up into the open, running from shell hole to shell hole, among sporadic explosions, under the random rattle of machine gun fire, past still smoking craters, over uncountable silent dead, and moaning wounded.

* * * *

Candles guttered in the crowded dugout. Colonel Rowland continued, "The two companies from the 17th Connaught Rangers are due to join us here by midnight, and attack with us. You'll have guides in our old front line trench, Mr Campbell, to bring them forward from there."

"Aye, sir . . . yes, sir."

"The artillery barrage will begin at first light, when the spotters can see the targets. The heavies will be directed specifically at the German pillboxes and wire . . . We will attack in two waves, at seven-thirty ack emma. Our first objective is the new German front line trench, but there will be no delay on that, and troops will advance straight on to the second objective, which is the German reserve trench . . . lines of advance will be by compass, bearing 20 degrees magnetic . . . that line will be adhered to at all costs . . ."

He went on . . . creeping barrage . . . rate of advance . . . necessity of keeping close behind the barrage . . . forming waves . . . wire . . . unexpended portion of the day's ration, if any (the men haven't had any rations, or fresh water, all day, Boy thought, as he listened, taking notes, an army message pad on his knee) . . . intercommunication . . . success signals . . . It was all a repeat of the scene the day before, except that that had been by daylight, and this was in the dusk, in a German dugout . . . and so many faces, grown familiar, had gone . . . Dodson, Burke-Greve, Beldring, Jackson, le Fevre, Nichols, Foy, Scott, Jerram, all dead . . . Kellaway, Garvey, Gates, Churchill-Gatty, Stroud, Buchman-Smythe, wounded . . . and the men—over five hundred.

The German dugout still smelled of German cigar smoke, German officers' equipment still hung on nails from the beams, the crowded British faces wavered in German candle light—Campbell, the old Scotsman he'd barely seen, come here under a cloud for getting drunk with an O.R. in the Depot Mess—he'd done all right today, though: Fred Stratton, confident, assertive, a new man . . . young Dale, gawky as a scarecrow but otherwise very Sandhurst, didn't need to shave yet—he'd done well, too . . . a York and Lancs subaltern just out from home, and almost dumb with the shock of what he'd seen . . . Father Caffin, *there* was a good one; he'd be pleased to see the Catholic Connaughts when they came up . . . but he was just as good with the Kentish and Cockney Protestants of the Wealds . . .

137

What had happened today? He ought to find out. Everyone ought to know, to make sure it didn't happen again. On this part of the front it had certainly been a disaster, only the stubborn courage of the men shining through the murk of failure. But it was all going to repeat itself tomorrow . . .

His uncle said, "Any questions?"

No one spoke and Quentin said, "Dismiss, then, and good luck tomorrow. I'll be round soon after midnight, when I've seen the Connaughts in, and made sure they understand the orders."

The officers rose from the bench and ammunition boxes and sandbags they had been sitting on, saluted, and filed out into the trench. There was no moon, and starlight gleamed dully on the bayonets of the sentries along the firestep—one-third of all men were on sentry duty, the rest sleeping at their feet in the bottom of the trench, their rifles cuddled in their arms.

The Yorks and Lancs subaltern had been appointed Boy's second-in-command, and the two now stumbled along one behind the other, trying not to tread on sleeping soldiers, edging round traverses, squeezing past N.C.O.s patrolling the trench, until they reached the dugout in the middle of Boy's sector where he had established his headquarters. Sergeant Thompson was waiting there, and Boy said, "I'll give all N.C.O.s orders in ten minutes, Sergeant, here."

"They're eating now, sir. We found a string of Jerry sausages, and a sack of bread—black bread, it is."

Boy led into the dugout, dropped the gas curtain into place, fumbled for a match, and lit the solitary candle that stood in a bottle on the table. He sank down wearily onto the backless chair on one side of the table, the subaltern onto the other, facing him. He was about twenty. He stared fixedly at Boy, his mouth working, and finally burst out in a marked Lancashire accent—"It will be joost the same as t'day! We'll all be killed!"

Boy said, "Not all . . . some."

"Boot . . ."

"It's a dangerous war," Boy snapped. Privately he thought that if the Germans were guilty of atrocities, the British generals certainly were for the planning of today's attack. Any other soldiers would have shot their officers in the back and run. Perhaps it would be better if they had. Then the brass hats back there would have had to face the facts. As it was, nothing went through . . . pale, frightened, hungry, thirsty, filthy, the British infantry stuck it; and the brass hats could report . . . victory.

"Smarten up," he said sharply to the subaltern. "The N.C.O.s will be here in a minute and I don't want them to think we don't believe entirely in what we're going to do." God, he thought, my voice was exactly like Uncle Quentin's when I said that.

* * * *

Quentin Rowland sat on an ammunition box in the dugout where he had given his orders. It seemed much larger now, with only himself, Father Caffin, and Campbell in it. A half empty bottle of German champagne stood on the battered table between two guttering candles. He was puffing on his last fill of tobacco, and his arm still hurt, but he felt a slow, solid content. The battalion had done magnificently. No other soldiers could have done it . . . just citizen soldiers, too, for the old regulars he'd commanded at Mons and Le Cateau and First Ypres were long gone. In spite of the tremendous artillery preparation, in the end the work had had to be done with bare hands. Tomorrow they'd finish this part of the job . . . and the day after, the next . . . and then the next . . .

Campbell, sipping the sweet champagne, watched the colonel with an artist's concentration. This was Fiona's husband, whom she despised, the man who didn't understand her . . . no imagination, she had said a hundred times. No understanding of her, she had meant; but he must have no imagination at all, or how could he sit there, in obvious contentment, with five hundred of his men and more than half his officers dead and wounded, the great attack dead. But there he was, and whatever the men had been through, he'd been through it with them. None of them were going to say a word against him, or hear one said. None of *them* were going to accuse him of lack of imagination . . . Why? Because they didn't have any themselves? That must be it, otherwise how could they face the memory of what they had seen, and the certainty of more of the same tomorrow, and tomorrow . . . for weeks, months, perhaps?

He said, "Sir . . . at first, when we left our trenches, the battalion on our right was doing very well. If they'd gone on they would have got behind the Huns who were enfilading us. But they stopped. Did they have to do that, sir?"

The colonel said, "It was in the orders . . . pace of advance not to be altered or exceeded in any circumstances, nor objectives changed."

"But, sir . . ."

The colonel interrupted, "If we don't stick to exact orders and timings, we lose all formation . . . There's no real communication once the battle has begun, whatever arrangements they make with Very lights, flags, coloured patches on the men's backs. If they were regulars, perhaps one could allow some flexibility . . . but as it is— stick to orders. It's the only way, in the long run. A few weeks at the

Depot, a few weeks in the trenches, is not enough to prepare men for this sort of thing . . . especially the officers. There'd be chaos." He puffed on his pipe and leaned back against the dugout's cold, wet wall.

The priest said, "Would there not be an advantage in attacking at night, Colonel . . . as you were going to do, before Brigade sent up the new orders?"

The colonel said, "I don't think so, Padre. I was going to because I couldn't get artillery support. This is better."

The priest said, "My brother thought night attacks would be the best way to attack anyone, these days. He was trying to get Pearse to make a night attack on the Curragh. The darkness would even things up, he said."

Archie saw the colonel's head jerk up, "Attack the Curragh? Why, that. . ."

The priest said gently, "My brother was a Sinn Feiner, colonel."

The colonel sat silent a moment, then said, "So's my sister."

The priest said, "I know. They call her Lady. My brother was in the Rising. He was courtmartialled and shot."

The colonel said, "Margaret deserved to be. She escaped."

For a long time no one spoke. Archie thought, the colonel's staring at me, or through me. He felt nervous. Did he know? Had Fiona told him that her ex-lover had come to the Wealds, and been posted to the 1st Battalion? She'd sent Archie three notes while he was at the Depot in Hedlington, but he had not answered them; and she had not spoken to him the night of the concert; but she hadn't given him up yet. He knew that from the look in her eye that night.

The priest said, "Night attacks may not be possible with these men, colonel . . . but nor is what we did today. After another day or two like that there'll be no British Army left."

The C.O. glowered at him and said shortly, "We'll obey orders."

The priest looked as though he was going to say something more on the same subject and Archie cut in—"Sir, I noticed that when the Germans counter-attacked they came out of their trenches in dribs and drabs, little groups here, others there . . . some came running, some dived for a shell hole and started firing. They made difficult targets for our machine gunners, even for the riflemen and Lewis gunners."

"We go in straight lines," the C.O. said, "for the same reason that we don't make large night attacks. The men are untrained. It requires a lot of training and good leadership at the platoon level, to let troops act in small separated groups like that."

"The Germans opposite us . . ."

"They did two years military trainii.g in peace time—all but the very youngest," the C.O. said. He took the pipe from his mouth and pointed the stem at Archie. His slightly protruding blue eyes were bloodshot with fatigue, but his voice was still strong, "You're an older man, Campbell, and now you're adjutant, and you, Padre, are officially a non-combatant . . . otherwise I wouldn't be discussing these matters with you. But you must both understand that no officer or man in this battalion must be permitted to express doubts or criticism of a plan, once ordered, whether by me, or by my superiors."

"Yes, sir," Archie said.

The C.O. said, "We must prepare our battle plans with the greatest care . . . you know how we rehearsed the attack on tapes, behind the lines. The orders must be clear, and allow no alternative choices. You've seen a battle now. You saw how quickly everything became disorganized, even with all our rehearsal . . . battalions, companies, platoons, men—all muddled up. Imagine how much worse it would have been without those definite plans and clearly defined tasks."

He resumed puffing at his pipe. Archie thought, he may be right. He's been out here nearly two years, and this is his profession. But surely there was a fault somewhere in that line of thinking? And surely he was underestimating his own men in one way, while holding the most sublime faith in them in another? If German conscripts could be taught to act independently, while supporting each other to a common end, why could not British bankers, farmers, machine tool operators—the men who made up the battalions of the New Army?

He stood up, "I'll try to sleep a couple of hours now, sir, unless you want me."

"No. Curl up in that bunk. I'll wake you at ten and then I'll take a nap myself until the Connaughts arrive."

Archie finished his champagne and said formally, "Good night, Padre. Good night, sir."

"Good night, Campbell . . . you did well today, and once you've learned how to write orders, I'm sure you'll make a good adjutant."

"Thank you, sir."

Archie climbed into the bunk and closed his eyes. He was beginning to feel personally fond of Quentin Rowland, for what he was not as much as for what he was. What would Fiona make of that? . . . Over the top again tomorrow. And tomorrow . . . Not much use worrying about what Fiona might think, or do, when neither of them was likely to be present to know of it.

The Daily Telegraph, Saturday, July 1, 1916

THE WEEK'S FINANCE

Much that has happened this week has formed a propitious prelude to the removal of the last of the minimum prices. That removal will make marketable hundreds of millions of investment securities hitherto protected or fettered, as one chooses to look at it, by artificial limitations on price . . . There are staunch people who will sell everything they have got for the sheer pleasure of putting the proceeds at the service of the State, and there are others who have been fretting for the opportunity to sell to discharge liabilities or wind up estates . . . the released stocks that come on offer will be easily absorbed. For we have seen Consols rising steadily until they yielded only a shade over 4 ⅛ percent, indicating that buyers were thinking less of present return, subject to heavy tax, than of capital increment which they hope to obtain by and by without tribute to the State. Anybody may be excused just now for projecting their thoughts beyond a troublesome present to a hopeful future, and that seems to be the attitude of investors . . .

FUNDS FOR THE WAR

Though the Government is drawing large sums from the general body of investors, it is evident enough from the change produced by the raising of Treasury Bill rates that the public is not, and has not been, the factor in enabling the Government to finance the war for months without recourse to a formal loan . . . Corporate war profits are financing the war to a great extent, and private and individual war profits are being employed in a more or less capricious fashion, with far too little regard to the main point in view, which is for everybody the hastening of a satisfactory end to the war, and for investors that and its corollary, the easing of the rate of taxation.

Cate thought that the kipper he was masticating did not taste as good as it ought to. Perhaps it had not been well kippered . . . or perhaps those offhand references to war profits had taken away his appetite. He himself was facing increasing difficulties as landlord to his tenant farmers; so were they. Overshadowing the financial difficulties and labour problems at home was the vast tragedy being staged across the Channel, with its daily sacrifices of blood and flesh. "War profit" ought to be an obscene phrase, but there it was, set out in black and white in a respectable newspaper. And God knew that what it stood for was real, and indeed common. Look at Hoggin, turned from a

Hedlington barrow boy to a millionaire and a national figure by the war, and by his shrewdness in seeing where he could use it for his advantage. And Hoggin was only one of hundreds, thousands . . .

But . . . but . . . how could such things be avoided, without the Government taking over the whole economy of the country, and in effect, turning the nation into an army, each person with his allotted role and salary? They'd have to take over all the wealth, too . . . all the factories, all the land . . . Would it come to that? Probably not. Just more taxation . . . if only *that* could take all war profits, and put them to good use.

The whole subject left an unpleasant taste in his mouth, and he turned the pages of the newspaper. Was all the news bad, or evil? Ah! he relaxed, folded the paper and propped it up on the toast rack:

GREAT ROSE SHOW
VISIT OF QUEEN ALEXANDRA

Mirvaux, Somme, France: July 1, 1916

10 Guy Rowland watched the leader's aircraft swing left, and, in his turn at the flank of the little group, swung his D.H. 2 round, following as the last of the three, now flying in line ahead. The windsock at the edge of the grassy field showed a gusty wind from the south-east, blowing almost across the field. Landing would be tricky, especially in a D.H. 2. He'd only flown one once before—yesterday, after taking delivery at the factory—when a couple of circuits and bumps had shown him that she was a tricky little machine to fly.

The flight leader, Captain Fanshawe, waggled his wings and turned down on his landing run. Lieutenant Osborne, in second place, and Guy in third, kept on course, completing another circle of the field at five hundred feet altitude while Fanshawe landed. Then from the same point where Fanshawe had peeled off, Osborne followed suit. Guy kept on turning . . . Good heavens, he could hear the guns, even over the sound of the engine! Partly that was because the D.H. 2 was a pusher, so the roar of the cylinders was blown to the rear. He glanced to his left. Nearly twenty miles away the simple sweep of the horizon was obscured by the murk of shell bursts—a pall over twenty miles long and a mile deep—British and German guns of every calibre hammering at each other and at the infantry in a fury of flying steel and earth. The wind whistled past his ears, the land below was neatly marked out in the long parcels of French villages, the wheat stood tall in the fields to the north and south of the landing field. Smoke curled up from the chimneys of the little village near the runway, behind the

144

clustered tents . . . seven thirty in the morning, the sun up, a beautiful day.

He came to the turning point and tilted his wings sharply—too sharply. For a moment he thought the little beast had got away from him. He lined up the runway in the gun sight . . . crabbing . . . corrected with a little right rudder . . . nose up again to slow her a bit—with a rotary engine like the D.H. 2's Gnome Monosoupape the momentum of the whirling machinery only permitted throttle control between 70 and 100 percent of full power; below that, the engine had to be switched off . . . a gust of wind caught him and whipped the nose twenty degrees off course. He was about fifty feet up. He corrected, roared on low over the grass . . . *when* would she come down? He cut the engine, nosed down, and hit the grass with a resounding crunch and a groan from all the wooden parts of the plane. Bouncing twice more, ten feet the first time, five feet the second, he rolled at last to a stop a bare five yards from the hedge that marked the end of the airfield. Two brown cows, tethered in the orchard inside, gazed mournfully at him over the hedge. Sweating, he again gave full power, and by alternately cutting and racing the engine—the process called blipping—taxied to the end of the line of D.H. 2s lined up at one side of the field.

Fanshawe and Osborne were nowhere in sight, in fact no other officers, only a small, slight man wearing tartan trews, his hands behind his back, standing by the wooden hut where the windsock flew. Outside the hut, Guy noticed as he taxied past, was a large white board inscribed *Headquarters 333 Squadron, Royal Flying Corps*. The man in trews watched him as he swung his machine into place, switched off the biplane's engine, climbed down onto the lower wing, and thence jumped to the ground. Taking off his goggles and leather helmet he walked toward the hut and the figure waiting outside. As he came close he saw that the man in the trews was also wearing the cutaway tunic of the King's Own Scottish Borderers, the wings of the Royal Flying Corps—and the crowns of a major. This must be the famous "Sulphuric" Sugden, the squadron commander.

Guy came to a halt, saluted and said, "Lieutenant Rowland, reporting for duty, sir, with one D.H. 2, serial number 37 from Airco. She's in good condition, sir."

"She was, perhaps, until you landed her. And you, I understand from your posting orders, have been instructing at Shoreham? And you taught the students how to land? Or just how to take off?"

"Yes, sir," Guy said again. He wanted to say it was gusty . . . the D.H. 2 was fairly new but already notoriously tricky . . . He kept his mouth shut.

The major said, "Get back in that unfortunate aircraft and make three circuits and bumps."

Guy saluted and returned to the D.H. 2. A fitter was already there, pouring in petrol. He said, "I'm taking her up again. I won't be long."

"Very good, sir. I'm Belcraft, your fitter. Jenks, your rigger's having breakfast." He ran round to the front of the plane and helped Guy climb back into the cockpit. Then, while Guy checked petrol level and mixture control, he waited behind the propeller.

Guy called back, "She's switched off! Turn!"

Belcraft took hold of the big mahogany and ash laminate propeller and labouriously turned it once, then again, and again, walking away from it each time. The engine had now sucked in the air and petrol mixture. Guy called out, "Contact! Start her!"

Belcraft approached the prop again, caught it, and swung hard, using all his body, turning away. The engine, still hot, caught at once, belching blue smoke, the cylinders whirling. Guy waved his gloved hand as the machine began to move.

Fifteen minutes later he came in blipping the engine, cut six feet above the beginning of the field and floated down for his third perfect three pointer in succession. As he taxied off the runway he saw that the propellers of the eleven D.H. 2s on the field were turning, including the other two new ones ferried over this morning.

"Major said you were not to fly," Belcraft shouted up through cupped hands. "Report to the adjutant!"

Guy ripped off his goggles and sat still in the cockpit, watching as the D.H. 2s lined up in threes and, three abreast, roared down the dry grass, took off, and climbed slowly to the east, toward the battle, toward the shaking earth and the black murk. The aircraft was trembling under him from that tremendous thunder as he sat, cold with pique and frustration.

When they were all airborne, out of sight, the hum of their engines faded, he climbed down and walked slowly to the Headquarters hut. Inside, he saluted the Lieutenant in King's Dragoon Guards uniform, with no wings, seated behind a desk labelled ADJUTANT. The man stood up, and came round the desk with a rhythmic creak from the wooden leg inside one of his perfectly cut and polished field boots. "Welcome to 333 Squadron," he said, his hand extended, "or Three Threes, as we usually call ourselves."

His eyes met Guy's, and for a long moment stared, astonished. Then he lowered his eyes. Guy put out his hand—"I'm Rowland, sir. I made an awful mess of landing—brought over a D.H. 2 from Airco and . . ."

"I know," the other said, "the C.O. told me." He returned to the other side of his desk and sat down. Guy knew why he had stared, at first. Guy's right eye was a brilliant icy blue, his left a soft warm brown; all his life he'd been used to that sudden start and stare as people realized that there was something strange about his face, and then recognized what it was. The adjutant said, "You weren't in time for orders, so you'll have to wait for the next show . . . probably this afternoon.   Let me tell you, on behalf of the C.O., that we're not fussy about dress in Three Threes—but we are very strict indeed about obeying battle orders. You can fly a show in your pyjamas if you like—plenty of them do, on the dawn patrol—but if you take off after a Hun by yourself when the battle plan is to act in concert, you'll find yourself grounded . . . I'll show you to your tent—you're alone in it for the moment. Neither of the fellows who were in it before will be using it again . . . one crashed yesterday, a cylinder exploded and he crashed . . . yes, it was a Monosoupape. The other fellow was shot down by Boelcke the day before . . . You've met your fitter and rigger?"

"Not the rigger yet, sir."

"Get some breakfast, and have a look at these." He handed over a wad of typed and cyclostyled sheets. Guy glanced at the title of the top sheet, "Standing Orders for Battle, 333 Squadron, R.F.C." and dated March 31 of this year. If there was a chance of a show this afternoon, he'd better do some reading.

*　　*　　*　　*

They sat at lunch round a long table in what had once been a barn attached to the farmhouse on the opposite side of the airfield from the squadron headquarters and huts. No one sat at any fixed place, nor came in together, but in dribs and drabs from half past twelve on. Before that, they had gathered in the farmhouse parlour, now the mess anteroom, and talked, read letters and newspapers, looked at the communiqués posted up on the notice board and stood round, drinking lemonade.

Guy went in to lunch by himself. He did not know anyone—he had only met Fanshawe and Osborne yesterday at Airco—so he sat silently near one end of the table while the mess waiters brought him roast lamb, green peas and excellent small potatoes. His neighbour at the table growled in disgust as he cut into his portion of lamb— "Underdone! This isn't beef."

The officer opposite said, "That's the disadvantage of having a French chef. It's not bad if you pretend not to notice the colour."

Guy enjoyed lamb however it was done, as long as it was tender, and this was; he ate slowly, eyeing his fellow officers of Three Threes, the squadron famous throughout the R.F.C. for that number. It was the result of a War Office clerk, typing out raising orders for new squadrons, typing 32, 33, and then 333, before continuing 34, 35, 36, 37. Naturally, once the orders had gone out it was unthinkable to change them, so . . . 333 it had remained.

There were nearly all at the table now . . . twelve pilots; the adjutant; the quartermaster, an ex-sergeant major of the Royal Welch Fusiliers; and Major Sugden. Most of them wore the uniforms of the regiments from which they had been seconded to the Royal Flying Corps, with their pilot's wings on the left breast above the tunic pocket and, here and there, a medal ribbon or two. Guy noticed three wearing the white-purple-white of the Military Cross, and two the blue-red-blue of the Distinguished Service Order—the C.O., and a baby-faced lieutenant. A few, like himself, wore the double breasted tunic of the R.F.C. itself, always referred to as the maternity jacket. One or two wore riding breeches and field boots, but most wore slacks. All their Sam Browne belts were hanging in the hall of the farmhouse.

Guy's neighbor said, "Were you one of the fellows who flew in the new D.H. 2s?

Guy said, "Yes," just stopping himself in time from adding "sir." His neighbour was only a lieutenant like himself; and Guy had been instructing lieutenants, captains, and even one major in flying. Back at Shoreham he had had no particular awe of them; but this was an entity, a fighting squadron of the Royal Flying Corps, and a crack one.

"Ever flown one in action?"

"No."

"Well, you can throw them around the sky and they'll hold together but they may spin in, so be careful when you're below three thousand feet. And they're cold. Jesus, they're cold! I hope to God we've got something else by October . . . preferably September."

"We'd better have," the man opposite said. "Jerry will have thought up something better than the Fokker E by then."

Another said, "And the Gnome Monosoupape's a bloody menace. We lost . . ."

"I know," Guy said, "I'm in his tent."

He returned to his plate. His father had dinned into him that officers never talked about shop, women, or politics in mess. Those rules did not seem to apply here . . . not about shop, anyway.

An airman came in through the barn door, which had been permanently sealed shut, by the smaller door cut in it for human purposes, started for the table at a run, then stopped, searched the group with his eyes, and, finding the slicked-back grey hair of Major Sugden, went to him and handed him a message form. The C.O. read, looked up, banged on the table with the handle of his knife and said, "Quiet please, gentlemen . . . We've been ordered to make another sweep of the battle front. The Boches have sent in two squadrons of E IIIs in an effort to clear the area so that their photographic and artillery spotter planes can get forward. We'll take off at . . ." he glanced at his wrist watch ". . . one thirty pip emma, that's in ten minutes. Rendezvous eight thousand feet over Albert, then up the main Bapaume road to ten miles behind the German front, then south-east to the Somme—all in stepped up echelon of flights, in order B, C, A, D. Tactics—as for flight actions, unless we run into a squadron or more of Boches in formation, when we'll attack in squadron formation, following my lead. That's all."

Guy took another mouthful of lamb, cleared his plate of peas, and went out. His rigger had already painted his individual number—3—in green on both sides of the nose of the cockpit, where it matched the green colors of D Flight which decorated the wheels and the propeller boss. He had learned from the Standing Orders that A Flight's colour was red, B's blue, and C's yellow; and the Squadron commander's black.

He climbed into the cockpit and began checking his instruments. He was going into action. In half an hour he might be dead. He felt a peculiar sinking sensation in his stomach and after a moment recognized it; it was what he always felt when first called on to bowl, as he was walking across the turf, rubbing the ball in his hand, measuring out his run. He fastened his safety strap, looked at the petrol gauge—full. He pulled his goggles down. The sergeant of the flight was waving his arm in a circular motion and Belcraft repeating it—Start engines! Guy checked his contact switch and shouted "Contact!" Belcraft went to the rear and caught hold of the propeller. An airman came running out of the line of tents, waving a revolver. He reached the side of Guy's aircraft as the engine caught and the propeller began to whirl, the cylinders coughing smoke and a reek of burned castor oil thick on the hot summer breeze. Belcraft took the revolver and handed it up to Guy, "You have to take your revolver, sir. Squadron orders!"

Guy waved a hand in acknowledgment and stuffed the Webley into its holster on his Sam Browne. B Flight was taxiing out, blipping their engines, three abreast, plus Major Sugden's machine on the right of the line. The wind had increased, still blowing from the south-west, but a point more up and down the field. Take off should be easy, except for the dust rising in little whorls behind the taxiing machines. B Flight lined up and took off: C filed out onto the line, turned, engines roaring . . . off! A—off! No, the right hand man's engine had cut, the propeller whirling to a stop—a final cough—dead. A dozen fitters and riggers ran out, reached it, lined up behind the lower wing, shoved, strained. The machine was trundled off out of the way. Hard cheese on someone, Guy thought. His D flight was on the move—one behind the other, in line, all turning left together. Oil pressure steady, ailerons and rudder tested . . . The Flight Commander raised his hand, looked right and left, dropped it. Guy opened the throttle wide and the D.H. 2 started to roll, grass flying back, the air still full of dust and dried grass from the passage of the leading flights. The wings of the machine in the centre began to rise above the wings of Guy's. He eased back on the stick. He was airborne, climbing on course, due east, falling into station as left hand man of the flight, above and a little behind number 1, while number 2 was in the same position the other side. The sun filtered brightly through strange, thin, long bands of cloud.

The flight climbed, the sun glistening on the pale yellow varnish of the wings, the other flights visible ahead. The spire of Albert church was straight ahead, the meanderings of the Somme off to the right. Here, behind the battle line, the fields were green, studded with copses, the underlying chalk of the Somme uplands clear through the grass or crops, every lane and road white in the strong light. Guy glanced at the map spread on his lap then quickly up, as he heard a strange sound, like the roaring of a train in a tunnel . . . another . . . again . . . several of them, each a rushing roar. Suddenly a glint ahead caught the light and for a moment he saw it—a heavy shell which had just passed him with that strange rushing sound, now for a moment flying in the same direction, on its arching course to its destination, easily visible from straight behind. The roarings ceased as the flight passed above the zenith of the shells' arcs. Almost at once the D.H. 2 began to bounce and surge, drop fifty feet, rise violently, lurch from side to side. Guy sweated as he struggled with rudder and ailerons to hold his machine steady. Then he realized that he was alone. Looking right, where the others had been, he saw them, still close, but diving toward a group of three small flying objects two thousand feet below—Fokkers. He nosed over to follow. They ought to get some of those Boches—coming out of the sun, from a superior height. The wind howled past, the fabric screamed and sang. Below, one of the Fokkers burst into flames, the others turned violently away. That must have been his Flight Commander's work. He tried to coax one of the swerving Fokkers into his sights, his thumb ready on the machine-gun trigger that was in the head of the joy stick, but it kept dodging, and also gaining on him, increasing the range. The other two machines of his flight were climbing back into the sun to rejoin the rest of the squadron, dark, silhouetted shapes above there. He pulled the stick back and followed, taking his thumb off the trigger. Close, but no luck. Well, it was his first day, and he had enough petrol for another hour's flying at least, depending on the wind.

The squadron finally made its rendezvous over Albert, and headed north-east up the Amiens-Bapaume road. They crossed both sets of trench lines, and for a moment, looking down, Guy imagined he saw, amid the smoke, lines of pygmy figures, the glint of steel catching the sun . . . his father might be down there. But it was only his imagination, he knew, for he would not make out any figures from eight thousand feet. One day soon, he must go up to the line and see and feel for himself what that side of the war was like. It was easy to read about, to look at photographs—but hard to understand, in your heart.

He glanced round. It was ten minutes since they had left Albert, and it hardly seemed to have moved—there it was, not four miles back. What on earth . . . ? On the way up to rejoin the flight after trying to get the Fokker he had experienced that same turbulence, at about six thousand feet . . . and now the squadron was making very slow progress toward the east. It could mean only one thing—a strong east wind was blowing at this altitude. Well, it would be easy to get home today. His Flight Commander kicked into a violent turn, and a second later a big shadow flashed over Guy. Instantly he pushed the stick over and kicked the rudder controls. He heard a muffled clatter, and saw the yellow streaks on his tail, and three, four others concentrating on his flight. The Germans had been spotted just in time, probably when diving out of cloud, and now the whole of 333 Squadron was engaged, the nearer sky full of weaving aircraft. Guy dived, as another burst of tracer missed him close, then swung over into an Immelmann turn. For a moment he had a Fokker swimming up into his sights. Just as he was ready to press the trigger, he felt the presence of another Fokker above and behind him, pulled the D.H. 2 into a climbing turn, flipped over on his back, and fell away in a spin.

After a few seconds he passed into cloud, and steadied the machine. He climbed back through the swirling vapour, jerking, bumping . . . out into sunshine . . . Not a sign of aircraft . . . Yes, there was one, about a mile away, near the same height as himself, flying on a crossing course. He recognized it at once as a D.H. 2, from the pusher engine, marked dihedral of the upper wing, and the fuselage shorter than a Vickers Gunbus. He waggled his wings and settled in beside it in echelon. It was No. 3 plane of A Flight. Whoever he was, he would be Guy's senior. The pilot raised an arm in the beginning of a signal, flying no more than sixty feet to Guy's right, when suddenly he leaned over, stared down, and pointed. Guy looked and saw,

silhouetted above the now distant earth, several machines, black crosses plain, a parasol-like structure over the single wing, the wing set
about mid-fuselage. They were Fokker Es, but not E IIIs, such as
they'd just had the dogfight with—E Is, perhaps . . . Two against
seven. The two D.H. 2s dived together, side by side, the sun straight
behind, no clouds within two miles.

The rear Fokker came into Guy's sights . . . the tail . . . the centre of the fuselage, the pilot . . . the pilot's head, looming larger and
larger . . . deflection one degree ahead . . . he pressed the trigger
and at once released it as the German pilot jerked upright, then
slumped forward. The Fokker fell away, but already he was on the tail
of the next . . . the ring and bead sight steady . . . a one-second burst
. . . again the slump, but this time the Fokker flipped over on its back,
the wing nearly touching his undercarriage as he passed over it. No
sign of his flight companion now, but another Fokker, near the head of
the formation, was in flames . . . They were breaking up, scattering.

He selected one, dived briefly to gain speed, and came up underneath it. To his left another Fokker was turning in to attack. He'd be
too late. Guy's short burst went into the cockpit and engine from
below. The Fokker turned lazily on its back, smoke trailing, and circled toward the earth.

He settled down in a stern chase of one of the remaining Germans.
He was almost within range . . . now the German would dive . . .
head for cloud . . . turn to attack. He did nothing, flew desperately
on. Guy's sights came on, from directly behind, and the German at-
tempted a loop . . . but Guy, climbing faster on the inside of the loop,
pulled his stick back a trifle harder. He pressed the trigger. As the
Fokker fell off the top of its loop, he shouted aloud, "Got him!" glaring
at the plane with teeth momentarily bared . . . just as he used to run
half-way down the pitch when he had clean bowled a batsman, letting
go the involuntary shout, and baring his teeth.

He glanced at his petrol gauge . . . less than a quarter of a tank
. . . twenty minutes flying. Two Fokkers were still in the air, fleeing
for their lives. Once more he settled to the chase. He was gaining . . .
two hundred yards . . . one hundred and fifty . . . well within range:
he closed his hand lovingly round the stick, his thumb caressing the
trigger . . . fifty yards . . .

The reason why he had won four such easy victories burst on him.
These were pilots from some advanced training unit, not a Jagdstaffel.
The very high east wind in the upper air had blown them farther west
than they expected, and there, still ten miles behind their own lines,
Guy and his companion had found them.

The German's head was clear and close. For a moment he turned, drawn, mouth open, terror evident in every line, very young, younger even than Guy. He couldn't bear it. He lifted the D.H. 2's nose up and pressed the trigger, sending a long burst six feet above the Fokker pilot's head. The Fokker swung sharply, turned over, and spun down. Guy eased into a circle and watched the German go down, spinning slowly like a huge maple leaf . . . "Right rudder!" he heard himself shouting. "Right rudder! Stick forward!" He remembered a pilot, one of his pupils, on his second solo, freezing up like that over Chanctonbury Ring. He had been in the air himself at the time, and had watched the B.E. 2 until the final shock, the towering flames. Now the Fokker went in: there were the flames, the smoke.

He swung the D.H.'s nose west, staying at eight thousand feet, and the man from A Flight joined him. The stream of the upper air hurled them on at 170 miles per hour ground speed, until, nearly over Mirvaux, they dived down through severe turbulence, and landed with both tank gauges showing empty. Then they taxied to their separate places in the line of D.H. 2s. As soon as he had stopped his engine the other pilot scrambled out of his cockpit and raced toward Guy, shouting at the top of his voice, "Five! My God, five Huns on your first day!"

Guy sat, the propeller whirling to a stop, kicking back once, stopping. His fitter and rigger were there, half a dozen of the squadron officers running up, catching the frenzied excitement of the first, shouting, cheering. Guy felt his stomach churn, his forehead break into a cold sweat, and with a single heave he vomited all over the cockpit, the instruments, the control column. Tears burst into his eyes, and he sat, shaking, retching, groaning, weeping.

The first man was on the lower wing—"My God! Rowland! Are you hit?"

Guy shook his head. He smelled vile. He hated himself. He croaked, "Keep off . . . get away . . . leave me alone."

Belcraft was there, on the wing, his hands out—"Here, sir . . . Don't worry about that . . . I'll clean it all up . . ."

"No, you won't!" The voice was harsh. "Anyone who is sick in an aircraft of this squadron cleans it up himself!"

"Yes, sir," Guy said, looking down at Major Sugden's grim face.

He climbed out and jumped feebly down—"Get me a bucket and mop," he muttered to Belcraft.

Sugden, surrounded by a crowd of officers, said, "Is it true, what O'Grady was saying—that you shot down five Boches?"

"Four, sir. They were trainees . . . must have been . . . blown west by the wind up there. I had the fifth in my sights when I realised . . . I fired over his head."

"You can't have!" O'Grady exclaimed, "I saw him go down."

"He was terrified," Guy said, "went into a spin—didn't know how to avoid me, didn't know how to get out of it."

Sugden turned on O'Grady, a lieutenant with black hair, greenish eyes and a long Irish upper lip—"You saw the others?"

"Yes, sir. I got one myself, with my second burst. Then my gun jammed, but I stayed with Rowland to make the Huns think there were two of us."

"And you're positive he got them . . . four?"

"One after the other . . . he had a long chase to get the fourth, but he got them all, all right. Closed to fifty yards or less before firing, just like Ball."

Sugden said, "Come and see me in the office, Rowland, when you've cleaned up that machine, and yourself."

"Yes, sir."

*　　*　　*　　*

The squadron flew two more sorties that day, the first day of the Battle of the Somme, and Guy made no more kills, though he damaged a Fokker E III over Peronne and others saw it flying lower and lower toward the east, trailing smoke. His own machine came back with bullet holes in the fuselage from each sortie, some very close to where he had sat in the cockpit, and as he landed for the last time, in the dusk, Major Sugden spoke briefly to him—"I'm claiming four Boches for you today, Rowland. You did well . . . though you should have shot at that fifth trainee. He might have survived, to kill you one day—or your best friend. You're a good scout pilot, obviously. You go in close and make sure of your kill. Your rigger told me you barely fired a belt in all. But when you meet real Jasta pilots, remember they'll have the guts and skill to be firing back at you."

"Yes, sir," Guy said. He thought, but I'm not going to miss a Hun just because he's firing back at me. I'll dodge, dive, do anything to escape if he has the jump on me; but if I have him in my sights, I won't lose him, ever.

A droning sound grew rapidly louder and a lone aircraft appeared low in the east. Guy stopped, watching, standing at the far side of the airfield. He stared at the plane, wondering. It was a Fokker E III hopping the hedges, skimming along the airfield with guns silent . . . one plane, alone . . . Mechanics, riggers, fitters, and pilots dived for cover. Guy stared intently. The machine turned tightly and roared back, low over the field. The pilot threw out a white package tied to trailing red ribbons. Hopping over the hedge, the Fokker vanished in the eastern gloaming.

Guy walked across the field. The adjutant was there limping toward the package. He picked it up, adjusted the monocle in his left eye, and opened the package, as Guy and others gathered round him. "That was von Rackow," he said. "Notice the yellow wing ends, outside the black crosses? And that was his E IV—same as an E III, but with three guns instead of two . . . Ah, what have we here? A package, labelled 'Personal effects of Lieutenant Bristol, R.F.C.' with a note addressed to 'The next of kin of Lieut. Bristol'—it's open . . ." He read aloud—"Dear Sir or Madame, Your son was a skilful pilot and a brave man, but his machine broke up under my fire. He died instantly and I honour his memory—Werner Von Rackow: . . . Here's another letter, addressed to Major D.Q. Sugden, D.S.O., O.C. 333 Squadron, Royal Flying Corps . . ."

Sugden arrived, mustache bristling, and the adjutant said, "Perhaps you'd better read it, sir."

Sugden tore open the envelope and read aloud: *"Dear Major Sugden: One of your officers today butchered five student pilots. I will be waiting for him, alone, 2,000 metres (6,600 feet) over Peronne at 7.30 tomorrow morning. Only one of my guns will be loaded. Respectfully yours, Werner von Rackow, Captain, Jagdstaffel 16."*

Sugden muttered, "What's he so angry about? How was Rowland expected to know that they were students?" He glanced up at Guy— "If you attempt to make that rendezvous, Rowland, you will be returned to England as unsuitable for active service." He stuffed the letter into his pocket and turned to the adjutant—"Get four machine guns from the nearest Ordnance Depot, and arrange to train a dozen fitters and riggers to fire them. It was chivalrous of von Rackow to bring over Bristol's effects, and the note, but I don't want them to get any ideas. The next Boche who flies down my airfield is not going to get home to his."

*   *   *   *

August 1, 1916

The great battle still raged between the Somme and the Ancre. Lieutenant Colonel Quentin Rowland, wounded again, this time through the stomach, was on his way to the railway station in Amiens, there to be loaded, with many others, onto a hospital train and taken to a Base Hospital. The ambulance bumped and rattled over the pavé, his wound hurt, his whole belly ached, but, lying in a haze of morphine, he did not think he was dangerously wounded. Doc Sholto, the R.M.O., had told him that the bullet—received in front of Contalmaison early this morning—had apparently gone clean through without touching any vital part.

*   *   *   *

Guy Rowland sat in the C.O.'s office, listening to Major Sugden. He had made three more kills during the month, raising his total to seven. Each time he had vomited in the cockpit of his D.H. 2 as soon as he was safely landed.

Sugden said, "I am giving you this leave so that you can see your grandfather, Rowland, and help the R.F.C. . . . because he is a Member of Parliament. I want you to impress on him that our most urgent problem is to get a workable synchronized machine gun. The Boches have had one for months, and it gives them a great advantage in design. Our designers have to build pushers, which, if they're single engine, must have twin booms and their concomitant problems."

"I found that out for myself, sir."

"You have designed aircraft?"

"A little. Single-engined pushers seemed to suffer from structural weakness and inefficiency of the propeller. It was all right, in theory, with multi-engined pushers out on the wings—they were aerodynamically as good as tractors."

"That's interesting . . . Well, make your grandfather appreciate—and have the Prime Minister appreciate—that the very best brains in the country must be put to this. We don't have much time. Now the D.H. 2 is superior to the E III, but Fokker's not going to sit still. I don't think he can push his E design any farther. He'll bring out something faster . . . more maneuverable, and it will knock us out of the skies, until we get a machine that has better flying characteristics than the D.H. 2, which means a tractor engine—which means synchronized guns—at least two of them . . . something like the new Sopwith that 70 Squadron got just before the start of the offensive."

Guy stood up, thinking the squadron commander had finished— "Anything else, sir?"

Sugden said, "Wait a minute. Tell him you've got the M.C. Not for your exploit with the student pilots, but for the way you attacked those four Boches on the 16th, when they had Gorringe cold, gun jammed and engine missing on most of its cylinders."

"Thank you, sir."

"You're a bit schoolboyish sometimes—I don't mean in Mess, that doesn't matter a damn—but in the air. How old are you?"

"Nineteen and nearly a half, sir."

Sugden sighed, "Well, you've got to act like eighteen, but think like forty, in the air. That's all."

Guy saluted, and went out, adjusting the forage cap to the proper angle on the side of his head. Four o'clock and the squadron's Crossley was waiting for him. His grandfather and the other two visiting M.P.s were in the Hotel de France in Amiens. He ought to get a good dinner out of it, at least . . .

The car started, Guy sitting beside the driver. For a while they talked, then Guy remembered that the adjutant had handed him two letters just before he went in to see the C.O. He pulled them out of his tunic pocket and glanced at the handwriting. The first was from Aunt Alice. He read quickly—Granny was in the hospital again, but no operation possible. Grandfather hadn't wanted to go on the tour of the Front with the other M.P.s, for Granny's sake, but she had insisted. Uncle Richard's aircraft company was doing well, big aeroplanes flying low over the town every day so that people hardly looked up any more; the American girl, Betty Merritt, was working for the company, helping design the aeroplanes, what a wonderful thing for a woman to do . . .

He opened the other letter. It was from his mother: Virginia was working as a common private or whatever they called them in the Women's Legion, cleaning lavatories and scrubbing floors; but she said she was happy. She herself was still in Hedlington, and unhappy: Guy would know why. She had seen the man she had told him about, but he would not speak to her. Was there anything he needed—socks, gloves, scarves, what about a sheepskin flying jacket?

What I'll need in a few weeks, flying a D.H. 2., is a polar bear's coat and trousers, Guy thought sardonically . . . Poor Mummy, apparently she knew where the man she loved was, but would not tell him or Virginia or anyone else. Guy thought he would like to meet the man some time. He ought to regard him as a cad and a rotter, ruining his father's marriage; but he couldn't. People weren't always responsible for themselves or their actions, and allowances had to be made. One had to understand, or try to . . . one had to think like forty.

At the main road the driver had to stop the Crossley and wait while a column of seventeen ambulances passed, also heading for Amiens. Then they followed behind. Guy thought, he had not yet had an opportunity to go up the line. He knew that his father's battalion was in the battle area. He'd go tomorrow, as soon as he'd said goodbye to Grandfather, instead of spending the day here, overeating and drinking.

They followed the ambulances until they turned off towards Amiens railway station, while the R.F.C. driver continued to the Hotel de France.

The evening passed pleasantly enough for Guy—a happy reunion with his grandfather, sherry with him and the other two M.P.s, while he told them about the war in the air and the absolute need for synchronized machine guns; an hour's mild flirtation with the vivacious young French woman behind the reception desk, then to his hotel room, and his thoughts . . . up the line tomorrow; next day, in the air again, and again the killing. His lips tightened and his eyes gleamed, leaning over the basin, staring at his own face in the mirror. This was the face that had gloated over the poor mad Hedlington Ripper, when he'd killed him on the steep slope down into the town, under the full moon. He had felt the same as each Fokker turned and died, its pilot with it. He leaned closer to his image and whispered, "Butcher!" Later he went to bed and tried to go to sleep, but, until three o'clock in the morning, failed.

*   *   *   *

Daily Telegraph, Friday, August 4, 1916

CASEMENT HANGED
"I DIE FOR MY COUNTRY"

Casement was hanged at Pentonville Prison shortly after nine o'clock yesterday morning. His last words, uttered just before the bolt was drawn, were "I die for my country." Ellis was the executioner.

A large crowd, composed mostly of women and children, assembled in the neighbourhood of the front entrance of the prison, in Caledonian-road. When the bell, announcing that the execution had taken place, began to toll, cheers were raised. The cheering was taken up by scores of people, and hats and handkerchiefs were waved . . .

Cate read it all again slowly. It was over.

It had not begun. Once, he would have felt so. Even his wife Margaret, all the years they had lived together, had not been able to make him see anything more in the troubles of Ireland than the squabblings and internecine bickerings of a small and unstable people, whose fate had unfortunately been linked by geography to that of England. The full majesty of the British legal process had been invoked in Casement's case; and there was no other way. Obviously, he could not be court-martialled and summarily shot, since he had not been caught with arms in his hands, waging war against the King. But now, from behind the grim walls of Pentonville, Casement would speak to future generations. You could dismiss the Connollys, Pearses, Plunketts, MacDermotts, and Clarkes as wild Irish fanatics, most of them dangerous radicals, too. Sir Roger Casement had been a British Consul, a knight, and a notable diplomat. Perhaps Casement should have been reprieved as a gesture of goodwill, in the name of the Irish soldiers now fighting and dying in France. Or perhaps it was the Pearses and Plunketts who should have been spared—given a stinging metaphorical cut across the palm and told to stand in the corner and be good boys in future.

Poor Ireland! No wonder the song called it the "most distressful country," and such it would remain if its leaders were to continue to be murderous fanatics and ignorant Roman Catholic bog priests. Definitely Casement should have been spared, to counter-balance the forces of superstition and ignorance.

Chill at heart, he wondered whether Margaret would meet her fate on an English gallows? Or whether by a burst of machine gun fire in some sordid Irish ambush or counter-ambush; and whether the finger on the trigger might not be their son's, or her brother's. Again, as so often now, he turned the pages of the newspaper, looking for something that was not tainted by the universal brutishness of the war. At last he found it, and read with spirits rising. Here was the old determination, the old true heart of England! Here was faith, and fellowship, high chivalry, and untarnished courage:

SOUTH POLE EXPEDITION
A TERRIBLE JOURNEY

Reuters' Agency states that three members of the Shackleton Expedition reached London yesterday from South Georgia. . . . They were three of the volunteer crew of five who accompanied Sir E. Shackleton on his journey by whale-boat from Elephant Island on April 24 and eventually reached South Georgia. They are full of enthusiasm for Sir E. Shackleton, whom they almost worship. They say that but for his leadership not one would have survived . . . The journey . . . which lasted fifteen days, is described as a terrible experience. Constantly they had to hack the ice from the boat to prevent her from being engulfed. They had sufficient rations, but were very short of water . . . There were continual hurricanes and bad weather, and even as they set out from Elephant Island the whale-boat and its occupants were capsized . . . The men had their first square meal on South Georgia, where they secured some albatross weighing 14 lb each. Each man consumed half of this, bones and all.

Hedlington: Thursday, September 7, 1916

11 *I am the resurrection and the life, saith the Lord: he that believeth in me, though he were dead, yet shall he live: and whosoever liveth in me shall never die.*

The coffin lay at the foot of the altar, covered in wreaths of autumn wildflowers and hothouse lilies. Harry Rowland bowed his head and let the slow tears flow. Through the blur in his mind he could see Rose in her coffin—though it was all of oak, fastened down—as she had been when they first met in the beauty of her youth.

I know that my Redeemer liveth, and that he shall stand at the latter day upon the earth. And though after my skin worms destroy this body, yet in my flesh shall I see God:

Richard stood next to his father, his wife Susan on his other side. It was raining outside, and he could see the streams of water running down the stained glass in the rose east window of the church. Susan heard the service, but did not listen. She was almost certain now that she was pregnant. She'd wait for one more missed period, then she'd have to tell Richard; but how?

We brought nothing into this world, and it is certain that we can carry nothing out. The Lord gave, and the Lord hath taken away: blessed be the name of the Lord.

Susan's adopted children, Tim and Sally, stood next to her, then John and Louise Rowland, Louise with her handkerchief to her eyes. Louise had been a little afraid of her mother-in-law all her married life, and had found her hard to approach, but there had never been any wavering in her respect for her. Louise heard a rustling and snickering and glanced down, frowning, at Tim and Sally. Susan had heard too, and was looking down. Tim was tearing corners out of the hymn book in front of him and rolling them in his mouth to make spitballs. Sally was trying to choke down her giggles. She caught Louise's stern eye and gagged. Tim swallowed his spitballs, turned red in the face and began to cough.

John Rowland heard the commotion the children were making, but his mind was far away. The battle in France, which had started early in July, was still raging. The casualties were beyond all reason. It had to be stopped, somehow, and every right-thinking man and woman must do all he or she could to see that it was. Louise would not agree. She, like many others, would think that he had turned pro-German, a traitor. So would his own son, Boy.

I will take heed to my ways: that I offend not in my tongue.
I will keep my mouth as it were with a bridle: while the ungodly is in my sight.

Quentin and Fiona stood in the pew behind. Quentin was in uniform, and tomorrow would return to France, to his battalion. He had been ready to go four days ago—the day his mother died. The War Office had extended his leave at once—because his father was an M.P., he supposed. England made him feel uneasy. He wanted to get back, and the sooner the better, for the battle was still raging by the Somme. His wound was healed for, as Sholto had predicted, the bullet had gone through without damaging any vital organ.

Fiona, at her husband's side, stared at the coffin. Like Louise, she had been a little afraid of her mother-in-law, but had also loved her, for they were both Celts—and they had understood each other. And now her attempts to make her very English family understand how the Scots and Welsh and Irish felt were ended. The persuasion was now in the hands, and arms, of others—many with violence, not reason, in their hearts. She turned her head slowly, while listening to the curate assisting the canon read the Psalm. When she came into the church she had noticed an odd-looking man by the door, dressed in blue serge, wearing a bowler hat, a man with a heavy face and sharp, little eyes—a policeman in plain clothes, she could swear. Scotland Yard would be thinking that perhaps Margaret would take the risk of coming over, in some sort of disguise, to pay her last respects.

The worst pain she suffered now was hearing Quentin talk of his new adjutant, Archie Campbell. It wrenched her bowels that Archie should prefer life in the trenches with Quentin, to what she had offered him. She was a woman and she had offered Archie her whole self—her body, her love, her life; instead he had gone into the mud with the soldiers, at Quentin's side. Quentin couldn't understand him, of course. "Drinks too much," he'd said, "but his heart's in the right place. And he's learning . . . It isn't as though we were having ceremonial parades every week, or providing full dress guards of honour for the Viceroy . . . this isn't soldiering, in France . . . it's a dirty, filthy street fight." He had not said a word to her about why she was still in the flat, and not gone to join her lover in London, as she had told him nearly a year ago that she would. And he had not once asked who the lover had been.

Lord, thou hast been our refuge: from one generation to another.
Before the mountains were brought forth, or ever the earth and the world were made: thou art God from everlasting, and world without end.

In the second row pew the other side of the aisle, behind the domestic staff of Laburnum Lodge, Bill and Ruth Hoggin stood beside the Earl and Countess of Swanwick. Hoggin had not known Rose Rowland well, but this was an important funeral in Hedlington and everyone who was anyone was here; so he had to be; and, by luck and good management, he had wriggled in next to the Swanwicks. Lady S had all but ignored their existence when they entered the pew, Ruth bobbing and curtseying as though she was greeting Queen Mary, but that didn't matter. The earl had got himself onto the Joint Select Committee looking into the food business—in return for promising to vote for something Asquith wanted, probably; and—here Hoggin pretended to blow his nose to smother a chuckle—the Committee had invited him, Bill Hoggin, to act as one of their technical advisers. So Bill Hoggin, expert, would be advising them about the doings of Bill Hoggin, food purveyor and manufacturer. And Horatio Bottomley, editor of the influential *John Bull*, was ready to eat out of his hand, for a consideration, of course. And the H.U.S.L. shops were coming along famously. It was enough to make a cat laugh.

Three young people stood together behind the elder Rowlands—Naomi, a driver of the Women's Volunteer Motor Drivers; Guy Rowland, a Lieutenant in the Royal Flying Corps; and his sister Virginia, a worker in the Women's Legion. The embroidered wings on Guy's tunic were beginning to fade, but now the white-purple-white ribbon of the Military Cross shone below them, bright and new. He watched the rain running down the rose window and thought, hope it clears a bit before four, as he was due to fly a new Hedlington Leopard twin-engined bomber to France, leaving at that hour. They had sent his squadron a telegram about the death of his grandmother, but he had not expected to be able to attend the funeral—the Somme battle was still raging, and the R.F.C. stretched to its utmost to maintain air superiority over the battlefield; but Major Sugden had called him in last night, and said curtly—"General Trenchard heard about your grandmother. He wants you to attend the funeral. In uniform. And don't forget to mention to your grandfather that we cannot carry the fight to the enemy unless we have aircraft at least as good as his. And we now know what we're going to be up against—the D. 1."

Guy thought, we do; or at least we can make an informed projection, on the basis of what Intelligence had learned from neutral sources, and what the few German pilot prisoners have hinted at, usually in their cups, while being wined and dined in the mess of the squadron that shot them down: a Fokker biplane, with two synchronized machine guns, a top speed of about 110 m.p.h. and a ceiling of near 17,000 feet—the Albatros D. 1. Jasta 16 would get them any moment now, then von Rackow would be sending over more challenges for the Butcher to come out and fight. He bit his lip, tightening his jaw muscles. He'd got to find some way that the C.O. would allow, to identify himself so that they could have it out.

Naomi kept her eyes on the coffin as she listened to the curate's strong, young voice and rather exaggerated Oxford accent reciting the Psalm. She would have to be on her guard with Colonel Rodney Venable. His long face was so intelligent, and so were the brown eyes under the thatch of his eyebrows . . . widely read, widely traveled, grandson of a viscount . . . had been in the 17th Lancers, used to play polo with Uncle Christopher's brother Oswald . . . but . . . but there was something in his look whenever she drove for him that made her flesh creep; and she could not say whether the frisson was of disgust, or expectation. She shook her head. He had not yet said or done anything improper, as between a colonel in the Intelligence section of the General Staff at the War Office and a female Volunteer. If he did, he must be told that she was in uniform to do her part in winning the war, not to be near men.

Guy's sister, Virginia, on the other side of him, furtively wiped her eyes, keeping her handkerchief rolled up in her hand. She had loved her grandmother, loved her father, did not understand her mother, adored her brother; and now, at seventeen and a half years of age, she was happy for the first time in her life. The girls in her detachment outside Aldershot were nearly all from the lower classes—mill girls, factory hands, girls escaped from service in big houses in the depths of the country. They were open, direct, crude, and she loved being with them. She still had much of her puppy fat, and had sworn, the day before she got the telegram about Granny, to start dieting. For Battery Sergeant Major Stanley Robinson, D.C.M., ex-Royal Field Artillery, had taken her out to the cinema, and said she was pretty; and, apologetically, that he would like to take her out again, if she wouldn't mind, him being only an O.R. and her a father a colonel, and all. She, too, felt a frisson—Stanley Robinson, only one arm, his left gone . . . old, of course, must be twenty-seven, twenty-eight . . . but so kind to her.

Now is Christ risen from the dead, and become the first-fruits of them that slept. For since by man came death, by man came also the resurrection of the dead. For as in Adam all die, even so in Christ shall all be made alive . . .

Bob and Jane Stratton stood behind the Swanwicks and Hoggins. Like many other women in the crowded church Jane dabbed frequently at her eyes. Rose Rowland had been a great lady, and a source of strength to her and her family from the earliest days, when it had been a matter of having babies and finding doctors for colic, to these latter times, when there had come other, darker troubles. Her sciatica ached badly today, and now the knuckles of her right hand, long swollen with arthritis, began to stab with pain. She winced and tried to compose herself. She must not allow any physical pain to take her mind off the loss she had suffered with Mrs Harry's death. Without her, Bob would be in prison now, instead of doing his job, and, perhaps—she prayed—escaping from the sinful and unnatural lusts that had held him.

Bob kept his head bent. Mrs Harry had frightened him as, he knew, she had frightened many others. Still, without her, Mr Harry wouldn't have been the man he was and, though she never came to the factory he and the shop foremen knew that her presence was there, in the influence she had on her husband. And she had saved him from gaol . . . at a price. Seeing Dr Deerfield five times a week was worse than having a wisdom tooth pulled every time, without gas. The things the doctor wanted him to remember, and say out loud, were downright filthy!

In the back of the church a baby set up a long wail, and Bob winced. Why did Mary Gorse have to bring the child to church? It must be about two months old, a girl, and they'd christened it Henrietta. Well, if it had to be brought, better Mary bring it than Violet.

Having the baby had turned her into a real woman. Mary's next girl, Betty, was ten now. She'd be smooth and hairless and thin. He felt an erection growing in his trousers and prayed, No, no, God help me, no!

And so it is written, the first Adam was made a living soul; the last Adam was made a quickening spirit. Howbeit, that was not first which is spiritual, but that which is natural: and afterward that which is spiritual. The first man is of the earth, earthy; the second man is the Lord from heaven.

Frank and Anne Stratton stood beside Bob and Jane, heads bowed. Anne tried to let the idea of peace and rest for Mrs Harry occupy her mind; but all she could think of was the cold of the open grave by the lych-gate. She stole a glance at her husband. He was thinner than he used to be, but carried himself straighter, and still wore the reddish beard that he had grown when he was Pioneer Sergeant. That beard meant a lot to him, but it made her nervous. Still, he was here, recovered from his wound and never, never to go to France again, or even to get into uniform—pensioned.

Frank's eyes strayed now, from the canon standing with clasped hands behind the coffin, to the Mayor of Hedlington reading the lesson, then across the aisle, to the three young people in uniform. His gaze rested there, on Guy Rowland in the maternity jacket of the Royal Flying Corps. Mr Guy was a great pilot, they were saying, but how good were his mechanics, on whom his life depended, too?

Therefore, my beloved brethren, be ye steadfast, unmoveable, always abounding in the work of the Lord, forasmuch as ye know that your labour is not in vain in the Lord.

The canon stepped forward, making a motion with his hands. The undertaker's professional pallbearers moved down the aisle, all in black, bare headed.

Man that is born of woman hath but a short time to live, and is full of misery. He cometh up, and is cut down, like a flower; he fleeth as it were a shadow, and never continueth in one stay.

The congregation led by Harry Rowland, leaning on the arm of his daughter, Alice, followed the coffin down the aisle.

In the midst of life we are in death; of whom may we seek for succour, but of thee O Lord, who for our sins are justly displeased?

Mary Gorse walked in the middle of the throng shuffling slowly down the aisle and out into the open. The rain had slackened but was still

falling, slanting down on the south-west wind, rustling the horse chestnut trees, still heavy with leaves, that bordered the churchyard, glistening on the spines of the yews by the lych-gate and on both sides of
the church door. Henrietta, her granddaughter, had stopped crying
and lay asleep in the crook of her right arm. Her first-born son,
Fletcher, was somewhere out there in the rain, still, living like an
animal in the woods. The police had come for him three weeks ago,
and told Mary he'd deserted from the Depot, up in Minden Barracks.
He'd not be comfortable but he'd not be starving or dying of cold,
either: Probyn had taught him everything he knew about the country
. . .

The tenor bell began to toll its six strokes, for the death of a
woman, a long pause between each. The head of the procession
reached the graveside, and the pallbearers waited, heads bared to the
rain, the coffin resting on the edge of the grave, ropes tied to the
carrying handles at each corner.

Ethel Fagioletti wept quietly. Mrs Harry was dead, who had given
her sweets when she was a little girl, who had shown her how a woman
should behave in hard times. She wished Niccolo could be here, and
wept harder, realizing that Niccolo, too, might be dead. The colonel,
Quentin, had assured her that he had been alive when he left the
battalion . . . but that was five weeks ago. And the colonel had said
that he was a good soldier, and had actually killed Germans at the
colonel's side, with a bayonet.

The pallbearers took hold of the ropes, and first lifting, brought
the coffin over the centre of the grave, then steadily lowered, while the
curate, picking up a handful of wet earth, dropped it on the coffin top.
The canon intoned:

*Forasmuch as it hath pleased Almighty God of his great mercy to take unto
himself the soul of our dear sister here departed, we therefore commit her body
to the ground.*

Ruth Hoggin sniffed, choked, and held her breath. Mrs Harry had
been a great lady . . . hard to know, perhaps, but then, as a Stratton,
it was not her place to know her that well. It was hard to think that Mr
Richard and Mr John and the colonel and the Commander had all
been little boys once, needing a mother's love . . .

*Earth to earth, ashes to ashes, dust to dust; in sure and certain hope of the
Resurrection to eternal life through our Lord Jesus Christ.*

Stella Merritt leaned more heavily on her husband's arm. She had not
known her grandmother well, and had been afraid of her. All her life

she had felt that Granny was able to sense her transgressions or sinful thoughts however hard she tried to hide them; and this feeling had been intensified in recent years, when the transgressions were not of failing to clean her teeth properly, or eating with her mouth open, but to do with the lusts of her body, the awareness of her beauty and of men's desire, the irresistible impulses towards whatever excited or carried the chill perfume of danger. She glanced across the grave and caught Dr Deerfield's eye. The hint of a smile touched his lips, then the tip of his tongue slid out, caressed the upper lip lasciviously, and slid back. That was the signal he gave her when, over lunch or tea, in some public place, he wanted to tell her that he desired her body, that they would soon again be enjoying the forbidden fruit, passionate mating . . . How could she, she thought, loving Johnny so much? How could she *not*, though, when even now the memory of that lecherous lick was soaking her underwear, even at her grandmother's graveside? They had been lovers for over three months.

Her husband patted her gloved hand with his, and prayed under his breath. The rain was increasing, Stella would catch cold; but, of course, she had to be there.

Lord, have mercy upon us.
Christ, have mercy upon us.
Lord, have mercy upon us.

Tim and Sally Rowland, the adopted children, were crying loudly, almost howling. Richard frowned down at them, murmuring, "Quiet!" They were really unpleasant little brats, and were crying now not because they were really sad at his mother's death, but because they thought it would earn them sympathy and approval from the family, perhaps even some money or sweets. Richard tried to remember what she so often said: the children had had no chance in life, knowing only the harsh world of the streets, and of men coming to use their mother's body, for money. Only love could help them. He'd keep trying.

Almighty God with whom do live the spirits of them that depart hence in the Lord, and with whom the souls of the faithful, after they are delivered from the burden of the flesh, are in joy and felicity.

Christopher Cate stood with his son Laurence on one side, Stella and Johnny on the other, and Mrs Isabel Kramer behind Laurence. He had admired his mother-in-law, and wished he could love her. His wife, his own wife, Margaret, the dead woman's eldest daughter, had not loved her . . . at first, she had told him, out of Rose's inability to share any real intimacy with her; later, because she came to believe that her mother, a descendant of the High Kings of All Ireland, had not fought enough to free Ireland from British rule. Now she was gone.

The grace of our Lord Jesus Christ, and the love of God, and the fellowship of the Holy Ghost, be with us all evermore.
Amen.

*   *   *   *

Richard stood with his father and sister near the French windows in the morning room of Laburnum Lodge, all with champagne glasses in hand. Rain streamed down the glass, spattered on the shallow stone steps outside, and pattered on the leaves of the tall trees along the wall. They had spoken of the woman recently buried, discussed family matters that she had raised on her deathbed—the disposal of rings and jewels among her daughters and the wives of her sons: special mementoes for the female staff, a pearl necklace for Jane Stratton. Then, for a minute they had been silent, in their own ways bidding her goodbye. She had lived, and was dead.

Harry said, "Churchill commiserated with me in the House yesterday. I don't think I like him or trust him, but I can't help admiring him . . . noticing the announcement of her death in the paper, working out who she must have been, taking the trouble to find me . . ."

Richard said, "I thought he was with the army in France. Quentin said he'd met him."

"Yes, but that was early in the year. He told me that his battalion was disbanded to make reinforcements for other battalions, and he decided to come back to Westminster . . . where an honest man needs a gas mask more than he does on the Western Front, he said." He shook his grey head wonderingly.

Richard saw his opportunity to broach a subject that he had for some time been meaning to bring up: "Father, a long time ago, when we founded the Jupiter Motor Company, I asked Dormouse to work for me. Now I'm going to ask her again—I think she's wasting her talent and education." He hesitated, not wishing to add bluntly—"looking after you, when there are half a dozen servants to do it"; but his father nodded and said, "I agree. Before the war, it was all right, perhaps . . . what better work for woman was there, than to be mistress of a household? But now—" he shook his head. "Women are doing things that one would have dismissed as impossible, or out of

168

the question for them—and doing them well. And so releasing men for the Front."

Alice said, "That's the only reason I hesitate to take up some full time war work—that and my House Parties and Tipperary Room. I can find someone to take them over from me, but I shudder to think that I shall, in effect, be personally sending some man to France . . . It's good of you to think of me, Lamps," she added, smiling up at her brother and using his old nickname, from the thick-lensed spectacles he had always had to wear. "But I have made up my mind to apply for work at Rowland's—the Shell Filling Factory."

Her father looked at her and said, "That's dangerous. They have had no accidents there, since it was converted, but there have been in other parts of the country. And Bob tells me the women suffer greatly from headaches."

"It's the fumes of the TNT," Richard said.

Alice said, "Well, I feel that I must take my share of danger and discomfort—and headaches." She ended with a small laugh. She looked at her father, "I will continue to live here, but we'll have to ask Mrs Stallings if she will be housekeeper as well as cook. . . . Willy will be conscripted, and Brace already has been. We can let Laura and Carrie go—they'll have no difficulty finding other work. That'll leave Judith and Martha to help Mrs Stallings, and Parrish as butler and houseman."

And Wright, the chauffeur, Richard thought, and McCracken the gardener, too old to be conscripted: Dixon the under gardener had gone . . . all this would leave three men and three women to look after the Governor and Alice. It would have seemed quite inadequate before the war; now, we looked at these matters very differently.

*   *   *   *

Naomi stood with her cousins, Virginia and Guy, Rowlands all. Naomi and Guy were tall and lean, the young man hawklike, the girl lithe and alert: Virginia was of average height, plump, with a heavy bosom. Naomi's eyes were brown, Virginia's pale grey, Guy's mismatched— one blue, one brown. Naomi was talking animatedly, with eager gestures—"So I wriggled under the car . . . it was a Humber—and flashed my torch up into the engine to see where the oil drip was coming from. The major was on his knees beside me in the mud, calling, 'Come out, miss. You shouldn't be under there. It's not right.' It's not decent, either, I thought, because of course I was wearing a skirt, so I had to worry about not showing too much leg while I was rolling about under the engine. I called back, 'Would you know what to look for, sir?' and he said, 'Well, no, miss, but someone else might.'

169

'There's no one within ten miles, sir,' I said—we were in the middle of the Hartford Bridge Flats, on a side road—'This is my job.' At that moment I saw the source of the leak—a loose nut at the base of the sump, and got out my adjustable spanner and tightened it and came out—face covered with oil and grease, skirt filthy. The major said, 'You know your job, miss.' "

Guy said, "Good show! Do all the girls in your detachment know their mechanics as well as you? After all, not many of them can have been raised in a car manufacturing family."

She said, "None. But they are good mechanics and drivers, they really are. And all they—we—ask is that you men treat us as that, not as comforts for officers, or something . . . something fragile. What about you, Virginia? How's life in the Women's Legion?"

Parrish came past then, with a silver tray loaded with full champagne glasses. Naomi took one, but Guy muttered, "No, thanks. I'll be flying in a few hours," and Virginia said, "I'm feeling silly already . . . It's different for us, Naomi, because we work mostly with Other Ranks. Our section cooks and housekeeps for a big barracks with a thousand men in Aldershot. We cook, wash up, clean the floors and windows, run the laundry . . . all the things that women would do if it were an ordinary household in peace, but in the Army men used to do them before the war—before we were formed. Officers aren't allowed to go out with any of us, as we're the equivalent of privates."

"So am I," Naomi murmured.

"Yes, but the people you work for are all officers. Ours aren't, and we are allowed to go out with them, when we're off duty, of course." Her colour heightened. "I went out with a Battery Sergeant Major a week ago. He won the D.C.M. at Loos but his left arm and a bit of his shoulder were blown off and he has an artificial arm now. He's sort of permanent sergeant clerk at the headquarters."

"Is he nice?" Naomi asked. "Rich? Madly in love with you? And a duke incognito?"

"Oh, don't be silly!"

"Be careful," Naomi said. "Pursuiters can become bores . . . How are the girls in France, Guy?"

"How should I know?" Guy said, grinning. "A girl behind the desk in a hotel in Amiens gave me the eye once—but I was with Grandfather and two other M.P.s, so what could I do? And the farmer's daughter where our mess is, at Mirvaux, is—well, I think 'available' would be the right word."

"Guy! You are awful!" Virginia said, gazing up at him with sparkling eyes.

Guy continued—"But she must weigh eleven stone, and looks extraordinarily like one of her father's cows. I don't want to find myself kissing Bossy in the dark, by mistake. But she's really very affectionate, I believe. Her name's Claudine, but we call her Poitrine, for two obvious reasons."

Naomi laughed briefly, then said, "Seriously, do you have any romantic attachments? I thought handsome young R.F.C. pilots couldn't avoid them—there, or here."

Guy said, "I'm fancy free." He looked from one to the other of the two girls, "I want my first love to be important, and . . . worthy. I suppose men and women can play at love, as they can play at games. I want mine to be serious, and lasting."

Neither girl spoke for a time, then Naomi said, "Don't be too cut up if it doesn't happen that way, Guy. I don't think we can always control these things."

*   *   *   *

Christopher Cate stood with Isabel Kramer, champagne glasses in hand, by the fireplace, where a small coal fire burned in the grate to disperse the damp of the day. They had not spoken for some time, but just stood, their backs half turned to the room, looking into each other's eyes.

At length Cate said, "I would like to ask you to marry me, Isabel, but as you know I am not free to do so."

She said nothing, but her expressive face was losing its composure, her lower lip beginning to tremble.

Cate said, "If I were able to get a divorce, would you be my wife?"

She said, her voice shaking, "Of course, Christopher. You are the nicest man I have ever met . . . and, as I am a brash American, I'll say it before you do—I love you."

Cate stooped down toward her, longing to kiss her on the lips, then checked himself. He said, "I wish I could ask you to live with me at the Manor until I can get a divorce—if I ever can. At night, now, I dream that I am seeing you across the breakfast table, as man and wife—sleeping in each other's arms—scrubbing each other's back in the bath . . ."

She said, "And I dream that I can be a helpmeet to you in every way. I know—" she rested a hand momentarily on his sleeve—"that you are having financial troubles, with the war taxes and prices. I would like to help here, too."

He said grimly, "Only a miracle can make it possible—what we both desire. Visits—even extended visits such as you have made, are accepted by the village . . . and would be, even if we had taken advantage of the situation to enjoy the intimacy I think we both desire.

171

They would understand that, approve of it—especially as they know my position with regard to Margaret. But, for you to live in the Manor would be . . ." he stopped, searching for the words.

She finished for him, ". . . a stain on the position you hold, and the example you must set, as squire of Walstone. I understand, my dear. Of course I do. Garrod now makes opportunities for us to be alone, when I am staying at the Manor. And I am sure she hopes that we have spent the night in one bed, yours or mine. But if I were to *live* here, she would have to acknowledge me as your mistress . . . and it is not proper that the squire of Walstone should flaunt his mistress in the face of his people, in their village."

Cate said, "You understand perfectly. That is why you would make such a perfect mistress—in the other sense—of the Manor, hence of the village . . . For a divorce I have to prove that Margaret has committed adultery. Which will be very difficult unless she helps, provides the evidence, really—which would be collusion. But my solicitor told me that the judges are becoming much less strict in demanding proof of adultery. Like anyone else, they live and operate in a climate of public opinion, and that's been changing rapidly, particularly since the war began. Most of them will now grant a divorce if an association is shown, from which adultery can reasonably be inferred."

Isabel sipped her champagne; then looking up from her 5'4" to Cate's 6'3" said in her flat down-Maine accent, "Will you spend a weekend with me, my dear? As man and wife. It doesn't matter where, as long as it's not in Walstone."

Cate felt silly, light headed, about to jump over the moon, sixteen years old and gasping at the sight of his first girl's hair spread on dandelion-gold grass. He said, "I will."

A hush fell on the assembly and they both glanced round. Parrish was standing in front of Harry Rowland, bowing slightly. He straightened and declared in a loud voice, "Luncheon is served, sir."

*   *   *   *

They sat at the long table, extra chairs crowded in among them, the younger people standing, waiting, for they were to eat at tables set up in the drawing room; but first their grandfather wanted to make an announcement to all the family, gathered for this solemn occasion.

Harry adjusted his spectacles on his nose, brushed his beard and found a paper in the pocket of his black frock coat. He peered at it, cleared his throat, and looked up—"My sons . . . daughters . . ." he choked, recovered, continued—"my family . . . when your mother was dying, she gave me a message for you, all of you . . . two messages. She could not write, but whispered . . . I wrote them down, as she gave them to me." He looked down at the paper—"This is the first

172

. . . *I love you all. Forgive me for my faults as a wife, mother, mother-in-law* . . . She had no faults as a wife but that is what she said. *Forgive each other. Love each other. Pray that the war may be over soon. Forgive our enemies.*" There was a long pause, then Harry spoke again, "This is the second . . . *Ireland must be free. Understand that Margaret is only doing what I should have done, if I had not chosen another path of life. Understand, and you will not hate. Work for this, and you will earn more for England than victory in war. Erin go bragh. Goodbye.*"

*   *   *   *

Guy Rowland and Johnny Merritt walked Hedlington Airfield in the rain, Guy wearing a khaki trench coat and Johnny a mackintosh. At the east end of the field, before turning back, Johnny said, "Hold hard a minute, Guy . . . Seeing you in uniform, with that ribbon, makes me feel more of a shirker than ever. But, you know what I found out last week? I'm colour blind . . . not badly, just can't tell blues and greens apart . . . so the R.F.C. wouldn't have me. I'd have to join the Army."

Guy said, "Don't do it, Johnny. Not our Army, anyway. America will come in soon—I don't think she can stay out, however much she might want to—and then you wouldn't worry, would you?"

"I would not," Johnny said. "The day America comes in, I enlist . . . But it's here and now that I feel such a shirker."

Guy said, "When America declares war, enlist. Meanwhile, keep on making these aeroplanes for us. That's a fair bargain, Johnny . . . The north side of the field is reasonably hard, except for that one patch over there. What will we weigh at take off?"

Johnny smiled and shook Guy's shoulder, "Thanks . . . It depends on whether you want a full load of petrol."

"To fly to Amiens? No, but orders are we should always take off full, as we might run into bad weather and have to come back, or go another hundred miles looking for an open airfield . . . but it will be that much more difficult to get her off this soft ground if she's fully loaded. There won't be any passengers, will there?"

"No."

"Good. You don't want me to crack up one of your beautiful bombers, and I certainly don't want to find myself nosing into that slush with five tons of aeroplane on top of me."

"All right." They walked past the control tower shed and into the passage way between the big construction hangars. The wooden skeleton of a fuselage passed, carried on two wheels, pulled by a plough horse. "Ancient and modern," Johnny said. "That's on its way from the fuselage shed to the assembly shed." He walked into another shed, Guy following. "This is the chassis forging unit . . . see, the root section of both wings, attached to the chassis, the two sets of landing wheels." He slapped the wing stub—"This is where the outer wings are attached . . . the bolts attaching them go here . . . Then they can be folded back for more economical storage—just like the Handley Page 0/400. Ginger brought that idea over—and many others, of course."

They walked out and into another shed, this one full of frames from which complete engine units, less the spinners and propellers, were suspended.

"Rolls Royce Eagle IIIs, aren't they?" Guy exclaimed. "I thought Handley Page was going to get the first allotment."

"So did they, but we managed to get some . . . Our Leopard Mark II's going to have Libertys. Come along . . . tail units are assembled in the back of the chassis shed . . . The main planes need a separate shed for trueing-in on the jigs. It's quite an operation and we're working on ways to cut down the time spent . . . Here's our works foreman, Frank Stratton. You know him, of course?"

Frank Stratton put out his hand eagerly. "Saw you in the church, Master Guy . . . Mister Guy . . . but didn't have a chance to speak to you . . . Could I have a word with you, in private, sir?"

Guy glanced at Johnny—"All right? We've done our business, haven't we?"

Johnny said, "I'd like to have half an hour with you, Guy, going over the plans for the Mark II. So do Betty and Ginger. We'll wait for you in the drawing office."

Guy nodded and walked off with Frank at his side. He said, "Hadn't we better go inside somewhere? It's wet out here."

Frank said, "I'd rather talk outside, sir. I won't be a minute . . . Sir, I want to get back to France."

Guy stopped and stared at him, rain running down their faces. He said, "But I understood that you have been severely wounded, and invalided out, unfit for any form of military duty."

"That's right, sir . . . I've been out of hospital seven months, foreman here nearly six months . . . I can't stand it any more . . . when I hear the guns at night and think of the blokes out there, in the mud, and us eating our beef and drinking our beer, and women everywhere, acting like prossies . . . and them in the regiment, out there." His voice trailed away to burst out suddenly, "My wife'll cry her eyes out, but I've got to go. England's a . . . a shithouse, sir."

Guy began to walk on, thinking. He said, "Did you mention this to my father when you were speaking to him?"

Frank said, "No, sir. I wanted to, but . . . my wife would have heard."

Guy rubbed his face thoughtfully. He said, "You'll never get back

174

to the Wealds, Frank. It would be suicide on your part to go—and murder on mine to help you—because you'd have no chance in the trenches. The Royal Flying Corps is the best corps in the world . . . as good as any regiment, I don't care whether it's the Guards, the Rifle Brigade, the Royal Welch Fusiliers, the Black Watch, anyone. You'll never fly, but you're as good a mechanic as any in the world. Our success in the air depends on the mechanics as well as on the pilots. Would you like to be a fitter in 333 Squadron of the R.F.C.? It's a Scout Squadron, now equipped with D.H. 2s . . . my squadron?"

Frank said, "Mr Charles used to tell me I ought to transfer to the R.E. or the R.F.C. . . . but I didn't want to, because I belonged in the Regiment. Now I can't belong, can I, not in France?" Guy nodded, though he knew the question was rhetorical. Frank said, "I'll come, sir. I'll be your fitter and you'll be one pilot whose engine never goes dud on him. Can I come with you now?"

Guy laughed and slapped Frank on the shoulder. "My major would have me for breakfast, and you for lunch! I have to explain what a wizard mechanic you are, and then I have to get my grandfather to see the right man at the War Office. And then, suddenly, you'll find yourself on your way to France, wearing the uniform of a private in the R.F.C. . . . but you'll be a sergeant before long, or I'll eat my cunt cap." He grinned. "That's what we call these." He touched the wet forage cap on his head.

Frank said eagerly, "So did we in the Regiment, sir . . . I suppose I'll have to shave off my beard for the R.F.C.?"

"I'm afraid so," Guy said. "We don't have Pioneer Sergeants in the Royal Flying Corps. Now come along and join us in this talk we're going to have about the Leopard Mark II."

*　　*　　*　　*

The engine whistled imperiously for the Litchfield tunnel and the roar of the train increased as the rattle of the wheels and the rush of the wind bounced back and forth between the sides of the carriages and the walls of the tunnel. The six officers in a first class compartment of the London & South Western Railway stared blankly ahead, except for one who had been reading a book and chuckling to himself. None of them knew each other, and had not felt any need to make conversation since leaving Waterloo over an hour ago. Besides, if one initiated a conversation, he might be snubbed.

Quentin closed his eyes. His mother was dead. He had been afraid of her, but at least she had taught all of them to face life with heads up. He had seen his son, looking bronzed and fit, but older than his nineteen and a half years. He had seen his daughter, and noted her new low-class accent. He had seen his wife. She had been polite, remote, never mentioned the man she loved, or what had happened. He had waited for her to say something, so that he could tell her he still loved her. She never did.

Well, he was on his way back to the battalion, at last. He knew they'd been in two major shows since he was wounded, and wondered how many more once familiar faces would have vanished. How had the shows been planned, and how had they gone, really? You couldn't trust what you read in the papers. It seemed disloyal to question the tactical doctrines on which all the Somme attacks had been made so far—think of the consolidated experience of all those generals and colonels, men who had been commanding companies in action in Afghanistan and Africa while he was a small boy . . . and all those brass hats with their staff tables . . . and the artillery fire charts, which he could not make head or tail of . . . and eighty-page orders, with twenty appendices. Still the German lines were bent but not broken, and the ground reeking with the unburied dead. He gritted his teeth. They'd just have to go on till the Germans couldn't stand it any more . . .

It would be good to talk to Campbell again. That fellow had led an interesting life. He was a bit of a radical in some ways, but you could learn a lot, listening to him . . . he could draw marvellously, too. His sketches of the men—in the line, on fatigue duty, limping back wounded, wiring at dusk—they really *were* the men . . .

Daily Telegraph, Saturday, September 16, 1916

GREAT ATTACK BY BRITISH ARMY
NEW ARMOURED CARS

Sir Douglas Haig, in his report sent off early yesterday afternoon, records the opening phases of another tremendous attack by the British Army on the German positions in the neighbourhood of Combles.

A special feature of this attack was the employment for the first time of a new form of a heavy armoured car, which appears to have fully justified expectations . . .

CAPTURE OF FLERS
FROM OUR SPECIAL CORRESPONDENT: BRITISH
HEADQUARTERS, *FRANCE*.

Friday 2 p.m.
To-day our troops, in a great assault, have broken through the enemy's third line of defense. It is reported that Flers is in our

hands, and that the infantry is advancing further in the direction of Morval. On our left we are at the moment in the outskirts of Martinpuich, and thence to the right we have moved forward along the whole line, encircling High Wood and occupying the main part of Bouleaux Wood.

Our men are filled with the spirit of victory, and in several parts of the line the enemy is fleeing back to his next line of trenches. Prisoners are coming in fast . . .

"A new form of a heavy armoured car," Cate thought. That sounded interesting. From everything he had heard and read, the problem in attack was the number of bullets that could be fired by machine guns these days. The more men you massed to attack, in the hope of overwhelming the enemy by sheer weight of numbers, the more men you put up as targets for their machine guns. Each gun fired 600 rounds a minute, Quentin had told him; and their range was 2,000 yards, or over a mile. Suppose you had forty such guns in a mile of front—and the Germans seemed to have at least that number, in places—why, they could fire 24,000 rounds a *minute*. In that minute the attacking soldiers could move forward perhaps fifty yards, weighted down as they were with so much equipment, tools and arms . . . If the German trenches were two hundred yards away they'd have to face 96,000 bullets . . . So, if it were possible to mass 96,000 men on a single mile of front . . . you'd lose them all in two minutes. These new cars, armoured to protect the men inside from bullets, could presumably advance over that two hundred yards in half a minute . . . but he had read a great deal about mud, even in the chalk of the Somme area. The heavy cars would get their wheels stuck in the mud, and the heavier they were, the thicker their armour, the more guns they carried, the deeper they'd sink in . . .

Well, better brains than his must have been thinking of answers to these problems for months, and one of Johnny Merritt's aeroplanes from Hedlington was buzzing overhead like a giant bumblebee, and a hen had escaped from the chicken run to lay an egg in the hedge beyond the lawn, a fact which she was now proudly cackling to the world. He turned the pages—ah, the Page for Women, which the Telegraph published every Saturday. One had to get away from the war sometimes or one would go mad . . . six drawings of autumnal coats and dresses . . . the skirts were about ten or twelve inches off the ground, he noticed . . . a long article about "Equal pay for equal work—Is this pure justice?" The writer seemed to conclude it wasn't . . . Butter and eggs going up in price . . . Fish dear all week, oysters very reasonable . . . hares not likely to be below 4s to 4s 6d . . . after

177

harvest, ducks at their best, but a high price compared to normal times must be paid . . . Some recipes—Novelty suet pudding; Short paste or bread dough pudding; Yorkshire pudding with fruit; a potato cake; Stale Bread Sweet; Bread and apple pudding; Nursery pudding—ah, was this what Nanny used to force on him, as a boy, sometimes? . . . "Dredge slices of stale bread with sugar and toast on both sides. Then place the slices in a dish, and cover with stewed fruit of any kind or a mixture of cooked fruit." Sounded like it, indeed . . . the only sweet he'd hated worse than trifle, and . . .

He heard Garrod come in and said, without looking up, "Some more coffee, please, Garrod . . . and tell Mrs Abell the kedgeree is excellent."

"Yes, sir." She brought the pot to him and poured coffee. "Sir . . ." Her voice was low but firm. He looked up, quailing. He knew that expression. No escape, not for a minute.

"Who is it?"

"The Englands, sir. Young Harry's been killed. A week ago . . . They got the telegram this morning, and a letter from Colonel Quentin half an hour later. Killed instantly by machine-gun fire near High Wood, the colonel said. He said he died doing his duty as a brave man and a good soldier and . . ."

". . . all ranks of the battalion join Mr and Mrs England in their bereavement," Cate finished. "I'll go down right away. He was nineteen . . ."

Southern England: Mid-October, 1916

12   Stella Merritt sat in the cottage's small drawing room, staring at the lawn, and, beyond the hedge, the roofs of Beighton below. A bottle of Bristol Milk sherry was on the table at her side, and a tulip glass, half empty, beside the bottle. From the other reception room across the entrance hall she heard Laura the maid humming as she flapped a duster over the furniture in there. Mummy would have been on her like a ton of bricks for the way she cleaned—or didn't. It was the same with Mrs Hackler, the cook. She wasn't a good cook, and Mummy would have sacked her long since . . . but then who'd cook for her, and for Johnny when he came home? Except that so often he didn't come home till after ten o'clock. She rolled the sweet wine round her mouth, and swallowed. That made her feel better, the warm glow spreading from her throat to her chest, her stomach and eventually to the tips of her toes.

She felt restless, dissatisfied, unhappy. She was betraying Johnny with Charles Deerfield, which was wrong. She should stop that, but . . . Johnny didn't make love to her very often, considering. Captain Irwin had done it three times in the one night in that pub, and he was thirty-six then. Charles always did it twice, after lunch, when they met. Johnny was only twenty-four but he came home so tired, and got up so early to study papers and designs that often she couldn't tempt him, morning or evening . . .

She jumped up, poured out a full glass of sherry and downed it in one gulp, then went to the corner, picked up the telephone, wound the handle, and called a number in Hedlington. The voice at the far end said, "Dr Deerfield."

"Charles? I must see you. Right away!"

A pause: then—"Come to my office at eleven-thirty."

"All right."

She went to the door and called, "Mrs Hackler, I have to go into Hedlington."

Mrs Hackler came out of the kitchen drying her hands on her apron—"What shall I do with the partridge, then?"

"Keep it for dinner, I'll be back for tea."

Mrs Hackler retired sulkily to the kitchen. Stella put on hat, veil, gloves, and long, warm winter driving coat and went out to the little shed they had had built to house their car, a Rowland Sapphire. It was there in the shed because today she had driven Johnny to Walstone station for a day's work in London, and was to meet him at seven in the evening—unless work delayed him till the last train, or overnight.

Young Sam, the gardener—gardener's boy, he would have been before the war—was there raking leaves and piling them on the bonfire in the corner of the little garden. He worshipped Stella, the Sapphire only a degree less, and at sixteen was strong and growing fast into manhood.

She called, "Sam!" He looked up, "Yes, m'm?" She smiled—"Would you start the car for me, please?"

" 'Course, m'm." He dropped the rake and came over, striding fast. The doors of the shed were already open and she climbed up into the driver's seat. When the car was started she said, "Thank you, Sam," and drove out, and away.

Dr Deerfield's white-painted door bore a brass plate, reading *Dr Charles S. Deerfield, M.D.* and, below that *Alienist*. It was closed but not locked, and she let herself in. He was working at his desk in the corner behind the couch where, he had told her, his patients lay, while he tried to find the roots of their problems; or rather, as he had often explained, tried to get them to identify those roots for themselves.

He stood up and came toward her with arms outstretched. She held him off, bending her back—"Charles, we've got to end this."

He paused then, eyeing her quizzically—"You've said that before."

"I know . . . but I mean it . . . it doesn't make me happy, the way it used to. Nothing does."

Gently he lifted her veil, saying, "Not even the sherry?"

She shook her head, "No . . ." It was no use. She just would not come here again. She closed her eyes. But this time, this last time . . . Her lips parted softly as his pressed down on hers, and she felt his body firm against her, hardening more at the groin, the male staff pressing against the material of her skirt, ready to pierce her. She groaned involuntarily, and tried to say something; but his mouth was insistent, and she was leaning back in his arms, stumbling. The edge of the couch was behind her knees and she half fell, half lay back on it. She opened her eyes . . . this was the moment she liked to see for herself . . . him bending over, pulling up her skirt till it was bunched round her waist, taking off her drawers, pulling them down. She raised her buttocks, breathing fast . . .

Five minutes later he rose, wiped his genitals with his handkerchief and sat down beside her, stroking her hair—"That was good, yes?" She nodded. His hand wandered to her pubis and stroked the tight blond curls there—"So, nothing works any more?"

She said wearily, "No. And I won't come here again, Charles." She got up, pulled on her drawers and let her skirt fall. "That was the last time." Her head swam momentarily and she stumbled and almost fell. Charles said, "Ah, you had a few little drinks before you came?"

She said, "Yes . . . Why did I let you seduce me?"

He was about to answer flippantly when he paused, and considered, and said slowly, "Because I represented danger. Which I no longer do. I have become like Johnny to you . . . safe, boring. But I think I have something for you that will be more exciting than sherry ever was . . . more exciting even than making love, the first time."

She listened, eager in spite of herself. What on earth could he mean?

He said, "Next time Johnny goes away for the day, warn me and come here early."

"But what . . . ?"

"Release from all your worries—not as sure as death, but much more pleasant . . . a trip to the Moon. You'll love it . . . Heroin."

*   *   *   *

It was hard work. The sweat formed steadily under Alice's mob cap and dripped into her eyes and down her cheeks. Mustn't think of it as sweat, she told herself, half smiling—horses sweat, gentlemen perspire, ladies merely glow. But this wasn't ladies' work, standing at a long table filling 18-pounder shells with amatol from buckets. It was a messy business and all the time cleaners were swabbing the cement floor to lay the dust that formed when spilled amatol—trinitrotoluene stabilized with ammonium nitrate—dried off back to its natural powdered state. On the table at which she and a score of other women worked were boxes of transit plugs, wooden hammers, and little cotton exploder bags already filled with powdered TNT. As she filled each projectile with its high explosive amatol, Alice, and every other woman working at that table, tucked in its exploder bag and screwed in its transit plug, which would be replaced at the actual firing site by the proper nose fuze . . . Barrows and trolleys, rubber-wheeled, passed, loaded with completed shells and pulled by sweating men. Outside the plant doors armoured lorries waited to take the shells to ammunition trains, loading at Hedlington railways goods yard, which would take them to Ordnance Depots scattered round the south of England, or direct to the Channel ports, for loading in ships and onward transit to the Western Front, where they would be destroyed . . . and destroy.

All the women working in the plant had to wear rubber-soled shoes; no jewelry was allowed, of any kind, not even a ring or one of the new lady's wristwatches; no other metal object could be worn or carried. When the women reached the plant for work they went first to a dressing room where they took off their outer clothing and put on, instead, over their underwear, khaki-trousered overalls, buttoning to the neck, a blue mob cap entirely containing their hair, and thin rubber gloves. There was only one naked light in the plant—in the canteen, where the workers could buy one cigarette at a time, to be smoked in the canteen itself. The amatol was melted purely by steam brought in by pipes to the various loading chambers through hundreds of feet of lagged piping from the boiler room, in a separate building. The loading chambers had strong walls and flimsy roofs, so that any blast would be funneled upward, not outward.

Alice had only been working a week, but still, toward the end of each day she not only felt tired, but had the beginnings of a headache. It was so today, and she found herself wondering how long to six o'clock and the end of her shift. There was no clock in any of the loading chambers, to give the workers no temptation to look up from their tasks, and so perhaps allow a shell case to go unfilled. Around her she heard the muttered gossiping of the women: that was forbidden, since there was supposed to be no talking except such as was called for by the work. But Bob Stratton didn't seem to care, so the various shop foremen and forewomen didn't enforce the rule, either . . . "proper scragger that Agnes Chittle is" . . . "So I told her she wasn't *my* foreman, strite I did, the old miaow!" . . . "Where's Bessie today? 'Aven't seen 'er since the dinner whistle. Is she sick?"—"Nah, aht on the pigtrot, if yer arsk me."

It was difficult to concentrate for eight hours on end, with a lunch break, on work as repetitive and unrewarding as this. Most of the other women working here were younger than she . . . naturally, for most women of her age were married and by now occupied with the care of children and a house. And they were mostly of the lower class—again, naturally, for the upper class being better educated—though often only through governesses, and in such skills as French poetry, water-colouring, and flower arrangement—looked for war work suited to their talents: they became nurses, drove staff cars and ambulances, or organized other women . . . as she herself had done, she acknowledged, when she had been running a Tipperary Room and her House Parties. She liked her fellow workers, and had learned much from them, even within the week, about courage and determination. After the whistle went at the end of the shift, many of the women headed for the nearest pub and had a drink before going home—usually a port and lemon, sometimes a small gin, often a tankard of porter. Alice had never been in a pub in her life till now; and she was beginning to enjoy those evening visits, and look forward to them. The women were so like men in that hour—voices raised, singing, back slapping . . . *My Bob's been made Leading Seaman . . . Fifteen shillings they fined 'er, it's a bleeding shyme . . . In 'ospital six months and them doctors ready to bury 'er every day, then she ups and walks out . . . No, they never married . . . Thirty-six hours I was, with me first, and no doctor—lost her, poor little mite . . .*

The whistle on the roof started its shrill blare and a foreman came down the aisles. "Six o'clock, six o'clock! Tidy up, tidy up!"

Alice stooped to scrape up some amatol she had spilled on the table and took it, in the carton provided, to the bin at the end of the room; then back to her place, tidied her piece of table, and joined the crowd of other women going towards the exit doors.

Ten minutes later she was walking out of the main gate, thinking of the lemonade she would have at the Star and Garter up the road. A woman and a man were standing beside the factory gate, in the road, shouting and waving pamphlets. "Stop the war! Join the Conscientious Objectors! Stop the slaughter of your brothers, husbands, fathers!" She paused, listening. She recognized the man at once as Bert Gorse. He used to work in the factory when it made motor cars, then he'd gone to work for Richard and then there'd been a scandal, and pictures in the papers, because he had shot off his own big toe to avoid military service. And the woman: ah, it was Naomi's friend from Cambridge, Rachel Cowan, who had spent the night in gaol with Naomi for allegedly assaulting the police outside the barracks.

"Stop the war! Stop the slaughter in France! . . . Come to the meeting tonight . . . seven o'clock, outside the Town Hall!"

Rachel's voice was shrill and carried far. Few of the women workers took a pamphlet, several spitting on the ground at the feet of the agitators. Alice went up to the woman and took a pamphlet. She said, "You are Rachel Cowan, aren't you? I got you out of the police station last spring."

The other woman said grudgingly, "I remember."

Alice raised her voice, "Naomi's in London with the Women's Volunteer Motor Drivers. She's well."

Rachel said, "I'm glad to hear it. Tell her . . . Oh, don't bother. She knows . . . Stop the war! Stop the slaughter! Come to the meeting!"

Alice passed on, as a woman behind her shouted, "Shut yer trap, ye dirty bitch! 'Ow dare you, while our men's fighting out there?"

"But don't you see?" Rachel cried, "we're trying to . . ." Alice heard the woman behind her spit, then an arm hooked into hers, and the same voice said, "Come and 'ave a drop of stout with me, luv. Need to wash the taste of them shit-eating bastards out of our mouths, eh?"

The Star and Garter was full to overflowing when they forced their way into the public—like rugby football players, Alice thought; and who could have imagined she'd ever be shoving like this, giggling, arms linked with her friend's, whom she'd never seen before, both pushing together, other women laughing, shouting. "Two 'arf pints milk stout," the woman yelled. "No, make it pints, ducks."

"Oh, I couldn't . . ." Alice began.

"'Course you can! Thirsty work, filling them bleeding shells." She leaned over two other women and took the pints, black filled, foam topped, from the barmaid. "'Ere . . . down the 'atch! Where's *your* old tin can?"

"I beg your pardon?"

The woman looked at her more closely, and said, "Ah, you're a proper miaow, ain't yer? I asked, where's yer old man, yer husband?"

"I'm Alice Rowland," she said, smiling. "I'm not married."

"Cor stone the crows!" her companion exclaimed. "Mr Harry's daughter? Never expected to be 'aving a drink with the likes of you."

Alice raised her huge glass, "Well, here we are, anyway. Thank you."

"Thank *you*, miss!" The two women drank. Alice could not get the picture of Rachel Cowan and Bert Gorse out of her mind. Perhaps she should go to the meeting and at least hear what they had to say. The war had become so dreadful, the casualty lists quite unbelievable. She had heard it whispered that the British Army had lost 60,000 men killed and wounded on the first day of the Somme battle—*sixty thousand in one day!* And that battle was still raging, three and a half months later.

Her companion said, "'Course, I wish the men was 'ome. It's lonely back 'ere for us women, ain't it? 'Tain't right, some 'ow . . . but we don't want 'em back and they don't want to come back till we've shown the bleeding 'Uns wot's wot and 'oo's 'oo, eh? . . . Miss, look, there's a pal of mine, Jimmy Pierson, 'e's an up'olsterer. Married, of course, but 'is wife don't come to the pub with 'im . . . Jimmy!" She raised her voice—"Come 'ere!" The man was small and alert-looking. He had been talking to another man, taller, darker, wearing spectacles, rather pale of face. Both were in their forties, Alice thought, and so safe from conscription.

The one addressed as Jimmy bussed Alice's companion heartily on the cheek, and said, "'Ello, ducks . . . This is my friend, Dave Cowell . . . Mister David Cowell, M.A., I'd 'ave you know."

The other man smiled, a little shyly. "I'm a schoolmaster." He looked at Alice, and the other woman quickly said, "This is Miss Alice Rowland."

The schoolmaster said, "I thought I recognized you. You came to the school with your father once, when he was giving away prizes."

She felt an unaccountable need to talk to him about the conscientious objection and anti-conscription movements. She said, in a low voice, hoping her companion would not overhear, "Did you see those Conscientious Objector people outside the Shell Filling Factory just now?"

"Yes," he said, "I'm going to their meeting."

"Why?" she asked.

He had a serious face, rather melancholy in repose, but becoming animated when he spoke. His accent was from the Midlands— Birmingham, or the Potteries—and his M.A. was almost certainly not from Oxford or Cambridge, but perhaps from Birmingham University . . . not a gentleman, though a scholar, and looking quite out of place in the din, the dense tobacco smoke, the clink of glass here. He said, "The war's grown too big for anyone to control, apparently. Perhaps it must be stopped, before it destroys everything that makes life worth living. And if it is to be stopped, campaigns of this kind may be the only action that can do it."

On an impulse she said, "May I come with you?"

Then he looked more closely into her eyes. His own were brown, and soft, and suddenly Alice felt a stirring in her body, and she remembered the Petty Officer the night of the dance last year. Her heart turned over, and she answered his look, her lips a little parted, waiting.

*   *   *   *

Rachel said, "That was a good crowd we got this evening, Bert."

Bert limped over to the fireplace and put on another two lumps of coal. "Not bad. I got twelve names and addresses afterwards."

"That makes how many so far, in Hedlington?"

"Thirty-nine, counting us. And do you know who was in the crowd? Miss Alice Rowland, old Harry's daughter. She was with Cowell, the schoolmaster, he teaches chemistry at the Grammar School by the prison. I knew him before the war."

"What were they doing at the meeting?"

"How the hell should I know? She's an old maid and always will be. He's married—two girls, I think."

"Don't be too sure that Miss Alice will die an old maid . . . She told me that Naomi's in London. There was a picture of her in the paper at her grandmother's funeral. I cut it out."

"She was a great friend of yours, once, wasn't she?"

Rachel did not speak for a time, then said, "We still could be, if we met. We were very close . . . But she's an enemy of the working class, an enemy of socialism—she and all her family. We couldn't spend five minutes together now—since I've been with you, since I've come back to my own class—without having a fight . . . We've got to get this group organized now, Bert. Call in all those people who've signed up, and work out what to do next."

"Work out what to do, *then* call them in and tell them," Bert said.

"All right. But we need a place to meet, indoors. This'll have to be our office—" she swept her hand round the two-room flat above a stable in North Hedlington where she and Bert had lived together for the last six months—"but we must find a meeting place."

Bert said, "Town Hall—they won't let us use it. Oddfellows—ditto . . . Big banquet room at the South Eastern, ditto."

She said, "What about a school?"

Neither spoke for a minute, then they said simultaneously, "Cowell!"

After a time Rachel said, "He's not a headmaster. So he doesn't have the power. And he didn't sign up. . . . And, Bert, before we decide on any course of action, we should get advice from others, who've been doing this longer. There's a group called the No-Conscription Fellowship, in London. Let's go up and talk to them—join them, perhaps."

"How are we going to get to London without any money?" Bert asked angrily. "I can't get a job 'cos I shot my bloody toe off. The landlady's trying to throw us out of here 'cos she's found out we're not married."

Rachel said hesitantly, "I have a little money saved up. And . . . why don't we get married, Bert? It would solve that problem, at least."

Bert said shortly, "Not on your bleeding life!"

"But why not? Are you against marriage?"

Bert said, more quietly, "No, but there isn't anyone who has the *right* to marry me. Why should I give the government the right, or the Church, when they're both capitalist oppressors?"

She said, "I was only thinking of convenience. I don't want to leave this place." She thought, what I do want are love, and peace, and an opportunity to make the working people's lives better; and I'm longing for a sense of security with this man; every woman is, probably, but will any have it, as long as the war lasts?

Bert said, "Well, if we get married, it'll be by standing in the field somewhere, or in a factory, with a hammer and sickle in our hands, and declaring that we're married. I'm against the Church and the State."

Rachel said sharply, "You're *against* everything, Bert Gorse. What are you *for*? Try to find out, and tell me, and we'll get on better."

* * * *

Betty Merritt waltzed carefully in Ginger Keble-Palmer's arms. They were in the Cat & Mouse, a cellar under a house in Albemarle Street, and now full of officers in uniform and many women, mostly with men, but some unattached. She said to Ginger, "I'm surprised the police don't raid this place. They must know that they serve drinks after hours, and harbour prostitutes."

Ginger started, "What? Good heavens, do you think those girls are, what you said?"

Her expression changed and she muttered in Ginger's ear, "Not all. The woman dancing with a naval officer, just behind you, is the Marchioness of Jarrow—Florinda Gorse that was." The band changed to a foxtrot and Ginger wailed, "I don't know how . . ."

"Take it easy," she said. "I'll teach you. Go soft . . . follow me . . . one two . . . left right, chassé . . . change step . . . back, turn, change step . . . good." After a few minutes, she said, "Let's sit down for a bit. I'm thirsty."

They sat at a little table at the back of the room, under a small, lighted sign reading GENTS. Betty eyed Florinda while Ginger ordered drinks—a small brandy and soda for himself and a glass of white wine for her. She must make an opportunity to speak to her. Florinda would know about Fletcher.

Meantime, she needed desperately to talk to someone about Stella and Johnny—but not to Ginger. He was one of the nicest young men she had ever met—brilliant at his work, unassuming, thoughtful, and shy—especially with women. She'd have to find a girl for him, the right sort of girl . . . but he wasn't sophisticated enough to be able to give her advice in this matter of Stella. Stella, Betty was sure, was drinking secretly . . . and visiting Hedlington more often than necessary. Why? She certainly wasn't shopping, for she had not bought any new clothes since the wedding. So what was it? Stella needed a baby; that would give her something to do about the house, apart from all the other things a baby meant, or should mean, to a couple in love with each other. Johnny was certainly in love with her, that was for sure.

The band blared a chord and everyone in the room fell silent. The M.C. stood at the edge of the band's little stage and said, "Ladies and gentlemen, and now—the Most Noble, the Marchioness of Jarrow, better known to one and all as . . . Florinda!"

Florinda walked out of the dark beside the band and stepped up onto the stage. The bandleader looked at her, gave a beat and the band began to play softly a sentimental ballad from *The Merry Widow:*

> *There once was a Vilia, A witch of the wood,*
> *A hunter beheld her alone as she stood,*
> *The spell of her beauty upon him was laid;*
> *He'd look'd for the magical maid!*

Gradually the clink of glasses died, the rustling increased and then faded as men and women sat down on the dance floor, holding hands, and were still.

She sings well, Betty thought; and she's beautiful, breathtakingly lovely, the lights glowing in the auburn hair piled on her head, and held by a diamond tiara . . . the dress black silk, very plain, no ornament but a diamond brooch at the neck of the dress, black silk stockings, diamante shoes with high heels, "princess" heels they called them . . . every inch a marchioness: Fletcher's sister.

The song ended and Florinda curtsied slowly to waves of applause. She sang *Four Indian Love Lyrics* then, and finally, *Keep the home fires burning.* Then curtsying again, she walked back into the darkness. Betty jumped to her feet, muttered, "Wait here, Ginger," and followed. She found Florinda leaning against the wall in the farthest dark corner, and said, "Lady Jarrow . . . I'm Betty Merritt."

"I know." She seemed tired.

Betty said, "Can you tell me where Fletcher is?"

Florinda's voice was suddenly hard—"No."

Betty said, "I . . . I just hope he's all right. I can't bear to think of him lying out in the woods in the rain and cold, especially now that winter's coming."

The Marchioness leaned forward, and said, "Oh! So that's it!"

Betty said, "We spent a lot of time together, when he was in the barracks. Then he deserted and I haven't heard a word."

"Perhaps he wants to get rid of you," Florinda said.

"I don't think so," Betty said unhappily, "but I wish he would write."

"Perhaps he doesn't have any paper or a pencil," Florinda said. "Listen, Miss Merritt, I don't know where he is at all, but I think Grandpa could find him, if he wanted to. Go and see him."

"Thank you," Betty said, and turned away. She rejoined Ginger and said, "Let's go home now. The smoke's suffocating me in here." They went out. Thank God, it wasn't raining. Ginger's car was parked in Piccadilly and soon they were crossing the river and heading out through darkened streets towards Hedlington. After a long silence Ginger burst out, stammering—"I love you, B-B-Betty. I-I-I've been wanting to tell you for m-m-months."

Oh dear, she thought. She put out a hand, resting it lightly on his arm. She said, "You are very, very sweet to say so, Ginger. I think you're the nicest man alive, and . . ."

"W-w-will you . . ."

She interrupted, "Don't say anything more. Please."

They crept on through the blackout, their car lights no more than dim blue ghosts in the black, damp night. At last he dropped her in front of No. 104 Station Road, where she had the ground floor flat of three rooms, including a large kitchen. Before getting out of the car she turned to Ginger and said, "Thanks—for everything. See you at the factory. Go on now . . . please!"

She jumped down and watched as the tail light faded. Then she hurried up the steps to her front door and fumbled in her bag for her key. A figure stepped out of the dark to her right, came up the steps, and muttered—"Betty."

She gasped, "Oh! . . . Fletcher! What are you doing here? Are you all right? The police are after you. There was a notice in the papers the other day." She stared, and saw that he had a beard.

"I'm all right. Lend me five pounds."

"Of course." She searched hurriedly in her bag, took out all the notes and silver, not counting, and pressed them into his hands. He said, "Thanks, Betty. I'll pay you back some day."

She peered at him, trying to see his face. Did he have lice, or fleas? He did not smell dirty or feral, not at all like an unwashed male . . . only a little earthy, but that was right, for him.

She said, "What are you going to do? You can't spend the rest of your life in the woods."

"I'm thinking," he said, "about me, and the poetry, and the war. And about you."

She waited for him to say something more, but he did not, so at last she said, "Well . . . I miss you. Always will . . . Come back soon . . . and good luck."

She felt him take her hand, raise it, and kiss the palm. Then he said, "I'll tell you soon's I've made up my mind."

Then he slipped down the steps, and vanished into the dark of the town.

*   *   *   *

Florinda Foudray, Marchioness of Jarrow, sang once more, at about two o'clock, at the Cat & Mouse. The house applauded, but she returned in a strange mood to the table where her escort, Billy Bidford, waited for her.

He said, "You were marvellous, Florinda!"

"I wasn't," she said curtly. "Not even as good as the first show—they're drunker, that's all." She emptied her glass and the waiter stationed behind their table came forward at once, bottle swathed, uncorked, and ready. Billy Bidford was a millionaire motor car racer, polo player, and flyer when not serving his country as a lieutenant in the Royal Naval Volunteer Reserve; and the Marchioness, though usually very pleasant to the staff where she sang, could lose her temper without apparent cause.

She said, "I'm sick of this place. Let's get something to eat."

Billy stood up at once, after leaving some Treasury notes on the table, and gave her his arm. At once half a dozen other young men round the room rose to their feet. A young captain of Seaforth Highlanders said, "Excuse me, your Ladyship . . . I was hoping to have the honour of a dance with you."

"I'm sorry," Florinda said briefly. "I'm tired." She looked again at the Highlander's face, and put her hand on his sleeve. "Tomorrow night, but earlier."

"Thank you, ma'am," the Highlander said. "I will be on my way back to France by then."

Poor devils. She was too tired to give any of them anything of what they needed, not even vivacity, a woman's pertness. She put up her arms, placed them round the Highlander's neck and kissed him with open mouth on his lips. She whispered, "Good luck . . . and thank you."

Then she walked quickly out of the club, Billy following, neither speaking, down Albemarle Street, across Piccadilly and into the Ritz. Half an hour later they were sharing a supper of devilled bones and Black Velvet. Billy was her beau of the moment—one of them—but not possessive. She wasn't ready to accept that from any man yet—certainly not from the sodden, old fumbler who was her husband. She had given him every opportunity to consummate the marriage—helped him as much as any woman could; nothing happened. The peer's penis remained despondently limp. Poor old bugger.

When they had eaten, it was three o'clock. Bidford kept a room in the Ritz, year in and year out, and had done since he was at Eton. He said, "Shall we retire, madam?"

She looked across the table at him—curly dark hair, amused blue eyes, the pea jacket with the wavy gold stripes fitting him like a glove. She considered his suggestion. She was a great lover. She knew that, and it irked her, because she wanted to be a great artiste, and after all the acting and singing lessons she was what she had been in the beginning—a talented amateur. So what was her role in life to be? A cunt for hungry, fearful men facing death, for old men trying to recreate the amorous fury of their youth, a lovely female object for the taste of such as Billy and Cantley?

"All right," she said.

But a waiter came to them, bent over the table and whispered, "M'lady, telephone, for you . . . in the night porter's office."

She said, "I'll be back in a mo'," and followed the waiter out and down the marble halls.

The night porter handed her the telephone and left the little cubbyhole. She put the earpiece to her ear and spoke into the mouthpiece—"The Marchioness of Jarrow speaking."

"M'lady . . ." she recognized the butler's voice. "M'lady . . ." the old voice cracked—"His Lordship is dead . . . I was taking him up another bottle of whisky an hour ago and found him . . . sprawled across the floor. Doctor Pickett came at once, but he was dead . . . They told me at the Cat & Mouse you'd probably be at the Ritz ... ."

"Thank you, Medley," she said. "I'll come at once."

She must get her jewels and bank books out of the Berkeley Square house before the new Marquess could come up to London. They were hers, freely given by her husband; but his son—a haughty man of forty or so, devoted to fox hunting in Leicestershire, hated and despised her as a whore after the old man's money. Well, she thought, as she walked back to the supper room, I'm not a whore, and I wasn't after his money, only trying to get to where I think I belong in this world.

At the table she said briefly, "He's dead, Billy. Get me a taxi, please."

"I'm sorry," he said.

"Why be?" They were walking back down the hall. "He's given me over a million, and a lot of jewels—about another half million . . . I've had my eye on a nice flat in Half Moon Street for some time. I'll call you at the Admiralty as soon as I get settled in. Or will you be back at Dover with your M.T.B.s?"

He said, "I wish it was so—but I have several more months to do in that damned rabbit warren."

Then they were at the door, and the night porter had hailed a taxicab. Florinda climbed in, waving goodbye to Billy Bidford. Alexander William Templeton Eastman Foudray, 4th Marquess of Jarrow, was dead; so she was no longer the Marchioness, but the Dowager Marchioness, or, in the more common modern usage, Florinda, Marchioness of Jarrow.

*　　*　　*　　*

Susan Rowland sat at the table in the nursery—it had been a spare bedroom until they had adopted Sally and Tim—one of the children on each side of her. Sally held the book and read slowly.

"*He was different from his brothers and sisters. Their hair already betrayed* . . . what's that, Mummy?"

"Betray . . ." Susan searched for the right words. "Here it means, 'show' . . . He might have written, *Their hair already showed the reddish hue* . . . Go on."

"*Reddish hue inherited from their mother, the she-wolf* . . . that means their dad was a dog and he fucked a wolf?"

"Sally! I've told you over and over you must not use that word . . . or the others. Yes, her father married a she-wolf. You remember that . . . Go on."

"*While he alone, in this particular, took after his father. He was the one little gray cub of the litter.*"

Susan suspected that neither Sally nor Tim knew what a litter was, but their attention was wandering. They didn't like to have to work at things. Sally read on, stumbling—"*He had bred true to the straight wolfstock—in fact, he had bred true, physically, to old One Eye himself, with but a single exception and that was that he had two eyes to his father's one.*

"*The gray cub's eyes had not been open long, yet* . . ."

"Pay attention, Tim. You're supposed to be reading along with Sally, but to yourself . . . Take over now."

Tim read better than his sister though often mispronouncing words—"*Already he could see with steady clearness. And while his eyes were still closed, he had felt, tasted, and smelled. He knew his two brothers and his sisters very well* . . . ha ha!" Tim burst out giggling, "*He tasted his sister.* I wouldn't like to taste Sally! I'd rather taste another slice of bread and dripping, ha ha!"

"Don't be silly! Go on."

The hands of the nursery clock crept round. They must have their full half hour. None of her friends or Richard's relatives could understand why she had not hired a nanny or governess to teach the children. But she had been taught that parents raise their children themselves, instead of handing them over to hirelings. And she must teach these orphans something that wasn't in books: pride in themselves. It was no use trying to make them forget their earlier circumstances. They knew what whores were, and they knew their mother had been one. They understood that they had had different fathers. They had come from a world warm but dirty, cosy but careless, sinful but forgiving. Here, they were going to be ladies and gentlemen, following a code that must not be broken.

"After that he recoiled from hurt because he knew that it hurt."

She looked at the clock. "That's enough, Tim . . . Run out and play now." They jumped up, nearly upsetting the table, and tore out of the room and down the stairs, whooping and yelling. She winced, then smiled. That noise, this excitement of children, was why she had adopted them, after all . . .

She walked slowly along to the main bedroom and into the bathroom, and stared at herself in the mirror. Forty-one, and now, at last, after eighteen years of marriage, and the adoption of two children—pregnant. Two periods missed, some episodes of what must have been morning sickness. She must go and see Dr Kimball. And she must tell Richard. She dreaded the moment.

She unfastened her stays, kicked off her shoes, and lay down on the bed . . . just a few minutes, before Sally and Tim came in again . . .

She awoke to a banging on the door and the high excited squeak of Peggy the younger housemaid, "Oh, Mrs Rowland, come quick!"

She rolled to her feet and into her shoes, struggling with her stays, calling, "Come in! What's happened? Is it the children?"

"Yes, m'm . . . I mean, no, m'm." Susan smelled smoke, and heard distant shouts.

"Farmer Handle's haystack's on fire, m'm, and they did it, Sally and Tim!"

"Oh dear!" Susan exclaimed. This was really awful, with what she already had to tell Richard. Farmer Handle's farm lay two hundred yards up the lane, his fields abutting Hill House at the back and on one side. She ran fast toward the towering smoke and the columns of yellow and red flame. She arrived panting and out of breath as Stella Merritt galloped into the farmyard, astride a big bay, swung to the ground, stared a moment at the stack and called, "Mr Handle, you'd better get a hose onto the barn there, or that might catch."

Farmer Handle hurried off. His wife and a couple of Women's Land Army girls stood watching, the girls shielding their faces with their hands. Police Constable Whiteside was there, one massive hand on each adopted child's shoulder.

Stella said, "On my way home from cubbing . . . How did it get started?"

Susan gasped, "Oh, Mr Whiteside, I can't believe that the children . . ."

Sally and Tim broke in together, "We done nothing, Mummy! We was playing with matches. We didn't mean no harm!" They burst into tears together, as at a signal. Susan hated them in that instant, for their ability to cry on command; for their total inability to feel what, in others, made one cry.

The constable said heavily, "They done it, m'm. They swear they was just playing with matches . . . but Mr Handle says the flames were going strong in four different places when he first saw it . . ."

She looked, and saw, and went slowly to Mr Handle. She said miserably, "I'm sorry, Mr Handle . . . We'll pay for any damage."

Handle was normally a kindly man; but he'd lost a son on the Somme, with the 60th Rifles, and he faced her with stony eyes— "Better send them young devils back where they belong—the streets, or the gaol."

*   *   *   *

Volunteer Naomi Rowland peered into the slanting rain through her goggles, her gloved hands tight on the wheel. She felt exhausted and strained. Her period had ended the day before yesterday, and it had dragged her down . . . and she had had to drive to remoter Norfolk with Colonel Venable and some man, a foreigner, whom the War Office didn't want anyone to see . . . and the Humber had broken down on the way out yesterday; and she hadn't slept well in the little attic room they had allotted to her at the Hall—some sort of very secret Intelligence organization occupied it—where they had dropped off the foreigner; and she'd eaten—poorly—with the Women's Legion girls who ran the kitchen; and now she and the colonel were on their way back to London.

"You're doing well, Volunteer Rowland," the colonel said. He was sitting beside her on the front seat, wrapped up, like her, in greatcoat, cap, goggles and big gloves, the rain driving against them. She hadn't asked him to sit in front: it embarrassed her. A lot of things about No. 3 Group embarrassed her. She had a suspicion that their Deputy Superintendent, the woman in charge of the Group, regarded them as a pool of pretty, young things, to be lent out to important generals and staff officers. She had once stumbled on another Volunteer being kiss-ed in the music room, behind the piano; so heaven knew what else might be going on.

"Do please relax, my dear," the colonel said. "It's a terrible night. The road's muddy. It's three hours at least to London, and it's almost dark . . . but we're alive, and well. Somewhere along the road I will stand you to as good a dinner as we can find. I shall sit at another table, and send you notes, about the wine, perhaps? Any idea where we are?"

"Just passed Stratton Strawless, sir. We'll be in Norwich in twenty minutes."

She heard a sharp, cracking, metallic sound from under the car. A moment later there was a quick rattling, flailing between the car and road. The engine lost all power and the car ground to a standstill. She sat a moment at the wheel, tears coming into her eyes. Why her? Why this, tonight?

The colonel said, "That sounded bad."

"I've heard that noise before," she said despondently. She climbed out and down and, lying on her back, torch in hand, pushed herself under the car . . . no mistake. She pushed herself out again and brushed down her greatcoat, now sodden and stained with mud. "Universal joint gone, sir," she said.

"At half past seven on an October night, outside Stratton Strawless, Norfolk . . . and within half a mile, if I recall aright, of Nash's grave."

"Which Nash?" she asked, standing in the rain beside the car. The colonel was mad. She found herself giggling.

He sounded baffled in the dark of the car, "Ah, there you have me. Nash, the architect? Nash, the dandy? Nash, the satirist? There's a telephone at the grave, too." He climbed slowly down from the car, turning up the collar of his greatcoat, pulling his red banded hat well down on his head. She began to laugh.

He said, "The telephone's not strictly at the grave, Volunteer Rowland, but at an excellent pub next to it. I have more than once enjoyed a stirrup cup at the Swan with Two Necks, which as you doubtless know is a corruption of . . ."

"The Swan with Two Nicks," she cried, "because the Vintners' Company marks swans belonging to them with a nick on either side of the beak. Swans with no nicks belong to the King. I've forgotten who owns swans with one nick."

"So have I," he said. He stepped close, enfolded her in his arms, bent his head slightly and put his lips to hers.

She stood frozen, the rain dripping off the peak of his cap onto her nose. His lips were warm. She realized that for years she had been suffering from a nameless yearning, a longing to share, to give—what? The night she had spent in Rachel Cowan's arms at Girton had not abated it, or told her what it was, only what it was not. She relaxed her own lips, raised her arms, clasped them round his neck, pressed

195

closer, forming her body against the length of his. They kissed ardently for a long time, then he stood back.

"Come, my dear. Give me your bag."

"I can carry it. It's very light. Just my nightie, toothbrush . . ."

*　　*　　*　　*

They ate together, at a small table set up by the fire in the inn's small dining room, waited on by the innkeeper's fat and rosy-cheeked wife, who clearly suspected some intrigue; but they had taken separate rooms, and he behaved with perfect courtesy during the meal . . . a half bottle of burgundy with the veal cutlet, a brandy for him afterward, talk by the fire . . .

"Why did you leave Girton, my dear?"

"It felt . . . stifling," she said eagerly. He really wanted to know her, not just . . . "The war made it worse, because men were going out doing such exciting things."

"What do you propose to do with yourself when this war is over? Have you thought?"

"I've thought," she said slowly, "but I haven't come to any conclusions. I'd like to run a business, I think, once I'd learned something about it."

"You don't think you'll marry, settle down in the country, and grow children and roses?"

She said, "I suppose it might happen, but I certainly don't feel like that now . . . Why did you . . . do what you did, just now?"

"Naomi, I don't think you realize how very attractive a young woman you are . . . intimidating to a very young man, perhaps, with your height, and rather stern manner . . . but to me, irresistible! You have character, brains, intelligence, courage . . . I can't fault you, except that you're only what, twenty?"

"Twenty-one."

". . . which will obviously correct itself soon. I've desired you since the first day I saw you. We have things we can give each other . . . you—that's obvious. It takes years off me, makes the world young and rosy, just to be with you . . . me—well, I think you have reached womanhood without knowing exactly what it is, in your body."

She nodded, muttering, "How did you know? Is it so obvious?"

"As obvious to me as the fact that you've recently had a period, and it's dragged you down."

She blushed a little; but was glad he had said it. Pretence was falling away; that was what she had always asked of men, and so far not found.

"I offer you experience, Naomi . . . an affectionate hand, a guide in the paths of love."

She looked up—"I'm a virgin."

He nodded. "Shall we go upstairs, my dear?"

There, soon, it was very much as she had hoped it would be, but had feared it would be otherwise, that she or the man—it was her husband, in the imagining—would act wrongly, carelessly, coldly, mechanically.

She awoke in his arms in the dawn light, warm, tired, proud. He had done it. She was his woman. She turned to him, bit his ear and whispered, "Rodney, I love you . . . I always have, secretly. I must have. I feel like a goddess . . . and you've done it. I love you."

"Don't say it," he muttered, "don't say it."

Daily Telegraph, Tuesday, October 17, 1916

PADDINGTON LABOUR TROUBLE
GOODS TRAFFIC HELD UP

No change has taken place in the unprecedented situation at the Paddington goods depot of the Great Western Railway. Practically the whole of the staff, some 2,000 in number, are still pursuing the tactics known as "going slow" . . . The men appear to think that they can force the company to reinstate the three carmen who were convicted in a case of stealing and receiving flour if they persist in their policy of holding up traffic by doing the minimum amount of work. The company, having made the offer that if the appeal to Quarter Sessions lodged by the carmen succeeds they will reinstate them and make good any loss of earnings, are not prepared to grant any further concessions. So the matter stands. It is understood that the appeal will not be heard until January, and the depot staff contend that unless the men are allowed to remain at work they may in the meantime be claimed under the Military Service Act, as they would no longer be entitled to exemption . . .

The men, who have just received an extension of their war bonus, bringing it up to 10s per week, are themselves sacrificing money by their policy, for they are paid what may be called a "Work bonus" for all goods they handle above a certain minimum weight. Yet it is stated that porters on the goods platforms are now pushing barrows containing about half the load they would usually tackle, and are content to move, as a railway official put it, "at something like a snail's pace."

Johnny Merritt folded the cutting carefully away into the envelope already addressed to his father, and returned to the letter he was writing:

The enclosed cutting is a symptom of a very serious disease in Britain—and a warning to us. It is from British common law that we have inherited the principle that every man is presumed innocent until he is proven guilty. Yet the Railway Company have fired the men while their appeal is pending. The only risk the Company would run by keeping them on the payroll now is that they will lose the men's pay and benefits if they lose their appeal. But how much is this, against the loss they are now suffering? And what a good impression it would have made on the rank and file of the men? And the union leaders would hardly have dared in that case to come out openly and say they are taking this action to save the jobs of convicted thieves. This is all a fine example of the narrow-mindedness of British management.

The other side of the picture is that the British unions will not only do all they can to protect their members against unjust or unfair management practises—they will also protect them, if they can possibly find a way to do so, against the laws of the land—from conscription, from punishment for theft and even murder. They have always been powerful here, and in spite of their publicly expressed fears, the war is giving them much increased power. I am convinced that a time will soon come when they will openly challenge the Government, by defying some law, constitutionally passed, by mass action. I never thought I would be writing this, but I urge you and the board of Fairfax, Gottlieb to give very careful consideration before enlarging operations in this country after the war, as I know is being discussed.

There are many reasons for labor's attitude here, mostly going back a long way—as everything does in this country. But one big reason is, I believe, the British class system, which locks the British working man into a certain place in society. He can not hope to become president of his company, let alone of his country; his children cannot hope, except in very few cases, to go to college and become doctors, lawyers, professional men. Our unions making, say, Pullman cars, take the attitude that every one of their members should be able to ride in one; a British union in the same position would take the attitude that if their members can not ride in Pullmans, no one ought to be able to.

All this makes for an extraordinarily stable society, especially in the rural areas where the problems and attitudes are really quite different; but it is something I am finding it harder and harder to handle. Once I intended to join the R.F.C. or any other British outfit. I know now it wouldn't work, for me. Guy and Laurence and Mr Cate belong in the system—it's theirs—and if anyone can make it work, they can. So, when I can finally get away to the war, it will be in and for the Army of the good old U.S. of A. . . .

Stella sends her love and says that . . .

Hedlington: Tuesday, October 17, 1916

13 Johnny Merritt worked steadily through the pile of papers that filled the IN tray on his desk, muttering frequently under his breath. His father had told him that the businessman's worst enemy was not his competitors, but the government, always poking its nose in where it was not wanted, always demanding information which would at once be filed and forgotten. The British were just as bad—worse perhaps, and with less excuse, for here there was a war on. What he ought to be doing was studying Ginger's new design for the folding wing of the Mark II Leopard. It had considerable differences from the modified Handley Page designs he had brought with him; and Johnny was not quite sure whether the differences added up to a net plus, or not. It would be a little lighter, certainly, and use fewer bolts; but probably less strong, and that was a risk which could not be accepted. One or two Leopards losing their wings in flight would finish off the company, let alone the unfortunate aircrews in them at the time. It was a matter of accurately assessing and precisely measuring the stresses and strains on the materials employed—Betty's job; and she was good at it.

He picked up a War Office memo to all manufacturers of aircraft: Subject—surface of rudder pedals . . . to be made of, or covered by some non-slip material, either . . .

The door burst open and his secretary hurried in—"They've downed tools, sir," she said. "Mr Stratton sent me a message."

"Where?" he said. "Which shops?"

"All of them, I think."

"Did Frank say why?"

"The boy said it was because of the expert—Mr Franklin."

"Oh God!" Johnny exclaimed, getting up. "I told . . ." He bit off the sentence. It would be disloyal to pass the blame onto Richard, though Miss Bamfylde knew that he had strongly opposed the hiring of the time-and-motion-study man, because she had taken the notes of the meeting.

Frank Stratton came into the room, followed a few seconds later by Mr Franklin, the efficiency expert.

"Is everybody out?" Johnny asked.

Frank said, "Nearly all the men—not the shop foremen, of course. Only half a dozen women."

"Can we keep the plant going?"

Frank shook his head emphatically, "Not a hope, Mr Johnny."

"I suppose it's because of Mr Franklin?"

Frank said, "That's it. We've no union men here, and very few who even want to have a union. It started in the first shop Mr Franklin went into—the fuselage shop. I was there . . . the nearest men looked at him, then at each other, then downed tools . . . One said to me, 'We're doing our best, and we won't have any outsider who doesn't know an aeroplane from a baby carriage'—begging your pardon, Mr Franklin—'telling us different.' "

Mr Franklin was a small man carrying a big notepad and pencil, with more pencils of different colors stuck in the breast pocket of his jacket. He gave a small, thin smile, "I do know the difference, actually, Mr Stratton . . . That's what the workers are afraid of."

"We'd better ask Mr Richard to come down," Johnny said. "Please get him on the telephone for me, Miss Bamfylde."

*   *   *   *

Richard Rowland was in a bad temper. This morning he'd received the bill for Mr Handle's hay rick, and it was not small. And this morning, too, Tim had scratched his initials in the paint of the car—a sacrilege. Susan had been pleased the boy knew what his initials were, now that he was officially a Rowland; and that he could write that well. She was determined to see the bright side of everything the little monsters did. And now, this strike at the factory!

He snapped, "We'll send out dismissal notices to all men on strike—and women—effective forty-eight hours from now. If they aren't back at work by then, the men will be conscripted. I'll see that they are. I have plenty of influence with the board here in Hedlington."

The others in the room—Johnny and Frank Stratton—were silent for a while, then Johnny said slowly, "Do you think it would be wise actually to make that threat, Richard? They know we have to send the board the names of anyone we fire, or who quits."

After a time Richard said, "You're right. They know, and if we don't make any threats they can't accuse us of intimidation. But . . . can Franklin do his work when the machines are idle?"

"Some of it," Frank said. "I'd have to be with him."

"Well, I'll tell him to carry on, with you. I'll draft the dismissal notices with you now, Johnny. That's all."

Frank said, "Mr Richard . . . I think we should ask the War Office to send down a pilot to talk to the blokes here about what the R.F.C. is doing in France. The day Mr Guy came for the funeral, and flew back, he didn't have time to speak to us, but everyone knew he'd been here. They were all talking about it, and nearly everyone had found a way to see him—pretending to be sick, or having to go the lavatory, or to the windows for a breath of fresh air, any excuse . . . It didn't help production that day, but it did for the next week."

"Good idea," Richard said. "I'll telephone them."

"Another thing, sir . . . Even if the men come back to work, the government is going to use a finer and finer comb in all the factories, if you see what I mean. It can't lose men the way it has in France this summer without them needing more out there. And they'll have to come from the factories . . . to be replaced by women. If we want the best women—the most educated, the most intelligent and hard-working—we'll have to pay them better than we are."

Richard snapped, "I'll think about it . . . Sorry, Frank. You're probably right. What about equal pay for equal work?"

Johnny said, "It'll cost us a bit to start with, but it seems the right thing to do . . . if it *is* equal work. They must do their own setting up, and so on."

"We've already established that. All right. I'll have the accountant work out the exact cost, and we may have to ask Fairfax, Gottlieb and Toledano's for more working capital. I know we can cable your father in New York, Johnny, but can we cable David Toledano out in Palestine, too? He can make his father understand what our problems are and why we need the capital."

Johnny said, "I'm sure we can cable David—through the War Office, if necessary. Your father could fix that."

"Yes . . . We must start a training programme to fit women for more of the top positions . . . Perhaps a woman will be works foreman before the war is over. How would you like that, Frank?"

Frank grinned—his face thinner than before, his shoulders a little bent—but the same wonderful smile—"We'll have to wait and see, Mr Richard."

*   *   *   *

Betty Merritt waited till after eight o'clock that evening before going to her brother's office. Ginger had long gone home to his little flat in Hedlington. The workers had been sent off at noon, without prejudice. Mr Franklin and Frank Stratton had left about half past five. The only lights burning in the whole factory were those in the drawing office, and the managing director's office.

At a few minutes past eight Betty turned her light out, picked up her bag, and walked out and down one of the factory's little "streets." The night watchmen—a pair, armed with long staves and torches—flashed their lights in her eyes, and then said, "Good night, miss."

Johnny was leaning back in his swivel chair, reading what appeared to be a printed folder, of small print, from some Government department. He glanced up as she came in, then went on reading. She sat down opposite him.

"Time you went home, Johnny."

"In a minute, sis. This is the last thing I have to do."

She said firmly, "It's past eight o'clock, Johnny. When did you get home last night?"

He put down the pamphlet, rubbing his eyes—"Oh, about ten."

"And the night before?"

"Can't remember . . . early, I think . . . seven?"

"Seven's not early, Johnny, and you know it. Stella's getting very lonely. When have you sat down and talked to her? Taken her out for a picnic . . . dinner and the theatre in London . . . just been with her, attending to her?"

"I don't know. There's a war on, Betty. The R.F.C. needs this bomber and we've got to get it to them."

"Not at the expense of your marriage," she said firmly. "Johnny, some older, more experienced women could stand the loneliness, probably. Stella's barely twenty, and," she drew a deep breath—"I'd rather you heard it from me than overheard it somewhere—she's drinking a lot."

Johnny dropped the pamphlet, which he had still been holding, as though meaning to continue his perusal of it as soon as his sister left him alone. "Good God!" he exclaimed, "you can't mean it! Oh, I know she has a glass of sherry before dinner. I encourage her to."

"She has several glasses of sherry every morning," Betty said, "and several more every afternoon. I've been round many times in the last few months, and every time she's been, well, a little sozzled. I suppose she takes a couple of aspirins and goes to bed about tea time, and is about recovered by the time you come home."

"I can't believe it," Johnny said heavily.

"You must. But it's only caused by loneliness. She's lonely for *you*, Johnny, for her *man*." She emphasized the word "man" slightly.

Johnny said, "I'll go home right away, and I'll really try . . ."

"Put aside one afternoon a week. Swear you'll never touch factory business, or any paper or document to do with it, on Sundays."

"I'll work it out, sis. You're right."

"Another thing . . . has Stella ever told you that she would like to have some work—a job?"

"No," he said. "She's sometimes talked about what fun it was being a V.A.D. before we were married, but that's all."

"I think you should encourage her to find some work—something that will keep her interested—driving an ambulance, going back to the V.A.D. . ."

Johnny shook his head slowly, "She's my wife, sis," he said. "I don't want her out all day, and she doesn't want to be. She'd have said so, otherwise."

Betty realized that she was up against a deeply ingrained male attitude, or prejudice; at the moment, it was no good arguing.

She said, "Well, think about it. I'm going home."

"Do you need a lift?"

"No, thanks, my car's here. Good night, Johnny." She leaned over, kissed him on the forehead, and went out.

*   *   *   *

Half an hour later Johnny drove the car into the little garage, locked it in, and hurried to the front door. It was unlocked and he strode in, calling, "Stella, darling! I'm home!"

"Johnny?" He heard her call from the drawing room. Her voice sounded strange and he hurried in, pausing at the door. She was in an armchair, dressed in her nightgown and a silk peignoir, legs sprawled, pom-pommed mules on her feet. Her eyes were wide open, her mouth hanging open.

"Have you been drinking?" Johnny said.

She appeared not to have heard, but stared on over his head, a beatific smile on her face, her breath coming and going in small rhythmic shudders.

He dropped to one knee beside her, "Are you all right?"

She leaned forward and smacked a kiss on his forehead. "I feel wunnderful," she said, slurring the syllables. "Havn' been drinking . . . not a drop since . . ." long pause, ". . . ten o'clock 'smorning."

"Are you sure you feel all right?" Johnny said anxiously. "Isn't this early for you to be going to bed?"

"Just feel so good," she said, "so good . . . so good."

"I'll make supper, darling. Mrs Hackler's gone home."

The wide eyes focussed on him. Her arms came out, grabbing him round the neck. She flung wide her legs and pulled him on top of her, mumbling, "Don't want supper, want you . . . so good . . . so good . . ."

*   *   *   *

At that moment Richard Rowland was passing the Cottage on his way home to his own home, Hill House, three hundred yards farther on. As he switched off his engine and came out on the drive to walk to the front door, he paused a moment—listening. In the still night the guns from France were quite plain—tonight a definite sound, rather than the shuddering of the air which they usually were. The great Somme offensive was still grinding on—in the same place. He went into the house.

Summers met him at the door and helped him out of his coat and hat. "Dinner will be ready whenever you are, sir," he said confidentially. "Mrs Baker said it would do no harm to hold it until you came home. It is shepherd's pie."

"Thank you, Summers."

He walked into the drawing room, where Susan was knitting by a small coal fire. She looked up—"The inspector came from the children's courts. He said there won't be any trial, or investigation, or whatever they do when children under age commit a crime. We'll have to pay for the damage, but I told him you already had. And he said we must keep a closer eye on them until they really grow out of their background . . . what they learned in the slums."

He said, "We certainly must. What if they put an iron bar on the railway line next, and derail a train and a dozen people are killed?"

Summers came in and poured him a glass of Amontillado. Susan said, "I'll have a glass tonight, Summers."

"Certainly, madam." The butler filled another glass and withdrew, closing the door silently behind him.

Richard said, "It's been a bad day—paying Handle . . . trouble at Hedlington Aircraft . . . Christopher told me he's going to have to sell one of his farms, at least, if prices go up any more." He drank from the tulip glass—"*This* doesn't solve any problems, but at least it puts a rosier light on them . . ."

"Richard, I have some news for you."

He froze, the glass half way to his mouth—"What have they done now?" he asked.

"It's not the children . . . I'm going to have a baby. I saw Dr Kimball today and he's positive. Early May next year."

Richard lifted the glass to his lips and slowly drained it. His mind churned, trying to grasp what she was telling him. "It's not possible," he said at last. "After eighteen years it . . ."

"It is possible, and it has happened," she said. She looked up at him, "Aren't you pleased?"

He dropped to his knees beside her, "Susan! Of course! After so long I'd given up hope . . . I can't believe it . . ." He bent forward and kissed her on the cheek—"My dearest . . ."

She bent, stroking his hair. After a while he stood up. He saw that she was crying, a half smile on her lips, the tears running silently down her cheeks.

A realization suddenly struck him and he burst out—"We needn't have adopted Sally and Tim!"

She said, "No, we need not have, but we have."

"Can't we . . . send them back? We don't need them any more. Heaven knows what they'll do to the baby."

She said, "No, Richard. They must still be treated as our children in every way."

Richard strode up and down the room, his mind in turmoil. He had grown to hate those slum kids. But he was in a trap, and must live in it for the rest of his life. The only way was to make it bearable— work with Susan to turn those monsters into decent people, a young lady and a young gentleman. He rang the bell for the butler and when he appeared said, "Summers, we have some champagne cold, do we not?"

"Yes, sir. Veuve Clicquot, 1907. Half a dozen bottles and one magnum."

"A bottle will do—with dinner, Summers. And we'll eat in quarter of an hour from now."

"Very good, sir."

*   *   *   *

They were gathered again in Johnny Merritt's office—Johnny, Richard Rowland, and Frank Stratton, with Miss Bamfylde sitting mouselike on a chair behind Johnny's shoulder, where he sat at the big desk. A watery sun shone on the airfield and the thrashing elms along the road beyond. Two Leopard Mark II bombers waited at the end of the field, engines running and propellers whirling, but only a subdued growl could be heard through the glass. The clock on the wall showed half past nine in the morning.

Johnny said, "The wind's pretty strong."

Richard said, "For the pilot from France? I expect they've had to fly in worse weather than this over there . . . Are the men coming?"

"To the meeting, yes, Mr Richard," Frank said. "The notices have been up all over town, and the Town Crier was calling it yesterday

205

afternoon . . . I went to a few pubs last night and saw a lot of our blokes. Nearly all of them said they were going to come. Bert Gorse and his woman were going round the pubs, too, telling men not to come, to sit tight and we'd have to give in. They'd have done better to stand them a few beers . . . but they don't have the ready."

"You bought beer for some men? Let me know how much, and we'll pay you back," Johnny said. Frank nodded.

Richard said, "Well, what's your suggestion, Johnny?"

Johnny said, "I'm inclined to give them best. After all, they have been producing very well. Efficiency has been increasing steadily, month by month. They seem to be happy—thanks to Frank. Can Mr Franklin really increase our output?"

"He's done it—or other members of his firm have done it, wherever they've been employed," Richard said. "I have the figures to prove it."

"I know," Johnny said, "but is it worth it, here, now, for us?"

Richard looked at Frank—"Frank?"

Frank pushed his bowler to the back of his head and stroked his newly bared chin—"When this factory was being put up, I was in hospital. And I knew nothing about aeroplanes . . . nothing. Soon's Mr Richard came and asked me about being works foreman here I started reading everything I could get my hands on . . . I learned about aerofoils, lift, drag, chord, dihedral, stagger, elevators, fins, rudders, ailerons . . . how to true a fuselage, brace wire attachments, true up a main plane . . . I read till my eyes were ready to drop out of my head. When I got here I saw right away that the different parts of the factory weren't in the right places . . . not in the *best* places, one with another, for the whole work to be best done with the least waste of time and energy, if you see what I mean."

"We do," Richard said. "Go on."

"I can do what Mr Franklin's supposed to do. It'll take me a month, and maybe it won't be as nicely written out on paper as Mr Franklin's would have been—but it'll be near as good, and a lot cheaper . . . and I think the men will stand for it—if we explain at the meeting that all we want is to turn out more aeroplanes for the R.F.C. . . . and raise pay a bit all round. S'pose after I've done my job we turn out twelve percent more bombers every month than we did before, with the same number of workers and machines . . . then we should raise everyone's pay."

"Twelve percent?"

"Close to it."

"I think we must hold something back in a contingency fund for emergencies."

"I like the idea," Johnny said.

Richard stared out of the window, watching the two Leopards take off, one after the other, into the wind. They disappeared from view and he looked back into the room—"All right. I'll say that . . . Should the pilot speak before or after me?"

"Before, I think," Johnny said. "He'll put them in a good mood—patriotic, too."

"That's all then. We have a few minutes and I think I'll go and get a cup of tea at the . . ."

"One moment, sir," Frank said. "You see I shaved off my beard?"

"Certainly, Frank—I think it suits you."

"Well, that beard was because I was thinking, in my head, that I'm really still the Pioneer Sergeant of the 1st Battalion of the Regiment . . . that I would be again, one day. Last night I got a letter from Mr Guy, in France, and another from Mr Harry, your dad—I'm to join the R.F.C. and go to France, to Mr Guy's squadron. It's all been fixed. I meant to give you my notice today, but I can't leave you till I've done this job. Then I'll go."

Richard said, "Are you sure you'll be able to stand it out there, Frank? You're not A. 1 you know, and never will be."

"When I think of what the lads have to put up with in the Regiment," Frank said, "I can't do no less."

Johnny said, "Have you told your wife? She'll take it hard, I imagine, thinking she had you safe and sound for good."

Frank's voice trembled, "That's the only bad part of it. She knows . . . I told her this morning, when I'd shaved—she nearly jumped out of bed when I turned round from the washhand-stand and kissed her—she thought it was a stranger burst into the bedroom, with no beard, see? But it can't be helped. I must go."

There was another long silence, then Johnny said, "You make me feel even more ashamed of myself than I usually do."

Richard cut in quickly, "*You're* doing your best for us here, doing just what you are doing . . . You have a job here any time you want it, Frank. Any time. Remember that."

"I will, sir. Thank you . . . Here he comes!"

They ran to the window. A biplane marked with the roundels of the Royal Flying Corps burst out of the drifting clouds at the limit of view from the window, and all of them, including Miss Bamfylde, hurried out and into the open air, heedless of the brisk chill in the wind.

"What is it?" Richard asked as the machine flew along the far side of the field, about a thousand feet up, down wind.

Johnny stared, "Sopwith . . . Is it the new Pup?"

Frank said, "No, sir. It's a One and a Half-Strutter. R.F.C. two-seater. The Navy have the single-seater."

207

The workers were crowding out of every shed and shop, running toward the field, lining up like a football crowd along the imaginary lines that marked the edge of the landing zone. The aeroplane's nose dipped and the machine dived toward the earth. A collective gasp went up from the crowd. The nose rose and with the engine strumming like a nest full of angry bees, the aeroplane curled over in a graceful loop, and at the top of the loop eased over into a half roll—completing the Immelmann turn and, being now pointed up wind, immediately started its descent, bumping and heaving in the gusty wind, to make a three point landing a hundred yards short of the tower and finally to blip to a standstill, the engine coughing, the propeller swinging, jerking, stopping.

The pilot eased himself out of the forward cockpit as Frank roared, "Jevons! Manville! Smith! Go and hold the wings down!"

The pilot jumped to earth and ran toward him, tearing off his flying helmet and goggles. It was Guy.

"Hullo, Uncle Richard," he shouted. "Hullo, Frank . . . Johnny." He shook hands all round. "When your request reached R.F.C. headquarters out there, Boom Trenchard told my major to send me . . . keep it in the family, sort of . . . but I have to be back for lunch."

He looked round at the crowded men and women, all cheering and clapping and smiling. He raised both hands in acknowledgment. He's just a kid, Frank thought, but there was a hard line to his jaw, and crows' feet round his mismatched eyes, and a curl to his nostril that were not those of youth. He would be a hard master to work for; but it would be worth it.

Guy said, "If someone will give me a cup of tea and a Bath bun—better still, a Chelsea bun—I'll be ready to tell you anything you want to know . . . that is, if I know it myself."

*   *   *   *

"They've gone back to work at Hedlington Aircraft," Bert Gorse said disgustedly. "Mr Richard just gave them a ruddy carrot—ninepence a day more now, and promises of more if production goes up . . . Frank Stratton's going to do what that efficiency bloke was supposed to."

"He'll do a good job," Rachel said, "and the men like him—the women, too, though he's shy of them . . . Guy Rowland made a big impression on them all. The women near mobbed *him* when he left. Well, we did our best. Didn't get much help from the party, though."

"They're too busy trying to stop the war altogether, or at least make all the governments come out and say what they're fighting for, to bother about helping us stop a little bit of it."

"We'll just go on. I spoke to Cowell, in the Star & Garter this evening. Alice Rowland was there, with him."

"Is she sweet on him?"

"How do I know? Looks like it . . . She left early and I asked him whether he would help us get the use of a school for our meetings. He said he'd try if we got some well known figures, respectable people to join . . . people the police will act careful of."

Bert riffled through the pile of letters and newspaper clippings on the table—"Here's what he wants—Mr John Rowland of High Staining."

Rachel looked round in astonishment—"Why, that's Naomi's father!"

"Well, he's written saying he's not a socialist but he does think that a way must be found to end the war before all that we are fighting to preserve is destroyed—that's his own words."

"Their son, Boy's, been at the front since near the beginning," Rachel said. "That's what's getting on his nerves."

"Well, it's one name for Cowell."

"We must get more . . . people who've lost a son . . . Look through the *Courier* for the past six months . . . they publish all the local casualties . . . Then I'll go and see the parents, at home. Say we're so sorry about their boy, and other boys, still being killed over there—for what? Won't they help us stop the slaughter?"

"A lot of 'em still slam the door in your face," Bert said. "The more they've lost the more they feel they mustn't stop till Germany's paid—been ground into dust . . . 'Course we're being ground into dust at the same time, but they don't think of that."

Rachel said, "We must join the No-Conscription Fellowship, Bert. You know I spoke to their leader, Clifford Allen, and also Bertrand Russell, when I went up to London, and now Russell's written that they would welcome us joining."

Bert interrupted with morose heat, "What we've got to do is get some money. I'm damn near starving."

"How much came in in subscriptions?"

"Ten pounds, twelve and fourpence. But we owed rent, had to pay the gas company, buy more paper and ink. There's only a quid and a tanner left."

Rachel said, "We can ask the people coming to the meeting to bring money . . . but we'd have to tell them it's to keep us alive, not for the work. They won't like that." She had an idea suddenly—"The day return fare to London's only three and fivepence. We can spare that . . . I'm going to go and see your niece, Florinda, and see what I can get out of her. She has millions."

"Garn!" Bert exclaimed. "Florinda won't give you anything. She's all for the war . . . seen the pictures of her in the papers, with Captain the Lord this, Commander the Honourable that . . ."

"I'm not so sure," Rachel said. "It's worth trying. She doesn't want Fletcher killed, after all."

"Fletcher'll get shot by the bleeding narks," Bert said.

"*If* they find him," Rachel said. "I have to go out now. I'll be back in by supper time."

"Hold hard, Rachel," Bert said. "You remember the other day you told me I was against everything, but what was I for?"

"I remember," she said.

"Well, I been thinking. I'm for the working man in a union."

"Not the working woman?"

"I suppose so," Bert said grudgingly, "though what the women are doing now is diluting the factories and blacklegging, so the unions are not as strong as they should be."

"You're not for socialism?" she asked.

Bert said slowly, "I don't think so. I've tried, because of you. You believe in it, all that stuff, about Fabianism and parliamentary socialism . . . it may help, but *I* think the only important thing is to get working men—all working men—into strong unions—*then* we could stop the war tomorrow, if that's what we wanted to do, and to hell with parliament and democracy."

She said, after a while, "Thank you for thinking about it, Bert . . . and for telling me. If we can understand each other better, we'll be happier, won't we?"

*   *   *   *

The two portly men dining in a secluded corner of the Savoy Grill tucked into their roast beef with relish. They had already demolished some real turtle soup, half a cold lobster each with mayonnaise, roast pheasant with Brussels sprouts and chestnuts, all washed down with three bottles of Mumm's champagne. The younger one, black-haired, red-faced, healthy-seeming in spite of his gluttony, pointed his fork at his companion—"Then that's settled, eh, Mr Bottomley? You'll accept a directorship of my company . . ."

"Certainly," the other boomed unctuously. "A privilege . . . honour . . ."

Hoggin continued, "And you'll come to our Edgware Road H.U.S.L. next week, and I'll show you round, so's you can write a piece about us in *John Bull*."

"I will, indeed . . . and please call me Horatio, Bill . . . But I'll be just! I owe that to my public . . . I shall tell it as I see it."

"We don't want no more than that," Hoggin said. "Can't ask for more, can we? Just the truth, the whole truth and nothing but the truth." The old fart knew the game, all right.

Hoggin said, "That Joint Select Committee's just about to report that there's never been any hanky-panky in the food business, an' we're all honest, patriotic blokes, just like them."

Bottomley said, "My article will be timely, then . . . I shall urge them to turn their energies elsewhere . . . such as getting *business* men into the government, like you, or me."

"That they should," Hoggin said—thinking, not bloody likely, when there's so much money to be made outside.

The waiter carried away the plates and brought steamed canary puddings. They ate those, and the waiter brought Angels on Horseback savory for Hoggin and Soft Herring Roe on toast for Bottomley. The waiter brought fruit, port, sherry, madeira. And coffee, balloon glasses, cognac, and a huge box of cigars. Hoggin lit his cigar slowly, puffed thoughtfully in the direction of the ceiling, then fished in the pocket of his tailcoat and brought out a fat envelope. "Our address . . . details of the H.U.S.L. shop you're going to look at, a little something for expenses . . ."

Bottomley picked the envelope off the table and slid it out of sight with a dexterity obviously born of much practise. Five thousand quid was in there, Hoggin thought; well, it was worth it.

He leaned across the table. "The young lady's been well taken care of, 'Oratio. You just take her home."

"Only one? What about you, my dear fellow?"

"Oh, me, I stick to my old trouble and strife. Don't know why . . ."

The headwaiter appeared, a vision of female loveliness close on his heels—a young woman with golden hair, a retroussé nose and cold, blue eyes, radiant in a daring gown of electric blue.

The two men stood up. Hoggin said, "Allow me to introduce you to Miss Jenny Jenkins, star of the musical comedy stage . . . Miss Jenkins, Mr Horatio Bottomley, editor and owner of *John Bull.*"

She sat down in the chair the head waiter had pulled back for her. Hoggin caught her eye. Another hundred quid gone there . . . it was worth it; and she'd earn it, with old Bumley belching and farting on top of her half the night, and probably with whisky cock, too.

Daily Telegraph, Monday, October 30, 1916

AMERICAN PRESIDENCY
STRENUOUS CAMPAIGN

From Our Own Correspondent, *New York*, Sunday Evening.
Both political parties here are straining every nerve to win the

> Presidency to-morrow week, and they have spent about £ 200,000 each on propaganda. No election since the days of the Civil War has excited so profound an interest, and none in which the issues are admittedly of such transcendent importance.
>
> For the first time in a Presidential contest State questions seem subservient to international, and there is a growing recognition among the leaders here that Mr Wilson was right last Thursday when he declared "this is the last big war in which America can keep neutral" . . .
>
> . . . Oratorical broadsides were delivered on Saturday by Messrs Wilson, Hughes, and Roosevelt. The last named . . . drew the largest crowd . . . to the delight of his followers he denounced Mr Wilson as insincere and hypocritical.
>
> If Wilson admits we cannot keep out of future big wars, why have we kept out of this? he shouted. Insincerity and hypocrisy, when successful in high places, work ruin to the nation's soul, and never have we had a greater degree of insincerity and hypocrisy than is contained in such a plea for re-election by the President, who has himself practised the coldest and most selfish neutrality when all those things that in the abstract he condemns were in concrete committed at the expense of Belgium, the Armenians, and Syrian Christians. (Loud Cheers) For a man to say he will do something in the future he is afraid to do now is abstract cowardice. (Hear, hear)

The Americans seemed to be going at it hammer and tongs, Cate thought. Since the dates when each election would be held were known ahead, the campaigns could begin as soon as any candidate chose. Indeed, it sometimes seemed that the country was in a permanent state of election fever, politicians and statesmen concerned with getting themselves re-elected rather than with the business of the country. He thought Mr Wilson would probably win this coming election on November 7th, partly because a president in office seemed to have a big advantage over there, and partly because—for all Mr Roosevelt's excoriations about "abstract cowardice"—he had kept the United States out of the war, thus saving many lives and making much money for many of his countrymen. Neither situation held true in England, where holding office was rather an invitation to be judged, and removed, by the people and one's fellow politicians; and—as of this moment, certainly—for a politician to advocate peace by negotiation would surely result in his defeat, even disgrace. England's blood was up . . . that diminishing reservoir of it not spilled and still spilling on the heights above the Somme.

He returned to the paper:

FAMOUS GERMAN AIRMAN
CAPTAIN BOELCKE KILLED

Amsterdam, **Sunday.**
A Berlin telegram states that during an air fight yesterday Captain Boelcke, the noted German aviator, came into collision with another aeroplane, and was killed in landing in the German lines. It was only the day before that Captain Boelcke shot down his fortieth aeroplane. REUTERS.

Ah, Cate thought—the war in the air! That is something new, and different. There they die, too—as Boelcke had, and as Guy might—but meantime, what an epic, fought over new horizons, with hitherto unknown feelings, emotions, and powers! Some day a great poet would write a new Iliad about that long-drawn-out seesaw struggle in the skies over France, and these names—Mannock, Bishop, Boelcke, Ball, Guynemer, Nungesser and even Rowland, would be as familiar in legend as Achilles, Agamemnon, Hector . . .

London: Friday, October 20, 1916

14 Tom Rowland stepped down onto the platform and stretched. The wartime Flying Scotsman was not a fast train, or a comfortable one, and today it had arrived half an hour late at King's Cross. He had been travelling over twenty-four hours now, first the ferry to the mainland at Dingwall, then the overcrowded little train to Inverness . . . change . . . change again at Edinburgh . . . here at last, nearly half-past six o'clock.

He beckoned to a porter—they were getting fewer every time he came ashore, and some were women. This was a man, but so old and frail Tom felt ashamed to indicate his suitcase on the rack in the compartment, and say "That's all, and I want a taxi, please."

He settled back as the taxi wound slowly south and west through heavy traffic toward his flat in Half Moon Street. He'd been wondering for months now, ever since the dates of this leave had been firmly fixed, what he was going to tell Jones about Charlie Bennett. Jones was the "gentleman's gentleman" who "did" for him three hours every morning. Tom had not been paying him while he was at sea, except for a fortnightly visit to dust and check that the flat was in good order. Jones had had no difficulty in finding another employer, for people were coming and going far more than they used to—because of the war, of course. He would not be there now . . . nor would Charlie, but in the morning . . . He scowled out of the taxi window at the muted lights of wartime London—he almost hoped for a Zeppelin raid so that he would know what it felt like. Perhaps he'd say Charlie had saved his life and he was rewarding him with these few days in

214

London. Jones would not be fooled. So, did it matter? Yes, damn it all, it did matter. How could he hold his head up, speak directly to Jones ever again if the man knew that he was a . . . damn! damn! damn!

The taxi drew to a halt. The driver came round, saying, " 'Ere y'are, sir." It was seven-fifteen.

Tom hurried up the stairs and let himself into his flat. Everything looked in place . . . there was the group of his term at Osborne . . . an enlarged photograph of H.M.S. *Agincourt,* in which he'd served a commission on the Mediterranean station . . . the reproduction of "Whistler's Mother," another of Turner's *Fighting Temeraire* . . . a copy of Hoppner's *Nelson.*

He took off his cap and hung it up; then his greatcoat. Charlie was due at eight. Should he change first? Charlie would be in uniform—had to wear it when travelling. If Tom stayed in uniform it would be hard for either of them to forget that they were a commander and an ordinary seaman, from the same ship of His Majesty's Navy. He went into his bathroom, turned on the bath, and began to undress quickly.

Clean at last, he stepped out of the bath and began to dry himself. The doorbell rang. He stood a moment, frozen: then swallowing and suddenly trembling, he wrapped the towel round his waist, went through the drawing room into the little entrance hall, and opened the door. Charlie Bennett stood outside, in uniform, his duffel bag resting beside him. He came to attention, his eyes widening and said, "Sir . . ."

Tom cut him short—"Come in, Charlie."

He closed the door behind the young man, then lead to the drawing room. In the middle of the room he turned, his hands out. The words he wanted to say would not come. All he could get out was "Charlie . . ."

"Sir . . ." Charlie had let go of the duffel bag. His hands came up to meet Tom's, his eyes shining.

"Tom's my name," Tom whispered.

"Tom . . ."

They held each other tight, cheek pressed against cheek. Then Tom broke free—"I'll run you a bath . . . that's your room . . . undress . . . would you like a drink? There's some beer in the pantry . . . whisky there . . . the siphon . . ."

"Ah'd reet love a bo'l of beer, sir, Tom," Charlie said shyly. Heavens, his Geordie accent was strong, Tom thought; no one's going to believe we can possibly have anything in common, except—this.

He fetched the bottle of beer, and sat on the bed, developing a powerful, slow, firm erection, while Charlie undressed, drinking Bass from the bottle neck, until at last they both stood naked, and erect, embracing.

*   *   *   *

Next morning they sat in the drawing room, both wearing civilian clothes—grey trousers, shirt without tie, odd jacket. Tom kept his in the flat, while Charlie had brought a set down with him in his duffel bag, after spending two days with his parents in Dipton, County Durham—having first told them that his leave was very short, instead of the ten days it actually was.

Tom raised his glass of sherry toward Charlie, who was drinking Bass, this time out of a heavy cut glass tumbler—"To the Immortal Memory."

Charlie looked puzzled and Tom motioned toward the picture of Nelson—"It's October 21st, Charlie—Trafalgar Day."

"Aye, of course," Charlie said guiltily. "I knew it was about now." He drank and lowered his glass.

Tom said, "People don't understand the conditions of modern naval war. At Trafalgar they went into action at two miles an hour. Once the fleets had engaged, they could not disengage until one or the other was defeated. At Jutland we were closing at forty miles an hour. A ship could be out of range or back in the mist before you'd have time to bracket."

Charlie nodded, but Tom wondered whether he was really listening. Did he care? Did he have the education to understand what was being said, and the implications of it? He continued—"Modern fire at long range is always plunging—like throwing a stone over a high wall, to land on a saucer the other side—a moving saucer . . . which was throwing stones back at you."

"The Germans gave our battle cruisers a good hiding," Charlie said.

Tom said, "I'm afraid part of the trouble is that our battle cruiser design has been at fault. There's not adequate protection against flashback down the barbettes to the magazines. That's what happened to all three of them—*Queen Mary, Indefatigable,* and *Invincible.*"

"Some of our shells was duds, too," Charlie said. "Same in the army. My brother's in the Durhams out there, and he says that a lot of our shells aren't exploding, on the Somme. Cor, that's a battle, innit? Been going on over three months now . . . proper slaughter house, that is . . . D'ye think the Germans'll come out again, sir? . . . Tom?"

Tom said slowly, "I don't, though it's always a possibility. That's why we'll have to keep the Grand Fleet in being until the war ends

. . . I have a feeling our next battle isn't going to involve the big fleets at all. The German leaders will see that if they devote all their naval energy to making more U-boats, and concentrate on our sea trade, they may bring us to our knees."

"Bluidy submarines, skulking under water," Charlie muttered. "Wish I could get my hands on some of them buggers."

*　　*　　*　　*

The clock on the mantel chimed six. It was dark outside. They had had a quiet day, not leaving the flat, at lunch eating some cold meat which Jones had gone out to buy for them. Jones had kept his face impassive—called Charlie "Mr Bennett"—acted just as though Charlie had indeed been a friend of Tom's own age and class.

"Well, what shall we do now?" Tom asked. "Too early for dinner," he added hastily, remembering that the lower deck liked to eat at ungodly hours. With his parents at Dipton Charlie had probably had high tea at five or soon after, and then a bite of supper before going to bed.

"I've never been to London," Charlie said. "I'd like to see Buckingham Palace and the Tower of London and Madame Tussaud's and the Crystal Palace, and . . ."

"So you shall," Tom said, smiling affectionately at the young man's enthusiasm. "We'll start sightseeing tomorrow . . . and go to the theatre, too."

"I'd like that!" Charlie said, jumping up excitedly. "A real theatre!"

Tom said, "I'll see what's on."

*　　*　　*　　*

They sat in the gallery at the Villiers, high above the upper circle, peering steeply down at the distant stage through the haze of tobacco smoke. Tom had never sat in the gods in his life—always in the dress circle, or stalls, near the front; and always in evening dress. But Charlie had never thought of going elsewhere—he had been to the theatre three times, repertory in Newcastle-on-Tyne. Tom was learning much that he did not expect to when he arranged to spend this leave with Charlie. Charlie's view of Buckingham Palace was reverent, but practical—"Cor, Tom, how do they get all those windows cleaned, without the window cleaner gawping in at the King and Queen, eating their suppers, maybe, or getting into a bath?" And, at the Tower, scorn for the Beefeaters—until one of them told him sharply that he had been a Chief Petty Officer in his time. Tom was learning how the ordinary people of England really felt, and acted, close to, being for the moment one of them, not one of their masters.

The show was a frothy review revue called *Maisie and Company,* which had already been running for over a year. It deserved its success, Tom thought—good songs, good dancers, good acting in its skits, and several very funny comedians. Most of *Penrith*'s officers had seen it when on leave, and its tunes were played for hours every day on the wardroom gramophone.

Russell Wharton was in it now, Tom had seen when he went to the ticket agency in the morning. And Russell Wharton's name in the cast was, he admitted, why he had chosen this show rather than another; for Russell Wharton was known to be "one of *them,*" a follower of Oscar Wilde; which actually meant, Tom could now admit "one of us." He had watched Wharton through opera glasses whenever he was on stage until Charlie had said, "Let me have a look, Tom!" Raising the glasses to his eyes, he'd stared a moment, then muttered softly, "He's . . . nice. He's looking at us."

Tom said, "Let's go backstage, after it's over, and tell him how much we liked his performance."

Charlie said, "That'll be good." He caught Tom's eye.

The curtain fell on the last act, the players took their bows, and the audience filed out. Tom and Charlie walked round the side of the theatre to the stage door and went in. A man with a cigar in his mouth said, "Who do you want?"

"Mr Wharton," Tom said. The man rolled his cigar to the other side of his mouth, glanced at Charlie, and said, "Second door on the right, up there."

They went to the door, and Tom knocked. The familiar voice, clear, high, a little nasal, called, "Come in."

He was seated at his dressing table, removing his makeup. He looked at them in the mirror in front of him and said, "Did you like the show?"

"Very much," Tom said. And, almost simultaneously Charlie said, "It was wunnerful, Mr Wharton . . . I'm Charlie Bennett."

"Tom Rowland," Tom said, taking Wharton's hand.

"Major Tom Rowland?" Wharton said slyly. "Your hair is so short . . . back so straight . . . but do I not detect the ruddy touch of the sun, the rough caress of the sea wind . . . Commander Rowland?"

Tom nodded.

"And . . . Able Seaman?"

"O.D.," Charlie said, blushing.

"How nice for you . . . but I suppose your admirals are so stuffy and pompous you can hardly get a moment together."

"We're on leave," Tom said.

Wharton's face was free of makeup at last and he said, "Have you had dinner?" Tom shook his head. "Care to join me for a bite of supper, then? Us, I should say, because Ivor Novello will be there, too."

Why not, Tom thought? But perhaps a press photographer would take a picture of them and . . . It was no good worrying about everything that *might* happen. He said, "Thanks. We'd like to. And it'll be interesting to meet Mr Novello. The sailors must sing 'Keep the home fires burning' more than any other song."

"Good! You like spaghetti, Charlie?"

"Never had it," Charlie said, grinning. "My mother doesn't cook any dago food, and nor does the Navy—just beef and potatoes."

Wharton smiled at him and said, "I'll be five minutes. No, don't go
. . ."

* * * *

They sat round a small table with a red and white checkered tablecloth. It was near midnight, and they had been there over an hour and drunk four bottles of Chianti between them. Charlie, unused to wine, had fallen asleep, his head on the table. Wharton, Novello and Tom held little glasses of grappa, their heads close. They were all a little drunk.

"You mustn't mind," Novello said. "You mustn't feel guilty about it. The Greeks lived this way . . . and they are the founders of our civilization."

God, he is beautiful, Tom thought, so young, his eyes so deep and dark—a genius, too. "I wish I could feel like that," he mumbled, "but
. . . I feel that I'm a freak."

Wharton said, "People think we only have to meet a nice girl, and we'll see the light . . . but it's in us. You have to be proud of it—it's you, it's the way you intend to live your life, and that's all."

"They'd throw me out of the Navy in a flash," Tom said.

"Why not? There are plenty of other ways to earn a living. We help each other . . . I know half a dozen fellows who would take you in."

Novello said, "Do you love the Navy?"

Tom said, "I've been in it since I was twelve . . . that's a long time
. . . made good friends . . . it's my career."

"But you must have always felt—this?"

Tom said slowly, "Yes . . . but I pretended I didn't . . . tried to commit suicide once, when I first really gave in . . . with him." He nodded at Charlie's reclining head.

Novello said, "Seriously, what talents do you have? What would you turn to if you *were* kicked out of the Navy?"

219

Tom said slowly, "I don't know . . . I look at all the dress designs I see—women's dresses—and think I could do better . . . I work on them with a pencil . . . then, of course, I have to tear up the paper, or burn it somehow . . ." Novello shook his head wonderingly—"I once designed a dress for my sister. She said it was beautiful, but I don't know . . ."

Novello looked at Wharton and said, "Arthur Gavilan."

Wharton nodded, "Just the man."

Novello said, "Have you ever heard of Arthur?"

Tom said, "Yes. He designs clothes for a lot of duchesses and countesses, doesn't he? And always wears velvet suits?"

"That's the man. Arthur makes a fortune because he has taste—because he knows materials—because he knows what a woman ought to look like—and because he treats them all as rather stupid animals . . . a firm hand, clear instructions, no back talk and, of course, no affection, let alone love. We'll introduce you to him."

"Well, thank you, that's very kind of you," Tom said. He felt excited. He would be going to go into a designer's studio for the first time in his life.

Wharton said, "You'll get on fine. Arthur *loves* the Navy. His drawing room's full of pictures of Jellicoe, Beatty, Battenberg, Jackie Fisher, Hood, Rodney, and of course Nelson—every admiral even you've ever heard of." He glanced at his gold wristwatch—"I have to be going. Give me a call tomorrow, or the day after." He handed over a card, and Tom, glancing at it, saw a Dean Street address and a Gerrard telephone number—"Don't join the Army—join us."

Novello said, smiling, "I must go too. And when you fix that date for Tom with Arthur, Russell, include me." He walked out, waving.

On an impulse Tom said to Wharton, "Have you been called up?"

"Oh yes, but they couldn't take me—bad heart—rheumatic fever when I was a kid. But I do my bit—been to France four times with troupes . . . a lot of charity appearances for soldiers here at home. I was down in your home town once—Hedlington. We had a good crew, with Harry Lauder, Jenny Jenkins, and Florinda, Marchioness of Jarrow, whom you've doubtless heard of. She's a widow now."

"Oh," Tom exclaimed, "I know her slightly. She was very pretty as a young girl."

Wharton said, "Still is. And not afraid to show her legs and tits. She'll never be really good, but everyone likes her, audiences too. Most women of that sort are hard as nails, but she's not . . . Good night."

"Good night," Tom said, putting out his hand. "And . . . thank you, really. You've made me feel much better. I don't feel that I'm in some terrible prison any more."

"That prison's your mind," Wharton said, patting him on the shoulder. "And now you'd better wake up Charlie."

*   *   *   *

Four days later Tom awoke in the early light and, as he had done every morning of the leave, turned to look down at the young sailor's head on the pillow beside him. Once, when he was a lieutenant he had brought a girl from the Gaiety chorus here, on a Saturday night; and had tried, without success, to do what he had brought her here to do; and in the morning, awakened before her, and stared down at her tousled woman's hair all over the pillow and the swell of her naked breasts, and felt, how strange, that she should be in my bed with me.

But each morning, with Charlie, it seemed right that the young, close-cropped head should lie there, snoring gently, breathing evenly, a little flushed, his neck so thick like a young bull's. Russell Wharton's words kept echoing in his head—Don't feel guilt, remorse, shame . . . It's natural . . . The Greeks did it . . . everyone does it. It was hard to accept, but, this first time that he had ever actually accepted homosexual behaviour in himself, it *had* seemed natural, and right; and he had *not* felt shame, guilt, or remorse. This was the only way he could live.

He slipped out of bed and, pulling on his dressing gown, went to the door, picked up the newspaper, and took it to the drawing room. Jones would be here in an hour. He should get Charlie up soon, and send him to his own room, as they had done every morning. Or should he? As a first step to a new way of life, why not stop pretending, leave Charlie's bed plainly unslept in?

He went to the little kitchen, put on the kettle, and sat down to look at the headlines . . . the Somme battle seemed to be winding down at last, in increasingly bad weather . . . mob riots continuing in Athens . . . Sinn Fein outrage in Cork: police constable shot in back and murdered. He read on . . . the constable lured with another into a narrow alley by cries of a woman apparently in distress; then shots fired, one constable killed, the other wounded; the notorious traitor, Mrs Cate, believed responsible, as second policeman thinks he recognized her when she and others were fleeing the scene of the ambush.

He read the item once more, then put the paper down . . . poor Margaret. Yet the situation in Ireland disturbed him. It had been hard to believe that a man of Sir Roger Casement's eminence had turned traitor, but now it was being whispered that Casement was also a homosexual pervert. He stirred uneasily. That was the way the world thought: homosexuality was more detestable than treason.

The kettle began to sing, and Tom made tea. Charlie came in, rubbing his eyes and yawning. He was wearing a pair of pyjamas that Tom had lent him, for he did not own any such garments himself. Like the other sailors, he slept in his purser issue drawers and singlet.

"Smelled tea," he said. "Cor, my head hurts. *An'* I stuck to beer, like Mr Wharton said to."

"Yes," Tom said, laughing, "but you insisted on having a couple of whiskies with the beer, didn't you?"

He looked affectionately at the young man. They'd learned much about each other in these six days; and Tom had found increasing pleasure in opening new windows for Charlie, bringing him to the edge of a way of life that he had not been exposed to in Dipton, or on the lower deck of H.M. warships. The two visits to Arthur Gavilan's salon, and the one to his luxurious flat, had been particularly wonderful.

Charlie said, "It was that rabbit that upset me. It smelled right horrible!"

"Rule's famous jugged hare," Tom said, laughing again, "and if we had another week, we'd eat roast grouse at Wilton's and roast pheasant at Boulestin's, by Covent Garden. And oysters at Prince's . . . They're all in season."

"Fish and chips for me," Charlie said, sipping the tea Tom had poured for him. He looked up—"I have to go back tonight."

"I know."

They fell silent.

After a time Charlie said, "You remember what I said to you after you fell in the sea?"

Tom nodded: the young sailor had said, "I love you, sir," and then rushed out of the cabin, tears in his eyes.

Charlie continued, "I mean it still . . . I wish we could be like this all the time. I could learn to cook and clean the place up better than that Jones with his bun face, pretending he doesn't know I'm a plain matlo."

Tom said, "I love you, too, Charlie. We mustn't give this up, whatever happens. After the war . . ." He stopped.

Charlie said, "We might be at the bottom of the North Sea, feeding the herrings." He cheered up, "What shall we do today? Madame Tussaud's, eh? It'll give me the creeps, so's I can stay awake all night on the train up."

"All right, Madame Tussaud's this morning, and a football match in the afternoon—rugby. Look in the paper and see who's playing."

Charlie turned the pages—"A Harlequins side against a London Hospitals side, at Twickenham, it says."

"That'll do us well."

"Never seen rugby before."

"Then . . . it'll be goodbye until I rejoin the ship, in two days time. I won't come to King's Cross with you."

" 'Course not . . . Here's Jones." Tom did not move, but reached for the paper, and shook it out to read, as Jones let himself in at the outer door.

*   *   *   *

Daily Telegraph, Monday, October 30, 1916

SOMME FIGHTING

From Perceval Gibbon, British Headquarters (*France*) Saturday. Men wounded in this week of white-hot fighting in the blasted fields between Les Boeufs and Le Transloy speak chiefly of the mud. They are to be found in the casualty clearing station behind the battle. The great tents lead one into the other—long, shadowy halls where the wounded lie to each side. Such tents I have seen a hundred times in Russia, but never such wounded. The Russian wounded man has always the childlike side of him most developed. Then it was, Well, where have you got it? "In the leg, sir—and, God help me, it hurts a lot." But here, "Got a puncture, sir. Machine gun bullet while we was going over the top . . . Yes, sir, a rest was all I wanted . . . No, it don't hurt nothin' to speak of!"

A child who lay between two hairy men-of-war told me about (the mud). He looked like a pretty girl, with the high roses on his thin cheeks and his tumbled hair and his blankets drawn to his chin. He thrust them back to rise on his elbow and show himself a bonny boy of nineteen. "I was up to my waist when we started to go across," he said. "I'd never have got out at all, but two chaps gave me a hand and just hauled me out of the mud . . . I didn't get five yards." "Whereabouts were you hit?" I asked him. He smiled. Mark that, he smiled! "Neck, right arm, back, and both legs," he replied, still smiling. He hesitated, "I've only been out six weeks," he added, like one who makes excuses.

Cate put the paper down, wondering how the writers, whoever they were, of whatever eminence, always managed to sound patronizing. Uncommon courage was obviously commonplace out there; the newspaper correspondents in their efforts to give colour to the bald communiqués, made war read like a village cricket match, complete with the proper village characters—the brawny blacksmith, the young yokel who was brighter than he let on, the simple son of the soil . . . He looked across the table at his companion. Isabel Kramer was wearing a plain, English woollen dressing gown of royal blue, matching her

223

eyes, over her nightgown, with, on her feet the sort of tartan wool felt-soled slippers that children wore. The dressing gown was piped with white, and she had done it up to the neck. The room was warm, for the hotel had central heating. The windows were closed, the tall curtains pulled back to reveal a long view down the grey, wind-tossed waters of the Mersey. A merchant ship was being pushed out into the stream by two tugs; and, a mile to seaward, two destroyers were steaming slowly in, their smoke pulled away to the north by the wind. It was raining.

Cate said slowly, "I don't think I have ever felt so *happy*."

She answered, "Nor I . . . though I loved my husband very much. You make a woman feel she is truly wanted . . . needed."

"In this case, it is true," he said. He put out his hand to her, and she rested hers on top of it—"I hope I was not too . . . excited, for you."

She smiled—"Not too much, my dear Christopher. I was proud of you . . . as well as being much moved, as you could obviously tell for yourself . . . We must not pretend that this sensuous side of our love is in any way inferior to the rest—the respect, the shared interests, the affection. Without it, I fear I would be in danger of being swept off my feet by some other man who could arouse it in me . . . for I know well that it is there. You too, surely?"

Cate nodded, "Yes. I could be swept into something I did not really want, simply by the lust of the flesh."

"Which, the Church thinks, we women were created to release. Though I hope we have some other uses, too!"

He laughed. "Dearest! . . . What would you like to do today? Whatever we do we must not waste our time. We only have forty-eight hours."

She said, "I'd like to put on a raincoat and hat and walk in the streets with you . . . look in shop windows . . . buy a little something here, something there . . . find a little French or Italian restaurant— if such a thing exists in Liverpool—and gaze adoringly at you while we have a light lunch . . . and I'll also try to persuade you to let me help you financially, though I know you won't, you obstinate *man* . . . pigheaded *English*man! And then we'll come back . . ." she leaned forward and whispered, "to bed! I'll feel your strong arms round me . . . your strong body in me . . . I am yours. I need you as much as you need me."

Cate gazed at her, his eyes watering. He said, his voice unsteady, "We can't marry till she's dead. You saw what she's suspected of having done, the other day . . . But they won't catch her."

Isabel's eyes, too, were damp. She said, "The war's changing so much. Death is waiting for all the young men . . . a wildness is in the air, a frenzy—eat drink and be merry for tomorrow you die! Everything's changing in this wonderful, tight, little island of yours, darling. Do you think it will change enough, fast enough, for the people of Walstone to accept me at the Manor, if they know that we simply *cannot* be legally married?"

She waited, dabbing her eyes with a little cambric handkerchief. Finally he answered her: "The people might accept, in time. But I couldn't. Not for you, or for me."

She got up, came round the table, silently laid her head on his, and let her tears roll down her cheeks onto his forehead.

Caesar's Camp Copse, Beighton Down, Kent: Monday, October 30, 1916

15 Fletcher Gorse eased himself an inch or two deeper into the badger sett, so that the rain ran directly onto the ground off the leaves he had arranged over the top of it, instead of first onto the brim of his old cap, and then down. Since it started raining a couple of hours ago the aeroplanes from Hedlington airfield had stopped coming over with their thunderous roar, and that was good, too. It must be like being a magician, a god, to fly in one of those machines with their long wings and the two engines growling and the two propellers whirling . . . perhaps the fellows in them couldn't hear the sound, in some way, and flew along in silence—but on the ground, looking up, the noise hammered into your head . . .

> *Of Man's first disobedience, and the fruit*
> *Of that forbidden tree whose mortal taste*
> *Brought death into the world, and all our woe*
> *With loss of Eden . . .*

He spoke the lines again, under his breath . . . "mortal taste?" What did that mean? Mortal was being human, certain to die . . . so the taste was certain to die? 'Course not—it was the fruit of the Knowledge of Good and Evil, that parson talked about in church every year, so it meant that the taste would bring the certainty of dying . . . He wondered what the Garden of Eden had really been like . . . a land flowing with milk and honey. Something like the Weald down there below, but not so cold in winter, perhaps. There'd have to be rain

226

sometimes, otherwise the crops wouldn't grow, stood to reason. And the cows wouldn't give milk without good grass, and the bees needed plenty of wildflowers to make honey . . . He brought out a stub of pencil from one jacket pocket, a piece of paper from another, and wrote, resting the paper on the palm of his hand . . . worst thing about living in the woods was it was hard to write . . . "wild sweet honey". . . "wild honey". . . words, words, visions. . . scribbles, staring, doze a little, with the visions in his head, the words flashing, fading . . .

He felt behind his waist in the narrow confines of the sett, and found a leather satchel and in it a slab of cheese and a few hard biscuits. This sett, dug into the long earth dyke that some said Horsa had made fifteen hundred years ago, was well hidden, and he had half a dozen other such hidey holes on the Downs and in the Weald; but all of them showed the traces, in the earth and dead leaves, of his coming and going. A good dog, like the Duke back home there with Granddad, would pick up his scent. He had to shit where he could, for one thing. Eating hadn't been a problem. He killed rabbits with his catapult. Dandelion leaves were good, though they made you piss like a cow . . . fish taken from the Scarrow, eggs from a barn . . . there were girls down there in the Weald, farmers' daughters, maids in the big houses, who'd listen to his tap on their window, and let him in, and next evening come by where he'd told them, and leave a loaf, cheese, hard-boiled eggs . . . Summer passed, to autumn. At times he felt that he was near some answer, but no certainty came, and he would go back to sleep until dark, and then move silently across the land, seeing with wide eyes in the dark, walking with sure foot through bramble and tussock between the boles of trees, across the short grass of the fields, dew or rain pearling his pale red mustache and beard.

He stiffened. He'd heard something. Drat the rain! . . . It was one person, walking through the copse, twigs cracking under his feet. Now he'd stopped. He heard a voice call anxiously, "Fletcher? . . . Fletcher?"

He recognized the voice at once—Laurence Cate, squire's son. Come from squire to beg him to go back? Might do it at that, for Mr Cate. And though he'd come here for solitude, and to think, he'd had about enough. It was beginning to seem that if there were any answers, they weren't here, but in France. Everything he saw from where he was hid seemed to be going towards France—men in big lorries, crammed trains, aeroplanes in the sky, heavy rain clouds, geese . . . all going to France; and at night the earth fretting under him, so that he could not sleep.

Fletcher wriggled out of the sett, and, kneeling against the bank, peered over. Laurence was standing in a clearing about fifty feet away, by the twisted beeches that marked the centre of the copse. He'd reached his full height now, nearly as tall as his Dad, about six foot two, maybe . . . thin, long face, sandy hair like squire, face anxious now, puzzled, helpless.

He called, "Here!" Laurence heard, turned at once, saw him and walked toward him.

"I have to talk to you," Laurence said. "Peggy, the maid at Hill House, told me where she'd left some cheese for you. I knew she was sweet on you, so I thought you might have visited her, and . . . she trusts me."

"Sweet on you, too," Fletcher said, smiling.

Laurence blushed—"A little perhaps . . . I told her I wasn't going to give you away for anything." He fell silent. After a long wait Fletcher said, "Well?"

"I want to join you," Laurence stammered. Then he spoke fast, stumbling over the words in his anxiety to get them out—"I'm supposed to report to the barracks on Thursday. I can't do it! I know I'll funk whatever I have to do, and hundreds of men will be killed and blown up because I didn't do what I was supposed to."

"Seems like hundreds get killed and blown up when the officers *do* do what they're supposed to—so what's the difference?"

Laurence shook his head violently—"I'm not meant to be an officer . . . but I can't say it to my father, or anyone but you. I'm his son, a Cate of Walstone. I *have* to be an officer . . . I have lots of money on me, saved up my allowance for two months . . . took money out of my savings account . . . We can disguise ourselves . . . go somewhere wilder . . . Forest of Dean . . . Sherwood Forest . . . Dartmoor . . ."

"Don't know any of them places," Fletcher said. "Wouldn't be no girls I knew, either." He held out a piece of cheese. Laurence shook his head, silent again.

After a while, both standing close by the bank in the rain, Fletcher said, "You'm not dressed proper, Mister Laurence, nor the boots. Come back here Wednesday, about this time, dressed like you're going shooting . . . with a mackintosh coat, too. What day would that be?"

"Wednesday, November 1st—All Saints Day."

"Ah, so tomorrow's Hallowe'en. Granddad says the village used to be full of ghost and goblins that night, and everyone stayed home with the doors locked, till parson came round and swore he'd ex . . . some long word . . . anyone who didn't come out to evening service that night." He laughed—"See you then, here, about this time."

"Thank you, thank you, Fletcher. It'll be . . . marvellous!"

228

Fletcher nodded, waving a hand in farewell. Laurence disappeared among the stooped beeches and tall elms and lusty oaks of the copse, walking along the line of Horsa's Bank.

Fletcher picked up an earthenware bowl set out in the open, drank some rain water, and again backed into the sett . . . Proper mess this was, with Mister Laurence wanting to be with him. Couldn't be done really, 'cos there was no room for two fellows in the sett—less in his other hiding places—and though Laurence was a good poacher, and knew the country almost as well as Fletcher and his granddad, if *he* disappeared there would be a big hunt put on. Squire didn't see his own son as clearly as he saw everyone else . . . 'twas human nature, that was.

So, there it was. Mister Laurence was going to be an officer—couldn't help it. And he was going to be a poet of the war—couldn't help it. The job now was to let Mr Laurence down easy; and for himself, get back into the Army without bloody silly court martials, colonels yelling at him across the orderly room table, provost corp tying him to a wagon wheel, or any of that codswallop. He settled down to work out a feasible plan.

*   *   *   *

His mind made up, he wriggled out of the sett, picked up his satchel, slung it over one shoulder, and walked out of the copse and southward off the down. In the slanting rain of late afternoon he set off across country for Walstone Manor. There he worked round the outside of the big house until he was at the French windows of the music room. He tapped on the glass. After a while the curtains inside were drawn back and Laurence Cate stood in the window, peering out. The light shone on Fletcher, and he waited while Laurence unbolted the window: then he stepped through into the warmth and light. Laurence closed the windows and drew the curtains behind him.

Fletcher said, "Is your Dad here?"

"No. He's in Liverpool . . . Are you in trouble, Fletcher? I thought . . ."

Fletcher said, "Mr Laurence, I been thinking, since you came up to the Down—I'm going back to the Army."

Laurence's face fell. Fletcher looked directly into his eyes and spoke earnestly. "There's no way round it, in the end. Sooner or later we have to go. You have to lead the men, because you're a Cate, and I have to write poetry about it."

Laurence said, "You want to go to France now?"

"I reckon I always did. It's not only the poetry out there, but . . . you know, the war will end some day, and everyone come home, and

229

talk, and I—nor you—would understand them. We'd be like China-
men or Zulus, less we go."

"I see," Laurence said at last. "Well, perhaps we'll meet out there.
But won't they court-martial you for desertion, when you go back?"

"They'd like to," Fletcher said, "but they won't . . . Will you take
me to your room, Mr Laurence?"

Laurence didn't say a word but led out of the room, along the hall
and up the stairs. In the room Fletcher went to the washhand-stand.
took up Laurence's open razor and shaving soap—both newly
acquired—and began to shave carefully. Ten minutes later his face
was clean shaven except for a luxuriously sweeping but neatly trim-
med auburn mustache. Then, taking the scissors, he snipped away till
his hair was fashionably short. Now he said, "Can I wash myself here,
and borrow some of your clothes—something too small for you, 'cos
you're taller than I am . . ."

Laurence found some suitable clothes in his wardrobe, laid them
on the bed, and said, "I'll wait for you in the music room."

"Thank you. I won't be long. . . ."

*　　*　　*　　*

Laurence waited, heavy of heart. As he had feared all along, there was
no way round it: he had to go. He wished his father could have
understood, and found some honourable way for him to serve England without going into the trenches, without putting on uniform,
even. But his father had been preoccupied, since 1914 really, with the
problems of the land, of the village, of taxes—it was certain that he'd
have to sell one of the farms now—and recently, with Mrs Kramer.
Laurence liked what he had seen of the American lady, and wondered
whether she was in Liverpool with his father. He thought that she understood him better than his father did. Once or twice she had said
things that could be interpreted as guiding his father to see him in a
different light. If they'd been married, perhaps she could have found
a way out for him—but it was too late now.

Fletcher came in, and Laurence started; though it was barely half
an hour since he'd left him, it was still difficult to accept him as
Fletcher Gorse, with that big mustache, and now wearing a pair of
tweed trousers a little too long for him and a hacking jacket with shirt,
collar, and tie.

"How's that?" Fletcher said, smiling.

"It's wonderful," Laurence said. "But . . . I've been thinking. Were
you under orders for France when you ran away?"

Fletcher shook his head and said, "No, and I always meant to come
back, once I'd sorted things out in my head a bit."

Laurence said eagerly, "Then it's not desertion! You have to mean never to go back for it to be desertion."

"They're not going to throw me into no cells, nor send me to no Glasshouse. I want to get to France just as quick as I can, and that would just waste my time, wouldn't it?"

"Then what . . . ?"

"You hardly recognized me just now, even though you'd seen me shaving. An' they won't at the barracks. I'm going to enlist—F. Whitman . . . I'd like to call myself Shakespeare, but I daren't. They'll never catch Private Gorse, because he'll be under their noses, as Private Whitman."

Laurence began to laugh. Fletcher said, "They're too busy dealing with squads to look at people, up there. Everything's changing too fast—recruits arrive, drill sergeants come and go, teach ten different squads a day. They'll never catch on. Will you tell my granddad, when you can, please? They'll be watching his cottage, so I can't go there."

"We're in the same boat, sort of," Laurence said. "Our mail's being opened here, because of Mummy—my mother. They hope she'll write to one of us one day and give away where she is."

"I'll be going now," Fletcher said cheerfully. "I don't want anyone thinking you've been harbouring a deserter in the Manor. Goodbye, Mr Laurence. If you see me at the barracks, just remember I'm Private Whitman—though we won't be able to say much, except I can say 'Yes, sir,' 'No, sir.' " He laughed, and, as Laurence opened the French windows, slipped out into the darkness.

Daily Telegraph, Thursday, November 2, 1916

WAR ON SHIPPING
LOSS OF THE *MARINA*
SUNK WITHOUT WARNING

From Our Own Correspondent, *Cork*, Tuesday (Midnight) Thirty-nine survivors of the torpedoed liner *Marina* reached Cork at ten o'clock to-night. They were met by Mr Wesley Frost, United States Consul, and the Americans, who number fifteen, were conducted to the Queen's Hotel, where their depositions were taken, while the remainder of the survivors were lodged in the Sailors' Home, Cork, for the night . . .

From interviews with the Americans it is clear beyond question that their ship was torpedoed without warning at 3.45 o'clock on Saturday afternoon. The torpedo struck the ship amidships on the starboard side, causing a tremendous explosion. Then the submarine went round and fired a second torpedo into the port side amidships. The vessel broke in two, and sank in fifteen minutes after the first explosion. About a dozen of the crew were in bed, but they got into the boats. The men in the stokehold, however, were drowned. Out of the fifty-two Americans on board seven were drowned. Captain Brown waited to save the ship's papers, and in the confusion, when he jumped for a small boat, he missed it and was drowned.

The survivors were tossed about for 17½ hours, and in the third and last boat they were adrift in a huge swell, for 31½ hours. They were in extreme peril when they were picked up, as the storm was increasing.

PRESIDENT'S INQUIRY

Long Branch (New Jersey), Tuesday
President Wilson, on being informed by Press messages that six Americans had lost their lives by the sinking of the *Marina*, telegraphed to Mr Lansing, Secretary of State, at Washington, to expedite the securing the facts of the case. Mr Lansing replied that, in addition to asking Mr Page, the American Ambassador in London, for information, he was having informal inquiries made in Germany. REUTERS.

The train rattled through a station and Cate looked out for the station sign board. He did not travel to and from London often enough to know them by heart, or sense just where he was by the passage of time . . . Otford, a row of oast houses looking like cowled monks in the slanting rain, and the engine whistling for a level crossing . . . only three or four stations to go, and he'd be home; well, at least in Hedlington, and someone would be there to meet him.

He returned to the paper: this sinking of the *Marina* would play some part in the election over there. The Germans seemed bent on antagonizing America, but . . . he'd talked about the whole American situation with Isabel, and she'd advised him to read the English newspapers with a grain of salt, if that was a viable metaphor. She said that they—the English papers—following the policy of the British Government, were doing everything possible to bring the United States into the war on the Allied side. Every accident or mishap to an American, or to American property, provided it was caused by the Germans, was played up to the hilt, and often actually exaggerated. The same news might not be published at all in American newspapers, or, if it were, might be played down because—as he must appreciate—a large part of the American public did not at all wish their country to become a combatant . . .

A station passed in a rocking blur—Borough Green: very close now. He closed his eyes briefly and saw her as they had parted at Euston, in a dark corner of the great bustling station, her lips warm on his, her eyes closed. The train slowed, steam hissing from the engine's safety valve and steam chest.

Hedlington: Saturday, November 4, 1916

16 Alice thought Naomi looked so pretty in her evening uniform, with six inches of khaki silk stocking showing under her skirt, the mid-heel shoes instead of the boots and gaiters, her hair piled high instead of hidden under the felt hat. Her face, always a little stern, had seemed vulnerable since she had arrived, half an hour ago from High Staining, where she was spending her weekend's leave with her parents. During that half hour, while Alice finished dressing for the dance, she had thought the girl was unusually silent. She had tried to bring her out—asked questions about the other girls—the officers—her quarters—the work—was she enjoying herself, did she feel it was worthwhile? But Naomi's answers had been brief, and as though relayed through a telephone from a long way off; Naomi herself, the young woman, was somewhere else.

Now, as Naomi engaged gear in the big, old Rowland Ruby, she said abruptly—"I have fallen in love, Aunt Alice."

Alice felt the throb in the girl's voice: tension, emotion . . . the Town Hall was barely ten minutes drive; not nearly enough for her to get out what she obviously needed to. Alice said quietly, "Drive out on the London road for a bit, dear. We're in no hurry."

Naomi turned the car at the next cross street and headed for the main London road. After a while, as the headlamps threw a faint light forward and onto the boles of trees marching alongside, Alice said, "Tell me about it. You must feel so . . . *good.*"

Naomi said, "I wake up every morning full of a feeling . . . I can't tell you . . . the sun seems to be inside me, not outside, even if it's

234

pouring cats and dogs. I can see his face, smiling, in the air . . . I can feel his arms round me . . ."

Oh dear, Alice thought. This war . . . !

Naomi went on—"At night I go to bed, hating myself, despising myself . . . feeling like a traitress to everything I believe in."

"But, my dear, why?"

Naomi turned her head a moment to look her aunt in the eye. "He's married."

"Oh dear!" Alice said aloud. "My poor darling . . . How dreadful for you."

She wondered whether they had . . . well, the word was adultery, since he was married: had they committed adultery? The thought stirred her. She knew she would have done whatever the petty officer needed, last October, if there had been a place, the opportunity. She was feeling something of the same sense of acquiescence now, wondering whether David Cowell would be at the dance.

She said gently, "Who is he?"

Naomi said, "A colonel . . . full colonel, in Intelligence at the War Office. I didn't like him at first . . . self-protection, I suppose. Then . . ." she drew a deep breath. "We spent the night together last month, for the first time."

"Oh dear," Alice said.

"I've been falling deeper and deeper every day . . . and feeling lower and lower. Our Deputy Superintendent likes to have her girls be seen with officers—the more senior the better. I've had opportunities to meet him. He can get a hotel room anywhere without trouble, just pretends he's on Intelligence work . . . but he has to lie to his wife. I've met her when I've picked him up at his house, on duty. She seems so nice . . ."

Alice said, "He may have done this sort of thing before. Some men do, you know."

"I suppose so . . . Yes, I think he has. But I don't care. I don't care, as long as he loves me, and wants me . . . Oh, Auntie, what am I to do?"

Alice said, "We've come far enough out now, Naomi. Let's turn back."

As Naomi backed the car into a lane, and then headed back toward Hedlington, Alice tried to think clearly. Should she make Naomi promise never to see the man again? The man must be rather a cad, as the Governor would say, and probably wouldn't release his hold on her . . . She herself could write to him . . . at the War Office? To his home, once she had found out where it was? No, that would hurt the wife. She'd have to go and see him in person. *What if she were pregnant?*

She said, "You should go away, Naomi. Or you could ask to be posted to another Group, in Scotland."

Naomi said, "It wouldn't be enough. I'd still see him. It couldn't be so often, but I'd get there somehow, and he to me, or we'd meet halfway . . . Don't you see, Auntie, I have no shame!"

Alice thought, it isn't just a question of distance, but of interest. Naomi had to have her spirit engaged as this man had engaged it.

"The war!" she exclaimed. "You must join the F.A.N.Y.s."

"The First Aid Nursing Yeomanry!" Naomi said. "Would they take me?"

"If you're a good enough driver and mechanic . . . and a lady, which you are."

"Not now," Naomi muttered.

Alice said firmly, "My dear, I fear that ladies, real ladies, commit adultery at least as often as other women . . . in certain circles, such as those round the old King, a great deal more often . . . I know a senior lady of the F.A.N.Y. and your grandfather knows her husband even better. Before you leave High Staining tomorrow evening to return to your Group, you must write a letter to the address I shall give you, and bring it to me at Laburnum Lodge before you catch the train. Then I shall telephone the lady and tell her that you passionately wish to join the F.A.N.Y. and go to one of their units in France."

They were passing down the dim streets now, pedestrians still dense on the pavements, many soldiers walking toward the Town Hall for the Soldiers and Sailors Dance. Naomi said, "I don't know."

"You must," Alice said firmly. "You'll kill yourself with worry if you don't."

"I can't do it," Naomi said. "I'll die if I don't see him again."

Alice paused, then returned to the attack—"Are you afraid of going to France?" she snapped. "You think it won't be as comfortable as the nice, big house in London you have been telling me about? That you might get shelled . . . wounded . . . killed?"

Naomi said with some heat, "Of course I'm not afraid, Aunt Alice!"

"You are! You're afraid you can't control yourself! Do what I say, join the F.A.N.Y. and go to France! . . . Are you pregnant?"

Naomi said, "No . . . I knew yesterday . . . I wished, I prayed that my period would *not* come . . . I know you're right, Auntie, but don't you see, *I'm in love, for the first time, totally.* I *can't* cut myself away from him. I just had to tell someone how . . . *awful* it is, as well as wonderful. But you don't understand."

Perhaps I do, or soon will, Alice thought unhappily but said nothing.

They drew up in front of the Town Hall, where Naomi found a

space at the pavement to leave the car. They got out, Naomi helping her aunt. A girl of medium height, in uniform, carrying herself well, walked past them, turning at the big main doors to glance round, then exclaiming, "Miss Rowland! Don't you remember me? Elizabeth Seddon."

"Of course! Niece of the Misses Frameley."

"I'm on leave from the F.A.N.Y.—Number Four Convoy. We run a Field Ambulance for the Belgians just outside Calais. The British Army wouldn't touch us in the beginning, but now there are rumours that an English Convoy will be formed soon, to serve with our own Army . . . about time, too!"

"How exciting! Do you know my niece here, Naomi Rowland?"

"We've met once or twice," the other girl said briefly.

Then they went on in, separately.

*   *   *   *

The dances for soldiers and sailors from Minden Barracks, from Chatham, from the camps and hutments dotted round the countryside, or home on leave from France and ships at sea, were now regular affairs, one Saturday a month. The women of Hedlington, of all classes, were urged to attend, to dance with the men, talk with them, share the (nonalcoholic) beverages and simple food supplied, and enjoy the music of the band—all free, since all costs were borne by various charitable organizations many of which liberally benefitted from the generosity of Mr Bill Hoggin. Mr Hoggin had recently been the subject of a long laudatory editorial in Horatio Bottomley's *John Bull* magazine, and that, together with the bland report of the Parliamentary Joint Select Committee on the food industry, had effectively blown away the bad odor which had hung around him since the beginning of the war; already a multi-millionaire he was now well on his way to becoming a national hero as well—except to the men in the trenches: there, "Hoggin's" was still a term of contempt and anger.

Alice came to the dances regularly, because she met women whom she had known from her Tipperary Room and House Parties. Often they were sad reunions, for the women, who had once talked together of what they would do when their husbands came home, now had no husband.

Alice danced two dances, then sat out along the wall. Many younger women had come—so pretty, so flushed and excited: older women, such as herself, would not be in much demand. She was glad of it: the work at the Shell Filling Factory was tiring, and, as her father and brother had warned her, it gave her an almost week-long headache.

The woman sitting next to her was swept away by a dashing sea-

237

man of the Royal Navy, and she glanced past the empty chair at her new neighbor and cried, "Ethel Fagioletti . . . Stratton . . . Fagioletti . . ."

The woman rose, half curtsying—"Miss Alice . . . I saw you coming in."

"I haven't seen you for ages. My father told me you had been divorced."

Ethel blushed and lowered her eyes and whispered, "Niccolo wanted it. I didn't do anything wrong. I love Niccolo, and now . . . now . . . he's in France . . . He's not a soldier, miss . . . he's not even English, really. He had another woman, and . . . I didn't have any babies."

"What a shame," Alice said, thinking, well, that "other woman," to another wife, was Naomi. What was happening to the decent women of England?

"I love him . . . and he'll be killed . . ." Ethel fumbled in her bag, pulled out a large handkerchief and sobbed quietly into it.

"There, there, don't cry," Alice said. "If he's out there, he can't be with the other woman, at least, can he?"

Ethel mumbled, "I never thought of that . . . He's too delicate for the trenches. He'll catch his death, in all that mud and water, and no roof over his head."

Alice said confidently, "He'll come home."

Ethel said, "My mother makes me come to these dances, so I can meet other men. There was a Mr Willibanks wanted to marry me, after I was divorced . . . still does . . . but I don't want any other man. So what's the use of coming?"

I'm not surprised, Alice thought; Ethel looked woebegone and mournful, tears staining her face, her blue eyes watery and little colour in her face. She wasn't young or naturally beautiful enough to carry that off, in spite of her fine bosom.

A soldier approached and Alice said cheerfully, "Well, here's someone come to dance with you. You don't have to think of marrying him. Just enjoy the dance." The man, a middle-aged corporal of Royal Engineers, took Ethel away, as if performing an arduous duty. Alice looked round her again.

A young private of the Wealds, with a luxuriant, sweeping reddish mustache, came up to her and said, "Would you like to dance, miss?"

She said, "You don't have to take pity on me. Look at all those pretty girls your own age, along that wall. Why don't you ask one of them?"

"I'd like to dance with you, Miss Alice."

She peered more closely, rising to her feet—"You know me? Have we met?"

He said, "I seen you often, when you come down to stay at High Staining or the Manor. I'm Fletcher Gorse, miss, only I'm Fletcher Whitman now."

"I remember! You deserted . . . but you've re-enlisted under another name?"

He smiled and nodded, moving her gracefully and easily out onto the floor in a slow waltz. "One of the sergeants guessed, but he's keeping his mouth shut. And Mr Laurence knows, of course."

"Laurence Cate?"

Fletcher nodded—"He's an officer recruit. The sergeant majors drill them on the square, same time as us, and call 'em names, too, only they have to say Mister at the beginning and "sir" at the end, when they've called them everything bar a darling in between."

"Mr Cate said you write very good poetry."

Fletcher said simply, "I do, and it's getting better. . . . That's Colonel Quentin's wife, isn't it?" He jerked his chin toward a plain chair near the door. Alice glanced over and recognized her sister-in-law Fiona, sitting upright, her face remote, long, aristocratic, cold. Not many young soldiers would want to tackle *that,* Alice thought.

She answered Fletcher, "Yes, that's my brother's wife. Would you like to dance with her?"

Fletcher said, "No, miss. She's not here. She's with the Colonel and the lads in France, perhaps . . . And I have a lady coming I promised to dance with. Here she is."

A lithe young woman in a simple afternoon dress, without hat, swept in through the door close to where Fiona sat. Alice recognized Betty Merritt as Fletcher eased her to the side of the room, released her, and said, "Thank you, Miss Alice."

She sat down, a little breathless, and watched with interest as Fletcher walked across the floor with a peculiar challenging glide, to stop in front of Betty Merritt. For a moment she held her head up, meeting his gaze face to face; then she lowered her eyes and seemed to melt, and in a moment they were out on the dance floor, curving gracefully in and out among the others, their heads close, lips curved in smiles, bodies moving in the perfect synchronization of inner harmony.

*   *   *   *

Naomi stood beside Miss Seddon, drinking coffee . . . Lance Corporal Seddon, she corrected herself. The F.A.N.Y. used military ranks, instead of shying away from them, as the other women's organizations did. And they, alone of all of them, were in France; and, as Miss Seddon had been making quite clear to her in a crisp, cool, detached way, they were not at all interested in forwarding women's

239

causes, such as the suffrage, or seats in Parliament; they were interested in winning the war.

"We're in Lamarck at the moment," Miss Seddon said, "but we're moving into Calais itself any moment. I didn't want to take leave but Captain MacDougall said I was run down from a 'flu and I had to take ten days at home . . . And I wouldn't be at this dance if my aunts hadn't insisted. How it helps win the war for me to have my toes trodden on and my bosom breathed heavily down by sex-starved private soldiers, I don't know."

Naomi wished Lance Corporal Seddon would ask her about the Women's Volunteer Motor Drivers, so that she could tell her what was wrong with it. But the Lance Corporal was supremely uninterested in the W.V.M.D., and when a sailor came up, cap in hand, and asked her for a dance, she went with him, nodding briefly at Naomi, left alone at the coffee table.

*   *   *   *

A shadow fell across Alice's lap and she looked up. Her heart missed a beat and the smile faded slowly from her face, as she saw David Cowell looking down at her. He said softly, "Male civilians are not encouraged to dance at these affairs, but the circumstances are exceptional. I've brought two daughters, so . . . will you dance with me, Miss Rowland?"

She put up a hand, and let him help her to her feet, not quite sure she could do it alone. The dance was a foxtrot, and neither of them knew it well, but . . . He drew her slowly closer. Their bodies touching, she could feel his movements: it was easier thus to follow the steps of the dance. He said, "That's my Josephine . . . in the blue dress, she's nineteen . . . I don't see Esther, she's twenty-two . . . she has a fiancé at Hedlington Aircraft Company, but he doesn't mind her coming to these affairs. My wife's not feeling well, so . . ."

"You came . . . You dance very well, Mr Cowell."

His speech was not as precise as normal, and his face was a little flushed. Had he had a drink or two before coming to the dance? He said, "You dance very well, too, Miss Rowland . . . May I call you Alice?"

She said, "Why not?" feeling a little faint, and warm all over. His Midland accent was more noticeable now that he was, well, a little tiddly. So why was she encouraging him to familiarity, and letting him press his body steadily against hers in this indecent new dance, that was making her breathing come unevenly and causing a tingling in her nipples and between her thighs?

240

He said, "Do you know about birds, Alice? Will you call me David?"

"David . . . A little. My nephew, Laurence Cate, has tried to teach all of us in the family something about birds."

"I go out most Sundays, on my bike . . . to Sheppey, or the Downs . . . sometimes a long way, beyond Canterbury."

"How nice," she said. "It must be wonderful to know all the birds and their calls."

He said, "Would you like to come with me, Alice?"

Obviously his wife didn't go on these bird-watching expeditions with him; or the daughters. He went alone. She would be alone, all day, in the country, with a married man.

She was thirty-seven, and there was a war on. Look at what the young women were doing, here and in France. Why should she be passed by?

She said, "I'd love to, David."

"Sunday after next. You have a bike?"

"Yes."

"Meet me a mile out on the road to the airfield . . . that corner where young Guy Rowland, your nephew, killed the Hedlington Ripper . . . ten o'clock . . . We'll have lunch in a pub somewhere—just bread and cheese and ale, it'll be."

"I shall love it."

"Oh, and binoculars, and a little notebook . . . I'll bring a book I have on birds, for you to keep."

"That'll be very kind of you."

Goodness, how stilted and proper she sounded, with her nipples now openly throbbing and hard as stones in her bodice. His eyes met hers, and they were very soft as he said, "I haven't known you for very long, Alice, but . . . you are one of the nicest women I've ever met . . . kind, gentle, sympathetic . . . and very nice looking."

"Not that," she said, bridling in spite of herself. Men felt they had to pay that sort of compliment; what she needed, they didn't understand, was a sense of personal affection, which might even become love.

"Truly," he said, "I want to be with you as much as I can. It can never be enough."

She flushed with pleasure. It was a mercy that he was over forty, and had not enlisted of his own accord. Besides, surely they wouldn't take him if he had to wear those big glasses, nearly as thick as Richard's?

"I—" she began, when a commotion in the hall made her pause and look round. A dozen men and women were coming in through the big doors, flung wide, the cold breath from the autumn street

241

pouring in with them. A little man at their head ran, limping, through the dancers to the bandstand and yelled at the musicians, "Shut your noise!" The band wheezed and groaned to a halt. She recognized Bert Gorse, and now, beside him on the bandstand, the girl who had been Naomi's friend at Girton, Rachel Cowan. The soldiers and sailors all stopped dancing, holding their partners. She saw anxiety in all their faces. Was there some terrible crisis in the war, and they all called back to their duty at once, in the middle of the night?

"Soldiers! . . . sailors!" Bert Gorse shouted. "Don't go back to your regiments, your ships, your barracks! We've got to stop the war! Who's keeping it going? The rich men, the owners, Hoggin and the likes of him! We could end it tomorrow and be no worse off than we were in August 1914 . . . except that we'll never get back the men they've killed—husbands, sons, fathers . . . the sixty thousand they did for the first day of the Somme!"

The crowd on the floor began to growl, becoming not a collection of individuals, men and women linked in separate pairs by arm and hand—but a slowly fuzing, welding entity, fuming, snarling . . . *Bloody conchies! . . . shirkers . . . traitors . . .*

Rachel had taken over from Bert. She was addressing the women, in a high-pitched desperate cry, almost a scream—"Women . . . don't let your men go back! Join us in the struggle to stop the war, stop the profiteering, stop the useless slaughter! Don't do any war work . . . don't . . ."

Alice felt a pamphlet pushed into her hand, and turned to stare into the face of her brother, John Rowland. She looked down at the paper, and saw the huge black headline STOP THE WAR!; and, below, in smaller, smudged print: *Join the Hedlington No-Conscription Fellowship & Anti-War League*—with an address, and a telephone number.

She gasped, "John! Have you joined these people?"

The crowd sound was increasing fast, a roaring bellow of male bass and female treble, so that John had to raise his voice, though he was only a foot away—"Yes, Alice. The war must be stopped, before it destroys all our sons, and England itself."

Some men were beginning to break for the platform now, others herding their women out of the melee toward the door, where a police constable had appeared, looking majestic but puzzled. Two sailors and a soldier grabbed Bert by the arms and threw him bodily off the platform. Two women seized Rachel's hair and pulled hard in different directions, while hairpins flew. Another woman, hurrying up, took out the long hairpin that had held up her bun and began to jab three inches of it in and out of Rachel's buttocks, screaming, "That's for my 'usband, Regimental Sergeant Major Nelson, dead for the likes of

you!" Everyone was shouting, "Take that, you nasty little fucker!"
"Bitch, bitch!" "Traitor!" "Owww! Oh! Ah!" On the floor men were
kicking Bert in the ribs with heavy boots.

"Put your arm round me, John, quick!" Alice cried. "Pretend we
were dancing!"

She saw David Cowell take position back to back with her brother
and experienced a warm glow of pride. He would fight to protect
John.

Naomi pushed to them through the mob, gasping, "Daddy! What
on earth are . . . ?"

"I came with the pacifists," he said quietly.

"You didn't tell me!"

"I didn't want to trouble you. Or have an argument, which would
upset all of us. My mind was made up."

"But Daddy . . . how can you, when the men are dying by thousands in France to win the war?" The poor girl was in tears, Alice saw,
her voice trembling.

"That is exactly why I must," John said. "Your mother does not
agree with me. We are really each doing what we think right, for Boy's
sake."

"But Boy would . . ."

She broke off. Lance Corporal Seddon had pushed her way into
the crowd of men kicking Bert Gorse, and now barked, "That's
enough now! Stand back! . . . You, stand back! Do you want to be
charged with murder?" The police constable's burly figure loomed
close as he strode forward, and the men obeyed. Bert lay on the floor,
writhing in agony, his face a ghastly green-grey, his nose dripping
blood, blood staining his mouth, his lips bloodied. He pulled himself
to a kneeling position and began to retch.

Rachel, beside him, croaked, "Savages! Bloody, murdering savages!" She caught Naomi's eye and stared, not recognizing her
through her own bruised and bloody eyes. Then she whispered, "See,
this is what your class lives by!"

Naomi put out a hand—"Rachel . . ." She wanted to say, let me
help; let's talk about it later; you've really asked for trouble, coming
here, but . . .

Rachel turned her back. Lance Corporal Seddon said, "You have
some strange friends . . . Don't move him yet . . . let him lie down."

Gradually the crowd dispersed. Rachel said to Lance Corporal
Seddon, "You saved his life."

"Unfortunately," Miss Seddon said coldly, and walked away.

Daily Telegraph, Monday, November 6, 1916

FUTURE OF POLAND
LATEST GERMAN SCHEME FOR
A NEW KINGDOM

From Leonard Apray, *Rotterdam*, Sunday.
Germany's bestowal of "sovereignty" on Poland is a surprise. This is true, notwithstanding the fact that a long time ago rumours spoke of such a move being contemplated . . . In the Allied countries, of course, no sensible person will take Germany's Polish "gesture" seriously. But many of the Pan-German party take it as seriously as—well, they take themselves. For a large section complete annexation, not sovereignty, of Poland is regarded as one of the essentials of Germany's "war objects," namely the so-called protection of East Prussia. This large and influential group includes Prince Bülow and nearly all the other open or secret enemies of Herr Bethmann-Hollweg.

There is no question that an announcement of the new scheme in the Reichstag, whilst doubtless receiving a large amount of approval, would also have provoked another stormy attack on the Government. This, after the recent damaging experiences, Herr Bethmann-Hollweg dared not face. The latest echo of the experiences alluded to is a remarkable article by Maximilian Harden, who makes an attack, covert but evident, on Dr Helfferich, the Home Secretary, demands in effect a peace offer by the German Chancellor and declares that Europe's horrors cannot be ended by force of arms.

Cate thought, Poland . . . one knows of it as a nation, a country; one knows roughly where it was; one knows of Poles and reads about Poles: Paderewski was a Pole, so were Pachmann, Pilsudski, Conrad, whose real name was Korzeniowski; Chopin had been . . . but when did Poland last actually exist? There had been three dismemberments at the end of the 18th century; after the last of which Poland ceased to exist as an independent country. Then the Congress of Vienna had recreated it—Congress-Poland—with its own constitution but really united to Russia. But soon Russia and Austria and Bismarck's Germany had once more swallowed it piecemeal. This latest move of Germany's was obviously aimed at turning Polish resentment and latent patriotism into fervour for Germany, and as a consequence, increased antagonism to Russia, which had made no such declaration in favour of re-establishing a sovereign Poland; though what sort of "sovereignty" Poland would actually receive, if Germany won the war, was a big and unanswered question.

The real interest of the article lay in the last sentence. Herr Harden's whole article had not been translated and reprinted, so one could only guess at its full content; but if an influential German was publicly demanding that Germany initiate a move toward peace . . . well, who knew what might come of it?

*   *   *   *

Garrod came in and refilled his cup. "Thank you, Garrod," he said. She returned to the sideboard with the coffee pot. Watching her, he said, "You have a sister in Eastbourne, don't you?"

"Oh yes, sir," Garrod said, turning, "ten years older than me, she is. Widowed five years ago."

"I remember. You went to the husband's funeral . . . Would you like to spend Christmas with her this year? It'd be a change . . . a rest."

Garrod looked shocked—"Why, sir, my place is here for Christmas, with Miss Stella and her husband coming, and Mr Laurence home."

"He'll be at the barracks in Hedlington," Cate said. "Most officers have to spend Christmas with the men . . . What about inviting your sister to have Christmas here with us, then?"

Garrod said, "Why . . . why, thank you, sir. That would be very nice. I'll have another bed put in my room." Cate thought a tear was forming in Garrod's eyes, and wondered if he was seeing straight; Garrod never cried or became emotional. She continued—"It'll cheer her up a bit, sir. Her eldest son was killed last week. The last day of the Battle of the Somme, the papers said. Thirty-eight he was—been a carpenter all his life, until this war came. Left four children, sir, but I'm sure he died happy. He was doing his duty."

The Western Front:
Wednesday, November 22, 1916

17 The rain fell steadily on the British trenches, on the German trenches, on No Man's Land, and on all the men, living, wounded, and dead, in them. The earth was torn and misshapen, hills and vales alike scarred, gouged, blackened by four months of shell fire. The south-west wind blew the stench of putrefying bodies toward the Germans, and their sentries often wore gas masks after the sun (if there was sun) had been shining for two or three hours, causing a visible miasma of decay to rise and hover, like a poisonous gas, over what had once been the lovely curves of the downlands by the Somme. The battle of the Somme had been officially declared over on November 1st, four months to the day after it began. The British line had advanced a mile, in places.

In a front line British trench opposite Thiepval, under two groundsheets tied together and fastened on one side to the parados, and on the other to sticks stuck into the soggy floor of the trench, a large ration box, upended, had been covered with an oilcloth, once white, marked out in squares; four bore the devices of club, diamond, heart, and spade: one a crown, one an anchor; and the seventh was bare, but on it stood a tiny table with bead legs, and on the table a box big enough to hold, and shake, five dice. Round the box six soldiers of the 1st Battalion, the Weald Light Infantry, wearing steel helmets, slung rifles, and groundsheet capes, stood or sat on other boxes, playing Crown & Anchor.

Private Lucas shook the dice in the box, chanting in a low voice,

"Lay it down, me lucky lads . . . You come on bikes, you go away in Rolls Royce motor cars . . . Jessop, are you sure you can afford one 'ole tanner? . . . The Old Firm, the Best Firm, all the way from the Scrubs! Lay it down, Ikey Mo . . . the old Mudhook's badly backed . . . Any more for any more?"

In a single movement he dived off the ammunition box into the stained chalk of the trench floor. A moment later the others followed as the rumble of a heavy shell became apparent to them, too. As they groveled the shell burst, five yards behind the parados.

The shelter was in ruins, the "table" overturned, the oilcloth and dice box in the mud. The soldiers began to pick up the pieces and set them all in order once more.

"Just six more hours," Bob Jevons said. His voice was trembling and his hand shook as he set up the little dice table.

"That bugger came too fucking close," Private "Ikey Mo" Leavey said. He blinked and licked his lips continuously.

The youngest of the six, Private Cyril Jessop, who'd given a false age to enlist early in the year, said, "None of them fuckers is going to get me till I've had my greens."

"Don't worry, we'll fix it," Stan Quick said. "Pity Harry England caught a packet, he could smell a willing cunt a mile away."

Private Brace frowned. He'd only been in France a month, and his mind was still attuned to the ponderous decencies of Laburnum Lodge, where he used to be houseman for Mr and Mrs Harry Rowland.

They knelt again. Quick said, "Can't understand why you haven't had a piece of skirt already, Cyril. You must be seventeen."

Lucas began his chant again, "Lay it down, me lucky lads, the more you put down the more you pick up . . ." Jevons stiffened. Five shells rumbled over, to burst a hundred yards to the left and a quarter of a mile back, somewhere on the reserve trench area . . . "The old firm, the firm you can trust, all the way from Pentonville . . . Any more for any more? Lay it down me lucky lads lay it down, thick and heavy . . . Right, up she comes . . . Two jam-tarts, the Mudhook, Kinkie, and the Curse . . . Double on the Tarts . . . Lay 'em down, pick 'em up—see Jessop, you always win with the old firm . . ."

The sentry behind them muttered, "Officer coming!"

"Who is it?"

"Mr Jonson."

"He'll pretend not to see. Rare good young officer."

2nd Lieutenant Benjamin Jonson passed. He pretended not to see the Crown & Anchor game, the soldiers pretended not to see him, decorum was observed. The game continued.

"Lay it down me lucky lads lay it down, look, there's nothing on Kinkie . . ."

". . . all I want is some cabbages, eggs, bread, a chicken . . . anything fresh."

"Up she comes . . . Two of the darling Majors, *and* two Mudhooks, and a Shamrock . . . Thick and heavy! Up she comes . . ."

"'Ere, 'ere, look where you're putting your bleeding boots."

Lucas looked up at Ikey Mo Leavey's angry exclamation. A private soldier staggering down the trench had cannoned into Leavey, knocking him onto the oilcloth. The other soldier had now fallen back against the rear wall of the trench. "He's drunk," Lucas said. "Half seas over. Wonder where the lucky bastard got the rum."

"Who is he?"

"Never seen him before . . . must have come along the trench from A Company."

The soldier slid slowly down the back wall, his hands slipping off the revetments, and fell on his back in the mud and water in the bottom of the trench.

The sentry above muttered, "Officers coming!"

"Who?"

"Gawd, three, four . . . old Rowley . . . a brass hat . . . the Regimental . . ."

Lucas swept the stakes off the oilcloth and into his pocket. He whipped the oilcloth off the "table," rolled it up and stuffed it under his tunic. The little dice table and box he put inside the ammunition box "table." He hissed, "Sit down on the firestep! We're talking, see?"

"What are we going to do with this bloke?" Brace asked.

The drunken soldier lay on his back, a beatific, twisted smile on his face. Lucas ripped off his groundsheet cape, covered the drunk's upper body and face with it, then sat down again, the rain dripping off his steel helmet onto his tunic and the box respirator slung on his chest.

Mr Campbell the adjutant came round the traverse into the bay, followed closely by a lieutenant general in a red-banded gold-leafed cap, Lieutenant Colonel Quentin Rowland, and Regimental Sergeant Major Dalley. The lieutenant general had short, white hair and a fierce, upswept white mustache. He barked at Lucas, "What's your name, my man?"

"Lucas, sir."

"Service?"

"Twenty years, four months."

"Good man! That's what the New Armies need—a leavening of real soldiers."

248

The general was about to speak to Private Brace when he noticed the groundsheet-covered body on the trench floor a pace or two ahead. He slowly stiffened, his right hand rising to the peak of his cap in salute—"I, Lieutenant General Sir Bailward Shannon-Watson, salute the gallant dead!" he intoned. He held the pose a long ten seconds, then snapped down, and moved on.

The groundsheet covering the "corpse" rose and fell away. The drunken soldier boomed blurrily, "What did the old fucker call me?" A shell rumbled close. The R.S.M. appeared to slip, falling on top of the drunk, effectively hiding and stifling him. The general and his party stiffened and crouched. The shell burst behind the next bay. The corps commander and party moved on. The cry came back down the trench, "Stretcher bearers! Stretcher bearers!"

Jevons said, "Jesus . . . only five hours to go in the line, and some poor bugger . . ."

Lieutenant Campbell passed back down the trench, hurrying. Lucas said, "Was it bad, sir?"

Campbell shook his head. "Just two. Mr Jonson and Lance Corporal Corbett, killed. No one wounded." He hurried on.

The soldiers sat down. "Want to start the game again?" Lucas said. They shook their heads. Only five hours . . .

Jevons started chuckling, and, imitating the general's potato-in-mouth accent, boomed, "I salute the gallant dead . . ."

Lucas said, "He looked a fool, all right, but you'll remember this day, Jevons, because of him. That's the first lieutenant general I or any of us ever seen in the front line."

*   *   *   *

They came out of the fading twilight, snaking down the communication trenches toward the west, until near Authuille the trench system ended and the men rose painfully like demons from the earth, to trudge on top of it through the slanting rain toward the battalion rendezvous, two miles farther on.

The C.O. waited, tapping his field boots with his swagger stick, his thick head a little thrust forward, legs apart. Behind him stood Campbell, his adjutant, watching, wishing he could make a quick sketch now, something to catch the sense of the heavy sky pushing down on those gleaming inverted steel bowls, the shoulders bowed under the weight of their packs, their weapons, the sky, their days in the line. There was a humming and murmuring in the ranks, that sounded quite different from the sounds the battalion made when going up the line. Then it was intermittent between long, tense silences—muttered exclamations, a command, a rifle dropped, a steel helmet clashing on a bayonet. Now it was continuous, like bees.

249

The companies fell in on their markers, in close column of platoons. German "coal scuttles" rumbled far overhead to land in muted thunder on British heavy artillery positions farther to the rear.

Campbell watched the platoons coagulating into the dense mass of a battalion formed up in close column and after a while summoned up his courage to speak—"Sir . . . do you think we had better open up, in case some German gunner puts a shell into us?"

Quentin Rowland said, "The Germans can't see us here, Campbell. It's too dark."

Campbell thought, it's still light enough for a spotting aeroplane to see; perhaps even a Boche captive balloon, using night glasses. Quentin stepped forward and the second-in-command shouted, "Weald Light Infantry . . . shun!" He turned and marched up to Quentin— "Battalion present and correct, sir."

Quentin raised his voice—"We're going north, to the Ypres sector, into general reserve, for ten days at least. You've done well here. The brigade commander has congratulated me on your performance while in the line . . . We must continue to uphold the standards of the regiment." His voice rose ten decibels—"Men will shave every day! Men will keep their arms, clothing, and equipment clean! Discipline will be maintained! . . . Yesterday I heard a private soldier calling a lance-corporal by his Christian name. Needless to say, the lance-corporal no longer has his stripe, for permitting such familiarity . . . Until we return to the line, saluting will . . ."

A rumbling filled the dusky air, and a German heavy exploded over the hedge twenty yards from the right rear flank of the parade. Campbell, ready to duck as he heard the rumble, realized that not a man had moved—until after the shell burst, when three men in the platoon nearest to the burst staggered out, one falling, his hands to his chest, the others crawling on their knees.

"Look after those men, Major Green!" Quentin shouted. He paused, then continued—"Saluting will be insisted on . . . Move to the right in column of fours—form fours—right!"

Eight hundred men sprang to attention, formed fours, turned right, and once more snapped their rifles out at ease. Boy Rowland, the leading company commander, shouted, "By the left, quick— march!" and his leading platoon strode off at the light infantry step, 140 paces a minute, rifles held parallel to the ground at the point of balance, sliding along level with the ground.

"Right wheel!"

The column swung onto the pavé of a road. Campbell, marching a yard behind the C.O., felt a lump in his throat. What divine lunacy! Like the Somme itself, the whole experience . . . the sheer madness, the terror, the heaped mountains of corpses . . . the universal, endless shelling . . . perhaps there was after all no way to survive it, except to ignore it, pretend it wasn't there, keep to the Waterloo standards.

"March at ease!" Quentin passed over his shoulder.

* * * *

The battalion was in billets at Eecke, a Flemish hamlet just inside France, fifteen miles behind the front line near Ypres. A pond covered with duckweed and hidden by thick hedges lay beside the lane out to the north of the village. A wintry sun shone on wet pasture, heavy cows grazing, muddy plough furrows in the field beyond. Private Lucas sat on a stump beside the pond, a cut willow twig in his hand, a piece of khaki thread from his housewife tied to the end of the twig, a bent pin baited with a worm on the end of the thread. He had his pipe in his mouth, and his soft fore-and-aft cap set at a sharp angle on the side of his head.

High in the sky above four aeroplanes swooped and circled in long, gracious curves, flashing silver or red, brief trails of exhaust smoke following the curves of their passage, now and then a murmured tattoo, like kettledrums, mingling with the nearer sounds of the pond. Private Jessop, lying on his back, sucking a blade of grass, said dreamily, "That's the place to be . . . the Flying Corps . . . clean fresh air, dry clothes, nice farmhouse to live in miles back—can't even 'ear the ruddy artillery . . . saucy mademoiselle to bring you morning tea in bed . . . her tits boiling over out of her dress, too . . ."

Lucas said, "Fore you join the R.F.C. go and have a look at what 'appens to 'em, when they ain't lucky. There's a Jerry crashed yesterday, just off the road 'alf a mile t'other side of Eecke. Pilot's still in it . . . they 'aven't 'ad time to scrape 'im out of 'is seat yet."

Jessop said, "But them blokes, the R.F.C., act like lords and ladies used to when everyone wore armour. Why, you know what Mr Rowland, Old Rowley's son, did last week? The gup is that some German ace's wife had a baby and our blokes in the R.F.C. got to 'ear of it, so young Rowland went up in the dark, dropped a packet of baby clothes, all pink, 'cos it was a girl, then went 'ome . . ." He rolled over, "You'll never catch anything here, Snaky. There ain't nothing in this pond to catch."

Lucas said, "When you've fished as many village tanks in the Shiny, as I have, and come back with a fish, you can open your trap. Besides, I like fishing. It lets you think of nothing . . . plain fuck nothing, and that's what a soldier needs most."

"Couldn't sleep last night," Jevons said, "woke up half a dozen times, in a muck sweat, dreaming I was lying out there in front of

High Wood and no one could hear me shouting for help. I was hit in the belly, too, in my dream."

"That's why I fish," Lucas said. "It's as good as sleeping, only you don't dream."

Jessop said, "When are you going to get me a woman, like you promised?"

"We will," Lucas said, "but we've got to get your strength up first. Fucking a woman's very tiring, me lad . . . especially your first. A lot of blokes get 'eart attacks and never recover."

Jessop turned pale but after a time said, "I don't care if I do drop dead. I'm going to 'ave a woman first."

"All right. Day after tomorrow . . . soon's we can find just the right one."

"Why not tomorrow?" Jessop asked aggrievedly. "My balls are ready to burst."

"Tomorrow there's a concert."

"The Divisional Concert party? I seen them four times already. 'Oo wants to look at A.S.C. corporals with 'airy legs pretending to be beautiful women?"

"No, this is a concert party from Blighty—Florinda's in it."

"The Marchioness of bloody Jarrow," Stan Quick said reverently. "And to think that when I was fifteen she let me kiss her in the bushes be'ind 'er granddad's cottage."

"And then you felt 'er titties and . . . ?" Jessop began eagerly.

"I tried," Quick said, "but she just laughed and ran away. But she'd made me feel good, so I didn't mind."

*　　*　　*　　*

Quentin Rowland was reading letters, sitting in the comfortable little upstairs bedroom in the village curé's house. The first letter had been from his daughter, still scrubbing floors in Aldershot; she had been to the cinema with Violet, Ivy, and Maggie, jolly nice girls, jolly interesting work, felt she was doing something for the war . . . enclose a snap: she was still fat, but her expression was more contented, arms linked with three other girls outside what looked like a Nissen hut . . . The next letter was from Christopher Cate: Laurence had been commissioned a 2nd Lieutenant in the Weald Light Infantry on his 18th birthday. He was dead keen to get to France, but would probably stay in Hedlington for some time, as there had been questions asked in Parliament about sending out eighteen-year-olds.

Quentin looked up, frowning. Bump . . . bump . . . bump . . . rhythmic heaving against the wall with its flowered red wallpaper. The crucifix hanging on it swung out and back in rhythm—tap . . . tap . . . tap . . . Vow of celibacy, indeed!

. . . John was selling off some of his cows so that he could follow the government's instructions to convert to arable and grow wheat; he was losing money on it, of course. If taxes went any higher, they'd all be in trouble . . . Had he seen in the papers that the Parliamentary Inquiry into the Food situation had made its report? And wished to thank its expert advisers Sir Jacob Isaacs, Lord Rownbush, and Mr William Hoggin for the unstinted gifts of their valuable time and invaluable experience and knowledge . . . Old Mr Kirby had had a minor heart attack in the hunting field, and had been forbidden to ride to hounds any more. Either way, it would probably finish him off . . .

There was a knock at the door and he called, "Come in." His adjutant, Lieutenant Campbell, came in, saluting. "You told me to come for you twenty minutes before the service, sir."

Quentin heaved up out of the chair—"Oh yes. Thanks." He jerked his head at the wall—"Listen to that!" They listened to the sounds of concupiscence, together with stifled grunts—"Ten o'clock in the morning, in bed with that woman . . . the blighter never shaves except on Sunday before Mass . . . he lives like a king, when most of the villagers are starving, or near it . . . He's ignorant, superstitious, selfish . . . How do the R.C.s do it? How is it that the only padres that are any good—the only ones the men like, whether they're Protestants, Presbyterians, Methodists, or Jews, it doesn't matter . . . are Roman priests?"

Archie said, "I don't know, sir. Perhaps the Pope has given them a dispensation—if they go with the troops into the line, all their other sins and peccadilloes are forgiven."

"This curé doesn't intend to go anywhere near the line . . . Has Father Caffin taken our R.C.s off to Hazebrouck?"

"Yes, sir."

"We'd better go. I asked the general to tell the Bishop that our men needed a real telling off, from the pulpit. I'm not going to have Frog villagers complaining about stolen chickens and us not able to find the culprits. Why, they'll be thinking they can get away with rape and murder next."

"Yes, sir," Archie said. The soldiers were going to catch it from the Bishop, were they? He had a feeling that the 1st Battalion of the Wealds could take it.

* * * *

The battalion was paraded in a hollow square, without hats or helmets, the men's heads bare to the gently falling sleet. A big table, covered with elaborately embroidered altar cloths, was set up as the focus of the square. The Suffragan Bishop of Headcorn, making an ecclesiastical tour of the Front to elevate the troops' spiritual substance, began to intone the service of Commination:

Brethren, in the Primitive Church there was a godly discipline, that, at the beginning of Lent, such persons as stood convicted of notorious sin were put to open penance . . .

Snaky Lucas thought, there *was* a fish in that pond, and I got him. Showed them youngsters . . . have to think about a woman for young Jessop. He had his eye on one: that plump woman who ran the baker's shop at the end of the village. An old sweat in D had told him she'd take a man upstairs for two francs . . . she was about forty, a bit old for Jessop, but that was better than some jumpy, little slut who'd scream bloody murder, her never having had anything bigger than her own finger up her slit.

The Bishop's surplice glistened in the sleet, his bared white hair was pearled with it, and it mantled the shoulder of his gold silk stole. His voice was deep and strong:

Cursed is he that curseth his father or mother

Amen the soldiers mumbled. *Amen,* Quentin Rowland cried in a loud clear voice.

Cursed is he that removeth his neighbor's landmark

Good God, Archie Campbell thought, the Church of England is incredible. Did the men really deserve this, just because someone had stolen a few chickens? And were they really likely to be removing their neighbor's landmark at this time and place in history? But the C.O. had asked for them to have the curses laid on them: they knew why, and probably approved.

Cursed is he that perverts the judgment of the stranger,
the fatherless and the widow
Amen.
Cursed is he that smiteth his neighbor secretly
Amen.

But what about smiting him openly without guile, with high explosives, incendiary bullets, poisonous gas, Archie thought?

Cursed is he that lieth with his neighbor's wife
Amen.

Archie glanced covertly at the profile of his C.O., Fiona's husband. The delights of Fiona's body, the passions of her female parts enfolding him were well remembered but he could no more make love to her, ever again, than he could fly. The ridiculous words of the old-fashioned, out-of-date commination service had suddenly stuck a knife under his ribs.

Cursed is he that taketh reward to slay the innocent
Amen.
Cursed is he that putteth his trust in man, and taketh
man for his defense, and in his heart goeth from the Lord
Amen.

Lucas cocked an ear. He'd been half listening. The old bugger had a good voice, good enough to be a sergeant major. Hadn't got *him* with any of those curses yet . . . Pa and Ma dead; never thought to slay a kid; bazaar whores weren't no one's neighbour's wives . . .

Cursed are the unmerciful, fornicators, and adulterers, covetous persons, idolaters, slanderers, drunkards, and extortioners.

Amen, Lucas said, with feeling. That was a good last salvo . . . got nearly everyone there, one way or another.

He muttered to Private Jessop, next to him, "See what you're letting yourself in for, young 'un? Still want us to find you a woman?"

Jessop grated his teeth, and, head bent in prayer, muttered, "'Course I fucking do."

*   *   *   *

They were working on two railway sidings outside Hazebrouck, unloading ammunition from a train that had brought it from Le Havre. They were loading it into lorries of the Army Service Corps, which were backed up along the sidings. It was dark and cold, without stars or moon, only gas lights at wide intervals, dimmed against air raids, hissing on tall poles at the limit of the railway's property.

Lucas and Jessop stood in the doorway of a Chemin de Fer du Nord goods wagon, marked like all the others of its type with the legend *Hommes 40 Chevaux 8,* picking up boxes of British small arms ammunition. The two men picked up a box between them, by the rope carrying loops at each end, swung it to the door and out and down, where Fagioletti and Leavey, reaching up, caught it, and swung it into the lorry parked a couple of yards away. At the next wagon Jevons and Brace, Quick and another soldier were working at the same task.

255

Corporals and lance-corporals were in the work gangs, sergeants supervised. Lieutenant Colonel Quentin Rowland stood near the middle of the siding with the Regimental Sergeant Major and a captain of the Army Service Corps. Quentin said, "What make are these lorries? Never seen anything like them before . . ."

The A.S.C. captain said, "They're J.M.C., sir—Jupiter Motor Company—American engines, the rest made in England and all assembled at Hedlington."

Oh, Quentin thought, so that's what Richard and the Yanks had designed. The machines looked high and stark and ugly to his eyes; he said so. The A.S.C. officer said, "They'll never win a Concours d'Elégance, sir—but we like them . . . everything get-at-able, all parts interchangeable . . ."

Quentin grunted. Then, "Are you sure you don't have any men for this loading and unloading?" He glared suspiciously at the captian.

"Not one, sir," the young officer said defensively. "Anyone who's not driving is on maintenance, or sleeping."

"My men have to sleep, too," Quentin growled. He hated to see his men working on this kind of fatigue during what was supposed to be a rest period. "These men are trained soldiers," he continued, glowering at the dim shape of the Service Corps captain, "not coolies."

The captain said nervously, "I believe there is an Indian Labour Corps somewhere in France, sir."

"We need more . . . coolies, labourers. . . . Conchies! If we aren't going to shoot them, *they* should be doing this!"

" 'Ark at old Rowley," Jessop muttered as he and Lucas swung out another box of .303.

" 'E's right," Lucas said. "*Hup!*"

"Gawd, I could do with a beer."

"They don't have . . . *hup* . . . no bleeding beer in—*hup*—this bleeding country—*hup* . . ."

Down below Leavey muttered, as he caught the boxes and sent them crashing into the bed of the lorry, "Who's that . . . near the light?"

His partner, Fagioletti, glanced round, then turned back in time to catch the next box of .303—"The Adjutant—Mr Campbell."

"What the 'ell's 'e doing?"

"Drawing . . . drawing *us!* You'll be in the papers, Ikey Mo!"

Lucas said, "Our gallant British Tommies working cheerfully at the common task, to defeat the 'Un . . . One dago waiter, and one Whitechapel Jew tailor."

"We're all fucking Wealds," Ikey Mo Leavey said without heat. "Fucking thirsty, just like Private Fucking Lucas, our hexpert in the French language."

Archie Campbell sat on a stack of railway sleepers near the edge of the circle of light thrown by one of the lights. The working men threw giant weird shadows on the ground and the insides and floors of the wagons they were working in. The violent but graceful movements, the rhythmic thump of the boxes being hurled and stacked in the lorries added something, of rhythm, of a diffused but common sense of purpose.

The C.O. came and glanced over his shoulder. After a moment he said, "That's pretty good, Campbell. Could I have one?"

"Of course, sir. Take any one you like."

"I'd like to frame it," the C.O. said.

"I hope to use these as notes one day, sir, and make oil paintings out of some of them . . . I've been drawing up the line, too."

"So I noticed. Didn't know you were this good, though."

Archie saw that the C.O. had taken a drawing he'd done earlier in the evening when the battalion had just started working, against a background of an old engine under steam, its crew leaning out of the cab and staring.

The labour continued. At midnight the battalion broke off for tea and biscuits, served at the siding by their own cooks, come down with the cook wagons from Eecke. Then they took an hour's rest, the men catnapping where they could, lying in the coal dust and clinker of the siding. Then work began again, this time to transfer ammunition for the 18-pounders of the field artillery. Shells for these guns were "fixed," that is the propellant and projectile fixed together and ready, fuzed, only to separate when the gun was fired. The shells came in boxes of four, weighing 150 pounds.

"Cor stone the fucking crows," young Jessop muttered, as he and Lucas lifted the first box of shells. "This'll fucking rupture us."

"Not me," the old soldier said. "Take it easy. Use your legs and back to lift them, not your belly and arms . . . And you don't get to be a man by using nasty words, but by . . . fucking women . . . killing men . . ."

"I killed plenty of men, by High Wood and Bazentan," Jessop said briefly; and in the unearthly light of the gas an innocent observer would not have guessed that he was barely seventeen—the lines of fear and triumph were etched into his face, the eyes narrowed, even in the dim interior of the wagon, the corners of the mouth hard.

"And you'll get to fuck a woman tomorrow . . . Take it easy, man, easy . . . swing slow, steady . . . like that . . . that's better."

Below, Leavey gasped, "These buggers weigh a ton, I swear!"

"Two tons, more like," Fagioletti gasped. "Damn fucking fuckers!" Whatever sort of language his comrades used, Fagioletti would use more, and stronger. From the day of the assault near Mametz he had felt a thawing in these hitherto unknown foreigners, strange soldiers, who were now his countrymen and comrades. He wanted to get closer, and this was surely the way to achieve it.

A voice called from nearby, "Private Fagioletti!"

Fagioletti stiffened—"Sir!" Since his hands were not there to catch that side of the next ammunition box, it swung loose hitting Leavey on the shin with tremendous force. Leavey fell to the ground with a yell. Captain Kellaway appeared round the back of the lorry.

He stooped over Leavey—"Are you all right?"

Leavey staggered to his feet and hopped around—"Don't know yet, sir . . . It hurts like . . . a lot . . . I'll be all right."

"Sit down a bit," Kellaway turned to Fagioletti. "Have some sense, man. You don't salute officers when you're supposed to be catching a box of 18-pounder shells. Which confirms my thought that there are jobs you are better suited for than rifleman in a platoon. I've decided that my batman, Wiley, deserves a stripe, and the C.O. agrees. Would you like to take his place?"

Fagioletti caught his breath. Three, two months ago he would have given his right arm for the job. He knew how to look after an officer. Soon a more senior officer would notice his skill, how smooth and professional was the service in Captain Kellaway's dugout . . . the colonel would have him transferred to be a waiter at the headquarters mess . . . the brigadier general . . . Sir Bailward Shannon-Watson . . . Sir Douglas Haig . . . he'd be wearing a white jacket, walking softly on thick carpets, serving chilled champagne, caviare . . .

The others were looking at him. They were just beginning to accept him, as one of them, a soldier of the Wealds. He had never felt such acceptance in his life before. He said, "Thank you, sir, but if you don't mind, I'd like to stay with the blokes . . . in the platoon."

Kellaway nodded. "I'll find someone else . . . Leavey, go and see Doctor Sholto at once, at the far end there. And don't come back for an hour. Tell the R.S.M. I sent you." He raised his voice—"Sar'nt major!"

"Sah?" another voice answered from up the line of wagons.

"Send a man from the spares to this end. Leavey's been hurt."

He strolled on, appearing and reappearing between the pools of darkness.

Work continued. As the earliest dawn streaked the east, and the guns in the Ypres salient opened up their regular morning thunder, the 1st Battalion, the Weald Light Infantry fell in along the siding and marched out onto the pavé, at the ceremonial step. Almost at once, "March at ease!" Quentin commanded, and lit his pipe. Coming down the road in the opposite direction was what looked like a football crowd, a mob, out of step, wearing all kinds of uniform.

"French, sir," Campbell said.

"Good God!" Quentin said. "No wonder it's taking so long to win the war."

Campbell, marching beside him, hesitated, then said, "They just don't do things the same as we do, sir . . . These men may have served a spell at Verdun."

The French came on at a rapid shamble, the rifles and long needle bayonets a wavering forest above them. As the two columns neared each other, opposite the railway station, the French burst into simultaneous deep-throated song:

> *Il est cocu, le chef de gare,*
> *Il est cocu, le chef de gare!*
> *Il est près d'sa femm' qui vient d'accoucher*
> *Il est près d'sa femm' qui vient d'accoucher*

Quentin began to chuckle—"The station master is a cuckold!" He couldn't understand the rest of the words but those were clear enough and the tune very catchy. The battalions passed, and he and the French major exchanged salutes, smiling. An upper window in the station building flew open and a man's head and shoulders appeared, wearing a red flannel nightgown and tasseled night cap. He was visibly dancing with rage, shaking his fist and screaming, *"Elle est défendue, cette chanson-lá . . . Imbéciles! Cretins! Criminels! . . . Défendue, défendue . . ."*

The Weald Light Infantry took up the song, the tune exact, making noises that sounded more or less like the French words: *Eel ay cockkoo le chef d'garr!*

The station master, for such it was, stared as though he could not believe his eyes and ears . . . British, singing the hated, legally forbidden song! He pulled in the metal shutters and slammed the window down.

*   *   *   *

The field was soft from overnight rain, and it was hard for the men to march well, at any step, let alone at 140 paces a minute. Quentin Rowland, watching the companies march onto their markers, kept his face impassive. They were doing their best; it wasn't good enough.

The battalion formed line of companies in close column of platoons and stood at ease. The fourteen men to receive decorations were standing in a row, facing Quentin, ten paces in front of the front rank of C Company. He raised a hand, and Campbell stepped out from behind him, walked forward, then mimicked the action of climbing out of a car . . . have to have some fresh brushwood put down there tomorrow early, or the general's car might get stuck in the mud. Lieutenant General Sir Bailward Shannon-Watson, K.C.B., C.M.G., D.S.O. would not be pleased.

Quentin bellowed, "Weald Light Infantry . . . general salute! Prese—eeent *arms!*"

The battalion sprang to attention and jerked the rifles to the present in two motions, the right heels kicking back behind the left as the left hands slapped the rifle slings.

"Order arms!"

Campbell began to walk down the front line as in a formal inspection, Quentin following him, sword drawn and upright. He had had all officers' swords dug out of the 2nd line transport, and insisted that officers should wear them for all drill parades in this period out of the line. It was good for morale, and it emphasized what some of the New Army officers were inclined to forget or gloss over—that they *were* officers, with separate responsibilities and lives from the men's.

He glanced at the men as he passed . . . not bad, considering. "Dirty cap badge!" he snapped. "Take his name."

"Gottim, sir!"

Quentin continued—"Dirty boots . . . that man's safety catch is off . . . sight not down, there . . . he didn't shave properly . . . that man has a packet of Woodbines and a box of matches under his helmet, Captain Kellaway."

Kellaway stared, "Private Lucas, sir? But . . ."

"Take your helmet off," Quentin snapped. Lucas, wooden-faced, lifted his steel helmet six inches straight up into the air, revealing a packet of Woodbine cigarettes, and a box of lucifers resting on the flat, close-cropped hair of his head.

Kellaway's jaw dropped and Quentin walked on behind Campbell, keeping his face straight. Lucas had been in his platoon in '06; he always carried his fags there.

The inspection ended. Quentin and Campbell returned to their places. Quentin called—"Company commanders!"

When they had all doubled out, with the battalion second-in-command, and stood in a row before him, swords vertical in their right hands, Quentin said, "We'll do it again. And this time the march-on must be better. The general won't be here to see it . . . but I will."

*　　*　　*　　*

"Now listen," Lucas said, "'er name is Fonsard."

"I can't get my tongue round that Frog stuff," young Jessop said. They were sitting in the back room of an *estaminet,* one of the four

260

in Eecke, drinking van blong. It was six o'clock in the evening, dark outside, no lamps in the street, all the house windows covered with brown paper outside and dark curtains inside. The place was full of soldiers, and thick with tobacco smoke from cigarettes and pipes.

"Dago and I'll go with you," Lucas said. "We walk in and Dago says, what he has to say."

Fagioletti said, *"Madame, voulez-vous coucher avec nous*—and we all put down our two francs. You sure that's right, Snaky?"

Lucas nodded—"I talked with Lakri Woods in D. We put the money down while you're talking, an' you know what that does to a Frog . . . And that's enough of that van blong, Jessop. You can drink a lot of van blong, or you can fuck Madame Fawnsar, but you can't do both . . . Then you go upstairs with her. You know what to do?"

Jessop said, "'Course I know what to do!"

"Well, it just comes natural," Lucas said; but in himself, looking at the boy, he wondered. The woman was a bloody Frog whore, and she'd just want her money and get onto the next man. That was a bloody shame, for Jessop, when you came to think of it. Couldn't be helped.

"Time to go," he said.

"I've got to piss," Jessop said. He went out of the back door to urinate on the pile of manure in the yard, as everyone else did.

Lucas leaned over to Fagioletti—"Listen, Dago, you tell the woman not to hurry Jessop, see? It's a 'orrible thing for a man if he can't get it up, especially the first time. Then he thinks he never will. There was a bloke in B Company in 'Pindi with me, near as young as Jessop, who put his rifle muzzle in his mouth and his big toe on the trigger because of that . . . blew his brains all over the barrack room wall, and we had to clean them off. Don't want that to 'appen 'ere, do we?"

Fagioletti swelled. Snaky Lucas, one of the oldest soldiers in the battalion, was engaging his, Niccolo Fagioletti's help, in a matter affecting a soldier of the battalion, his battalion. "I'll tell 'er," he said, "though I don't know the French for hurry . . . yes, I do too— *dépéchez-vous . . . non dépéchez-vous.*"

They rose from the table as Jessop came back in. The bill was paid and they went out into the darkness. The bakery door was shut. The three soldiers opened it and walked into the light. Madame Fonsard was of medium height, fortyish, with big, sad, blue eyes—a faded northern blonde with work-hardened and cold-chapped hands. She smiled tiredly at them—*"Bon soir, messieurs. Que voulez-vous?"*

Fagioletti stepped half a pace forward and took out two francs and put them on the counter. Lucas and Jessop followed suit. Fagioletti said, *"Madame, voulez-vous coucher avec nous?"*

The woman's smile faded. She looked at the door, hesitated, and said, *"J'ai peur de la police . . .* your regiment polis."

"Tell her I know the Provost Corp," Lucas said. "Spoke to him at dinner. All fixed."

Fagioletti translated as best he could. Madame went to the door without a word, closed and bolted it, and said, *"Qui vient le premier?"*

Fagioletti pushed Jessop forward, muttering, *"C'est la première femme pour lui, madame . . . non dépéchez-vous."*

"No 'urry?" she said, the smile half-reappearing. She looked at Jessop and took his hand, "Come wiz me."

They listened as the clump of Jessop's boots and the pad of the woman's soft slippers faded up the stairs. Lucas beckoned and pointed upstairs—"Boots off!" he hissed. Quickly they took off their boots, and, holding them in their hands, crept upstairs. Two stairs creaked but no one came out of the rooms at the top. They heard faint voices from the room on the right, and Fagioletti stooped to the keyhole. Lucas bent close.

"She's undressing," he said.

"What color's her bush?"

"Wait a minute . . . dark brown."

"What's he doing?"

"Taking off his shirt . . . trousers . . . prick's limp as a piece a cooked macaroni . . . she's lying back on the bed . . . putting up her legs."

"Bloody 'ore!" Lucas whispered furiously. "We told the bitch to go slow! First sight of one of them things between 'er legs can frighten a boy out of his wits . . . looks as if it's a bloody hairy spider going to eat your prick. I've a good mind to go in and . . ."

"Hsssh! Wait . . . Jessop's crying. He's sitting on the bed . . . I can see his shoulders shaking . . . She's sitting up now. She's stroking his head."

"Never had a two bob whore stroke *my* head! Let me see!" Lucas bent, looked and leaned away. "My God, she is! He's resting his head on her tits . . . she's stroking his cheek . . . kissing him on the lips . . . putting his hand on her bush . . . very gentle . . ." He pulled away from the keyhole and stared at Fagioletti. "She's crying, Dago."

He bent to look again. This time he stayed a long time. The boy was growing a full, proud erection. The woman was pressing her wet face to his cheeks, sighing, affectionate, kind. Lucas stood away and up. "She's not a two-bob whore," he said. "She's a widow . . . twice, Lakri said. Come on downstairs, Dago. When Jessop comes down we'll tell him we've changed our minds, and he can have our turns."

"And our money, to pay for it?" Fagioletti said anxiously. He didn't want to offend Lucas; but he needed those two francs.

"She won't take any money," Lucas said.

"Can't be French," Fagioletti said.

Lucas said, "And we don't really want her, do we? You got an old woman back home? Save it up for her. Let Madame Fawnsar turn our brave boy into a fine upright British soldier. A lot of other women will be grateful to her, if he doesn't get his balls blown off first. C'mon, let's go and play Housey-housey."

*   *   *   *

Company Quartermaster Sergeant Spencer, of C, was calling the numbers, and this card he was calling Regimental House: that is, when the number he had to call was "One" he didn't call the usual "Kelly's Eye, number one," but "Pontius Pilate's Bodyguard"—the nickname of the Royal Scots, the 1st Foot of the British Line. He never called the actual number out at all; if you didn't know the numbers, nicknames, and connected anecdotes of every regiment in the Army, you were never able to fill in your card. Lucas had undertaken to teach Fagioletti what he knew, for a consideration—a packet of Woodbines every day for the next seven days.

"The other Minden Light Infantry," Spencer called. "The Chowkidars . . ."

"God, what's them?" Fagioletti muttered.

"Fifty-one—King's Own Yorkshire Light Infantry: they was at Minden with us . . . Forty-two, the Black Watch—Chowkidar's Hindustani for a watchman."

". . . Right in front of the Red Marines . . . they marched away and left the girls in a family way . . ."

"Forty-nine, Royal Berks," Lucas said, "the Marines march between them and the Scruffy Half Hundredth, Royal West Kents, when they're on parade with the Army . . . Ninety-five, the Rifle Brigade's old number, ain't got one at all now, that's their regimental march . . ."

"Silver Wreath . . . The Back Badge . . . Die Hards . . ."

"Twenty-four, South Wales Borderers, they have a silver wreath hung on their King's Colour, something to do with the Zulus . . . Twenty-eight, Gloucesters, fought the Frogs back to back somewhere . . . Fifty-seven, Middlesex, what their colonel said to them at Albuera . . we was there, too . . ."

Spencer droned on; the bent soldiers scribbled and listened, listened and scribbled. "I'll never remember all this," Fagioletti groaned. "How do you learn it?"

"What else is there to do spending bloody hours in wet canteens in Aldershot, bazaar rum shops in Calcutta, red 'ot barrack rooms in Khartoum? You told me 'ow you used to learn customers when you was a waiter—name and face and family and everything? Well, you do this the same way."

I will, one day, Fagioletti muttered to himself, through gritted teeth. At the moment though, Spencer might as well be speaking Dutch or Hottentot.

A triumphant yell arose from a corner of the room, by a window—"House!"

Lucas looked round—"Hatfield, in A. Nineteen years, he's got in . . . Wonder 'ow young Jessop's getting on . . . 'Ere, get us another card. Spencer'll call this straight."

Fagioletti went up to buy a card for the next call, thinking, even "straight" isn't all that straight in the Army; for "11" was "Ladies legs," and "66" was "clickety-click" and many other numbers were defined by cockney allusions or rhyming slang.

*   *   *   *

Cyril Jessop awoke in Madame Fonsard's arms at midnight, to an unearthly rumble and rattle and roar in the street. They jumped out and went together to the window, and stood, arms wrapped round each other, watching. One after another in the damp moonlight twenty monstrous metal beasts, grinding forward on wide caterpillar tracks, guns or machine guns sticking out of their flanks, engines roaring and coughing blue smoke rumbled through eastward. Every house trembled, every window rattled, every man, woman and child, awakened, rushed to windows and doors, and watched in awe and deep-seated fear that could not be assuaged by the knowledge that these fearful engines were on their side. Friendly was a word no one could say: those things could never be friends to any human being.

"Tanks," Cyril said at last. "We've been hearing of them since September, but I never seen one before . . ."

She pulled him back toward the high bed, *"Viens,* Cyril . . . you are a wonderful boy . . . you stay all night . . . an' come *demain, le lende-main aussi . . ."*

But the bugles blew at 4 a.m., sounding first the Battalion call, then Company Commanders. The Corps, including the battalion, had been ordered up the line, to the Arras front, to start its march at noon.

Daily Telegraph, Saturday, December 2, 1916

EAST AFRICA, Friday

Further particulars have been received relating to operations since October 19 between Iringa and Ngominji (thirty-two miles south-

west of Iringa), and in the vicinity of Lupembe and the Ruhudje River.

On the date mentioned above the strong German force, under the command of Major General Wahle, dislodged from Tabora by the advance of British and Belgian columns from north, west, and southwest, came into contact with the British troops at and south of Iringa . . . Severe fighting ensued at several points of contact. The enemy attempts to break through near Neu Iringa were repulsed and on October 30 the British columns on the Ruhudje River gained a conspicuous success, driving the enemy opposed to them over the river, with the loss of over 200 killed or wounded, 82 prisoners and a quantity of arms and materiel . . . Meantime the main body of the western German force divided into two parties, one of which proceeded to invest the British post at Lupembe. This post, held by native troops less than half the strength of the attacking German column, maintained itself for six days when (on Nov. 18) the investing force was caught between converging British columns and driven northward, abandoning a field gun. The remainder of the main German force was isolated in Hembuke Mission Station (68 miles N.E. of Neu Langenburg) where it was forced to surrender on November 26, to the number of 7 officers, 47 other Europeans, and 449 seasoned and fully trained native soldiers . . .

During the period October 19 to November 23 alone, 71 German Europeans and 370 native soldiers were killed and buried by our columns or otherwise accounted for . . . The remnants of General Wahle's force having lost the bulk of its artillery and machine guns, and suffered casualties probably amounting to over 50 percent of its original strength, is making eastward for Mahenge.

Tabora? Ngominji? Lupembe? This was like an Alice-in-Wonderland geography lesson. In the headlines of the past weeks he had read such headings as ROUMANIAN GOVERNMENT LEAVES BUCHAREST FOR JASSY . . . BRITISH NAVAL PLANES DROP BOMBS ON DILLINGEN . . . ORSOVA AND TURNU-SEVERIN LOST WITH ALL WALLACHIA . . . ALLIED TROOPS TAKE DOBROMIR . . . KUT EL AMARA . . . ERZERUM . . . KIONGA . . . JEDDA . . . BIARAMULO . . . GORIZIA . . . MONASTIR . . . but where *were* Jassy, Turnu-Severin, Biaramulo and the rest of them? Where *were* those other places whose names had been burned into the conscience and consciousness of all Englishmen these past five months . . Butte d'Arlencourt, Mametz, Contalmaison, Fricourt, Bazentin le Petit, Les Boeufs? Perhaps they existed only for the time and place that they had been fought in and over, as, some philosophers believed, objects existed only when observed.

1915 had been the year of disappointment. 1916 looked like being the year of blood. At the end of 1915 there had been a general feeling in Britain that the commanders in France did not know their business.

265

The feeling was probably correct, and Field Marshal French had gone. Now there was agreement that the trouble lay deeper, and was more universal. If progress was to be made against an enemy as powerful as Germany, it was the upper ranks of the country—the direction of the war—that must be examined, and if necessary taken to pieces and re-assembled, better—with new parts, new ideas, new motive power, and above all, new policies.

House of Commons, London: Thursday, November 30, 1916

18 The House was in committee, the Chairman of Ways and Means in the chair, the great silver Mace gleaming under the table. The voice of the Honourable Member for Bury droned on:

May I ask whether it would not be for the convenience of the Committee if we were to adopt the Government Amendments *en bloc*, then recommit the Bill, and work upon it from the White Paper?

The house was half empty. Harry Rowland, seated well back on the Government benches, stifled a yawn. It wasn't an exciting process, but the business of the country could not always be like a battle or a mass fencing match—such as the debate on the 8th: the Great Palm Kernel debate, they were already calling it in the gutter press. He was glad that it could not be so. He had only been a Member for a year, but he recognized that the Commons was like a good club, where bitter political enemies flayed each other on the floor of this holy chamber, then shared roast beef and a glass of wine in the House's dining room.

That debate of the 8th was Carson's doing . . . and Carson's also the decision to press it to a division after Bonar Law had warned him that the government would consider it a vote of confidence; and a narrow squeak it had been, with only 73 Conservatives voting for the Coalition government—of which they were a part—out of 286 in the House. That debate, and the division, had aroused intense feelings far beyond the House. It might have been some foreign country, not England, so bitter were the expressions being used inside and outside Parliament.

The honourable and gallant member for Sunderland, Colonel Sir H. Greenwood, was on his feet:

. . . it must have a Minister who does not want any advice other than he can get from his own officials, and who is prepared to come to this House, and face the fire with his own decisions, and, as the hon. Member has just said, take the gallows if he fails and a peerage, possibly, if he succeeds. (Laughter)
A voice: A peerage if he fails! (Renewed laughter)

The plain fact was, Harry thought, that a sharp split had developed in the Cabinet, and in the country, which transcended party affiliations. The split was over the war, and its conduct. The battle was being waged not only in this Palace of Westminster, but in every private house, club, and pub in the Kingdom: and it had been brought about through the machinations of Alfred Harmsworth, Lord Northcliffe, the owner of the biggest newspaper chain in the world—the Amalgamated Press. Northcliffe thought that the war was being waged unskillfully, weakly, and without determination. Many parliamentarians agreed with him, notably Sir Edward Carson, the Ulster fire-eater; Winston Churchill, another fire-eater; and even David Lloyd George, the Minister of War since Kitchener's death.

Dr Macnamara said that in view of the feeling of the House that there should be a Pensions Minister, the Admiralty felt bound to withdraw its request for exclusion. It accepted, without reserve, the full authority and control of the new Minister . . .
The amendment was therefore withdrawn. The clause, as amended, was agreed to.

The clock above the Chair indicated a quarter to nine in the evening. Harry's stomach was rumbling ominously. He rose, bowed to the Chairman, and left the Chamber.
In the House dining room he sat down at a small table by himself. A waiter glided up at once and he ordered a pair of lamb chops with vegetables, and a half bottle of Beaujolais. When the food was brought, and he began to eat, a shadow fell across his plate and he looked up. Winston Churchill was standing beside him, beaming down, a glass of brandy in hand. He said, "Did I ever tell you I met your son, when I was in exile in France, Rowland?"
"Quentin," Harry said. "He did mention in a letter that he had met you." He waited. It was obvious that Churchill was paying attention to him, an insignificant backbencher, because every vote would count in the coming struggle for power. Like most conservative-thinking

people, of all parties, he had felt a deep distrust for Churchill, but this war had changed many things, including one's point of view. If Churchill had mismanaged the Dardanelles expedition—which no one could yet say for certain—he had certainly shown an offensive spirit; and he had courage, brains, and determination, which was much more than one could say of most politicians.

Churchill said, "Not long afterward, my battalion was disbanded—lack of manpower—and I found myself once more in these halls of discord . . . Mind if I join you for a few moments?"

Harry gestured to the other chair—"If you don't mind my eating. These chops are excellent, but there's nothing worse than congealed lamb fat."

"Mind if I light up?" Harry shook his head, his mouth full. Churchill opened his cigar case and selected a long, fat Havana. As he lit and began to draw on the cigar he said, "I suppose you know that affairs here will come to a head at any moment?"

Harry said cautiously, "What affairs, Churchill?"

"In the government . . . regarding the Prime Minister's position . . . It's been a bad year for the country. Jutland . . . it was a strategic victory, all right, but Jellicoe didn't destroy the German fleet and that was what the country was expecting. The Somme . . . do you know what the total casualty figures were, from July 1st to November 1st, when Haig declared the offensive ended? Four hundred and fifty thousand! The people are appalled. You know how deep and mournful an impression those casualty lists have on one—those endless columns of fine black print, the realization that each of those names, packed like sardines on the page, represents someone's father, brother, lover, husband. It would be different if we could show some great, decisive result. We would accept the losses then. We could raise our heads, and let our tears crown their triumph . . . But what in fact do we have to show? A few square miles of scarred and poisoned earth!"

Harry said slowly, "Yours is one point of view. I suppose you think Asquith should go. Northcliffe certainly does."

"For purely patriotic reasons," Churchill interjected.

"Perhaps . . . But I am not sure that I can accept the vicious attacks that his newspapers have made on the Prime Minister over the Somme offensive, and other matters connected with running the war."

Churchill said, "Since Northcliffe owns the *Times,* with its great authority, and the *Daily Mail* with its enormous circulation, he is a very formidable enemy . . . Yet Mr Asquith does have two powerful weapons at his disposal, which I and others have long been urging him to use. The first is the secret session of the House. Then Members could learn the truth of affairs, instead of gleaning what they can from, on the one hand, the jejune communiqués of the generals and admirals, and on the other, the insidious and hostile suggestions of Lord Northcliffe . . . but Mr Asquith will not hear of it. Why, I do not know."

He drew deep on his cigar, and swallowed some brandy with evident satisfaction. Harry said, "And the other weapon?"

Churchill said, "He has the power to requisition a newspaper—any newspaper—and turn it into the official mouthpiece of the government, the State Monitor, if you will. He could seize the *Times* for that purpose tomorrow, and so strike that weapon from Northcliffe's hands. But I fear, sir, though Mr Asquith has been my friend and colleague for a long time, that his metal is not tempered for war. He is a man of peace."

And you are not, Harry thought to himself: you, and Carson, the man calling for open rebellion in Ulster, and Lloyd George, who had taken on the whole House of Lords, and beaten them. He said, "About the Somme . . . isn't it true that the French . . . ?"

"Ah, Rowland, I know what you are going to say," Churchill cried, stabbing the air with his cigar—"that we had to save the French from disaster by attracting German forces away from Verdun. That is true, as a strategic fact . . . but did it need to be done by *these* means, which amounted to wholesale slaughter of *our* men rather than theirs? Sixty thousand men lost on the first day! Figures that stagger the mind, chill the soul!"

Harry swallowed the last of his meat and, wiping his mouth, said, "I suppose Haig could find no better way."

"And we can find no better general, apparently," Churchill said, suddenly gloomy. "But we must! Rowland, it is the soldiers we have to think of, and they are now no more than the expression in uniform of the people of these islands . . . they have grudged no sacrifice, however unfruitful, and shrunk from no ordeal, however destructive . . . struggling forward through the mire and filth of the trenches across the corpse-strewn crater fields amid the flaring, crashing, blasting barrages and murderous machine-gun fire, conscious of their race, proud of their cause, they seized the most formidable soldiery in Europe by the throat, and slew them, and hurled them unceasingly backward . . . No attack, however forlorn, however fatal, found them without ardour. No slaughter, however devastating, prevented them from returning to the charge. No physical conditions however severe deprived their commanders of their obedience and loyalty. They were unconquerable, except by death—which they have conquered. They have set up a monument of native virtue which will command the wonder, the reverence, and the gratitude of our island people as long as we endure as a nation among men."

Harry, staring mesmerized into Churchill's face, so close, saw tears welling in the other's eyes; and as a tear ran down his own cheek and splashed onto his plate, he realized that he too was weeping.

Churchill's voice was hoarse, "Rowland, we must not let those men down. The conduct of the war must be put into other, stronger, more ruthless hands. We have no higher duty, no stronger loyalty, than to put control of the war into the hands of those who will bring victory. May we count on your support?"

Harry thought, he means, will I stab Asquith, my leader, in the back, if I am asked to by the conspirators—Carson, Lloyd George, Churchill himself?

He said, "I don't know, Churchill."

"Think, Rowland!" Churchill said, getting up, waving the cigar. "Think of the consequences if this nation loses the war, through inept direction . . . Think." He nodded and walked away between the tables, pausing to mutter a word here, pat a shoulder there . . . mostly backbenchers, Harry noted. The offensive was under way.

*   *   *   *

Alfred Charles William Harmsworth, first Baron Northcliffe of the Isle of Thanet, had a heavy face with a big nose, high cheekbones, bags under his eyes, and a wide cruel mouth—a strong face. He was sitting at the head of the long dining room table in his house in St James's Place. Eleven Members of Parliament sat at the table with him—seven Liberals, of the Prime Minister's party; and four Conservatives, unwilling allies in the Coalition Government. All four Conservatives had voted against the government in the Great Palm Kernel debate. The table had been cleared of everything but the cut glass decanters of port, madeira, and sherry. A cigar box, clipper, and lighter in the shape of a flaming grenade were being passed round from hand to hand. The servants who had attended the lavish dinner had left the room. The Members and the Press lord were alone.

Northcliffe was expansive—hands waving or thumping the table—pausing now and then to sip his port: "We're going to form a Committee to run the war . . . Lloyd George, Bonar Law, and Carson . . . Asquith can stay as Prime Minister—but he'll have nothing to do with controlling the war. The Committee will do that."

A Member on Harry's right, a man he didn't ever remember seeing before, said, "What will the P.M. have to do, then?"

Northcliffe waved a hand—"Supervision of political affairs . . . general control over the Committee, unless they outvote him."

271

The Member shook his head: he was tall and bald, and sounded like a lawyer—"I don't see how Asquith can accept it. If the Committee is to run the war without his real control, then he is Prime Minister in name only. For of course all wars are political as well as military."

Northcliffe's baggy eyes wandered over the speaker. He said, "You have given me the clue, the answer to our problem. Bonar Law tells me that in his opinion Asquith will accept the Committee in principle, but make it clear that he must exercise control . . . which can mean anything he chooses to make it mean. That is what we do not want . . . it would be fatal for the country. Perhaps we need a forceful leader in the *Times,* accepting the Committee ideas as the right one, since of course it means that the Prime Minister has, quite properly, been deprived of all control of the conduct of the war . . ."

Another M.P. broke in, "Asquith will take umbrage, and refuse to accept the Committee."

Northcliffe smiled wickedly, "Any man with a spark of self respect would do so."

"And then you will be in a position to bring the rebellion into the open?"

Northcliffe nodded and poured himself another glass of port. He said, "If we are to topple Asquith—and if we don't we shall lose the war, I insist you understand that—we must not make out the recent great offensive on the Somme to be more of a victory than it was. I have given orders to all correspondents and writers for my papers—and of course the leader writers above all—that the Army's casualties shall receive more notice than its advances, though the latter are not to be denied . . . *if* they really occurred. The people must not be allowed to believe that Asquith has, in any sense, however remote, been the architect of a great victory in France."

Harry felt unhappy. He stared at Northcliffe, who was now animatedly talking to the M.P. opposite him. What did that mean—take more notice of casualties than advances? In plain fact it meant manipulating the news for a political purpose . . . but was that any different from manipulating it for a national purpose, as had certainly been done early in the war . . . to influence American opinion, to prevent disheartenment, to deny the enemy useful information?

When Northcliffe looked up from his conversation, Harry said, "Don't we risk causing the Army to lose heart that way?"

Northcliffe smiled winningly, "I agree with you, Rowland, but what I am advocating is the Army's own policy! Charteris told me and Sir Douglas emphasized it, the last time I was over at G.H.Q.—that they don't want optimistic or favorable reports published. If they are, the people will think everything is going well, the Army has everything it needs. But the Army wants to paint itself as always lacking for essentials, especially men, machine guns, shells, and now the new machines, the tanks . . ."

"That is better than the early days," another M.P. said, "when you knew—or soon learned from men coming back on leave—that the official communiqués were much too rosy, if not complete lies."

Northcliffe said, "That hasn't ended. Asquith has been labeling every little advance a great victory . . . We must break up soon, gentlemen. I am returning to France the day after tomorrow, and I hope that I—I hope that *England*—may count on your support when the time comes." He rose, dramatically raising his glass—"I give you a toast . . ."

The Members of Parliament rose, looking at each other. Northcliffe was very emotional, a little mad, Harry thought. What did the French call it? *Folie de la grandeur?*

"I give you a toast . . . To a new Prime Minister, now . . . and Victory, in 1917!"

They drank, muttering words under their breaths; but the only word that Harry thought had been spoken by everyone was "victory." He pulled out his watch and peered at the face. Ten thirty—just time to catch the last train to Hedlington. Tomorrow he'd start digging into what his constituents thought about Asquith and the conduct of the war.

*   *   *   *

As Wright helped him down from the big car, Harry bundled himself deeper into his overcoat against the raw buffet of the wind whirling down Jervis Street. "Thank you, Wright," he said, "I won't be long."

"Very good, sir," the old chauffeur said, touching his cap. He was bent with rheumatism, Harry noted; and said, "Get back in the car. Keep warm," and turned to cross the pavement toward Number 85. The door opened as he reached for the knocker, and Bob Stratton stood inside, Jane at his shoulder.

"We saw the car, through the curtains," Jane said. "Come in, Mr Harry. Let me take your coat . . . there. How's Miss Alice? And I hear Mr Charles is home on leave."

"Boy is a captain now," Harry said proudly. "He's been at High Staining with his father and mother for the last four days, but he's coming up to have dinner and spend the night with us at Laburnum Lodge tonight."

He followed Bob into the front parlour, where he was surprised to see Fred Stratton, in lieutenant's uniform, standing by the centre table. "Fred's home on leave, too," Jane said from behind him.

"Good evening, Mr Rowland," Fred said.

"Nice to see you safe and sound," Harry said. It was cold and correct here in the front parlour, the heavy curtains drawn against the November damp, the aspidistra wilting on the centre table on its doily, the framed photograph of Bob and Jane's wedding (they looked like stuffed dummies), the photographs of the children at their weddings on the tallboy against one wall, a sickly lithograph of Jesus walking on the water opposite.

Fred looked well, more sure of himself, less surly; Jane's hands and knuckles were in a terrible state with the arthritis, and her back stooped from rheumatism; Bob was looking older, but well . . . Harry wished he could ask for his overcoat back, but Jane might be insulted. He'd better get to business right away. He said, "I sent Judith round with the note because I wanted to have your opinion on a very important matter, Bob. And I'm glad you're here too, Fred . . . The question is, do you think the present government, under Mr Asquith, is conducting the war as well as it should be, or could be?"

He waited, thinking that Bob Stratton always looked like a stranger in his own home, and much more vulnerable than in his "real" life at the plant, for here he was not wearing his bowler hat. At last Bob said, "I don't rightly know, Mr Harry . . . but we're losing an awful lot of men, and not getting any nearer Berlin, as far as I can see. There isn't a week passes without one or two of the women at the factory coming to work with black armbands . . . or I find them crying at the benches . . . Of course, the censors out there read the soldiers' letters and take out anything the generals don't want us to know about . . . but men come back on leave, and no one can stop them talking then . . . Perhaps it's the generals that want sacking, not Mr Asquith."

"That's what a lot of us think," Fred cut in. "The generals and the brass hats—the staff."

Harry said, "But in the last resort, no one can sack the generals—the top ones—except Mr Asquith."

Bob said, "I suppose that puts it back in his lap . . . Then there was that battle when we lost so many ships, and didn't sink all the Germans . . . and Lord Kitchener drowning, that made everyone feel bad."

Harry said, "We can hardly blame the Prime Minister because Lord Kitchener's ship struck a mine."

"No, but I'd feel better if Lord Kitchener was still there in London. Then I'd know the best was being done, but . . ."

Harry looked interrogatively at Fred. Fred said, "They ought to get after Tinker and Hoggin and Maconochie and all those people who make rations . . . Make the French charge us fair for what we have to buy there . . . See that there's some decent places to rest, and good food, when we're out of the line . . . and no fatigues . . . hire niggers for that, so we can rest."

Harry said unhappily, "All those things add up to some incompetence—lack of care for our men . . . but if they were all rectified tomorrow, would we beat the Germans?"

Fred said forcefully, "No, Mr Rowland, because the Germans are bloody good, excuse me, fighting men, and so are their officers, and their generals. They fight hard but they fight fair . . . When we've been up the line for a few weeks, and haven't seen a drop of rum, or a food parcel, or a money order, a lot of the men would just as soon invite the Germans to come over and help us sort out our back areas, and the French, and then we'd all go over and do the same their side."

Harry tried again, asking Jane this time; but the result was the same: nothing definite, a feeling of mismanagement, but none of crisis; no despair or even anger—just unhappiness.

The cold began to work through his thick serge suit, and after thanking them, he left.

*   *   *   *

Bert Gorse opened the door to him, and stood staring, open-mouthed. At length—"Mr Harry!" he gasped. He stood back, recovering from his surprise—"Rachel, our M.P.'s come to see us."

In the cramped room, with the primitive printing press set up in one corner, Rachel Cowan rose to her feet. Harry said, "I know you are of a different political party than mine, and I know that you are both active in the pacifist movement. But you are English, you are my constituents, and I feel I must consult you . . . What do you think of Mr Asquith's conduct of the war?"

Rachel looked at Bert, Bert looked at Rachel. Rachel said, "We think the war must be ended."

"On any terms? Total surrender on our part? Hand over our fleet to Germany? Give up our colonies and empire, accept a German Viceroy here in England?"

"The German people will rise, too."

Harry turned to Bert and said, "You agree with Miss Cowan?"

Bert said, "The war is being used to destroy the power of the unions—the working man's only weapon and defence."

Harry grew angry against his will. "The working men of this country want to win the war just as much as anyone else. And you know very well that one of the first acts of the Germans, if they win, would be to abolish the trade unions altogether."

Bert, seeing Harry Rowland suppressing anger, controlled himself and spoke very carefully. "Mr Rowland," he said, "when working men first stood together here for decent wages, decent terms—you had them hanged, shot, gaoled, sent to Australia. If the Germans win this war, your lot's position would change—*you'd* get hanged and shot and sent off somewhere, and Germans would take your jobs and places. But the working man wouldn't be worse off—they can't hang all of us, and we'd fight them for decent wages, decent laws, decent conditions, fair rewards, just as we'll fight you when the war's over. So, for us, it's going to be the same after the war whoever wins—a fight for the working man's rightful place in power, and his rightful share of the riches he creates . . . so why not stop the war now, when there'll be more of us left to fight the real fight?"

Harry could hardly believe his ears. He stood up slowly, saying, "You are talking treason, Bert. Your own men would lynch you, if they could hear."

"Now, they might," Bert said, "because your lot are still pulling the wool over their eyes, about patriotism and what the Huns'll do . . . but after the war, it'll be different. You'll see, Mr Harry."

*   *   *   *

Harry sat with his two grandsons, Capt. Boy Rowland and 2nd Lieut. Laurence Cate, and Johnny Merritt, at the dining room table. The meal and all its appurtenances had been cleared away. Alice Rowland and Stella Merritt were in the drawing room, for they had left the men to their port.

Each man had a full glass in hand. Boy said, "Uncle Quentin very nearly had me transferred to another battalion, because he was afraid that promoting me would look like nepotism." He held the glass up to the light and exclaimed, "What a marvellous color port is, isn't it, Grandfather?"

Harry noticed that the young man's hand trembled. Boy saw it at the same time, and quickly lowered his hand to rest the glass on the table.

Harry said, "I've had a very interesting letter from Guy—he may be home on leave soon, by the way . . . He has sixteen kills now, not counting captive balloons, and his squadron commander has allowed him to paint his tail fin—the stabilizer, isn't it?—red, so that von Rackow will know him if they meet. Von Rackow's sworn to kill him, but the squadron commander said that Guy would never be out alone, so the distinctive marking might draw von Rackow into a fight at a disadvantage."

Boy said, "Wish our war could be like that . . . Single combat, knights of the air, chivalrous salutes. There's nothing chivalrous about a 9.2-inch howitzer shell."

276

Harry leaned forward. "I'm very glad to see you here, Boy, but I also asked you to dinner for a reason—all of you . . . I'm a Member of Parliament. Ultimately, I and the other M.P.s are responsible for the conduct of this war. Do you think we're doing our job as well as is possible?"

Boy hesitated a long time and Harry said, "We have to learn *somehow,* Boy. I can see why the censorship must include even us, but it does make it very difficult to get the information we need to make the right decisions."

Boy said, "Uncle Quentin would have me shot if he heard me saying it, but . . . I don't think our generals are always as good as they ought to be. They do their best, I suppose, but . . ." He shrugged his shoulders. "The men trust Haig. He doesn't talk much. He tries to unbend but can't . . . He inspected us once when we were in divisional reserve, and stopped in front of one private soldier in my company and stared at him a long time. Finally he snapped, 'Where did you start this war?' And the man stuttered and stammered and finally blurted out, 'Please, sir, *I* didn't start it.' Haig never smiled, just moved on expressionless, and asked another man ten places down how long he'd been in France . . . It's the staff we can't stand. We never see them, so all their plans are based on guesswork, or wishful thinking. Uncle Quentin swears he'll shoot one of them one day . . . Of course, *he* wouldn't, but the adjutant, Archie Campbell, might well do it when he's had a drop or two."

Harry tried to put his question again—"But what do you in the trenches think of Mr Asquith, and the present government?"

"We don't," Boy said. "We're too busy trying to keep alive . . . and move forward. The Germans may be barbarians and baby eaters, Grandfather, but they're good soldiers . . . brave, well trained, well disciplined. They fight like tigers."

"Do you still have shortages of shells? Ammunition? Food? Comforts for the troops?"

Boy said, "There aren't shortages like there used to be in '15— except that all battalions are always under strength. Rations aren't bad, but we can't cook them properly. We soak Army biscuits a day or two—they'll crack a brick otherwise—pour in milk, jam, cook the lot in a sandbag until it's hard and then cut off slices—sandbag and all . . . Comforts—half of what's sent to us is stolen by the people on the lines of communication. And when we go out of the line there's only the *estaminets,* and the French, and the brothels . . ."

Harry said, "I've had a lot of letters from churches, women's organizations, and so on, telling us we must make the Army abolish the brothels. Every M.P. has."

Boy said, "I don't suppose it will make much difference. The

French women will carry on somehow—they make too much money at it. It's necessary, I suppose, but it's so degrading . . . The French overcharge the men for everything. I heard the brigadier general tell the C.O. that the French were charging us—the British Government—for every train that is run on their railways for us— troop trains, ammunition trains, hospital trains—everything. And we're only there trying to help them defend their country. It's a question of whom we hate the most—the French, or our own brass hats."

Harry tried once more, "So you . . . by you I mean the fighting men out there, don't have any particular feeling about Mr Asquith's government?"

Boy considered once more and finally said, "No, Grandfather. They're too far away."

That's no answer, Harry thought; then, a moment later, he thought, but it is. He turned to Johnny Merritt and said, "I haven't seen as much of you recently as I should have, and as I'd like to . . . what do *you* think of the higher conduct of the war here?"

Johnny looked down, collecting his thoughts. He's thinner than he ought to be, Harry thought; and looks tired, and several years older than he is . . . works too hard . . . or perhaps Stella's wearing him out in bed . . . or both . . . Stella had looked beautiful tonight, as always, but somehow remote, and as though not present with the rest of them, not hearing what was said, slow moving in another world of her own.

Johnny said slowly, "I think everything's been done in too *gentlemanly* a way . . . Mr Asquith's a gentleman, but this war isn't a gentleman's sport. Conscription should have been brought in a long time ago—universal conscription, of men, money, industry, capital, labor, land . . . no more pretence of 'business as usual.' How can anything be 'as usual' when you see those casualty lists in the paper every day? I would say that Mr Asquith is the man responsible—who else can be held responsible, but the Prime Minister?—and that he should be made to resign."

"Whom would you like to see in his place?"

"Winston Churchill, or Lloyd George," Johnny said.

"Thank you, Johnny. I value your opinion all the more because, as an American, you see us from outside ourselves . . . Pull the bell for Parrish, will you, Laurence."

Laurence got up and pulled the long velvet rope that hung by the side of the mantelpiece, connected by wire to one of the row of bells on the wall in the servants' hall.

When Parrish came in, Harry said, "You three go and join your aunt in the drawing room. Take the decanter. I want a word with Parrish."

278

When the young men had left, he turned to the old butler—"What do you think of the war, Parrish?"

"Terrible, sir," the butler said sadly. "All those young gentlemen . . ." His voice trailed away. "And thinking that Captain Charles has to go back to it. And Mr Laurence will go too, soon."

Harry said, "Do you think it . . . that our leaders are running it as well as they should?"

"I'm sure I don't know, sir."

"Do you have confidence in Mr Asquith?"

"He's the Prime Minister," Parrish said, "and if the people in Parliament don't think he's doing right, they'll have an election and ask the King to make someone else Prime Minister. I'll do whatever they tell me to do . . . if I can."

Harry said, "Thank you, Parrish."

"Thank you, sir. Good night, sir."

As he entered the drawing room he heard his daughter saying, "Well, gentlemen, I have to get up at dawn tomorrow, so I'll be going to bed."

"She's going bird watching," Laurence said. "Wish I could go with her, but it's a private club, Auntie says."

"Wait a minute," Harry said. "I want to ask you a few questions." He knew how the work at the shell factory exhausted her during the week and said, "It won't be long, and it really is important."

Alice sat back in her chair, putting down her book. Boy refilled his grandfather's port glass. Johnny sat on a sofa holding Stella's hand: Stella appeared to be asleep. Harry said, "I shall have to make some important decisions in the House any day now—important for our survival as a nation—and I am trying to get all the information I need to help me make the right ones. What do *you* think about the conduct of the war?"

Alice fondled the ears of the dachshund lying beside her chair, and said thoughtfully, "I don't think it is being run as well as it can be . . . but who is responsible for that, I don't know."

Boy said, "When a battalion does badly in France, the brigadier general doesn't ask who was at fault—he sacks the C.O."

Harry said, "And Mr Asquith's the C.O. of the country, in that sense?"

Boy said, "I think so."

Alice said, "The women in the factory are mostly ready for a change, as far as I can tell. They're all dead determined to win the war, but when they've had a glass or two of port and lemon in the Moon and Bloomers, they . . ."

"In the *what?*" Harry cried, scandalized.

Alice blushed, "Oh, I am sorry, Father, but that's what all the

279

women call the Star and Garter, and I've just picked it up . . . well, when they've had a drink they cry, and ask why winning has to cost so much. If Mr Asquith has to resign, I don't think there will be any public uproar, certainly not among that class."

Harry drank some port, "But it's so . . . sordid. One gets buttonholed in the corridors of the House . . . rumours are passed from table to table . . . insinuations whispered in the bar . . . And Mr Asquith is an honourable man. How can I desert him for such as Churchill, the self-seeker? Carson, whom many feel is as guilty of treason as Connolly or Casement? Lloyd George, the libertine radical?"

Boy stood up suddenly and took his glass to the fireplace, turning round so that the fire warmed his back—"Excuse me, Grandfather," he said, "but this is another thing I dream of in the trenches—of warming myself at a fire." His face became grim, and suddenly ten years older. The three stars on each shoulder glittered in the overhead light. Like the tunic itself, the white and purple ribbon on its left breast was faded now. He said, "I can't tell you how wonderful the men are, Grandfather, Aunt Alice . . . Oh, they get afraid, we all do . . . they don't achieve everything even they expect to, let alone what the generals and the bloody brass hats—excuse me—think they ought to. Life out there would be impossible for me without my men . . ." His voice broke and he half sobbed: ". . . My men . . . oh, my men . . ." He drew a big khaki handkerchief from his sleeve and blew his nose—"Sorry . . . What I'm trying to say is that they deserve the best we can give them. They'll take anything, endure anything, do anything, till the end . . . but it's up to us to lead them as well as we can, from the Prime Minister down to the newest 2nd Lieutenant."

After a long silence Harry said gently, "Well, Boy, what do you think about Mr Asquith? You must understand that I'm as torn as you must be—as you are, we can see—between determination, pride, and sorrow for what you have to order your men to do, and suffer. I am old and . . . I can't stand it. Please, Boy, please . . . help me!"

Boy said, "I've been home three days now, and I feel that the country is not really engaged to the full in the war. It's like coming to another planet, but it should not be. It should be like going from one part of the nation at war to another . . . a part where there'll be girls, good food, hot baths, warm fires, rest, quiet . . . but also the same sort of feeling there is over there . . . determination, dogged guts, a sense that we're all in it together, and are ready at any moment to give everything we have . . . the present, the future . . . our lives."

*   *   *   *

The blind soldier came to Harry in the night, tapping into the room with his white cane, clear as though illumined by gas lights in the darkness of the bedroom, this slight figure, stooped in hospital blue, the blackened glasses covering both eyes. He stood at the foot of the bed, and to Harry's frozen horror, did just what he had done in the Town Hall the day of Harry's election. He took off the glasses, revealing ulcerated blue-white eyeballs and spoke the same words that he had spoken then: "Do you know what you're doing? At all?"

Harry woke up screaming, his hands in front of his face. Slowly he lowered them. The blind young soldier had gone. It was a dream. Alice came hurrying into his room. "Father! . . . Are you all right?"

He let out his breath in a long sigh. "I had a nightmare."

He lay back. Did he know? At all? He repeated to himself the blind soldier's last words, that time, when the Mayor was blustering at him for his intrusion—"I'm only asking them what they must have been asking themselves, if they cared." Then he had turned again to Harry and repeated that dreadful question, *"Do you?"*

*   *   *   *

On Monday Harry went up to London early, worked on committees till one and then repaired to the House dining room for lunch. Again Churchill came past his table, stopped, sat down without invitation, and said, "Have you heard the news?"

"About Mr Asquith? Yes."

Just as Northcliffe had promised at that dinner, there had been a leader in *The Times* strongly supporting the proposal of a War Committee to run the war—without interference from the Prime Minister.

"He will resign today or tomorrow," Churchill said.

"It's what you wanted," Harry said, a little coldly.

Churchill cried, "My dear Rowland, some of us, who can regard ourselves as friends of both the Prime Minister and Mr Lloyd George, have spent the best part of the last forty-eight hours trying to persuade Mr Asquith that the War Committee would work, with Lloyd George at its head, and himself staying on as Prime Minister—they have different strengths—different, but complementary . . . wheel horse, lead horse."

Harry was not fully appeased. He said sullenly, "What post will you be awarded in any new cabinet?"

Churchill puffed on his cigar, looking at him quizzically through the blue smoke. He said at last, "You are a loyal man, Rowland, and it does you credit."

Harry said, "I have thought—and suffered a great deal in the past few days, and I have made up my mind to support any move to bring

281

Mr Lloyd George to the head of our affairs. But I do not like the way the present position has been brought about."

"Ah, politics is not always played in clean fresh water, especially when one has to swim with such as my Lord Northcliffe . . . But you are wrong about one thing. I shall have no responsibilities in any new government. It will have to rely heavily on the support of certain key conservative figures, in both Houses. Those figures have prepared a manifesto, declaring that a new government can count on their full support . . . on one condition."

He waited, a half smile on his curved plump lips, his expression cherubic. Harry had to ask—"What's that?"

"That neither Lord Northcliffe nor myself shall have any position in it!" Churchill crowed triumphantly. "Au revoir, my friend."

Harry watched him go, still wondering—genius, or charlatan?

* * * *

Andrew Bonar Law, leader of the Conservative Party, sometime First Lord of the Exchequer and Prime Minister of Great Britain, stood in morning coat before his sovereign, who was wearing the uniform of a Field Marshal. The King said, "I suppose you know why I've sent for you?"

"It is rumoured that Mr Asquith has been to the Palace to tender his resignation."

The King said, "He has. Because, he told me, the public interpretation put on the War Committee proposal made his position as Prime Minister untenable. So he turned it down—the War Committee idea . . . and that led to Mr Lloyd George's resignation, as the War Committee was his brainchild."

"That is so, sir."

The King stroked his beard and looked at Bonar Law. He's worried, Bonar Law thought. This is a constitutional crisis, of a sort. In peace time, His Majesty could prorogue parliament and call an election, but that was not to be thought of now, except in the direst emergency, when events might in any case forestall the process.

The King said, "Will you form a Ministry?"

Bonar Law said, "I am sorry, sir, but there is only one possible Prime Minister at this juncture in our affairs."

The King said, "I don't like him . . . a howling demagogue . . . terrible reputation with the ladies . . . well earned, I am assured . . . gloated over the way I had to knuckle down, and promise to create Peers so his damned tax bill could pass . . ."

Bonar Law said slowly, and with all the earnestness he could muster, "Sir, he has boundless energy. He can see affairs in large, even so huge a monster as this war. Alone among us, the people believe that he can control events by sheer force of personality, rather than the other way round. If I may say so, sir, it would be a disaster for the monarchy if, at this moment, you sent for anyone else."

"And for the country, as you see it?" the King said.

"Yes, sir."

The King turned away and up the room, came back. He said, "I'll send for him."

Bonar Law inclined his head an inch in the formal bow given to royalty on such occasions, said, "Thank you, Your Majesty," and backed out of the room. A Private Secretary who had remained silent throughout the interview held the door open for him at the last minute.

The moment the secretary closed the door behind Bonar Law, another door at the opposite end of the room opened, and Queen Mary sailed in, her pale violet gown sweeping the floor, a tall, silk-veiled hat of the same colour on her piled hair, an umbrella also of violet in her hand. A Lady-in-Waiting followed. The Queen said, "Who is it to be, George? Mr Bonar Law or that man?"

"That man," the King said.

The Queen said, "Thank heaven for that. He is the only one possible, now." She turned on the young woman beside her—"Make sure that you never find yourself alone in any room with Mr Lloyd George, Maud. And tell all the other Ladies-in-Waiting."

Maud said, "I think they already know that they must be . . . alert, ma'am, in those circumstances."

The Private Secretary bowed, the Lady-in-Waiting curtsied, and both left the room. The Queen went to the fireplace and hoisted high the back of her skirt to warm her behind through her petticoat, at the fire. The King cried, "Good heavens, Mary, that's . . . indecent!"

"It's freezing in here," his wife snapped. "The whole Palace is freezing."

"I don't think it's too bad," the King said defensively, "and we have to save fuel."

The Queen said, "It's all very well for you men in thick serge, but we women freeze unless we wrap up like mummies, and then you complain because we look like German frumps."

There was a knock at the door. The King waited until the Queen had dropped her skirt back into place, then called, "Come in."

Daily Telegraph, Wednesday, December 13, 1916

PEACE OFFER BY GERMANY

In the Reichstag yesterday the German Chancellor announced that Germany, and her allies, Austro-Hungary, Bulgaria, and Turkey,

had proposed to the hostile Powers to enter into peace negotiations. The step had been taken "conscious of their responsibility before God, before their own nation, and before humanity."

The Quadruple Alliance had accordingly handed to the representatives of the neutral Powers a Note, to be handed to the hostile Powers, proposing that negotiations shall begin "forthwith."

If, in spite of this "offer of peace and reconciliation," the struggle should go on, the four Allied Powers were resolved "to continue it until a victorious end"—but they "solemnly decline every responsibility for this before humanity and history."

Germany and the allies have sent identical Notes to the Pope in the same sense, and asking for the "precious support of the Holy See."

The text of the two notes formed the greater part of the Chancellor's address, which was otherwise mainly concerned with boasts about German victories and economic stability, and contained no statement whatever as to terms of peace.

NO INFORMATION

Reuters' Agency was informed at the Foreign Office last evening that his Majesty's Government had so far heard nothing of the reported desire of the Central Powers to negotiate for peace.

The Press Association says in official circles in London yesterday afternoon absolute reserve was maintained in reference to the Berlin announcement of peace proposals.

. . . it was considered significant that Mr Arthur Henderson, in his speech at Clapham on Monday night, should have deprecated all idea of premature peace. That attitude has, in fact, been declared over and over again by spokesmen of the Entente Powers . . . It is generally felt that no peace proposals are likely to be entertained except on terms which commend themselves to the Allies as likely to ensure the achievement of their minimum demands, viz. that Europe shall be saved from the risk of any recurrence of such happenings as those which have occurred since August 4, 1914.

So here it came, just as he had thought it would and just as that German writer had said it should a few weeks ago. Cate wondered whether the death of the Austrian Emperor Francis Joseph last month, after a reign of sixty-eight years, had helped or hindered the proposal. The old man was generally believed to have worked toward moderating the extreme—sometimes hysterical—positions and pronunciamientos of the Kaiser; so he would probably have been a supporter of the peace initiative. His death had put his grand-nephew

Charles on the thrones of the Dual Monarchy, and however strong a personality he might be—personally, Cate knew nothing about him—it would take him months or years to attain a stature where he could exert much influence on Potsdam. It was also clear that the British Government, indeed all the Entente Powers, were going to regard the German proposal with as much caution as though it were a delicately fused bomb.

Garrod came in and said, "More coffee, sir?"

He shook his head. "No, thanks. I've finished." He stood up, folding the paper. Garrod said, "Begging your pardon, sir, Hilda and Tillie say they want a whole day off every week."

Cate thought, why is she asking me? But of course Margaret wasn't here . . . These domestic problems had been put to him for many, many months now, but still he could not get used to them. He said, "With only me here, I should think that would be all right, wouldn't it?"

Garrod sniffed. She herself had never had even half a day off for the first twenty years of her service. She said, "For the same wages, sir?"

Cate said, "Oh, yes . . . You know, if we don't give them that, we'll lose them both to the factories."

Garrod said, "We don't need them both, really, sir."

Cate said, "I suppose not, but Tillie's been with us a good many years now, and Hilda, well, I feel she's too young to go out into the world alone."

"She's twenty, sir."

"Good heavens, I suppose she is. She was only fifteen when she came to work here . . . I can't believe it was five years ago—before the war."

"Yes, sir . . . Jill's had her puppies, sir, in the kitchen, if you want to see them."

Cate said, "Of course." He followed Garrod along the passage to the kitchen, to find the other two maids crouched beside the dog basket in a corner, with Jack, the male blue roan cocker spaniel, standing to one side looking nonchalant, while Jill lay on her side in the basket, seven tiny blind puppies crawling over her belly seeking her dugs.

Cate looked at the puppies, then at the bitch, who hung her head; then at Garrod, then at Jack. Garrod shook her head discreetly. Jack had good reason to look nonchalant: he had clearly had nothing to do with the puppies' conception. "Naughty girl," Cate said softly, wagging a finger. The maids giggled.

Hedlington, Kent: Tuesday, December 5, 1916

19 Guy Rowland sat with his mother in the drawing room of their big Hedlington flat. "You saw Virginia," she asked listlessly. "How was she?"

"Great," Guy said. "They let me take her out in work hours. She's loving it all, Mummy."

"I suppose their officers, or supervisors, or whatever they call them, at least, are ladies?"

"I believe so, but Virginia doesn't want to become one, though they've suggested it to her."

His mother nodded and looked back into the fire. Guy wondered what she did with herself. With no husband or children at home, housekeeping could not take up much time, especially as she still had Mrs Orr and Ivy, though Ivy was now married—to a soldier in France. She didn't knit, or sew, or paint, just sat, walked, shopped, but everything listlessly.

He said, "I've seen Daddy once since Granny's funeral. I took a day off and went up the line and spent the day with his battalion. Old Sulphuric likes us to do that. He was looking well then, though I don't understand how anyone can stick it there for . . ."

She interrupted, "Why would he do it to me? Why?"

Guy said cautiously, "Who, Mummy? Do what?"

"Archie . . . I told you last Christmas I was in love with another man and was going to leave Daddy—we have had no real marriage for years, nothing in common. I've been very unhappy, you know that."

"Yes, Mummy."

"Then, when you'd left for the R.F.C., I went up to his flat, and

286

he'd gone—vanished . . . I guessed he'd got drunk and joined up. I thought it would be in the Argyll & Sutherland Highlanders—he *is* a Campbell. I telephoned their depot, but got no satisfactory answer." She stared into the fire. "I waited, waited, dying . . . *why* would he not write, at least? Then one day in May I saw him, here in Hedlington. He was walking down High Street, near the South Eastern, in the uniform of a 2nd Lieutenant of the Wealds!"

Guy dared not look at his mother. His father's adjutant was an older man called Archie Campbell, who told him he had been a painter. He must be the man who had been his mother's lover . . .

She said, "When he got a commission he could have applied for any of the Highland regiments. In this war, even the Camerons would have taken him. He *must* have applied for the Wealds. It's too much of a coincidence otherwise, with sixty regiments to choose from, not to mention the gunners, sappers, A.S.C. . . . And now he's Quentin's adjutant! His closest, personal staff officer!"

"He can't have applied for that," Guy said. "Daddy must have chosen him."

She said, "I don't understand any of it . . . I don't understand men. And the war's made them all worse, stranger."

Guy said cautiously, "Do you think Daddy knows, or suspects, that he's the man you wanted to go away to?"

She shook her head, "I never told Quentin his name . . . If he's killed, he'll come back to me . . ."

Guy thought, she means, if Daddy is killed; but what if Campbell is the one who is killed?

* * * *

It came out of the clouds seven thousand feet above Peronne . . . a biplane, two struts each side, big white numeral 16 painted on the fuselage, body green with patches of brown . . . camouflage paint . . . yellow wing tips outside the black cross, spinner and wheels painted yellow . . . an Albatros D II—Werner von Rackow. A trail of black smoke spiralling down the sky behind him marked the funeral course of Guy's last opponent, another D II . . . A learner pilot? No, a woman . . . a girl! He'd killed a girl, blown her head in two with the stream of his machine gun bullets from a hundred feet above and behind . . . Crash! Flames spreading like red blossom down there, like a cancer, over the trenches, the towns, the railway lines, in the fleeting winter sun . . . heavy shells rumbling by . . . von Rackow was circling wide, closing in, but still out of range. He waited. The Pup only had one gun but it could turn inside a D II . . . The hairs on his neck crept and he kicked the Pup into a tight climbing turn. A stream of tracer bullets passed close over his head, and into the fabric of the wings. Two D IIs streaked by below and disappeared into the vast silence, no sound of his own engine, von Rackow had turned sharply and was coming at him, guns flickering. Guy swung inside, tight, tighter, the blood pounding in his head . . . the D II was sliding into his sights now . . . now! His thumb closed on the button . . .

His scream still echoed in the room. Sweat was running down his face, and his pyjamas were soaked. It was dark. He switched on the light and went out. His mother was in the passage, her hands to her cheeks—"Guy, darling! What's . . . ?"

"I'm all right, Mummy," he said, and went into the drawing room, took a bottle of brandy out of the sideboard and drank deep direct from the bottle, then went back to bed, past his mother, and waited, a long time, for sleep to come.

*   *   *   *

Guy sat in Probyn Gorse's cottage while the old man mended rabbit nets at the table and the Woman washed and gutted a rabbit in the sink. "Don't know what's going to happen to us all, the way things are going," Probyn growled. "Squire's had to sell Lower Bohun, so now Shearer don't own it any more than he did before, nor does Squire—the bank does."

"Why did Uncle Christopher have to sell?" Guy asked.

"Get more cash, to keep up the other farms, pay taxes . . . Shearer's going to have to cut down half his hops . . . and he'll be paying the bank more interest on the loan and mortgage than he was paying rent to Squire. What's wrong with being a tenant, tell me that!"

Guy drank some of the beer he had brought from Walstone's smaller pub, the Goat & Compasses, as he passed, riding a hired motor cycle. He said, "Well, the, ah, game preservation must be going well."

"Naow! Too easy!" Probyn snorted. "Rabbits swarming, 'cos there's a shortage of cartridges . . . gamekeepers gone off to the Army . . ." He glanced up, "What are you now, Mister Guy? Captain? Major?"

Guy laughed, "A plain lieutenant."

"See any pheasants out there?"

Guy nodded, "Plenty, but they're very wary with all the noise. The earth rumbles and the trees shake and they don't understand it . . . How's Florinda? That's her stage name, isn't it? Just 'Florinda?' "

"Dunno. Ain't seen her for two, three months."

"Does she write?"

"No. She'll come down one day and tell me what she's been up to."

"Fletcher?"

"In the barracks, down there. Only he's called Whitman now. Don't know when he'll be going to France, but he's rare fed up with them barracks, I can tell you that."

"Have you had any more contacts with Lord Swanwick, or his pheasants?"

Probyn put down the net and looked at Guy. He said earnestly, "Lord Swanwick's fallen on hard times, Mr Guy. His keepers have all gone now, all the old ones. He has one man, don't know a pheasant from a badger, and afraid to go out at night in case he catches cold . . . the birds are going to be very poor next year, 'cos no one knows how to look after them . . . Lord Swanwick's trying to pretend everything's the same—inviting lords and ladies down for a shoot every other weekend . . . still Master of the Hounds, but they're no better than a pack of mongrels now . . . farmers shooting foxes in front of his eyes . . . I'm right sorry for him . . . 'cos it ain't his fault, see? Things are changing too fast . . . too fast for him and too fast for me. I don't like to see women working the ploughs, that I don't. Or driving the baker's vans . . . brewers' drays, even . . . taking tickets at the station . . . and the noise, aeroplanes, motor cars stinking the roads, and frightening the cows out of their milk . . . and sometimes, the earth shaking . . . *the earth!*"

Guy said nothing for a long while, then he said, "Let's hope it's over soon, Probyn."

*   *   *   *

He rode the motor cycle to the front door, swung round with a jab of the brake, and stopped in a sideswiping shower of gravel. The door opened and a disapproving old housemaid appeared, saying sharply, "Now, young man . . ."

A small figure with thick glasses and a jutting thatch of grey eyebrows pushed past her, his hand out—"I never thought I'd welcome the sound of one of those infernal machines . . ."

"It's a . . ." Guy began.

Rudyard Kipling raised a hand, "It's a Triumph Model H—the military model—550 c.c., three-speed Sturmey Archer gearbox, side valve, belt driven, of course . . . What's that leather cylinder on the rear mudguard?"

"There's a spare driving belt in it, sir. The Royal Engineers said they had to have it for their despatch riders."

"Well, come on in, my boy. I know you have to go after lunch, so we mustn't waste time. Let's have a look at you . . . lieutenant . . . D.S.O. . . . M.C., those wings look good . . . Your father must be so proud of you. I suppose he's out there?"

"Yes, sir."

Guy followed Kipling into Bateman's, the famous author's refuge from fame and, since September 1915, from the world. At the end of that month, in the Battle of Loos, Ensign John Kipling of the Irish Guards, a contemporary and friend of Guy's at Wellington, and just past his eighteenth birthday, had been posted as "missing believed killed"; nothing more had been heard of him. He was Rudyard and Carrie Kipling's only son.

Then Kipling took him into the book-lined, paper-strewn study and said, "Tell me, Guy . . . I've been out there, of course, but I am still far from understanding, *feeling* it, as I felt the North West Frontier, and somehow I must learn what John learned. He could have told me."

"He could have tried, sir," Guy said slowly. "But I don't know whether he or I or anyone else can succeed."

Kipling reached out with both hands, "Try, my boy, try . . . Dear God, I must understand, somehow."

*   *   *   *

Guy sat by the fire in his Uncle Tom's flat, thinking. He had had a good breakfast and Jones had just gone; but he had not slept well. Things he had seen haunted him—barefooted, hungry children begging in Piccadilly; and the faces of women mobbing him outside the stage door of His Majesty's, because he was a hero of the R.F.C. They were hungry, not loving . . . He remembered Florinda Gorse, when he was ten; she'd loved him, and showed it in those big green eyes . . . He might go down to Aldershot later this morning, and take Virginia out again. She'd probably be excused duty because of his wings and the ribbon of the D.S.O. That ribbon would accomplish wonders, as he had been finding out ever since he left the squadron.

And from Aldershot he could go over to the Royal Aircraft Establishment at Farnborough and get some mysterious tool that Frank wanted—swore he would never be able to tune the engine of his Pup properly without it . . . Well, how did the other riggers tune theirs then?

Frank had said earnestly, "Ah, they're tuned all right for *them*, Mr Guy . . . as well as they can be without the micrometer . . . but not well enough for you."

He'd laughed, glad that the C.O. hadn't heard that. Major Sugden, like the R.F.C. in general, did not believe in the star or ace system: and nor did Guy. . . . But he was having phenomenal luck; already there was only one pilot in the squadron with more kills. The Germans knew it, and recognized him as an ace, even if the R.F.C., Sulphuric Sugden, and Guy himself refused to.

His eye fell on the name John Rowland in the paper and he started. He was looking at the Letters to the Editor. This one read:

Sir: We have now been at war for twenty-eight months. We have lost two hundred and twenty thousand of our young men, killed. Another one million have suffered wounds. The same is true, in differing proportions and numbers, of France, Germany, Russia, Austria-Hungary, Italy, Turkey, and every other warring nation. Yet what has been achieved? Nothing. The question must now be asked, what do we hope to achieve? The dead—and those yet to be sacrificed—demand to know what they died, or will die, for. In the name of common sense, let all thinking men call upon all governments, including our own, to make a clear and unequivocal statement of their war aims.

Yours etc
John Rowland
High Staining, Walstone, Kent.

Guy put the paper down thoughtfully. Someone had helped Uncle John write that. It was too forceful and direct for him, words did not come that easily to him. The letter made sense, yet he was surprised that the *Telegraph* had published it, for it was saying slow, stop, let's search our minds and find what we really want out of this war, and what the other fellow really wants, then perhaps we can work out a compromise. But the war was going full blast, full steam ahead now, and would not be stopped.

He'd like to go to the theatre again, but not in uniform . . . He couldn't face that again. He looked at the list of shows . . . *The Bing Boys Are Here, The Happy Day* . . . pantomimes—*Charley's Aunt, The Thief of Baghdad, Jack and the Beanstalk* . . . *The Merry Widow, The Second Mrs Tanqueray, The Boy;* a revue, *Stand Up and Sing* with Miss Evelyn Laye, Tom Walls, Ralph Lynn, and Florinda . . . Florinda! That settled it. He'd go tonight . . . but dash it, tonight he'd promised to dine with Naomi at her Group's big house in Belgravia. It would have to be tomorrow, after he'd come back from Hedlington.

*   *   *   *

Guy sat in the draughting office of the Hedlington Aircraft Company, his feet on the edge of a table, a huge sheet of thick drawing paper spread on his lap. His R.F.C. side cap hung on a hook behind the door. Beyond the window, its panes streaming with rain, the airfield was a dull greeny grey, marked with deep brown ruts where aeroplanes had been landing and taking off until the field controller closed it to prevent more such damage to the surface.

Guy glanced up from the diagram and said, "Have you worked out the stress on each wheel of the landing gear?"

291

Betty Merritt, standing behind him, said, "2.376 tons—when she's standing still."

"The landing stress would be much more than that . . . depending how softly the pilot can put her down."

Ginger Keble-Palmer said earnestly, "I know. One day we're going to have to have some sort of hard, permanent runways for heavy bombers . . . but these're going to fly from Norfolk and Lincoln, where it's usually dry."

Betty said, "Aircraft are getting heavier all the time. The Handley Page 0/100 is 13,974 pounds, just a little more than our Lion. I agree with you about hard runways, because the R.F.C.'s not going to accept that their machines can't fly because of *anything*—nor will the ordinary Army generals accept it. They must be able to fly by night, and in all weathers. That means better instruments, but it also means permanent hard runways."

"They'll be a long time coming," Ginger said. "Think of the expense!"

Guy returned his attention to the designs. What he was looking at was the first conception of the idea, which would one day, after a thousand hours more work in this draughting office, and then in the machine tool shops and the wood shaping shops, become a four-engined bomber, designed to fly non-stop from East Anglia to Berlin and back, with a payload of 7,500 pounds of bombs.

Betty said, "I went to Cricklewood, and Handley Page confirm that they have a plan for a four-engined bomber, too. They're no farther forward with it than we are with this. What *are* we going to call it? Handley Page will use some austere set of numbers, but . . . us?"

"Elephant?" Ginger suggested.

Guy said, "We already have one . . . everyone's nicknamed the Martinsyde G.100 the 'Elephant,' because it's so big for a single seater. What about Buffalo? They're big, strong animals."

"That would be nice," Betty exclaimed. "We love the buffalo in America."

"That is a bison," Guy said. "You Americans can't tell one bird or beast from another. Johnny used to talk to me about robins, which turned out to be thrushes with orange breasts . . . and lions, which turned out to be pumas. Now buffaloes . . ."

"Oh, Guy!" she exclaimed in exasperation, "one day you'll go to America and they'll take you down a peg or two."

Guy said, "I'll look forward to it . . . Four machine guns is pretty good. But I think you're badly going to need another in the tail . . . here." He put his finger on the tail assembly. "Can you extend the fuselage say four feet behind the stabilizers? And put in a little cockpit, with twin machine guns on a Scarffing, so that the gunner can take on enemy attacking from straight astern—that's where they'll come from, mostly, you know. It'll do awful things to the centre of gravity, but perhaps that could be worked out."

Ginger said, "I wonder. Extra structure, two guns, with ammunition and mountings and a gunner, puts up the weight by at least 500 pounds, and we're already up to twelve and a half tons, 29,900 pounds. The centre of gravity will be moved aft, the wrong way."

"Then instead of lengthening the fuselage, could you move the stabilizer and fins four feet forward? That wouldn't add so much to the structure weight . . . the only extra would be the cockpit seat, gun ring, and the guns . . . and the gunner. He's going to be very lonely out there, but I do think it would make a great improvement to the fighting power of the machine."

Ginger said, "It changes a lot of the aerodynamics, and you'd still have some C of G problem. We must work it out. We might get away with one gun. We have time. We'll get all we can out of the Leopard and Lion series . . . then we'll show the War Office the design for the Buffalo."

Betty said, "And Handley Page will show them the design for their VG/1700/X."

Guy rolled up the paper and handed it to Ginger. Ginger said, "I've got to go out for a few minutes. Back soon."

Guy stood up, stretching, and turned to Betty. "Johnny still working as hard as ever?"

"Yes. Between you and me I think he leaves Stella alone too much. She doesn't look well—very listless, yawny."

Guy shot a look at her but said nothing. He said, "Family all right?"

"Yes. My Aunt Isabel comes down to spend a weekend at Walstone Manor at least twice a month. It makes me very sad." Guy nodded; that problem did not need explanation. "My father's well, he writes. He's still hoping Mr Wilson can keep us out of the war. I hoped the opposite until this summer. But I don't know how we could take something like the battles this year."

Guy nodded again. He could still see in his mind's eye the abomination of desolation that was the infantry's front—the slimy slopes of earth, the seas of mud and urine and excreta in which men waded and wallowed, and slept—the look in their eyes.

"And you?" he asked. "How many pursuiters have you got now?"

She did not laugh or turn off the joke with another. She said slowly, "I think I'm falling in love, Guy."

He said, as seriously, "That's good, isn't it?"

She said, "Johnny told me so much about you before I came over that I expected to fall for you . . . You won't approve . . . It's Fletcher Gorse. A member of your British lower classes."

Guy said, "Poets are *hors classe*. And I've, er, had close personal relations with his sister."

"Guy! How long ago was this? Wasn't everyone terribly shocked?"

"Ten years. And as to shock, it mostly happened while I was spending some of my hols at the Manor. Mrs Cate never noticed what I did or who I went out with."

Betty laughed. "Well, Fletcher's a private in the Wealds, in Hedlington—under a false name. It's too complicated to go into, but he's here, and I see him most Sundays, when he can get a few hours' leave. He's eager to get to France."

"So Probyn told me."

Betty said, "He's a *great* poet! I've read some of his work, and it's good, it really is . . ."

"I'm sure it is," Guy said, patting her on the shoulder. "And I wish you both all the luck in the world—especially him . . . I'm seeing Florinda tonight. She's the star of *Stand Up and Sing*."

Betty stared, open-mouthed. Then she said, "She's not the star. Evelyn Laye is."

"Ah well." Guy put his cap on the side of his head. The right eye was like blue ice in his head, the left brown, warm and melting—"Let the generals clasp the stars to their bosoms, we subalterns have to content ourselves with the ladies of the chorus, or thereabouts."

He saluted Betty formally, then blew her a kiss and went out.

*   *   *   *

Guy sat in the back of the pit stalls, wearing an imperfectly fitting tweed suit of Uncle Tom's. Outside the theatre, as he was queueing up to buy his ticket, gorgeous young women in silks and furs had sniffed as they passed, because he wasn't in evening dress; and beautiful young men in khaki or navy blue had glowered, because he wasn't in uniform. Some girls were still giving out white feathers and he half hoped one such would pick on him tonight . . . but nothing happened. A sort of pariah, he imagined himself surrounded by an invisible aura of disapproval and scorn. It was better than the fawn and gloat. He determined to enjoy the show. He glanced at his neighbors—both men, both tall and thin: the one on his right was a civilian, of about twenty-five, very pale, with spots of high color on his cheeks: he looked ill. The one on his left was a captain of the Royal Welch Fusiliers, the black flash of his regiment conspicuous on the back of his tunic, below the collar: he was about thirty, and he had an M.C.

Stand Up and Sing began. It was not very good, its moronic scenario interrupted at frequent intervals by songs, dances, and performances by the whole chorus. But it was pleasant enough except when they became patriotic, and sang about the beastly Huns, the Kaiser *they* were going to hang, *their* boys in the trenches, and such; then Guy's throat constricted, for the difference between this—this scent of perfume and cigar smoke, these petty lusts, over-drinking, over-eating— and what he had seen on the uplands of the Somme, brought him near to vomiting.

The Welch Fusilier captain muttered angrily, "Blighters!"

Guy said, "I beg your pardon?"

The captain glanced at him and whispered, "Look at them! The house is crammed, tier upon tier . . . grinning and cackling at the show . . . while those prancing harlots shrill the chorus . . . listen!"

We're sure the Kaiser loves our dear old tanks!

"I'd like to see a tank come down the stalls," the captain said viciously, "lurching to *Home Sweet Home,* perhaps . . . then there'd be no more jokes in music halls to mock the riddled corpses round Mametz, Fricourt, Bapaume."

Guy's other neighbor, who could not have helped overhearing, leaned across and muttered, "Great! I wish I could express what I feel half as well."

The Fusilier said, "I thought you must have been out there. Gassed?"

The other whispered, "Yes. Ypres. January. 60th . . . invalided out, in October. Left lung napoo, t'other not so good."

"Lucky you," the Fusilier said; then the man behind them made a ssshing noise and the lady beyond the gassed man rattled her programme angrily, and the three were silent.

At the interval they went out together and found the bar. They ordered drinks and introduced themselves—"Sassoon," the captain said. "Came up to town from Clitherland to see a show. Can't imagine what led me to pick this one."

"Bentley," the gassed man said.

"Rowland," Guy said, "R.F.C."

Sassoon said, "Wise man, not to wear uniform." He turned to Bentley—"Damn good regiment, the 60th."

Bentley laughed and said, "Yes, but I'm not in good odour with them, I fear."

Sassoon raised an eyebrow. Bentley said, "I think the war ought to be stopped. I think it's being continued for personal, petty, and political reasons that are no longer valid, when you consider the appalling slaughter over there. They can't accuse me of cowardice—I got an M.C. at Loos . . . so they say my mind has been affected. I don't mean just the chaps I used to know in the 60th—I mean my father, family, everyone . . ."

"I have an uncle who agrees with you," Guy said.

Sassoon said, "And I'm not sure I don't agree with you myself . . . but the war will go on . . ."

The bells rang for the end of the interval; and they returned to their seats.

Guy felt depressed. Everyone in the theatre except him, and perhaps Sassoon, seemed to be having a good time, but he was not. Why stay? At the second interval he muttered goodbyes to Bentley and Sassoon, and went up the aisle, heading for the cloakroom, to get his overcoat—Uncle Tom's. The rain had stopped while he was in the train up from Hedlington, and it wasn't a bad night. One of the women who ushered patrons into their seats caught up with him at the top of the aisle, and said breathlessly, "Are you Guy Rowland?"

He said yes, and she handed him a note she'd kept tucked into the deep cleavage of her abbreviated dress. "From Florinda, sir," she said.

Guy opened the note—"Saw you coming back from the bar after the first interval, from the wings. Come and see me after the show— F."

He stood a moment, thinking, while people pushed past him, none too politely. Then he gave the usher a half crown and went back to his seat.

*　　*　　*　　*

They sat in the Savoy Grill, facing each other across a small table half hidden from most of the diners by a potted palm. Schneider himself had taken them to the table, and had assured Lady Jarrow that they would not be bothered. The menus lay between them on the white table cloth. The table waiter was opening a bottle of Roederer Cristal. He poured a little; Guy tasted and nodded—"Fine, thank you." The waiter three-quarters filled both glasses and withdrew. Guy raised his glass—"To your success, Florinda."

She drank, and looking him in the eye, said, "Are you sure you can afford all this, Guy?"

He said, "Not every night, but we don't get badly paid, and there's nothing over there to spend it on. Don't worry."

She drank again, then said, "How good am I?"

He looked at her. The eyes were deep and green, the hair stunning auburn, with gold highlights. She wore one huge emerald ring,

296

an emerald necklace and a very severe black dress. He said, "You have a good voice, but it doesn't come out quite naturally . . . I know you're full of beans . . . lots of energy, very lively . . . but all of that doesn't reach the audience."

"Wooden? Stilted?"

"A bit. Not badly. They applauded."

She nodded—"I heard . . . Sometimes I think that all I need is more training, more practice, more experience. Then I watch some girl step in off the street for a tryout and the moment she opens her mouth or dances five steps, we all know she's got it. I haven't. All I've got is money—millions of it."

"How nice!" Guy said, smiling. "And you've got your health. I wish we could walk the Down again, from Hedlington to near Canterbury, as we did birds' nesting one day, remember?"

"'Course I remember! Wouldn't go in for any more of those peeing competitions with you, though. I've learned we women can't win—unless it's 'no hands,' perhaps."

He laughed heartily, causing nearby diners to turn round, frowning when they saw the young ruffian in the tweed suit. "The same Florinda as ever," he said, instinctively putting out his hand to cover hers. She turned hers over, and gripped his.

When at last the table was cleared, and each held a balloon glass of Remy Martin brandy in hand, Florinda said, "I want you to come home with me, Guy . . . but not as a trophy. A lot of women just want that."

He felt warm from the champagne and brandy. Time had not passed, nor the war come, nor the nightmares. He was with Florinda, the girl, a year and a half older than himself, who had showed him just how girls were different from boys, in their bodies, their actions, their feelings, their logic. And he had protected her from an angry dog, and carried her across a river before she could swim—it was barely two and a half feet deep but she was frightened then, or had pretended to be. They had been intimate friends and, in the way of extreme youth, lovers.

He said, "Why, then?"

She said, "I don't know. It's like old times, except that we're grown up. Then, we used to hold hands, and kiss a little, didn't we? Why?"

"We wanted to. It was the best we could do to show what we felt."

She nodded—"Now we can do more."

*   *   *   *

She awoke in the middle of the dark night. There was a clock on her dressing table but she could not read it without switching on the light. He was moaning beside her, and she felt him wet with sweat. His cries became more frequent, uttered between clenched teeth, with grunts and fierce gasps. "Fire!" he said suddenly, loud and clear—"Left deflection, two . . . no, you don't, you bugger . . . Got you!"

He sat up in bed, eyes wide, the brown one nearest to her, staring at the ceiling. She switched on the light then. He blinked, covered his eyes. His chest and belly heaved, and he suddenly leaped out of bed and ran stumbling into her bathroom. She heard the hard sound of him retching and vomiting, and swung her legs out of the bed to go and help. She swung them back again. He'd want to be alone.

She heard running water and fifteen minutes later he came back, pale, smiling the slight sardonic smile she had known so well. He slipped back between the sheets and said, "Sorry."

She said, "Poor Guy."

He said, after a while, "It's the killing. While I'm doing it, I like it . . . more than that, it's like sex—coming—a compulsion . . . When it's over, I can't stand it, or myself . . . They call me The Butcher, behind my back, some of them. It's supposed to be because I killed five German student pilots my first day in action. If that was really why they do it, it'd be damned unfair . . . but it isn't. It's because they *know*, somehow, that I like it. I'm dangerous, I've got a disease, that'll kill . . ."

She waited, but he did not say any more. He didn't want to. When he did, he would.

She leaned her breasts against him and said, "Was that your first time ever, with a woman?"

He said, "I've been to bed with the farmer's daughter, where our squadron is, half a dozen times. Her name's Pauline, but we all call her Poitrine for two obvious reasons."

"'Sno' fu'in' obvious t'me, mite," she said, in cockney with strong glottal stops.

"Sorry." He kissed her cheek—"Poitrine means 'bosom' or 'breast' in French . . . I think several other chaps have been with her, too. She's not a tart, but she can't say no, and I think she wants a baby . . . plus a rich English husband to go with it. I feel like a cad when I go to her, because I don't love her, but I think of this—" he caressed Florinda's wet and swollen sex with two gentle fingers—"and I can't resist it."

She said, "There's a name for that condition—cuntstruck. Thank God men get it! . . . But remember, darling, that every woman in the world has one . . . and we aren't all nice . . . That farm girl will get pregnant soon enough."

"Not from me. I take it out. I should have with you, except that you wouldn't let me. And I'd marry you, only you're so rich."

"Garn, I'm not good enough for you, Guy Rowland! You're going to marry the Honourable Lady Ermyntrude Cuntworthy-Prickforth

. . . face like a horse and t'other end about the same, only *so* well bred, doncha know? And don't worry about putting a bun in my oven. I'm wearing a rubber thing over the mouth of my womb—it's called a pessary. You must've felt it when you went deep . . . And you did, 'cos you've got a lovely, big, stiff cock—luvverly!" She kissed his ear. He slid his fingers slowly up and down the silken petals between her lips.

She said, "I wonder if this is what I'm meant to do, the rest of my life. Look after hungry men . . . tired men . . . frightened men . . . I think I'll leave the stage and work in the military hospitals, the convalescent depots . . . when I'm among men, I can *feel* them wanting me, Guy. I don't mean just wanting to fuck, but yearning, what Adam must have felt when he first saw Eve . . ."

"Will you write to me?"

" 'Course I will! Once a month. And you write to me, see?"

"I will . . . probably more than once a month. I feel things, remember, imagine . . . well, you saw what effect it has on me . . . and there's no one out there I can talk to about it."

"You try to tell me that and they'll put blue pencils through most of it. They don't *want* us to know what it's really like, and that's a fact." She had slipped slightly out of her upper class accent, deliberately, he thought, to emphasize the close, undemanding love of their childhood. She didn't want to lose that, he thought, in the present fires of lust and passion.

She slowly lifted her knees, and spread them, her eyes on him. He raised himself, growing frantic for her, and slid into her as she buried her teeth in his shoulder and, muffled against his bleeding skin, gasped rhythmically, "Guy, Guy, Guy, love me!"

Daily Telegraph, Thursday, December 14, 1916

HEADQUARTERS (*France*) **Wednesday (9:30 p.m.)**
Hostile patrols which endeavoured to enter our trenches last night east of Armentières were driven off.

There has been the usual artillery activity throughout the day at different points along the front.

We carried out bombardments of the enemy's trenches in the neighbourhood of Festubert, Neuve Chapelle, and Ypres.

EFFECT IN WALL STREET

From our Financial Correspondent,
New York, Tuesday Afternoon.
The very mention of the peace proposals from Berlin excited a bearish element in the stock market, and traders' fears were further

> fostered by a Washington despatch intimating that a forecast of
> such proposals had been cabled yesterday. In the absence of defi-
> nite information, the stock market sold off rapidly, declines in war
> stocks ranging from 1 to 30 points, but the entire list, rails in-
> cluded, was affected. To see prices trembling in just two hours, one
> might have thought that peace was already here, and that the Amer-
> ican prosperity of the last two years, based on the war, had finally
> disappeared.

Cate thought, those two items of news are really obscene, read together like that. "The usual artillery activity" meant so many soldiers
killed, so many maimed. "Bombardment of the enemy's trenches"
meant the same, only the soldiers would be Germans. And the first
hint that someone in a position of authority was suggesting that the
artillery activity and bombardment, not to mention the patrolling and
attacking, might be made to cease, by negotiation, had caused a near
panic in financial circles. Of course that was in America, not here.
What would actually happen to American prosperity if they entered
the war? It could not fail to increase, with the tremendous home
orders for war materials that there would be, in addition to the present
ones from the Allies. So what worried the financiers over there was the
chance that the war might end before they got into it, thus instantly
cutting off the huge war commerce.

He looked out of the window—slight rain, chilly wind, low clouds,
bare earth, the wind blowing the smoke eastward from the chimney
pots of Walstone below. He'd been sitting indoors, looking at accounts
and statements and feed and fertilizer prices for too many days. He'd
put on his raincoat, have Marquis or Willow saddled, and go out
visiting . . . go and see the Garths and their new baby; of course the
first one had been Fletcher Gorse's—you could see the resemblance
with startling clarity now that the little boy was nearly two . . . then
perhaps call on old Commander Quigley and see if he could tell him
what could be done about these beastly submarines. He probably
wouldn't learn much: last time he'd mentioned the subject the commander had croaked, "Why, hang the crews from their own yard-
arms, Cate! They're pirates!" . . . Magistrates' court this afternoon,
so before he went out he'd better spend an hour studying the docket,
and thinking about each person involved, what he knew of him, what
might have made him do what he was accused of—if he had . . . Oh,
and on his way home a glass of ginger wine at the Beaulieu Arms, and
inquire after Miss Parsley's rheumatism, and the Haversham boy's
existence: he was in France, with the Grenadier Guards.

Walstone, Kent: Thursday, December 14, 1916

20 Bill Hoggin leaned forward, pulling earnestly on the fat Havana cigar in his mouth, being careful not to blow the smoke in the Earl of Swanwick's face. Books lined the room, the library of Walstone Park, from floor to ceiling, except where here and there space had been left for oil paintings of previous earls as Masters of Foxhounds, the horn of office tucked between the second and third buttons of the pink coats.

It was not warm in there—no part of the great pile was warm, in winter; but beads of sweat formed continuously on Hoggin's heavy jowls and trickled down between the rolls of fat at his neck and the stiffly starched white collar. He said, "We're nearly ready, my lord . . . the Articles of Association are ready for signing—drawn up by the best solicitors in London. Lloyds and Midland are each putting up one third of the capital and I'm doing the third. We'll be going public inside six months."

"I like the name," his lordship said. "Hustle . . . American, I suppose?"

"No, my lord, it's the initials of Hoggin's Universal Stores Limited—H U S L, pronounced HUSTLE. But we do 'ope, hope people will think it's American. American things is very fashionable these days."

"Can't understand why," the earl muttered. "Cowardly cads . . . and now some of *our* people are becoming too proud to fight. Look at John Rowland! But you don't know him, do you?"

"I've met him, milord. You see, my Ruthie's the daughter of Bob Stratton, who worked for old Mr Harry Rowland all his life, till Row-

301

land's had to convert to shell filling. I know them all, a bit—the Colonel, Mr Richard, who's making the American lorries now, at J.M.C., Mr . . ."

"Bloody Americans, getting rich, while we bleed to death to make the world safe for them and their damned democracy!"

"Quite right, my lord, that's what I always says, too . . . but people don't seem to think about that when they choose gramophone records, or go to the cinema, or buy tinned food . . . We've got store sites in half a dozen places already—Birmingham, Bristol, Newcastle-on-Tyne, Sheffield, Portsmouth, Plymouth, Reading, mostly grocer's shops which I bought out . . . You see, till now it's been all my money, 'cos I wanted to show the bank people that it was a good idea and it would work. I've done it, and we're getting the money much cheaper, and much more of it, than if I'd gone to them six months ago with just the idea. And when we let the public in, we'll really start to expand . . . I've got options on sites in Leeds, Manchester, Norwich, 'Ampstead, Kensington, Paddington . . . 'ad a bit of luck in Hull, too—big warehouse blown up by Gothas last week, bought the site dirt cheap yesterday."

The earl puffed on his cigar—"With so many shops, surely you will have great difficulty finding enough assistants. Heaven knows we do here."

"It's not the same, my lord. Girls nowadays don't realize what an honour and what an education it is to work for the Earl and Countess of Swanwick . . . but they'll work for me, because I'll pay them well, and our shops are all in the cities."

"All women?" the earl said, raising an eyebrow.

"Every last one of 'em. We can't get *many* men, so I thought, 'ell, we won't have any. Less arguing, see?"

"The managers, too?" the earl gasped.

"Most of them," Hoggin said emphatically. "You wouldn't believe how many women we had applying when we advertised . . . women who could read, write, do algebra even. Some of 'em had been running the catering for hospitals, factories, hotels. We'll get them, my lord, don't you worry . . . We won't have no bleeding ladies, though, begging your pardon, my lord . . . There's ladies can run anything—look at the way Her Ladyship runs this place—but they generally don't know much about saving the farthings, and they like the best things . . . best food . . . best bread . . . best eggs . . . We're not going to sell the best, just the cheapest."

His Lordship looked with distaste at Hoggin and said, "That's all you're aiming for, in all the H.U.S.L. shops—just the cheapest, without regard to quality?"

Hoggin said, "We're after the people what before didn't buy much in the groceries at all . . . didn't buy tinned beans, but fresh ones and cooked 'em themselves . . . didn't buy tinned meat . . . made their own jam and marmalade . . . Every one of our stores is going to look the same, and everything's going to be in the same place, so the women'll know where to go even in another town. There's going to be big signs: Tinned Meat here, Tinned Soups here, Tinned Fruit here—now mind a lot of those will be our own brand, Hoggin's Jam, Hoggin's Bully, and they'll always be the cheapest . . . An' there'll be a counter for meat, and another for fish, and another for veg and fruit, an' p'raps another for things women are always running out of in the kitchen, like matches, soap, hand towels, knives, ladles, so we'll 'ave a little bit of hardware, too. They've got a whole chain of stores like this over in America—call 'em Piggly Wiggly."

"Good God!" the earl said.

"An' we won't be buying a gross of tins at a time, like Wardle did in Hedlington before I bought him out—but five thousand cases . . . 'cos we'll buy for all the H.U.S.L. shops from a central office, and distribute in our own vans."

His Lordship said, "I wish you luck . . . though I can't honestly say that the Countess or the housekeeper will ever patronize any of your shops."

Hoggin carefully rested his cigar in the ashtray set on a weighted green band astride the leather arm of his chair. "You won't have to buy anything, my lord . . . but I 'ope you'll be seen and photographed visiting some of our stores, because I'd like you to accept the post of Chairman of the company's board of directors."

The earl said, "Well, Hoggin, that's very . . ."

"Two thousand a year screw . . . stipend," Hoggin said. "Plus one percent of the net profit after taxes—when we make one . . . That'll come to a lot more than two thousand bradburies or I'm a Dutchman . . . but we won't make real profits till 1918, I think."

"And you'll be . . . ?"

"Managing Director, twenty thousand a year, plus ten percent of the profit . . . You won't 'ave to do a thing, my lord, except visit the stores . . . have your name on all our paper and advertisements, 'The Right Honourable the Earl of Swanwick, K.G.' It'll look good!"

"I haven't got the Garter!" the earl snapped. It was a sore point with him. His grandfather had worn the blue ribbon, all the more valued because there was "no damned merit about it"; but succeeding sovereigns had not seen fit to make either his father, or himself, members of England's oldest order of chivalry.

He said, "I don't know, Hoggin . . . It's trade, after all."

303

Hoggin swore under his breath, picked up the cigar, carefully relit it, creating a vile stink, and said, "My lord, I know you've been having trouble with taxes, rents, expenses of all kinds. I've been proud to help you 'cos I think you're a great English gentleman. Where would we be without the likes of you? No better than Frogs or Dagoes!" he declaimed. "I paid for the repairs to the roof here."

"I know," the earl muttered.

"I been contributing to the 'Ounds . . . supporting the Wire Fund . . . making personal loans . . ."

"I know."

"And you've 'elped me, knowing the people you do in Parliament. You did a lot to make that bloody silly parliamentary committee see sense . . . There's a lot of lords with their names on the paper of companies—breweries, soap factories, sausage makers, everything. And the title still means a lot. It means *respectability*, my lord! It's worth money."

"I know," the earl said. "I've always despised those fellows." He shook his head angrily. He still despised the idea, but the blighter was really trying to do him a good turn. Two thousand a year wouldn't solve his debts, but it would help, and if H.U.S.L. expanded successfully, there'd be more. He said, "All right, Hoggin. Where is the head office going to be?"

"In my house for the time being. We've only got the one baby, and the place has ten bedrooms, so we're going to use them as offices . . . and there are four big rooms downstairs."

The earl nodded and thought, now he'll leave and I can interview that fellow who answered my advertisement for a gamekeeper: he could hardly be worse than the old fool he'd got now. And then he'd ride over to Beighton and find out what in blazes was giving the bitches diarrhoea, and . . .

But Hoggin said, "There's another matter, my lord."

"What's that?" the earl said. His mind wandered again. Have to find a cheaper source of meat for the hounds . . . horsemeat was getting too expensive, too much demand for it—a lot of it certainly being shipped to France for the Frogs to eat, bloody barbarians.

"The missus and I would be honoured if you and Her Ladyship would honour us by partaking of tea with us, some time before Christmas."

The earl was startled . . . tea? with Hoggin? The fellow must be joking. But Hoggin said, "How about a week from today, then? You'll let me know? Thank you, my lord, thank you! One more thing . . . I want to make a contribution to the government, to the war effort—a considerable contribution . . ." The beady eyes were fixed on His Lordship's now: the voice had dropped and taken on a rasping edge

. . . "Big enough to make sure it receives proper recognition. When I'm ready, I 'ope I can count on your advice as to 'ow, how to do it, so it hachieves my hobject."

Swanwick followed his guest to the front door and watched him climb into his Rolls Royce and be driven away by his liveried chauffeur. Then he returned to the library and sank heavily into his chair. He had hardly been able to believe his ears. Hoggin, after a knighthood! He began to shake with laughter—his first genuine laughter for years—at the ridiculousness of the idea: then the laughter turned bitter, and faded away, as he realized that these days the idea was anything but ridiculous, with enough money to back it. Sir Bill Hoggin! Bloody farce! It was beginning to look as though the British nobility was at last going to go under, after so many centuries, in a sea of taxes and ridicule . . . Lloyd George had a huge private fund he didn't account to anyone for, but he himself didn't know the Prime Minister well, and cordially disliked what he did know. He'd speak to Balfour, who was a gentleman, and Balfour could approach Lloyd George, on Hoggin's behalf.

*   *   *   *

Hoggin was sitting behind a big old-fashioned desk in what had once been the morning room of The Yews, on Gorston Road in Hedlington, two houses up from Laburnum Lodge, the residence of Mr Harry Rowland, M.P. for Mid-Scarrow. A thin gloomy man with a long face and protruding teeth stood in front of him, his hands washing each other with invisible soap. Hoggin said, "Well, the Parliamentary Inquiry's dead, old Bumley's yelling that I'm the greatest public benefactor since whoever put in the drains, but we're not out of the wood yet. There's still the police."

Milner said, "I know. I'm sure they're trying to find out where I got my extra money from."

"You won it on the geegees and they can't prove different."

"Anyone can tell 'em that if I put as much as a tanner on a horse, it falls down at the start."

"They can't prove anything. You just keep your mouth shut . . . And from now on everything's going to be respectable . . . no more wide boy tricks for me. You make more money straight. It's hard to believe, but it's true."

"You'd better hold a job for me in one of your stores," Milner said. "They've been looking for a chance to give me the sack ever since those receipts disappeared from the condemned food files."

Hoggin looked at him for a while, silent, then said, "You give me an idea, Milner, me boy. You're coming into H.U.S.L. as General Inspector. You know all the tricks. Now you'll see that no one plays

305

them on me—none of the managers, the clerks, the suppliers, *no one*. You'll be watch dog, all the way down the line, from the docks to the stores."

Milner's habitual gloom lightened—"Thanks, Hoggin. Just tell me when to start . . . How much?"

"What are you getting now?"

"Nine pounds fourteen a week."

"Fifteen quid—and a percentage of what you catch—fraud, theft, embezzlement . . . Get out now, the Heinz salesman is waiting."

Milner went out. Miss Meiklejohn, the secretary, who had a little desk in the hall outside, with typewriter and telephone, ushered in the head salesman in Britain for the Heinz Company.

Hoggin said, "Sit down . . . Name's Hansberg, right?"

"Richard H. Hansberg," the other said in a strong Midwestern American accent—"I've received your letter and brochure about H.U.S.L. We at Heinz will be happy to supply you with anything in our line—in spite of the German submarine campaign."

Hoggin said, "What discount will you give me on orders of five thousand cases at a time?"

The salesman was fiftyish, with pince-nez and a rosy complexion that yet managed to look unhealthy. He said, "The Heinz Company does not give discounts. Our prices to wholesalers are already as low as a reasonable profit margin will permit."

Hoggin said, "How much for five thousand cases of baked beans then? Delivered to our warehouse."

"Where's that, Mr Hoggin?"

"Don't know yet. Either Birmingham or South London. We've got our eye on a couple of places."

Mr Hansberg said, "The price today would be four and a penny a case . . ." He looked at the ceiling a moment—"A thousand and twenty pounds, sixteen shillings and seven pence."

"Nine hundred even," Hoggin said.

Mr Hansberg said, "I am sorry, Mr Hoggin, but it is against company policy to . . ."

"Then don't waste my bloody time!" Hoggin roared. "I know where I can get baked beans at three and seven pence the case."

"Not as good as ours, Mr Hoggin."

"I'm not after good stuff," Hoggin said. "Get out!"

Mr Hansberg rose to his feet, looking as though he had walked into a brick wall, turned, and went out, with head bowed.

Miss Meiklejohn came in—"Mr Blossom, from the Acme Boot Factory."

Hoggin stood up and advanced with hand outstretched—"Ah, Mr Blossom . . . Sit down . . . Care for a spot of whisky? Quite, quite

. . . Well, we're both busy men, I know, so let's get to business. The plain fact is, we want to buy your factory, tear out all that you've got inside, and make the buildings into warehouses."

"That'll be a fairly expensive proposition," Mr Blossom said, "though you'd get a good price for the machinery."

"Just scrap-iron rates," Hoggin said briefly. "It's thirty years out of date. And we're bidding on the buildings at warehouse rates—so much the cubic foot."

Mr Blossom seemed to sag in his chair. "But . . ." he stammered, "we're a going concern."

"Going under, more like," Hoggin said. "You owe the banks near forty thousand quid, and your sales 'ave been dropping for two years—since the war started. And the balance sheets is like what they call a novel, ain't they—works of imagination?" He gazed meaningly at Blossom. Blossom looked at the ceiling, the floor, the walls, anywhere but at Hoggin.

Hoggin spoke more kindly. "Look here, Blossom, suppose I slip you ten thousand, in cash. You put it in your pocket, we close the deal, then you resign. Let someone else clear up the mess."

After a time Blossom said, "All right."

Hoggin said, "Bring the papers, all ready, a week from today, no, tomorrow week—we'll sign them, and when you leave you'll find your little attachy case heavier than when you came in, get it?"

Mr Blossom nodded and went out. Miss Meiklejohn came in. "Your wife wishes to see you, sir."

Hoggin said, "My wife? Who? . . . Oh, Ruthie . . . What the hell does she want? Can't she see I'm busy?"

"I'm sure I don't know, sir," said Miss Meiklejohn, sniffing. She was thirty-five and genteel.

"Orright, show her in . . . Ruthie, what the 'ell do you want, and look sharp about it, I got Mr Hawke of Hawke, Hawke, Snot and Phlegm coming with a lot of contracts."

Ruth Hoggin, nee Stratton, stood her ground before the desk. She was small and big busted, and, as Miss Meiklejohn looked refined, Mrs Hoggin looked mousey. She said, "When you came home, before lunch, you said you had invited Lord and Lady Swanwick to tea next week. Did they say they would come?"

"They didn't say no," Hoggin said. "They'll come."

"I can't believe it," she muttered, agitatedly running her hand through her thin hair.

"It's true."

"Well, then I must have a new dress and hat. I don't have a thing to wear . . . and I must get my hair done that morning."

"Wot the hell," he began; then, "Oh, all right. Go to Jonas and

Johnson and get yourself a nice dress an' hat and gloves and all the rest."

Ruth said, "I am not going to wear anything from Hedlington. I am going to London . . . to Barker's."

Hoggin stared at her—"Barker's in Kensington? Why, that'll cost you . . ."

"You can afford it," she said. "I'll go tomorrow so that I'll have time to alter the dress a bit if it isn't a perfect fit. I shall need twenty-five pounds."

"Twenty-five pounds! Why . . . !"

She waited, and at last he opened his wallet and gave her the money, secretly proud of her. He liked people who stood up to him.

She turned to go but he said, " 'Arf a mo' . . . how's Launcelot? I haven't seen him for a week."

She said, "Well, he's still asleep when you get up in the morning, and he's been put to bed when you finish work. He's all right . . . a bit thin . . ."

"I hear him crying a lot, don't I?"

"He's teething," she said. "He only has two more to come in, but they're giving him trouble. Come up and talk to him now, Bill. You really should."

Miss Meiklejohn marched in—"Mr Hawke is waiting, sir."

Hoggin growled, "Let him wait . . . Tell him I'm going to spend ten minutes with my baby son . . . No, tell him I'm having a shit, crap, whatever you want to call it, and he's welcome to join me if he doesn't want to wait."

"Really, sir," Miss Meiklejohn stammered, and "Bill!" Ruth cried; but Hoggin was out of the door, calling over his shoulder, "Come on, Ruthie, I don't have all day."

*   *   *   *

Bill and Ruth Hoggin stood in the window of the drawing room of The Yews, watching the snow fall with mixed emotions. Ruth was wearing her new dress, floor length, soft purple, of pure silk, with a high collar and a sash of a lighter shade of purple, almost heliotrope, and a hat of purple felt, with an ostrich feather dyed the same heliotrope as the organdy sash. Her gloves, halfway up her forearms, were of the same heliotrope. "They won't come," she muttered, half to herself. "It's snowing too hard, even if they ever meant to."

If they didn't come, all her work, all the extra cleaning and polishing in the house, the arranging and rearranging of furniture, would have gone for nothing. But, if they didn't come, she would not have to face the ordeal of entertaining them, knowing she would do something wrong—everything wrong. Why, oh why, did Bill have to invite them?

Hoggin, standing with hands clasped behind his back, his belly pushing out in front with the gold watch chain curving across it, suffered from no such dichotomy; he hoped that the earl and countess would brave the snow and come. If they didn't, he would ask them another day; for he was determined to let Hedlington and the world know that he was an intimate of that most noble family.

At a quarter past four Ruth said, "They're not coming. I wonder they didn't telephone . . ."

Hoggin grunted, and at eighteen minutes past four the maroon-painted Humber with the earl's coronet on the door swept slowly in through the opened gates, and Hoggin and his wife hurried out into the hall, to stand five paces back from the front door, where Harbinger the butler waited. The moment the bell rang Harbinger swung open both doors, admitting a whistling wind and a flurry of snow that stippled the first ten feet of the hall with white dots and flakes.

Harbinger turned and announced: "The Right Honourable the Earl of Swanwick and the Countess of Swanwick."

The Hoggins went forward together, Ruth's knees shaking. She found herself dropping a curtsy before the gaze of the Countess, while Hoggin bowed from the waist. Harbinger had already taken Lady Swanwick's fur coat and was helping the earl out of his overcoat. The earl gave the butler his hat and rubbed his hands together— "Damned cold out there, Hoggin!"

"It's so kind of you . . . to . . . come," Ruth stammered. "I didn't think, we didn't think . . . with the snow . . . and all . . ."

Lady Swanwick said pointedly, "The wind seems to come right through the door doesn't it?"

"What? Oh yes, of course . . . This way." Ruth led back into the drawing room, where a huge coal fire burned in the grate. Lady Swanwick sat down, her eyes wandering round the room—large oil portraits of "ancestors" obviously bought at antique dealers . . . landscapes . . . fox hunting . . . heavy gilt frames . . . Louis XV furniture, second hand . . . didn't all match . . . They'd have done better to choose some less ornate style and carry through with it. The room was a hodgepodge of opulence, like poor Mrs Hoggin's dress . . . that hat! Looked like Barker's at its worst. The poor woman was so nervous.

The earl, warming his hands in front of the fire, said, "Did you read what that blighter's done now, Hoggin?"

Hoggin was puzzled, "What blighter, me lord?"

"Lloyd George. He's released a lot of Sinn Feiners who were taken in arms against us during the Easter Rising."

"Why would he do that?" Hoggin asked.

"To please the bloody Yanks," the earl said.

The countess intervened, "Now, Roger, we didn't come here to talk about such unpleasant subjects . . . Don't you have a little boy, Mrs Hoggin?"

"Oh yes, m'lady . . . Launcelot."

"How old is he?"

"A year and ten months, m'lady. I was going to have Nanny bring him down for a minute, when we've had our tea."

"That would be nice."

Ruth drew a deep breath and said, "He's going to Eton College, m'lady. After that, I suppose it'll be up to him, then, to decide what he wants to be. Once he's been at Eton College, he can be anything."

The earl had heard and broke in, speaking to Hoggin, "What's that? Your boy going to Eton?"

Hoggin said, "Ruthie's got her heart set on it."

The earl said, "Have you entered him? Written to the school, telling them you have a son and you want him to enter in such and such a half?"

Hoggin said, "No, my lord, we haven't done that yet. It can wait till he's a bit older, can't it?"

"Good God, no," the earl said. "He'd start in the summer of 1928, but he should have been entered within a day or two of birth. There'll be no place for him. You might have afforded to wait a year if you had family connections, but . . ."

"'Course not!" Hoggin said. "This ain't none of *my* doing. It's Ruthie. He'll be like a fish out of water there, if you ask me."

Ruth said sharply, "Launcelot's going to Eton College, Bill! And he's going to speak proper, so the other boys won't laugh at him!"

The countess listened, fascinated: a war in the family—Hoggin wanting to stay in his own class, though apparently seeking a K, but with money to do what he liked: concomitantly, accepting none of the upper classes' duties and obligations—catch *him* leading a platoon over the top! . . . while the little mousey wife wanted their son to rise, knowing that if he did, she'd lose him, and he would accept the responsibilities his father was avoiding . . . fascinating!

Lord Swanwick said, "I don't think you have a hope of getting him into Eton now."

The countess thought, that little woman deserves help. She said, "There is one chance. Tell them about Collegers, Roger."

The earl looked doubtful—"Is he clever? Got to be damn clever to be a Colleger . . . a real inky swot."

"We don't know how clever he is," Hoggin said. "He hasn't made any speeches yet."

310

Swanwick said, "Oh? Yes, quite . . . Well, a certain number of boys are admitted to Eton every year, free, as a result of winning scholarships—by open competition. They're called Collegers because they live in the college buildings. There are about a hundred of them at school at any one time, as far as I can remember. All the other boys, about a thousand of them, are called Oppidans, and live in various houses in the town round Eton—*Oppidum,* Latin for town. Each house has its own housemasters. You call him 'm'tutor.' If your boy—what's his name?"

"Launcelot," Hoggin said, glowering at his wife.

"Launcelot—wants to go to Eton, he must win an open scholarship. Then they cannot refuse him. He'll be a Colleger, a scholar."

Hoggin said, "An' I won't be paying them a penny, though by then I'll be able to buy the plurry place, beg pardon, Your Ladyship. It's enough to make a cat laugh."

Ruth Hoggin said, "He will win the scholarship, my lord . . . Can you tell us the name of a good school where he can go first? So that he will be sure to win the scholarship. Or do you think it would be better if we hired tutors here?"

The earl said heartily, "Send him to school, Mrs Hoggin . . . dozens of such prep schools—private schools, we called them at Eton—all over the place . . . get his little bottom whacked and his face pushed in the mud, do him a world of good!" Ruth Hoggin paled. The countess murmured aside, "It doesn't have to be as brutal as that," while the earl barked, "Just make sure that none of the beaks are, well, you know, *those* . . . see that they don't starve the little beasts . . . Lot of those places serve potatoes till the boys are full, then a piece of meat not big enough for a good dinner for a mouse. The boys can't eat even that, so the school takes it back and makes mince out of it for tomorrow." He pulled out his watch and Ruth started—"Oh, shall we serve tea, m'lady?"

"Certainly," the countess said. "We built up quite an appetite on the drive here . . ."

*   *   *   *

The tea had been served and eaten and the ruins removed. Nanny Hopgood had brought Launcelot downstairs and led him into the drawing room, curtsying to the earl and countess as she came in. She was fifty and had served two generations in a noble house in Ireland, but now the nurseries were empty and would not be filled again in her lifetime, for the boys who would soon have become fathers were instead manuring the soil of Picardy, Flanders, and Artois. Ruth was humble before Nanny Hopgood's knowledge of society and how to raise small sprigs of the aristocracy; but Nanny Hopgood had sensed

311

the little woman's fierce devotion to Launcelot, and was careful never to dictate to her employer where the little boy's well-being was directly concerned: only in such matters as where she herself was to eat, her wages, her relationship with the rest of the staff . . .

Launcelot shook hands with the earl and countess, bowing jerkily before each. He was wearing a royal blue velvet jacket over a white shirt with a wide Byronic blue tie, and royal blue velvet shorts over long black silk stockings. There were pearl buttons on the sides of his shorts, and silver buckles on his shoes.

Nanny Hopgood led him out. As soon as she was sure he could not hear, the countess said, "A nice little boy . . . Such fine eyes—like yours, Mrs Hoggin." The young should never be complimented to their faces.

Ruth blushed with pleasure, wishing Launcelot could have heard what Her Ladyship had said. Really, it hadn't been so bad after all . . . with Harbinger and Mrs Bowes to arrange things, it had gone off very well.

The earl settled back in his chair, stretching out his hands toward the fire—"What do you think of Mr Wilson's latest proposal, Hoggin?"

"What proposal, my lord?"

The earl realized that Hoggin read nothing in the papers except what he saw as connected with or concerning him and his business— which was making money, not war. He said, "Mr Wilson—the American president—has invited all the belligerents to state their war aims. He thinks, he says, that they may not prove irreconcilable."

Hoggin scratched his head and said, "Well, our war aim is to beat the 'Uns, right?"

"That's what *I'd* tell him," the earl said. "The country won't swallow anything less."

"An' the war might be over in a couple of weeks or months," Hoggin said; and that would be a bloody disaster, he was about to add, but caught the countess's cold look, and remembered that her younger son was rotting in the slime somewhere over there. He said instead, "I mean, we've got to teach the swine a lesson, don't we?"

"That's what I say," Swanwick said.

The countess said, "It's time we went home, Roger, before the roads become impassable."

Ruth jumped to her feet, nearly falling over the hem of her gown—"Certainly, m'lady . . . It's been so nice seeing you . . . and thank you ever so for telling us about Eton College and the private schools."

"We'll give you some introductions, for the schools," the countess said. "Then you should go and look at a few for yourself and decide

312

which one would be best for Launcelot. Then enter his name—the good private schools have waiting lists, too."

Hoggin was on his feet, bowing, "It's been an honour, Your Lordship . . . Your Ladyship."

When Swanwick's car had swept round the drive, and disappeared, and the front door of The Yews been closed, Ruth turned to her husband, "What did Lord Swanwick mean when he said we were to make sure the schoolmasters weren't *those?*"

Bill patted her head, and said, "He meant to look out for like them scoutmasters what teach little boys what their cocks is for, and parsons what bumfuck the choirboys behind the altar."

"Bill!"

"Cheer up, Ruthie. Worse things 'appen at sea, and Christmas is coming."

He stopped in the middle of the hall, flung up one hand, and declaimed:

'Twas Christmas Day in the workhouse, that day of all the year
When the paupers' 'earts is full of gladness and their bellies full of beer.
Up spake the workhouse master, "To all within these walls,
I wish a Merry Christmas!" and the paupers answered . . .

"Bill!" Ruth cried, putting her hand over his mouth. She had heard the poem before.

Daily Telegraph, Friday, December 22, 1916

PEACE APPEAL FROM PRESIDENT WILSON
INQUIRY AS TO TERMS

We were officially informed by the Press Bureau last night that the following Note was communicated by the United States ambassador to his Majesty's Government on Wednesday last:

The President of the United States has instructed me to suggest . . . a course of action with regard to the present war which he hopes (will be taken) under consideration as coming from . . . the representative of a neutral nation whose interests have been most seriously affected by the war . . .

The President suggests that an early occasion be sought to call out from all the nations now at war such an avowal of their respective views as to the terms upon which the war might be concluded, and the arrangements which would be deemed satisfactory as a guarantee against its renewal or the kindling of any similar conflict in the future, as would make it possible frankly to compare them . . .

REASON FOR THE STEP

U.S. NEAR VERGE OF WAR.

Washington, Thursday.

Mr Wilson's Note came as a surprise to the official world at Washington. None of the ambassadors apparently had any idea that he intended to despatch one. Exactly when the Note was finished has not been disclosed, but it is known that it was cabled on Tuesday.

Mr Lansing, Secretary of State, to-day made a statement explaining that Mr Wilson's Note to the belligerents declared that the situation for neutrals was becoming increasingly critical, and that the United States itself was being drawn near the verge of war. The following is the text of Mr Lansing's statement:

> The reasons for sending the Note were as follows. It was not our material interests that we had in mind when the Note was sent, but rather our own rights, which are becoming more and more involved by belligerents on both sides, so that the situation is becoming increasingly critical. I mean by that we are drawing nearer to the verge of war ourselves, and therefore we are entitled to know exactly what each belligerent seeks in order that we may regulate our conduct in future.

Cate read the whole of the President's Note and the Secretary of State's statement with absorbed interest. What Mr Lansing was clearly trying to do was dispel the widely held belief that America's only interest in the war was to make money. What Mr Wilson was equally clearly trying to do was force the belligerents to state with precision what their war aims were. A part of the Note pointed out that "the leaders of the several belligerents have stated these objects in general terms. But stated in general terms they seem the same on both sides." Well, that was enough to raise the jingoes' blood pressure, but if you went back to the very origins of the war, it had some validity. However, when you defined that into, say, a German demand for large and rich portions of France and Russia (to protect herself against a war on two fronts); and England's demand that the German Navy be reduced to a cipher with no submarines (which would ensure that Britain could not be starved out); and France's demand for the return of Alsace and Lorraine; and all the Allies' insistence that a democratic form of government be imposed on Germany, and the Kaiser hanged . . . it was impossible. Nor would any diplomat of any skill show his real hand this early. They would all overstate their cases, with the intention of later giving away a little of this, which they didn't really want, in return for a little of that—which they did. But the inflated demands, once stated, would put a stop to all talk of accommodation or negotiation.

No, one side had to be forced to its knees, to a point where negotiation with all its terrors was clearly less bad than the alternative.

Only three days to Christmas. Boxing Day would fall on Sunday this year, so if he gave out the boxes that day, no one would be able to buy anything for little after-Christmas celebrations. He'd better calculate what the boxes would come to—it would make more of a hole in his account than he cared to contemplate; but he couldn't reduce them now, with prices going up everywhere. Then he'd go early into Hedlington, draw the money, come back at once, and distribute the boxes this afternoon, so the people would have tomorrow to make any purchases.

London: Wednesday, January 17, 1917

21 Colonel Rodney Venable wandered down the Admiralty corridor, pass ready in hand, because he knew he would have to show it again before he could have a word with Room 40. He'd given Admiral Hall, Director of Naval Intelligence, the information Army Counter-Intelligence had picked up about two Irish nationalists working in Plymouth dockyard. Admiral Hall had been pleased. He'd been in a strange mood, for him, Venable thought . . . euphoric, ready to go through the high ceiling.

The duty officer at the cipher room was a lieutenant R.N.V.R., whom Venable knew. He held up the pass and the lieutenant said, "Morning, Colonel."

Venable put away the pass and knocked on the door of the inner room beyond—Room 40—and waited. Then someone called—he recognized Montgomery's voice; he was a clergyman and had never lost the unctuous tones of the Church of England—"Who is it?"

"Venable," he answered.

"Wait a minute, please, Colonel."

He waited, what seemed a long time. He heard a door slam—a heavy door—probably one of the cipher safes . . . they must have had something really hush-hush on the table if they felt compelled to hide it from *him*.

"Come in, Colonel." The door opened and he walked in. The younger man, de Grey, sitting at a desk by the window, said, "What can we do for you, Colonel?"

"Oh, nothing. I've just given the D.N.I. some information which we knew would interest him . . . I thought I'd drop in and see if you fellows had anything for us before I go back to the War Office."

The older Montgomery looked at his colleague—both civilians, taken from their normal professions at the outbreak of war and now working as cipher experts in this most secret of secret departments of the Admiralty—indeed of the whole British government. Montgomery said, "Nothing at all, Colonel—that hasn't been sent over to your people through normal channels."

"Sorry to bother you then," Venable said. "No link turned up between Bertrand Russell's pacifists and the Germans?"

"Nothing that we know of," Montgomery said. "And I somehow doubt whether Bertrand Russell is linked with the Germans in any way, Colonel. I feel he acts from his own motives."

"So did the Sinn Feiners and the Irish Republican Army," Venable said, "but they turned to Germany for help—which made them traitors. Well, sorry to have bothered you."

He went out with a nod and a wave of his leather-gloved hand. The duty officer looked up, said nothing, and returned to his work. Venable strode down the passage. They were like dogs with a hidden bone in there. His loins stirred . . . Naomi, as soon after two as she could get there, to No. 43 Halsey Crescent in St John's Wood. He saw her long body, the breasts upthrust, swelling, her arms out, her deep brown eyes softening. Oh Christ, she was beginning to obsess him . . .

*   *   *   *

In Room 40 the two civilians began opening safes and taking out heavy cipher books, deciphering keys, and the papers they had been working on. They sat down side by side at a table by one wall, facing the wall. Montgomery said, "I wish we had had some sop to give Colonel Venable. He's no fool. He'll guess something important's going on."

"But not exactly what. And he'll be out of Intelligence here before long. Our counter-intelligence people have discovered that he's having an affair with a girl in one of the women's services . . . using flats the War Office keeps for interviews and to hide people they want to protect and so on, to meet her."

"Have we told the D.M.I. yet?"

De Grey shook his head—"No. We're waiting to see whether there is anything really dangerous in it—spying, double agents, links with subversives which he's not supposed to have . . . but probably not. Just the simple lust of an elderly Don Juan."

The clergyman sighed, "Poor Venable . . . Well, let us see what we have." They bent their heads together over two sheets of paper. The first one was headed:

Berlin to Washington. W 158. 16 January, 1917. Most Secret. For your Excellency's personal information and to be handed on to the Imperial Minister in Mexico by a safe route.

The second sheet of paper read, in Montgomery's handwriting:

NO. 1. WE PROPOSE TO BEGIN ON FEBRUARY 1 UNRESTRICTED SUBMARINE WARFARE. IN DOING THIS HOWEVER WE SHALL ENDEAVOR TO KEEP AMERICA NEUTRAL . . . ? IF WE SHOULD NOT . . . ? WE PROPOSE . . . ? . . . AN ALLIANCE UPON THE FOLLOWING BASIS . . . ? . . . CONDUCT OF WAR . . . ? . . .

CONCLUSION OF PEACE . . . ? . . . YOUR EXCELLENCY SHOULD FOR THE PRESENT INFORM THE PRESIDENT SECRETLY . . . ? . . . WAR WITH THE U.S.A. . . . ? . . . ? . . . AND AT THE SAME TIME NEGOTIATE BETWEEN US AND JAPAN. PLEASE TELL THE PRESIDENT THAT . . . ? . . . OUR SUBMARINES WILL COMPEL ENGLAND TO PEACE WITHIN A FEW MONTHS. ACKNOWLEDGE RECEIPT. ZIMMERMANN.

Montgomery said, "Let's try all the variants on the groups we haven't got yet."

De Grey said, "The D.N.I. thinks that missing bit after 'should not' will be something like 'succeed in doing so' . . . and the long gap after 'conclusion of peace' will be something to do with offering Mexico part of America—I can still not really believe they can be such absolute idiots."

The clergyman said soberly, "This is not a trap. It's a blunder that will win the war for us . . . but the D.N.I.'s going to have a very difficult job finding some way of publishing this without giving away that we can read their ciphers."

De Grey said, "I agree, but he specifically told us not to worry about that—just to decipher the rest of the message so that he can decide how best to use it."

*   *   *   *

Rachel Cowan, her hair pulled back in a severe bun, looked covertly round the gathering. She herself was sitting on the floor next to Bert Gorse. John Rowland was in an armchair behind them, his face wearing the permanent look of concern that had settled on it since he decided that he must support any initiatives for peace, even if his own friends and family thought his actions treasonable. Round the rest of the room—on the floor, in the few chairs, sitting on the edge of the desk, leaning against the tall bookshelf, were the rest of them—

members of the No-Conscription Fellowship come up from Kent, Sussex, and West Surrey to a policy meeting under the direction of Bertrand Russell. They were gathered in the top floor room which Bertrand's brother, Earl Russell, had allotted to him in his house on Gordon Square in Bloomsbury. The room was small at any time, and cluttered with books, papers, objets d'art, busts of noted philosophers, and portraits, including two of the Germans, Leibnitz and Frege.

Russell, small, clean shaven, thick wavy silver-grey hair, his expression and the whole cast of his face intense, like some emotional hawk, was wearing a dark suit, a high stiff collar with rounded points, and a plain dark tie. He was speaking, quickly, emphasizing his points with sharp, alert gestures. The other delegates listened intently. Next to Russell a young woman of great beauty with wavy dark hair and a vaguely theatrical manner, who was not a delegate, listened and watched with what Rachel considered to be open adoration; she had been introduced as Lady Constance Malleson.

It was two o'clock on this bleak, dark January afternoon. Bertrand Russell, now forty-five, stood in front of the fireplace, his hair streaming back from his forehead as though he were facing into a keen wind on some remote moor. Rachel listened, making notes, as he summed up the war situation.

Russell finished, "Well, that's the situation . . . Our national committee met yesterday, when we had had a chance to digest the Allied reply to Wilson. Allen proposed, and we agreed, that we must step up action in the direction of passive resistance. If we go and derail ammunition trains, blow up arsenals, scuttle ships, we will draw the full force of the government's police power against us—and we shall lose that sympathy which we now have, if only in a sneaking, secret way, from many who must openly support the war but in their hearts know that we are right to try to bring it to an end. Therefore—passive resistance. This is the appeal we drafted at our meeting—I have copies for all delegations. Take it back, have thousands of copies printed—it is quite short—and distribute it in public places." He handed round copies. "As you see, it appeals to all men and women to do nothing to further the prosecution of the war and to deny any such services that they are already rendering."

"What about air raid precautions, blackout?" the Surrey woman asked. "Should we refuse to comply—leave lights on in the house, use open headlights on cars?"

Russell said, "We thought about that, but we decided against those steps. They might draw enemy bombs, kill some people who would otherwise have survived . . . and lose us sympathy."

"What about nurses?" Rachel asked; realizing as soon as the words

319

had left her mouth that the answer would be the same as to the last questioner. Though the refusal of nursing services in military hospitals and convalescent depots would hinder the conduct of the war, it would arouse great antagonism, so—"No"; and thus Russell answered.

He said, "Organize public meetings. Distribute the pamphlets. Urge non-violent non-cooperation on everyone . . . Your meetings will be attacked, and the police will do nothing to protect you. You may be arrested on charges ranging from breach of the peace to treason . . . Persevere!"

"We're running very short of funds in Surrey," the woman said.

All the delegates murmured agreement. Russell raised a hand. "We're getting a few large contributions from a few rich people who are on our side . . . but most of the rich, and all the big companies, are against us. We are going to distribute about five hundred pounds nationally, the day after tomorrow. That's based on two shillings per member on your rolls."

Rachel thought, a hundred and forty shillings for us then, with our seventy members—seven pounds. Couldn't get much done with that.

Russell was speaking again—"Make collections at your meetings. Our people in the North have been surprised to find how much is slipped to them, even when a crowd has apparently been hostile." He paused—"That's all, comrades."

Rachel began to struggle to her feet. A hand reached down to help her up and she looked up into the eyes of a delegate from Sussex called Wilfred Bentley. He was tall and thin, and Russell had mentioned that he had been gassed earlier in the war. She said, "I'm so sorry. I hope it doesn't hurt too much—your lung."

He laughed—"Russell shouldn't have mentioned that."

She said, "It must have been awful for someone like you . . . I don't mean just the gassing, but everything—the violence, the killing, the brutishness, men acting like animals—worse—the debasement of human character."

He said earnestly, "The war is a debasement, Miss Cowan, but the men have not been debased. It's a privilege to have served out there, with them."

She was puzzled, and was making ready to ask him a question when Bert, at her side, said, "Come on. We got a bus and a train to catch, and the 'ell of a lot to do when we get 'ome."

Bentley wandered off, a hand raised in goodbye.

She said, to Bert, "That was rude of you, to interrupt. I was talking to Mr Bentley."

Bert said, "We got to go. Are you coming with us, Mr Rowland?"

John Rowland, standing close by, started. He'd been miles away in his mind, Rachel thought. "Thank you, no," he said. "I'm staying in town overnight. My daughter Naomi has obtained a weekend's leave and I am taking her to the theatre and giving her a few good meals."

"Give her my—regards," Rachel said, feeling awkward. She would have said "love" instead of "regards" a year ago. Perhaps love was what she still felt for Naomi . . . but much water had flowed under the bridges since those Girton days.

*　　*　　*　　*

John Rowland walked beside the Serpentine with his daughter, Naomi, in a cold east wind that blew flurries of snow across the surface of the water and eddied the dead leaves under the chestnut trees. His collar was turned up, and his scarf wrapped as high round his neck as he could get it, but the wind bit at his exposed ears and threatened to blow the bowler hat off his head, even the rolled umbrella out of his gloved hands. Naomi, beside him, walked as tall as he, her back straighter in the long khaki greatcoat, under it the swinging khaki skirt, and the black boots of her Corps, on her windblown hair the wide-brimmed felt hat, its badge, and a long hatpin stuck through to keep it on her head. She too was wearing gloves, but no scarf; that was not regulation.

John was talking about farming—"It never was easy, Naomi, now it's really difficult. And it's becoming too expensive. I think Shearer's very foolish to have insisted on buying his farm from your Uncle Christopher. One bad crop and he'll lose it to the banks. Before, Christopher stood between him and that kind of disaster."

"I thought Uncle Christopher had to raise some money somehow, to meet taxes and expenses."

John said, "He did, but he could have sold some of his securities and that was what he really wanted to do, but Shearer kept pressing him to sell him the farm."

Naomi said, "Tenant farming like that won't last long, after the war, Daddy. The relation that there used to be between the landowner and the tenants depended on things that are going, being blown up, over there in France . . . What happened at your meeting last night?"

John said, "It's been decided to start a national campaign of non-cooperation . . . passive resistance, is what I think they are going to call it officially."

Naomi said after a time, "Violence will be forced on you, I'm afraid, Daddy. And I don't think you will achieve anything. There aren't enough people who think as you do to affect the war . . . not even Mummy agrees with you." She laid a hand on her father's arm—"That's true, isn't it?"

321

John said, heavily, "Yes . . . Your mother can not see how good—how *Christian*—our cause is. She can only see that Boy must get all that he needs to fight the Germans. I—we—can only see that as long as the shells and guns and barbed wire—and men—are provided, the war will continue. And without a cause."

His daughter said, "I know a colonel in the War Office . . . drive him about quite a bit . . . He talks to me on the long trips. He says that the Germans are like sheep—sheep with wolves' teeth—and that unless they are crushed now, they will come back again at us in ten or twenty years time. And next time they'll make sure that we don't have France or Russia as allies . . . or America."

"He may be right," John said, "but we can't afford to think of what might happen in the future if we are destroying ourselves now—to such an extent that there may *be* no future for us."

"Colonel Venable doesn't think it's as bad as that. We are hurting them as much as they're hurting us . . . he thinks Lloyd George will want to just stay on the defensive in France, but make a big attack from Italy, which would end the war."

"If I could believe it . . ." John said. He thought, but even if I did believe it, I shouldn't change my course; I believe in a negotiated peace, so what am I doing, hoping surreptitiously for a knockout victory?

"Rodney thinks it might be a good idea, but . . ."

"Rodney? Who is he?"

"Oh, Colonel Venable. He makes me call him Rodney when we don't have any other passengers in the car. It's quite against regulations, but he insists . . . He thinks that the other allies won't hear of it, especially France."

The mallards were sheltering in little groups under the bank, and under the overhanging boughs of the willows. Dogs and children gambolled on the path, and a few stern Nannies braved the wind and the snow, wheeling young ladies and gentlemen westward toward the Albert Memorial, the Round Pond, and nursery lunch in S.W.7. John felt a momentary pang—his daughter, a tall-standing English rose, this grass, these trees, the wall of Buckingham Palace farther along there, the Iron Duke's mansion at the corner, all these men, women, and children in the Park—all English—even the dogs. Wasn't all this worth fighting for, to the end?

But all this, precisely, was what would not exist, or have no meaning, if the fabric which held it and shaped it was destroyed.

"What does Boy think?" Naomi asked him. "I suppose he knows what you're doing?"

John said, "He says he understands, but he has to fight until the

Germans are beaten. Couldn't say anything else, poor fellow, could he? But I think . . . I feel . . . that he hates it over there . . ."

"I'm sure he does," Naomi said, "they all do, except a few lunatics, but I don't think he'll give up."

John said, "Nearly time for lunch, and then a matinee, eh?" He turned and headed across the grass toward the back of the Hyde Park Hotel, where they were staying. Naomi said hurriedly, "I won't be able to go to the theatre this afternoon, Daddy. I forgot to tell you last night, when you picked me up . . . I have to go to the barracks at two for an urgent job—they're very short-handed . . . I should be free again by six."

"Then we can go to an evening show, eh?" John said. His daughter did not answer, her head and face hidden by the greatcoat's high collar, as the wind whistled past their ears, tugged at their hats and gloves, and bit through their socks and boots into their feet.

*   *   *   *

Rachel Cowan, pulling her hat well down on her head and thrusting five big hatpins through it, stared into the cracked mirror over the rickety washstand. She was getting to look like a rat—wary, mouth set, teeth bared: beware, keep clear, I bite. Well, that's what the hatpins were for—to stick into the police if they tried to push her about . . . or if the usual crowd of jeering soldiers, sailors, labourers, and women of all sorts, who attended their peace rallies, got out of hand, and the police gave up even their usual feeble pretence of protecting the peace group.

Bert Gorse was lying on the bed beside her, fully dressed, reading a newspaper. He glanced up. She said, "Nearly time to go, Bert."

Movement on the pavement outside the front door below caught her eye and she said, "Someone's coming! It's a soldier . . ." She peered down—"Can't see his face . . ."

Bert got up, went downstairs and jerked open the door—"'Oo the 'ell . . . ? Why, it's Fletcher. Come on in."

Rachel followed more slowly down the short narrow stairs. The house smelled of cabbage, and dust lay thick everywhere. She was a bad housekeeper; but when did she have the time? There were more important things in life for women to do than sweep and mop and brush and dust.

Fletcher said, "Thought I'd come by to say goodbye, Bert . . . Hullo, Rachel."

He looked beautiful, she thought, even in that horrible khaki. He somehow made the stiffness of the rolled puttees, gleaming black boots, and green-blancoed web belt look like the clothing of a forest hunter, a runner over the American plains.

"They sending you to France?" Bert asked.

Fletcher nodded—"Monday. Don't know which battalion yet."

"You'd do better to shoot your trigger finger off," Bert said, "or rob a bank and knock a rozzer on the head, then you'd spend the rest of the war in gaol instead of . . ."

"I got to go," Fletcher said.

"'Oo says you *got* to go?" Bert said. "Run away, like you did before. Only this time don't come back."

"*I* got to go," Fletcher said, "and if you write, don't forget I'm Private Fletcher Whitman . . . Well, cheerio."

"Where are you going now?"

"Out," Fletcher said, "with a young lady."

Bert said sarcastically, "You don't say? I thought it would be with a bleeding orangutan."

"Miss Merritt?" Rachel inquired. She watched Fletcher closely for any signs of gloating, the unpleasant male boastful look that says "I've got her, I can do what I like with her, she's in the bag."

Fletcher said, "Yes. We're going to the seaside, in her car."

"In February?" Bert cried. "You're mad, Fletcher."

"Coming back this evening?" Rachel asked.

"I don't have to," Fletcher said. "I've forty-eight hours leave. Depends on Betty, what she wants. I love her."

"Good bloody Christ," Bert murmured. "The Romeo of Walstone's fallen at last. I don't believe it!"

*   *   *   *

They walked slowly through the twilight, Rachel trying to keep her head up, her back straight, to look every passer-by in the eyes; but she was so tired, so tired. Bert, limping beside her, muttered, "My big toe that isn't there hurts worse every day."

"You ought to see a doctor," she said listlessly.

The peace rally had gone off as well as the others, and as badly. The same crowd had attended—a third of them members of the Fellowship, to clap and cheer, to take the pamphlets and pass through the crowd handing them out . . . the other two thirds the jeerers, with just a scattering of the people the Fellowship really wanted, the worried, the doubters, the appalled. Rachel had recognized some familiar faces—four or five men and as many women, whose main joy in life, and the outlet of all their fury, frustration and fear, was to attend these Hedlington rallies, scream abuse at Rachel, Bert, or other speakers, throw rotten fruit and vegetables, shove and jostle the volunteers, snatch pamphlets from them and trample them in the mud.

They reached the front door and saw a light on inside, shining through the fanlight. "Someone's in there," Bert said sharply. He hurried forward. "It's unlocked!" He jerked the door open and stopped suddenly. A police constable was facing him.

"Are you Mr Albert Gorse?"

"What of it?" Bert answered belligerently.

"And you are Miss Rachel Cowan?"

"Yes."

The policeman, who wore the striped sleeve band of a constable on duty, felt in his tunic pocket and produced a sheet of paper. "This is our warrant to search this house. We have reason to believe it is being used to print seditious material."

Another constable came out of the door of the front parlour and said, "It's not screwed to anything, George, but we'll need another man to carry it out, and a van to take it to the station."

Bert screamed, "Our press! You can't take our press!"

The senior constable said, "We can. And you are both under arrest. The charge is publishing seditious material. We are also confiscating books, magazines, and pamphlets which appear to be in the German language."

Rachel shouted, "They are documents explaining the German position, and appeals from German pacifists and Socialists to their own people, to stop the war!"

"That's as may be, miss," the constable said. "The judge will decide, won't he? Hold out your hands, please." The handcuffs clicked locked.

Rachel said, "I want to call a lawyer."

"At the station, miss . . . There, you'll be given every right you 'ave, under the law."

Rachel said, "Hurry up, then. Don't shout, Bert. And don't try to hit them, Bert. Our job is to get back here as soon as we can and get on with our job—stopping the war."

*   *   *   *

Johnny Merritt sat in a large office of the United States Embassy, Grosvenor Gardens. It was evening of a raw February day and the lights were glimmering through a foggy haze. Across the big desk sat Virgil Kramer, Secretary of Embassy—forty-five, square of face and build, with a ruddy complexion and iron grey hair *en brosse*. Johnny thought of him as "uncle" but his actual relationship was less easily defined: he was Johnny's father's sister's dead husband's brother.

"Glad you could drop by for a minute," the older man said. "Stella well?"

"Fine," Johnny said.

"How's business?"

"The Leopard Mark II's programme's finished. The Lion is doing well, and we've just had another order—forty. But I spent all day today at the War Office trying to get someone to understand that if the R.F.C. want a heavy bomber by next year—they must make up their minds *now*. It's very hard to get even the best of them, as flyers, as leaders of the air war, to understand the factory side of it . . . the time involved with design, tests, re-designs, re-tests, placement of orders, tool and die cutting . . ."

"Well, if you use Libertys for the Buffalo—that's what you're going to call it, you told me, didn't you?—we'll do all we can from the Embassy to help you. And that will be true even if we do get into the war ourselves. The Secretary of War had a paper prepared by the Department of the Army Signal Corps a month ago, and they came to the conclusion that until 1919 any aeroplanes we used, if we go to war, would have to be made for us by the other Allies—France and England."

Johnny leaned forward, "That's really what I came about, Uncle Virgil . . . *Are* we getting in?"

Kramer said, "I wish I knew, Johnny, I wish I knew."

Johnny said unhappily, "I can't stand it much longer. In 1914 I was rarin' to come over and fight for England and civilization. Dad persuaded me—sort of bamboozled and soft-soaped me—into the J.M.C., then this . . . and now that I know a lot more about the war than I did then, I'm not thanking God for the war. And I don't want to fight with the English. For them, maybe—we're all in the same boat there . . . but not *with* them. I'm an American. And, by God, the moment we declare war, I'm off. Nothing's going to stop me—*nothing*!"

"The Signal Corps, to fly?" his uncle asked.

Johnny shook his head. "That's what I'd have preferred. But I had my eyes tested last month—in case. Color blind. Oh, not serious—I can tell reds and greens apart and every other color, until you get down to pale blues and pale greens. It'll have to be the Army—infantry or artillery, I guess." He got up—"If you'll excuse me, Uncle, I have to catch a train. Stella . . ."

"Of course, man . . . Your Aunt Isabel's going to be at Walstone Manor this weekend, you know."

"I didn't. I expect she'll come over to see us. She usually does."

Virgil Kramer shook his head, "If she and Christopher weren't both such great people, it might be kind of funny, but it isn't . . . It's a tragedy—the sort of tragedy that only strikes men and women of unflinching courage, devotion to duty, and the highest moral standards . . . Goodnight, Johnny."

"Goodnight, Uncle."

*　　*　　*　　*

Fletcher Gorse and Betty Merritt walked the shore in silence. The pebbles, sloping down in an even bank to the sea, crunched and grated under their feet. The arch of darkness was spangled bright with stars, for the moon had not yet risen. The sea was a pale shimmer beside them, murmuring ceaselessly on the stones, limning them with a momentary white lace, that disappeared, whispered, reappeared, sighed, withdrew.

The pebbles shook and slid, the windows rattled in their sashes, the sea trembled, the earth beneath shook, all to the low, bass shudder of the guns on the Western Front.

Betty spoke in a near whisper as though someone close was eavesdropping on their privacy—"Do you want to go?"

"I got to," the young man said. It was cold, and he had not taken his greatcoat from barracks, but he did not notice. He had spent many hours out on colder nights than this, in thinner clothes, waiting to snare a pheasant, or climb a drainpipe to a girl's window.

"But do you *want* to?"

"I got to see it, to live there, in the war."

After a while she said, "You'll write wonderful poetry about it, Fletcher. What you have written already . . . what you read to me today, and before . . . is so wonderful. You are a . . . you're a great poet, Fletcher, like Shelley or Keats . . . or Whitman."

"I'll be greater," he said simply, "if I don't get killed."

After another five minutes, when they had nearly reached the great pier reaching out into the sea, the silhouetted bulk of armed, greatcoated, steel-helmeted sentries with fixed bayonets patrolling it now visible, he said, "I love you, Betty Merritt."

She began to cry, silently. A time later he realized that she was crying, and put his arm round her tenderly, and said, "Don't cry, love."

She sobbed, "I'm so happy." She stopped suddenly, turned and pressed her face into his tunic. He bent his head, lifted her chin with his free hand and kissed her on the lips. Willingly her lips parted, softened, her body grew soft, pressing against him.

"I'm not gentry," he said.

"It doesn't matter," she cried. "I'm an American! I don't believe in that rot. All men are born free and equal!"

"Only some of us freer and more equal than others," he said, grinning down at her in the dark.

They turned and walked back down the shingle toward the south.

His physical presence overwhelmed her, as it always did. But, she must think, forecast . . . how could they live together, as man and wife, if he never read anything but poetry, knew nothing of politics, music, theatre, even games? He was really uneducated . . . She'd think of a snug cottage, and he . . . of being out under a full moon stalking birds and beasts, nearly as wild as they. The guns shuddered in her flesh, urging her on.

She whispered, "We should be starting back soon, Fletcher . . . Would you . . . will you . . . come back to my flat with me? For the night?"

He said softly, "Hey, woman, you must let me ask that."

She said, "But you're going to France on Monday . . . I've been thinking of you in the flat, with me, alone, at night . . . for weeks, months, now . . ."

"If I weren't going to France, would you ask me?" he said.

She considered, for she wanted to answer honestly. She said, "I don't know. I feel . . . oh, how do I know what I feel, when I've never been with a man before, or wanted to? I know what my body wants, but . . . I was strictly brought up, Fletcher. I'd hate to hurt my father . . . I don't know."

He stopped and kissed her again then, long and slow and caressingly. Two soldiers passed, bayonets sharp against the stars, the pebbles rolling down, their voices a murmur, a subdued chuckle. He gently explored her mouth with his tongue. She smelled fresh, of the sea, and of the seaweed they had been playing with earlier, and of a faint expensive perfume in her hair. Words moved in his head, forming ideas, pictures, a translation and embodiment of his love.

He said, "Not to your flat, love. People would know and I don't want that—them looking at you, thinking, Fletcher Gorse fucked her."

She winced involuntarily at the harsh word. He continued: "Shall we try a hotel? They'll likely have a room and I hear the hotels don't ask soldiers in uniform for their marriage lines, if they're with a woman, these days." The rumble of the guns punctuated his light tenor voice.

She whispered, "It'll be my first time, Fletcher."

He said, "Not mine, love. I'll guide thee . . . What am I saying? It'll be my first time, too . . . with a woman I love. So we'll have to guide each other."

"In a world of our own," she whispered, "under the bedclothes!"

He understood her and said, "I'll love you, Betty, all night, and more, all day, till you know what sort of woman you are. But I can't quiet the guns, not by curtains nor window glass nor bedclothes nor nothing else."

Daily Telegraph, Saturday, February 24, 1917

AIRCRAFT WORK
HOW WOMEN ARE EMPLOYED

Women are now taking a large share in the industry which provides one of the greatest assets of the Forces on land or sea, in the form of aeroplanes, war balloons, sea-planes and other aerial scouts. Not only are they to be seen in those sections of the aircraft industry where their help might have been expected in pre-war times, such as in cutting-out, sewing, painting, and varnishing the fabric for aeroplane wings, but they are supplementing men in the essential engineering operations. The most important part of an aeroplane—its heart, so to speak—is the engine, the construction of which calls for the utmost accuracy. Women are now entrusted with much of this work, and are undertaking the milling of the top and the grinding of the inside of the engine cylinders, and they are also engaged on machining the connecting-rods, the valves, the pistons, and the holding-down bolts. These processes are often carried out to an accuracy of half-a-thousandth of an inch, that is, to one-eighth of the thickness of an average human hair, a measurement which can only be gauged by the most ingeniously constructed instruments. Women are further employed in the aceto-welding process where conscientious and intelligent work is imperative, since upon the soundness of the joints depends the safety of the machine and the life of the flying man. Such services may best be offered by those of the educated classes whose previous experience fits them for deftness of manipulation, keenness of observation, and accuracy of judgment.

Johnny took the cutting, which had been sent over to his office by Betty, with an admonition to send it on to their father, and laid it down beside the letter he was working on. The sound of aircraft engines made him get up and walk to the window. Snow was beginning to fall, and a Leopard was coming in to land. This one should have no difficulty, but another Leopard was up in the air, on a compass test flight to Salisbury Plain and back: that one might have a sticky time, if this got worse.

He returned to his desk, picked up his pen, and continued the letter to his father:

A couple of months ago the country was in the throes of the parliamentary crisis. Well, of course it has long been settled, and Mr Lloyd George is firm in the saddle. He is an interesting personality, with tremendous energy, a very quick and powerful intelligence; plus strong streaks of guile and ruthlessness, which are all to the good in the present circumstances. He has already kindled a new spirit in the British, and if he continues as he has begun he will be forgiven his faults.

The war is in a period of semi-calm, which many feel is the calm before the storm. The colonel I talk to at the War Office has got hold of the 1916 casualty figures—this is British Empire only, Western Front only—and they are appalling: 150,131 killed, 1,145,452 wounded, missing, and prisoners. (For this the King made Haig a Field Marshal!) Now consider that the French, Russians, and Germans have all had more; the Italians, Serbs, Rumanians, and Belgians equally heavy, in proportion—and 1916 begins to take shape as the year of the Apocalypse for Western civilization—all civilization, perhaps. I didn't think highly of Bertrand Russell and the other pacifists—regarded them as crackpots and traitors—but those figures make one think that they may be the only sane people on earth. However, as a practical matter it is certain that no one is in fact going to negotiate an end to the war.

In the light of the casualty figures, and the effort they represent, it is unlikely that the British will mount the first major offensive of 1917. The Germans will. It seems almost certain that we, the U.S. of A., are going to be drawn into it whether we like it or not; and it is impossible that we should come in on the German side. They have done so much against our interests, and British propaganda has been so smart in the U.S.A., that to join the Germans now is unthinkable. But Wilson might be reinforced in his own personal desire to keep us out if some catastrophe to the Allies can make their cause seem less attractive to us.

As for the German targets, the French at Verdun or the British at Ypres are the favorites. Verdun is 130 easy miles from Paris. A breakthrough there could be decisive—the French defeated, the British left to be dealt with at leisure.

I regard our entry into the war as long overdue, as you know. We will make no less money, as a nation—even as a business here—in fact we shall make more; but we shall be in a position to say, we have earned it, we deserve it; instead of acting rather like jackals or hyenas round a nobler beast's kill. My bet is that we shall declare war three months after the German assault starts—that is, when it has demonstrably been held. What the precise excuse or *casus belli* will be, no one can foretell; but I am positive one will be found. And, as soon as it is, I shall be entering the U.S. Army. I've sat on the sidelines long enough.

A faint drone of aircraft engines grew stronger, thick, deadened by the snow. The snow was falling faster and visibility could be no more than three hundred yards horizontal and about two hundred feet vertically. Johnny went again to the window and stood there, watching anxiously. He could see nothing now . . . just the grass and some parked bicycles in a rack directly below his window. The drone grew fainter . . . circling round to the south, fading . . . Why didn't he gain altitude and fly back to the Plain? Conditions here were murderous . . . but perhaps he didn't have enough petrol left, had no choice . . . The noise grew louder, then dropped, and steadied . . . louder . . . louder . . . the great shape appeared a hundred yards away, eighty feet up, blue flames flickering from its exhausts. At once the pilot put the nose down, and cut his engines. The bomber glided silently down, almost at once vanishing into the snowstorm. Johnny waited, nerves taut . . . no sound . . . no crash, no flames . . . just the silent snow. He'd landed, dead stick, near the west end of the field.

Johnny drew out his handkerchief, wiped his face, and returned to his desk. He'd like to tell Dad that Stella was in great shape—but she wasn't . . . sleepy and yawning most of the time, grumpy the rest . . . uninterested in anything, even sex. He couldn't tell his father that. Instead he'd tell Dad what he thought Fairfax, Gottlieb should be prepared for, in the way of expanding war production, when the U.S.A. became a belligerent.

At Sea: Friday, February 23, 1917

22 H.M.S. *Penrith* plunged her bow into the wall-like face of the wave, green and white water bursting in a bomb of spray straight up in the salt-laden air, to sweep back along the deck, smashing over the forward turret into the bridge structure, whirling past the reeling foremast and funnels, foaming along the quarterdeck and back into the sea. The bridge watchkeepers rocked on their heels, legs spread for balance, greatcoat collars turned up, salt-rimmed eyes searching the endless expanse of heaving water ahead.

The officer of the watch said, "Cape Wrath bears south, sir."

Captain Leach said, "Starboard fifteen . . . steady on west by south."

"West by south, sir . . . steady, steady!"

Penrith headed into the teeth of a winter gale, battened down, the lower messdecks already awash, water everywhere, every man soaked to the skin in the three hours since the light cruiser had passed the new Commander-in-Chief, Admiral Sir David Beatty, in H.M.S. *Queen Elizabeth*, the crew fallen-in by divisions on the upper deck from fo'c'sle to quarterdeck, all officers and ratings on the bridge except the officer conning the ship facing the battleship and saluting as the marine bugler sounded the "Alert." As the ratings on *Queen Elizabeth's* decks faced *Penrith*, officers saluting, the admiral himself had come to the corner of his flag bridge and raised his cap six inches off his head. So *Penrith* had passed down the Flow, through the Grand Fleet, while the Officer of the Watch, a junior Sub Lieutenant, a copy of the Navy List in his hand, muttered to Captain Leach which captains were senior to him and must be saluted, and which were junior, and would initiate the salute. Now, three hours later, an almost visible aura of excitement pervaded the ship, a lightness, like children let out of a dark schoolroom into sunny playgrounds. The Grand Fleet was Britain's right arm, her first and principal line of defence. When at sea it presented the most fearsome spectacle of disciplined power yet seen by man . . . seven squadrons of battleships, and battle cruisers, six of cruisers, over eighty destroyers . . . Yet every sailor of the Navy still hated service in it, because every sailor knew that after Jutland the German High Seas Fleet never would venture out again. Officers found guilty of minor peccadilloes anywhere else in the Service were sent to the Grand Fleet as a punishment. It was a prison, from which *Penrith* had just escaped, ordered to the North American and West Indies Station, at an hour's notice.

The Navy phone from the foretop, swaying wildly against the scudding clouds fifty feet above, whined tinnily—"Bridge—Object bearing green six oh . . . I think it's a ship's lifeboat."

"Port fifteen," Captain Leach said. He stooped to another voice pipe—"Tom . . . object sighted, off the starboard bow, probably a lifeboat."

"Right, sir."

In his cabin, Tom picked up his binoculars and hurried out onto the quarterdeck. There, he put the binoculars to his eyes, and tried with one hand to shield the eyepieces from the flying spray and water; but it was no use, there was too much of it, it filled the air and sky. Peering under his hand, watching the wavetops ahead, at last he saw it, rising, disappearing, rising, perched for a moment between sea and sky on the crest of a great wave, about a mile away, a white-painted lifeboat, no mast or jury sail . . . too far to see whether there were oars over the side, but he thought not . . . definitely a sea anchor out for she was riding mostly head to sea, though on the front faces of some waves, the steep fall was slewing her round.

"She'll capsize if that gets much worse," he muttered.

On the bridge Leach, too, peered forward under his sheltering hand, and after a moment said, "I don't like it . . . Number One, put the scrambling nets out on the starboard side. Away sea boat's crew, but don't launch. Stand by the nets until we see what we've got."

"Aye, aye, sir!" Lieutenant Commander Mainprice-King slid down the bridge ladder. At once the boatswain's pipes twittered, and the chief boatswain's mate began to bark orders that sounded distant and thin against the bellow and shriek of the wind and the smash of the sea.

The lifeboat came closer. "Half ahead both," the captain ordered into the engine room pipe: then "Twenty of port wheel, quartermaster!"

"Twenty of port wheel, sir . . . Twenty of port wheel on, sir."

"Starboard five . . . steady! Slow, both . . . Stop engines . . . Slow astern, port engine! Stop engines!"

The cruiser, stopped in the water, rolled heavily, wind and seas now striking her full on the port side. The mast head and foretop seemed to strike the crest of each wave as it passed by, but just in time the trough followed and *Penrith* righted herself and began a lurch to port. In the starboard wing of the bridge, looking back along the steel slide, Leach saw the lifeboat coming closer as the cruiser drifted down on it. It was full of men . . . and women . . . it must have been a passenger ship that had been torpedoed. They were lying in the bottom-boards, among swirling water, flotsam, coats, lifebelts. Boat hooks reached out from the scrambling net and Lieutenant Mountjoy and a couple of sailors dropped into the lifeboat. Leach saw Mountjoy stoop and take one of the people's collars . . . turn him over . . . pause . . . onto the next, the next . . . the next . . . Mountjoy looked up toward the bridge and even from that distance Tom saw that his face was white, his mouth set, either in fierce anger or to prevent himself from vomiting. He gave some order to the sailors, which Leach could not hear, and scrambled back up the net to the cruiser's deck. A moment later he appeared on the bridge.

"S.S. *Styria,* Liverpool, sir. Thirty-one men, nine women, six children. They're all dead."

"How?" the captain interjected.

"Exposure, sir . . . starvation and thirst, too, perhaps . . . the water barrel's stove in . . . I told the men to delay doing anything until I'd spoken to you. Their eyes have all been eaten out . . . faces scratched."

"Gulls!" Leach exclaimed. "I don't remember when the *Styria* was sunk. It must have been some time ago."

"What . . . ?" young Mountjoy began; Leach raised his hand—"I'm thinking." After a minute he said, "Bridge messenger!"

"Sir!"

"Get me the prayer book off the desk in my day cabin."

"Aye, aye, sir!" The boy sailor darted down the bridge ladder.

The captain turned to Mountjoy—"Weight all the bodies with a shell. I'll read the burial service over them from the deck. Have a man in the boat and as soon as I'm finished signal him to scuttle it . . . Oh, and have a Union Flag dropped over them while I read. Haul it back as the boat sinks."

Mountjoy saluted, turned, and left. Tom came up onto the bridge. Leach looked at him—"I think that'll satisfy the men's sense of decorum, don't you? What an utter swine the Hun really is."

Half an hour later, the burial service completed, the cruiser's propellers began to turn again, thrusting the vessel ever westward, her long lean bows pointed to Cape Race on the south coast of Newfoundland, and Halifax, Nova Scotia.

The captain returned to the bridge, prayer book in his gloved hand, his face grim—"Who's on watch?"

Lieutenant Onslow from the far corner said, "I am, sir."

"You know the course?"

"Yes, sir—west by south."

"Reduce speed to ten knots till this lessens. She's shaking to pieces."

"Aye, aye, sir."

"Tom, come to my cabin, please."

Tom followed his captain down the ladders and aft along the lower deck to the big stern cabin. He waited, cap in hand, until Leach had sat down and waved him to a chair.

Leach said, "I haven't had a chance to speak to you since we got the orders . . . They're going to institute trans-Atlantic convoys. That's the only thing this move of ours can mean."

"They've been running them for some time on the Harwich-Scheldt route, sir," Tom said.

"Started in December last," Leach said briefly, "and, since last month, on the cross-channel coal traffic—the French insisted. The Admiralty didn't want to do it, but the French were losing too much coal . . . Now it looks as if the Anti-Submarine Division have had their way and we're going to have all merchant ships convoyed, at least on principal routes . . . and they'll need cruisers for the trans-Atlantic run. Destroyers haven't got the endurance."

"And they'd have a very bad time in weather like this," Tom said, rubbing his hands together.

"You're soaked," the captain exclaimed, noticing the gesture—"Here." He opened a cupboard, took out a bottle, and poured a stiff tot into a glass—"It's malt whisky . . . pure malt."

Tom took a swig, let the golden fire trickle down his throat and emptied the glass—"Thank you, sir."

"It's about time . . . that they really accepted the convoy principle," Leach said. "Our losses have been staggering since the Germans instituted unrestricted submarine warfare . . . 200,000 tons of shipping sunk in January, but 500,000 tons in February, after they'd opened the all-out campaign . . . and the figures are still climbing

335

. . . I believe that Admiral Jellicoe warned the Cabinet some time back that if the trend wasn't stopped, we'd be starved out."

Tom said, "But Admiral Jellicoe doesn't think the convoy system will work."

"It appears that he doesn't have any other suggestions, so it has been forced on him."

The Navy phone spoke from the bridge—"Captain, sir."

"Yes?"

"Object sighted ahead . . . foretop lookout thinks it's another lifeboat . . . black painted . . . can't see anyone in it, sir."

Leach said, "Steer for it. I'm coming up." He turned to Tom— "More corpses . . . more girls with their eyes pecked out . . . How clean Coronel and the Falkland Islands battles seem now."

* * * *

An afternoon, evening, and night had passed. *Penrith* sliced into lessening seas at sixteen knots, 120 nautical miles west-north-west of North Rhona, heading to make a landfall off the southern tip of Iceland. The sun peered out now and then through driven clouds. Rain squalls blew down the wind, spattered the deck, and passed on. The surface of the sea was pale green where the fitful sun shone on it, dull green-grey in the cloud shadow.

Tom Rowland worked at the little desk in his cabin off the quarter-deck. Someone knocked, and he said "Come in," without looking up. The graph of tonnage sunk on the Harwich-Scheldt route, since the institution of convoys, was interesting, and indicative, though it did not cover a long enough period of time to be conclusive. He glanced up, to see Ordinary Seaman Charlie Bennett standing just inside the cabin door. He motioned with his hand and the sailor closed the door quietly behind him. He held out his hand and Tom took it, pressing the soft palm with his fingers.

Charlie said, in a low voice, "Any chance of leave when we get over the other side, Tom?"

Tom shook his head—"Probably not for two or three months . . . and then what can we do in Halifax? We can't lose ourselves there—it's too small." He wished Charlie wouldn't come in, on some pretext or other, so often. He had to come in now and then to clean the cabin, polish Tom's boots and shoes, lay out his clothes, and the like, but . . . sooner or later someone would notice; and above all he didn't want to put John Leach in an invidious position. He muttered, "Better run along, Charlie . . . Take my shoes."

"Aye, aye, sir," Charlie said, grinning a secretive, shared smile. He let go Tom's hand, opened the door, and slid out.

336

*　　*　　*　　*

The coast of Nova Scotia lay three miles ahead, pale grey under a pale sun. The sea was calm, as though half frozen, livid green in color. A Royal Canadian Navy seaplane made a final circle overhead and then returned toward the land. On the bridge of H.M.S. *Penrith,* Captain Leach said, "Next time we come in here we may be escorting U.S. ships. Thank God for Mr Zimmermann and his stupidity! From the reports that have been passed on to us, the Americans seem to have gone through the roof when the news broke about his telegram."

Tom said, "It's just in time, sir. We need the Americans badly now. There won't be any Eastern Front soon—Rumania knocked out, Serbia practically gone, Russia tottering on the edge of revolution."

Leach said, "Our fellows are going to have a hard time in France this summer."

Tom said, "A lot of people seem to believe we must try somewhere else. I believe the Prime Minister's one of them. They think the Western Front's turned into a slaughterhouse—and nothing more."

The captain said grimly, "There'll be as much bloodshed in London over that question as there has been in France, till it's settled one way or the other . . . Meanwhile, if the Yanks do come in they will eventually be sending troops to France, hundreds of thousands of them. Who's going to protect them?"

"Their Navy will do what it can," Tom said.

"Quite," Leach said, "but it can't anywhere near do the job. *We'll* have to, and if we fail, thousands of American soldiers are going to be drowned, which will not make the United States a very enthusiastic ally."

Tom said, "All ships must have more depth charges, sir—even cruisers, certainly light cruisers. After all, any sort of ship can attack a submerged submarine. It doesn't take great speed or maneuverability."

"Just enough speed so it doesn't blow its own stern off," Leach said, "and we've got to be able to fire the things off the beam, not just roll them off the stern. . . . I wonder whether anyone's trying to find out if eighty feet is really the right setting for the pistols. I talk with submariners whenever I get a chance and they all say that they wouldn't hesitate to go below eighty feet if they were being attacked—or in danger of it."

"Wish we could capture some German depth charges, and see how they do it," Tom said. "They've been specializing in war under the sea for a long time, it appears."

"It should have been obvious, years ago, that that is what they were up to," Leach said, "but it wasn't. We are a very stupid people, in some ways, Tom. We think the enemy must do what we want him to do, and then we are shocked and hurt when he does something different . . ."

"And the one time he did come out in line of battle—he got away."

Leach nodded—"The rest of this war is going to be fought down there—" he indicated the sea and its depths—"dirty work . . . It will be won by new inventions, Tom . . . new ways to trace submarines, perhaps even when their engines are stopped . . . new ways to attack them . . . depth charges dropped from aircraft, perhaps? Homing torpedoes?"

Tom said, "The last letter I had from my nephew, Guy—the R.F.C. ace—he said we should be bombing the submarine building yards. It makes sense—destroying the submarines is just as important as building more merchant ships, and if we can destroy them before they ever take to sea, so much the better."

"And building more merchant ships depends on our bloody dockyard workers." Leach said. "Always striking! I'd like to see them put in some of the ships they build—or refuse to—and sent out on the Atlantic without escort or convoy."

Tom said nothing, but thought—a good proportion of the Navy's own men came from just such backgrounds as the striking dock workers; they certainly had fathers and brothers among the strikers; those in the Navy did their jobs silently, efficiently, without fuss or trouble; those ashore moaned and struck and complained . . .

Leach took a turn along the bridge. When he came back he said, "Prepare to enter harbour!" His tone had sharpened; the conversation was over. Tom said, "Aye, aye, sir . . . Bennett, tell the Chief Bo'sun's Mate to pipe 'Hands prepare for entering harbour.'"

Captain Leach stayed on the bridge, silent, watching. Tom set off round the ship, Ordinary Seaman Bennett in his wake, observing the preparations being made on the upper deck. The First Lieutenant headed for the fo'c'sle to take charge of the cable party.

*   *   *   *

The cruiser glided between the narrow rock walls of the harbour entrance toward the little wooden city on the slope beyond. Black-backed gulls wheeled and swerved round her stern where the Surgeon, having nothing to do in the harbouring process, strolled back and forth on the quarterdeck. On the fo'c'sle one anchor was ready for letting go—in case of emergency—though the ship was berthing alongside. Salutes had been paid to an armoured cruiser, and received from two Canadian destroyers; berthing wires and springs were ready . . . the minutes passed . . . she got her cable . . . the main engines were rung off . . . the hands piped to "Secure." Captain Leach had long gone below, but now his messenger came to Tom, saluting—"Captain's compliments, sir, and he wishes to see you."

Tom straightened his tie, made sure his gold-leafed cap was on straight, and headed below to the captain's day cabin, which occupied the stern of the ship directly under the ensign. Captain Leach sat at the desk, his cap resting on it. He looked up and said quietly, "This is going to be unpleasant, Tom, for me just as much as for you. More, perhaps." His thin face was set, the blue eyes boring relentlessly into Tom's. Tom felt himself freezing, piece by piece, from the inside out, first the marrow in his bones, then the bones, then the flesh.

"Three days ago an anonymous letter was slipped into my greatcoat pocket, somehow, without my knowing it. I don't like anonymous letters—no honest man does—but in a disciplined service they do sometimes represent the only outlet for a man's frustrations . . . or for a truth to come out which the writer feels ought to be known, but never will be in any other way. I read the letter. It said that you were a—the word used was 'pansy'—and that you were doing indecent things with Ordinary Seaman Bennett—who is, I think, your seaman-servant."

His voice softened slightly as he continued, Tom rigid and cold in front of him—"What could I do? Appoint seamen to spy on you? Browbeat or bribe Bennett until he confessed? Not in my ship."

He got up suddenly and walked across the cabin, back, forward, not looking at Tom. Tom stayed rigid.

"I thought of asking you point blank. But what could you say? If you denied it, the doubt would remain. If you confessed it, I would have to send you both up for court martial."

Abruptly he sat down again behind his desk. He said, "I have signalled the C-in-C requesting a transfer for you. He has agreed, without asking questions. You are to return on the first ship sailing from here for England—Navy or merchant. In a confidential letter I am explaining why I want you taken out of this ship. From there on, what happens to you will be up to you . . . and to the 2nd Sea Lord, to whom this matter has been referred . . . Sit down, Tom."

Tom collapsed into an easy chair off the front corner of the desk. He knew that his face was white, his jowls pale green, as though he were about to be sick, or faint, or both. Leach held out a cigarette case—"Have one, Tom."

Tom shook his head wordlessly, staring at the middle buttons of the captain's pea jacket.

Leach said, "When you get to London, see someone, Tom. Try to get help . . . I've heard there are doctors who specialize in our minds rather than in our bodies . . . find out why people do certain things.

If you can't find that sort of doctor, see a parson, a priest . . . But for God's sake see *someone!* You're such a good fellow . . . and a good sailor . . . and officer . . . This has been the happiest commission of my service, thanks to you. I couldn't bear to see you destroy yourself . . . I have a pile of documents to go through. Just sit there till you're ready to go. I shan't need you for anything the rest of the day."

He picked up a pile of papers and shuffled them, and read, or pretended to. Tom sat, staring at the floor, the gold-leafed cap and the great crest of the Royal Navy, wreathed in gold laurel, resting between his pale, cold hands.

The Admiralty, London: Saturday, March 31, 1917

The Second Sea Lord and Chief of Naval Personnel, Admiral Sir Cecil Burney, G.C.M.G., K.C.B., R.N., stood by the fireplace in his spacious office, facing Tom across the table. The Admiral's Naval Assistant, Captain Buller, R.N., stood a little to one side. Tom stood to attention, cap under his arm.

The Admiral said, "I am posting you to the Anti-Submarine Division. Report there immediately you leave this room."

"Aye, aye, sir."

"I do not have the manpower to have you watched at all times, and if I thought that really necessary, I would have you dismissed the Service as not worth the trouble. But you will be watched—from time to time. And if the allegation made in the anonymous letter to Captain Leach turns out to be well founded, I shall act at once, and without mercy, for the good of the Service. You understand?"

"Yes, sir."

"You are to wear uniform at all times outside your house or flat."

"Aye, aye, sir."

"That's all."

Tom wheeled about and left the room.

*   *   *   *

The half moon hung yellow and serene over London . . . a bomber's night, Tom thought, standing in the window of his flat, a night for the Gothas or the Zeppelins . . . calm, quiet, subdued movement in the street below, a humming murmur from the great city. He had eaten, but felt hungry and uneasy, the coldness that had knifed into him in *Penrith*'s stern cabin still there, under all other emotions and feelings. Three days after that interview he had sailed in a Canadian minesweeper recently built in Halifax and going to join the Harwich force . . . a hard trip in the usual foul early-spring weather, two days skirt-

ing the ice pack and watching majestic icebergs drifting southward
into the shipping lanes . . . the skipper several years younger and
junior to himself, but of course still the captain, as Tom was sailing as a
passenger. He hadn't gone near Bennett since the interview. Without
a word being said, somehow another sailor had appeared as his servant, a grizzled old fellow really too experienced for such a job—he
would be wanted in a turret . . . but of course that was where he
would return, as soon as Tom left.

He pulled the curtains to and switched on the light, for he had
been standing in the dark. There, by the fireplace, his nephew, Guy's,
school friend, Dick Yeoman, had made a sexual advance to him, and,
if the telephone call from the Admiralty had not broken the tension,
he would have responded to the boy's invitation and, then and there,
acknowledged that he was . . . what he was. It had come soon
enough: he remembered Charlie Bennett's eyelashes, the black eye,
the first touching of hands, the tears in his eyes, the sense that they two
were alone among a host of hostile, indifferent strangers, that only
they understood each other, or could comfort.

He opened the drawer of his little roll-top desk in the corner and
took out the service revolver, a heavy blued Webley .455. Six cartridges, lead-balled, lay in a little box beside the revolver in the
drawer. He knew where to aim for, his hand was firm . . . firm as an
iceberg, since that day. The light glittered for a moment on the gold of
his cufflinks as he turned the revolver over in his hand . . . gold links
with the naval crown embossed on them in enamel, a gift from his
mother when he became a midshipman . . . there was the Hoppner
Nelson, a gift from his father when he got his first ship, a destroyer,
ten years ago . . . The revolver was heavy, serviceable, of the Service
. . . *The* Service: proud, implacable, unforgiving as the seas it ruled:
uncompromising master and mistress . . . This, or that, the Service
said—the revolver, or me, and all that I demand, of your life, your
love, your heart.

He raised the revolver to his temple, placed the cold ring of the
muzzle precisely in the correct place to blow out his brains, and
pressed the trigger. It took a heavy pressure on the trigger, but the
muzzle had not moved, nor the direction of the barrel. He could do it.
He lowered the revolver to his face and stared down the empty barrel,
into blackness.

He returned the revolver to its drawer, put on his greatcoat and
went out. At the corner he glanced round to see whether anyone was
following him. There was no one. He walked on toward Piccadilly.

*   *   *   *

341

They sat in the same Italian restaurant in Soho where they had been with Charlie Bennett and Ivor Novello. There were a dozen other people in the small room, men and women; but nearly all the men were sitting together in pairs, as were most of the women. Tom and Russell Wharton were eating *spaghetti a la vongole* and drinking Chianti. Wharton had not fully removed his theatrical eye make-up—perhaps deliberately, Tom thought.

Tom said, "They found out about me and Charlie."

"The beautiful Geordie boy? That's a shame."

"And now I'm going to be observed, from time to time. I suppose they think I'm susceptible to blackmail."

Russell Wharton said, "That's only true if you care, laddie. Look at me. Everyone in the theatre knows what I am and I don't pretend to be anything else. Of course, I'll never be knighted . . . can't have Sir Russell caught offering young soldiers a quid a night in the *pissoir* at Waterloo, can we? But on the other hand no one can blackmail me. I'd quote the Iron Duke at them—publish and be damned."

Tom drank deeply of the wine, thinking. He said, "So I can really only be blackmailed as long as I try to be a naval officer?"

"Or want to be," Wharton said. "That's the heart of the matter."

Tom said, "I thought of committing suicide, earlier this evening. Then I decided not to . . . and came to your theatre."

"Ghastly show, isn't it? . . . I guessed something of the sort, when you came to the dressing room. You looked pretty grim. So now you don't care what they say, or do?"

"I'm trying not to care," Tom said. "I tell myself I don't. But I do . . . What does your father think?"

Wharton laughed bitterly—"He doesn't speak to me . . . hasn't for twenty years. But what would we have to talk about if he did, eh? Listen, I'll help you, we'll all help. You have to step out of your skin and into another—ours. Meet people—people like us . . . Ivor, young Coward, Owen, dozens of others in the theatre alone, many more who decorate the big houses and flats, antique dealers, designers, gallery owners . . . You'll find a different atmosphere—different, and in my opinion, much more Christian, than you've been used to. A bit catty at times, both sexes . . . bitchy, to tell the truth . . . but on the whole, everyone does his best to understand the other fellow, and not hurt him where it matters. I'm having a party next Sunday, six o'clock—it'll go on till all hours. Come along . . . 47 Dean Street."

"Thanks," Tom said. "I'd love to."

"There's an entrance fee," Wharton said nonchalantly. He put down the fork with which he had been expertly twirling spaghetti against his plate, and looked up at Tom—"More like an initiation. Pick up a soldier."

342

"What?" Tom gasped. "It was only Charlie I was . . ."

"Are you sure?" Wharton said intently. "Think! Never been tempted by anyone else? I bet you have . . . You go and do it, tonight, and then we'll know you're really one of us. And," he added, picking up his wine glass and looking at Tom over the rim, "it'll help you break the umbilical cord to your dearly beloved mother, the Service!"

"But I'm in uniform!"

"That's just what I mean."

*　　*　　*　　*

It was morning, the sun up. The soldier had gone, pushed out early by Tom. Tom felt ashamed and soiled. Why had he allowed Wharton to challenge him with a schoolboy dare? Surely *his* friends did not all go round picking up soldiers as one would a tart? Surely they had more permanent relationships with each other, full of affection and shared interests besides sexuality? He and Charlie had loved each other in a way modified and shaped by their profession and the naval ties—and barriers—between them. He hadn't loved that young soldier, didn't know his name, didn't want to . . .

So why did he do it?

Because Wharton told him the only way to be free was to toss himself off in the Navy's face . . . and he'd done it. The defiance of decency, the deliberate public defilement of his uniform, had indeed freed him from something—but not yet from himself. He picked up the *Observer* and scanned the principal headline:

PRESIDENT WILSON CALLS SPECIAL SESSION OF CONGRESS
EXPECTED TO DEMAND U.S. DECLARATION OF WAR

Daily Telegraph, Monday, April 2, 1917

CONGRESS & GERMANY
TO-DAY'S MEETING
APPROACHING CONFLICT

From Our Own Correspondent, *New York*, Sunday.
In a minor degree, and allowing for the fact that 3,000 miles of the Atlantic divide, if not protect the United States from Germany, one might say Americans are to-day witnessing demonstrations and phenomena recalling the days in England just preceding the

343

British declaration of war. Mr Taft's remark that "once you set the heather on fire in the United States you never know how far the flames will spread" seems justified, for to-day patriotic support for the policy of national defence seems fairly well spread from the Atlantic to the Pacific . . . One thing is very obvious—that almost everything depends upon President Wilson's leadership and the terms of his message to Congress. It doesn't matter much whether Congress is asked to declare war or a state of war—the probability is the latter alternative will be adopted—but it does matter whether the President submits a war programme harmonising with the requirements of the situation . . . President Wilson alone knows just the form and scope of his forthcoming recommendations. The only thing certain is that he will not favour any legislation short of a proclamation that, by reason of the acts of Germany, a state of war exists between that country and the United States. No move by Germany can make any change, and since Bethmann-Hollweg's latest speech, no move is expected.

At last, Cate thought, at long, long last . . . poor America, after trying so hard to keep out, forced in at the bloodiest, beastliest time. The torpedoing of the American ship *City of Memphis* a couple of weeks ago had been another shove in that direction, after so many other sinkings and drownings before it, but the Zimmermann telegram had been the final straw. The Americans, judging by the excerpts from their newspapers, had gone mad with rage at the thought that Germany was proposing to give away bits of *their* country. It would be most interesting to know just how the text of the Zimmermann telegram had come into Allied hands, for surely the Germans must have taken extreme precautions to keep such an explosive communication secret.

The war, which Cate felt had been out of human control for some months or even years, was now really taking the bit between its teeth. Wherever you looked the news was not merely sanguinary—of death and destruction—but weird. The Czar had abdicated—the beloved Little Father, gone, and a republic set up in his place! But what was Russia without a Czar? Baghdad was under the rule of a British general . . . but where were Haroun-al-Raschid, Scheherezade, the Caliphs, the harem women of the Arabian Nights? In Ireland the out-and-out Sinn Feiners were actually winning elections: that was unheard of a year or two ago; at any time before the Easter Rising of 1916 and the subsequent executions, to be honest . . .

He started, spilling a little coffee out of his cup—Johnny Merritt had sworn a dozen times, in his hearing, that as soon as America declared war, he'd join the U.S. Army. That would leave Stella alone,

344

if he meant it. But did he? He'd better ride over to Beighton and talk to Stella about it . . . telephone first perhaps, as Stella often wasn't at home, these days—she liked to shop in Hedlington, and was also, she said, studying a lot in the Public Library: the poor girl was lonely, that was the truth, with Johnny working so hard. If he went off to war, she'd be much lonelier.

Washington, District of Columbia:
Monday, April 2, 1917

23 The high limousine reached the Treasury building and began the final climb up Pennsylvania Avenue toward the dome of the Capitol, brilliant white against the black sky. The President sat in the back with Dr Grayson, Colonel Hartz and Mr Tumulty, the passing street lamps picking out the rain spots from the April shower that had just passed, which pearled the hats and tunics of the escorting cavalrymen. His face was set but calm, and he made no acknowledgment of the cheers, shouts, and occasional boos from the people lining the route. Police were on duty every ten yards, and the District of Columbia garbage workers were sweeping up the broken glass, thrown fruit, torn paper, and other debris from the street fights and near riots that had raged all day near the Capitol, between the nation's pacifists, who had come to disrupt the President's planned speech to the Congress, and the anti-pacifists, who had come from all over, some in special trains from New York, to support the President in what was already obvious must be a call to arms.

The limousine rode steadily on, the hum of its engine drowned in the jingle and thump, the heavy creak of leather and the steady tattoo of the horses' hooves of B Troop, 2nd Regiment of United States Cavalry, riding as escort to the President, drawn sabres resting on their right shoulders, rifles thumping in the boots on the horses' off sides.

The car swung round at the foot of the great steps of the Capitol. Small deputations from Senate and House waited there to greet the President and escort him up the steps to the robing room, then into the chamber. They were flanked by the horses and men of A and F Troops of the 2nd Cavalry, which had been on duty all day keeping pacifist demonstrators out of the Capitol and examining the special passes without which, today, no one could enter.

The President climbed down, a sheaf of notes in his hand. The waiting Congressmen removed their hats, shook hands, then turned and led him up the wide steps.

Inside the House, Stephen Merritt waited, sitting in the visitor's gallery of the House of Representatives, flanked by Andrew Mellon and Andrew Carnegie, the latter bent and hunched under the weight of his eighty-two years, but the eyes still keen. The diplomatic corps were present *en masse*, all in full evening dress, rank on rank near the floor of the House. In the centre of the floor directly in front of the dais where the Vice President and the Speaker of the House waited behind their tall desks, sat the members of the Supreme Court, without robes; Edward Douglas White, Chief Justice of the United States, in the centre of the front row; Oliver Wendell Holmes to his left.

In response to a signal from outside, unseen by any but himself, the Speaker tapped his gavel on his desk and called quietly, "The House will be in order!"

A sudden silence fell. The Doorkeeper of the House, in frock coat and doeskin gloves, walked in through the open door. When just inside the House he stopped, and boomed sternly, "Mr Speaker, the President of the United States!"

The President walked steadily up the aisle between the cheering representatives, the diplomatic corps, the senators—nearly all these with small American flags in their lapels—past the justices, to the dais. There, he reached up and shook hands first with his Vice President, then with the Speaker. He turned. The Speaker again banged his gavel and announced "Members of the Congress, I have the high privilege and distinct honour of introducing to you the President of the United States."

Woodrow Wilson spread his notes carefully on the lectern under the reading light, adjusted his pince-nez high on his long nose, and began:

I have called the Congress into extraordinary session because there are serious, very serious choices to be made, and made immediately, which it was neither right nor constitutionally permissible that I should assume the responsibilities of making.

In the House the rustle of silk and shirr of broadcloth had died away. Looking round the gallery Stephen saw the faces as a

347

generalized impression, not as individuals—grim, anxious, exulting;
together with the mass on the floor it was the embodiment of the
power of the United States, both in theory and in practice—down
there the justices and senators, President and Vice President; up
here—himself and Morgan and Mellon and Carnegie; Morgenthau,
Vanderbilt, Baruch; Harriman, Taft, Rockefeller; Bell, Edison . . .

The challenge is to all mankind. Each nation must decide for itself
how it will meet it. The choice we make for ourselves must be made
with a moderation of counsel and a temperateness of judgment befit-
ting our character and our motives as a nation. We must . . .

Stephen listened intently. Carnegie was holding a wrinkled hand
to his ear, making an *extempore* ear trumpet. Mellon's heavy, handsome
head was up, the eyes staring fixedly at the President. Wilson was
speaking more forcefully, now and then raising his head to look from
side to side, not seeking applause but as though making sure the
Congress was attending to him.

There is one choice we can not make, we are incapable of making:
we will not choose the path of submission . . .

A clapping and cheering broke out all over the packed House. In
the centre of the floor the Chief Justice was standing, arms upflung,
and so remained for a long five seconds, he and the President the only
two on their feet. The cheering and shouting rose to a universal pan-
demonium. Everyone stood. La Follette of Wisconsin stayed seated,
alone, his arms folded tight across his chest, chewing gum, a sardonic
smile on his slightly working face.
    Wilson waited; after five minutes the cheering died down and he
repeated,

We will not choose the path of submission and suffer the most sacred
rights of our nation and our people to be ignored or violated. The
wrongs against which we now array ourselves are no common wrongs;
they cut to the very roots of human life.
    With a profound sense of the solemn, and even tragical character
of the step I am taking . . . I advise that the Congress declare the
recent course of the Imperial German Government to be in fact nothing less than war against the Government and people of the United
States . . .

"War," Stephen muttered to Carnegie. The old man nodded—"No
doubt about it. The Germans have managed to drag Wilson to the
starting post when no one else could."

We are at the beginning of an age in which it will be insisted that the same standard of conduct and of responsibility for wrong done shall be observed among nations and their Governments that are observed among the individual citizens of civilized States.

"Now that it's done, one wonders why it couldn't have been done sooner," Mellon muttered. "How many lives could have been saved . . . how much destruction averted."

Stephen said, "Not many American lives, or much American property. I think he was right to do all he could to save us from the war as long as it was humanly possible.

The world must be made safe for democracy. Its peace must be planted upon the tested foundations of political liberty. We have no selfish ends to serve. We desire no conquest or domination. We ask no indemnities for ourselves, no material compensation for the sacrifices we shall freely make. We are but one of the champions of the rights of mankind . . .

"A far cry from those speeches about 'drunken brawl' . . . and 'too proud to fight,'" Carnegie whispered hoarsely. Stephen did not respond. As a Republican he abhorred Wilson's domestic policies, but it was impossible to despise the man himself. It might have been Irish wardheelers and Southern despots who got him elected, but there was no doubting the depth and reality of his idealism.

It is a fearful thing to lead this great, peaceful people into war, into the most terrible and disastrous of all wars . . . But the right is more precious than peace, and we shall fight for the things which we have always carried nearest our hearts—for democracy, for the rights of those who submit to authority to have a voice in their own Governments, for the rights and liberties of small nations, for a universal dominion of right by such a concert of free people as shall bring peace and safety to all nations and make the world itself at last free.

Stephen pulled out his watch and peered at it. All that had to be said had been said. This was so much rhetoric. The President was good at rhetoric; now he had brought himself to face, and deal with, facts.

War, then! His grandchildren (if Johnny and Betty ever got down to having any) would grow up into a world almost unimaginably different from the one *he* had known as a child . . . although the war, for all its horrors, had caused some amazing and in themselves wonderful advances, particularly in the sciences. Look at aviation, look at medicine. It was only a few days ago that he had read a piece in *The New York Times* where the writer, a military expert, had pointed out that, according to current figures, the battle casualties in this war would far exceed those caused by disease—for the first time in history.

To such a task we dedicate our lives and our fortunes, everything that we are and everything that we have, with the pride of those who know that the day has come when America is privileged to spend her blood and her might for the principles that gave her birth and happiness and the peace which she has treasured.

God helping her, she can do no other.

Stephen rose, clapping . . . Carnegie staggered up beside him. All round the gallery the people were now visibly aroused. Faces that had been sombre and reserved were open, turning red, mouths agape. The Chief Justice was again on his feet, his white mane shining like a halo, his arms upraised. From the floor Southern senators and representatives set up the flesh-creeping Rebel yell of the Confederacy—in whose ranks the Chief Justice had carried a rifle fifty-two years earlier. The clapping became frenzied. War fever . . . Betty had told him about dachshunds being kicked to death in the streets of England—by the English, of all people! . . . anyone with a German name pilloried and spat upon. Stephen felt a gloomy certainty that it was going to happen here.

Mellon said, "Well, that's that . . . a brilliant stroke that, at the end—paraphrasing Luther at Worms, to win over the German-Americans. It only remains for Congress to declare war, which they certainly will."

"La Follette will hold it up for a few days, but that's all," Carnegie said. "Well, I must get back to Pittsburgh, so . . ."

He shuffled off. Mellon said, "There'll certainly be some form of compulsory military service."

Stephen said, "Yes. I have a son of military age. But he's engaged in work of what will I am sure be regarded as national importance."

Mellon said, "My Paul's too young—thank heavens!"

With brief nods, they parted.

*   *   *   *

Stephen leaned back in the heavily upholstered swiveling armchair of the parlour car, and drew thoughtfully on his cigar. At Union Station he had run into George Neidorf, president of the Lackawanna Southern, and a member of the board of directors of his own company, Fairfax, Gottlieb, investment bankers; and now George was sitting

Washington, District of Columbia: Monday, April 2, 1917

opposite him as the train drew out of Philadelphia and raced on through the blustery night toward New York on the Pennsylvania Railroad's quadruple-tracked main line. Stations passed as a blur of light . . . Frankford, Bridesburg, Tacony, Homesburg Junction . . . smoke from the new K4 Pacific far ahead blew back past the windows. The car rumbled heavily on over the rail joints.

The attendant came to their chairs, white napkin over his arm—"Any orders, gentlemen?"

Stephen looked up. "A small Scotch and water, please."

"Same for me," George said.

The porter said, "Right away, gentlemen."

. . . Torresdale, Cornwall Heights, Bristol, Morrisville. The engine whistled, the train slowed.

"Trenton," Neidorf said.

Stephen said, "As you know, Johnny's doing amazingly well with the Hedlington Aircraft Company. Of course, Richard Rowland's been generally supervising, but Richard himself assures me that that is all he has had to do. In fact, he said, their biggest problem—labour trouble—came when he did not listen to what Johnny advised."

Neidorf pulled on his cigar—"Whatever legislation the Congress passes will certainly contain some provision for keeping men vital to the civilian war effort—to production—in their jobs. We have surely learned that from the experience of the British. Johnny'll be safe."

"I hope so, but he's been itching to get into the war for two and a half years now."

The porter came with their drinks and the two men leaned back, drinking, staring out of the blind window, thinking their own thoughts; for both carried heavy responsibilities, public as well as private; and the war, which had seemed so far away, safely chained up across the Atlantic like some dangerous beast, was now at their throats.

Stephen said, "I think I must go over to England."

Neidorf glanced up in surprise, "Yourself? Can't it be done by letter or cable?"

Stephen shook his head. He said, "I want to see whether it's possible to expand the Hedlington Aircraft Company—and the J.M.C. perhaps . . . with a view to selling *our* government our trucks and aircraft, almost on the battlefield, instead of the government buying them from someone else here and shipping them across the Atlantic. The Royal Flying Corps seem to like our Leopard and Lion, but we can't get a definitive answer on the Buffalo—the heavy long-range bomber. Perhaps I can help there. I've done business with Lloyd George."

351

"They don't want to put any of their money into our dirty Yankee pockets," Neidorf said, grinning.

"Perhaps. . . . I'll go back to Washington as soon as war is actually declared, and talk to the Secretary of War about all this."

"Newton Baker?"

"Yes . . . I can give him the specification and performance figures he needs. Prices, too, for trucks delivered at a British port for shipment to France."

"The last report I read from Hedlington," Neidorf said, "Richard Rowland and Johnny were anxious about the supply of engines. They thought that the British government might commandeer all Rolls Royce Eagles—which Johnny needs for the Buffalo."

Stephen said, "That's another reason I want to see Newton. I intend to ask for an allotment of Liberty engines . . . As soon as I have answers from the Secretary, I'll go to England. Overfeld and Morgan have both told Richard they want to come back Stateside soon, and I'll try to persuade them to hang on over there for another year at least, or until the war's over."

"I'll pray for you," Neidorf said seriously. "That's not a very safe trip these days, Stephen."

Stephen said, "I know it, George. But, when you think what our young men will soon be facing . . . we have to face a few perils ourselves."

The train sped on . . . Princeton Junction, Plainsboro, Monmouth Junction . . . Newark . . . New York, Pennsylvania Station.

April 6, 1917

Stella Merritt sat in a deep chair by the fire in the cottage's drawing room, a book rested in her lap, her eyes closed. Johnny looked at her fondly, his own book on his lap. She was a little flushed, perhaps from the port that she had been drinking—three small glasses since dinner. He felt guilty and responsible, for although he had tried, he had not in fact succeeded in giving her appreciably more of his attention. So she had been lonely. So she sipped sherry all day—he knew that, because he had to buy the sherry; and in the evenings, port. Sometimes she was on top of the world when he came home, other times dull and lethargic.

He glanced at the little ormolu clock on the mantelpiece. Ten o'clock. The telephone in the hall rang and he got up. Stella stirred uneasily as he went out. He took the receiver off the hook—"Johnny Merritt."

"Good evening, Mr Merritt. Stanley Barstow here."

"Ah, yes," Johnny said. "What is it?" Barstow was a clerk at Reuters' head office in London, a man Johnny had contacted by chance early in 1916, and later retained to pass on at once urgent war news, particularly about ship sinkings that might affect the delivery of American engines to the Jupiter Motor Company.

Barstow said, "The American Congress declared war on Germany at a quarter past two o'clock, this afternoon, Eastern Standard Time."

"What was the vote, Mr Barstow?" Johnny asked.

"82 to 6 in the Senate and 373 to 50 in the House of Representatives. The resolution ends with 'To bring the conflict to a successful termination all the resources of the country are hereby pledged by the Congress of the United States.'"

"Nothing about compulsory military service?"

"No, Mr Merritt."

"Well, thank you, Mr Barstow . . . You'll keep me informed?"

"Yes, sir. Either at your house or direct to the factory, as you ordered."

Johnny replaced the receiver and walked slowly back into the drawing room. He went to the fire, and stood there a long time, thinking. Then he bent down and shook his wife. At last she woke up. He said, "Well, it's done. We've declared war."

She mumbled, "War? Oh, America . . . good." Her eyes closed again.

Johnny said, talking almost to himself, "It's come at last. I'll be miserable leaving you, but you know I've got to go. We've talked about it a hundred times, haven't we? . . . I must call Richard . . . It's been hard to keep one's self-respect. I've never told you this before but, last September, at the height of the Battle of the Somme, I was in the train to London, reading about the fighting. There was a young officer in the carriage—British, lieutenant. Just as we were nearing Victoria I read about some particularly bloody engagement and blurted out 'Some fight!' The British officer was getting up, putting on his cap, and he said softly, 'And some don't.' . . . Hey, are you listening, darling?"

"'Course," . . . but she did not open her eyes.

He looked down at her. The eyelids were a little puffy, the cheeks, too; her complexion wasn't the perfection of rose petals and cream that it had been; but she was still the most beautiful woman he had ever seen.

He said, "I'll go to London tomorrow, and book a passage on the first ship I can."

She mumbled, "Going . . . where?"

"You *know*, darling. To America! To join up and fight."

Stella began to cry, quietly, passionlessly, the tears rolling silently down her cheeks, her face almost unmoving. She said, "I'm pregnant."

Johnny stared, aghast. He dropped to one knee beside her—"You're sure? When?"

She said, "I've missed three periods. The baby's due in the middle of October."

"Have you seen Dr Kimball?" She shook her head. "Then, how do you . . . ?"

"I know," Stella said. Couldn't tell Johnny that Charles Deerfield had examined her, and assured her of the fact, and the date.

Johnny felt an even heavier sense of guilt descend on him and weigh him down; but he could not escape his duty, renege on his own promises—made to himself as well as to others. He said, "I must go, my darling. *I must!* . . . Betty will be here. And Aunt Isabel . . . and Mrs Rowland, Fiona . . . Louise." An idea struck him and he said excitedly, "Why don't you come over with me? You can live with Daddy in Nyack, and have the baby there, or in New York, with the best and most modern medical attention in the world! And perhaps I'll have a few days leave before they ship me overseas. . . ."

"I want to stay here," she said, almost snapped.

He was about to respond, when he held his tongue. This was her country; it was quite understandable that she would want to wait out her pregnancy and have the baby here close to her father and among her family.

She said, "What will you join?"

He said, "When I get over I'll find out from Mr Baker—he's Secretary of War, and an old friend of ours—he's been a house guest at Nyack many times . . . just which outfit is likely to go first, and I'll join that, wherever it is."

Stella struggled to her feet, as Johnny stooped to help her up, and mumbled, "I'm going to bed."

Johnny glanced at the clock—a quarter past ten. He made it a rule to read official reports, and technical papers on aircraft construction until eleven every night, otherwise he would fall behind, so rapidly were advances being made in the field. But, good heavens, he wasn't going to be in the field any more! He'd go up with Stella, and they'd rejoice together over the baby to come, fruit of their love and passion. But she said, "No, no, Johnny . . . Come up at eleven."

She went slowly up the stairs. Johnny watched her go and then sat down. What now? From force of habit, he picked up the book he had been reading, *The Aeroplane Speaks* by Captain Barber, R.F.C., and tried to concentrate.

In their bedroom Stella undressed. Charles had told her she was pregnant a month ago. But whose was the baby—his or Johnny's? How could she find out? Would anyone ever find out? Her head ached and her tongue was dry, her eyeballs burning. Charles had been cutting down on her heroin ever since he had discovered her pregnancy, saying that she must be free of her addiction as soon as possible, or the baby would be born with it, and could die soon after birth from withdrawal symptoms. But damn him, he must give her some more . . . more than this last dose which she was carefully preparing to swallow. Four months ago he had been giving her injections of it—paradise! She swallowed and lay down, lay back. She knew what was coming— dear God, not for the last time, not that! . . . a perfect drowsy content, no need to struggle, to wonder—no desire to search for finality in the thrust of a man's body in hers, perfect confidence in Johnny's love for her and hers for him, all right to make love to Charles, too, he'd look after her when Johnny went away, give her more, whatever he said . . . more . . . more. She felt superb, glowing, warm . . .

Sunday, April 8

Isabel Kramer, her nephew, Johnny Merritt, and his sister, Betty, walked briskly on Beighton Down into the teeth of a spring wind from the north-east that tugged at the women's heavy tweed skirts and the hair piled under well-anchored tweed hats. Isabel swung a walking stick in her hand, for she was not as sure footed as she used to be; and in any case was happier on horseback than on foot.

They skirted Caesar's Camp Copse on the south side, and Betty peered in, trying to imagine Fletcher living in there, for so many long months. It looked pretty now, with pink and yellow buds bursting on the boughs and the leaves sprouting green and the tall elms swaying in the wind, the earth rain-soft and dark.

Isabel said, "What are you going to do, Betty?"

Betty answered without hesitation—"Stay here, Aunt Isabel. I have a job—work—and a responsibility to Mr Rowland."

What she had said was true enough; but, far stronger in her mind was the fact that whenever Fletcher Gorse could get leave, or if he were wounded—this was where he would come . . . to England, and in the end to Kent, to Walstone, down there in the Weald, beside the meandering Scarrow. But her aunt did not know about Fletcher. If she did, would she understand, or would she see only the difference in their social class, and education? Betty could hardly blame her for that; too often, she found those differences weighing on her own mind—and she was Fletcher's lover, and he hers.

Mrs Kramer said, "Would you consider moving in with Stella . . . until Johnny comes home again?"

Betty shot a quick glance at her aunt. Was she asking her to keep an eye on Stella? Prevent her drinking too much? Stop her going to Hedlington so often?

Johnny said, "That would be nice—for Stella, I'm sure. But perhaps Betty prefers to be her own mistress."

They passed out of the shelter of the copse and the wind blew stronger again, whistling through the short grass and moaning in the scattered thorn bushes. Far to the east a shepherd in a long, heavy coat moved his flock slowly toward them, his crook on his shoulder, his dog a small black and grey shape floating from flank to flank behind the grazing Southdowns.

Betty said, "I do value that—being independent—but, yes, I'd be very happy to live at the cottage with Stella as long as I'm needed. You understand that I'll still be working at Hedlington Aircraft."

"Of course you must, child," Aunt Isabel said. "Stella and Johnny wouldn't dream of preventing you. Stella doesn't need a nanny, or a keeper . . . just a friend, a friendly relative."

I hope you're right, Betty thought. She had felt it necessary to stake out the boundaries of her commitment to Stella; though, privately, she did not expect to be going out much until Fletcher came back to take her in his arms . . . and . . . she half closed her eyes, seeing him . . . to carry her into that land of total giving, total accepting, that they had entered in the little hotel on the Deal front, facing the winter sea.

Aunt Isabel looked at the gold watch pinned to her lapel and said, "We've been out over an hour, and it'll take us at least a half an hour to get back to the car, and then another fifteen minutes to the Manor."

"Turn down here," Johnny said, "head for those three thick bushes. I've been up here often, with Guy and Laurence and Stella, before . . ." He trailed into silence.

Christopher Cate was waiting for them in the doorway of Walstone Manor, his long face a little grave. He said, "You've all got a nice colour . . . A telegram came half an hour ago for you, Johnny." He held out the pink envelope, still sealed. "The telegraph boy went to the cottage, of course, and Stella told him to bring it on here."

They scraped the mud off their boots on the footscraper, and then the doormat, and went into the old house. Laurence Cate was standing by the fire, tall and good looking in his uniform of a 2nd Lieutenant of the Weald Light Infantry. He had been at the Regimental Depot in Hedlington for four months now, and would be sent overseas as soon as he reached eighteen and a half, next month. Johnny

nodded toward him and then opened the envelope. He read aloud—
"It's from Dad:

Am coming to England soonest attempting book passage SS *Baltic*
sailing New York [*deleted by censor, that must be the date of the ship's sailing*]
important plans for Hedlington Aircraft and J.M.C. under study
make no plans of your own till my arrival inform Betty hope she will
return with me for job in Newton Baker's office inform Richard Rowland of contents of this cable much love to you and Stella—[*signed*]
Stephen Merritt."

Betty said in a clear, distinct voice, "I am not going back to America now."

Isabel Kramer said soothingly, "I'm sure your father will understand when you get a chance to speak to him."

Johnny said, "I have a passage booked on the *Sylvania*, for next
Wednesday the 11th, and I'm not going to miss it."

Isabel looked at Cate and raised her eyes briefly to the ceiling.
The young had the bits between their teeth and nothing would stop
them now.

Johnny said, "I must be getting back, sir. Are you ready, Betty?"

Betty said, "Yes. I'll drop you off at the cottage and then go on
home. Phone me to tell me when you want me to move in, after you've
spoken to Stella."

"If I'm leaving on Wednesday, you can come in on Thursday,"
Johnny said.

"Telephone me, though."

"All right."

Then they went out, with Laurence, who threw over his shoulder,
"I'm going down to talk to Probyn about the golden oriole I saw on
Beighton Hill this morning early, Daddy."

"Are you sure that's what it was?" Christopher called after him.

"Quite, Daddy. There's no other bird, even migrant, as brightly
colored, and of that size."

Then they were all gone. Isabel turned and put her arms round
Christopher's neck, pressing her body gently against his. He stooped,
kissed her on the mouth, and leaned away—"They are so sweet and
brave . . . and young," Isabel murmured. "God grant that they all
come out safe and sound."

"Safe, perhaps, with luck," Cate said. "Sound . . . I'm not sure
that anyone who goes through this war, fighting, will ever be really
sound again."

After a while Isabel said, "I had a cable from America, too, Chris-

357

topher. It came yesterday morning, just before I left the house to catch the train here."

Christopher waited, looking down at her, their hands now locked, face to face, standing a foot apart.

She continued, "It was from Stephen, too. He asked me to come home with him, when he goes back, and keep house for him."

Christopher said, "Well, my dear, you must do what you think you must. I shall love you wherever you are, whatever you do."

Isabel said, "Peter van Dehofer lives in Grandview, just down the river. He has asked me to marry him a dozen times since Wilson died."

This time Christopher eased his hands free of hers and walked up the room, turned, and came back—"My dearest Isabel," he began slowly, "my case seems hopeless. Unless Margaret commits adultery, and I can prove it, without collusion, I cannot get a divorce. Even if Margaret were to be caught, and sentenced to death, and the sentence commuted to life imprisonment—I still could not get a divorce."

"You could in the United States," Isabel said, her eyes on his.

His lips tightened. "You know I cannot leave Walstone," he said. "You *know*. Why do you torment me?"

She said, "Because I'm a woman, Christopher. I just had to tell you what I am *happy* to give up. I wouldn't marry Peter in a thousand years, now that I've met you. I am happier seeing you once or twice a month, our moments of love stolen almost in public, than to live day and night with anyone else. And all this is because you are what you are . . . Now, just humour me, dearest, because I'm a woman, and an emotional American. Tell me you love me."

Christopher stood close, without touching her, and whispered in her ear, "I love you, I adore you . . . with my body I thee worship . . . with my soul, too, but don't tell the rector . . . I want you, I worship you." He sank his teeth slowly into her ear.

He heard the knock on the door and Garrod's "Tea, madam . . . sir." She came in bustling, carrying the silver tea tray, preceded by a waft of buttered crumpets and a tinkle of china. She set down the tray and looked up, "Nice and hot, madam, and not too strong, just the way you like it."

"Thank you, Garrod," Isabel said, smiling back. And Christopher smiled. Garrod had seen, of course. Seen and understood. And being what she was, had not gasped "Excuse me," or dropped the tea tray or slunk out again, closing the door carefully behind her. Her master was in love, and she knew it. And was happy for them both. All the village knew, too, and was happy. And, Cate thought, every one of them understands perfectly clearly the nature of the insoluble problem that prevents our enjoying the full happiness that is held in its double padlock.

*　　*　　*　　*

The telephone in Betty's front room rang just as she was patting her hair into place before starting to cook her dinner. It was her brother. His voice sounded strange and awkward: "Betty . . . I've spoken to Stella. She's very grateful to you for offering to come here but she swears she'll be all right by herself . . . She's pregnant, and . . ."

Betty cut in, "Oh, Johnny, how wonderful! When's the baby due?"

"Middle of October. I know she wants me to stay, but I can't, Betty, I can't. You do understand, don't you?"

Betty said quietly, "I understand, Johnny."

"Perhaps, later, when the baby's nearly due, she won't want to be alone here. Perhaps . . ."

"I'll make it quite clear to her that I'll come whenever she wants me," Betty said.

She replaced the receiver and stood a moment, staring at it. So Stella was pregnant, at last. It couldn't have come at a worse time, with Johnny going off to the war, but in the long run it might be the best thing that ever happened to her. Meantime, it was clear that she, Stella, wanted to be alone, to live her own life—whatever that now was.

*　　*　　*　　*

In the First Sea Lord's spacious room at the Admiralty, Admiral Sir John Jellicoe, Royal Navy, faced Rear Admiral William S. Sims, United States Navy. Sims had sailed before the American declaration of war, and arrived in England three days after it. The biggest chart on the wall showed the loss of tonnage to German U boats, month by month. It was a steadily rising red line. On the same graph there was another line, in blue—also rising, but not as fast as the red one: this was the monthly tonnage of shipping being turned out of the shipbuilding yards. A third line, in green, also rose, but at a still lesser angle: this was the sinking of U boats.

"Half a million tons in March," Admiral Sims said.

"And it'll be over eight hundred thousand tons this month, if the trend continues," Jellicoe said gloomily. He was the finest naval tactician of the time. His handling of the enormous Grand Fleet at the Battle of Jutland had been brilliant, and must have resulted in a decisive victory if he had been as well served by his scouting admirals and commodores as he deserved. But this war under the sea seemed to be outside the scope of his mind.

359

"Looks as if the Germans are winning the war," the American said cheerfully.

Jellicoe said, "They will unless we stop those losses."

"We will," Admiral Sims said. "With convoys."

Jellicoe looked up. "I've been forced to accept them. I must say I don't like the idea. Blockade and patrol are the classic answers, but . . . perhaps the Prime Minister's right. Here, come along to our Anti-Submarine Division and you can see how it works, in theory."

The two admirals walked along the passage and up a wide flight of stairs. Jellicoe opened the door of a big room on the third floor and looked around. Commander Tom Rowland glanced up from his desk and at once came forward.

The First Sea Lord said, "Where's Admiral Duff?"

"In conference, sir. And Captain Fisher."

"Well, this is Admiral Sims, United States Navy. Who's in charge of the trans-Atlantic convoy planning?"

"I am, sir—Commander Rowland."

Sims stuck out his hand, "You're my man, then, Commander. Admiral Bayly has already told me how he works it, in practice, out of Queenstown. Now you show me how and where you get the ships and convoying vessels into Admiral Bayly's hands, and I'll see how we can best fit in with you. We're slow, but we're not stupid."

Jellicoe laughed, and said, "Well, I'll leave you in Rowland's hands . . . Bring the admiral back to my room when he's had enough here."

"Aye, aye, sir."

Daily Telegraph, Saturday, April 28, 1917

PREMIER'S CALL TO THE NATION
FOOD ECONOMY VITAL

It was as one watched the guests arrive that one realized the significance of the ceremony in the Guildhall yesterday. At the heart of the Empire, a stone's throw from the Bank, there assembled men from its outermost parts, and as one looked at them and remembered the reason for their presence in our midst at this time it was borne in upon one that this conferring of the freedom upon the Prime Minister was a ceremonial act of the City's faith in Britain's cause . . .

. . . the ceremonies followed their accustomed routine . . . Then came the Prime Minister's turn to reply . . . If one might describe the spirit of his speech in a sentence, it was confidence with an "if." The "if" was the spirit in which, in the coming weeks, the public faces its proper responsibilities in regard to the food supply. Here are some of his most striking points:

More cargo ships would be brought to our ports in July than in March, even though we continued to lose from submarine activity at the rate we are now doing.

A year hence there will be three, if not four times as many ships as were built in the preceding twelve-month period.

We shall have three million more acres in cultivation for the harvest of 1918 than we have now, and without a ton of food "from abroad" no one could starve us.

The people must vigorously ration themselves, just to be absolutely safe, proceed as though the submarine problems were insoluble.

"I have never seen a human problem which is not soluble, and I do not believe this is an exception."

It was one of the essentials to speedy victory that Ireland should be converted from a suspicious, dangerous, surly neighbour to a cheerful, loyal comrade.

Cate read the long speech with interest, and, with equal interest, the list of guests. It would be nice, some time, to attend such a gathering and feel—indeed, know—that you were at the very heart of the Empire, in some sense a part of it; but they also serve who only . . . inspect dry rot in tenants' cellars. And worry about the French. It had long been obvious that their new Commander-in-Chief, Nivelle, would mount a great offensive as soon as he could in the spring. It had, equally obviously, been launched a week ago, and continued on successive days. The newspaper communiqués had started by being boastful, rapidly becoming chary, cautious, and now all but silent. What had happened? Something bad, that one could count on, in this war.

House of Commons, London: Thursday, May 10, 1917

24 The Right Honourable Member for Caernarvon, Mr David Lloyd George (Lib.), called "I spy strangers." The Strangers' Gallery was cleared. The House met in Secret Session. The Right Honourable Member for Dundee, Mr Winston Churchill (Lib.), then said, in substance, a new campaign is about to open. Since the beginning of the year two events have occurred, each of which has changed the whole situation and both of which must be taken into account in the policy of the Allies. On the one hand an Allied Empire whose standing Army comprised over seven million soldiers has been crushed by the German hammer. On the other a nation comprising one hundred and twenty millions of the most active, educated, and wealthy citizens, commanding intact almost limitless resources of every kind, has engaged itself in our cause . . . If time is given nothing can stand against Great Britain and the United States together . . .

There is one other factor beside time which is vital: Sea Communications . . . We do not know, we do not wish to know, how many ships are being sunk each week by submarines. We know that the number and proportion is most serious and is still increasing. Here then is the fatal crux. Let the whole energies of Britain be directed upon this point . . . Let every resource and invention be applied. Let the anti-submarine war claim priority and dominance over every other form of British effort. Let us make sure we can bring the American Armies to Europe as soon as they are fit to come.

Meanwhile what should be our policy on land? Is it not obvious, from the primary factors which have been described, that we ought not to squander the remaining Armies of France and Britain in precipitate offensives before the American power begins to be felt on the battlefields? . . . Let the House implore the Prime Minister to use the authority which he wields, and all his personal weight, to prevent the French and British High Commands from dragging each other into fresh, bloody, and disastrous adventures. Bring over the American millions, and meanwhile maintain an active defensive on the Western Front, so as to economise French and British lives, and so as to train and perfect our Armies and our methods for a decisive effort in a later year.

(Various members then intervened in the debate.)

The Right Honourable Member for Caernarvon, Mr David Lloyd George (Lib.) . . . I accept in principle my Right Honourable friend's statement of the main factors affecting our policy. I must, however, decline to commit this government, or myself personally, against a renewed offensive on the Western Front during the current year.

(The Prime Minister then surveyed the war situation on all fronts, and at home. On resuming his seat, he was loudly cheered by nearly all sections.)

*   *   *   *

Stella had had lunch with her aunt by marriage, Fiona Rowland, and was now feeling a little muzzy from the wine Fiona had given her at the meal, and the sherries beforehand. Fiona, she noticed, had taken no sherry, or wine, but two small glasses of whisky, neat. But of course Aunt Fiona was Scottish, and had probably been given whisky as soon as she was old enough to sit at the grown-ups' table for dinner.

Mrs Orr, the cook, came in and said, "I'll be going out shopping now, m'm. The new saucepans, m'm."

Fiona said, "I remember. Thank you." The cook bustled out, closing the drawing room door quietly behind her. Fiona leaned back in her chair, crossed her legs at the ankles, and said, "So you're pregnant. Are you happy about it?"

Stella said, "Of course, Aunt Fiona! I only wish Johnny could be with me."

Fiona said, "But the baby's not going to be Johnny's . . . is it?"

Stella stared, entranced, at the other woman. Fiona seemed to be moving, swaying. There were two Fionas, overlapping. Stella said at last, "How do you know?"

Fiona said, "I have the sight, child."

She's mad, Stella thought. But Aunt Fiona had always been strange, given to prophetic utterances which often turned out to be correct.

Stella felt herself crying, the tears rolling silently down her cheeks. She stammered, "I was . . . s-so lonely . . . I . . . ."

Fiona said, "Don't tell me . . . I wish I could have had a child by *my*

363

lover. God knows I wanted one, and begged him to give me one . . . but mostly he used those rubber things, and even when he didn't, nothing happened."

Stella's tears slowly dried as she stared in mounting astonishment at her aunt, Guy and Virginia's mother, Uncle Quentin's wife. She said, "You had a . . . a lover?"

Fiona rose abruptly from her chair and stood by the window looking out at the bright yellow blossoms of a laburnum and the pink candles of a horse chestnut, glowing like fire in the light spring rain. She said, "For ten years—until he joined the Army, last Christmas. Why did he do that? He could have been excused. If he had tried . . . or become an official war artist. But he joined up, and now he's in the same battalion as Quentin. He's Quentin's adjutant, his personal staff officer!"

Stella said wonderingly, "Does he . . . do they . . . know?"

Fiona said, "Quentin doesn't." She was silent a moment, then said abruptly, "Do you love him?"

Stella said slowly, "I don't know, Auntie. I don't think so. But when I'm with him, I think I do."

"That's true with all men who show interest in you, isn't it?"

Stella said, "Not every man . . . It's when they're exciting. They make me feel bolder than I really am . . . I love Johnny so much, but . . ." She shrugged; she was becoming irritated and unhappy and her mouth was dry. Aunt Fiona could not understand, and she could not explain. She'd leave as soon as she decently could, go home and have a little sherry and a little sniff. What to talk about for the next ten minutes?

She looked round. The walls of the room were hung with small water colors, some oils, and a few pen and ink drawings, all of wartime scenes in France. On a sudden intuition she said, "Are those pictures by . . . him?"

Fiona said, "Yes. Some, Archie gave to Quentin, others, I am to keep to the end of the war, when we'll give them back to Archie." She laughed bitterly—"There'll be no end of the war for one of them . . . perhaps neither. Have a look at them—a good look."

Stella rose and circled the walls examining the paintings. She didn't know much about art, but the Manor was full of good classic English oils, family portraits, country scenes; and her father used to take them all to the Royal Academy summer exhibitions . . . These were very good, very strong. The condition of the war over there was apparent in every line . . . Here was a soldier, stretched out beside a road, weariness in every line of his face, in the exhausted fall of his hand across his rifle beside him . . . Here was a soldier talking to a girl,

in a bar—what did they call it? *estaminet*—just the two heads, the girl obviously flirting, the soldier's face yearning, trying not to show it—she
knew that look in men, too well—bottles and glasses sketched in, all
seen through a bluish haze of tobacco smoke . . . And here was Uncle
Quentin, as she had known him all her life . . . a little thinner than he
used to be, his mouth set, his popping blue eyes more wrinkled at the
corners, staring past the painter, binoculars in his hands, held high,
ready . . . She licked her lips, and stifled a yawn.

"They're awfully good, Auntie," she said, "and now I'm afraid
. . ."

"They're the best things he's ever done," Fiona said angrily, "and
do you know why?"

"No, I can't think."

"Because Quentin's perverted him, so that he feels more for those
men, the soldiers, than he does for anything or anybody else. He's
painted me a dozen times, clothed, nude, head and shoulders. None
was half as good as these. He knew. . . . But now he sees the soldiers
as Quentin always has, as a lover should, as a mother would . . . he
was my lover, but *I* could not arouse that insight." She laughed
again, high and bitter—"He used to make love to his models . . . I
was never jealous. He didn't love them, he loved me. I would never
lose him to any of them. Now I *have* lost him . . . to my husband!
What do you think of that?"

Stella waited a minute before saying, "I really think I must be
going now, Aunt Fiona."

El Paso, Texas

The ancient Hupmobile taxi wheezed to a stop outside the open iron
gate with the big white-painted arch over it proclaiming HEAD-
QUARTERS 16th U.S. INFANTRY. "Not allowed to pass here 'less
I'm carrying an officer" the driver said in a Tex-Mex singsong. Johnny
scrambled out, pulling his heavy suitcase after him, and stood a moment, stretching in the sun. The buildings of the barracks shimmered
in the heat, white waves of sun glared off the gravelly dust of the
parade ground. A company of soldiers in faded khaki, their campaign
hats ringed with the blue cord of the infantry, marched and
counter-marched, the dust swirling round their leggings, rifles
steady on the right shoulders. Johnny listened to the barked commands of the sergeants—"Left face! . . . Left shoulder—arms! . . .
About—face!" . . . sergeants calling the cadence, bawling impreca-
tions and oaths . . . silence again, but for the tramp tramp of the
boots.

From behind him the driver called, "Hey meester, pay opp so's I can go. I seen more of these sonsabeetches than I want to awreddy."

Johnny turned and gave the man his fare, passed under the arch and trudged up the dusty road, lined with whitewashed stones, that led to a building set between two white flagpoles, one flying the flag of the United States, the other the crested blue flag of the 16th U.S. Infantry. After a while he paused to rest, lowering his suitcase, finding a handkerchief in the breast pocket of his Brooks Brothers seersucker suit, and mopping his forehead. Another man passed him, this one carrying nothing, a squat young man about five foot seven inches tall, and almost as wide, his face dark brown and square as the body, on his head a tall black cowboy hat, domed, an eagle's feather in the beaded band, from under which hung down on both sides shiny locks of straight black hair. He was wearing a pair of old torn khaki drill trousers and a cotton shirt of the same color; and on his feet deerskin moccasins tied with a thin strip of leather—an obvious Indian. Johnny picked up his suitcase and trudged on, the Indian now a few paces in front of him.

As they neared the building with the flags, Johnny saw a sentry standing at parade rest outside the door, under a thatched awning. The Indian had stopped, staring from side to side. Johnny stepped in front of the sentry, and said, "I want to enlist. Where do I go?"

The sentry jerked his head over his shoulder—"In there, second door on the right."

The Indian had listened, but not spoken. Now, as Johnny picked up his suitcase, and entered the building, the Indian followed. They turned down a narrow passage, hot and airless. Johnny knocked at the second door on the right. No answer. They waited. Johnny knocked again. A deep voice from behind the door roared, "Come in!" Johnny opened the door. The room contained a table covered with papers, and behind it a chair, occupied by a huge man in his forties, in uniform, three chevrons on each sleeve. He must be six foot two or three, Johnny thought, and over two hundred and thirty pounds. This terrifying apparition bawled, "This is the Army, you dumb hayseeds, not a ladies' piss house. What do you want?"

"I want to enlist, sir," Johnny said.

"Don't call me 'sir,'" the sergeant snapped. "I'm Sergeant Leary and I'm the poor son of a bitch who has to train recruits." He turned to the Indian—"You want to enlist, too, Chief?"

The Indian nodded. The sergeant said to Johnny, "What do *you* want to enlist for?"

"We're at war, for democracy," Johnny said. "I think it's every able-bodied man's duty to . . ." He said no more; whatever it was, it

366

would sound pompous. The sergeant turned to the Indian—"You, why do you want to enlist? You a patriot, too? You're a Navajo, aren't you?"

The Indian said nothing and the sergeant shouted, "Don't you speak English? I got enough troubles without trying to teach poor bastards who don't understand what I'm telling 'em!"

The Indian said, "No food. Four days."

The sergeant, whose Irish accent was becoming more marked as time passed, said, "You walked in from the reservation? In four days?"

"Gallup, in wagon," the young Indian said. "Rode Santa Fe freight, Belen . . . two days, freight to here . . . No food at home."

Johnny listened in horror. If he'd known, if the man had told him, he could have stood him a meal, at least. There was a taco stand right outside the gate . . . It was too late now; the sergeant was pulling a sheaf of papers toward him. "O.K.," he said, looking up at Johnny. "Name?"

"John de Lisle Merritt . . . River House, Nyack, New York . . . and in case of injury you'd better notify my wife, Mrs John Merritt, The Cottage, Beighton, Kent, England."

"By special cable? Any more addresses? What about your club? . . . All right then. Grade school?"

"Eh?"

"Did you get through grade school, dummy?"

"B.A. Harvard, 1914, sir—sergeant."

"Christ!" the sergeant said, "and you're married. You must have murdered someone to be enlisting." He turned to the Indian—"Name?"

"Chee Shush Benally."

The sergeant laid down his pen—"Mother of God, spell it—slowly."

The Indian said nothing, and Johnny cut in—"Perhaps he doesn't know how it's spelled, if he can't write."

"When I want your help, rookie, I'll ask for it . . . Say that again, Chief."

"Chee . . . Shush . . . Benally."

The sergeant wrote painstakingly, muttering, "I suppose that means Rain-on-the-Mountains or Two-Dogs-Fucking."

The Indian spoke unexpectedly, "Red Bear's Grandson."

"Eh? O.K., there's half a dozen other Indians in the outfit and three of them are Navajo, I know. You won't be seeing anything of them till you're fit to wear our uniform off the post here . . . Raise your right hands . . . Swear after me . . . Sign here . . . Make a mark, Chief, an X—like this, see . . . All right, now you're sojers in the United States Army. You're recruits in the best goddamned regiment in the Army, which means in the world. And the latrine rumour is that we'll be heading for France soon, because Black Jack Pershing knows us, and he knows we're the best, so he has asked for us."

"That's true," Johnny said.

The sergeant glared at him—"Did I ask you to open your big mouth, rookie? . . . How do you know?"

"The Secretary of War, Mr Baker, told me. That's why I wanted to enlist in this regiment, particularly."

"Oh, is it?" Sergeant Leary said. "Well, next time you write, give Mr Baker Sergeant Leary's compliments and tell him his little friend's starting his very first K.P. this very evening . . . Now, listen to what I'm going to tell you, and you'll be O.K. There are three ways of doing anything—the right way, the wrong way, and the Army way. You do it the Army way, always! . . . Johnson!"

An old soldier came in, chewing on a dead cigar—"Take these men to the supply sergeant and have them fitted out. Then they go to the Recruit Barrack, beds 47 and 48, both in Corporal Jalnik's squad. Then take them to the mess hall and have Cookie give 'em some chow. They're starving . . . least, the Chief is. Don't suppose you've ever known what it is to be even a bit hungry, eh, Harvard?"

Johnny thought carefully and said "No, sergeant. Not yet."

The Western Front

The headquarters of the 1st Battalion the Weald Light Infantry were in the ruins of Feuchy, beside the Scarpe on the Arras front, with B and D Companies in the front line of trenches, and A and C in reserve. Most of the brigade machine guns were massed on slightly rising ground in the south sector of the front, under brigade control, where they could enfilade the brigade's front. The brigade had two battalions up, two back. The 1st Wealds were left forward, the 9th Leinsters right forward, the 11th Devons left rear, and the 24th South Wales Borderers right rear. The corps had occupied these and many more trenches of the area between April 6th and 10th, when patrols had revealed the unbelievable—the Germans had abandoned them without a fight, slipping off eastward in the night.

Lieutenant Colonel Quentin Rowland was in his battalion headquarters dugout, until 1915 the cellar of one of the little village's larger houses. He was sitting at a makeshift table, puffing at his pipe, half listening to the soft brogue of Father Caffin, just outside the dugout, telling a story to the battalion runners. "So Doctor Geoghegan took his little black bag and drove the trap round to Mrs Murphy's cottage and asked, 'An' how's the diarrhoea this morning, Mrs Murphy?' and Mrs Murphy sez, 'A little thicker, thank you, Doctor.'" The soldiers chuckled, the priest began another story, Quentin frowned . . . damned Irish . . . damned Germans . . . damned war . . . He took his pipe from his mouth and said, "The Boches must have known about our offensive and just pulled back, so that we'd hit empty air. Clever swine."

His adjutant, Lieutenant Archie Campbell, looked up from the Army form he was filling in, reporting the number of skilled blacksmiths and plumbers they had in the battalion, and said, "Yes, sir . . . There wasn't much secrecy about that French push . . . or ours, since we were conforming."

"Pity we didn't patrol harder," Quentin said. "Then perhaps we'd have caught them on the move . . . with one foot off the ground, so to speak."

Archie said nothing. His commanding officer often talked more or less to himself.

Quentin said, "Well, they won't slip away next time we attack. They'll have to hold the Hindenburg line."

"It'll be a tough nut to crack, sir," Archie said. "Concrete machine-gun posts, tunnels fifty feet down for the men to shelter in until our bombardment lifts. That last Intelligence report from interrogation of P.O.W.s was very interesting."

Quentin said, "One thing I don't understand, is why they didn't include that little rise on the right of our sector, Hill 44, in their line. They could have done it perfectly easily, but . . ."

A series of deafening crashes shook the ground about them. Bricks from ruined walls tumbled onto the cellar's corrugated iron and earth roof. Five in the afternoon, Archie thought, strange time for the Hun to have a hate. The colonel was on his feet, reaching for his steel helmet. His gas mask was already slung on his chest, the leather Sam Browne buckled, the Webley .455 in its holster. "Better take a look-see," the colonel said. "Come along."

He walked up the cellar steps until his head and shoulders were above ground. Archie quailed a moment, then followed and stood beside him. All round, shells were bursting with a continuous roar, fountains of mud rising, falling back, splashing on the heavy earth. "Hitting our front lines," the C.O. muttered.

The telephone in the cellar rang and Archie ran back down inside, glad of the excuse—"Hullo . . . battalion headquarters here." It was Captain Kellaway, commanding B Company—"Heavy artillery fire on our positions, Campbell . . . and now the Germans are assaulting

369

across our front, aiming at D, I think . . . I'm putting up the S.O.S. Very lights."

"How many enemy attacking?" Archie shouted, for he could hardly hear above the sudden din.

"Looks like a battalion, at least. It's . . ."

The line went dead. Archie swore and ran up the steps. "B Company reports a German battalion attacking D, sir," he said. "There goes the S.O.S!" A red Very light rose and burst and hung in the bright sky, followed by a green and another green. The British artillery began to fire, shells of light and medium calibre whistling overhead.

"Why aren't the machine guns firing?" the C.O. said. He raised his binoculars, stared a moment, then muttered, "I can see Germans. The whole hill's gone . . . Here, we'd better get forward."

With Archie at his heels he ran across a patch of open ground and dropped into the communication trench. The German artillery had blocked them off on all sides, so no reinforcements could come forward. Well, they'd taken the words out of his mouth . . . staged an attack to correct what experience had shown them was a tactical fault in their line.

C Company, now commanded by his nephew, Boy Rowland, was standing to, as he passed. Boy was there, white faced, hands shaking but face set, standing on the firestep, looking forward.

"Watch your right flank, Boy," Quentin snapped. "They've got Hill 44 . . . probably wiped out all the machine guns . . . the swine must have attacked before their barrage lifted."

"I think they walked right into it," Boy said. "Must have lost a lot of men to their own guns, but they were into our machine guns before anyone was sure that they'd left their trenches."

"Hold tight," Quentin said, "they want Feuchy, and they're not going to get it."

He hurried on up the muddy trench, with its dugouts all facing the wrong way, but deep, well revetted and roofed, and still smelling of German tobacco, German socks, German garlic sausage. Ten minutes later, struggling past many wounded lying in the bottom of the trench, Caffin and Campbell at his heels, 5.9 shells still crashing and exploding all round, he found Kellaway on the firestep, a rifle in his hand, aiming and firing at unseen targets. He scrambled up to join. him, and as soon as he could see over the top, gasped, "My God!"

The ground in front was full of Germans, coming with bayonets agleam, groups here, running forward, groups there tumbling into shell holes for cover. A single machine gun from the Leinsters had seen what was happening and opened fire across the front. Archie

Campbell was at his side, thrusting a rifle into his hands. He rested it on the sandbags and began to fire.

"They've overrun D, sir," Kellaway shouted, between the rapid crack crack of his shots. All along the trench the soldiers were firing, not the murderous rapid fire of the old regulars of Mons and Le Cateau, but good enough. Five Lewis guns rattled in short, vicious bursts.

Ten Germans reached the British wire, which had been cut in several places by the savage bombardment. Campbell got one, Kellaway another, and Quentin had a third in his sights when a potato masher bomb, landing just in front of him, spent splinters clanging off his helmet, half stunned him and threw mud into his eyes. He fell back into the trench, wiped his eyes, picked up his rifle and rejoined the others. In the minute or so that he had been down, the German attack had withered. The few visible were dead, hanging over the wire, kneeling with their faces in the mud, lying on their backs, arms thrown out . . . one crawling blindly on hands and knees, his entrails dragging. A soldier to Quentin's right took aim and fired. The crawling man dropped, at peace.

Quentin said, "Take a look round, Kellaway . . . Plenty of ammunition?"

"For a few hours, sir," Kellaway said.

"Just hold hard. They'll attack again . . . Come along, Campbell. Got to find out what happened to D."

Swine, he thought, as he worked his way along the trench, attacking without a real barrage, at five in the afternoon . . . clever swine. That machine gun from the Leinsters had saved their bacon, in B Company . . . too late to save D, apparently.

They came to a knot of men facing a traverse, rifles aimed at the point where the trench itself turned at the traverse. Lieutenant Fred Stratton was there, with a sergeant and half a dozen private soldiers. Two dead Germans lay in the trench bottom, near the traverse. He said, "What's the matter, Stratton?"

Stratton did not move. He was pressed back against the parados, his revolver drawn and aimed, his eyes never leaving the traverse ahead. "Germans in D Company trenches, sir," he said briefly over his shoulder. "Those two came on and were round the traverse almost before we knew it. We got them, but . . ."

A group of potato masher bombs, four or five almost together, whirled over the traverse and landed in the trench. As they exploded the sergeant dropped, screaming, a private soldier fell back against the parapet, slowly slipping down. A German officer came darting round the traverse, Mauser blazing, soldiers hard on his heels. Quentin whipped up his rifle and fired. The officer fell. German bullets, fired from the hip, smacked by Quentin. Stratton's revolver was barking, the heavy lead bullets slamming into the Germans at five paces. Quentin shouted, "Bayonets, Wealds, bayonets!" and rushed forward, stabbing fiercely. For a few moments the bay was a scene of total turmoil, men pushing, shoving, stabbing, shooting, falling, dying in the confined space. More Germans stormed round the traverse. From the other direction Captain Kellaway arrived with a dozen men, each man's pockets full of Mills bombs. They threw them over the traverse into the next bay, where the Germans were coming from. As they burst in a long boo-boo-boo-boom-boom, the Wealds finished off the Germans in their own bay. No more came round the traverse.

"Any wire here?" Quentin asked.

Stratton said, "Some, sir. We were going to do some rewiring out there tonight."

"Bring some rolls here. Block the trench at the traverse, where you can cover it . . . Watch your reserve trenches, Kellaway, they may try to come in through there . . . Any communication at all with D?"

"No, sir . . . Battalion headquarters called me to ask where you were. They say they can't get D by any means."

"Assume they've been wiped out, then," Quentin said.

He walked back along the trench, thinking. His right front company had gone, his left front holding, but with difficulty. German artillery was still isolating the battalion from help . . . they'd have to help themselves. Could he get through to the guns? Counter attack with A and C, to recapture D's position? . . . Do it from B's area, laterally along the trenches, not up across open ground from the reserve area?

"Sir . . . sir!" he stopped, looking up. It was a corporal, covered in mud. He must know the man . . . couldn't think of his name. The corporal said, "Captain Rowland sent me to tell you the Germans are in behind us, sir." He was gasping, short of breath, and had obviously been running and struggling forward for some time.

Quentin said, "Where's the nearest field telephone?"

"Here, sir."

He seized the handle and cranked, sitting on the upturned ammunition box where the telephone had been set up, its wires running up and out over the open ground to the rear. "Hullo . . . Hullo . . . C Company . . . C Company . . ." No answer. "A Company."

A tinny voice answered, "A Company."

"Colonel Rowland . . . C reports Germans behind them. Go over and arrange to help C cut them off . . . Send a runner back to the Devons, telling them what's happening, and for them to tell brigade."

"Right, sir . . . The shell fire's very heavy to our rear and our left."

"It's all round us," Quentin said grimly, "but we've got to try to get a message out. It's vital. Do you understand?"

"Yes, sir."

Quentin put the instrument back in its cradle.

The battalion headquarters position in the cellar was no good now—too close to the Germans in the old D Company area. The Boches might well be actually in it by now. Swine, probably drinking his whisky and eating his bully at this moment. What was best to do? Cut off on three sides by Germans, and on the fourth by the Scarpe. No communication with the artillery, so they could only fire on prearranged S.O.S. targets, on Very light call . . . but the S.O.S. targets might not be appropriate now . . . Well, brigade must be getting an inkling of what was going on from the Leinsters, at least . . . But then, it would take them hours to confirm it, make a plan, issue orders, act. Meanwhile, the only thing was . . . dig in . . . hold tight . . . what was the motto of the old 57th Foot, the Middlesex, their colonel's rallying cry at Albuera? "Die hard, 57th!" That would serve the Wealds now.

But was that really the best course of action open to him? To hang grimly on, in defence? What were the Germans thinking? They had made a surprise attack, and had succeeded, at least in part. They must be in process of reorganizing themselves. It was near dusk . . . They should be attacked, as soon as possible . . . Artillery support—nil. But wasn't that just how they had achieved their surprise, just now?

He hurried toward B Company and found Kellaway at the same spot, but down in the trench, studying a map. He said, "Kellaway, I'm going to counter attack."

Kellaway's eyes were dull with fatigue. "Yes, sir?"

"Using your company and some of C and A . . . a platoon from each. At dusk."

"What will be our objective, sir?"

"The positions the Germans came from—there." He gestured to the east.

"The Hindenburg line?" Kellaway said, his face falling.

"Not the whole line, in depth. Just the outposts. They won't be well defended—the Germans never hold their front in strength and they certainly won't be now."

An hour to dusk. It would take time to bring the platoons forward . . . warn A to send another platoon to take over these trenches, which B would be vacating when they assaulted . . . Couldn't afford to let the Boches think they'd got you down . . . ever, ever . . . had to fight back . . . kick 'em in the face. He found his pipe and tobacco pouch and lit up.

Archie Campbell, sitting a few feet away, watched his commanding officer in awe. Damned old fool . . . narrow minded butcher . . . why not just sit tight, wait for the Huns to come, and when you had killed all you could, put up your hands? What more could anyone do, out-numbered and outmaneuvered as they had been here? Instead it looked as though the two of them, and many other good men and true would enter eternity somewhere out there on the shell-torn earth between Feuchy and the frowning, sunken fortresses of the Hinden-burg Line . . . which the Germans called the Siegfried Line, he had noted in the Intelligence reports. He lit a cigarette and tried to tell himself it tasted as good to his dry lips and tongue as the C.O.'s pipe tobacco was certainly tasting to him.

*   *   *   *

The sun had sunk half an hour ago, still the long twilight of the young northern summer persisted. The men in the front line trench waited, heads down, breathing deep. They were not as densely packed as in a normal attack, there were not enough of them for that. The air was still and calm but for the steady whistle of German shells passing overhead to burst in the box pattern that surrounded the Weald Light Infantry's position. Private Fagioletti tried to control his breathing and the slight shivering of his right hand where it held the forestock of his rifle. Beyond him Leavey and Bob Jevons murmured to each other in low tones, but Fagioletti could not hear what they were saying. Beyond again, the old soldier Snaky Lucas waited, his steel-helmeted head leaning against the chalky front wall of the trench. Then came Sergeant Bygrave, the boy Cyril Jessop, Fletcher Whitman, Brace—no one had learned his Christian name in all these months—then a traverse. What lay beyond, Fagioletti had no idea. More of the battal-ion's men—Captain Kellaway, the colonel perhaps: Fagioletti had seen him an hour or so back, coming down this trench with the captain, peering over the top, saying something to the captain, going on, later returning.

They were going to attack. The sergeant had pointed out their objectives, the places they were supposed to capture—a few humps two hundred yards out across the broken ground. Looked nasty. Not as bad as Fricourt and Mametz, though. A lark towered into the twilight bursting with song, and fell, in silence. The guns continued their monotonous rhythmic emphasis. It was dark.

"Ready, lads!" Sergeant Bygrave called quietly.

Private Lucas leaned back, took a stub of cold cigarette from his lips and put it behind his ear. Fagioletti swallowed twice. He wanted to shit . . . not again . . . he bloody well wouldn't do it!

No whistle blew, but the sergeant said, "Now!" On top, Fagioletti could just make out the irregular line of men to his right, edging through the twisted, tortured arms of the wire . . . no one on his left. He was the left hand man of the whole attack. His bayonet shone clear against the dark of the lower sky by some apparent phosphorescence in the blade. The helmets to his right were dully gleaming bowls. Not a sound from Jerry . . . Fifty yards gone . . . still nothing. He stumbled over something, saw it was a body, two, amalgamated in death—Germans . . . On again . . . nearly half-way there. The shadows were moving away from him and he muttered in Venetian, "Non stà lassarme!" and broke into a stumbling run until he had caught up with the line again. More wire . . . he searched frantically for a place where it was broken and found a lane—twelve feet wide . . . the Jerries must have come through here in their attack . . . Then the noise began. Bullets clattered by, bombs burst. He heard his platoon officer, Mr Stratton, bellowing "Get in!" Then a German-helmeted shape was rising from the ground before him and his rifle jerking in his hand as he pulled the trigger . . . again . . . and again, as more shapes staggered out. He was jumping down into a trench, landing hard, stumbling . . . about to fire again, when he recognized the outline of a British steel helmet, and Lucas's voice, curt—"Down, Dago!" Beyond, shapes and shadows were scrambling up out of the back of the trench and Whitman was firing steadily at them. The German machine gun that had opened up just as they came through the German wire had been silenced. There it was, on the parapet now, one gunner hunched dead over it, the other fallen backward into the trench bottom. British soldiers were pulling the dead man off the gun, swinging it round to face the rear, sitting down in firing position behind it.

Lieutenant Stratton called, "Sergeant Bygrave!"

"Here, sir!"

"Clear the trench—that way—about a hundred yards. No farther. I'll be along in a minute."

"Very good, sir . . . Fagioletti, Lucas . . . Whitman, Brace, Jessop . . . Bombs ready! Dago, you start as point. Ready? Move, man!" They scurried round the first traverse . . . Fagioletti in the lead, his blood curdling with fear, his legs like lead. The sergeant was on his heels, Lucas close with a bomb in each hand, his rifle slung. Star shells rose from the German artillery, climbed, burst, and cast brilliant light over the whole earth but Fagioletti did not lift his eyes from the narrow trench ahead of him. Next traverse. He paused, held his rifle out, a round in the breech, finger on the trigger . . . Lucas lobbed two grenades over the traverse. As soon as they burst, Fagioletti jumped round . . . no one there . . . run to the end of the bay . . . Same again: two grenades, the heavy clangour of their explosions, jump round the traverse . . . no one . . . on . . . twice more . . . the bays were forty feet long, some less . . . on, two grenades, round the traverse . . . two bullets smacked into the sandbags by his head. As he saw the Germans and pulled the trigger his fear suddenly became fury. He charged forward, screaming in Venetian. The swine were trying to kill him! One of the Germans who had fired was leaning against the back wall of the trench, his chest ripped open by grenade splinters; the other was running. Fagioletti first shot the running man in the back, then bayoneted the other, the dying man, pinning him through the throat to the trench wall. Savagely he jerked his bayonet free. Potato masher bombs whirled in, landed with dead thumps and exploded. He heard screams, gasps, groans, looked round in the light of new star shells . . . the sergeant wounded in the head and down, Bob Jevons down, dead.

"Come on!" he yelled. "*Avanti!* You got some more bombs, Snaky?"

Lucas said, "Wait'll I get the sergeant's. You take Jevons' . . . Ready."

Whitman said, "Jessop and Brace and I have got a dozen."

Fagioletti led to the next traverse: Lucas threw two grenades over into the next bay: they stormed round. The German artillery kept the trenches bright with star shells, trying to find out what was happening . . . charge! Whoever had thrown the potato mashers had gone.

Fagioletti scrambled on, panting, teeth bared. Lucas said, "I 'eard Mr Stratton say a hundred yards. We've done that."

Fagioletti snarled, "We can clear the whole trench. Come on!"

Lucas said, "'Old 'ard! Are you trying to win a fucking V.C.?"

Fagioletti subsided, out of breath, against the trench wall. He found he was soaked with sweat, his hands shaking like a palsied man's. He said in wonder, "Look, Snaky, my hand's shaking, see . . . but I'm not frightened!"

Lucas said, "Then you're a bloody fool." He swung round, bayonet out, finger on the trigger, and Fagioletti, hearing sounds from the bay behind them, said, "Ready with the grenades, Whitman! Who goes there?"

"Mr Stratton," came the answer, shouted over the traverse. A moment later he appeared, with four men. "Good work," he said briefly. "Sergeant Bygrave's bad."

Lucas said, "Fagioletti here led us, sir."

Stratton said, "Good man . . . You're an acting corporal, Fagioletti, from now. I'll ask the C.O. to confirm you as soon as we get back to our own trenches . . . Hold this position, corporal, till just before dawn. Then we will retreat the way we came. You'll get orders at about three. Dawn's at four. These men are under your orders. My headquarters is back down the trench, where you started from."

"Very good, sir," Fagioletti said.

His head was swimming. Fred Stratton, his brother-in-law, who had hardly spoken a word to him, except to tick him off, since he came to this platoon, had made him a corporal. A two-striper, in the 1st Battalion of the Weald Light Infantry! He'd get more pay . . . but what could you spend it on? All the same, two stripes on his arm!

"Better post double sentries, Dago," Lucas said.

Fagioletti steeled himself—"You call me 'corporal' now, Snaky. Old Rowley'd be down on us both like a ton of bricks if he heard you."

"Right you are, corporal," Lucas said equably.

"Why did you tell the officer I led the charge? The sergeant detailed me for it. We were all in it. You're the one who ought to be corporal . . . twenty-one years you got in!"

Lucas spat accurately over the parapet onto an abandoned German helmet with a jagged hole in it, and said, "Me, take a stripe? Don't be bloody daft, man!"

*   *   *   *

The Germans counter-attacked to regain the lost positions at eleven o'clock that night. The artillery preparation was brief, and only a part of it was aimed at the trenches actually held by the British. The attack itself was curiously haphazard and tentative for a German assault, Quentin thought. The hundred men he had taken forward in his attack beat it off with ease and small loss to themselves, using mainly the Germans' own captured machine guns, and the light of a few white Very lights. They received no help at all from the main British position behind, neither artillery nor machine guns. The hundred men and half a dozen officers were in a world of their own.

Quentin lit his last fill of tobacco. The German field telephone was quiet again. It had linked the German troops in these trenches and the Wealds had simply taken it over, cutting the wire that had led to the German rear, and now into the new No Man's Land. In a deep dugout, acrid with the smell of German ersatz acorn coffee, Archie Campbell lit a cigarette. He was tired, almost too tired to feel fear. The Germans would come again—they always did. Ammunition was running low. What hope did they have, isolated out here?

Father Caffin got up from the box he was sitting on and murmured, "I'll be going round the trenches, Archie. 'Tis a hard time for the bhoys, waiting like this."

He went out. Good man, Archie thought: nothing on earth would induce *him* to go out there unless he had to—ordered out by the C.O.

He looked across at Quentin and wished he had his sketch pad with him. He'd sketched the colonel several times, and knew—eerie feeling—that the drawings were being sent back to Fiona. He'd caught him in some typical attitudes, the character showing very clearly . . . this was perhaps the best of all, the plump cheeks lit by the candle, the eyes closed, in repose; not very intelligent, but calm, sure of duty done . . . Immortal, in a way. But of course he wasn't immortal: any moment a shell might destroy him . . . all of them.

Here it came! A whoosh and a roar like an express train, the 5.9 digging into the earth twenty yards away, bursting, the candle flame shaking. The C.O. opened his eyes as another shell landed twenty yards off in the opposite direction. The tempo of the shelling did not increase as they waited, listening.

The C.O. said, "Not preparation fire . . . too slow. Harassing . . . My pipe's gone out." He relit it, carefully blowing out the match and dropping it into the empty German coffee tin on the table.

The shelling continued, steady, slow. Archie felt it was searching for them . . . one here . . . pause . . . one there . . . where are you? . . . crash! No? Well, let's try here . . . crash! . . . crash! . . . Sooner or later, I'll get you . . .

They were going to die. He wished to God he had a bottle of whisky.

A man couldn't die with *this* on his conscience. He drew a deep breath, forced his hands to lie still on the shaking board that was the table top, and said, "Sir, I was your wife's lover."

Quentin's protuberant blue eyes turned slowly on him, peering through the blue tobacco smoke. A frown creased the domelike forehead. He said, "Don't be ridiculous, Campbell. Have you been hit on the head, and didn't tell me?"

"No, sir. I can't lie to you any more . . . live the lie . . . I was Fiona's lover for nine, ten years. She wanted me to marry her."

After a while Quentin said, "Are you the fellow she said she was going to live with some time ago? November, 1915, it was."

"Yes, sir."

Another long pause—then: "Why didn't she? I never understood."

Campbell spoke eagerly, anxious to get the load off his mind, the cloud off his conscience—"I didn't want to marry her . . . or anyone. She only *thought* she loved me because she thought you *didn't* . . . that you didn't understand her."

Quentin drew on his pipe, looked away, looked back—"Not a very decent way to treat a lady, Campbell . . . take advantage of her and then refuse to marry her."

"Sir, she was married to you! She'd never have been happy with me. I didn't know what to do, when she told me she was going to leave you . . . I joined up."

Quentin picked up the field telephone, wound the handle, and said, "Kellaway? Everything all right? . . . Good . . . If the shelling stops, stand to at once." He replaced the instrument, wound again, and said, "Stratton? C.O. here . . . Are you all right? . . . Good . . . Keep a close lookout all round. If the shelling stops, stand to at once."

He returned to Campbell, "Why did you apply to come to this regiment? Or was it pure chance?"

"No, I applied. I had to meet you, man to man. We had met before actually—three times, at art shows Fiona dragged you to—but you didn't remember, why should you? . . . I had to face the same dangers you were facing. If I did, and survived, I thought I might be able to marry Fiona after all . . . but not otherwise."

Quentin said, "She doesn't love me . . . never has . . ."

"I'm sure that if she can only be made to appreciate how much you . . ."

Quentin continued, "If you promise to marry her, I'll divorce her . . . give her evidence so that she can divorce me, I mean, of course. Can't have her name dragged through the mud in the divorce courts."

"Sir," Archie said, "I couldn't, now. She's your wife and when all this is over she'll understand what a wonderful husband she has. I could only make her unhappy."

"You should have thought of that in the beginning," Quentin said severely. Then—"You do not want to marry her? At all?"

"No, sir. I don't want to see her again. I'm sorry for what I—we—did wrong, and I . . . that's all."

Quentin shook out the dottle from his pipe into the tin can. He thought he must be dreaming, talking to a lieutenant, a temporary officer, at that, about his marriage, and Fiona, and their future . . . Campbell was an older man, of course—nearly his own age. It wouldn't have seemed strange if they were both out of uniform. He felt an immense lightening of spirit. Fiona was not yet over her infatuation, apparently, but there was a chance, if Campbell kept his word, that sooner or later she would be. He must just keep on loving her, and hope that one day she would return to him.

Campbell said, "I've been very happy in the Wealds, sir. Please don't have me transferred out of the regiment altogether."

"Out of the regiment?" the C.O. growled. "What are you talking about? You're not leaving this battalion. You'll stay here. I'm not going to start training another adjutant . . . I'm going round our trenches. Stay by the telephone here. If any message comes from brigade, send to find me at once. It will be important. They might tell us not to retire—that they're going to break through and reinforce us . . . I'll be back in an hour."

"Very good, sir."

*   *   *   *

Quentin was on his way back to his command dugout. All was well, the moon was still bright and would last most of the rest of the night, being five days past full. That might mean trouble, if the German machine gunners spotted them as they started their withdrawal, but it was a chance he'd have to take. Withdrawal after daylight would be impossible—and if they stayed they'd be wiped out by the next German counter-attack, this time properly organized, and with heavy artillery support; for the fall of the German harassing fire—still in progress—showed that by now they had plotted quite precisely what area of their trenches was held by the British.

But there was also the chance to give the Boches a bloody nose, if reinforcements came up; or perhaps even to hold onto these advanced outworks of the Hindenburg Line. That attack at dusk yesterday had taken the Hun by surprise; now if only the brigade could get through with some message, bring up reserves, wire, more machine guns, put the artillery onto pounding the Germans opposite—this could be consolidated, held . . . But no one had got through, neither the men the Wealds had sent back nor those the brigade had sent forward—if any.

He was three bays from the headquarters dugout when a sentry on the firestep, facing the front, turned round sharply and said, "Someone coming from be'ind!" He swung up his rifle as Quentin leaped up onto the parados—the German firestep a few hours ago—and peered out, revolver outthrust. He saw a figure stumbling, crawling on, and in the moonlight clearly recognized the British steel helmet. "Don't fire!" he snapped at the sentry. "One of ours."

The stumbling man at last reached the trench, slid down into it, struggled back to his feet and peered up—"Who's there? Is this the Wealds?"

"Yes, I'm the C.O.," Quentin said eagerly. "Are you from brigade?"

"Yes, sir."

At last, Quentin thought! We're in touch again. To the runner he said, "You're wounded."

"Not bad, sir. Through the arm . . . had to drop my rifle, though."

"Doesn't matter."

"Saw some Jerries back there, so I crawled round them . . . ran into some of our blokes, too . . . don't know what push they was from . . . They didn't know where you was, so . . . kept on . . ."

"Good man!"

"The message is in my breast pocket, sir . . . can't get it out."

Quentin eagerly fumbled with the man's pocket button, found the message and started for his dugout, turning only to say to the nearest soldier, "Look after this man."

They were through! Anything was possible now . . . he could almost hear the clink of bayonets as reinforcements came up . . . the deeper heavier beat from the guns . . . must remember to put that runner in for an M.M., at the least, for what he'd faced and overcome to bring the message up . . .

He reached the double-blanket-shielded door of the dugout, carefully passed through the light and gas blocks, and entered. Campbell and Caffin jumped to their feet as Quentin cried exultantly, "A message from brigade!"

He unfolded the message form and read:

MOST URGENT
To: OC 1 WLI
From: G.H.Q., B.E.F.

Ref. I.O.D. Lucknow Letter 729573 dated August 1, 1914 and reminders. If Lieutenant C.J.C. Rowland 2 WLI att 1 WLI does not pay Rs. 64–10–1 into Paymaster Funds immediately on account of pakhals lost April 7, 1914, and finding of Court of Inquiry held Lucknow Jul 6 1914 subsequently confirmed by G.O.C. Lucknow District, orders for Lieutenant Rowland's arrest will be issued by Brigade commander concerned.

Quentin's head slowly sank and his shoulders hunched. Slowly he composed himself. This was the Army. Orders must be obeyed. After a time he said to his adjutant, "Give this message to Boy when you can, Campbell. Tell him to give you a check, at once, and you send it on."

"Yes, sir . . . Then we'll retire to our old positions fifteen minutes before dawn, as you ordered?"

"Yes . . . Damn it, damn it!"

*   *   *   *

The brigadier general was angry, his face red under the red banded hat, his neck muscles swelling up as he banged the table in his headquarters, two miles behind the front line—"Why did you not have sentries posted?" he snapped.

"We did, sir," Quentin said. "They saw the Germans as soon as they left their trenches, and called the Stand-to."

"Why couldn't you halt the attack, then?"

381

"They came on too fast, sir, before their barrage lifted."

"You were taken by surprise, then?"

"Yes, sir," Quentin answered after a momentary hesitation. The general wasn't being quite fair. All standing orders had been obeyed—their own, brigade's, and division's. The Germans had just come too fast, and in too great numbers, using the ground well . . . and the British artillery response to the S.O.S. had been a few seconds slower than it should have been . . .

The Brigade Major, a beautiful young man from the 4th Hussars, stood behind the general's desk, trying to look sympathetic, but only succeeding in looking debonair and bored.

The brigadier general said, "How we ever got your battalion out of the mess you had it in, I don't know. But with luck—much more luck than you deserved—we did. I had to report to the divisional commander what was happening—as far as I could make it out. He was not pleased."

Naturally, Quentin thought. It had all been very messy, for nearly twelve hours, until finally everyone seemed to have infiltrated back into the positions they'd been occupying before the Germans broke the peace.

The brigadier general said, "I was seriously thinking of relieving you of command of your battalion, Rowland, but there are extenuating circumstances. And your action in attacking and capturing part of the German front line was most commendable . . . By itself, that would have merited me recommending you for a D.S.O., but . . . well, consider yourself lucky you're still in command."

"Yes, sir. Thank you, sir."

"That's all."

Quentin saluted, turned about, and marched out. Campbell was waiting for him and walked back at his side as they headed up the muddy shell-torn pavé for the front. Pollarded willows followed the course of a little stream, here poplars lined the road, there a broken brick wall and a calvary marked a crossroads. Just ahead, the path sank into the earth and became a trench.

Campbell said at last, "What did the general say, sir?"

"Said we'd been surprised."

"That's a lie!" Campbell exploded. "We were just overwhelmed."

"He was pleased about our counter-attack. If it hadn't been for that, he would have stellenbosched me."

Campbell broke out violently, "The bloody fool! He was the one who was taken by surprise, with nothing allotted to protect that flank, and the brigade's machine guns put so far forward they were overrun in the first wave!"

"Don't speak of superior officers like that, Campbell," Quentin said. He trudged on, but felt better. The men had done well, whatever the general said.

Half an hour later they came to battalion headquarters, back in the cellar of the ruined house in the centre of Feuchy. A clerk was waiting at the table, with a sheet of paper held in one hand. He saluted— "Casualty list, as reported by companies at ten ack emma, sir . . . And 2nd Lieutenants Cate and Harbeston have just reported for duty, from the Depot, sir."

Quentin took off his helmet and hung it on its peg. To Campbell he said, "I'll see them in a few minutes—when I've had a look at this."

He sat down and began to study the list . . . most from D Company which had been overrun in the beginning. They must have put up a stiff fight, though . . . died hard . . . Then B, which had done the counter-attack: not many from A or C. He began to read:

Killed: Major Green D.W., Lieutenant Reeves J.R., 2nd Lieutenant
    Bevington, P.

Died of Wounds: 2nd Lieutenant Marlowe, C.

Killed: Sergeant Bygrave, M., Sgt Braddock, R., Cpl Brooks, G., Cpl Lemon, T., Cpl Smith G.J., Ptes Scannel, Bartholomew, Shelley, Garner, Farley—old soldier, Farley: was in his platoon in South Africa—Galvin, Cantrell, Faraday, Daly, Bitting, Bracken, Watt, Nealy, Jones, Jevons, Garrick, Constable, Trevithick, More, Donne . . .

He found tears clouding his vision. Out there, they were the anonymous dead. To him they were his flesh. "Oh my men, my men," he gasped . . . and everything was back as it was, by the Scarpe, except the dead.

He read on: Bunyan, Turner, Gibbon, Darwin . . .

Daily Telegraph, Tuesday, May 29, 1917

NEW SUCCESSES OF THE ITALIAN ARMY
BRILLIANT RESULTS

From Our Own Correspondent, *Rome,* **Monday.**
After six days of battle the Italian Army is still fresh and almost intact, as before the offensive. Never have such brilliant results been obtained with so few losses, and never have the enemy's losses in killed and wounded been so serious . . . The Austrians have suffered very heavy losses in machine guns, which have been destroyed or captured, but they withdrew their big guns while the battle was in progress. Through a gap made near Medeazza Italian

troops are pouring round Mount Hermada, whose fate is sealed. The Austrians are hastily constructing other defences east of Hermada and closer to Trieste . . .

Well, good, Cate thought. The Italians and Austrians seem well matched to each other; but they'd better look out if the Germans sent some divisions down there. Everything he had read and heard made it clear that the German soldier—officer and man—was a great fighter. Many individual Austrians might be too, of course—but then there'd be Croats and Slovenes and Montenegrins and Hungarians with no stomach for the business, particularly since the unifying grandfather figure of old Mutton Chops, Francis Joseph, had gone.

He put down the paper. There was to be a meeting of the Mid Scarrow War Problems Committee this afternoon. The agenda that he'd been sent already looked as though they'd be at it a long time— increasing amount of rape and molestation of women on non-corridor trains; care of old people living alone, when so many of those who would in normal times have been looking after them had left home to work in factories hundreds of miles away; day care for children of mothers working in the munition factories.

Sufficient unto the day: he turned to his mail—three letters: one from Naomi, one from Guy, one from Charlotte, his brother Oswald's widow; he hoped she wasn't inviting herself to Walstone for a visit: wouldn't read that now—it might spoil his kedgeree . . . Naomi was feeling very restless in London and had just about made up her mind to transfer to the F.A.N.Y. He used his butter knife to open Guy's letter and settled down to read, with pleasure.

The Western Front: Wednesday, June 6, 1917

25 Guy Rowland adjusted his goggles and looked quickly round the sky . . . a summer morning over Artois, climbing eastward, altitude ten thousand feet; scattered cumulus cloud to the south, over the Somme; below, the zigzag lines of the trenches, the wide dark carpets of barbed wire, in between and for miles to east and west the pockmarked earth, a patient dying of smallpox. The sun shone on the torn roof of Arras cathedral and the great cobbled "places." Nearer to hand, flying in tight stepped-up echelon of Vs, were the other S.E. 5 As of Three Threes; to the north, and lower, two squadrons of Bristol F 2 Bs.

He was flight commander now and, keeping an eye on his squadron commander, he noticed that the major's machine was climbing a little more steeply than his own. He eased his throttle forward, and pulled the control column a fraction closer to his belly. The little biplane answered like a rocket and in a moment he found himself surging past the level of the major's left wing tip. The goggled head turned, and he could imagine the punitive glare in the concealed eyes. "Sorry," he said aloud, knowing that no one could hear; and eased his craft back into position. These little blighters were very light on the controls . . . wish he'd had more time to get used to them, but they'd only arrived three days ago, and yesterday everyone had had to take his own machine up, individually, to try it out and get the feel of it. Obviously he himself had not succeeded very well. But what bliss it was to have a liquid cooled V-8 engine, and a real working throttle, with total command of power, instead of that mass of machinery whirling round in front of you, and only the most elementary control of it!

From the corner of his eye he caught an unusual change in the pattern of the Bristols and quickly looked to his own rear. The S.E. 5 A was equipped with two machine guns, a Vickers synchronized to fire forward through the arc of the propeller, and a Lewis gun mounted on top of the upper wing. A dexterous pilot, having stalked an enemy aircraft from below could, while flying his machine with one hand, pull down the butt of the Lewis gun with the other, and send a stream of bullets into the German from underneath.

The sky beyond the Bristols was dark with what looked like a flock of big birds, brightly coloured—Albatros D IIIs, the machines that had caused the Royal Flying Corps to name this past April, 1917, "Bloody April." His squadron commander tipped over and dived straight toward the Albatroses. Already a Bristol had got one of them, a long trail of black smoke spiralling up from a twisting, falling Albatros. Guy felt the familiar cold settle in the pit of his stomach, the steady warmth in his hands and feet on the controls, his eyes sharp as a falcon's behind the goggles. He felt the rush of air, heard the roar of the Hispano Suiza engine's 200 horse, saw the sun glinting on the green paint on his engine nacelle . . . Twelve thousand feet, into the sun, turning tight, gathering speed . . . a hundred and fifty . . . hundred and seventy . . . He picked out an Albatros and, going straight at him from above and a little behind, fired a short burst at the pilot's head from two hundred feet. The head disappeared, the Albatros flipped over onto its back and screamed headlong toward the distant earth. Guy pulled the S.E. 5 A into a climbing turn, hung vertically on his propeller for a moment, then fell away into another short dive, this time head to head with another Albatros. He saw the flashes of the other's tracer passing low overhead, but held his course. When the two machines were barely a hundred yards apart on a collision course, the German pulled up his nose. Guy breathed an ecstatic, sighing, "Got you!" as his thumbs closed on the trigger—again a short burst, this time into the Albatros's belly as it passed over him. He turned savagely, knowing that he had not wounded the other mortally, and at the end of the turn came out level, four hundred yards behind the Albatros, which was flying starboard wing down. He jerked himself up and down in his seat, swearing, "Faster . . . faster . . . you swine . . . faster!" An S.E. 5 A was 28 m.p.h. faster than an Albatros: it shouldn't take long. Steadily he closed on the wounded Albatros. He had him in his sights . . . something wrong with the fellow's aileron controls . . . pilot wounded, too, perhaps . . .

Something reflected in his goggles, a touch of colour, shouldn't be there. He thrust fiercely at the stick and kicked the rudder over. The S.E. responded in a spiral dive—a shadow roared over . . . yellow spinner and wheels, yellow wing ends outside the black crosses, red stabilizer . . . von Rackow's own Albatros. He'd been commanding Jasta 16 for three weeks now, and had from that day painted his stabilizer red, the same as Guy's . . . So, von R., with four, five, six more of his Jagdstaffel around him. Nearly got him that time. Guy pulled the S.E. out of the spin and began climbing. There they were, circling a thousand feet above . . . a few S.E.s were climbing with him . . . it would be a tough fight, with the Germans having the height, and the Three Threes broken up by the earlier encounter from their usual close order, mutual support fighting formation.

The Albatroses waited for them, like a mid-air version of a scene he remembered from an American film, where the U.S. cavalry waited in the middle of the prairie and the Indians rode out toward them . . . He found von Rackow's plane again easily enough from the red stabilizer . . . Damn, two of the other Three Threes were going for him, from underneath . . . couldn't see the flame from the guns, but they were in attacking position. Von Rackow turned tight, inside the S.E.s, and fired from a beam position. Guy swore, tight lipped, as he saw an S.E. stagger and seem to stop in mid air . . . it carried the number "2" in blue—that was Graham . . . but his attack had made von Rackow vulnerable to his companion, No. 3—and to Guy himself. Range . . . too long for certainty, but in another two seconds von R. would be out of danger. Guy pressed the trigger and saw his tracer pass over von Rackow's cockpit. He lowered his nose a touch and fired again . . . some hits, too far aft, and von Rackow was falling away in the same sort of dive that he had saved himself with a few minutes ago.

He dived after him. Von Rackow broke away half a second before Guy had expected him to and in a flash was coming up on Guy's tail, almost in position to open fire. Guy flung the S.E. into a turn so tight that the fabric juddered and the wooden frame members creaked. In the middle of his full turn, wings vertical, von Rackow passed through his sights, and he fired—missed astern—at once kicked the S.E. into a reverse turn as tight as the one he had attacked from. Where was von Rackow? . . . he jerked his head round, not in front . . . neither flank . . . ah, behind, nearly on his tail again . . . stick forward, hard, tracer flashing into the canvas of the wing over his head, full right rudder . . . down . . . The German had him cold, couldn't shake him off . . . wished he could get back and tell them what modifications needed to be made to the S.E. 5 A to enable it to beat the Albatros . . . speed was fine, but needed more maneuverability . . .

Why had he not felt the bullets smashing into him, or seen the engine burst into flames in front of him? He looked round and saw von Rackow a hundred feet behind, the twin guns aimed straight at him—but the muzzles black, and von Rackow jerking furiously at the gun levers . . . Guy laughed. Guns jammed!

He swung the S.E., turning tight inside the Albatros. Von Rackow couldn't properly fly his machine and unjam his guns at the same time, and in a few seconds Guy was inside him, then above. Von Rackow gave up on his guns and climbed away. Guy followed, aimed his machine, pressed the trigger . . . but a fraction of a second before, the Albatros turned sharply, and he missed . . . again . . . again . . . His petrol gauge marked nearly empty. Angrily he tried one last burst—again von Rackow jinked at the last moment. Guy turned away, heading for home. Von Rackow, receding to the east, waggled his wings in sardonic farewell.

*   *   *   *

Corporal Frank Stratton climbed up on his wing as soon as he switched off the engine, and said anxiously, "You all right, sir? There's twenty holes in the upper wing and there must be twenty more in the fuselage."

Guy pushed back his goggles and climbed stiffly out of the cockpit. One kill . . . Frank was holding the bucket ready . . . ready for him to vomit into, the sign that the whole squadron knew by now meant that the Butcher had killed. But he did not feel as he usually did. The long duel with von Rackow had altered his emotional view of the fight. He was exhilarated: von Rackow could fly, all right—better than he could, no doubt about it even allowing for the Albatros's superiority in maneuverability. Von R. should have had him before his guns jammed. There were several seconds there when he'd had Guy helpless in his sights, the range short, the air still and clear.

"I got one," he said.

"Good news, sir! That makes you 37 . . . and at least one Hun every day this week!"

Guy started walking toward the long hutment, recently erected, which housed the headquarters offices of the three squadrons that used Ambrines—333 equipped with S.E. 5 As, and two squadrons of Bristol Fighters. He said, "I'll come back when I've made my report."

"Very good, sir." Frank saluted, watched his pilot for a few moments, then returned to the machine, for which he was mechanically responsible.

When he reached it, he stood a moment, staring at the starboard side, counting the bullet holes in the canvas, then walked round and counted those in the port side . . . then in the wings, then in the aluminum sheet of the engine cowling. Fifty-two in all. They'd need a big roll of canvas and a big pot of dope. Where was that lad Farrar with the step ladder?

The rigger's voice was close behind him—"Here y'are, Corp. I was in the bogs . . . had to go . . ."

Frank glared at him disapprovingly. Wonder the squadron commander didn't say something about the length of his hair, must be four inches long, wavy, and thick with lavender oil; but he was a good man with the fabric—worked in a tailor's shop before the war, he said.

Frank indicated the S.E.—"Someone put a lot of holes in our machine, so you patch them, while I look at the engine and the controls, make sure no harm done there."

He climbed up onto the wing, thence into the cockpit and began carefully working all the controls—rudder, ailerons, control column—feeling the firmness and accuracy of the response. He'd check them all by sight, by actually running the cables through his hands, later, and then make sure no bullet had hit a stressed strut: but this to start with. All good so far. The Germans who'd put all those bullets into Mr Guy's machine had fired high. Mr Guy never made that mistake. If you aimed a little low, you'd still hit some other part of the fuselage, but if you were high, all you'd hit was air.

He climbed out and down, moved the step ladder and climbed up to examine the propeller; then he unfastened the engine cowling and, getting Farrar to start up the engine, watched it, as the propeller whirled. All well, no damage to the cylinders, plugs . . . fuel pipes sound, exhaust clean, firing sweetly . . . no, one of the cylinders sour . . . No. 5 . . . He pulled a notebook out of the pocket of his grease-stained overalls and made a note with a stub of pencil . . . then stopped the engine, climbed back to the ground, and made more notes.

A shadow fell across the notebook and he looked round to see Guy Rowland staring at the S.E., his flying helmet and goggles in one hand, stroking his chin with the other. He said, "How is she?"

"Number 5 cylinder—or the plug—is sour. That's all—an' the bullet holes, of course."

"We're going on a sweep at three this afternoon."

"She'll be fixed by then, sir . . . Farrar, be careful with that dope. The surface has to be smooth, you understand?"

"O.K., Corp."

Guy Rowland said, "There are two things wrong with this plane. One is the maneuverability has to be improved, somehow. The other is that there's something wrong with the engine, but I'm not enough of an engineer to put my finger on it."

"I gave it a top check over last night, sir, and . . ."

"Ah, that's why you have those bags under your eyes. I thought you'd been out on the tiles with a mademoiselle."

"I'm a married man, sir," Frank said, grinning. Mr Guy liked to tease him about being a Romeo, but he'd never looked at another woman but Anne, and Mr Guy knew it.

He said, "Well, sir, I think it's the reduction gear . . . I don't know why the Hispano Suiza people don't re-gear the engine so that it doesn't need reduction. I'd like to see them put a Rolls Royce Falcon in, same as the Bristols have."

"That looks pretty big for an S.E. 5."

"It is, sir, so they'd have to modify the cowling . . . change the engine bearers, recalculate the centre of gravity . . . but none of that should give them any trouble at Farnborough."

"Well, I'll talk to the C.O. about it, and try to persuade him to put these ideas to Wing." He nodded and turned to walk away. Frank came up beside him saying, "Sir . . . is there any chance of leave soon?"

Guy stopped and looked at the corporal. Frank knew that the R.F.C. was being stretched to the limit of its men and machines. It was unlike him to ask for leave when he must know that it was all but impossible. There were many domestic emergencies which in more normal times would merit the grant of leave . . . not now, though. The war demanded all.

He held Frank's eyes. "Trouble at home, Frank?"

"I don't know, sir." Frank's open face was disturbed—"There was a letter from Mother in the post bag yesterday. She said I must come home . . . she said she'd tell the R.F.C. about my being 4 F really, and not fit for active service, if I didn't."

"Did she say why it was so important?"

"No, sir. But I wish I *could* go home for a couple of days and see what's the matter . . . Mother's practically crippled with the rheumatism and arthritis and all. Dad has to look after her about as much as she looks after him, Ruthie says. That's my sister, sir—Mrs Hoggin."

Guy recognized that Frank didn't really expect to get leave. What he wanted was someone to talk to; and here he, Guy Rowland, was closer to Frank than any of the other corporals or sergeants in whom another man might have confided, in preference to an officer.

He said, "I'm afraid you won't get any leave now, Frank. It's not even worth applying, unless . . ."

"Oh, no, sir, I understand." He laughed ruefully. "I suppose I'm just feeling a mite homesick for Anne and the kids—" he laughed again—"Even to see Victoria—that's a motor bike my Dad's making in his shed, to go a hundred miles an hour. I used to work on it with him before the war . . . not much though. I bet I could get a hundred and five out of her, if he'd let me, but . . ." he shrugged—"He's my dad, and he's set in his ways."

"Aren't they all?" Guy said.

They walked on until Frank Stratton said, "Well, I'd best be getting back, sir. She'll be in tiptop shape in no time . . . and you can bag another Hun for tea."

Guy laughed, waved his helmet and goggles in the air in response to Frank's punctilious infantry-type salute, and went to the officers' quarters—ten huts, each with two quarters in it, each for two officers. He had the end quarter—alone.

In the room he dropped his helmet and goggles on the bed, picked five letters off the table and sprawled back in a battered wicker chair by the empty grate. The windows were open, and a robin was sitting on the window sill watching him, its head cocked. He found a Nice biscuit in his pocket, broke off a crumb and threw it at the little bird. The robin dodged and flew down outside, following the crumb. Guy began to open the letters.

His sister, Virginia: thrilled to hear he had shot down twenty-eight German aeroplanes, not counting twelve balloons. It was a swizz that they never mentioned his name in the papers, or showed his picture. They'd have to do it if he won the V.C., wouldn't they? She was so proud of him and had his picture up in her barrack room and all the other girls thought he was so handsome. He'd better be careful if he ever came to visit her again, as she couldn't guarantee his safety (ha ha) . . . She'd been home on leave. Mummy spent most of her time moping round the house. She ought to get a job, there were plenty she could do, but she just sat and moped. The girls in her Section were marvellous, friendly, helpful, they all stuck together, and she'd never thought it could be so much fun with other girls, after Cheltenham Ladies College. And she was going out every Saturday with Battery Sergeant Major Stanley Robinson, D.C.M., who wished to be remembered to Guy and respectfully wished him all good fortune. Lots of love and kisses X X X X.

From No. 9056748 Private John D. Merritt, Co.D., 16th Infantry Regiment, El Paso, Texas . . . He was in the Army now, a dogface, earning all of $25 a week, what did Guy think of that? Only half the other enlisted men, old regulars, could read or write, and when he'd foolishly let slip that he had been at Harvard they'd given him a hard time, until he fought the one who'd been riding him the hardest and broke his nose. But they were good fellows. He'd never known any people like them before, meeting them was like going down into the cellar of your house and finding a whole different breed of Americans down there, who'd quietly been feeding the furnace and fixing the plumbing without anyone upstairs realizing what they really looked like. They'd show the Krauts something when they got over. And that wouldn't be long as (*deleted by censor*).

From David Toledano, Royal Field Artillery, in Palestine, obviously . . . enjoying the climate, bathing in the Mediterranean . . . had enough leave recently to visit the Valley of the Kings and Thebes: magnificent, awe inspiring . . . life likely to change its tenour now that Allenby is coming out as C-in-C. We hear he is nicknamed the Bull, and we expect him to live up to it, and lead us charging off against the Turks . . .

His father: proud of him . . . the battalion in the line again after a short rest . . . saw aeroplanes flying over all the time and often wondered if he's in one of them . . . the battalion was in good shape though something must be done about (*deleted by censor*) before winter comes. The battalion had a good many casualties the last time it was in the line, but remained in good spirits. Your Affec. father . . .

From Florinda—this one he'd kept till last: she was performing at three hospitals a week, all over the country. Getting so tired of sitting up in trains all day, all night, always looked like something the cat brought in, in the mornings, and the trains always late . . . thought about him a lot, couldn't realize it was six months since he was here, how time flies, and now she'd better stop, bloody train to catch in an hour and couldn't find her music and she had the curse, what a life, love, love, love. . . .

He held the letter and stared sightlessly out of the window. Nothing about other men there. But what right did he have to be told about that? Did he want to be, if there were? He must remember that she wasn't Probyn's granddaughter any more, but a very rich peeress and actress, very beautiful—miles away, in space, and circumstance. The robin watched him from the window sill, waiting for more biscuit. Guy saw nothing, but an abstraction of sky, cloud, and earth, unfocussed, framed in the oblong of the window. The robin flew in and landed on the table beside him. Then he noticed it and, feeling in his pocket, held out his hand, full of biscuit crumbs. The robin hopped onto the ball of his thumb and began to peck away with great satisfaction, and no fear.

*   *   *   *

The four S.E. 5 As of D Flight, 333 Squadron, Royal Flying Corps, flew north through scattered banks of heavy cumulus cloud in V formation, the flight leader, Lieutenant Guy Rowland, D.S.O., M.C., at the point of the V. They were at 8,000 feet, the air cold for the time of year. To the left, slag heaps, pithead towers and wheels, and the enormous straddling black shape of Tower Bridge marked the mining towns of Hulluch, Loos, Lens, and La Bassee. The flight was keeping about five miles on the German side of the trench lines. A south-west wind of twenty knots at that altitude made the machines crab slightly to keep on course. It was evening, the sun low, squalls coming up.

Guy flew with no thought on the business of flying. By now, that—the maneuvering of the control column and the rudder pedals, was instinctual, as were his periodic glances at the compass and altimeter. His attention was concentrated in the encircling sky . . . the line of observation balloons to the west—the German ones very close, the British beyond, over the slag heaps and pitheads . . . two R.E. 8s, Corps aircraft, doing artillery spotting and ranging for the British guns—tempting targets for Jasta 16, those R.E. 8s. Von R's men liked to pounce out of the clouds on the practically helpless R.E.s, shoot a couple down, then fly back, speeding on the western wind, to their bases.

Major Sugden's orders had been unequivocal—"Sweep just the German side of the line at eight thousand, from Arras northward to Armentières, then back at twelve thousand. Attack and destroy anything you meet on your patrol, except balloons . . . Our object is to demonstrate to the infantry that we control the air over the front line fighting area. As you know they have recently been attacked by German aircraft. I hope you catch some of them at it . . . particularly in our gun areas."

The little fighter flew into a white, damp, swirling blindness of cumulus, lurched and heaved through it and after two minutes burst out into sunlight. Guy swept the sky . . . no change . . . there must have been strong updraughts in that cloud, for his altimeter read eight five. He pointed the nose gently down, and the two others followed close. Into cloud again, bump, watch the altimeter carefully now, still rising, with nose down. He broke again into sunlight, seeing straight ahead, five hundred feet below, the black crosses and yellow spinners of twelve Albatros D III fighters. No need to signal—nose down—attack! Throttle wide . . . he had one in his sights, just beginning to turn away. He fired at a hundred and fifty feet, and the Albatros exploded into a huge ball of fire, so large that he flew through it, the flames momentarily scorching him, the smells of burning fuel acrid in his nostrils . . . He was through, an Albatros closing up on his tail, tracer bullets beginning to clack past. He swung the S.E. round in a tight, flat crab motion. The Albatros, expecting an Immelmann,

passed close to the right as Guy held the S.E., kicked it back and
waited till the Albatros slid into his sights . . . a long burst . . . got
him! No, damn, the man was falling off, Guy's sights slipping back
toward the tail . . . he'd put a lot of holes through the fabric there,
but it didn't catch fire. The German turned on his back and started to
spin down . . . doing it on purpose, Guy muttered, it won't help . . .
he followed, thumb ready on the trigger, twisting and turning . . .
The fellow was down to three thousand . . . two . . . one . . .
screaming east, as fast as he could go, he'd burst his engine from
over-revving . . . even so, Guy gained on him steadily, slowly . . .
There was nothing the fellow could do to get away . . . He flew on,
closing inexorably, unaware of the time, any of his instruments, only
the fleeing German ahead. At last he was close enough. Why didn't the
man turn and fight? He'd have a chance of doing some damage at
least. But he didn't. At a hundred feet range and barely twenty feet
above the ground, Guy fired a one-second burst. The Albatros nosed
over at a hundred and ten miles an hour and flew into an open field,
disintegrating into a thousand pieces that bounced back into the sky,
cartwheeled across the field, burst through hedges. One of the pieces
was the body of the pilot, it too breaking and scattering as it bounced.

Guy climbed back and up. No damage that he could see, controls
all answering well. Time to turn for home. The sun was sinking beneath the horizon. Where was the rest of his flight?

He saw the Albatros from two miles away, coming out of the
setting sun at him . . . no other aircraft in the sky, all gone home, like
birds, to their roosts . . . all but that single Albatros and his single S.E.
They must be at least twenty miles behind the German lines, so the
Albatros could maneuver any way he liked, while, unless it came to
desperation, Guy must try to work back westward—or face imprisonment for the rest of the war, even if he won the dogfight. He flew on,
climbing as the Albatros maneuvered to cut across his course.

He knew it before he saw it: yellow wing tips . . . von Rackow
again, come to get the Butcher. Rain began to stream past him, and
the temperature dropped abruptly. He hadn't enough petrol—he'd
never get home—but he had no choice.

Guy turned suddenly and attacked. Von Rackow was ready and
twisted away two seconds before Guy was ready to fire. Guy swung the
S.E.'s nose again to the west, still climbing . . . must have some height
for emergencies . . . Why not just run for it? He might just get home,
or at least crash-land on his own side of the lines. He had the speed
advantage, and von Rackow would only get one chance, as he passed.
Guy threw the S.E. into the same flat turn that he had used before, in
his second fight of the evening, and for a moment had von Rackow by
surprise, the Albatros's cockpit flashing across his sights as he pressed

the trigger. The tracer slashed just behind the pilot's body, perhaps four or five bullets into the fuselage—nothing serious. Then von Rackow had hauled the Albatros round, water vapour trails streaming from his wingtips, until he too could fire a burst. But Guy was turning hard and it went behind him; he pulled up and heaved round; so for a few minutes they circled, like wary dogs. This time it was von Rackow who attacked, jerking his Albatros into a savage turn and at once opening fire. Guy kicked on full rudder and skidded horribly out of the way . . . glimpsing the tracer streaming behind his shoulder . . . pulled up the nose, went over into an Immelmann and at the end of the half-roll found the German coming up at him, the muzzles of his Spandaus red and yellow fire. His own thumbs were on the triggers . . .

A tremendous blow on the side of the head made him reel in the cockpit . . . von Rackow was turning again, no time to wonder where he was hit, how badly. He rolled over, spiralling. Von Rackow didn't believe it and was lining up for another attack. Guy turned to face him, firing as he turned . . . something wet on his cheek, inside the flying helmet, dripping onto his hand when he leaned forward, head hurting . . . fearful smarting pain along the side somewhere . . . He jerked the S.E. out of its spin, fired again . . . more hits, but no visible sign of damage. Clouds everywhere now, rain, grey vapour scurrying past, the S.E. jumping all over the sky, sun gone . . . God, lightning behind von Rackow!

He could barely see now, for the blood running in his eyes, and turned blindly, kicking the rudder this way and that. There he was . . . yellow, seen for a moment, red stabilizer. He pressed the trigger, tracer flashing yellow fire in the dusk. He prayed for the red blossom of flame to erupt from the Albatros's engine, but it flew on, turning tight, out of his sights, gone . . . he wiped desperately at his goggles with his gloved hand . . . tore off the gloves, tore off the goggles, wiped his face, his hand red and sticky. He saw von Rackow, coming at him again out of the black rain, and pressed the trigger button . . . the Vickers fired . . . he lifted his thumb off the trigger . . . the gun kept on firing. Oh God, trigger jammed, runaway gun! The belt was flying through the gun and he could not stop it. He had used the last of his Vickers ammunition, there was no possibility of being able to use the Lewis, and he ached all over with fatigue. The engine began to cough. Lightning flashed and he saw the Albatros plain. It was still shooting, while his own engine clattered and panted as if in despair. More lightning, and the engine failed—picked up—failed again. The S.E.'s nose dipped as power was lost. The propeller windmilled uselessly in front of him. He was done.

He pushed the stick forward to gain flying speed, so that he could have some control over the machine. Any moment now von Rackow would complete his turn, and—finis! He looked round, saw the Albatros coming at him, raised his hand in salute, and waited, trying not to cringe. The Albatros did not fire but passed by, very close, so that he could see the pilot's thin blonde mustache under his goggles. "Get on with it," he shouted. He could just make out the earth below . . . a field, a farm building, near one corner . . . hard to judge his height. Why bother? Von Rackow came round again . . . sights on. Guy waited.

Again the Albatros swung past, this time close above, and Guy, looking up, saw that the struts of one of its landing wheels were shot through. Well, von Rackow would catch it when he landed . . . cartwheel at least, and with luck, catch fire . . . meanwhile, he was down to five hundred, the wind whistling and roaring loud now that the engine was silent . . . still raining—that, too, loud in his ears. Nose down a little more, he must keep up flying speed in the tight turns he'd have to make if he wanted to land in that big field . . .

If? He wiped more blood off his face and looked round. The Albatros was following him down . . . about a hundred yards back. Playing cat and mouse? Waiting till he thought he was at least going to make a safe landing, and then cutting him to pieces with those Spandaus? That wasn't von Rackow's reputation . . . but with Germans, you never knew.

He braced himself for the landing. Perhaps his own undercarriage was shot through . . . more likely his tail or upper wing struts damaged . . . one way to die wouldn't be much different from another. Just don't let it be a bad wound, crippling. The field rushed up in the dusk. Which way was the wind blowing? Impossible to tell in the near darkness, better assume it was south-west, as it had been when he took off, and still was when he'd seen the smoke from chimneys toward Lille. He glanced quickly at his compass, once more brushed blood from his eyes and face with the back of his bare hand, and watched the earth take shape and form close ahead. Buildings loomed—no lights—nose down a touch more. He skimmed over a hedge and at once lifted the nose. The S.E. settled at once with a heavy bump, then rolled forward through some crop, dull green in the dusk, over hard earth, slightly ridged . . . He was down. Now von Rackow would fire . . . He heaved himself out of the cockpit, stumbled onto the wing, slipped and fell to the ground, struggled up and began to run toward the dark shapes of the buildings. The sound of the aircraft engine which had been in his ears all the way down—von Rackow's engine— was now loud overhead, the Albatros a big dark silhouette against the lightning-shot clouds. The wings swept round and there was enough light for Guy to make out the yellow wheels and spinner. He stooped and turned, watching . . . von Rackow was coming down . . . Perhaps he could make him prisoner. He found his revolver, drew it and again started to run, this time toward the place where the Albatros would land.

From twenty yards off he watched it swoop over the hedge just beyond where he had done so himself . . . then he heard the engine being cut . . . then a splintering crash . . . One wing dipped into the earth, the Albatros swung round and over, a giant moth thrashing in the night, groaning and screaming in pain. Guy stumbled forward. The Albatros was lying on its side, one wing torn off, the other crumpled. The pilot was crawling out of his cockpit. Guy pointed the revolver and shouted, "Hands up, von Rackow!" The German crawled on, and Guy cried furiously, "Hands up!" Something bright and metallic caught his eye and he saw that it was a belt of ammunition from one of the Albatros's Spandaus, trailing down from the gun. Then he felt a peculiar sensation of lightness, his body rising in the night toward the clouds, rain dripping from him, and . . . he was fainting . . . what? . . . what . . . ?

He was on his back, swimming up to consciousness, the earth cold beneath him. A dark human shape was kneeling beside him, the bluish glint of a revolver in his hand. Guy groaned, his head aching worse than it had since he was hit. The figure said, "How are you? I imagine it hurts."

Guy felt his head and found a raw gash along the right cheek, starting just by his eye and going through the flap of his ear. It was still bleeding, but not much—the side of his head was a mess of congealing blood and raw skin.

Von Rackow said, "Do you want your revolver back? I've emptied it . . . You don't give up easily, do you?"

"You're von Rackow," Guy said weakly.

"I am, and you're Guy Rowland . . . the Butcher. Thirty-seven kills, isn't it?"

"Thirty-nine now," Guy said. "And why didn't you shoot me down when my gun ran away—and my engine stopped?"

"Because *I* had used up all mine, too. That burst that hit you—I saw your S.E. practically leap in the air . . . were the last rounds I had. I knew you were wounded, too, and I thought I'd take you prisoner if you could manage to land without crashing . . . then I was the one to crash. Broke my wrist." He held up his left arm to show the hand dangling from the wrist.

Guy said, "I saw that your undercarriage was damaged, and knew you'd crash, wherever you landed."

397

Von Rackow said, "Well, I should have had you a couple of times before that, but to tell the truth I'm not the best shot in the world. I'd have a better score than our Rittmeister Herr Baron if I were . . . You're out of petrol?" Guy nodded, then winced. Von Rackow said, "We'll find out later . . . where are we?"

Guy sat up, von Rackow held out his hand and helped pull him to his feet. Guy said, "Somewhere between Lille and Douai, but a little farther east . . . I can hear the guns, but they're miles off . . . I'm going to wash my face if I can find any water."

The storm was passing over, stars emerging one by one. The two young men walked together toward the building. It was a barn, empty, straw piled in one corner, a cattle trough outside, spades and pitchforks stacked inside, with a wheelbarrow and a full haycart. Guy found his handkerchief and wiped his face clean of blood, nearly fainting again with the pain as he did so. Von Rackow said, "Do you have a first field dressing?"

Guy nodded and found it. Von Rackow said, "You'll have to open it, then we can work together to put it on."

Carefully in the faint starlight, with the sweet smell of hay about them, they opened the little package, applied the disinfected pad to Guy's cheek and fastened the khaki bandage strips round his jaw and head to hold it in place. Then Guy said, "You should have a splint . . . Look, I'll take your shirt off . . . mine's soaked with blood . . . and make a splint . . . break off one of the pitchfork tines—they're all wood . . ."

Carefully he took off von Rackow's tunic, with the Pour le Merite medal, and the Iron Cross ribbon disappearing between the buttons. Then the shirt; and as it came off, von Rackow wincing with pain as the sleeve slipped over his wrist, Guy caught the dull gleam of a gold ornament hanging round the German's neck on a gold chain, next to his skin. He could see clearly what it was, and said, "That's a swastika. It's an Indian symbol . . . I didn't know it was popular in Germany."

Von Rackow said, "It isn't. They've never heard of it in Germany." Guy saw he was smiling, his teeth white and close and the eyes snapping—"That little good luck charm has *C.J.C. Rowland* inscribed on the front . . ."

"Boy!" Guy exclaimed.

"Quite . . . On the back is *To Boy with love from Naomi* . . . His lady friend?"

"His sister," Guy said. "They're my cousins."

"He gave me that at the Christmas Day truce in 1914, when I was still in the infantry. Is he . . . ?"

Guy said, "As far as I know."

"If he lived through the Somme battles he's a lucky man . . . as that swastika charm has made me. And it was given to me by an enemy!"

Guy remembered something, and said suddenly, "Your ammunition isn't finished. You let me live because of this."

"Nonsense, my dear fellow! Do you think I'd let a beastly *Engländer* go free?"

"I saw a full belt in one of your guns, just now."

The German did not answer for a time, then he put out his good hand, "I am a sentimental fellow. I wanted to meet you."

Guy said, "Thanks . . . I'm sorry about those fellows my first day."

Von Rackow said, "I am sorry I was so . . . angry. Of course, you were only doing your job . . . but one of them was the brother of a lady I am very much in love with and hope to marry. We had known each other all our lives."

"I'm sorry," Guy said.

After a time von Rackow said, *"C'est la guerre."* And Guy said, "Sit down till I get the splint and tear up your shirt to the right size. Are you warm enough?"

"Quite," von Rackow said. "And soon we'll be warmer still."

Twenty minutes later, the damaged wrist held in a splint, von Rackow said, "In the wreckage of my beautiful Albatros is a large flask of French brandy. Also a length of German sausage, and some rye bread. I often have a snack while flying."

"I eat biscuits," Guy exclaimed. "Bourbons or Nice . . . sweet ones. And how do you speak English so well—Werner, isn't it?"

"Mother's English," von Rackow said, briefly—"Let's get the flask."

They walked together to the smashed Albatros and soon extracted the food and drink, returned to the barn, sat down, and in intimate silence drank water from the cattle trough, sipped brandy, and ate sausage, rye bread, and sweet biscuits.

"My head feels better now," Guy said. "Not good, just not unbearable."

Von Rackow nodded. Now, having spent two hours in the starlight they could see each other almost clearly, and distinguish all but the smallest changes of expression.

Von Rackow said, "Do you know what this war's about?"

Guy thought for a while and said, "Treaties, I suppose. Belgium . . ."

"We are told it is for our survival as a people," von Rackow said, "but I think it is more an expression of energy. Ever since I was a small boy I have felt that we are somehow constricted . . . bound in."

Guy said, "And we wouldn't let you expand."

"No. Because that meant sea power . . . which you dare not grant—though you will have to grant it to the Americans."

Guy said, "Well, if that's true, we've lost or are going to lose our sea power . . . and you're going to lose all chance of expanding."

"And more treaties are being broken every day—the Hague Convention by us, the Treaty of London by you and the Americans . . . and countless thousands of soldiers and sailors and civilians are being shot or starved or drowned to death . . ."

Together they said, "For what, then?"

Von Rackow was the first to speak again—"What can we do about it?"

Guy said, "Nothing. We've decided to make this a test . . . *a l'outrance* . . . and the people want it. Even the soldiers do. There's talk of a negotiated peace at home now, but . . ."

"In Germany, too, since Bethmann-Hollweg suggested the possibility."

"My uncle—Boy's father—is in the pacifist movement, I know . . . and a lot of people are asking, why go on with the slaughter? But the moment anyone mentions actual terms, everyone says 'Not on your life.' "

"Same in Germany," von Rackow said. "So, slowly, we'll bleed to death . . . and the world with us . . . What on earth do you think it will be like when the war does end—whichever way it does?"

"I can't imagine," Guy said. "I was seventeen when it began . . . I can remember what it was like then, as though it were yesterday . . . myself, my sister, mother, maid, the flat, Turf, Wellington, jallyhoes, everything . . . And I can see this—the war, here, now . . . but the future, no. I try, but no picture comes. It's blank."

"The world is going to need help, or it will never recover," von Rackow said. "And where's it going to come from, if we're all knocked out?"

"America, Werner," Guy said. "They're not going to suffer much—there isn't time, now. They'll have to help the rest of us afterward, for their own sakes."

Von Rackow said, "It's people who are going to need help, as well as nations . . . and much more urgently. Wouldn't it be wonderful if we—you and I . . . could do something together, for people? We would symbolize the new world . . . the war gone and forgotten, old enemies, new friends . . . healing wounds, healing minds . . . free from hate as well as fear."

"I wish I could help the infantry now," Guy said. "I feel guilty every time I fly over the trenches . . . I've been in them. My father's in them now. Boy's in them . . . the ordinary men, the private soldiers

. . . what they suffer and endure . . . on both sides, French, Russians, Germans, Italians—all infantry . . . in the mud, the cold, freezing . . . and for what? How much does a German private get? No comforts, no women, except those beastly *maisons de tolérance* and the fat bloated whores who work in them . . . wounds, disablement, death."

They did not speak again until nearly half an hour later von Rackow said, "I'm going to sleep in the hay now, Guy."

Guy got up from the cart and said, "Me too." His head was aching and burning and he said, "Can I have another swig of the brandy?" Von Rackow handed over the flask wordlessly and Guy drank. Then together they went to the back of the barn, and lay down side by side in the hay, and went to sleep.

* * * *

In the first light of before dawn they went out together, having awoken an hour earlier and lain there in the hay, talking in low tones about their homes and families, about Florinda Gorse and Maria Rittenhaus and their homes in Kent and the Altmark.

Together they examined the smashed Albatros. "The fuel tank hasn't burst," said Guy.

"Good German workmanship. If it had I would probably have fried."

They looked at the S.E., and after a few minutes von Rackow said, "It really seems quite serviceable, though I put a lot of holes in you. You must have the luck of the devil. All it needs to get you home is a few gallons of petrol."

"I've got an aeroplane," said Guy, "and you've got petrol."

"You have stated the technical problem very clearly. Do you suppose we can do anything about it, like looking for a container in the barn, before the farmer wakes?"

"Worth trying, if you're prepared to explain to your people." Guy's head was splitting, and he was only an unskilled helper to von Rackow's efficient transfer of petrol from the German to the British plane. At last von Rackow had to help him up into the cockpit. "Sure you're all right to fly?" he asked; then, "And what on earth are you going to tell old Sulphuric?"

"Don't know . . . I'll think of something . . . say my engine stopped because of dirty plugs and I spent the night cleaning them, then she started . . . or, I landed beside a crashed plane, out of fuel, but passed out and couldn't go and look for a bucket till near dawn, to transfer petrol from it . . ."

"Well, good luck." Von Rackow turned the propeller half a dozen times, and called up—"Ready?"

Guy cried "Contact!" and switched on. Von Rackow bent over and turned the propeller with an awkward jerk of his body and good arm. The engine spluttered once and died. Again . . . again. At the third swing the cylinders caught. Von Rackow came up to the edge of the cockpit. Guy leaned out and shouted, "I'm not going to fire at you again, Werner."

Von Rackow shouted back, "Nor I . . . Now get back to hospital or you'll get gangrene."

Guy shouted, "I'll tell Boy I met you . . . Good luck!" He waved his hand, pushed the throttle forward, taxied to the end of the field, turned into the slow morning wind. A farmer was coming up the lane behind, driving four brown cows. Smoke rose from a cottage half a mile away beside a dense copse. Guy pushed the throttle wide and the S.E. bounced and jumped across the shallow furrows, the farmer gazing in astonishment at the darting English plane, the wrecked Albatros and the German officer waving one hand in the air, the other dangling. The S.E. climbed away, heading west. Von Rackow watched it disappear and then walked slowly toward the cottage.

*   *   *   *

> *A young aviator lay dying;*
> *And as 'neath the wreckage he lay—he lay,*
> *To the mechanics there standing around him,*
> *These last dying words he did say—did say . . .*

The long hut shook to the roar of the singers, twenty young men of Three Threes, stamping their feet on the rug-covered concrete floor, full wine glasses raised, spilling over, faces red, mouths gaping, eyes bulging.

> *Take the cylinders out of my kidneys,*
> *The connecting rod out of my brain—my brain*
> *From the small of my back take the crankshaft*
> *And assemble the engine again—again!*

"And again!" Bunny Fuller screamed. He jumped onto the top of the rickety table where magazines and newspapers were stacked and waved his champagne glass—"All together! And more feeling in that repeat, chaps! The poor bugger's dying there, *dying*! Let's see some tears! Start again!"

> *A young aviator lay dying,*
> *And as 'neath the wreckage he lay . . .*
> Piano, con brio, lento . . . he laaaaay!

Guy swallowed, giggled, drank, and sang again. Under the plaster the scar on his right cheekbone was raw and red, and the hole was not healed in his ear. Apparently the phosphorus on the tracer bullet that hit him had cauterized the wound, helping to prevent gangrene; but the bullet had cut a branch of the right mandibular facial muscle, which would leave him with a permanent slight droop to the right side of his mouth. General Trenchard had visited the ward, and said, "As they're going to let you out, you'll be in time for a joint celebration in your mess tonight—Major Sugden's second bar to his D.S.O. . . . and your first. And you've been promoted to captain, at Major Sugden's request. Congratulations." The tall man had smiled, a small frosty smile, and left.

And now here he was, the Butcher no more, but Guy, good old Guy, wearing the three stars of a captain. They were chairing the Major round the room on their shoulders, bellowing *For he's a jolly good fellow* . . . for the fourth time. Old Sulphuric could hold his drink . . . they'd all been at it since seven, and here it was near four a.m., and getting light . . . Dawn Patrol being taken by 56 today.

"Let's debag Bunny! Off with his bags!" the cry arose. Bunny Fuller jumped down from the table top and raced round the room pulling over chairs behind him as he went. The pack followed, giving tongue like foxhounds. Tiny Entwhistle had his hunting horn out, and was blowing the "Gone awaaaaay." Major Sugden subsided into an armchair, where a grinning mess waiter brought him a glass of brandy and soda . . . Crashes and shrieks from the grass outside the mess hut—Bunny's voice raised, "You rotters . . . my best bags! Four quid gone down the drain . . . oh, ouch . . . aah!" The hunting horn blared the kill. "Break 'im and eat 'im," Tiny brayed.

The hounds trooped back, bearing Bunny Fuller's torn trousers aloft like a fox's brush. Bunny himself was carried in slung by several men like a dead deer, his shirt tails flapping.

A roar of sound boomed across the grass and a Very light, fired at close range, shattered one window pane, flashed through the room and broke a pane opposite on its way out, where it bounced on the grass, exploded, and lit up the whole area with lurid red light. It was quickly followed by another, this one green.

The young men of Three Threes hurled themselves to the floor— "It's the bloody Bristols," shouted Jimmy Brentward from the floor. "Come to break up our party!"

"They've got one of their own," another yelled. "Mainwaring's V.C.! Up and at 'em!"

They all jumped to their feet, hurling glasses behind, onto the floor, at the wall, anywhere, and burst out through windows and doors

403

to join in combat with the officers of one of the Bristol Fighter squadrons.

"Sic 'em, sic 'em!" Major Sugden shouted. A fist ploughed past Guy's ear, tearing off the plaster. His wound reopened, spurting blood. "Up the Three Threes!" he yelled and hurled himself onto the heaving pile of bodies on the grass.

Five minutes later he struggled out, panting, in the strengthening light of dawn, clutching a piece of kilt material . . . No one in Three Threes wore the kilt, so he'd got an enemy's, at least. From the far end of the field a bugle blew the Stand-to. The distant hum of aircraft engines increased to a roar. The pile of bodies gradually untangled. A man cried in an aggrieved voice, "Some cad's been bloody well bleeding on me! Look at my shirt!"

Twelve S.E. 5 As appeared in the west, and swooped down on the field in a single V. The celebrants staggered about and waved and shouted as the squadron leader of the dawn patrol raised a gloved hand fifty feet above them, then gunned his engine and at the head of his squadron climbed away toward the front line, Germany, and the east.

Daily Telegraph, Saturday, June 2, 1917

WOMEN'S WAR WORK

Interesting information concerning the wide extension of the employment of women in industry . . . is given in the report for 1916 of the chief inspector of factories. Miss Anderson, the principal lady inspector, says it appears that the one absolute limit to the replacement of men by women lies in those heavy occupations and processes where adaptation of plant or appliances can not be effected so as to bring them within the compass even of selected women of physical capacity above the normal . . .

As to whether substitution has progressed as far as it can and ought in the present national emergency, it is suggested that in many cases progress has been made proportionately to the pressure brought to bear by military tribunals, and that so long as men's labour can be got, few employers will experiment with women's, though once the experiment is made, satisfaction is expressed with the result. In the country generally, apart from a few localities, the supply of women appears to be almost unlimited. Large numbers of women have been transferred to the congested areas of Coventry and Woolwich without in any way affecting local demands.

Miss Anderson adds: "The national gain appears to me to be overwhelming, as against all risks of loss or disturbance, in the new

> self-confidence engendered in women by the very considerable proportion of cases where they are efficiently doing men's work at men's rates of pay. If this new valuation can be reflected on to their own special, and often highly skilled and nationally indispensable occupations, a renaissance may there be effected of far greater significance even than the immediate widening of women's opportunities, great as that is."

Cate pondered a moment. What *would* be the effect of the war on the relationship between the sexes when the present revolution had run its course? Miss Anderson had not, perhaps, stressed enough that soon the advance in mechanical aids to labour would bring all but a very, very few tasks within a woman's strength. Nor had she mentioned that when the war was over, and men were again available for work in the factories and farms, employers would give them preference because they would be much less likely to leave because of marriage, child bearing and raising, moving to another city with a husband, and in many cases, looking after aged parents. He was also not quite sure how many men would appreciate women who had the self-confidence to say, "I can do your work just as well as you" . . . with the corollary, perhaps, that the man could start to mop and sweep and cook while the woman earned half or more of the family wages. Women had, of course, given orders to men for centuries. Lady Swanwick didn't have to send for the earl when she wanted to tell Chapman something: but it had usually been in a domestic setting. If women stayed in industry, they would not be content to be permanently allotted the bottom rungs. They would demand to be able to climb, and reach the top, like men . . . It would not be easy for men to accept that; and generally, the lower the class, the less it would be accepted. He himself occasionally cooked a meal, when he felt like it and Mrs Abell would let him; he had even washed dishes with Tillie when the staff was depleted by flu; but he knew that Frank Cawthon had never done either in his life . . . and that was true of nearly every man in the village.

Meanwhile, he had a problem, to do with a woman, that was quite traditional, and much harder to solve. His life was empty without Isabel Kramer as his partner in it. He did his duty, but that wasn't enough. He must try again to see what legal recourse might be possibly open to him. He'd telephone Ogle . . . no, better write to him, setting out the circumstances of the case in detail; and ask Ogle to seek Counsel's advice—the best available. Could he afford Marshall Hall? Or Hewart? Probably not—but he'd get one or other of them, just the same.

England: Early June, 1917

26 Colonel Rodney Venable awoke to the bed shaking and heaving, the pictures rattling on the wall, an indescribable tremor in the air. Beside him Naomi Rowland gasped, "Wha', what's that?" Then they were both bolt upright, holding the edges of the bed.

"Gothas . . . or Zeppelins," Venable said. "But I didn't hear a siren or guns."

"It felt like a big explosion very deep, or an earthquake."

They went back to sleep after a while, but Venable kept waking up and finally near four got up and lit the gas mantle. The strong white light illumined Naomi's soft young face, the strong eyebrows, the direct eyes, just opened and looking at him. She looked away. He knelt beside the bed, on her side, "Do you know how beautiful you look . . . sleep still in your eyes, your shoulders bare?"

She said nothing and he climbed into the bed beside her, putting his arm round her, his hand cupping one breast inside the cotton nightdress. He whispered, "Do you know how much I love you, my dearest Naomi?"

The soft weight of her breast in his hand worked its inevitable magic and his penis rose, stiffening and growing. He pulled up her nightdress and slid his other hand up the inside of her thigh, gently among the curly hairs, toward the parting of her sex . . . it would be pouting, slippery soft for his entry: but it was not. She was nearly dry, the lips pursed. She was lying on her back, legs almost together. He began to caress her clitoris with his finger, whispering endearments into her ear, stroking a nipple. It would not stand up to his touch, to his plea.

"Don't be frightened, Naomi," he muttered. "I have the rubber things this time . . . and you did have your period, didn't you?"

She nodded. Sexually nothing was happening to her or in her. The tried and true was not working: she was not softening, nor swelling, nor parting, nor becoming wet. He said, "God, I love you. When the war's over we'll run away . . . to America . . . I have plenty of money. I know Frances will give me a divorce."

"No!" she said suddenly, forcefully.

"But darling, I don't love Frances any more. I can only think of you."

He tried to part her sexual lips but they remained closed and though he could just touch the inner fold of them, dry.

She said, "It's no good, Rodney. It's over."

He paused, shocked. "Naomi, you can't . . . Is it another man?" She was so much younger than he; it must be some dashing handsome subaltern with an M.C., and wound stripes.

She said, "There's no one else. I feel ashamed of myself, that's all, skulking in dirty little hotels in back streets, or houses like this . . . or rooms belonging to heaven knows who—some friend of yours? And your wife . . . She's been so nice to me whenever I've had to pick you up or drop you back at your house . . . And what we had, is gone. You must have noticed."

She said it as a statement, and Venable acknowledged that she was right. For two or three months her body had not responded as that of a young woman in love, or at least possessed by sexual passion, should respond. Their lovemaking had been uncomfortable at best, almost painful at worst . . . tepid flesh, dry lips, anxious striving—where before there had been a liquid melting together.

Her voice was softer—"You've done so much for me, Rodney, taught me what love is . . . at any rate what sex is, and ought to be . . . how tender a man can be, at the same time as being so strong . . . wines, foods, the best in life . . . But there's never been love, has there, really—except from me, at first? I was infatuated, then."

Venable said slowly, "There is now—from me . . . With me, it's been just the opposite from you. At first, you were only another young woman to conquer, to possess, to teach, to mould a little perhaps . . ."

She interrupted softly, "That first night, in Norfolk, I said 'I love you' and you said 'Don't say it' . . . You were right, but I really believed it then."

He said, "Well, now I've been caught in my own net. I'm hopelessly in love with you."

She slipped out of bed and for a moment stood, the gracious curves sliding into one another, from light to dark, from smooth to rough, from outthrusting to inward sloping. Then she began to pull on her clothes, speaking from time to time: "I'm sorry, Rodney . . . there's nothing . . . I must go to France . . . I have already applied to transfer to the F.A.N.Y. . . . I have to get away from you . . . I hope you will understand . . . Until I'm free of you, I'll never find real love."

"You won't find it in the F.A.N.Y.," he said; then with a touch of the sardonic humour that made him so wonderful a companion— "Unless you choose the Sapphic mode."

She said earnestly, "No. I tried that once. At Girton, another woman was in love with me, and we spent one night together. It wasn't . . . right . . . What time is it?"

He looked at his wrist watch—"A few minutes past six."

She turned off the gas light and opened the curtains, revealing the early morning light strong on the row of houses in the mean street west of Paddington. She said, "I'll catch the first train I can to Hedlington, and spend the rest of my leave at High Staining . . . Goodbye, Rodney."

She picked up her overnight bag, looked in the stained mirror to adjust her hat, and tucked away a few stray strands of hair. He came forward, hands out. She backed away—"I'm sorry, Rodney, I can't. It must end . . . here, now."

"Goodbye, then," he said. "And God be with you, whatever you do, wherever you go."

The door closed behind her. Venable sat down on the bed in his pyjamas, looking out at the hard day.

The door opened without a knock and two men came in, both wearing plain clothes. He recognized one as Brigadier General Attwell, head of the Counter-Intelligence Section in the Directorate of Military Intelligence; the other he did not know. The general said, "Morning, Rodney . . . been interrogating a suspect? Guarding some valuable contact from Hun counter-agents?"

Venable knew from the other's tone that he knew. He said, "She's a good girl, sir. It never interfered with duty."

"We've been checking on that for nearly six months," the general said. "You're right. She's a good girl, in one sense—the sense that matters these days, I suppose—which means we've wasted a lot of manpower on your account. But what you've been doing is against regulations—these apartments and houses are for intelligence work, not love affairs. You have also laid yourself open to being blackmailed. And worst of all, you've been acting foolishly . . . The D.M.I. wishes to see you in his office at eleven o'clock sharp this morning. With belt and sword."

Venable said, "Very good, sir. I'll be there."

The general's voice softened, just as Naomi's had a little while ago. He said, "I suspect you'll be on a boat to France within forty-eight hours, Rodney. That's not so bad, is it? You've had a pretty good run with the fillies, in your old age."

"She was just a filly to begin with," Venable said. "But now . . . I want to marry her."

The general said, "Frances wouldn't let you. You'll be much better off in France, believe me."

"Perhaps, sir," Venable said, thinking—I'll be near Naomi . . . must find out what F.A.N.Y. unit she's going to, where it is . . . visit her . . . Oh hell!

The two men turned to go and Venable said, "By the way, sir, there was a tremendous explosion about twenty-five past three this morning, but no sign of an air raid. Do you happen to know what it was?"

The general said, "As a matter of fact, I do. Nineteen mines, containing four hundred and forty tons of explosive, were set off under the German lines at Messines, near Ypres, at 3.10 a.m. It took the blast twelve minutes and some seconds to get here. It's the start of another big offensive in the Ypres sector. May go on all summer, and longer. You'll be in it, with luck."

*   *   *   *

Stella Merritt pecked nervously at Dr Charles Deerfield's plump cheek, sat down, and tried to keep still. Her skin felt dry and itchy, and her head was aching. Charles was running a hand through her hair, the hand now sliding down onto her breasts. They felt uncomfortable, her nipples tender and scratchy, her mouth hot. She yawned, cleared her throat, yawned again. Charles was pulling her to her feet, toward the couch. God, the door was open. He was saying, "No one there . . . the street door's locked . . . don't worry."

She jibbed, pulling back against him—"You promised to give me some more heroin."

"We'll talk about it afterward," he said.

She thought, he holds it back, so that she would do anything for him, lick his boots, grovel.

Deerfield said, "Take your drawers off, my dear."

She cried, "Oh yes . . . but give me an injection first."

"Drawers off first," he said, smiling. He was so close she could smell his breath, and a faint perfume of eau-de-cologne, hear his thick breathing. "Damn you," she sobbed, pulling off her drawers.

"On the couch . . . there, there!" She lay back, knees raised and parted wide, eyes tight shut. He was coming in now, moaning in her ear. She clenched her teeth, it felt good, but the other was sitting on top of it, the throbs of sexual lust lost in the aching need all over. "Hurry up," she gasped.

He kept on, sliding in and out with luxurious control, licking his lips, savouring her flesh, her agony of need.

"Hurry," she cried again, but he would not, or could not, and she burst into tears, struggling under him, jerking this way and that, biting desperately at his ear, his chin, his shoulder. That made him thrust deeper and faster, his breathing became a series of shuddering gasps, and at last it was done, and he was still on top of her spreadeagled body, dragging breath into his lungs.

"Now, now!" she cried. "You promised!"

He did not move for a while, then slowly got up and went to sit in a chair facing her. She lay in the same position, her sexual parts exposed, her dress fallen back on her thighs, shivering.

He said, "We opened a Pandora's box when we started giving you heroin, didn't we? It was my fault. I wanted you so much . . . but the heroin wasn't necessary for that, was it?"

"Hurry, hurry," she cried. "Give me a pill, an injection, a sniff even."

"We've got to cut down or your baby will suffer. You don't want that to happen, do you?"

"I don't care," she moaned. "It's too far away . . . this is here, now."

Dimly she saw him stand, go to a corner cupboard, get out a syringe. He said, "I'm going to reduce the doses. This is a sixteenth of a grain . . . Relax."

The needle pricked and she winced. Slowly Deerfield pushed the plunger home, slowly the drug entered her vein.

The lights grew dim, bright, from white to yellow to gold. The itching and dryness began to slip away into a bad, but momentarily vanishing dream. She was back in reality, happy, secure, expanding wonder and love filling her. She realized that Charles was approaching her again and from a thousand miles away heard him say, "Let us make love again, now, before you float away altogether." She held out her arms to enfold him, opened wider her thighs to receive him into her warmth and love. She could take in the universe.

*   *   *   *

It had rained the night before and the footpath on Chetney Marsh was slippery with mud. Alice Rowland and Dave Cowell leaned their

410

bicycles against the wooden base of the little windmill and headed north, then east on the footpath as it wound on between tall reeds and marsh grass. The sun was sinking, and scattered bands of cloud, turning to orange and pink, heralded a dramatic sunset. They had arrived before ten in the morning, after the twenty-mile bicycle ride from Hedlington, and spent the day between Chetney Cottages and Deadman's Island, at the far end of the marsh.

They came to the bank of Long Reach and settled down, binoculars ready, Alice facing south along the water toward the road and railway bridges at Swale Station, and Dave Cowell up toward Deadman's Island and across the Reach toward the houses of Queensborough in Sheppey.

"Not a bad day, it's been," he muttered to her as they sat on the ground, back to back, leaning comfortably into one another.

"It's been wonderful, darling," she whispered, "like every day we've been able to spend together . . . I hate to see the sun beginning to sink now, though I used to like sunsets—because I think of these days with you . . . the lovely birds, the wonderful sky . . . even in the rain . . . the fresh air, of forest, or down, or marsh."

"And the goodbye," he said, heaving his back against hers so that they rubbed together for a second.

"That, too . . . especially," she whispered. She had long since ceased blushing when she thought of physical love. It was now a part of her, an absolutely necessary part, that shone in her always, like an inner sun, even when she was alone, even when she was filling shells in the factory.

He said, "Sixty-one different, from nine families, and . . ."

She interrupted him—"Dave! My side, swooping near the windmill!"

Dave turned and knelt beside her, his glasses to his eyes. "Harrier," he muttered under his breath—"Coming closer, sweeping the edge of the Reach . . . lost him."

He put the glasses down and turned to her, eyes shining—"I couldn't tell the colour for sure, and the sun's almost gone, but it didn't look brown enough for a Marsh."

"Montague's?" she asked. "That's pale, too, isn't it?"

"Light greyish blue for both of them. Montague's has a distinct dark bar on wingtips and tail, pale grey head . . ."

"There he is again," she interrupted—"Coming over the marsh on the Sheppey side."

Cowell lifted his glasses: "It's definitely not a Marsh . . . I've seen them before. They nest in Suffolk and come over sometimes in summer, about this time . . ." He paused a long time, his head moving

411

steadily to keep the binoculars focussed on the big bird. "Hen Harrier," he said at last with triumph. "No dark bar, and he definitely has a light patch on the rump. This is the tiercel." He leaned back against her with a sigh of pure pleasure. "That's the first I've ever seen, dear. They mostly breed and live in Scotland—very few in England or Wales. You always bring me luck!" He turned round and found her mouth with his, closed his eyes, and kissed her. Her lips parted softly. In the shadowless light, the water still and salt in the quiet air, without a word spoken, they rolled over like animals at play onto the thick grass beside them, he fumbling for the bottom of her skirt, she helping him. Their breaths coming faster, gasping love into each other's ears, they began to mate. The Hen Harrier continued his hunting course toward the estuary of the Scarrow.

*   *   *   *

Margaret Cate sat with Michael Collins in the small back room of a stone house in Tulla, County Clare. Collins was one of over a hundred prisoners from Easter Week, 1916, recently released from English prisons by Lloyd George. Another of the released prisoners was Eamonn de Valera.

Margaret said, "I don't think de Valera's right to take part in the election. It's being run by the English—for the English Parliament. We should boycott all their institutions . . . especially this convention."

Collins said, "Ach, the convention's only being held as a sop to the Americans but I think Dev's right. We're all being treated like heroes now—we were thunderstruck—quite different from when we were being led off to gaol the day we surrendered . . . What de Valera's doing is making Sinn Fein respectable, gathering supporters, who'll likely stay with us if we do have to go into the streets again."

"He's telling the people that a vote for him is a vote for our independence, and freedom," Margaret said, "but he doesn't say how he's going to get them."

"Ah, if he mentions violence, he'll lose the people he wants to attract," Collins said. "We don't want to talk about violence now, Lady . . . when the time comes we'll just do it! Most people will follow along with whatever we have to do, by then."

"Sinn Fein clubs are certainly springing up everywhere," Margaret said grudgingly. "We have more support, in numbers, than we've ever had . . . I just wonder how much they'll be worth, when the time comes for something harder than dropping a vote in an urn."

Collins said earnestly, "Look, Lady, let's get de Valera elected. You know and I know that he'll never take the oath of allegiance . . . We're going to demand independence and the only real question is whether we're going to demand it from a post-war peace conference, as a small nation—same as Serbia or Montenegro, or even Poland . . . or demand it in the English Parliament. If either or both of them say no—then we go out in the streets, and the fields . . . the way you wanted to last year . . . What's the time?"

"About ten."

"I have to go to Limerick to set up a Volunteer escort service. On Election day the other side's bully boys will be attacking any car they think is one of ours . . . and we'll be ready for them."

Margaret watched him go, then returned to her business, of cleaning the arms—rifles, pistols, and shotguns—stacked in various parts of the house, against the day when votes failed and guns were again called upon to speak for Sinn Fein.

*   *   *   *

Christopher Cate walked through the twilight of Walstone, wearing a light tweed suit and cap. Isabel Kramer tripped neatly beside him in a light dress with a straw hat, the brim not excessive, the colours of her clothing bright but not garish. The sun had set in a blaze of gold and red, but there was still strong light from a clear sky. Hunting swallows raced up and down the Scarrow beside them, and the clock in the Saxon tower of the church was striking nine.

The village constable passed, strolling portentously in the opposite direction, and raised a finger to his helmet in salute. Cate touched the peak of his cap and stopped, "Evening, Fulcher. No serious crime over the weekend, I hope?"

"Nothing, sir," the constable said. "There was some soldiers creating a commotion in the Beaulieu Arms about dinner time Saturday. Danged if I know why they don't get drunk in Hedlington, 'stead of coming all the way down here to do it."

"Perhaps they hope to meet some nice country girls, Mr Fulcher," Isabel said.

Fulcher's tone softened. "Ah, Mrs Kramer, the girls here won't look at them when they're drunk. They know that."

"Well, I hope you weren't too hard on them," Cate said. "They'll all be off to France soon enough."

"Set 'em out to dry in Ormer's hayfield by the river," Fulcher said.

"Good man . . . Good news from Tip, I hope."

"No bad news, anyway, sir. He's with the Grand Fleet still."

"Then I don't think any harm will come to him. The Germans won't come out again." He nodded and moved on, passing Quick the postman's house on the other side of the narrow street. Henry Quick and his wife Flora were standing in the doorway, talking to Miss

Morelock, the schoolmistress. Cate stopped and raised his cap. The three turned with respectful greetings—"Good evening, Mr Cate . . . Good evening, Mrs Kramer . . ." The schoolmistress added, "That's such a pretty dress you're wearing, Mrs Kramer. Is it American?"

"Yes," Isabel said, laughing, "and it must be twenty years old . . . but fashions come round in circles, don't they, Miss Morelock? If you just look in your old trunks you'll find an up-to-date Paris creation again."

Good, Cate thought, everyone knows her by now; and she knows everyone, which is not so easy; but she's done it. He turned to Quick. "How's Stan, Henry?"

"All right so far, sir," the postman replied. His wife's face was sad, as she added—"We pray for him every night."

"We must all pray," Cate said.

They walked on. "Pray for peace, too?" Isabel said in a low voice— "They deserve it . . . the soldiers need it. What do the people here think of John and his pacifist campaign?"

"About the same as Louise does," Cate replied. "The English countryman is a tolerant person. He's had a lot of practice at it. They've all known John a long time and they don't think he's suddenly become a Hun because he's joined the peace movement. Mostly they don't agree with him, either."

"Not even the Englands there, with one son gone and the other likely to at any moment, if they start another Somme battle?"

"Especially not them, or those like them . . . Hullo, Probyn, any news from Fletcher?"

"Never heard of him," the wizened figure in the deerstalker hat said, stopping and touching his forelock.

Cate slowed down—"I know what his new name is . . . What's his news?"

"Lots of shelling . . . thinks the generals are going to start another big battle any moment now . . . and they're going to make a regular mess of it, like always . . . They've made him a sniper and he's killed a lot of Germans. Mostly officers, but he's afraid he killed one poet . . . just felt it was . . ."

"Has he sent you any poems from the Front?"

Gorse shook his head—"Gives 'em to a captain . . . he was in this captain's company afore they made him battalion sniper. The captain sends them to some bloke in London, an editor, like, who prints books."

"A publisher," Cate said. "That sounds hopeful. Fletcher will be famous yet, Probyn. How's Mrs Gorse?"

"Got a bellyache, Squire. She'll be all right tomorrow . . . Has Garrod found another girl to take Hilda's place?"

Cate shook his head—"We're not trying to, Probyn. We're all right as we are. Hilda's in Coventry, working in an aeroplane engine factory. She wrote to Tillie."

"Flighty, that's what she is," Probyn grumbled. He moved on, with another touch of his hand to his cap.

Old Commander Quigley passed, peering shortsightedly. "Oh, hello, Christopher . . . and Mrs Kramer, isn't it? The lady from Yankeeland. Our ally at last." He cackled heartily. Isabel Kramer moved easily round Christopher. The old Commander liked to pinch ladies' behinds. "The Huns keep sinking ships with their damned submarines," Quigley said. "Swine—lurking under water like sharks. We'll get 'em, though . . . drown the whole lot of them."

"We'd better," Cate said. "The figures of tonnage sunk are alarming."

"But improving, improving!" the Commander croaked.

Cate and Isabel moved on. A voice called—"Christopher . . . Squire!" Cate stopped, turning. It was the rector, stocky, upright, white haired, seventy-seven years old—"How's that boy of yours? In France, isn't he?"

"Yes," Christopher said. "To his hearty relief. They had kept him back in the Depot partly because he was still rather young and partly because he seemed to have developed quite a knack for teaching the recruits shooting and patrolling. He's stalked birds with his binoculars all his life, so I expect that was it."

"But he didn't shoot the birds," Isabel said in a low voice.

The rector said, "I expect they all find it a bit different out in France . . . You know, last time he was down here, he came to see me?"

"I didn't know," Cate said.

"Well, he came and talked to me . . . said he might like to come into the Church after the war. Had he ever mentioned that to you?"

"A long time ago," Cate said slowly. "Before Christmas, 1915, when he was home from Charterhouse. I told him that his great-great-great-grandfather had been squarson."

The rector said, "It would be wonderful if he could follow me . . . He'll have to hurry, though. Kimball's told me I'll kill myself if I go on hunting, and I know I'll die if I don't—not that the hunting's been even fair, these past two years . . . It was good to see you at evensong," he said to Isabel.

"Thank you, Rector. You have such a lovely church . . . and we all have so much to pray for."

Cate said, "We'd better be moving on, Rector. I have to put Mrs Kramer on the train."

The rector toddled on. Isabel said, "Laurence might want to leave

415

Walstone, you know." Cate thought, Laurence not want to live in Walstone? What would happen to the Manor? Isabel said, "It is a possibility, Christopher. In fact, Laurence may be thinking of joining the Church *in order* to get away."

Cate said, "I can't believe it. Surely, when he comes back, out of the trenches, he'll want to come home. This will seem like . . . what it is . . . his place, his land . . . Walstone."

Isabel said, "It's possible that these things, this portion, which to you are just love, are oppressive responsibilities to him."

The Manor trap rattled past, the new girl who had replaced the stable boy at the reins. She raised her whip in salute as she passed, then the gold glow of the twin lamps receded in the twilight and Isabel said, "Let's not talk about that any more. We have so little time . . . We'd better go to the station now, dearest."

They turned down the lane that led to the railway station. Others were going the same way—soldiers down from Hedlington returning to barracks, relatives returning to London . . . Sunday evening, young summer, the Weald of Kent. The trap was standing in the station yard, the horse tethered to the rail at the far end.

"She must have taken my suitcase onto the platform," Isabel said.

They walked through the little booking office and onto the platform. The rails reflected red light from the up starter signal, the heavy trees lined the open trench of the railway, the evening was hushed and still. They saw the girl with the suitcase, talking to a pair of soldiers, but walked past her, silent, to the end of the platform. There, under the white glow cast down from the open underside of the up home signal, she turned and whispered, "Darling—how long, how long?"

"I don't know," he muttered.

"My body yearns for you . . . I'm parched."

"I could come up to London . . . or Liverpool again."

She touched his hand with hers—"It isn't enough, dearest. I want peace, a place . . . my place, beside you."

"You know it can't be, yet."

She dropped her hand, and tears glistened in her eyes. The stationmaster, Frank Miller, bustled by on his way back from some distant errand, and said, "Evening, Mr Cate . . . evening, Mrs Kramer—going back to London now?"

"I'm afraid so."

Cate said, "Any news from the boys, Frank?"

"They're all right, sir . . . they *was* all right, middle of May. That's the last letter we had . . . sort of postcard, really, from Alf, with printed words like 'I am well,' 'I am sick,' 'I have been wounded,' 'Hoping this finds you as it leaves me'; and then you cross out words, like. Those boys never was much of a hand at writing, especially Gerald. Miss Morelock used to say they'd best go into some job where they could shout, instead of writing . . . Mister Laurence well, sir?"

"As far as I know."

The signal above them dropped with a metallic clang. From the east, an engine whistled high and long out of the dusk; a barn owl swooped across the rails and vanished silently into the woods opposite.

The lovers walked back down the platform to where the stable girl waited with Isabel's suitcase.

*　　*　　*　　*

Rachel Cowan let herself into the little house near eleven o'clock. It was dark but not dense, impenetrable dark—it never was, in England, in June, for the sun was never far below the horizon. Bert was in the front room, where the new printing press had been installed, smaller and older than the first, and liable to frequent breakdowns. He was drinking ale from a bottle, and there was a newspaper thrown on the floor beside him.

He said, "I thought you was supposed to be home by tea time."

Rachel said, "I'm sorry, Bert. We got to talking." She didn't want to upset him; she didn't want to tell him what she had been doing, either. It would be a sort of desecration.

"Talking about what?" he asked, raising the bottle to his lips.

"The peace movement, of course," she said. "Ways to make the government come out in the open . . . more places where we can employ passive resistance without hurting ordinary people."

That was true, as far as it went. The meeting had again been held in Bertrand Russell's rooms. Russell had been there, again with the beautiful young Lady Constance Malleson.

And Wilfred Bentley had been present, the red spots obvious on his cheeks, coughing thinly, holding a handkerchief to his mouth, dabbing his forehead, but the smile always there, the eyes steady, the spirit unbroken, hatred for no one . . . if there were more Christians like him, she might become one herself.

She said, "Bertrand Russell congratulated us on getting out of prison, and said we really ought to be congratulated just as much for going in."

"Can't see *him* going to prison," Bert said. "Too bloody aristocratic for that."

"He'd go," she said indignantly. "You know he would. He's not afraid of them. John Rowland was there . . . Naomi's going to France soon, he told me, and he's expecting his son, Boy, home on leave soon . . . Wilfred Bentley was there, and . . ."

417

Bert said, "He's always there, always talking."

"He's going to become a socialist soon," she said. "He says he's learning more with us, at these meetings, about the true state of society in this country, than he had learned at Winchester and Balliol, and in all his years before—he's twenty-seven."

Bert said, "So you just sat on your arses talking from eleven in the morning to seven, eight, nine at night, eh?"

It was just as she had feared. Bert was laying philistine hands on a wonderful experience. The meeting had ended at two in the afternoon, and Wilfred Bentley then asked her to share a late lunch with him. After hesitation—she should get back to Hedlington, her work, Bert—she had agreed. They had eaten in a little restaurant near the south end of Bloomsbury Street. They talked, before, during, and after the meal. Then they walked to and into Regent's Park . . . she had found herself listening as though to two other people—a short dark Jewish woman with short legs, her East End accent only half blanketed by two years of Girton, and a tall young country gentleman and officer, fair haired, unfailingly gentle and polite, with the quiet, confident accents of Winchester and what regiment did he say? Some number, it was. (He had said very earnestly, "You are making a mistake to attack the Army as such, Rachel. All of us are proud of our regiments. The 60th has given me something nothing can take away, not even death. We all feel the same. Many of us are disillusioned about the war, even about England, and think peace ought to be, and can be made . . . but we're proud of our service, our comradeship in the Regiment.")

" 'Ave a beer," Bert said.

"No, thank you. I'm not thirsty."

Bert drank, looking at her over the rim of his glass. She ought to tell him what she had been doing—walking, talking, discussing, listening; but he would say that it was a waste of time. They ought to go out and shoot a peeler, he'd say. And she'd have to tell him she'd been with Wilfred . . . through the afternoon, in a taxi to the West End, through the evening, dining at some expensive restaurant, strange foods she had never known . . . "Profiteers' Heaven, this place," he had whispered in her ear. What did he see in her? It was just their shared commitment to the cause. Waiting, standing close, at the farthest end of the platform on the Chatham side of Victoria, too? And the kiss under the signal light, the sudden flooding passion making her knees shake, the aching loss of goodbye—these, too?

Bert said, "I can see you had a good time, love. Wish I could . . ." he shook his head, ". . . but I'm not cut out for that sitting round, talking, talking . . . Oh, those people are all right, an' they've got

418

guts, but they don't understand me, and I don't understand them. We don't speak the same language, see? . . . I won't be going to the meetings any more, I'll . . ."

"Oh, Bert," she cried, stricken.

"I'll work with you here," he said, "but my place is in the factories, at the union office. I s'pose we're both fighting the same war, but you and your lot will be in the headquarters and offices . . . I'll be in the trenches."

*   *   *   *

Susan Rowland hurried out of the drawing room in the middle of a sentence and from the foot of the stairs shouted, "Sally! Tim! Come downstairs this minute!" She waited until the two faces appeared at the banister above her. Both dirty, she noted, though it was barely half an hour since she had personally supervised them washing themselves.

"Come down," she commanded. "What were you doing to make such a noise?"

They shuffled down toward her, Sally whining, "Only playing with the toys in the day nursery, Mummy."

"You must have been throwing them at the wall and then jumping on them," she said severely. "I can't think how you haven't awakened Dicky. Now run and play outside, it's a lovely day."

They sidled past her and out of the front door. She returned to the drawing room, where Mrs Baker waited patiently, notebook and pencil in hand, standing by the open window. She said, "They'll wear you out, m'm. It's a wonder you don't get a nanny. Of course, they don't mean any harm, but they'll wear you out, just the same."

Susan wondered if it was true that the children didn't mean her any harm. Raising those two to be ladies and gentlemen in these times was not easy. Sometimes she felt a glow of real warmth coming from them, toward her or Richard, even toward the staff—particularly Mrs Baker . . . then they would do something despicable, mean . . . and she would again be convinced, as Richard was all the time, that their interest was always selfish. They only liked Mrs Baker, he said, because she was the cook.

She said now, "You know I think a mother ought to raise her children herself, Mrs Baker, if she is able to. I only wish I could feed Dicky."

"There, none of us can help that," Mrs Baker said comfortably. "If God don't give the milk, there's no call for us women to feel we done something wrong . . . Lunch today is cold mutton, but I haven't bought anything for dinner yet."

419

Susan said, "There was a good recipe in the *Daily Telegraph* Page for Women, a few days ago . . . risotto—here, I cut it out. Shall we try that?"

Mrs Baker held the slip of newsprint as though it were a snake and read aloud suspiciously—"Take one ounce chopped onion, half a pint of rice, one ounce fat, half a pint or more of stock . . ." She read on and then looked up—"Is this Eyetalian, m'm?"

"I suppose so, originally, but it sounds good. Let's try it."

"All right, m'm," Mrs Baker said grudgingly and stuffed the slip of paper into the pocket of her apron. "For lunch tomorrow I thought a bit of braised tongue with madeira sauce and spring greens."

Susan thought, oh dear, that sounds rather rich but Mrs B. had given in over the risotto, with an effort, so she'd better agree. She said enthusiastically, "That sounds excellent, Mrs Baker."

They talked on another ten minutes, then Mrs Baker said, "It's getting a lot of work down there now, m'm, since that flibbertigibbet Peggy went to the shell factory in Hedlington. Don't know what girls are coming to these days—living by twos and threes in flats in Hedlington and working in a factory instead of living at home, or going into service, and learning something that's useful when they marry and have kids of their own."

Susan said, "I'll try to get another maid, but it really isn't easy. They just don't want to live in the country."

"You could pay 'em more," Mrs Baker said.

Susan spread her hands unhappily—"Mr Rowland won't let me offer more than the standard rate. He says that would be inflation."

Mrs Baker said, "I don't know about that, m'm, but I do need help in the kitchen, what with the baby, and Tim and Sally. Joan's got all she can do upstairs, I know that."

The mention of Sally and Tim struck a nerve in Susan's brain and she said, "I wonder what they're doing."

"Well, if there's nothing more, m'm . . ."

"Yes, yes," she said. "Thank you. That's all for now."

Susan hurried out of the room, down the hall, and out of the front door. The lawn was empty, no sign of the children. Had they sneaked down to Handle's farm again? Kathleen was polishing the car outside the garage. She called—"Kathleen, have you seen the children recently?"

"No, madam," the chauffeur called back. "They came out about half an hour ago, and watched me for a few minutes—then they went away. I didn't notice where to."

Susan walked back into the house and stood in the hall a moment, thinking. She felt uneasy, as though something terrible was about to happen. She heard a faint sound from above and at once hurled herself at the stairs, her fears concentrated into a central knot—Dicky, Dicky, something wrong with Dicky, the fruit of her womb. As she neared the top of the stairs she saw Sally and Tim sneak out of the nursery and across the passage. They saw her and broke into a run, diving into the day nursery. She burst into the night nursery, screaming as she saw the cradle, the five-week-old baby in it hidden under a heavy pillow. She wrenched the pillow away and threw herself to her knees. The baby's face was blue, his eyes starting out of his head. She plucked him up, held him to her, and breathed slowly into his mouth, then squeezed his chest, breathed again. Oh God save him, save him! The little body hung limp in her arms. Again, again . . . he moved, gasped, coughed, sucked air into his lungs . . . After he had breathed normally for ten minutes and the color had returned to his fat cheeks, she carefully laid him down in his cot and walked across the landing to the day nursery.

They were in there, sitting side by side on the sofa, their faces taut. She walked over to them and hit each of them as hard as she could on the cheek with the flat of her hand. Sally rocked, gasped, and came back upright. The force of her blow knocked the smaller Tim clear off the sofa to the floor. He moaned once, then climbed quickly back up beside his sister. She said, "You know why I did that?"

Sally said coldly, "Yes, Mummy."

"Why did you do it? Why? Tell me. When you hear the words you may understand what a terrible thing you tried to do."

"We tried to kill 'im," Tim said. "Wish we 'ad." It was the first time in months that he had dropped an aitch, Susan noted.

"Why do you want to kill him?"

"You love 'im more'n you do us," he said in the same small hard voice.

Sally said, "When he grows up, you'll get rid of us. We know."

Susan stood back, staring down at them. Tears sprang to her eyes and she knelt in front of them, crying, "You're wrong! You'll always be our children. This will always be your home. But it's got to be Dicky's, too."

They stared at her. She could not know whether they understood, or believed. Only time, and deeds, would show. She said, "Now go outside, and stay outside until you're called for lunch."

She followed them downstairs, watched them go out in unusual silence, and turned into the drawing room. She went to the telephone and picked up the receiver—"Give me the *Hedlington Courier*, please . . . classified advertisements, please . . . I want to advertise for a children's Nanny at thirty shillings a week and all found . . . Yes, I

421

said thirty shillings a week. Ready?" She began to dictate the wording of the advertisement.

*   *   *   *

Bob Stratton surveyed Victoria on her platform. He'd run her up to ninety-five yesterday, on the Canterbury road and she'd hardly seemed to be trying, running smooth as a bird, quiet, too—all the improvements he'd made this past four years and more come to their best, and working together—that was important, for sometimes you made one thing better but it didn't fit with something else, which got worse. The Thompson Bennett magneto was great, and the new sparking plugs of compressed mica worked fine: he'd mistrusted them—but they were lighter, no doubt of that, and every ounce counted; and if the aeroplanes could use them, at their higher speeds and all kinds of temperatures, they should be better for motors on the ground; and, so far, they'd proved so . . . wish he could find a way to use aircraft cylinders . . . but there were too many problems . . . it was like attacking a nest of rats, soon's you got one killed, two more popped up.

He climbed astride the machine, started it, and sat there, the engine ticking slowly as it warmed up, his fingers automatically moving the choke and air levers . . . The reason Victoria had run so good yesterday was that he'd made up his mind not to go to that Dr Deerfield any more, and that was the truth of it. Near eighteen months he'd been going, five times a week, regular as clockwork, and what good had it done? It wasn't right, trying to cut into a man's mind like it was a bit of wood, or an old book you'd picked up . . . as though you could see what was in there . . . and not just what *was* there, but what *had* been there, forty, fifty, years ago. Had he ever seen his mother naked? Why should a man remember a thing like that, sixty years on? She'd been in her shift, stooped over the bed, and the shift rode up and there was a tuft of hair sticking out between her legs at the back, high up, and like thick lips, hanging open. It had frightened the wits out of him. What had she got there? A rabbit, cut open? What was she doing with it? 'Course he was only two then, maybe three . . . and he'd learned soon enough what it was, but that wasn't the same. It never gripped him again, in the belly, so that he broke out sweating, wanting to be sick, like that time, with Mother, God rest her soul . . . Had he ever thought of his mother sexually? What a question to ask a man, his mother long since in her grave? Never, never never . . . Cuddled up in her titties, yes, that was it, he'd thought of that, often and often, as a boy . . . a young man even. Did he fear women, grown women? Had he ever had a sexual relation with another man, a boy? Did he like boys, prefer looking at them to girls?

It was a sin, really, trying to see into a man's mind, that only God could make, or know.

He opened the throttle and the engine growled louder, the rear wheel spun faster on the sunken counterwheel. . . . Dr Deerfield was a Hun, that was the truth of it. Couldn't make a man an Englishman by giving him a piece of paper and changing his name. Just a dirty Hun, asking dirty questions . . . and costing a lot of money, too.

He closed his eyes, the engine roaring. There it was, plain as a pikestaff in front of him, a little girl's cunny, smooth, fat, the lips folding in, big . . . twice as big as a grown woman's, that was the God's truth. His breathing came unevenly, gasping, the engine throbbed more heavily to the touch of his hand. He felt an erection growing inside his trousers and cried out, with no blasphemy—"Oh, Jesus Christ! Oh, God Almighty!"

Shaking, he throttled the engine back until it stopped, then climbed down, covered Victoria with her dust sheet, and went out of the shed and the garden, by the little door beside the shed. The lane was empty, but it was a fine summer evening. There'd be some girls playing hopscotch at the corner, and there were always two or three looking for rags and bones and tins in the refuse dump by the Scarrow. He made sure that he had two shillings in his pocket and walked faster. One way or another, the ache in his groin, the bursting lust in his heart for that fat slit would kill him anyway. A man could only go so far against what God had made him.

Daily Telegraph, Monday, June 4, 1917

SOCIALIST DEMANDS AT THE LEEDS CONVENTION
SOLDIERS' COUNCILS

The conference convened by the United Socialists Council was held at Leeds yesterday, and attended by 1,500 delegates. Mr Robert Smillie presided.

A telegram of greeting was read from Petrograd in the following terms:

The Executive of the Soldiers' and Workmen's Deputies sends salutations and fraternal greetings to the conference of Socialist and Workmen's organizations at Leeds, and hopes to meet representatives of the Labour Conference between July 15 and 30. The Executive Committee finds Stockholm most convenient as a place for the conference . . .

Resolutions were passed hailing the Russian revolution; calling upon the Government to announce its agreement with the declared foreign policy and war aims of the democratic Government of Russia; to establish political rights for all men and women; and to grant a general amnesty for all political and religious prisoners. The chief interest centred in a resolution demanding the setting-up of Workmen's and Soldiers' Councils in this country. This resolution was carried by a large margin.

Mr PHILIP SNOWDEN moved a resolution urging the convention to identify itself with the declared policy and aim of the Russian Government of peace without annexation or indemnity . . .

Captain TUPPER: Can the voice of the seamen be heard? (Uproar)

Mr FAIRCHILD seconded Mr Snowden's resolution, declaring that . . . indemnity was a device of capitalism to further its own process of exploitation.

Captain TUPPER expressed his regret that his amendment had been disallowed, because it would have raised the question of merchant seamen who had been foully murdered when bringing food to this country . . . Seamen wanted to know who, in the event of there being no indemnities, was going to reimburse the widows and orphans for their loss. (Voices: the shipowners) . . .

A delegate, standing on a chair, protested against this "gammon" about seamen being torpedoed, and added that the Germans were not such enemies of our seamen as the shipowners were. (Cheers)

At this enlivening stage the convention adjourned for lunch.

Mr C. G. AMMON moved a further resolution calling upon the Government to carry into immediate effect a charter of liberties establishing complete political rights for all men and women, unrestricted freedom of the press, freedom of speech, a general amnesty . . .

The Hon. BERTRAND RUSSELL said he spoke on behalf of a thousand men who were in prison because they believed in the brotherhood of mankind. By their refusal to serve they had shown it was possible for the individual to stand, in the matter of military service, against the whole power of the State. That was a great discovery . . .

They were mad, Cate thought, not mad like a village idiot, but snarling, hating mad, like cornered wolves. Were these the people John had to associate with because of his sincere feeling that an end to the war must be negotiated? How could Russell's intelligence stomach that howl about British shipowners being more dangerous to their crews than German U-boat captains? Or was it not belief or intelligence that motivated them, but only what that Russian doctor had won a Nobel prize for discovering—conditioned reflexes? They heard the word "owner" or "lord" or "capitalist" and started slavering at the mouth—in this case foaming would be the right word.

He felt unhappy. Relations between the classes in England had not been perfect, especially in the northern and midland cities, but they had been better than in almost any other country; now the war, conscription, the slaughter, the manifest profiteering, and food shortages, had combined to make some Englishmen as bad as continental anarchists shouting for blood, upheaval, overturn, ruin, above all—hate.

He returned to the paper. Unpleasant reading though it made, he'd better learn about it, if only to know what was in store for the country when the war ended, and these new hatreds instead of the old national antagonisms, occupied the stage. He had a sad, heavy feeling, that it would be less bloody, but far more unpleasant.

The telephone rang and a moment later Garrod came in—"Mr John on the telephone for you, sir."

Cate went into the passage and picked up the telephone—"Hullo, John." He stopped short, realising that John might be calling because they'd received bad news about Boy.

His brother-in-law's voice was jubilant, happier than he had heard it for nearly a year now—"Boy'll be home on the 26th, Christopher!"

"Wonderful!" Cate exclaimed.

John's voice was not so cheerful—"If nothing happens in the meantime, of course."

Walstone, Kent: Late June, 1917

27 The two men worked side by side down the field under a hot sun, their scythes sweeping in long, slow strokes, the blades whirring as they bit into the stalks of the green grass and the purple clover and the white moon-daisies. Behind each man, a woman, working with a rake, spread the cut grass to hasten drying. The men were wearing white shirts, sleeves rolled, and old straw hats, the older a Panama with a pink Leander band round it, the younger a stiff straw with the orange and black band of the Wellington 1st XV. The women wore pinafores of blue or green with deep bonnets, the ribbons tied under their rounded chins, for they were both young. Sweat ran down the faces of all four.

Hard work, Boy Rowland thought, but he was glad the horse-drawn mower had broken down, for he was enjoying the steady thrust and pull of his muscles, the ache of them reassuring him that he was alive, as surely as the sweet smell of the grass and the stirring of it in the breeze. And it was going to make hay for his father's cows, the serious Friesians in the next field, some of them peering over the hedge like heavy inquisitive young women, at the workers.

The scythe blade struck down the sweep of grass instead of felling it. Boy straightened and reached round to the whetstone in its leather case on his belt in the small of his back. His father straightened simultaneously and did the same. Their eyes met. John said, "Sure you're not tired, Boy?"

"Not a bit, Father." He passed the stone up and down the blade. "I was just thinking, this is good work . . . I'd never get tired doing this."

426

"You would," his father said seriously. "We can do it without you, you know. Helen's a good scythesman."

Boy glanced round at the taller of the two young women. She looked up from her raking, "Better than you," she said with a grin.

"I'm out of practice," Boy protested. "You've been doing this for . . ."

"My third year," Lady Helen Durand-Beaulieu said. "But I didn't do much scything the first year. One of the men was still here then."

"We'll have a competition, after the war," Boy said, bending again to his work. After the war . . . the remark fell into the still, summer air, and lay, silent, dormant, waiting.

A thrush and two blackbirds worked along the hedge, their song trilling and rising with the morning. A family of rabbits watched, nibbling, from the warren at the far end of the field, only scuttling into their holes as the scythers came close, turned and started back up. Half-way down the hedge, on that side, a picnic hamper held glasses and a jug of fresh lemonade, covered with a cloth. They stopped and drank, all four, when they came to it. Carol Adams, big bosomed and ruddy, her plump face shining with sweat, stood closer to Boy and said, "Let me take the scythe for a bit, Boy."

"I'm all right," he said. He liked her . . . he liked all the farm girls, these two and Frances Enright and Joan Pitman, up in the barn now. It was like being lord of a little harem, though of friends, who happened to be women, who sounded and acted and smelled different. What music their voices were, so sweet in his ear! . . . Carol had managed to stay close to him ever since he'd come home, though today Lady Helen was raking for him. He thought that if he wanted to he could seduce Carol, and go back to France at least knowing what it was like to make love to a woman. She seemed—well, it was an ungallant thing to impute to a young lady, but she seemed hungry . . . her eyes and mouth telling him of desires that were not in words.

"Back to work," his father said, and they took up scythes and rakes and again bent their backs, and worked, as the sun climbed to its zenith. Then John said, "It must be nearly noon, Boy"; and Boy glanced at his wrist watch and said, "Two minutes past."

They shouldered rakes and scythes then, and walked together up the field, through the gate, into the lane, and up toward High Staining. "We'll get it done this afternoon, Mr Rowland," Helen said. "Especially if I can take over from Boy." She looked at him with her head cocked, her lips parted.

"That's a da . . . dashed insult," Boy cried. "You'll be pooped by tea time."

427

"You think I'm just a poor weak woman?" Helen said. "Race you to the house!"

"Done! Ready?" He walked up level with her.

"Hey!" his father cried. "Give us that scythe and rake. You can't run carrying those. It's dangerous."

They handed the tools over, and Boy said again, "Ready? . . . You'd better have a start, Helen."

"Rats!" Lady Helen said. "Steady? . . . Go!" She flew off, her skirts billowing, her feet flying, her heavy boots pounding on the flinty surface of the lane. Boy was slower off the mark, then ran with all his might . . . but did not gain on her. The house was two hundred yards away . . . one hundred . . . he was still three paces back . . . how did she do it? She was holding up her skirt with one hand now, showing her knees. He drew up to her shoulder and with a last pounding effort up the drive reached the front door two paces ahead of her. They leaned there, gasping, face to face. Words came into Boy's head . . . See? . . . I told you so . . . You are a weak woman after all, aren't you? He said nothing. Their eyes were nearly level, for she was tall— and now they met, and locked. Boy saw her face changing, slowly falling into a deep calm, the teasing flirt gone, the effort of the work and the race erased. He knew that his own face was changing the same way. His lips parted, as hers did. Surely she would at last look down, away . . . but no, they stared and stared into each other, seeing deeper and deeper. At last she sighed a long sigh and whispered, "Boy," and he said, "Helen."

A moment later she said lightly, "I would win if I took my skirt and petticoat off." Then his father and Carol Adams came, and they went into the house for lunch.

*   *   *   *

Boy sat alone with his father in the study, a glass of port before him. His father had forsworn wine until peace should be declared, obtained by whatever means. His mother and the girls were in the drawing room. The two were alone—for the first time, Boy thought, since he came home on leave.

"I don't know how long this lull will last," Boy said. "There'll be another big push soon. The only question is, where."

"Not on the Somme, I pray," his father said. "The ground there is already sodden with our young men's blood . . . I do not understand why we have to attack, Boy, if attack is so costly, in the face of machine guns and barbed wire. Why can we not let the Germans attack, and destroy them as they seem to be destroying us?"

Boy stared into the red of his port glass. Why not? It was hard to explain. He hated and feared those "pushes" as much as anyone, but he believed the war could not be won by the defensive alone. He said, "It's the second stage of an attack that is the difficult one, for the Germans as much as for us. We can break into each other's front and even reserve trenches—but by the time we're ready to break out and through, they've had time to bring up fresh troops. If only we could fly a division or two right across the trenches and land behind them . . . or perhaps the tanks could do it . . . though how well they can function when the weather breaks for the winter, I don't know. I saw a good many stranded in shell holes and even ordinary fields and brooks last winter. We need more of them, too, I think—many more. And now these damned strikers and conchies are stopping or slowing down production of them, and other things we need."

He realized then that he was talking about one of his father's peace efforts; he would be hurt . . . well, he would have to be. There were the facts.

His father said sadly, "We are trying to save your life, Boy, and the lives of thousands—millions—like you . . . young men of all the warring countries, who must be saved to become the husbands and fathers of the future . . . the artists and inventors, the poets and painters and diplomats. We simply can not go on as we have been. That's why we pacifists do what we do."

Boy said, "We must go on, Father. We're not afraid. I mean, of course, we're afraid. It's hell, out there, a lot of the time. But we aren't going to let anyone beat us. If they can stand it, so can we."

"There seems to be no middle ground," his father said. "I can see only the ruin, and you can see only the defeat, as you would call it."

"Did you go to that big Socialist Convention in Leeds last month?" Boy asked.

His father shook his head. "No. We have some socialists among us in the No Conscription Fellowship . . . a strong influence, in fact . . . but the movements are quite distinct. They are anti-militaristic, we simply want peace . . . How are the French doing? Our military contacts—we have some in high places—tell us that the main reason for a British offensive now is being given as the need to keep the French in the war until the Americans have had time to organize and take a real part."

"I should think that's true," Boy said. "The censorship doesn't let much come through, but it's obvious the French offensive in the spring was a complete failure. We all knew where they were going to attack, and what they were planning to achieve. General Nivelle told everyone—including the Germans, of course . . . After that, silence. But we heard in the *estaminets,* from men on leave in Paris and Rouen and Amiens, that whole regiments mutinied . . . a whole division, even."

"We've heard that, too. Your grandfather told me."

"We heard that one regiment was formed up in a square and then massacred by its own artillery, for refusing to obey the order to advance." He shrugged, "Most of us hate the French—all the men see is the overcharging, the profiteering, the typical French selfishness—but there's no doubt the French have had a very hard time . . . they lost a million men in August, 1914, alone . . . then there was the Aisne, Champagne, Verdun. So we'll have to bear the brunt now."

"Where do you think our attack will be?"

Boy laughed shortly. "We've tried the Somme, Arras, the mining area round Loos . . . there's only the Salient left—Ypres."

His father said, "I pray that we pacifists can have some effect before the battle is joined, if only to force the generals to take greater regard of their men's lives." His tone changed suddenly—"We're having a difficult time over all this, Boy—your mother and I. We . . . we . . ."

Boy said awkwardly, "I understand, Father. I don't . . . I can't agree with you, but I still . . . love you, both."

John said, "We are both thinking of you, in our own ways."

"I know."

"But . . . we are drifting apart . . . there is a chill between us where there used to be warmth. I don't know what we can do."

Boy was silent. At last his father said, "Shall we join the ladies?"

*　　*　　*　　*

John and Louise Rowland lay side by side in the high bed, propped up on pillows. The windows were open and the sounds and smells of the summer night wafted in over them, reassuring them that they were in England. Tonight, as for many nights, they had not heard the guns from France. Now, though he was speaking to his wife, John kept listening for them to herald the offensive his son had told him must be coming. Then the guns would speak, and be heard here in Kent.

He said, "Boy only has two more days with us."

His wife said, "I know. And Naomi's out there, too, now."

"They won't let the women get into any danger," he said, adding—"At least, no more than the rest of us. The Gothas drop their bombs everywhere."

She said, "Carol's fallen in love with him."

"With Boy?"

"It isn't real love, either. It's—you know—sex."

John said uneasily, "Well, I don't think anything can happen with so many other people about all the time."

"She'll find a place and a time, if he gives her any encouragement," she said ominously. "Remember what happened with Fred Stratton."

"I remember," John said, vividly recalling Carol Adams's thighs clasped round Fred's back, when he was foreman here, and the look of ecstasy on her face—"But I really don't . . ."

"*He's* in love with Helen," Louise said. "And she with him. And neither of them know it."

"He's hardly seen her, except at work, and . . ." John began.

"They've known each other all their lives," Louise said. "And now, well, war makes life seem very short to all the young people. Fires don't smoulder now—there isn't time—they burst into flame. We'd better be careful."

"If it's true," John said. "It would be very suitable, I should think."

"For us, perhaps," she said. "All we want is for Boy to be happy. And if he is ever going to take over High Staining, he couldn't choose a better wife than Helen. But Lord and Lady Swanwick have other ideas, I'm sure."

John considered a while—"You are probably right about that . . . But Boy may not be in love with Helen at all. He has been flirting with all the girls since he came home on leave—in a nice, proper way, of course. They all love him, a little, I think—even Frances. Why shouldn't they?"

"It's Helen for him, and he for her, you mark my words," his wife said. "Put out the light now, please."

*   *   *   *

Stella Merritt and Dr Charles Deerfield sat next to each other in deck chairs at the edge of the cricket field. The bulk of Walstone Park rose beyond the pitch, for Walstone's village team was playing, as they did twice every summer, on the Earl's own pitch, fallow deer watching from the deep, the grass beautiful to look at but uneven to walk on or bounce a cricket ball accurately on. The Earl and Countess and two score other spectators stood or sat on benches and deck chairs round the boundary lines or outside the marquee that had been put up for the game, another score under the giant elms beside the marquee. Lady Helen Durand-Beaulieu was there with her sister Lady Barbara, and two more of the High Staining farm girls—Frances Enright and Carol Adams. On Stella's other side there was an empty chair, where Betty Merritt, her sister-in-law, had watched the first hour of the game; after that she had excused herself. Stella wondered, not for the first time, how much Betty suspected about the relationship between herself and Charles Deerfield. She put the thought from her mind—it didn't matter; nothing mattered except escaping from this torture.

She muttered, "You've got to give me more. I can't stand it."

Deerfield was looking thinner than he used to, and his plump face was haggard. He said, "I can't, Stella! Oh God, I wish I'd never got into this with you. It's not worth it . . . nothing could be . . ."

"I can't sleep at night. Look at me."

Deerfield shook his head. He knew what she looked like—beautiful, but no longer virginal, dark shadows under her eyes, mouth set. People thought it was the baby—she was nearly six months gone now.

He said, "I've given you bromides . . . Look, there is a new hypnotic drug called Veronal, which might act better . . ."

"I want heroin," Stella said. "It's not only not sleeping. I hurt . . . it's like torture everywhere, in my head, my stomach, legs . . ."

"You're taking aspirin, a great deal of it."

"It's not enough . . . I sweat all night sometimes, and can't sleep till I get the little dose you allow, and then not for long."

"I'll give you codeine, for the pain."

"I want heroin."

"I've told you a dozen times, Stella, that if you don't detoxify yourself before the baby is born, it will be born addicted, and may die within a few days."

She stood up unsteadily, looking down at him. Her blue eyes were blazing, her teeth set, a thin film of perspiration sheening her skin—she said, "I'm leaving now, Charles . . . going first to the cottage to get a kitchen knife . . . then driving to Hedlington . . . to your office . . . If you're not there by then, to give me an injection—of heroin, a big one—I'll kill myself, on your doorstep. Then what will happen to your career?"

Deerfield looked up at her, aghast. Gradually, he gathered his wits. Perhaps it would be the best way out, in the end.

*   *   *   *

Boy strolled round the stumps to his place at cover point, as young Calder took the ball from the previous bowler and walked to the end of his run. The batsman had already been in for twenty minutes, with a score of 19, and appeared well set to finish the match and probably win it for a Weald Light Infantry team from the Depot in Hedlington. Boy settled into position, keenly aware of the powerful odor of mothballs surrounding him; his white flannels had been in the drawer for several years.

He looked at his watch. The shadows were long and the light flat and cool. The colours of the women's dresses were muted outside the marquee. Earlier he'd seen his cousin Stella here in a brilliant yellow dress, but she seemed to have gone. Pity, he would have liked to speak to her; he'd hardly seen her this leave . . .

432

The ball was hit straight at him. He awoke from a daydream, and caught it. Harry Swithin walked past him on the way to the marquee, grinning, "You looked as if you were catching a potato masher, Boy. I was expecting you to throw it back at me." He passed on.

Only one more day. The land was unbelievably green, the trees so heavy and tall. How was it possible to turn a tree like that elm into match sticks and sodden pulp? Helen was wearing a blue shirt. He picked her out, and felt his hands moisten, and his throat constrict.

The war was like that damned Indian Ordnance Depot claim for the lost pakhals—whatever you did, it came back. You could say that you didn't owe it; that it wasn't your fault; even, at last, that you'd paid . . . it would come back. The shelling abated, but always came back: the trenches receded in memory as you went out on relief, but they always came back—the smells, the corpses, the shit piled in the latrine buckets, the whiffs of gas, of rotting flesh, of dead rats, of maggots . . . the bitter cold, the body hanging on the wire in a frosty night, twenty yards away, staring at you, Private Hammond . . . (Hammond '57, because he had a brother in C, Hammond '91) . . . staring at you with wide eyes, for a day and a half until they'd been able to send a patrol out to cut him loose.

They were cheering, Ted England pulling up the stumps. He glanced at the little blackboard set up on an easel beside the marquee. It read 104—7—7. As Walstone had made 103 the visitors had won, with what must have been about the last ball of the game, for it was half past six, the time agreed upon for drawing stumps. He headed for the marquee, his eyes on Lady Helen Durand-Beaulieu. She was watching him, her dark blue eyes glowing, her parted lips creamy soft.

In a trance he found his blazer, put it on. The girls were waiting for him and after goodbyes they walked away together across the grass, under the trees, and onto the gravelled drive leading to the Walstone Gate and the Old Bridge. The bats were out over the Scarrow as they crossed the Old Bridge, and Boy felt a surge of sheer joy at living. He linked arms with the girls on either side and said, "What song do we all know?"

"Green grow the rushes oh!" Carol exclaimed, squeezing his arm. "That's a lovely song."

"Not that, it's his Regimental march," Helen said with a touch of sharpness—"Greensleeves!"

She raised her voice in a pure contralto, untrained, low, strong, a mature woman's voice, singing from the depths of her being:

Alas, my love, you do me wrong to cast me off discourteously,
And I have loved you so long delighting in your company.
Greensleeves was all my joy, Greensleeves was my delight

433

Greensleeves was my heart of gold, and who but my lady Greensleeves.
I have been ready at your hand to grant whatever you would crave
I have both wagéd life and land your love and goodwill for to have
Greensleeves was all my joy . . .

They all sang the chorus with her, Boy in his baritone, the other two in pleasant trebles. The harmony soared into the heavy foliage of the trees above, surged out across the fields, and entered the open windows and doors of the cottages along their road. Probyn Gorse, standing by his door, heard, and listened. Boys and girls in the summer night, he thought. Adam and Eve.

As they entered the village proper, P. C. Fulcher peered at them from a corner and said, "'Ere, 'ere . . . Why, it's Captain Rowland . . . and Lady Helen . . . I thought you must be folks from London . . ."

Boy waved a hand, "It's all right, Mr Fulcher. We'll be quiet now. We just felt good."

"Don't know what about, sir," the constable said. "I 'ear we lost to the soldiers."

"'Fraid we did . . . Here, girls, I feel like a drink, and here's the Beaulieu Arms, Prop. James Haversham, licensed to sell beer, wines, spirits and tobacco. We will enter that imposing portal and I shall stand you all drinks from my amassed pay, which at eighteen and sixpence per day, plus field allowance, lodging allowance and mess allowance, comes to nigh on twenty-five and ninepence per diem, and my lodging's been quite free most of the time, free—damp, and draughty."

Helen pushed him, as P. C. Fulcher chuckled. Helen said, "Go on in, and stop talking, Boy. I'm thirsty, too."

"Ever been in a pub before?"

"Two or three times. Your father and mother don't approve, nor do mine, but we working farm girls all go sometimes."

"Just to prove you're as good as men, I know."

They entered, Boy leading the way. The barmaid was old Parsley, a grey-haired maiden lady of about eighty, who'd served him his first pint of bitter in this same bar some twelve years ago. The Public bar, which they had gone into, was half full of farm labourers, a couple of farmers' teen-aged sons, but, at that moment, no other women. Boy said, "Everyone having bitter?"

"Cider for me," Carol said. "Scrumpy."

"Scrumpy for me, too," Helen said, "only half a pint, please."

"Two pints of bitter, please, Miss Parsley, and one pint and one half of scrumpy."

434

"Yes, sir." She peered at them. "Good evening, m'lady . . . I heard the cook left up at the big house."

"I'm afraid so, Miss Parsley. Mother's trying to teach Hazel how to cook, but she's not having much success. Father's learned how to boil an egg, though."

The old lady behind the bar chuckled and peered at the young women with sharp old eyes behind her gold-rimmed glasses—"Drink up, young ladies. There's only one way to take good British beer . . . fast! And scrumpy, too, m'lady . . . otherwise it tastes like . . ."

Helen raised a finger, "Shhh!" She turned to Boy and they raised glasses, all four, clinking them together. The farmers in the bar watched from the corners of their eyes, some amused, some approving, some disapproving. The girls were gentry, of course; they could afford to act badly, and it didn't matter—they were not the village. But let one of their own daughters come in here, in a band, with a young man, and there'd be some words spoken and tears shed later.

Probyn Gorse came through the open door and, before he was inside, called, "Pint of old and mild, Miss Parsley."

He glanced at Boy's party and nodded, "Evening, Captain . . . m'lady . . . miss . . . miss." So it was them singing, he thought; there was only one Adam . . . but which was Eve, to sing that mating song in the twilight?

The girls had another half pint each and Boy, feeling the need for something stronger, took a double whisky, with soda from the heavy siphon on the bar. Probyn finished his pint, laid money on the bar, and went out. Five minutes later Boy said, "We ought to be going on home now."

Carol Adams turned—"I suppose we'd better. Anyway, if I drink any more beer . . ."

Little Frances cut in unexpectedly—"You two go on. Carol and I are just getting going. We're shredding reputations."

Carol said, "Well, I don't know . . ."

Frances insisted—"We'll stay, Miss Parsley . . . two half pints please." She looked at Boy and he saw that she was blushing.

"See you later, then," he said, and went out, holding the door open for Lady Helen to precede him. In the street they turned left, without speaking, and walked out of the village. At the last cottage Boy slowed his pace. There was a sliver of moon in a pale twilight, and the softest of heavy breezes, sweet with honeysuckle from the hedges and new scythed hay from the fields. His heart was in his mouth and he could not properly control his breathing. Yet he had no idea what would happen . . . only that he did not want to reach home, or see his father

435

and mother, only to keep on breathing this instant, her hand now in his. But how, what? . . . She possessed him, soul and body.

She pulled him to a stop, turned him round in the lane, and put her arms about his neck, and her face under his, her lips parted. Slowly, at first wondering, at last accepting, he pressed down. Her lips opened, and as though she had been twined naked round him it was plain to him that her body opened. She stood away and said, "I love you, Boy."

He said, "I . . . I love you, too. I've never felt like this before, so I don't know . . . but it must be. It can't be anything else."

She took his hand again and led him a few yards up the lane, where a five-barred gate marked the entrance to a field—the field where they had been haymaking. She walked along the side hedge until they were well away from the lane, then turned again, and began to unbutton his blazer. "Spread it on the grass," she whispered. Swiftly, she took off her boots and stockings and then her breeches and drawers, finally shirt and short camisole, spreading them all on the long grass under the hedge, where the scythe blades had not reached. Trembling, Boy followed her example, until they stood face to face, naked in the hot summer dusk. She pulled his head down to kiss her breasts, then they kissed mouth to mouth, standing until their strengths flowed from their knees into their loins, and they collapsed slowly, like falling intertwined trees. Again he kissed her iron-hard nipples, slid his hand into the mysteries of her sex, and they ached and throbbed, and moaned together, crying Helen . . . Oh Helen . . . Boy, my darling . . . darling . . .

Behind the hedge Probyn Gorse listened with satisfaction. The Captain was doing right by the girl, and she by him. 'Twould have been a shame just to stand up and fuck like dogs, when there was so much love and so much innocence. They deserved each other. The moans grew to a climax, punctuated by a sharp cry from the woman—must have broken her maidenhead there, he opined. He looked through the hedge and for a few moments observed the heaving and thrusting of the two lithe young bodies, flesh white and firm and strong. Probyn leaned back, and waited for the climax, the outcry . . . and after, ah, good, the captain was not jumping to his feet, finished, impatient to be off. He was loving her, more than when he was in her. Women needed that whether they were duchesses or milkmaids. He was a good man, Boy Rowland. Only hope he comes back again, from France, so they could go on as they had started, till they were as old as he.

*   *   *   *

She lay on her back in his bed, naked, her arms wrapped tight around him, holding him to her, holding his weight on top of her. Her face was damp with the exertions of their lovemaking, and with her tears, that had flowed unchecked since the moment, after she had stripped off her nightgown and spread herself for him, when she had felt him enter her body. It seemed that the first night and this night and the day between had passed like a flash of the sun on a distant window. As soon as they had eaten their dinners, after the first love in the hayfield, they had gone to bed, and at eleven o'clock she had come to him . . . and stayed till dawn . . . worked all day . . . now again. Tomorrow—no, this day, for it was two o'clock in the morning—he must return to France.

He slid off her at last, and they lay side by side, he resting one hand on her sex, where she lay quiet, her thighs slightly parted. She whispered, "Scratch my back, darling."

"What?"

"Scratch my back . . . Mummy told me once that all women liked their backs scratched, and I said, I don't, and she said, you will one day . . . Now I understand. Go on!" Boy scratched away, while Helen made small noises like a happy pig, giggled, and wriggled her backbone and the skin of her back.

He said, "I suppose I ought to feel an awful cad for taking advantage of you . . . but I don't."

"I asked, and you gave."

Boy hitched himself closer to her, and whispered in her ear—"Will you marry me?"

"Of course. When the war's over."

He muttered, "It may never be. It's . . . immortal. We aren't. Father can't kill the war any more than the Kaiser can."

She said, "I couldn't bear to marry you, and think of you as my husband, and then lose you. Until it's over, and you're safe, you must be my lover, and I your mistress."

He said, troubled, "I'll be thinking of you all the time . . . What if you have a baby? And I'm . . . killed, or made prisoner?"

"Don't worry about that," she said. "It might have been better if we could have got married at the beginning of your leave, but . . . I didn't know how I felt then. Not till the race."

"Me, too."

"Then . . . I couldn't let you go back to France without giving myself to you . . . hateful phrase . . . I mean, I had to complete, in my body, what I was feeling in my mind—a locking with you, now and forever."

"Promise to write? Tell me everything. And if you get pregnant

. . ." She put her hand on his mouth and said, "Don't think about it
. . . And you write to me, and tell me what you are doing and how
you feel . . . really, not just what you're supposed to feel."

"I'll try," he said, "though the censors won't pass it. They want us
all to be three cheers for the war, but we aren't . . . we're just bloody
well going to stick it through."

She began to search his body with her tongue, looking up once to
whisper, "See how quickly we women learn?" She slipped her lips over
his penis and slid them down and up, then off and up, to kiss his little
nipples, and whisper, "It comes naturally . . . And there was a
dirty-minded Italian princess at the finishing school I went to in Paris,
who had a collection of postcards. We all thought they were terribly
depraved . . . but we looked . . . and remembered . . ." She took his
erect penis in her hand, and, slipping under him, guided him into her.
She murmured, "Am I as good as the French harlots?"

"I don't know," Boy said. "You're the only woman I've ever made
love to, and the only one I ever will."

Daily Telegraph, Tuesday, July 24, 1917

RUSSIA'S PERIL
NEW PREMIER'S TASK

The situation in Russia, both as regards the Army and the Government, gives undoubted cause for anxiety, but not necessarily for
despair. In the capital anti-Revolutionary forces are at work, and at
the front, particularly in Galicia, the morale of the troops has de-
teriorated to such an extent that "Complete disorganisation of the
Second Army is threatened . . ."

Whether the new premier, M. Kerenski, will be able, by sheer
force of character, to reorganise the Army and restore public order
at home remains to be seen.

APPALLING DISORGANISATION

Petrograd, Sunday.

The Executive Committee of the South-Western Front, that of the
Second Army, and the Commissary of the provisional Government
with this Army, have sent to M. Kerensky, to the Provincial Government, and to the Council of Workmen's and Soldiers' Delegates
the following telegram:

The German offensive which began on July 19 on the front
of the Second Army is assuming the character of a disaster
which threatens a catastrophe to revolutionary Russia. A fatal

> crisis has occurred in the morale of the troops recently sent forward against the enemy by the heroic efforts of the conscientious minority. Most of the military units are in a state of complete disorganisation, their spirit for an offensive has utterly disappeared and they no longer listen to the orders of their leaders, and neglect all the exhortations of their comrades, even replying to them by threats and shots . . .

Cate read on with increasing gloom. The headlines and sub-heads were not encouraging—VENGEANCE ON TRAITORS . . . PRACTICAL DICTATORSHIP. M. Kerenski—or Kerensky, the newspaper didn't seem sure how to spell his name—would need all that "sheer force of character" hoped for, and more. For this news today was only the latest in a series of disastrous reports that had been pouring out for over a week, of mutiny, revolts, defeats, and intrigues. Russia was too big and too Russian to understand, and those Russian names didn't help. The news of the U-boat campaign was almost equally gloomy, and much closer to home. But it was a lovely summer day, and he'd go and talk to John and Louise and try to cheer up them and the girls, over Boy's return to the front at the end of his leave. It had been wonderful for all of them to see him, even though he had been thin and pale and a little nervous—but he had had a good time, played some cricket, drank a lot of beer . . . and not said a word about the trenches.

He picked up the letter arrived today from Johnny Merritt, to re-read it—for it was interesting, and illuminating:

We landed at (deleted by censor) a few days ago, after a smooth passage—but our ship was attacked by a German submarine, whose torpedo missed. We'd hardly got ourselves settled into our tents at (deleted by censor) when our battalion was ordered to (deleted by censor) for a 4th of July parade, and to show the French that the Americans had really arrived. There we paraded opposite a French battalion—their men were much smaller than ours, but they looked tough—and war hardened. There was a ceremony—I saw Marshal Joffre—then we marched from the Invalides to the cemetery where Lafayette is buried. (Marie Joseph Paul Yves Roch Gilbert du Motier, marquis de Lafayette, in case you Englishmen aren't taught, was a French general who fought for us in our American Revolution against a country whose name escapes me; he is an American national hero.) I never heard the name of the cemetery but the march to it none of us will ever forget. Seen from above we must have looked like a long moving flower bed, entirely surrounded by other brighter flowers, also moving . . . women—they in turn flanked by darker, denser crowds of men and children. Our band was playing all the time, but no one

439

heard a note. The only sound I heard was, "Vivent les Teddies" (that's what the French call us) shrieked in my ear by a dozen ladies at different times.

Then we reached the cemetery and formed up, and there were more speeches, mostly in French. My Navajo friend Chee kept muttering to me, what are they saying? I understood, when I could hear, but none of it was worth translating to him, until General Pershing spoke a few words by the tomb, then motioned a Quartermaster Corps colonel forward. I don't know who he was, or why the general wanted him to say something; but what he said was the most eloquent speech any of us had ever heard or are likely to. He said, "Lafayette, nous voilà." That, I did translate for Chee . . .

Hedlington: Tuesday, July 31, 1917

28 Bob Stratton surveyed the vast filling shop with morose dissatisfaction. It had once been the main assembly shop of the Rowland Motor Car Company; now it was broken up into smaller rooms, and the overhead lineshafting had been replaced by lagged steam pipes . . . and everywhere there was the blue of women's mob caps, their hair piled up invisible inside them. As usual some of the mob caps were green, or grey, or brown. It was against regulations, but what could you do with women? You could see a man's cloth cap now and then, usually seen moving while the mob caps stayed in one place, for six of the ten men now employed in the factory, not counting himself, were supervisors or foremen.

He moved down the steps, his bowler hat set square and imposing on the top of his head, two pencils sticking up from the breast pocket of his blue suit, the watch chain and fob stretching across his belly, coat pockets bulging with a notebook, tape measure, rubber eraser, spectacle case with spectacles, handkerchief, some greased twine, pocket knife . . . Needn't be carrying that lot now that he was manager, instead of plant foreman; but he wasn't going to change his life's habits now.

"Good morning, Miss Alice," he said, lifting his bowler hat an inch off his head.

"Good morning, Mr Stratton," Alice Rowland said, without looking up from her work.

Bob strolled slowly on. It was right strange having Mr Harry's daughter working under him. Give him a funny feeling, like goose pimples, but she was a good worker, one of the best. Ought to be a section foreman, but she wouldn't accept it. He hadn't seen much of her face just now, but the last few months she'd been looking real pretty, and happy, even doing that job.

That job, he thought glumly—pour liquid amatol into shell cases, tuck in the exploder bag and nowadays the smoke bag too, and screw in the transit plug. Call that skill? He'd have a riot on his hands if he tried to make men do that sort of work. But women could do it . . . liked it . . . no skill, no need to think for yourself, just do the same thing over and over, carefully . . . be as careful at the end of an eight-hour shift as at the beginning.

"Mr Stratton . . . May I have a word with you?"

He turned, sticking his thumbs into his lower waistcoat pockets. It was Miss Dawlish, the gawky forty-year-old spinster who was assistant foreman of the Reception Section. He said nothing. The fact that he had turned had shown that he was listening.

She said, "You remember that I spoke to you about some of the women wearing shoes with heels last month, Mr Stratton?"

He nodded. The whirr of trolley and barrow wheels, the tap of wooden hammers on the transit plugs, made her shout in a high squeak, though they were only four feet apart. She screeched, "I have warned them, two, three times since, but they ignore me. You will have to dismiss at least one of them, as an example."

Bob looked at her with distaste. Upper class, sort of . . . father a bank manager, perhaps; what the working women called a miaow. Educated, of course . . . He said, "It's your job to see that orders are obeyed." He turned again, hearing behind him her plaintive voice screech still higher, "But I have no authority to dismiss or fine them, Mr Stratton. I can not . . ."

The voice died away. Bob walked on. The place smelled foul, of amatol and women, instead of oil and hot steel . . . Woman there wearing a ring, two rings . . . that was forbidden. The foreman here should see to it . . . one there with short thick blonde curls sticking out from under her mob cap—forbidden, too, and it reminded him of what he'd seen as a child: looked like his mother's bush. Ugly. Terrifying . . . Dr Deerfield had sent him two letters, said he was not cured, and he knew he was not; must have patience; please come back and resume your treatment. Treatment, bah? Call that treatment, lying on a couch and talking dirty about what you'd seen and smelled and touched and done when you were a kid, a baby, almost? In the second letter the doctor had even threatened to "report him" . . . Who to? Mrs Harry was dead, God rest her soul, and she was the only one who could have done anything. The only other person who knew why he was going to Dr Deerfield was his own Jane, and she'd never go to the police. Oh, and Mary Gorse, Willum's wife—she knew. And Violet, of course. But what could they do? If Mary opened her mouth, he'd sack Willum, and where else would *he* find a job these days? As for Violet . . . little slut, big breasts now, hair under her arms and down there, big arse, big cunt, big mouth—a woman.

The noon whistle blew, the women streamed down the aisles, took off overalls and caps in the changing rooms, picked up their lunch boxes, stepped over the CLEAN/DIRTY barrier and poured out into the factory's sunlit little yard. Bob followed. The few men usually gathered in one particular corner of the yard, if it was not raining; mostly he himself ate in his office, but today he would join them and they'd be like a little island of rock, among all this shifting sand and water of the women. Drat them, what a row they made, chattering shrill and high, sitting on the ground, on piles of planks, oil drums, leaning against the wall, eating sandwiches, drinking lemonade, gesticulating. The smell of perfume was overpowering . . . couldn't honestly say it really was strong, but that was the way it felt, to him.

Willum waved a large hand, "Come to eat with us, Mr Bob?"

Bob sat down next to him among the men and opened his box. "Surprised to see you turn up for work this morning, Willum," he said. "With Woolley playing down at the County ground."

"Only against the Chatham Dockyard, Mr Bob," Willum said disgustedly, "and Colin Blythe's not playing. 'Sides, I can't afford to lose a day's wages—saving up to buy little Henrietta new shoes, I am. She's a picture, she is, Mr Bob, wish you could see her."

Bob grunted, as he opened his lunch box. Henrietta was his own daughter, by Violet Gorse, Willum's twelve-year-old, now thirteen. None of these other men knew, and nor did Willum. Another baby had appeared in the house, and he'd accepted it, never wondering where it had come from.

The women were blossoming in the sun, the sound of female chirp and chatter growing louder.

"Can't hardly hear yerself think," Charlie Whitworth, on his left, muttered. Charlie was thirty-eight and if a woman could be found to do his job, off he'd go to the trenches. Bob knew he was making sure that none of the women in his section were learning anything in that direction.

After a time Willum Gorse said, "Good news from France, eh, Mr Bob?"

Bob grunted, "What news?" He didn't recall seeing anything special in the morning paper.

"About the big attack near Ypres," Willum said, pronouncing it Eepray, as he'd learned from soldiers back on leave; although others called it Wipers.

Bob grunted again. A big attack didn't mean a big success, still less

443

good news, just longer lists of dead soldiers in the paper. Any moment one of them might be Fred, and then heaven knew how he'd calm Jane, with her already hurting so much with the arthritis and the rheumatism.

"They wanted to make my Fletcher a corporal," Willum crowed. "He told us in a letter, but he said no."

Bob grunted again. He didn't know young Fletcher Gorse well, but from what he'd heard he was best at getting the girls on their backs. Still, it must take all sorts to run a war.

Jimmy Blaydon said, "You or your missus been to the H.U.S.L. shop, Mr Stratton? My missus says it's wonderful—everything cheap, and beef and veg and fruit and fish all there too . . . lots of smart girls to serve you . . . everything wrapped up in a jiffy, in shiny yellow paper with H.U.S.L. on it in red . . ."

Bob grunted, "No." Jane had talked about going to the H.U.S.L.—it had been Paradine's grocery shop before Hoggin bought Paradine out—but they'd never been. Ethel had, and liked it, said it was very convenient, but she thought the goods were poor quality; and that was enough for Jane. But he'd heard it was full all day, every day. When Ruth had married Hoggin he and Jane had thought it was a toss-up which of them—Ruth or Ethel, marrying that dago waiter—had done the worst for herself. Well, they'd been wrong about Hoggin, might as well admit it.

The whistle blew and the women trooped back into the factory. Bob went to his office and worked on indents and accounts with the secretary until four, when he made one more round of the shops, then got onto his bicycle and pedalled home to 85 Jervis Street. As he carried his bicycle up the front steps, the door opened and his daughter, Ethel, appeared. She'd worked in the factory for a time, the time when she was very depressed over Fagioletti divorcing her. But she'd stopped working two, three months ago, and stopped being depressed. Fagioletti might be in the Army in France—but he wasn't in the clutches of that other woman. She was looking cheerful now, as she said, "Did you have a nice day, Father?"

"No," he said. "Same 's usual." Too many women, he almost added; but didn't. He went into the back parlour. "Where's Mother?" he started to ask, then turned the question into a grunt. His wife was, as he well knew, in Bristol with her sister, who had been taken seriously ill and was expected to die at any moment. Jane had been away three days already.

Ethel said, "What would you like to your tea, Father?"

He thought and said, "A bite of cold meat and bubble-and-squeak, if there's any."

"Oh yes, we had cabbage and potatoes with our dinner and I know there's plenty left over. I'll make it."

Bob went upstairs, washed, came down and waited till Ethel brought him his high tea with the meat, bubble-and-squeak, and a big pot of tea, finishing up with a slice of bread and butter and strawberry jam. That finished, he looked at the clock on the mantelpiece. It read six o'clock. He rose heavily, wiped his mouth with the napkin and said, "I'll go down to the shed and work on Victoria a bit—a couple of hours, likely. She's nearly ready for another test."

Ethel sprang to her feet, "Oh, just wait till I take these things down for Ivy to wash up, and I'll come with you."

Bob grunted and walked down the passage to the back door. He'd been to the shed a couple of times since Jane went to Bristol, and both times Ethel had insisted on coming down with him. She had no interest in machinery—never had had. So why was she so keen now? Had Jane told her to keep an eye on her father? Didn't trust him, in spite of his promises that he'd never put the sign in the window again? Well, that he hadn't . . . yet. But going down to the wasteland, and watching the girls play hopscotch, and giving one sixpence to take down her drawers—it wasn't the same.

In the shed he set up the motor cycle on its test bed, and began his tests. Ethel arrived before he had started, and sat in the corner on a stool, knitting khaki socks—for whom, he wondered. They did not speak a word to each other. Bob ran the rubber exhaust extension out through its hole in the wall and started the machine, attaching it to the prony brake. His target was a torque of 32 foot-pounds at 3,500 revolutions per minute. This, translated into brake horsepower, came to 21.32—theoretically enough to thrust the weight of Victoria, fueled and ready, plus his own weight, in summer racing clothes, through the air and over the ground at 102 miles per hour.

The engine roared louder as he throttled up. It had no tachometer—couldn't afford the weight—but Bob could estimate the engine revs very accurately. He was now close to 3,000.

He throttled up again. Better hurry, or the friction in the brake at the pulley would be enough to set the blocks on fire. He was hunched in the saddle, crouched forward over the handlebars as though he was in fact racing forward at a hundred miles an hour instead of rocking and roaring on the stand. 3,200 . . . the counterweights began to rise.

"Father!" His daughter's voice was a shriek.

Bob throttled back. The counterweights sagged to the floor. He looked at Ethel. She was holding up her hand, shouting "Stop!"

He throttled all the way down until the engine sound was no more

445

than a deep mutter in the little shed. Ethel said, "There's a telegraph boy outside . . . Oh dear!" She suddenly slipped off her stool, holding her hand to her heart—"Suppose it's from the War Office . . ."

Bob said, "Only one way to find out." He went to the door and opened it. The telegraph boy handed him a pink envelope and a book—"Sign here, please sir."

Bob said, "It's for you, Ethel."

"Open it, Father," she whispered. "I couldn't . . . It might be Niccolo . . ."

Bob opened the envelope with his thumb nail, found his glasses and put them on. He read aloud: "Take room for us Grosvenor Hotel Victoria Arriving late July 31 six days leave Nick Fagioletti Corporal."

Ethel stood upright, her hands to her cheeks—"July 31 . . . when's that?"

"Today."

"Oh! Oh! He's coming back . . . and he wants me!"

"Don't you have no shame, going back to that dago after what he did to you?"

"He's my husband," she said simply. "*I* always knew he'd come back, after he'd got tired of that woman."

"Your mother will be cross with you. She thinks Fagioletti's treated you bad, and there's other fish in the sea for you. It isn't as if you had kids."

She said; "We will now, Father. I *know* we will. He's changed . . . he's a corporal!"

"Has been that for months, hasn't he? In the officers' mess, likely, because he's a good waiter."

She said, "I must go, Father . . . There's a train at 7.43 I can catch easily. I'll run up and pack a bag and then I'll go down to the station on my bicycle. It has a carrier."

She hurried out and away. Doesn't worry about what I'm going to eat till Jane comes home, Bob thought, grumbling to himself. Leaves me alone in the house with that Ivy, who can only think of when she'll be free to go to the cinema and see Mary Pickford.

He turned back to Victoria, but stopped with one hand on the handlebars. Jane in Bristol, Ethel on her way to London. Neither of them would be back for a few days. He'd take Victoria up to 3,500 revs tomorrow, or Sunday. Meantime . . .

He went out of the back gate, and headed for the wasteland where the children of the poorest played among the tin cans and broken bricks and ash and clinker refuse from coal fires.

*   *   *   *

Next day Bob left the factory at his usual time, bicycled home, ate his high tea, and at a few minutes past six went down to the shed, and set up Victoria; but, before doing that, he opened a drawer in his work bench and took out the picture of the Rowland Ruby, and stuck it in the window facing the lane at the back, the picture visible to the lane, the curtains drawn behind it.

He set up Victoria, connected up the prony brake, led the exhaust hose out through its hole, started the machine, and waited. The engine throbbed slowly and a little unevenly, until she was well warmed up. Then he climbed into the saddle, and began to open up the throttle. He had reached about 2,800 revs when he heard the knock on the door. He waited a moment, feeling a vein in his temple beginning to pound; then pushed the throttle lever closed. The engine's roar died away, and he slid off, went to the door and opened it.

She was eleven, wearing a torn dress that had once been yellow, black cotton stockings with holes in them, and boy's black shoes two sizes too big for her. Her face was smudged with ash . . . she was about five feet or five feet one, her face long and thin, the eyes alert and wide set, greenish, her hair long and brown and dirty, hanging to her shoulders on both sides. She'd been playing in the refuse yesterday and he'd told her he'd give her a shilling if she'd come to him, but make sure the picture was in the window before she knocked. She had looked at him with those green eyes wide—she knew, damn her, they all knew—and nodded. Now she held out her hand—long hand, long fingers—"Gimme the bob, mister."

He took a shilling from his trouser pocket and gave it to her, feeling his penis stiffen inside his trousers as he did so. "What's your name?" he asked, as she took the coin and dropped it into a pocket at the side of the dress.

"Ireenie," she said, and then, "My mother's an 'ore."

He said, "Lift up your dress, Irene." She looked him in the eye a moment, a half smile curling her thin lips, then slowly, lasciviously, raised the hem of the tattered skirt, up past her knees . . . above the top of the stockings . . . Bob's breath came faster, one hand caressing his beard, the other fumbling at his fly buttons. The penis sprang out, fully erect, at the instant that the hem of her skirt revealed her plump mount of Venus, the deep dark slit plunging down between her closed thighs.

"Here," he said thickly. He sat down on a stool and held out his hands. She came forward, step by step, the hem of the dress hovering just above the rounded top of her slit.

When she was close he put out one hand and touched it, sliding up and down. Not a hair, smooth, a little damp. He smelled his finger and

447

gasped . . . just like that girl . . . near sixty years ago. He pulled her toward him but she held back, the strange smile on her face. "What you going to do, mister?"

He said, "Put it in . . . this." He held his penis, and thrust the knob toward her.

She said, "Oh, I couldn't do that."

"Liar!" he muttered between clenched teeth. He released his penis, found another shilling and gave it to her—"Now . . . you've done this before, haven't you? Don't lie to me."

She laughed softly, her face six inches from his—"'Course I 'ave, mister. Wiv the boys, wen they got any money. With my dad, when mum's got the rags on. Or he says 'e's my dad, but mum ain't sure."

"Little bitch," Bob groaned. He lifted her bodily and lowered her, legs wide parted, onto his penis. It slid easily into her as she clasped him round the back with her legs. He thrust at her, the stool groaning, he groaning with it as the ecstasy rose in his loins. He became blind with desire as his seed started to pump into her, oblivious of the sneering triumphant smile on her face, the low laugh in her throat.

After a few moments she slipped off him and as he sat, gasping, struggling to recover the even rhythm of his breathing, she wiped off her slit with the end of her skirt and said, "Make it 'arf a crown, and I'll come any time, Mister. Ta, ta."

She slipped out and was gone. Bob slowly did up his buttons and heaved a great sigh. Oh God, it was beautiful, with them . . . she had the slit, but she was not a woman. Why did that Hun Doctor Deerfield ask him whether he liked boys? Of course he liked boys, but not this way. He didn't *like* little girls, come to that—they just drove him mad, and gave him this reward, this mighty sense of power—and, later, the mighty loneliness of guilt.

Victoria sparkled on the test bed, and he thought, There's time. Why not? She's warm already.

He started her again, took off the exhaust extension tube and prepared her for the road. Five minutes later he pushed her out of the back gate, mounted, and rode south. Once out on the Canterbury road he opened the throttle and streaked along under the south face of the Downs at forty miles an hour until, nearing the racing straight, he slowed, stopped, and made himself ready. He tightened the strap of his goggles, fastened all the buttons of his coat, and put on bicycle clips to keep his trousers from flapping in the wind of his passage. Then he climbed back into the saddle, slipped into gear and at once opened the throttle with a long steady pull, until the lever was against the stop. Victoria roared down the long straight, slightly downhill, faster and faster. At the foot, where the level began, the speedometer needle hovered over 98. Stooped low, the wind screaming in his ears, he held the handlebar grips firm against the jerk and bounce transmitted from the road. She was riding steady as a rock . . . all the hours of work had paid off . . . the needle steady on 96 . . . 96, 97 . . . his goggles suddenly flew off and the wind hit his eyeballs like blows from icy fists. He flinched, narrowed his eyelids, and held the throttle against the stop . . . 100. He eased the throttle sharply back and the frantic roar of the engine slowed, quietened.

He drove on, at 20 miles an hour, bursting with elation, struggling to control himself. He'd done 100 miles an hour! Because he'd got the Hun doctor off his back and out of his mind, and done what he had to. A man was a man and must do what he must. The little slut Irene would come whenever he could put the picture in the window, and no one—not even Mr Hunnicutt, the minister at his Wesleyan chapel, could say he was doing *her* any harm. She was what she was, always had been, always would be. No one could change that—least, not for the better. And Victoria, the real lady of steel and aluminum, had done it, even more than the girl, lifting him to ecstasy . . . 100!

He was going to be Bob Stratton, world motor cycle speed record holder . . . his face in all the advertisements for the oil and petrol and tyre people . . . Bob Stratton says . . . And that little slut's slit whenever he wanted it . . . and she'd bring him others . . . take a commission from them for it, of course, but that was her business.

A halo seemed to float over 85 Jervis Street as he wheeled Victoria in through the back gate. He had succeeded, and would now reap the fruits.

*　　*　　*　　*

When Alice reached Laburnum Lodge that evening after work, her head aching as usual, old Parrish the butler met her at the door—"Good evening, Miss Alice. I hope the sandwiches were satisfactory?"

"They always are," she said, summoning a weary smile.

She moved to pass the butler but he said in a low voice, "There's a party here, to see you, Miss Alice . . . says her name is Mrs Cowell. I put her in the morning room, as Mr Harry's in London. She's been here an hour. I hope I did the right thing, but you working in the shell factory and all . . ."

"Who knows what sort of people can now claim acquaintance with you?," the unfinished sentence hinted. Alice's heart sank, and she felt cold in her throat.

She went into the morning room. It was almost dark and she switched on the lights as she entered. A woman rose from a hard chair, her hands to her eyes.

"I'm sorry," Alice said. "Would you prefer I left the lights off?"

"Oh yes . . . Miss, please," the woman said in a low trembling voice. Alice switched off the lights and sat down opposite her in the gloomy room, and motioned her to be seated again.

"What is it?" she asked.

"I'm Dave's wife," she said. Alice saw that she was of medium height, plump, dressed respectably but rather dowdily, with greying hair. . . . "I know about you and my Dave."

Alice thought, I don't want to hurt her, but she said, "What do you know, Mrs Cowell?"

"He's your fancy man," she said. "My brother seen you, with him, in the wood, doing you know what . . . three weeks ago, it was. Dave doesn't go with no club to watch birds, he told me, but only to be with Miss Rowland. Is it true, Miss?"

Alice said quietly, "I'm afraid it is, Mrs Cowell."

The other woman said, "I was in the H.U.S.L. one day and Mrs Goodby said her husband got 'ome from watching the birds at three o'clock the day before, 'cos there weren't no birds out that day, but my Dave didn't get 'ome till seven, so I spoke to my brother about it, and he said he'd follow him, at a distance like, and see what he was up to . . ."

She droned on. Dave was not a gentleman in the accepted sense of the word, Alice knew; he had had a good education, but of the kind that leaves a man with a certain accent. Mrs Cowell was a simple country woman. So Dave had married beneath him, and now she was afraid of losing him.

Mrs Cowell said, "I didn't want to believe it till you told me it was right, what my brother seed." She whined on, about their daughters not knowing, she not suspecting, nor no one else, neither . . . Alice thought, she doesn't seem to have any animus against me, at all. Perhaps I can suggest that we share Dave—as we are doing, after all.

Mrs Cowell said suddenly, "You ought to get a husband of your own, Miss, really you ought."

"I know," she said sadly, "but no one's asked me."

"There must be lots of men would want to marry a nice lady like you, Miss, and with plenty of money. You shouldn't ought to have to come and take my Dave, should you?"

"No," Alice said, "I shouldn't. But I'm afraid I fell in love . . . What do you want me to do, Mrs Cowell?"

The woman leaned forward, putting her hand on Alice's knee—"If you see him again, Miss, he'll only lie again. Men can't help it, can they? But now you know I know, and you won't like that, will you, 'cause you're a lady, a nice lady. Everyone knows that."

"No," Alice said miserably, her head splitting—"I won't like it." After a time she added, "I'm afraid it's impossible."

"You can't send him packing?" It was Mrs Cowell's turn to look and sound despondent—"He's a nice man, Miss . . . a good man for me . . . look at what I am . . . but he's nothing for you . . ."

"He's all I have," Alice said, "but I meant, that it will be impossible for me to see him again."

Mrs Cowell sprang to her feet, "Oh, thank you, Miss, thank you. And I'll tell him how wicked he's been to make you unhappy like this."

Alice started walking to the door, accompanying the other woman. She said, "Tell him . . . everything will always be what it is today, between us . . . but I can never see him again."

"I'll tell him, Miss, don't you fear."

"You're sure? He must know."

"I'll tell him . . . and may God bless you with a husband soon, Miss."

*　　*　　*　　*

Bert Gorse laboriously totted up the totals a fourth time, and made another correction in pencil. He'd hated arithmetic in school, never got farther than adding and subtracting, of course, and every time he'd added up these bloody figures they'd come out different. He started again, licking the point of his pencil, his brows furrowed, and after five minutes achieved the same total he'd had the second time. That would be it, and if it wasn't right, they knew what they could do with it. He pushed the papers away, stood up, lit a cigarette, and began puffing furiously, walking back and forth across the little room like a caged animal, limping, pursing his lips, scowling at the floor, breathing out cigarette smoke through his nostrils. The printing press had broken down again, and he needed a part to fix it, and no one would sell it to him.

The post was in, two letters lying on the mat inside the front door, having been pushed through the slot by the postman. He picked them up—both for Rachel: one he recognized from her mother in Whitechapel; didn't know the other, an expensive heavy white paper, Rachel's name and address written with a thin pen, like one of those books they taught you to write from, copperplate almost.

He put them on the table and resumed his pacing. Rachel ought to have been back twenty minutes ago . . . He wished she'd give up the No-Conscription Fellowship and join him in union work instead. When you got right down to it, the Russells and Bentleys and Allens were the enemy—as he'd told her a dozen times. She used to agree, but now she was all for unity.

451

He looked again at the letters on the table, picked up the heavy white envelope, and sniffed it. No scent . . . postmark Winchester, Hants . . . Hadn't Rachel said that that Bentley lived in Winchester? This might be from him . . . felt like several pages . . .

He heard someone outside screeching, "Bert Gorse! Bert Gorse!" and went to the door and opened it. An old harridan standing the other side of the street was screaming his name. He said, "Shut yer trap, you old fart. I'm working."

She yelled, "The coppers 'ave taken your fancy woman to the station . . . an' she 'as a black eye and 'er face looks like a piece of mincemeat what's going bad . . . I seed 'er, heh, heh, heh!" she cackled, moving on along the pavement.

Bert went back into the house. So they'd arrested her again, and probably John Rowland, too; he was going to be at the demonstration. Well, no one should be surprised. The boss class was using every excuse—and making some up—to hit the pacifists, especially in the pocket if they could. The beaks would give her a stiff fine, wanting to drain the Fellowship's funds . . . but she wouldn't pay, and would go to gaol instead.

He stared at the letters, and after a short moment, picked up the white envelope, opened it, and began to read the beautiful script, "Dearest Rachel . . . the socialist movement . . . special problems of farming in such a state . . . must beware of a huge bureaucracy, which would inevitably take the place of capitalism's boards of directors, managers, foremen and so on . . . not convinced that the State the best entity to run, for example, the insurance business . . ." on and on, six pages of it, then: "When will we meet again? There's no central meeting of the Fellowship until September, and that's too long to wait. We have so much to give each other. Perhaps I could drive over to Hedlington one day and take you out somewhere for lunch. I would much like to see you in your natural habitat, so to speak. Give my regards to Bert. Affectionately, Wilfred."

Give his regards to Bert, the bugger . . . trying to steal Rachel away from him, with his "dearests" and "affectionately" . . . Of course, he might not know that he and Rachel lived together: they were always introduced as Miss Cowan and Mr Gorse . . . but did he know that he loved Rachel? She used to love him, too, but now she didn't. For how long had that been? Since about the time she met Wilfred Bentley. She must have told Bentley all this, and more, during those endless meetings she went to, while he stayed at home, working for the working man, limping up and down, his missing toe and now his whole foot aching.

He tore the letter up and threw the pieces into the waste paper basket by the printing press. He was going to lose her, and tearing up her letters wouldn't help. But he had to show her that it hurt. Only she'd never see the pieces in the waste paper basket because she was in a police station cell. He'd best go and see her . . .

*　　*　　*　　*

Alice Rowland worked steadily and carefully at her bench. You had to have patience, and concentration, in work like this, which the younger women seemed to find very hard. The girl opposite, a pretty eighteen-year-old, was yawning, stealing glances right, left, at the ceiling. Her own eyes held steady on the shell she was filling, but seeing the girl clear beyond with peripheral vision. It must come with age, Alice thought—this ability to maintain concentration at work that by no stretch of the imagination could be described as interesting, and was besides, in its way, an act of murder . . . or of madness, at least.

"Old Stratton must 'a got out of bed the right side, for a change," the woman to her left muttered. "Look over there . . . smiling, he is."

Alice did not look up, but heard the factory manager's familiar gruff voice, "Good work . . . keep it up, and you'll get a bonus, come Christmas."

Come Christmas, Alice thought; another Christmas alone with her father in the big house that had once echoed to the laughs and shouts of Tom and John and Quentin and Richard and Margaret and herself . . . to the sound of music as Mother played the piano after dinner and they all sang from the sheet music set up in front of her . . . the shrieks of charades . . . And this last Christmas, a secret meeting with Dave on the Down, in Caesar's Camp Copse, the snow falling lightly and they kissing as though they'd never see each other again, and at last falling to the ground, their intimate bodies finding each other, surrounded by clothes, wind, snow, cold, but there, together, locked, warm, aware only of love. It was such memories that must give her strength to keep her promise to his wife.

Her amatol bucket was empty, and the shell case she was pouring into only half full. She turned to refill the bucket, and suddenly the room was filled with a flash of brilliant light, followed at once by a roaring force that spread, lifted her, hurled her through the air . . . other women were flying with her in the still glaring brilliance, skirts awry, faces contorted, clothes burning, an arm, a severed head, blood all over. She hit something hard with a crash, and lay stunned, trying to breathe, unaware of any pain, only a dull roar in her ears, and the blinding light . . . now a smell, strong, sweet, familiar . . . roasting flesh. She reached out to pull herself upright . . . the machine she held onto was red hot, her hands sticking to it, skin peeling off, the

453

smell stronger. A weight lay across her legs, the room in near darkness now, filled with choking smoke. She tugged at the weight and forced it free. It was a leg—her own. Her skirt, underclothes, and overalls had gone. She lay naked, burned, one leg gone six inches above the knee, the thigh dripping blood, the leg itself in her peeling hands. She dropped the leg and struggled on, on one knee, through the dark and the smoke and at last, pain now screaming all through her, fell out into the open air.

*   *   *   *

Daily Telegraph, Wednesday, August 1, 1917

THE WAR
3rd year of the war: 52nd week; 1st day.
PRISONERS STREAMING IN
GUNS PURSUING ENEMY

France, Tuesday.
The tension of the past few days snapped at three o'clock this morning . . . The earth rocked under the drumlike tempest produced by weapons ranging between 50 cwt and twice as many tons. The night was damp, with visibility low and the coruscating horizon found a most lurid reflection in the murky sky . . .

The battle is raging furiously, and, as is inevitable at such times, rumours are flying thick as to the degree of our success.

Tuesday, (4 p.m.)
By ten o'clock this morning a whole British Army had made an advance to an average depth of a thousand yards . . . Prisoners are said to be streaming in, and I know that this is the case from the stories I have heard told by lightly wounded men as to the readiness with which the Germans surrendered.

We have crossed the Yser in many places . . . One division alone, in the course of a single day, and under fire the whole time, succeeded in throwing seventeen bridges over the river upon its front . . . It is small wonder to find the enemy sometimes lacking in stomach for the fight, for, in very truth, our attacks nowadays, when we are putting out the full weight of our resources, are a terrible ordeal to face. The boiling oil drums in themselves are enough to quench the most heroic spirits; realising which, our people do not economise expenditure in these projectiles. In places, however, the Huns have been fighting as sturdily as ever . . .

A thousand yards on the front of a whole Army! Cate didn't know how much that would be, but it must be measured in miles rather than yards. Prisoners streaming in . . . he shook his head. The 3rd year of the war was in its 52nd week, as the headline showed; and in those years Cate, and everyone else in Britain, had learned to read official military communiqués with considerable reserve. It was wiser, as the saying went, to wait till the other shoe dropped. All one could be sure of was that the Army was again locked in major battle, which would go on for weeks . . . months, perhaps.

Garrod came in and said, "There's Florinda and Probyn Gorse to see you, sir. Shall I tell them to wait in the kitchen till you've had your breakfast?"

Cate laughed. "Good gracious, no! Have the Marchioness of Jarrow cooling her heels in our kitchen? Bring them in here, please, and bring another pair of cups."

Garrod returned a minute later and held the door open as she said formally, "The Marchioness of Jarrow and Probyn Gorse, sir."

Cate got up and held out his hands to Florinda—"You look even more lovely than you do in the *Bystander* and the newspapers . . . How are you, Probyn? Sit down. Coffee or tea?"

They sat down one on either side of him, and Florinda said, "Coffee, please, Miss Garrod," and Probyn said, "Tea."

"This is an early call," Cate said, sipping his newly refilled coffee cup, "but welcome."

Florinda said, "I brought something to show you, before I go back to London. I want to know whether it's all right." She opened the heavy cardboard box she had been carrying, to reveal a blued telescopic sight, lying on tissue paper and chamois leather. Cate whistled softly, "For Fletcher?" She nodded. Probyn said, "It'll fit one of them Lee Enfields the soldiers use."

Cate looked at it and murmured, "Magnification × 6 . . . that's good. I was afraid, when I first saw it, that you'd chosen too big a magnification . . . he'll need a reasonably wide field, and good lighting—this has it. And it's beautifully made. German, I see!"

He put the sight down and Florinda said, "Could you test it, Mr Cate? I wouldn't want Fletcher to trust it, out there, if it wasn't right."

"Oh, I'll be happy to test it," Cate said, "but aren't you afraid it might be stolen in the post? Many good things are, on their way to the Front."

"I have my own couriers," Florinda said, smiling. Ah, Cate thought, of course she'll have plenty of pilots and officers at her beck and call. Her lips were slightly parted, the sun pouring through the tall windows into her auburn hair. She seemed to have gained an inch in the bust and lost two in the waist, and her skin was perfect. She was gorgeous, luscious. Yet Cate felt no stir of sexual longing for her, as he

455

often had in the past, and, at least a few times, had slaked in her body. For him now, sexually, there was only Isabel Kramer; and, looking into Florinda's eyes, he could tell that she was sending him the same message—of affection, understanding, a warm regard for what they had been and done: but now—her heart and body belonged elsewhere.

Flanders: Summer, 1917

29 The land rises gently to the Pilckem Ridge ahead, and the Gheluvelt plateau to the right. Little streams called *bekes* in Flemish flow down the centre of each shallow valley and depression. There are no woods or trees near the front lines, all destroyed by the artillery fire of the past three years. Miles of barbed wire, a hundred feet deep, cover each front. The ruins of Ypres Cloth Hall rise like a shattered cathedral out of the landscape behind.

On July 16th the artillery preparation for the great attack begins. Three thousand and ninety-one British guns open fire, and continue firing according to detailed programmes of targets until the assault. The guns are aided by 600 aircraft. The final barrage begins at 1 a.m. on July 31, all the guns firing at once, making the loudest noise till that moment created by man, and rivalling the explosion of Krakatoa. By then 65,000 tons of shells have destroyed the natural drainage of the whole area. The breeze is west, with dense clouds low overhead, about five hundred feet up. At 3.50 a.m. the British infantry climb out of their trenches and advance through the gaps cut that night in their own wire.

In the afternoon it begins to rain. It rains all day the next day, and the next. It continues raining.

*　　*　　*　　*

Excerpt from the diary of Brigadier General John Charteris, Field Marshal Haig's Chief of Intelligence:

August 4. All my fears about the weather have been realized. It has killed this attack. . . . Every brook is swollen and the ground is a quagmire. If it were not that all the records of previous years had given us fair warning, it would seem as if Providence had declared against us . . . It is so easy to think what might have happened had we attacked on the 26th or 28th and got the high ground before this monsoon had burst on us. We can not break off the battle now, even if we would. We have to fight forward to keep the Germans from attacking the French.

August 9. The rain keeps on and with each day's rain our task gets more difficult . . . the front area baffles description. It is just a sea of mud, churned up by shell fire.

* * * *

Captain Ramsburgh was a thin lantern-jawed officer from Newmarket, Virginia, by way of the United States Military Academy, West Point, New York. First Sergeant Patrick Leary, 6 feet 3 inches, 230 pounds, was from Benicia, California, via twenty-one years service in the 16th U.S. Infantry. Corporal John Merritt was from Nyack, New York, via Harvard University. The three shared a dugout near battalion headquarters of the 1st Weald Light Infantry, to which they were attached for instruction in trench warfare. Outside, it was raining, and water dripped steadily through the makeshift roof, falling with small metallic pings onto their steel helmets. The Germans were shelling the area at random. Inside, they were attempting to brew up coffee. Two days before the 1st Wealds had taken part in an attack in the Nollehoek sector. They had advanced two hundred yards. Yesterday they had beaten off a strong German counter-attack. The ground gained had been consolidated; but Nollehoek itself was still a mile away, up the gently sloping ridge.

Captain Ramsburgh said, "What do you make of the British fatigue system, Top?"

"No good, sir," Leary replied. "Why, every man spends half the night on fatigues when he's supposed to be resting up for his next spell in the line."

"How can we improve on it?"

"Use tractors to pull the loads farther forward," the sergeant said.

Ramsburgh said, "That would help, but tractors can't do trench revetment." He looked at Johnny. Johnny said, "Use labour battalions farther forward, sir."

Ramsburgh said, "H'm . . . This Weald outfit makes the sentries stand with their heads and shoulders clear of the parapet. Doesn't make sense to me."

Leary said, "I think it does, Captain. The Krauts like to fix machine guns to fire at the parapet level. If the sentry's showing his shoulders, he stands a chance of getting a chest or shoulder wound—if he's only showing his head, that's where he'll get it."

"But the other will produce more wounds, over all . . . we'll have to think about it . . . What was the main thing you learned from the attack, Merritt?"

"That no one can move in this mud," Johnny said without hesitation. "And the worst of the mud was apparently caused by the shelling. If they'd attacked with no shelling or very little, it wouldn't be so bad."

Ramsburgh said, "I don't know . . . I reckon that no attack will have a hope of succeeding without really heavy artillery preparation, and our Field Artillery doesn't have the weight of fire to give it."

"How can we, with nothing bigger than French 75s, sir?" Johnny Merritt said. "The 75's high explosive shell weighs only 11.65 pounds, with an actual H.E. content of 3 pounds of melinite, and the shrapnel shell's not much more—15.96 pounds, with 300 lead bullets. Compare that with . . ."

"Say, Harvard, have you been reading the Artillery manuals?"

"As a matter of fact I have, Top," Johnny said. "And when I get back Stateside, I'm going to apply for the Field Artillery. The first time I saw a battery on the move, I said to myself . . ."

Captain Ramsburgh interrupted—"We're not all that interested in your future plans, Corporal . . . We were talking about what we've learned from the British, so far."

"Our soldiers'll sure as hell mutiny if they get this Hoggin's Jam and Bully," the sergeant said.

A shell burst nearby, shaking the ground and bringing trickles of mud down the sides of the dugout. A head poked round the side of the gas blanket and the three Americans rose to their feet, crouched over, saluting. Lieutenant Colonel Rowland said, "I'm going to visit the Regimental Aid Post, Captain Ramsburgh, and then go round the battalion's trenches, if you'd care to come with me."

"Yes, sir. May I bring Sergeant Leary and Corporal Merritt with me?"

"Of course. And when we come back I've told my adjutant to show you all how we prepare trench maps and keep them up to date."

"Thank you, sir."

"Come along, then."

*   *   *   *

England: August, 1917

Jane Stratton sat in the parlour, her arthritically swollen hands folded in her lap, staring at the curtained window. She ought to be doing something, but what? Supervise Nellie cleaning the bedrooms? Going shopping? She couldn't face the crowds, the people . . . so many she would know, coming up with mournful faces . . . "So sorry, Mrs Stratton, our deepest sympathy . . ."

Listlessly she picked up the newspaper, glanced at a headline and put it down again. What did it matter what was happening in the world? How would it help her to live out her remaining days, a widow, to know that the Serbians were counter-attacking at some place with a name a yard long, or that Mr Lloyd George was visiting Durham to speak to the coal miners?

She heard footsteps coming downstairs and put her handkerchief to her eyes. Her daughter, Ethel Fagioletti, came in, head high, smiling, her face shining from recent scrubbing, smelling of Pears Soap. "It's time to go out shopping, Mother," she said cheerfully, coming to a stop in front of her mother's chair.

Jane dabbed her eyes. "How can you be so happy and smiling with your poor father not yet cold in his grave?" she muttered. She shivered involuntarily as she spoke, for Bob was in no grave. They had not found anything more of him than a few shreds of his coat, and his bowler hat, undamaged, on a rooftop a quarter of a mile off. A dozen of those poor women had gone the same way, vanished. So there was nothing of Bob Stratton in the grave: she'd wanted to bury just the bowler hat in the coffin, but the Reverend Mr Hunnicutt had regretfully refused permission, saying that the burial service was to be said over the bodies of departed souls, not their bowler hats. Jane felt obstinately that Mr Hunnicutt was wrong. The bowler had been a part of Bob just as surely as his hand or foot . . .

Ethel composed her face to a more serious expression and said, "I'm sorry, Mother . . . and you know how sad I am about Father, but . . . but with Niccolo come back to me, how can I help being happy, a bit? And we're getting married again."

"You're all the same," Jane mumbled. "Even Frank, sending that telegram to make sure that that motor cycle of your father's— Victoria—isn't sold until . . . And you should have had more pride than to go crawling back to Niccolo, after what he did," she added, feeling a surge of anger fill the empty void of her emotions.

"But I love him," Ethel said simply. "Mother, Niccolo wants us—him and me—to have our own house again. I must leave here soon, and go to London and find one. You must live with me, till the war's over. You'll never be able to look after yourself here, alone."

Jane said, "I'll not come to London. I'll not leave here."

"Well, we'll talk about it later . . . Come on now, the shopping."

"You do it," Jane said. "I don't want to go out."

Ethel put out her hand and took one of her mother's—"Come on, Mother! You shouldn't sit here, thinking of poor Father . . . come and buy a new hat."

"It'll have to be black," Jane said sharply.

"Yes, of course . . . and visit Anne and her children."

"That sister-in-law of yours is going out too much," Jane said. "People are talking."

"Come on, Mother."

Slowly, Jane rose to her feet; then put away her little handkerchief and said, "I must wash my face. I look dreadful."

*   *   *   *

Fletcher Gorse and Betty Merritt walked on Beighton Down, westward, with swinging strides toward the setting sun. He was wearing his own clothes, as he used to wear them here in summer, his uniform left at his grandfather's cottage—she a light summer dress, but with strong shoes and no hat, tendrils of her hair escaping to frame her face, now tanned by the day in the sun and reddened by the wind. They had not spoken more than a few words all day, since she had picked him up in her car at the cottage and driven to the edge of the Down. Since then they had walked nearly twenty miles, first east until they were level with Ashford in the Weald below, then back by different tracks, north of the Daneway. The larks were silent now on the Down, for the broods had long since hatched and the males had no cause to rise, rejoicing, towering against the sun, to announce in endless lyric outpouring the birth of their young.

He has not changed, she thought. Whatever horrors he has seen, and endured, have somehow passed over him . . . or entered only into the secret part of him that makes his poetry—not marked his face or eyes, as they did to so many others. She was content.

He said suddenly, but the words coming slowly, "There's greater things, out there, than Milton had in *Paradise Lost* . . . and very like, too . . . The armies of Satan thrown down—that's us, all of us . . . gathering on the edge of the burning lake . . . rallying to Satan's colours . . . with pain and hurt . . . and many of them afraid of the anger of God, I'll be bound."

He walked on five minutes. Then—"It's so big you can't see the end of it, any way you look . . . right, left, up . . . it reaches up to the sun . . . the size of it, it's like the Milky Way, circling round you, we're all lost in it . . . But it's so small, too. When I get a man's head in my sniper sights . . . the telescopic sight Flo gave me . . . it's not big, it's very small, just that man's eye, and the blue of it, and in the middle of the blue I can see him and his wife and baby. They're still there, for a

461

moment, after he drops . . . Other times, I'm looking at my mate's eye, and seeing through it, into him, and I can see deep into him because of the war. It's stripping him . . . the bit that he thought was brave, the bit that he thought was cowardly—whatever isn't really there, goes . . . what's left, is him."

They had come down off the Down and were heading south into the Weald, to the place where she had left the car in the morning. He said, "Captain Kellaway is sending my poetry to a publisher in London."

"I know," she said. "You told me."

"The first lot's going to be published soon—November, perhaps. The captain wants me to call it *De Profundis*."

"From the depths," she said. "Oscar Wilde used the same title to explain . . , what he was, really."

"The captain told me, but I don't want no Latin name . . . I'll think of something, soon's I get back."

"Are you going to use your own name, as author?"

Fletcher laughed then—"No, just 'Fletcher.'"

They stopped beside the car, and Fletcher climbed into the passenger seat. "Beighton—the Seven Stars," he said. "There's good cheese there and we won't have to listen to old Parsley."

"Certainly, milord," she said, scrambling up into the driver's seat. "Shall I be eating outside, or may I join you in the bar?"

He leaned over and kissed her on the cheek, "You try and get away from my side and see what happens to you, pretty Betty." She turned her face quickly so that his lips found hers, and they kissed, long and lovingly.

He leaned away, and said, "I'm changing, Betty. Growing into the world . . . the one we all live in, except some of us in Walstone don't know it . . . I've never met anyone like Fagioletti before—he's a corporal in B Company . . . Captain Kellaway . . . a lot of London fellows, there's all sorts in the Army now . . . even old Rowley, the C.O.—known him all my life, from far away, but he's different now . . . or I am . . . Mr Campbell, the adjutant . . . talks to me for an hour on end sometimes, when he finds me resting or reading. Snipers spend all day out in a post, without moving, but ready . . . so we always get the next day off duties. I've had a lot of time to think . . . and I think I'll be ready, and fit to be your husband when it's over."

She cried, "Oh, Fletcher, *why* can't we have more time together? It's not fair!"

"No, it's not," he said, "but we wouldn't have even this day if Mum hadn't got so ill with the influenza and Mr Campbell given me a special 72 hours leave. So we'd best make the best of what we do have. You'll spend the night with me in the cottage?"

462

She said quietly, "Of course, Fletcher . . . all the hours you have."

"What's happening to your work?"

"Ginger understands . . . He's my boss . . . though I think he's jealous, poor man. He's so nice, but . . . he's not you."

Fletcher slid out of the seat, jumped to the ground and went forward to crank up the engine.

"Switched off," Betty called; then—"Switched on!" Fletcher swung, the engine fired.

*   *   *   *

Tom Rowland walked along the Admiralty corridor toward the 2nd Sea Lord's office, whither he had been summoned. A letter burned in his pocket: it was from Ordinary Seaman Charlie Bennett, written from his home in County Durham. Charlie had consumption, developed not a month after Tom had left *Penrith*. Now, after two months in hospital, he was discharged from the Navy as medically unfit . . . Would . . . could . . . he come and see Tom?

Tom wondered whether the D.N.I. was intercepting his mail; and if so, if he had read the letter . . . perhaps that was what this summons from the 2nd Sea Lord was about. As to the letter itself . . . Charlie Bennett had conclusively shown him, Tom, what he was, sexually. They had sworn to each other their love. Faith between men must be as inviolable as it was supposed to be between man and woman. He would ask Charlie to come and live with him, and be his companion . . . Charlie would be his servant, too, obviously. There would be no need for Jones to clean the flat—Charlie would do it; and learn how to cook, and put out his clothes. In return, Tom would continue what he had started, in so small a way, last October—educating Charlie for the world he would now be living in, a world of art galleries and Green Rooms and haute couture salons instead of gun turrets, hammocks, and mess decks.

Inside the big room the Naval Assistant stood aside as Tom stood stiff backed in front of Admiral Burney's desk, his gold-braided cap under his arm. The admiral was speaking, "Admiral Fisher, and earlier Admiral Duff, have reported that you are doing very good work in the Anti-Submarine Division, Rowland. They say you have originality, application, and common sense—it's surprising how few people working on problems from the theoretical end have that last quality . . . On the other hand, the D.N.I. has informed me that you are associating with Russell Wharton, the actor." He paused, looking up.

Tom hesitated a moment. But if Russell was teaching him anything, it was that he must not cringe or lie: he was what he was, whatever the consequences. He said, "Yes, sir. He's a friend of mine."

"Close?" the admiral said. He's trying to let me off easily, Tom thought; he's leaving me the openings to say Oh, no . . . He said, "In the past four months, since I was posted here, he has become so, yes, sir."

The admiral's tone hardened, "You remember when you first came, I gave you a formal warning, in the presence of Captain Buller here, who made an official note of it."

"I remember, sir."

"In view of Captain Leach's reason for asking that you be posted away from *Penrith,* don't you think it is unwise for you to associate with a known homosexual such as Wharton?"

Tom said, "I am sorry, sir . . . he is my friend. When I am with him I am always in uniform, as you ordered."

He waited. Let them do what they would, or felt they must. He missed the sea, the sailors, and the comradeship of the wardroom; but in himself, he was a much happier and better functioning man. He could not have earned the head of the Division's commendation as the man he used to be—he would have been too much on edge, worried about himself and his nature.

The admiral said, "This is a warning, Rowland. We can't dismiss you, or court martial you, merely for associating with an actor . . . why in the name of God isn't it an actress? . . . but the D.N.I.'s people will watch you more closely. That's all."

Tom said, "Aye, aye, sir," wheeled round and marched out and back to his office in the Anti-Submarine Division.

*   *   *   *

Alice Rowland lay in the hospital bed, staring at the open window, and the heavy outline of the trees beyond. The humped bedclothes covered the basket that protected the short stump of her left leg, making her body seem that of some strange and monstrous animal . . . well, that's what she was now, after all. She felt far away, partly because every bone in her body still throbbed and ached, partly because she was almost due for her morphine injection, of which she was having two a day to deaden the pain of the shattered and separated thigh.

The ward sister came in leading a dumpy woman of middle age, simply dressed. Alice stared at her—who was this? The sister said, "Here's a friend to visit you, Miss Alice."

The woman said, "Mrs Cowell, miss . . . Dave's wife."

"Of course," Alice said. "It was so dark in that room, wasn't it?"

"I can only stay a minute, miss. I wanted to come and tell you how sorry we are about it . . . your leg. Dave said I must come, but I had to come for myself, too . . . Do you think it would help if Dave came to see you?" Her eyes were big and anxious. "I wouldn't mind, you know. I mean, things is different . . . All that matters is you getting well. So, if it would help . . ."

Alice put out her hand—"Thank you so much, Mrs Cowell . . . I think I'd better not."

The ward sister returned with another visitor. This was a young woman in expensive clothes, a rather short green dress, green suede shoes, and a wide hat with a gallant ostrich feather. The late sun shone through the auburn hair piled under the hat, and caught the glint of her green eyes. The sister said, "The Marchioness of Jarrow, Miss Alice." Mrs Cowell slunk away with a murmured, "Goodbye, miss."

Alice stared, and then said, "Florinda, of course! . . . You look so beautiful."

Florinda sat down in the bedside chair—"I thought of bringing you some flowers, but they're supposed not to be good in a hospital."

"I think they're nice even if they do drink some of my oxygen," Alice said.

Florinda said, "How are you, Miss Alice? Seems such a long time ago since you gave me a big doll for Christmas when you were staying with Squire . . ."

"Oh dear," Alice said, "you were . . . eleven, I think. I remember wondering whether you would think yourself too old for dolls." She looked surreptitiously at the clock. When would that doctor come? She hated the sting of the needle but afterward . . . ah!

Florinda said, "Hope you've had nothing but good news from your family, miss."

"So far," Alice said. Tom was safe in the Admiralty, but one could only hope, and pray, for Quentin and Guy and Boy—and soon, Naomi.

"Is there anything I can do for you?" Florinda asked. "Anything you want? I can easily get it in London, whatever it is."

And can afford whatever she wants, Alice thought; she was a good tactful girl, with natural taste.

"Nothing, thanks . . ." except morphine, she added to herself. Florinda rose from the chair. "I have to go back to London . . . Fletcher's going to have dinner with me before he catches the leave train for France . . . Don't forget, Miss Alice—anything I can do . . ." She waved her hand and walked out of the private room without looking back.

The sister came in again. Now, Alice thought, surely . . . "Mrs Merritt," the sister said. Stella came in, and Alice eyed her as closely as her condition and anxiety allowed. She looked tired—beautiful, of course, Stella could never be otherwise—but not at peace. She was, let's see, seven months pregnant, for the baby was due in mid-

465

October, and would be the Governor's first great-grandchild. It was a shame that Johnny would not be here to see his baby; he was in France with the American Army, Stella had told her, but had not yet been sent into battle.

Stella sat down in the chair Florinda had just vacated, and said, "I passed Florinda coming out—Florinda Gorse."

Alice said, "She was here." She was getting fidgety, her fingers playing with the coverlet. "How are you? You look tired."

"I am, a bit. The baby seems so heavy sometimes . . ." Her voice trailed away as she yawned. She blinked, stared at Alice and mumbled, "The doctor said I wasn't to stay more than five minutes."

"The doctor? Where is he?"

"In the next room . . . He said he'd be coming along."

Alice lay back. Soon! Stella said, "Johnny was in a place called Chaumont, but he said a group of them were going to our area—the British—any moment, to learn about trench warfare. Then, he said, he'll probably be sent back to America to become an officer."

"Good," Alice said. "Will he be coming through England on his way?"

"I'm afraid not. The American ships are landing at Brest and St. Nazaire, and going straight back from there."

The door opened and the doctor came in. Alice began to roll back the long sleeve of her nightgown. The doctor came to her bedside and said, "No need for that now, Miss Rowland. Only one nasty needle a day for you now, and soon—none!"

She tried to jerk herself upright—"I'm supposed to have two injections a day! You ordered them yourself!"

The doctor glanced at Stella and said, "That's true, Miss Rowland, but now, well, the pain is less and we are going to taper the doses down to nothing over the next ten days."

Alice heard herself screaming, "I must have it! I can't stand it . . . you promised . . . where is it, where is it?" She burst into uncontrollable sobbing.

The doctor's face was grave. As her sobs subsided he said, "Miss Rowland, morphine is a very dangerous drug . . . as are all drugs . . . cocaine, opium, heroin, all of them. They are habit forming, and we do not like to give them to any patient for more than a few days at a time in case the patient becomes addicted. In your case . . . do you hear me?"

Alice nodded miserably.

"In your case, the addiction has obviously come sooner than we expected. We had to take the risk because of the extremely serious and painful nature of your wound. But we must now treat you as an addict. You shall have your two injections a day, for a week—but

466

progressively smaller . . . then one a day, for three or four days. After that we'll discontinue the morphine altogether. You will have some not very pleasant withdrawal symptoms—pains all over the body, sweating, shakes, insomnia. I shall give you Luminal to help you sleep, and aspirin for the pains . . . or, if they become very bad, codeine."

Stella listened, sweating. It was like a broken gramophone record. Aunt Alice—a drug fiend—from having been given the stuff by a doctor. She herself now knew the majestic ecstasies and power of her own drug, her own mind. Could it be possible that Aunt Alice, mousey old Aunt Alice, could be experiencing the same?

The doctor said, "We shall need your co-operation, too, Miss Rowland. Between us, we'll set you free. Sister, bring me the syringe and ampoule, please."

Set you free, Stella thought. What if Aunt Alice didn't want to be set free? As she didn't . . . but the baby? She got up abruptly and left the room, without saying another word.

*　　*　　*　　*

Lady Helen Durand-Beaulieu was walking back from Walstone to High Staining, having posted a parcel to her brother, Captain Lord Cantley, with the Coldstream Guards in France, and another to Captain Charles Rowland, with the Weald Light Infantry; bought some stamps, and listened to some gossip from Miss Macaulay the postmistress. Probyn Gorse sidled up alongside her, appearing from heaven knew where. He touched the peak of his old deerstalker, murmuring, "Afternoon, milady . . . Been shopping?"

"Sending off parcels, Probyn," she said.

"Look a mite peaky, milady. Hope you're not coming down with the fluenzie."

"Oh no, Probyn, I'm quite all right," she said. She had been sick this morning, and her period was a week overdue. There was a strong chance that she was carrying Boy's baby. A few days would confirm her hopes for sure, or dash them.

Probyn said confidentially, loping along beside her at a pace that somehow kept easily abreast of her long strides—"This is just between you and me, milady, what I'm going to say . . . There's a certain young woman in this village is going to come and see you soon, if she's in trouble—she don't know for sure yet, if you know what I mean."

"I understand," Lady Helen said.

Probyn continued, "She doesn't know where to turn, 'cept you. She trusts you . . ."

Helen racked her brain. "It must be Hetty Watkins," she said. "She was my maid for a year when I came back from finishing school."

"No names, no pack drill," Probyn said mysteriously. "What I mean to say is, if she comes, you can send her to see my Woman. My Woman 'elps girls in trouble."

"It's against the law," Helen said.

"'Course it is," Probyn said with a touch of asperity, "but the law is a ass. We don't have no truck with the girl's dad, but my Woman will help *her*. So tell her, if she comes."

"I will," Helen said. Probyn touched his cap and turned away. "Give my regards to Mrs Gorse," Helen called after him.

"When I get home I will."

"Where are you going, then?"

"Fishing."

"Oh dear, not on father's water, I hope."

"I'd be ashamed to, with the keepers his lordship has now." Probyn disappeared into the hedge.

Helen walked on. Hetty Watkins, pregnant. Poor Hetty.

She started. Poor Hetty, indeed! Probyn's mysterious young woman who might be in trouble was clearly herself, Lady Helen Durand-Beaulieu. Had he guessed that she had fallen in love with Boy, and made love with him? Or did he *know*—by watching, perhaps? He had come into the Arms that evening after the cricket match, and left before they did. It was possible . . . it was probable. She felt indignant. Then she began to laugh. Hadn't that Italian princess showed her a Renaissance medallion of a satyr enjoying a nymph while Pan scattered rose petals over the two of them? Probyn was a sort of Pan, and so sacred a rite as theirs that first night really should not have taken place without a priest to bless it.

And, of course, Frances Enright had been an altar boy, deliberately keeping Carol Adams back in the Arms.

But she was not going to use Probyn's Woman's services, no, thank you. She paused in her stride. Well, perhaps she would, not to rid herself of Boy's child, but to give it birth in dignity and secrecy. Then she herself would raise it until he could come and claim them both. She set off again striding longer and whistling "Greensleeves" with unladylike energy, praying for the moment to come when she could feel the life moving in her womb.

*　　*　　*　　*

Virginia Rowland and another young woman worked on their knees, on padded sandbags, with brush and pail of soapy water beside them, wet cloths in their reddened hands. In an hour the cold cement floor of the mess hall would be spotless, first swabbed down, then scrubbed by hand. Then their Deputy Administrator would come round and say, in her upper-class accent, "That's well done." Then she'd take Virginia aside and say, "You really ought to accept the Senior Unit

Administrator's offer to send you to administrative school. You are, after all, a lady."

Virginia kept swabbing, inching forward on the sandbag. Nothing would make her agree to become an administrator, or even a Forewoman, and leave girls like June Adkinson, working here beside her, and join with those who had power over them. She'd been miserable as a girl—she could admit it to herself now—fat, no good at games, no good at work, a disappointment to her parents. Only her moments with Guy had been happy. Her stroke became slower as she thought of him, in his R.F.C. jacket, with the two medal ribbons . . . already! And the blue eye and the brown, both smiling at her.

She sighed and scrubbed faster. She'd never be like him, even in so far as a woman could be; and if you weren't like Guy, or Naomi, or even Stella in her own way, being upper class was just a lot of restrictions, denials and . . . rejections. This was the place for her. She thanked God for the war, which had given her the power to break away, and a place to go to. She whispered to herself "Sorry, I don't mean it—about the war." Then she thanked Him that she was here, scrubbing floors in Aldershot, a worker of the Woman's Army Auxiliary Corps, which had taken over the duties and most of the personnel of her old unit of the Women's Legion.

Beside her, June said, "Tha's daydreaming, Ginnie. Look, tha's missed a bludy great patch of the cement, there!"

Virginia smiled and went back over the place June pointed out. June was from Wigan, and had worked two years in the cotton mills before the war offered her, too, an escape. For the first year of their service together she had heaped all kind of scorn on Virginia—for being a lady, for her accent, for her general lack of knowledge of anything practical . . . but recently she had changed completely, and appointed herself Virginia's best friend and protector.

She said now, "An' you're not using t'regulation broosh. Old Basin Tits'll 'ave your blud for that."

"I lost it," Virginia said.

"Sum bitch stoal it, more like. You get on with t'work an' I'll get you a broosh from t'stores. Lansbury there owes me summat."

She got up and went out, returning five minutes later with a new, official floor brush. She smacked Virginia's behind before kneeling beside her. "Tha' needs a bludy keeper, Ginnie, that's t'truth."

They worked on, steadily and efficiently, with little speech. At four o'clock the bugles blew; and at five Virginia was free for three hours. Her Deputy Administrator checked her out of the gate of the collection of tin-roofed Nissen huts, surrounded by barbed wire, and said, "Remember, Rowland, back before eight, sharp!"

Stanley Robinson was waiting for her outside the cinema and at once bought tickets, and they went in together. She sat, as always, on his right, so that once the house became dark, he could hold her hand. The lights dimmed, their hands met and folded, the giant images flashed on the silver screen, the pianist began to pound out "The Flight of the Bumblebee." Mack Sennett and the Keystone cops raced across the screen from right to left on bicycles; there was a fight; they rushed back in a Model T Ford; a locomotive appeared, steam and smoke pouring out of every valve and joint; the car raced it to a level crossing, marked by a swinging lamp and crossed planks on a pole . . . They laughed till their sides ached, their hands always locked.

A newsreel followed the Mack Sennett . . . our Boys in France . . . a destroyer crew waving from the deck as the ship docked . . . A German Gotha aeroplane, or rather the smashed pieces of it, on a hillside somewhere in England, soldiers staring at it . . . the Queen opening a bazaar . . . the King visiting a Convalescent Depot . . . Guns firing somewhere in France . . . The grip of his hand tightened and he muttered, "Those are 18 pounders, my guns." She returned his grip, understanding what he was feeling.

Afterwards, in the street again he tucked her arm under his good elbow and she said, "Stanley! We're not allowed to show affection in public. Miss Charnley would give me fourteen days C.B. if she saw us."

"Some say good old Basin Tits," Stanley muttered.

Virginia squeezed his arm. The unspoken second half of the saying was "Some say fuck old Basin Tits." The girls of the W.A.A.C. knew all the swear words the men did, and more, and used them when no superiors were about; or, when they lost their tempers, used the words to the superiors' faces. Virginia sometimes used the words herself, but it made her feel warm that Stanley should keep his language decent in front of her.

He said now, "We'll pick up some fish and chips and eat them outside the Queen's Arms, with a bottle of beer, eh?"

"That'll be lovely," she said.

Outside the pub they sat on the grass in the fading light, eating off the stained newsprint in which fish and chips were always wrapped, licking their greasy fingers, smiling at each other. At last, "Half-past seven, Stanley," she said. "I must go, or Miss Charnley . . ."

Stanley rose unwillingly, then helped her up. They disposed of the paper in a dust bin and walked slowly toward the W.A.A.C. hutments at the lower end of Aldershot. A hundred yards from the knife rest, now pulled aside, that marked the entrance, and at night was pulled across to block it, he stopped. This was the first place he had kissed her—the first place and time she had ever been kissed.

She turned up her face, waiting for the kiss. He said, "Will you marry me, Virginia?"

She said, "Yes. When?"

He said, "I'll remind you again I've not the education I should have. My father's a corporation dustman in Leeds, you know that. And yours is a colonel . . . even though you *are* speaking less la-di-da the last few months. Your mum and dad'll be proper ashamed of you."

"I want to speak like you and June and the others," Virginia said.

"And me with only one arm and all. God only knows what sort of a job I'll be able to get when the war's over."

"It doesn't matter. I can work."

"Not if you have bairns to look after . . . not with *my* bairns, you won't."

"We'll find something."

"You'll write to your mother, then . . . best, take a forty-eight and go and see her, and tell her. I'll write to your father." She made a gesture of dissent, but he said firmly, "It must be done right, Virginia. If I was a toff, we might elope or something, but I'm not going to have any of your family saying 'That soldier ran away with our Virginia for her money.' Besides, it's the right thing to do. They're your father and mother . . . Then, when it's settled and agreed to, we'll get married in church, and you'll have a guard of honour of sergeants and bombardiers of the Royal Regiment."

She said apprehensively, "But what if Daddy or Mummy say no?"

"They won't," he said confidently.

*   *   *   *

Ruth Hoggin sat beside Miss Plummer, the elocution teacher, in the day nursery of the big house, Launcelot squirming on a high chair across the table from them. He was wearing a velveteen suit with knee breeches and white socks, and patent leather shoes with a single pearl button fastening the cross strap.

"How now brown cow," Miss Plummer said.

"How now brown cow," Launcelot repeated. Ruth beamed with pride.

"Rainy plain."

"Rain . . ."

Ruth cut in, "Miss Plummer said 'Rainy plain,' Launcelot."

Launcelot yawned and looked out of the window and fidgeted on his chair.

"Try again, Launcelot," Miss Plummer said, "say 'rainy.' "

"Riney."

"No, Launcelot, rainy. Say that."

"Rainy. Look, old Sharples, up tree." The little boy jumped down and ran to the open window. There he peered out, on tiptoe, waving one hand frantically at the old gardener, twenty feet up an elm tree on a long ladder.

Ruth said severely, "Come back, Launcelot, and sit down. You'll never learn if you don't pay attention and then what will they think of you at Eton College?"

Miss Plummer muttered in a low voice, "We must remember he's only two and a half, Mrs Hoggin. He is really very advanced for his age."

Launcelot came back unwillingly and climbed up into his chair. Miss Plummer said, "Say the words after me, Launcelot . . . 'High.'"

"High."

"Butter."

"Bu'er."

"Butter. Sound the Ts, Launcelot."

"Butt-ter."

"Better, but not quite right . . . What?" She sounded the H clearly.

"Wot . . . old Sharples fall's bloody noggin!"

Again Launcelot rushed to the window. The gardener teetered momentarily on his ladder, but recovered himself. Ruth said, "He uses such awful language . . . well, you know his father didn't have any proper education and Launcelot picks it up . . . though, mind, Mr Hoggin speaks much better than he used to, thanks to you. But he still swears . . . he forgets, that's it."

"Quite, Mrs Hoggin. I think it would be best if I took Launcelot for a little walk now . . . just the two of us," she added pointedly as Ruth made to get up as though to accompany them. "He needs to concentrate on one person, one thing . . . not try to please his mother as well as hear what I am trying to teach him."

Miss Plummer collected Launcelot and went out and down the stairs. Ruth followed more slowly, and, ignoring Miss Meiklejohn's startled look, walked past her desk into Bill's office. He glanced up— "Saw Launcelot going out just now . . . I'd have been torn limb from limb if I'd 'a walked out in clothes like those, when I was his age."

"That was different," she said. "Bill, we must have my mother to live with us."

Bill rose slowly behind his big desk, "Your mother! What the bleeding 'ell do you think . . . ?"

"She is all but crippled. Nellie's leaving to join the W.R.N.S. Ethel's going back to London, and Mother doesn't want to go there."

"She hates me, I'm dirt to her, the scum of the earth."

"Well, you used to use such awful language, and had nasty friends. Now it's different. You're an important man, and well off. And this is our house, not hers."

"But . . ." Hoggin said helplessly.

"We've got to," Ruth said firmly. "It's a daughter's duty to look after her mother and father when they can't look after themselves, and that's what I'm going to do."

She went out, closing the door behind her. Bill stared after her, then muttered, "Cor stone the fucking crows," and picked up the balance sheet of another H.U.S.L. shop.

*   *   *   *

The Earl of Swanwick stood by the open French window of the blue drawing room of Walstone Park, hands in pockets, looking out over the sweep of lawn, the heavy trees of the Deer Park, half a dozen grazing fallow does with two bucks, and his elder daughter, Lady Barbara Durand-Beaulieu, in the driver's seat of the little go cart she used to run small errands in the village. He said gloomily, "This offensive at Ypres is getting nowhere . . . for thousands of casualties. Bad as the Somme."

"How do you know, Roger?" the countess said, without looking up from the book she was reading, *Economic Housekeeping in Wartime*.

The earl said, "Heard it at the Carlton yesterday . . . someone had heard it from his wife, who'd heard it from the wife of a Cabinet Minister."

"They should remember what Kitchener said," the countess said, looking up now. "He didn't tell politicians anything about war operations because, he said, if he did they all immediately told their wives, except Asquith, who told other men's wives."

"Ha! Got rid of him, anyway . . . Lloyd George at least knows what he wants to do, and does it . . . damned swine . . . I worry about Cantley."

"We've been lucky so far," she said. "Since Arthur was killed none of our nephews have gone. And Cantley's not been even wounded."

"The title would go to that damned cowboy in Canada," the earl said with deepened gloom, "and he hasn't got enough money to keep up this place even if he doesn't want to stay with his cows or steers or whatever they have on ranches in Alberta. . . . Wish Cantley would get married. A Yankee heiress . . . or the daughter of one of our beer barons. They all have pots of money . . . I sometimes wonder if he, hrrmph, likes women."

"He liked Florinda Gorse," the countess said grimly.

"And now she has several million," the earl said disgustedly. "What the hell's England coming to? . . . Perhaps we could marry Helen off, but she'll never catch anyone if she stays at High Staining dressed in breeches and a cowman's coat and big boots, reeking of cow dung. My God, she must be working twenty hours a day now, with John in gaol."

"She was looking very pale under that dreadful suntan the last time we saw her," the countess said. "And she was obviously sad that Boy Rowland had had to go back to the trenches . . . She's in love with him."

"Boy? Good God! He doesn't have any money . . . well, they're not paupers and Richard's going to make a great deal out of that aircraft company, but John won't get much of it, if any . . ."

"Whatever Boy has will have to be enough, if they decide to get married," she said. "We can not stand in the way of her happiness just for the sake of keeping up the Park, or preserving our way of life . . . When *will* this terrible war end, Roger? How long, how long?"

"Until Hoggin has made another five million," the earl said viciously, "and Sir Launcelot is at Eton!"

The countess said nothing, returning to her book, trying to read the small print through blurred eyes.

*   *   *   *

Wilfred Bentley sat across the long table from Rachel in the big room at Hedlington Gaol where prisoners were permitted to receive visitors, at stated times, under the eyes of warders, standing by the room's two doors. Farther along the table, beyond two pickpockets and a burglar, John Rowland was being visited by his wife, Louise. They did not seem to be saying much, Rachel thought, just looking unhappily at each other.

Wilfred spoke in a low voice—"As you suggested, I visited Tim Vallance in the hospital—Lady Blackwell's. He has a bullet through the shoulder, not very serious, they say. He was telling us it's really bad out there now . . . they're losing thousands of men every day in futile attacks near Ypres. The men aren't all being killed by German bullets and shells, a lot of them are being drowned in the mud . . . drowned! Vallance spent four days and nights in a shellhole, wounded, and when our attacks finally moved past the shellhole and they found him, it took six men an hour to pull him out of the mud!"

Rachel said, "They can't keep all this secret. More and more men are going to be coming home to the hospitals and the convalescent depots. We must make them realize that now is the time to strike . . . refuse orders, refuse to go back."

Bentley said, "If only we could get enough men to do that, at the same time! Otherwise, the few who do will be court martialled and shot, and . . ."

Bert Gorse had come in, unnoticed by either of them, and was standing behind Bentley. He had heard what had been said, and cut in, "Might be best if we get hold of a lot of soldiers on leave or sick here, and fix a date which they can pass on to the blokes in France, so on that day everyone downs their rifles—except perhaps to shoot their officers and sergeants first. It's time to stop the talking. What we want is mutiny in the Army and the Navy."

Bentley said, "I don't know whether we all want that, Bert. Russell and others are doing something in what I think is the right direction. Look at this." From his pocket he drew out a pamphlet and held it up so that Rachel, behind the bars, could read it. The heading, in thick black type, was:

AN OFFICER FROM THE TRENCHES SPEAKS
by Captain S. Sassoon M.C.

[Rachel read on] I am making this statement as an act of wilful defiance of military authority, because I believe that the War is being deliberately prolonged by those who have the power to win it. I am a soldier, convinced that I am acting on behalf of soldiers. I believe that this War, upon which I entered as a war of defence, and liberation, has now become a war of aggression and conquest. I believe that the purposes for which I and my fellow soldiers entered upon this War should have been so clearly stated, as to have made it impossible to change them, and that, had this been done, the objects which actuate us would now be attainable by negotiation. I have seen and endured the sufferings of the troops, and I can no longer be a party to prolong these sufferings for ends which I believe to be evil and unjust. I am not protesting against the conduct of the War but against the political errors and insincerities for which the fighting men are being sacrificed. On behalf of those who are suffering now I make this protest against the deception which is being practised on them; also I believe that I may help to destroy the callous complacency with which the majority of those at home regard the continuance of agonies which they do not share, and which they do not have sufficient imagination to realise. [Signed] Siegfried Sassoon, Captain, Royal Welch Fusiliers.

"I know him," Bentley said, "or, at least, I've met him . . . in a theatre last December."

"If he's an officer, he'd be one of the blokes we ought to be shooting," Bert said.

Bentley said, "You—we—would be very foolish to shoot Sassoon, or men like him. They're on our side."

"Not on mine," Bert said. "On stopping the war, p'raps, but that's

not really what *we're* thinking of. We're thinking of *after* the war." He
finished abruptly, "I got work to do." He at once turned back—" 'Fore
I go, I meant to tell you—Dave Cowell's been sacked."

Rachel paled, "Sacked? From the school? What for?"

"Letting you use his classroom for one of your meetings, of
course."

"That's a disgrace!" Rachel said. "That's . . . persecution!"

"That's it," Bert said. "That's just what it is. Persecution. Now
p'raps you understand better why we say *everything's* got to be changed
in this country, not just the war ended." He went out, past the hard,
neutral scrutiny of the gaolers guarding the door.

Rachel said, "They really are swine."

Bentley said, "I don't know Cowell, but perhaps he's the sort of
man who could be useful to us."

"If we could find a job for him. He has a wife to support."

Then neither said anything for a while. After the long silence, both
staring at each other, Bentley said, "Did you get my last letter? It
should have arrived the day you were arrested. Bert should have
brought it to you."

She shook her head.

Bentley said, "I think he opened it . . . destroyed it . . ."

Rachel said, "I used to love him. Or thought I did. We were lovers,
for a time . . . I feel so sorry for him, sometimes, but . . ."

"You have no other place to go?"

She shook her head; adding, after a while, "I have to live in Hedlington. We don't have much of an organization here, but it's something, and I have to look after it . . . two, really, the Socialist Party
and the No-Conscription Fellowship. Dave Cowell's a Socialist, but he
didn't belong to the N.C.F.—just thought we ought to be given a
meeting place, in fairness."

He said slowly, "I have nothing to keep me in Winchester, except
five other members of the Fellowship, and they can find another
chairman. You're my teacher, my *guru* in socialism. Could I come to
Hedlington and help you?"

She said, "Yes . . . you could . . . it would be wonderful, Wilfred
. . . really wonderful."

She smiled at him then, through tears, and he smiled back at her.
There was much more to be said between them, of course, and they
both knew it; but the visitors' room in Hedlington Gaol was not the
place to say it.

*　　*　　*　　*

Christopher Cate and Isabel Kramer sat opposite each other in the 1st
class compartment, gazing into each other's eyes. Their luggage was

on the rack, neatly labelled as belonging to Mr and Mrs Cate, temporarily of the Mersey Hotel, Liverpool. The sole other occupant of the compartment was a tall, heavily built man, reading the *Times*. They had both recognized the 17th Earl of Derby, currently Secretary of State for War, obviously going home to mend political fences in his native Lancashire, but they did not impose on him. Ahead, the train engine was labouring heavily up the Camden Bank, a banker puffing from behind. Isabel's eyes shone behind the veil, a half-smile warmed the curve of her lips. She made a moue at Christopher, of a kiss. He glanced at Lord Derby, but the nobleman had not noticed.

The train plunged into a tunnel and the compartment was filled with an acrid cloud of coal smoke. The roar of the wheels on the rails and the clacking over the joints grew very loud. The lights came on overhead and Lord Derby pulled his window closed, muttering, "Hope you don't mind . . . just for a few minutes."

"Not a bit," Christopher said.

They sat in silence, hammered by sound until the train burst out into light. A station passed . . . steps going up to an overbridge, advertisements on each step—Iron Jelloids, Iron Jelloids, Veno's Lightning Cough Cure . . . Do you use Pear's soap? . . . A boon and a blessing to men, the Earl and the Owl and the Waverley Pen . . . a big ink blot, Stephen's Ink . . . The earl reopened the window. The engine ahead shrieked long and loud. The one behind had dropped off.

Christopher remembered something, felt in his pocket and handed Isabel a letter. "From Laurence. Came yesterday," he muttered. "Forgot to show it to you." Mustn't let on, of course, that they had met at Euston a quarter of an hour before the train time.

She produced a pair of spectacles from her handbag, raised her veil, and read. At length she handed it back, saying, "He's surviving, at least . . . better than I feared he would, to tell the truth."

"He hates it, though," Christopher said. "He's trying to hide it, but he hates it, really—the dirt, the smells . . . same as Boy, only more so. I wonder if he should have gone into the Navy, really. We did talk about it once, long ago."

"Perhaps," she said, "but . . . perhaps he should have stayed at home. Look what was in *my* mail this morning." She held out a pamphlet. Christopher read the heading: AN OFFICER FROM THE TRENCHES SPEAKS, by Captain S. Sassoon, M.C. He read on; at the end, he handed the pamphlet back to Isabel, saying, "I feel sorry for him, but I don't think he's right."

Lord Derby lowered his newspaper and said, "I could not help overhearing your conversation, sir, madam . . . and seeing the heading of that pamphlet, reflected in my glasses . . . You have a son in the trenches?"

"Yes, Lord Derby."

The earl took the recognition as no more than his right, which it was. There were precious few people in Britain who had not seen a hundred press photographs of that burly well-paunched figure with the face and rolled neck of a jovial butcher, a bowler hat a size too small for him perched on his head. The bowler was in the rack above his head now.

"This Sassoon has an excellent record . . . great gallantry. He has a Military Cross, as you see . . . was put in for a Victoria Cross . . . but he's been got hold of by the No-Conscription Fellowship people. That letter was polished up by Bertrand Russell."

"The philosopher?" Isabel asked.

"Yes, madam," Derby growled, "and traitor, if you ask me. They wanted to use Sassoon for their own purposes, and tried to do so. But fortunately another young officer of the Royal Welch Fusiliers, Robert Graves, intervened through highly placed friends, and we were able to have Sassoon sent to a convalescent home rather than have to court martial him."

"Graves?" Christopher said. "There was a boy called Graves at Charterhouse when my son first went there. I wonder if this is the same one."

"I couldn't say," the earl said. "Just thought I'd let you know that Sassoon is being used by people who want us to lose the war."

Cate said, "I see. But he does raise a point. What *are* our war aims? Is it possible that we could now achieve what we went to war for, by negotiation?"

The earl said heavily, "Not a chance, sir. After so much blood's been spilled, neither side's going to give up without getting revenge."

"Achieving *katharsis*," Cate murmured.

"Eh? No, the decision will be achieved on the Western Front. Has to be." With a final nod the earl raised his *Times* and behind its shelter resumed reading war propaganda, much of which he had himself helped to produce. Cate suppressed his smile: Wellington, and the Grenadiers hardly counted as a classical education; one had to make allowances.

He sat back, looking at Isabel with love and longing. The train hurried through Bushey, spray dashing past the windows as the Claughton picked up water from the troughs. Speed remained steady at 45 m.p.h. on the excellent London & North Western roadbed, climbing easily up the southern slopes of the Chilterns. Why should I be picked on, of all the men in the world, Cate thought, to love a woman and not be allowed to share my life publicly with her? Why do we have to meet in railway stations, and sleep in strange hotel rooms, instead of in my great bed in the Manor house of my village? Why can we not marry, at least, even if it is too late to raise more children from this woman's womb? The train hurried past King's Langley . . . Berkhamstead . . . still climbing, labouring, rocking, pounding . . . the vale spread away to his left, the ribbon of the Grand Junction Canal close, white lock gates, long narrow barges with brightly painted metal flower pots, a canal-side pub . . . swans on the water, last spring's cygnets beginning to get their adult white plumage . . . Why was his son in France, killing people he'd never met or, usually, even seen? The train passed over Tring summit and at once the beat of the Claughton's exhaust quickened, the wheels clacked faster over the joints, and the wind rushed faster past Lord Derby's open window, riffling the newspaper he held steady in his massive, imperially pale hands.

*　　*　　*　　*

The leave ship was crowded, the men on the decks below a seething mass, not much movement, just the gleam of the steel helmets strapped to their packs, the rifles slung on their shoulders, the smoke curling up from hundreds of cigarettes and pipes. The big overhead lights on the dockside were dark for fear of German air attack, the water below shining only from the starlight and the iridescence of oil on its surface. Naomi watched, leaning over the rail, her hat pulled firmly down on her head. She was in the uniform of the First Aid Nursing Yeomanry, on her way at last to join Number 12 Convoy, the new English Convoy, serving with the British Army east of Amiens, where she was to report to the Town Major for detailed orders and onward transport. At last she felt clean and free, the sea wind blowing stray strands of her hair, tugging at the hat with the big F.A.N.Y. badge. Rodney Venable had written to her half a dozen times from France—he didn't say how he had come to be sent out there, after so long in the War Office—but he did say it had been a privilege to know her and sincerely hoped they could renew their friendship soon. He had given her confidence, and taught her that there really was an attainable relationship between men and women, that did not depend on subservience or domination. But. . . . it was over. France lay ahead, and war, and after that . . . who knew?

A soldier near her on the rail said, "Good evening, Miss Naomi."

She peered and cried out, "Fletcher Gorse!"

His teeth shone momentarily, "Fletcher Whitman, miss. Private, 1st Battalion the Weald Light Infantry."

"Did you have a good time on leave?" she asked; and remembered that her mother had written in one of her letters that Betty Merritt was rumoured to have been seen in Hedlington with Fletcher when he was a recruit at the Depot. Well, good luck to them, if they could find anything to talk about together, when the kissing was over.

Fletcher said, "Sorry to hear about Mr John."

"Oh, he'd feel guilty if he wasn't in gaol, the way he feels about the war . . . and I've been praying every night that it won't be over before I get out there! But it must be dreadful for you, having to go back to—what you are going back to. I do admire you all so much."

Fletcher said, "It's horrible, miss, but they couldn't stop me going back, however hard they tried. Not if Field Marshal Haig himself said, Fletcher, don't come back. I've got to be there, to see and feel it, so's I can write the poetry."

"Oh, yes," she said. "You are a poet, aren't you?"

Fletcher said, "Yes, miss. *I will write the evangel-poem of comrades and of love.*"

The ship's siren boomed, her body shuddering to its tremendous throb, the water began to churn under the stern, and the dock, the shore, the land, England, home, receded, the gap of water widening, shining, gleaming dark and deep.

*   *   *   *

Daily Telegraph, Thursday, August 30, 1917

AMERICA'S REPLY
TO THE
POPE'S NOTE
WHY WAR MUST GO ON

The first of the belligerent nations to send a formal reply to the Pope's Note on peace is the United States. The answer, by direction of President Wilson, is made by the Secretary of State, Mr Lansing, and we are officially informed that its text is as follows:

Every heart that has not been blinded and hardened by this terrible war must be touched by this moving appeal of His Holiness the Pope, must feel the dignity and force of the humane and generous motives which prompted it, and must fervently wish that we might take the path of peace he so persuasively points out. But it would be folly to take it if it does not in fact lead to the goal he proposes . . .

His Holiness in substance proposes that we return to the status quo ante bellum, and that then there can be a general

condonation, disarmament, and a concert of nations based upon the acceptance of the principle of arbitration; and that the territorial claims of France and Italy, the perplexing problems of the Balkan States, and the restitution of Poland, be left to such conciliatory adjustments as may be possible in the new temper of peace . . .

It is manifest that no part of this programme can be successfully carried out unless the restitution of the status quo ante furnished a firm and satisfactory basis for it . . . The test, therefore, of every plan is this: Is it based upon the faith of all the peoples involved, or merely upon the word of an ambitious and intriguing government on the one hand, and of a group of free peoples on the other? This is a test which goes to the roots of the matter, and it is the test which must be applied . . .

Benedict XV was a good man, Cate thought, and doing no more than his spiritual duty in trying to bring about an end to the war. But Wilson and Lansing were right, too: Germany could not be trusted. Better to say—the American Note had made the distinction clear—the present rulers of Germany could not be trusted. So, the war would go on; and the attacks round Ypres, in the rain and the mud. The guns were firing day and night over there, but they could barely be heard these days, because of the dense atmosphere, the low clouds, the rain. The air was as heavy, as thick, as impassable, as the mud which seemed to have become the dominating factor of the offensive. He looked at the open letter beside his plate—*Dear Father Christopher*—he smiled; that was what Johnny had decided to call him, as he said he didn't like any of the other possibilities. It made him sound like a Roman Catholic priest, but that couldn't be helped . . . the salutation had a pleasant ring to it:

This is my last day with the 16th Infantry, and I am sorry to be leaving them, while keenly looking forward to becoming an officer of the Field Artillery. The colonel (of the 16th) was not pleased when I told him I would be applying for the FA, but he calmed down when he realized that I would be very unlikely to be posted back to this regiment, in any case, even if I stayed in the infantry. Also, that the FA is expanding even faster than the infantry, and desperately needs officers.

We have been back two weeks from our spell with the British, and have been able to pass on everything we learned, both as to what to do and what not to do. My Navajo friend Chee Shush Benally has applied to return Stateside with me as my striker (soldier servant). The major blew his top and said no, but Chee says he will come to my battery, wherever it is, when I get back to France, which should be before Christmas. And he will, believe me, whatever the U.S. Army thinks!

Unless I make a fool of myself at my interview with the F.A. colonel tomorrow it is certain that I shall be sent to Fort Sill, in Oklahoma, to be turned from a footslogging corporal to a red-legged shavetail; so my next letter to you will probably be from there. Stella writes that she is well, and the baby is not giving her any trouble. It must be very tiring for her, but I know you are all looking after her. Still, I wish I could be there when our baby is born.

Cate folded the letter and put it in his pocket. He saw Stella about twice a week, and wrote regularly to Johnny about her. Dr Kimball had examined her only two days ago, and said that the baby was in a good position and the birth should be normal in every way. Yet . . . yet . . . Stella was not her old self. The beauty was there, but not the old sense of life. He'd better ride over this morning, tell her what Johnny had said—she might have had a letter from him herself, of course—and generally cheer her up. Johnny wouldn't be back to France until the end of the year, he'd said. And there probably wouldn't be any major American action until the spring. That was six or seven months away . . . not much, in a lifetime of marriage; but a great deal, in this war.

Near Nollehoek, Belgium: Thursday, September 20, 1917

30 The blizzard of shells howled overhead without cease. Shells exploded in continuous thunder along the German front line trenches and barbed wire, two hundred yards ahead and thirty feet higher up the slope from the *beke*. The men of the Weald Light Infantry waited in the British trenches, bowed, jammed against one another like sardines, the bayonet points stabbing the thick air above them. Rain splashed down steadily, trickling off the rims of the steel helmets, soaking and weighting the rough serge of the uniforms, glistening on the backs of the hands, on the few upturned faces. They stood in a foot of mud, a brown glue, two inches of water now running on top of it, flowing along the trench in a turgid slow stream, carrying with it empty Woodbine packets, message forms, lost letters from home, turds swept out of the latrine bays or overturned buckets, bandages—anything that would float. Deep in the mud, out of sight, but known as soon as a man moved, were rifles, bayonets, mess tins, clips of ammunition, shell splinters, ammunition boxes, unexploded grenades and shells, heads, drowned rats, hands, entrails—a universal foul smelling half-solid slime.

The first light of day had come half an hour ago, revealing the sodden waste of No Man's Land, the Nollehoek ridge, low scurrying clouds, haggard faces, dark rimmed eyes, blinking, holding tight to sanity, sometimes not succeeding. Quentin Rowland looked at his watch. Five minutes to zero hour. "We'll get the bottom of the ridge this time," he said to his adjutant, standing beside him, "and Nollehoek next time."

Archie Campbell said, "Yes, sir," but Quentin frowned. Campbell had not sounded confident. How could the men be expected to attack with fire and fury if their officers didn't believe that what they were going to do had much chance of success?

Archie noticed his colonel's expression in the flat, dead light, and added, "We'll take our objectives, I'm sure, sir . . . but then they'll counter-attack. They always have."

"Yes," Quentin said, "and that's why we're going in with only one company up, and three in reserve, just to have a bigger force in hand when the Boches do counter-attack." He looked at his watch again, then glanced down the bay, where his nephew Captain Boy Rowland was looking at his. Boy's C Company would lead the attack. Boy drew his whistle from his breast pocket as his uncle watched, then, waiting ten seconds till the hands showed the precise hour, he blew the whistle. The men scrambled up the short ladders that had been placed there in the night for the purpose, and, slipping and sliding in the mud, snaked through the gaps in the British barbed wire, then, spreading out to right and left, began to advance, rifles at the high port.

Quentin followed to the top of a ladder, put up his binoculars and watched, exposed to the waist. Fountains of mud and earth began to rise all round him, obscuring and blurring his view, as the German artillery opened defensive fire on the British trench and No Man's Land. The clatter of machine guns became a continuous tearing roar. The men out there were barely thirty yards away, though they had been in the open for a minute or more. At each agonized step every man's leg sank into the mud almost to the knee, burying the puttee, plastering the trousers with mud. Painfully they dragged that leg out . . . put down the next. There must have been the sounds of sucking, of boots being torn off by the grip of the mud, but Quentin could hear nothing over the thunder of the artillery and the vast ripping-canvas crackle of the machine guns. On . . . men falling . . . he could clearly see Boy, in the centre of the sixty men who now comprised C Company, a few paces in front of them . . . four more minutes to go, at least . . . men down in the mud, heaving humps in the rain, then lying still. A cry burst through his gritted teeth, "Go on, Wealds . . . on . . . !" More men down, an officer turning in a slow, grotesque pirouette of death, falling at last sideways and lying twisted, without motion—"On . . . On!"

"Are they there yet, sir?" Campbell shouted up.

"Nearly," he called back. "Where's Kellaway?"

"Here, sir."

"Are you ready?"

"Yes, sir."

Quentin had never taken his eyes off the thin, painful progress of C Company. They had passed through the German wire where gaps had been torn in it by British artillery fire . . . they were disappearing into the earth now, in threes and fours . . . were they being shot down? He stared tensely through the eyepieces. No, they were jumping down into the German trench!

"They're in!" he shouted. "C's in . . . All right, Kellaway, go!" He hurried up the last rungs of the ladder onto the mud above. Whistles shrilled in the trench. Campbell struggled up to join him, then the R.S.M., two batmen, two runners . . . then Kellaway, his C.S.M., and the men of B, spreading out as C had; D Company was snaking up the communication trench to follow B. Quentin started walking forward, and at once fell on his face, his legs held by the mud. He struggled up, his tunic filthy and his face splashed with mud, and took another step . . . he was deep in the mud . . . another . . . the air chattered and moaned, and shouted and tugged at his flesh, at his soaked, mud-heavy uniform . . . one step at a time, teeth grated, he forced on.

*   *   *   *

Captain Charles Kellaway struggled painfully along the German trench, followed by his batman-runner, Private Codd. It was extraordinarily empty, except for the thinly spaced men of his B Company, standing on the makeshift firestep they had hacked out of the mud of what had been the backside of the trench until twenty minutes ago. There were some dead Germans, but few—a captain, hands clasped across his stomach, entrails bulging out, in one of the bays behind . . . two privates, both probably blasted by the same British six-inch howitzer shell . . . almost nothing in the dugouts as loot—no sausages, bread, wine, greatcoats—just a few worn and filthy blankets, two or three candles. A single jackboot was stuck in the mud in front of him: the boot contained a foot and leg, to the knee. Kellaway thought grimly, at least the Boches share the mud with us, even though they are almost above the range of the *beke's* flooding.

A shot rang out close to his head and he ducked instinctively, then slowly stood upright again. That shot had been going out, and in any case the trench was nearly seven feet deep, so he was well under cover. He looked up, saw the soles of a soldier and, peering on tiptoe, slowly made out the rest of him, lying almost invisible in the mud, covered in mud from head to foot, including his face, no helmet—only his hands clean and they too showing brown because he was wearing his khaki woolen mittens, the trigger finger ungloved. A German body lay sprawled in front of the man, who now fired again, round the dead

485

German's head. It was Private Fletcher Whitman, at work, sniping, using the dead German's body as cover. He sensed Kellaway's presence and, without moving, called back, "Got two, sir . . . but please don't stay there near me."

"Good work," Kellaway said, hastily moving on. Amazing man, Whitman, or, as Boy had told him he really was, Gorse. The men liked him, but were a little afraid of him, too, because he didn't act or move as they did. It was like having a leopard in your midst. He acted as though he wouldn't bite, or turn into a werewolf, but you couldn't be sure . . . for he was, after all, palpably a leopard, that had temporarily taken man's shape.

Turning the angle of the next traverse he stumbled into Boy Rowland, accompanied by his C.S.M. "Is this your boundary, Boy?" Kellaway asked.

Boy nodded, "This is my right. There's nothing on my left—not even Germans . . . I've never imagined anything like this . . . the mud . . . Christ, I wish we had some rum, whisky, anything, to give the men."

"Nothing's even reached Corps," Kellaway said. "The C.O. told me about an hour before zero that Corps had sent a signal—nothing, but we'll get the first lot that comes up, they promise."

Boy laughed harshly. Kellaway saw that he was shaking, as though from a light fever, and his eyes were bolting from his head—"Had bad casualties?" he asked.

"Very few, so far," Boy said. "I don't understand it."

"The Boche evacuated his front line," Kellaway said. "Well, we've got six of the brigade machine guns up. We're ready."

"Where's the C.O.?"

"He's set up battalion headquarters in the middle of my company area . . . D's beyond . . . A's still back in our old front line, to support us and cover our flanks."

Boy nodded again, and Kellaway turned back. Almost at once the tone of the day again altered. Every German weapon within its range seemed to open up at the same moment. The air was filled with chattering, battering, whining, the rolling thunder of bursting shells, mortar bombs screaming down from clouds in the rain. Again the mud geysered up and again the liquid earth rose, hovered, and splashed down. The walls of the trench began to give way, so that Kellaway and Codd scrambled on over mounds of mud, boots and arms sticking out, gesticulating, clutching, jerking. From the old British lines machine guns opened fire, the streams of bullets, every fifth one tracer, streaking past the left and right flanks of the Wealds' position. The rest of the brigade attack must have failed to reach the German lines, so here they were, three companies of the Wealds, both flanks exposed, left in air.

Whitman was firing steadily now, and as Kellaway passed called back, "They're moving up in their old second line trench, sir . . . probably going to attack us and C."

Kellaway stumbled and slid on; but ten yards farther, a German heavy hit the back wall of the trench fair and square, the trench collapsed, tons of earth rose, fell, splashing. The trench was blocked . . . another shell, the same, twenty yards up. And the Germans were on them.

Kellaway clambered up into the open and started firing his revolver, aiming carefully at the Germans struggling toward him through the mud from their second line trenches. The German artillery fire had lifted. Two British Vickers machine guns and a score of Lewis guns had good targets at close range. Most of the soldiers were out in the open, as long sections of the firestep had collapsed. Kellaway dropped beside one of his platoon commanders, young Cate, and shouted, "Are you all right?"

Laurence looked round at him with a puzzled expression. "Yes, sir . . . What's happening?"

"The Germans, there, attacking, man!"

The mud-coated figure lying beside Cate shouted, "I'll look after him, sir . . . shell shock!" He fired, and again, and again.

"Good man, Fagioletti," Kellaway shouted.

Cate didn't know where he was, Kellaway thought . . . but he had no time to worry about that now. Cate had a competent platoon sergeant and Fagioletti was one of the best corporals in the battalion in a tight corner.

The German attack was wavering, men falling, a few turning back, others dropping out of sight into shell holes . . . They'll drown in those, Kellaway thought grimly.

He slid back down into the trench and continued the way he'd been going, toward his right flank. Who had the platoon there? . . . Fred Stratton. He found him on the firestep, leaning his elbows on the mud, only his eyes and the bowl of his helmet visible above ground level, looking toward the Germans. Beside him two soldiers were working on a jammed Lewis gun. "How is it, Stratton?" Kellaway asked.

"All right," Stratton said, without turning. "The Huns are moving round Boy's left, I think . . . They'll be coming along the trench soon . . ."

The German shelling began again, heavies and field guns and mortars all firing at the captured trench. Kellaway shouted, "They won't move in till this stops . . . Have some men ready to help me if I have to back up C."

"We may be busy ourselves," Stratton said. "What a balls up this whole bloody show has been. We never had a hope."

"You'd best keep your opinions to yourself," Kellaway said. Stratton was right, of course. The men would be on the verge of mutiny if it weren't for the C.O. They were doing this for him . . . because he had faith in them, shared all their dangers, and more. They didn't want to disappoint him. And he could see, could understand . . . nothing!

The shelling continued, hour after hour. Kellaway passed slowly back and forth along his company's sector of trench. Here half a platoon sat in the gloom of a quaking concrete dugout, its mouth facing the wrong way, while two men took half-hour spells on sentry, watching for the Germans to renew their counter-attack. They sat silent in the mud, their backs to the dripping wall, their rifles held between their knees, their faces taut, the thunder and lightning continuous . . . Suddenly a man screamed, hurled his rifle across the dugout and began tearing off his clothes. Without a word a corporal and two privates seized him and held him down, while Kellaway watched, standing in the entrance of the dugout. When the man was quiet he said, "Thank you," and went out and on, through the mud.

In another place he found five men cowering behind the remains of a brick wall, that had been built into the trench by the Germans— the ruins of a small barn or shed, perhaps. The men were shivering and moaning, as though one had caught a fever and the others contracted it from him. They were huddled together, bodies jammed into one another's, their rifles lying in the mud beside them, tears streaming down their cheeks. Kellaway went back a few yards and found the platoon commander. It was Cate. He said, "Mr Cate, some of your men are in the last stages of panic up there. Go and shake them out of it. Take your sergeant."

"He's dead, sir," Cate said. His eyes still had a vacant, wandering look—"I killed a German."

"I hope you killed many Germans," Kellaway said.

"There was a flock of swifts, flying over the German lines," Cate said. "It's a little late for them still to be as far north as this."

Kellaway stared at the young man, thinking—he's not here, he's escaped to another world, where only birds exist, not this fury of madness. He wondered how he should treat him, and decided he must jerk him back to reality before he could do any damage to his platoon. He seized Cate by the shoulder and shook him violently, "You're in a battle," he yelled in his ear. "You're in command of a platoon of my company. Command it!"

488

From beside him Corporal Fagioletti cut in, "He was all right after you left last time, sir . . . killed a lot of Germans with a dead bloke's rifle . . . walked up and down, telling the blokes it was all right . . . brave as a lion . . . Then the sergeant was blown to bits, all over him."

Now, looking more closely, Kellaway saw blood and mucus and brains mixed with the mud on Cate's uniform. But the young man was recovering. His eyes were focussed and he was trembling; as would any man in his right mind, in these hellish circumstances. Kellaway said, "Do you know where you are, Mr Cate?"

"Yes, sir . . . we'll stop them, if they come."

"Good man . . . Fagioletti, you're platoon sergeant from now on . . . acting, of course. Only the C.O. can give you the real promotion."

"Thank you, sir. Don't you worry about the platoon, sir . . . Father Caffin was by an hour ago. Made everyone feel good, he did."

Kellaway nodded, and Fagioletti said, "Wish we could get some rum or whisky, sir."

"So do we all, but there isn't any."

Kellaway moved on along the trench. As soon as he was out of sight round the traverse Laurence Cate said, "We must see those men." He struggled up the trench, found the piece of broken wall, and the still cowering, still weeping men.

"Get up," he said gently.

"Can't, sir . . . can't . . ." one moaned.

Laurence stared unhappily at them. The shelling would never end. He could hardly make himself think, for the sound was inside his head, shaking his brains. The swifts had gone, there were no birds singing anywhere.

Fagioletti jumped up onto the low step where the men were crouched, and leaned over them with his rifle drawn back. "Up, you bastards," he cried fiercely. "Up!" He jabbed an inch of bayonet into one of the men's buttocks. The man yelled in pain, and stopped moaning. Fagioletti jabbed the others in the buttock, one after the other. They tumbled down into the trench proper. He jumped after them, and yelled, "Now, up on the firestep . . . you, there! . . . you, there! . . . Look at the Germans, not me!" He fired a shot just over the nearest man's head.

He turned to Cate, "They'll be all right, sir."

Cate leaned against the back wall of the trench, wiping mud off his face with a handkerchief. "Thank you, Sergeant," he said. A soldier slipped backward down into the trench and Cate saw that it was Fletcher, quite recognizable behind the muddied face.

"Hullo, Fletcher," he cried. "What are you doing here?"

Fletcher glanced at Fagioletti and said, "I'm a battalion sniper, sir.

Private Whitman." Poor Mr Laurence had forgotten, though he'd seen Fletcher only a day or two after he'd arrived from the Depot, and knew he was being called Whitman.

Cate said, "Did you get any Germans today?"

"Six by sniping and seven when they attacked, sir . . . and three more wounded, but I don't count them, 'cos they was holding up their hands, or swinging a pick up and down very slowly, from down in the trench."

"What do you mean?"

Fagioletti cut in, "Working a Blighty, sir . . . If they show an arm or a hand, they 'ope one of our snipers'll put a bullet in it—and that'll be a Blighty for them."

Laurence said wonderingly, "Do any of our men do that?"

"Not in the Wealds, sir," Fagioletti said virtuously, thinking of half a dozen who had, since he'd come out. Four finally got their Blighties from kind Jerry; the other two had bad luck—showed too much, Jerry sniper wasn't so sharp, bullet through the head; and of himself, who'd spent his first month out here trying that game, and failed.

Fletcher produced a tin of bully beef from his haversack, opened it, and offered it to Laurence Cate and Fagioletti. Both refused, and Fletcher began to eat, with an Army biscuit and his fingers.

Cate said, "What do you hear from home, Sergeant?"

"My wife's found a little house in Soho, sir—that's where I want to live—you can get good Italian food in the grocery shops there, and I still like that. And there's lots of restaurants I could get a job in, when this is over, if I can't get back to the Savoy . . . or I could open a restaurant myself . . . But she has had trouble with the boarders. She's had two, already, and had to throw them both out."

"What for?"

Fagioletti looked at Fletcher. Mr Cate was barely nineteen and very innocent. The men didn't like to swear in front of him for fear of polluting his ears. He said at last, "They both turned out to be loose women, sir . . . er, prossies. There's a lot of those in Soho."

Cate said, "Give me the address, for when I get home on leave . . . I'd like to tell her myself how much you've done for me, since I took over the platoon."

Fagioletti flushed with pleasure, and said, "46 Dean Street, sir . . . here, I'll write it down . . ."

The shelling continued. The hands of the watches ground slowly on through the afternoon, and the twilight, to the night.

*   *   *   *

Lieutenant Archie Campbell leaned against the wall of the trench in the darkness, the sky lit by flares and the orange bursts of shells. He was so tired he could not keep his eyelids open. His body ached and sagged. It was one o'clock in the morning. The Germans had counter-attacked once more, at dusk, trying to retake the positions they had evacuated. Their shelling had been continuous until the actual moment when their infantry assaulted; and then it had lifted only from the captured trench system itself; the curtain of shells and bombs had never ceased to fall on all flanks of the Wealds, isolating them from contact with any world or beings except themselves, and their attackers. Madness, hell, demoniac lunacy, Archie thought through the dark fog of fatigue. What he had seen during the hours of daylight was burned into his brain, through his eyes. Surely his eyeballs would be scarred for the rest of their existence in his body?

The attack was beaten off, but night brought no rest, or peace. Still there was the underlying sense of fury: the war was not impersonal or inanimate—it had a being and a purpose of its own . . . The three companies of Wealds, and the Germans, surrounding them on three sides, were in the same pit, separated from homes, headquarters, supplies, superiors, supports, plans, maps, intentions, just struggling in the mud, and in it, sinking.

The C.O. said, "I'd better go round again, Campbell . . . They may try a night attack."

His pipe was glowing faintly in the dark. There were no moon or stars, no sense of sky, only the brooding shifting darkness, and the rain.

The C.O. continued—"Must go and see B . . . Can't have men pretending to be shell shocked. They need bucking up, that's all."

"Yes, sir."

"Wish we had a rum ration. That would cheer them up . . . me, too, to tell the truth."

"Yes, sir." Archie didn't want to stay here, under this never-ending shelling, alone, with the R.S.M. and the remaining runners. He said, "Shall I come with you, sir?"

The voice from the darkness said, "No. Someone has to be at headquarters at all times. How often have I told you that?"

"Yes, sir."

"I'll come with you, colonel. 'Tis like the bottom of a grave here."

Quentin seemed to be about to say something, but didn't. Campbell watched his bulky figure disappear, followed by the slender Father Caffin and the C.O.'s batman, slow-moving humps in the night, going away along the trench.

Hells . . . shells . . . hells . . . When they got out he must get a few days' leave to paint this, before it faded . . . It must fade, or he'd go mad. No one could live with these memories as brilliant as they were now . . . if he did get out . . . if any of them got out . . . It was

491

a queer feeling to know Fiona might understand what they were going through, for she'd seen his paintings, of course. The C.O. would ask for one or two and send them home . . . He should ask him whether there had ever been any real marriage between them, in terms of personal affection and understanding. But they did not discuss her; only, the C.O. said, when he got a letter from home, usually from his father or one of his brothers—"Fiona is well." The gruff words, thrown away, were somehow very moving, coming from him . . . an acknowledgment that he had been her lover, and had understood her better than himself, her husband, had. But that was not a discussion . . . and there had been nothing more. After the war, they *must* spend a long time together, as man and man. If he could get the C.O. drunk, he might be able to make him see what kind of a woman Fiona was . . . how to treat her . . . what to say to her, when . . . He might get his head bitten off, but it would be worth it. He must try. He dozed off.

He awoke to find someone shaking him. It was Sergeant Hawkins, of A Company, with a private he did not know.

"Runner from Brigade, sir. He fell into our trenches an hour ago. He has a message for the C.O. Captain Weeks told me to bring him up here."

"Why have you been so long?" Archie asked.

"Mud, sir . . . We fell into a shell hole in No Man's Land, what was. Took us half an hour to get out . . . near drowned, we did."

By the unsteady light Archie could see that both men were slimy with mud from neck to knee—below that they were standing in the mud, as was he himself. He took out his torch, switched it on and, crouching, read the message:

"To 1 WLI . . . Withdraw to old position front line trench AAA artillery will fire box barrage round your present positions from 3.00 am AAA commence withdrawal at 3.30 am."

"What's this? What's this?" It was the C.O., stooping over him, Father Caffin behind.

"Message from Brigade, sir." He handed it up, keeping the light on it. Colonel Rowland read, then muttered, "We can hold out here. They ought to reinforce us instead of . . . Damn it, it's just like Feuchy, and what an opportunity they threw away then." He stopped short, realizing that he was criticizing his superiors in front of his juniors.

He turned to Sergeant Hawkins—"A Company in good order?"

"Yes, sir. They're back in the front line—the old one, still."

"The shelling wasn't too bad when you were crossing No Man's Land?"

"It wasn't like a walk in the Park, sir, if you know what I mean."

Quentin stood thinking, the light switched off. He said, "It's half past one now. Half an hour's box barrage will warn the Germans exactly what we are going to do . . . and give them half an hour to lay on a barrage that will wipe us out, when we move. It'll take fifteen minutes to get back to our old trenches . . . Could you take a message back, runner?"

"Yes, sir . . . Brigade Headquarters is still at Jack Johnson Farm, sir."

"That's another two miles, nearly," Quentin muttered. "There isn't time to ask the general to change our orders . . . Switch that light on again, Campbell. Give me a message pad."

He wrote on his knee, and then again; and gave the two messages to the Brigade runner. "Take this one to our A Company . . . And this one to the Brigadier General. You go with him all the way, sergeant. Off you go!"

When the men had climbed up and out of the trench and vanished in the noisy darkness, Quentin said, "We'll start our withdrawal at two-thirty. I've warned A Company to look out for us from then on."

"No artillery cover, sir?"

"No. Nothing. Just all three companies here get up and go back, at the same time . . . leave the trenches at two-thirty ack emma, exactly. Synchronize watches. It's . . . one fifty-four . . . now! Send the R.S.M. to C, you go to D, I'll warn B."

"Very good, sir."

*   *   *   *

Two days later:

As the shadow fell across the opening of the dugout Quentin looked up from the scraps of paper in his hands. They were message forms, spotted with mud and rain, some torn, all covered with names scrawled in pencil—the names of the killed and wounded in each company, submitted by company commanders this second day after the return from the German trenches. He could not see clearly, for his eyes were blurred, but could distinguish the red and black armband and the red gorget patches of a staff officer.

"A staff officer from Corps," he snapped. "We don't see much of your sort down here."

His adjutant, standing beside the visitor in the dugout entrance, said, "Colonel Venable, sir."

Quentin stood up, saluting. Now he saw that it was indeed a full colonel. He hadn't seen anyone that exalted since the offensive began

493

on July 31 . . . except, twice, his brigadier general and, once, the divisional commander; no one at all from Corps . . . Before the battle they used to be condescended upon by the occasional young lieutenant or captain, puffed up with self-importance by the gorget patches and red banded hat: since July 31—nothing.

The colonel was tall and suave, and pretended not to have heard Quentin's ill-natured greeting. He put out his hand, "I'm G.S.O. 1(I) at Corps. We'd like to talk to you about German morale and methods. We get reports, of course, but it's better to be able to ask questions, follow up leads. I have the division and brigade commanders' permission to take you back to Corps HQ now, to talk to us all afternoon, and spend the night with us—we can find you a comfortable bed—and send you back tomorrow about this time."

Quentin hesitated. He wanted to spend the day visiting his companies, seeing that the men had a good meal, go to Brigade Headquarters and once more press the general to get some rum or whisky, somewhere, somehow. The men deserved it . . . and damn it, they needed it.

Venable said gently, "I know you have many things to do, but we really do need your help . . . and it is an order, from the corps commander." He laughed, to soften the hint of steel behind the velvet glove.

"Very well, sir," Quentin said. "If I can have a few minutes to arrange things here." He turned to Campbell and began giving orders, while the colonel walked out of the dugout and up the steps and waited for him in the light September drizzle.

Fifteen minutes later Quentin joined him, and they started toward the rear, following the usual sequence that had obtained since the end of 1914 and the death of the mobile war—down communication trenches to the support line—back another half mile under ground level, then out, among battered houses and many shell holes. The Germans knew well where the trench system ended and regularly plastered all the exit points with long-range artillery, usually in the middle of the night, when ration parties and replacements would be coming up and wounded moving back. There was no shelling now, and a quarter of a mile beyond the end of the trench system they found Venable's staff car and chauffeur, climbed in, and started off down the wrecked pavé. After twenty minutes they came to a cluster of big khaki marquees in a muddy field beside the muddy road. A Red Cross flag flew over the biggest tent and Red Crosses were also painted on the canvas roofs. A convoy of a dozen motor ambulances were arriving from the west—the rear—as they walked up.

"Is that the Casualty Clearing Station?" Quentin asked.

Venable said, "One of them. This is 46 C.C.S."

"I'd like to go in for a while, sir . . . We had a lot of men wounded in the last push."

Venable hesitated, then said, "Of course. I'll come with you."

Quentin waited a moment, bracing himself. He had been a patient in a C.C.S. himself, and visited them as often as he could, when the battalion was not in the front line. But every visit was an ordeal, far worse than the slaughter of the trenches. That he could endure—the men shot, wounded, dying, torn to pieces, spattered over him; but he was there, and there were the Germans, and all his being was braced to endure. Perhaps it was this that had lost him Fiona, he thought—that he could see such suffering and not weep, or lose his reason. But when it was over, when he had to read the lists of their names . . . worst of all, when he saw them lying in the narrow beds, or sometimes, after a heavy engagement, on the bare ground. Farther back there were nurses, some softness, the melody of women's voices, the touch of their hands . . . not here, only the Royal Army Medical Corps doctors and soldier attendants. The R.A.M.C.—Rob All My Comrades, the men called them; for a soldier who went in with a silver cigarette case or a gold coin, even five francs in his pocket, or a signet ring on his finger, was unlikely to have them when he left—either back toward the front, or on to the rear, to the Base hospitals, the Hospital barges, ships, and trains, and Home . . . or to the cemetery always created next to any C.C.S. at the same time as the tents were set up.

He walked into the nearest of the big marquees and slowly down the middle between the rows of beds. The ground underfoot was wet earth, partly covered with duckboards. The air reeked of ether. "Any Wealds here?" he asked, as he went. His voice was lost in the low moaning of the tent, the flapping of the canvas walls and ceiling, and everywhere the fast shallow breathing, the rattling in men's throats, the moans as they moved, the sound of weeping, stifled sobs, groans . . . a sudden cry, cut off as the soldier in the bed beside him clenched his teeth.

"Any Wealds . . . ? Wealds . . ."

"Here, sir." He stopped, beside a bed where a man lay under bed clothes, all his head except his mouth hidden by bandages, and there the lips swollen and the teeth gone.

"Private Shaddle, sir. D Company . . . it's the C.O., isn't it?"

"Yes, Shaddle. How do you feel?"

"Oh, could be worse, sir."

"Well done. You'll be back in Blighty in no time . . . Wealds? . . . You're Smith, 96, C Company, aren't you?"

"Yes, sir." The man had a greenish tinge, his voice was weak, bandages crossed his chest, and froth bubbled on his lips. Lung wound, Quentin thought. He said, "Well done . . . You'll be back in Blighty in no time . . . Wickilam, where were you hit?"

"Foot, sir. Can't walk . . . 'ave to transfer to the Navy . . . or get a job selling tickets at one of them cinemas."

"Not too bad, sir . . . Never thought I'd like Hoggin's Plum & Apple, but the first rations we had when we got here was that . . . best meal I ever had."

Heavy breathing . . . a face staring up at the high canvas . . . "Aren't you Corporal Tompkins? Can you hear me?"

"He don't speak to anyone, sir. Just stares at the ceiling, shaking like . . . screams in the middle of the night . . ."

On, slowly, Venable silent at his heels . . . on, down the corridor of anguish, the valley of suffering. Men without arms, without legs, with life visibly draining from them, grotesque shapes in bandages, small faces haloed by death, a head with no face, two doctors and attendant bending over it, it struggling, mouthing words unhearable, unbearable. Quentin's eyes were smarting and bulging. He forced himself to walk on, slowly, calling, "Wealds? Any Wealds? . . ." through tent after tent, speaking, saying the same banal lies over and over again. He knew they were lies . . . still, it was right that they should be said, it was right that the men should see their commanding officer, and that he should offer them life, as he had sent them to death, and this.

Outside the end of the last marquee, he turned right, walked a few paces, then leaned against the canvas, his eyes closed, his hands clenched so tight that the nails bit into the palms.

At last he said, "Shall we go on now, sir?"

Venable said, "Yes . . . All of us ought to be forced to go through a C.C.S. once a week . . . us staff officers."

They walked through the mud and the rain to the big Rolls Royce staff car, and climbed in. The chauffeur, a young soldier, started up and they drove off, slipping and sliding at slow speed. Quentin said, "It can't be helped, sir. We all have a job to do."

Signs of war gradually disappeared. Houses and trees stood in their ancient splendour. Green lawns stretched down to overflowing *bekee.* Soldiers marched to and fro, spic and span, heads up, unbowed, carrying no weapons. The fields were green except where the large-eyed placid cows had churned the earth to mud round the entrances to the barns. A gravelled drive swept up to a great building with many windows. At the wrought iron gates military policemen in redcovered caps examined Colonel Venable's pass. They entered the grounds of the huge seventeenth-century château that was the site of Corps Headquarters.

*   *   *   *

After the afternoon of conferring with Venable, Quentin bathed himself and cleaned his uniform as best he could, in the privacy of the large room allotted to him in the west wing of the château; but he still felt shabby and soiled when he entered the Great Hall, now being used as the anteroom for the Corps Headquarters A Mess. Here the Corps Commander dined each night with his principal staff officers. The Corps Commander had insisted that they were all on active service, so the mess waiters had not been issued with white coats, but wore their plain khaki tunics; however, white cotton gloves had been found. The officers all looked so fresh, Quentin thought unhappily, and they all had so many medal ribbons, even young captains . . . he recognized a Legion of Honour here, a Belgian order there, a Russian decoration on another breast . . . three, four D.S.O.s . . . half a dozen M.C.s . . . You had to listen carefully to hear the distant murmur of artillery under the tinkle of the wine glasses.

Colonel Venable came forward, glass in hand, saying, "Let me introduce you to the B.G.G.S., Rowland. This is Lieutenant Colonel Rowland of the 1st Wealds, sir, whom I told you about . . . Brigadier General Mallory."

The B.G.G.S. put out his well-manicured hand—"Welcome to our little home away from home, Rowland. Venable tells me you helped him a great deal, this afternoon. Now, a drink . . . whisky do you? Waiter!"

Quentin felt puzzled—"But, sir," he said, "there can't be any whisky."

The B.G.G.S. said, "Nonsense, there's plenty of it. The best, too."

Quentin said, "I don't understand . . . We've had signals for three weeks, that there is no whisky available . . . no rum, even. And that as soon as any arrived from the rear it would be sent up to the front line."

The B.G.G.S. was tapping the fingers of his free hand against the side of his thigh, a distant expression growing more aloof every moment on his face. Colonel Venable cut in, "This has just arrived, Rowland."

The B.G.G.S. said coldly, "Nonsense. There's never been any shortage, here."

Quentin faced him. He still couldn't understand. This was another Englishman, like himself—a regular, been through Sandhurst . . . served in a good regiment . . . and he was saying these words, which amounted to . . . barefaced robbery of his men's simplest needs. He said, "We've been in the front line three weeks . . . mud, rain, shelling

497

. . . The attack on the Nollehoek ridge . . . all we asked for was rum, whisky, for the men. You kept it here."

The B.G.G.S. said, "Now, look here, Rowland . . ."

Quentin turned on Venable—"I have to get back to my battalion, sir."

Venable glanced at the B.G.G.S. who turned his back. Everyone stood up as the Corps Commander swept into the room, followed by one of his A.D.C.s, the Director of Medical Services, and the Commander, Corps Royal Artillery. Venable muttered, "Come with me." Once out of the room he said, "I'm sorry . . . Are you sure you won't stay? You—I mean you personally—deserve a good night's rest in a comfortable bed, a good meal, even a drink."

"I won't drink here," Quentin said. "I must go back."

"I understand. I'll get you a staff car at once." He picked up the telephone on a table in the hall and spoke a few words. "It'll be five minutes."

"I'll go and get my things."

"Yes . . . Oh, are you by chance any relation to a Miss Naomi Rowland, who was in the Women's Volunteer Motor Drivers?"

"She's my niece."

"She drove me about quite a lot when I was in the War Office. She occasionally mentioned her uncle in the Wealds and I thought it must be you. A charming young lady, and very efficient, too. My wife wants to keep in touch with her, but doesn't get any answer to her letters. We hope she's all right."

Quentin said, "As far as I know . . . She transferred to the F.A.N.Y.s, and my brother—her father—told me that she had been sent to France last month . . . to Number 12 Convoy, I believe. Anyway, with our Army, not the French or Belgians."

"Thanks, I'll tell my wife . . . And I really am sorry about the whisky. It's a disgrace."

Quentin looked him full in the face, and said, "Yes, sir. It is."

*   *   *   *

When he awoke next morning, late, the rain had stopped and a watery sun shone through drifting clouds of early autumn . . . A bite in the air warned of winter coming . . . the sooner the better, he thought, as long as the frost is hard enough to freeze the mud and keep it frozen. What hope was there of that, here? You'd have to go to Russia or Canada or somewhere to find cold as intense as that. Here, it would just harden the mud a bit in the night; by ten in the morning the ground would be like porridge again, only with the added discomfort of being cold.

Archie Campbell appeared in the dugout entrance, and said, "Good morning, sir. The mess sergeant wants to know whether you will be having breakfast. If not he'll clear it away. We've all eaten."

Quentin grunted, then said, "Yes. Ten minutes."

Campbell saluted, and disappeared. Quentin slid off the planks that were his bed and called for his batman to bring hot water. He washed, cleaned his teeth, then began to shave with one of his pair of open razors. The guns were firing to north and south, but not heavily . . . harassing fire, he thought. The nearest German shells were falling about four hundred yards away, up toward the front line. British shells sighed far overhead on their way to the German rear areas. He heard, for the first time for several days, the sputter and buzz of an aeroplane . . . might be his son Guy up there . . . could well be, for much of the R.F.C. had been concentrated behind Ypres, to support the offensive. In the last two weeks of July he'd never seen a Boche aircraft. Then—low clouds, rain . . . all the advantages of air superiority over the battle field lost.

He began to dress. He couldn't get the scene in the Corps Headquarters A Mess out of his mind . . . a land of milk and honey, everything neat and clean, whisky, brandy, sherry, and wine flowing; he might have been in the Savoy. But that was England, the people there were civilians, or officers on leave, and women. The Savoy *ought* to be a luxurious haven. But in France . . . driving back through the darkness, sitting silent in the back seat, he had felt a progressive lightening, a sense of escape, and of coming home. He'd like to talk to Campbell about what he'd seen, what had happened. But it wouldn't do to let junior officers lose faith in their seniors and the higher formations. Someone had to command the Corps and Armies and staff them. He certainly couldn't do it—didn't have the brains . . . and if he did have the brains, he'd probably be making sure he got his whisky, as they did. The B.G.G.S. must have thought he was being deliberately insulting, but he wasn't—he just couldn't understand; and when at last he did, he felt so bad, because he didn't belong there.

Along the trench the men were singing, softly, with immense *brio:*

> *They were only playing leap frog*
> *They were only playing leap frog*
> *They were only playing leap frog*
> *When one staff officer jumped up*
> *on the other staff officer's back.*

He went out, suppressing a smile, to have breakfast in the mess dugout farther up the trench. To his surprise he found Captain

Ramsburgh, the American officer who had been under instruction with the battalion some time back, at the makeshift table. He sat down as Ramsburgh stood up, saluting. Quentin said, "What brings you here, Ramsburgh? . . . Glad to see you, of course."

The captain said, "Our general sent me to your Army Headquarters on a mission—spent three days there . . . thought I'd like to drop in on you, sir, on my way back."

"Well, that's very good of you," Quentin said. The mess sergeant brought him sausages, bread and jam, and a mug of hot thick sweet tea. Hoggin's Plum & Apple jam, he noticed crossly. Surely that fellow could afford to make some raspberry or strawberry jam now and then? He said, "Don't you want breakfast?"

"I had some early, sir, back down the line."

Quentin began to eat. Ramsburgh said, "I've had a letter from Johnny Merritt, Colonel. He's arrived at Fort Sill."

"That's for officer training in the Field Artillery, isn't it?"

"Yes, sir."

"I'll write to his wife . . . but he must have done that himself."

"Surely . . . We never had a proper chance to say goodbye to your companies, Colonel, when we left. Sergeant Leary and Corporal Merritt can't be with me, but I'd like to do it now, for all of us—with your permission."

"Of course. Lucky for you they don't have any booze, or you'd never get back to your Regiment."

Ramsburgh's Virginia accent became a longer drawl—"I have overcome that problem, sir. I borrowed one of our ambulances for this trip and went scouting at your Corps and Army Headquarters yesterday. I obtained a dozen bottles of brandy."

"Did you, by Jove!"

"Yes, sir. And one's for you, if you'll do me the honour of accepting it—as from Leary, Merritt, and myself. Or, I might say, from the United States Army."

"Why . . . why . . . Thank you very much," Quentin said. "And you'll need a couple of men to help carry up that brandy. Ask the Adjutant for them."

Ramsburgh saluted and left the dugout. Quentin drank some more tea. It was troops' char as he'd drunk it a hundred times from his company cookhouse in India—pale brown, sweet, heavy with condensed milk, stewed enough to tan the lining of your stomach. He loved it.

Interesting fellows, these Americans, once you got to know them. Couldn't tell what their discipline was like just from seeing Ramsburgh with Leary and Merritt, obviously all picked men. They'd both often spoken to Ramsburgh before they'd been spoken to, which the Wealds wouldn't tolerate; but then, what they said, in his hearing at least, had usually made sense. And though Leary was much the same sort of person as regular sergeants in any Army he'd ever come across, Johnny Merritt was obviously not like most regular privates. He was an educated man and a gentleman . . . like many of the men whom conscription was putting in the uniform of the Wealds, he grudgingly admitted . . . Wonder where Ramsburgh got the brandy? And how? Could he have just stolen it. . . . Might have forged an indent . . . or got some brass hat to requisition it for imaginary sick Americans, on the grounds of inter-Allied friendship? . . . Ingenious fellows, the Americans. They'd make a difference when they started to join the battle in large numbers.

What to do today? Nothing . . . well, that was never true, if you were commanding a battalion—just nothing obvious that had to be done. He'd sit here a while, resting and digesting, then decide what to do.

Archie Campbell came in and said, "Do you want to write to the next of kin now, sir?"

"In a minute . . . It looks like a long list."

"It is, sir."

"It's time we got this war over with."

"There are quite a lot of people at home trying to do that apparently," Archie said, "by passive resistance to all war work and effort."

Quentin said, "I know . . ." Then, the words wrenched out of him by the need to tell someone, he added, "My brother's one of them. Boy's father. In gaol for it at this moment, or just out . . ."

Campbell said, "That must hurt you, sir."

Quentin looked up. Archie understood. He said, "Yes . . . How can he do it? Stab us out here in the back?"

"Perhaps he's trying to save us all, sir, including you and Boy."

"I don't want to be saved, and I'm sure Boy doesn't either," Quentin snapped. "We want to win the damned war and we're damned well going to do it. All we want is to do it quickly, and the first step is to get that damned Nollehoek-Passchendaele ridge."

"God knows we're trying hard enough, sir . . . the men are, at least."

Meaning, the brass hats aren't, Quentin thought. He ought to reprimand Campbell for that; but he didn't feel like it. Instead he said gruffly, "I'll be writing to my wife later. Any messages?"

Campbell said slowly, "I don't think there's any need to say anything, sir."

Their eyes met. Quentin thought again, he understands. Good

man, in spite of being a Scotsman, an artist, and overfree with women and whisky, when he got the chance. Well, that all went together, really.

Troops passed in a long single file up the trench, heading for the front line, marching painfully through the mud, chanting to the tune of "The Battle Hymn of the Republic":

> *The platoon commander had twenty-five men,*
> *The platoon commander had twenty-five men,*
> *The platoon commander had twenty-five men,*
> *But the brass hats buggered them all away!*
> *Bugger, bugger all the brass hats,*
> *Bugger, bugger all the brass hats,*
> *Bugger, bugger all the brass hats,*
> *For the brass hats buggered them all away!*

Archie Campbell and Quentin Rowland listened. Quentin frowned. Such foul language should not be permitted. He should . . . Campbell should . . . Ramsburgh would hear it and think . . . The men were Devons, not his. He did nothing.

> *The company commander had one hundred men,*
> *The company commander had one hundred men,*
> *The company commander had one hundred men,*
> *But the brass hats buggered them all away!*
> *Bugger, bugger all the brass hats . . .*

PIRACY CAMPAIGN
THE SHADOW OF DEFEAT
by ARCHIBALD HURD

The enemy has lost more submarines during the past few weeks than in any corresponding period of the war, and the number is increasing. The toll is causing growing anxiety in Berlin, as the tone of inspired articles in the German newspapers indicates . . . With what feelings do the German crews look forward to the coming months of cumulative distress? They were to have achieved victory by the beginning of May last—two months of piracy, as Herr Zimmermann, the Foreign Secretary, told Mr Gerard, and then in the third month, a German peace . . . If we hold out, as we must and shall hold out until April . . . the menace of the submarine will have become negligible . . . But the nation must also play its part; a rigid economy must be practised in the matter of food, and fuel, and light, and thus the pressure on tonnage, and the demand for labour, will be relieved, and the prosecution of the war continued with vigour. The nation must ration itself, and then we shall turn the corner with ease . . . The weekly average of loss (of big ships) in the three completed weeks of September has been just over 10, as compared with 26 in April, 18 in May, 21 in June, 16 in July, and 17 in August . . . We may raise our hats to the officers and men of the Navy, and to the crews of the merchantmen, whom the enemy, with all his frightfulness, has failed to cow . . .

Cate looked up from the paper at his brother-in-law, Commander Tom Rowland, down at Walstone recovering from a severe bout of flu which had kept him in bed for three days. "Have you seen this piece by Archibald Hurd, Tom?" he asked.

Tom said, "Not yet—but I know what's in it. Hurd asked me some questions when he was preparing it."

"Then Hurd's right—we do have the submarine problem beaten?"

Tom spread marmalade on a piece of toast. "Not beaten, but on the way to it. So far in this war we've sunk about seventy-five U-boats. The French, Russians, and Americans have sunk one each, too."

Cate leaned back and pushed the paper away. "It's obviously the most important battle of the war, yet it's—well, invisible. How is it being fought, really? . . . Oh, I don't want to be told anything secret," he added hastily.

Tom laughed. "There are some secret things about it, of course, but they're mostly technical—at what depth are we setting the depth charge pistols, for instance . . . but the general outlines are clear enough. For a time our best weapon was the Q ship—a merchant ship carrying a hidden gun, and trained gunners. That was when U-boats surfaced and used their guns to sink merchant ships, to save torpedoes, which are expensive, and very powerful, and they can only carry a few. But the Q ships can't do much when the U-boats don't surface, but simply fire torpedoes . . . We lay huge minefields, at varying depths, through which the U-boats must find their way to the trade routes. . . . but I'm afraid that until recently our mines were badly designed and made. We captured a German document which said flatly 'British mines don't explode,' but it's better now . . . We put wire nets across specific places, and channels. We patrol the seas day and night, with the object of forcing the U-boats to stay submerged— they use up a lot of battery power when they're running submerged . . . And we build more ships. At this moment two lines are about to cross on our graphs—the one showing British merchant tonnage being sunk, a line which is steadily going down—and the line showing the amount of British tonnage being launched—which is steadily going up . . ."

"And we can find the men to man them and officers to guide them?" Cate said. "That's the wonder of it, considering the risks they have to face."

"The merchant Navy's had a much harder war than we have," Tom said. "They have to dip their ensigns to us when we meet at sea, but believe me, we all take off our hats to them, too."

"That's just what Hurd says," Cate said. He watched as Tom spread another piece of toast. After six months in the Admiralty some of the distinctive red-bronze wind and sun burn of the sea had faded from his face; but he seemed more at ease in himself, more relaxed. He had before always struck Cate as being not exactly aloof, but held in tight control.

Garrod came in, felt the coffee and tea pots and brought him some coffee. She went out, and Cate picked up the paper—"Been to the theatre recently, Tom?"

Tom almost jumped, and his mouth tightened. Cate continued, wondering—"I'm thinking of going up to Town some day soon . . . do some business . . . perhaps see a show. I wondered if you could recommend one . . ."

Tom relaxed—"Oh, of course. There's . . ."

London: Thursday, October 25, 1917

31 Sipping his coffee, Harry Rowland felt a strange sensation of timelessness. Here he was in the Middle Drawing Room of No. 10 Downing Street, with the Prime Minister, the sun shining on Horse Guards' Parade . . . but much blood had flowed under the bridges since August, 1914. It was chiefly the physical presence of the Prime Minister that marked the passage of time—for this was not the suave Herbert Asquith, but the square dynamic figure of David Lloyd George, one hand clenched into a fist as he made his points, the mane of grey-brown hair always in motion as the heavy head turned this way and that.

"It's a conspiracy!" he said fiercely. "If I gave Haig the sack, none of the Army commanders would agree to take his place. Robertson backs him up in the War Office."

Harry glanced at the long-faced figure in uniform, his left breast aglow with medal ribbons, sprawled in an arm chair, the long legs in glassy field boots crossed at the knee, the long hands entwined. The figure, General Sir Henry Wilson, spoke—"It does not have to be one of the Army commanders, Prime Minister."

Lloyd George said, "Ah, we all know you'd like the job, Henry." He wagged an admonitory forefinger at him. "But once we've got rid of Haig, Robertson will resign—he must, he's totally committed himself to Haig and his policies . . . and that's where you will come in."

"Chief of the Imperial General Staff," Wilson murmured dreamily.

The Prime Minister said, "The man to succeed Haig will have to come from the Western Front. Otherwise the soldiers out there will

505

not have faith in him, won't believe he knows what he's doing. Any ideas, Craddock? Mackenzie? Rowland?"

The three back-bench M.P.s sat up a little straighter. Craddock said, "I don't know, Prime Minister . . . the men trust Haig. I hear that everywhere I go. They respect him, too."

Lloyd George said with intense animation, "But don't you see, that's just why we must get rid of him? He's leading the Army to ruin . . . If only someone—Army commander, Corps commander, anyone . . . would revolt, say officially this is murder, we could act."

Mackenzie said, "The men and officers I've spoken to, back home on leave, have spoken very highly of Plumer."

"I know they have," Lloyd George snapped, "and Plumer took Messines with a fifth of the casualties expected. He looks like a caricature of a British general—short little legs, white mustache, paunch, rosy cheeks . . . but he won't take it. We've sounded him out, privately. He's loyal to Haig, instead of to his country."

Harry said, "Churchill thinks highly of General Monash, Prime Minister."

Lloyd George swung on him. "Yes. So do others. Notably Haig . . . which is enough to put me off him, in itself . . . Not really, but we couldn't put a colonial in command of all our Armies in France, a colonial who's still only a major general. And Monash is not only an Australian, he's a lawyer, an amateur soldier . . . and a Jew. The generals would refuse to serve under him."

"The man who impressed me most when I went out in 1915," said Craddock, "was Trenchard."

Lloyd George said, "Another major general, and an airman."

I wonder if the soldiers would care what the commander-in-chief's rank or race was, Harry thought, as long as he achieved victory quickly and brought them home out of the bath of blood and mud in which they had been suffering for so long.

The Prime Minister glanced round at the clock on the mantelpiece behind him, and said, "I have a War Cabinet meeting in a few minutes . . . I asked you three here because I need the support of the House of Commons in what I must do . . . what I think is vital for the country that we do, that is—get rid of Haig. In the last resort I could dismiss him out of hand—but, as General Wilson and I have explained to you, it would be very difficult to replace him in those circumstances. I want you three to go out to France—not as an official House committee, but as individual M.P.s—and spend a week sounding out everyone you can get hold of, about who can be persuaded to replace Haig. If we're to have any men left, I must act by the end of the year, at the latest . . . Look around you, look at the women particularly. Their eyes are haunted, even as they go about their work in the houses, the factories. It's got to stop . . . Go next week. Henry here will see that you get accommodation, transport, guides, everything . . . I have to leave you now."

He walked briskly out of the big room. Wilson uncoiled his legs and stood up to his considerable height—"I must go, too. Call me on the telephone as soon as you've decided when to leave. I can make out an itinerary for you . . . one that will enable you to talk to the most useful people." He nodded and strode out.

Craddock, Mackenzie and Harry, all now on their feet, looked at each other. "Why us?" Craddock said. "Why not Carson, Churchill, Curzon, Bonar Law—cabinet members, front benchers?"

Mackenzie said in his soft Highland singsong, "*Because* we're back benchers, Craddock. The important names are all more or less committed to Mr Lloyd George, so whatever they report would be construed as having come from the Prime Minister. But he wants it to come from the Commons—the ordinary people of the country."

"He wants us to find a traitor in Haig's camp, is what it comes to," Craddock said, grumbling.

Harry said slowly, "In a way, but we do have a responsibility to the country . . . we all do, including the soldiers and generals out there, greater than any allegiance to Haig."

*   *   *   *

Four of them occupied the small private dining room at Rule's, Harry Rowland facing the Minister of Munitions, Winston Churchill. The women in the other two chairs were Churchill's mother, Lady Randolph Churchill, and Daisy, Countess of Warwick.

Churchill, the host for the hastily arranged luncheon, said, "May I have your permission to smoke, ladies?"

His mother nodded and the countess said, "Of course, Winston . . . and *I* shall have a cigarette."

Winston lit up, turned his brandy glass round to catch the light, and said, "When are you leaving for France?"

Harry said, "We haven't decided yet, but it'll be soon."

Churchill drank, sighed with contentment, and said, "It's a question of finding a general with *imagination*. For the life of me I can not understand why Haig used the tanks last September, on the Somme. I was midwife to their birth, and after all the genius expended in inventing them, all our efforts to keep them shrouded in secrecy, so that they could burst upon the Huns in mass, a thousand, two thousand, flooding the field of battle, irresistible . . . for Haig to use a paltry score in the insignificant and limited engagement at Flers is . . . words fail me!"

"I can't believe *that*," Daisy murmured.

Churchill continued, "So, which of our generals has imagination? Oh, they want to win the war all right . . . but they won't think beyond the Western Front, and violently resist any attempt of ours to do so."

Harry said, "France is the decisive theatre, surely?"

Churchill waved his cigar expansively. "Certainly. But we don't have to achieve victory there this year . . . or next. We can hold defensively until the Americans have had time to develop their full potential. We can build up our strength, and at the same time deprive the Germans of their peripheral allies . . . drive the Austrians back over the Dolomites and into the plain of the Danube . . . knock Turkey out of the war with decisive blows—and cheap ones—in Palestine and Mesopotamia . . ."

"But we've lost the Russians," Lady Randolph said.

Churchill said, "All the more reason to stand on the defensive in the West, Mother, to prepare ourselves for the assault that must certainly come when the Germans can remove nearly all their divisions from the East and bring them against us and the French. One can almost say, to a few days, when the great assault will be launched."

"How can that be?" Lady Warwick asked. Harry wondered, too. Churchill was a brilliant man, but surely this was . . . ?

"Late March," Churchill said, leaning forward. "Why? Because winter has already set in, and nothing can be done now until the snow has melted and movement is again possible. But by late spring next year the Americans will be in France in strength . . . say April. So—the Germans must attack as soon as winter is over, but before the Americans come . . . *ergo,* late March. So we must ensure that by then our Armies are at full strength, including artillery and ammunition of all kinds . . . If Haig cannot be restrained—or replaced—we will not achieve that. We will have instead an Army under strength through continuous heavy casualties, discouraged and demoralized by repeated failures."

Lady Randolph said hesitantly, "There is another alternative, Winston . . . a negotiated peace. When you read the terrible casualty lists you have to think that perhaps Benjamin Franklin was right—there never was a good war or a bad peace."

Churchill wagged his finger at his mother, "Your American ancestors would not have said that in 1776, Mother! Franklin himself was not saying it a few years later. Were we English to say it, a century ago, faced by the monstrous tyranny of Bonaparte? . . . I know Russell, and some of the other leaders of the pacifist movement . . . I believe he is an honest man, not self-serving, certainly possessed of great moral courage . . . but I think he is wrong, disastrously wrong. The first victims of any such peace—for make no mistake, there would be victims—would be such independent, brilliant spirits as himself. He can only live in the broad tolerant bosom of this nation, where he is no more than a tick, that has to be scratched at now and then." He rose to his feet, "I have to make a speech in the House about the production of tanks. The bill here's paid, of course." He looked suddenly hard at Harry—"Did I not read that a Miss Alice Rowland was severely hurt in the Hedlington factory explosion?"

"My daughter," Harry said. "She lost a leg."

"My dear sir, I am sorry. She has suffered for her country as surely as a soldier wounded in the trenches. Please give her my deepest condolences . . . and I wish I could say that I intend to punish whoever was responsible for causing that explosion, but I can not . . . he is beyond my reach."

"Do you know, yet?" Harry asked.

Churchill nodded. "I had the report of the inspector last month. The manager had been lax in enforcing the safety regulations. Some of the women were wearing earrings, improper ornaments, even ordinary shoes . . . But he was killed . . . I must go." He pecked his mother on the cheek, kissed Lady Warwick's hand, and went out.

Poor Bob, Harry thought. He'd been a good foreman, but managing was a different matter. It was a tragic irony, if what Churchill said was true, that Bob Stratton should have been in the end responsible for Alice's mutilation, when Bob and Jane had always been willing to do anything for her—certainly their favourite among his children.

Meanwhile, here he was, in a secluded dining room with two of the most beautiful women in England. Three, indeed, for lunching at a table for two, her back to them, was Lillie Langtry, with a plump theatrical man who looked like an impresario—or her agent, perhaps. All three ladies were well into middle age by now, Daisy and Lillie getting a little plump . . . but two of them had certainly been the late King's mistresses, and Jennie may well have been . . . some of Daisy's and Lillie's clandestine meetings with him had taken place in this very room, reached by those narrow side stairs. He ought to be able to tell someone about this, and have them hanging on every word . . . but now, who would be interested?

*   *   *   *

Harry Rowland sat at dinner, at home, with his two elder sons and their wives.

"How's Alice?" Richard asked his father. "Susan saw her a week ago, and she seemed depressed."

"She still isn't quite over the drug withdrawal, the doctor says,"

Harry said. "But I think it's mainly impatience. She wants so badly to get her artificial leg, so that she can start learning to walk with it. And she's started a correspondence course in bookkeeping. She's going to work for you at Hedlington Aircraft, isn't she?"

Richard said, "Yes. We have a good secretary, but we need a specialist bookkeeper, too, the way we are expanding. The first production Buffalo is going to fly within six months, test models earlier . . ."

"Is that the one that's going to drop bombs on Berlin?" John asked.

Richard said, "Yes. Probably with J & G engines. That's Jones & Gatewood, a firm in Connecticut which Stephen Merritt's bank bought out in the spring, and have converted to making engines exclusively for aircraft . . . so far all air-cooled radials—radials, not rotaries. We're expecting a dozen next month for trials and fitting to the Buffalo air frame . . . Oh, by the way, you know that motor cycle Bob Stratton was working on, to break the world's 1000cc and all comers' speed record? We flew it to France, to Frank Stratton, in a Leopard that we were delivering to the R.F.C. He's going to work on it, I imagine."

"He'll break the record, then," Harry said. "He's a better man with engines even than Bob was."

Louise Rowland, impatient at the men's talk of machines and engines, asked her father-in-law, "How's Mrs Stallings doing as housekeeper?"

"Very well," Harry said. "She can't do as much cooking as she used to, of course, but I'm not here most of the week so it works out all right."

He drank some wine, looking round from his position at the head of the table. Susan and Louise sat at his sides, John and Richard beyond them. Dinner was nearly over, and he saw Susan glancing at Louise, to catch her eye. He said, "Don't leave us, ladies. I want to talk to all of you. This war is not just a men's affair, as we have all learned, to our cost . . . The Prime Minister has asked me and two other back benchers to go to France and look over the situation there. I shall do my best to see Quentin, Guy, Boy, Laurence—and Naomi—but can't guarantee that I will have the time, or the opportunity. . . . Now, I want your frank opinions . . . What do you think of our war policy?"

No one spoke for a time, then Louise said, "We must beat the Germans in France. If we try to win by other means, we'll only have to face them again, later. That's what Boy said when he was home last."

Harry looked at John, whose face was sad and worried. John said, "I think we ought to state our war aims, and ask the Germans to state theirs . . . declare an armistice, one-sided if necessary . . . appoint

510

Commissioners for both sides to hammer out some sort of compromise between us . . ."

Richard said, "The stated war aims—and war claims—are going to be exaggerated. There'll never be an agreement."

"But there won't be any slaughter while we argue. And once it stops, no one will have the nerve to start it again."

"Leaving us just where we happen to be now—Alsace, Lorraine, and large parts of northern France in German hands, Rumania occupied, Serbia torn to pieces . . . All that will lead to another war, with still more horrible weapons, in twenty or thirty years."

"Perhaps," John said doggedly, "but anything's better than what's happening now."

Harry looked at Susan, "You haven't spoken yet. What do you think?"

Susan said, "I know it's horrible . . . but I think we'd better get it over with. I'm a Republican, but I think Mr Wilson was right—we must make the world safe for democracy, at whatever cost."

Richard said, "I don't think the trouble is in France, Father. It's at home—the unions sticking to peacetime restrictive practices . . . bad procurement procedures by management . . . No one thinks big enough. I'm ready to make five hundred four-engined bombers by next autumn, with a radius of action of 650 miles . . . They'd end the war in a month! But 30 bombers won't, nor yet 40."

John said, "It isn't only the slaughter . . . It's the brutalization, the degradation of our society . . . Bertrand Russell was telling us about walking on the South Downs, and afterward going into Lewes to catch a train back to London, and the station being full of soldiers, all drunk, mostly with prostitutes, everyone despairing, drunk, mad . . . because they were going back to France."

Louise said sharply, "At least they *were* going back, while Mr Russell—the aristocratic philosopher looking down his nose at the brutal and licentious protectors of his freedom—wasn't going back to France, just back to a warm bed with Lady Ottoline Morrell or Colette."

They were all silent, a little shocked by the vehemence of Louise's outburst. Louise added, more quietly, "Men who fight in France are to be forgiven their excesses, not sneered at by aristocratic cowards."

Harry said gently, "Perhaps, my dear Louise, we must also forgive the excesses of those who are working, after all, for peace. Even Winston Churchill, who positively revels in war—not the killing, but the sense of purpose, the energy, the *doing*—is willing to admit the nobility of purpose of such as Bertrand Russell, Clifford Allen, and their followers."

Louise said, "You're right, Father . . . I'm sorry, but . . ."

Harry interrupted—"Let's get back to the subject . . . my subject, at any rate . . . What do you think of Field Marshal Haig?"

Again it was Louise who spoke first—"I think he's the best man we have. The soldiers trust him . . . though Boy didn't think much of some of the other generals, under him . . . so we must trust him, too."

Richard said, "I agree, on the whole. I don't think anyone else could do better. He'll see us through."

Susan said, "I am not sure. If it's true that many of the subordinate generals are poor, why doesn't Field Marshal Haig replace them? Who else can do it, or should?"

Harry thought, I am no forrader than I was after listening to Churchill and Lloyd George. Reading Lord Northcliffe's newspapers didn't help, either. He'd have to make up his mind for himself. He said, "Ring the bell, please, John, and we'll go through and have our coffee in the drawing room."

But at that moment old Parrish came into the room, bent beside Harry's chair, and muttered, "Telephone, for you, sir."

"Who is it?"

"A Mrs Bodding," Parrish said.

Harry had never heard of her; but left the dining room with an apology and went to the telephone, in the hall. He put the receiver to his ear and said, "Harry Rowland speaking."

The voice at the other end was broad Woman of Kent, speaking unhurriedly, "Mister Rowland, I'm Mrs Bodding, the midwife in Beighton. Mrs Merritt's waters has broke and she's in bed now."

"What, what?" Harry said excitedly. He knew that Stella's baby was due—a few days overdue, in fact—but the press of national problems had pushed it to the back of his mind. "Has labour started yet?"

"Yes, sir. But the pains are still over a quarter of an hour apart. I've called on the telephone to Dr Kimball, but I don't think the baby will come quickly, mind. With first ones it usually takes longer."

"Good, good," Harry said. "Tell Dr Kimball to call me when he arrives, please."

"That I will, sir."

*   *   *   *

Harry waited in his library, standing, the door open, listening to old Parrish's discreet footsteps approaching down the hall, accompanied by the ponderous creaking of another, heavier, more powerful man, his boots smacking down with purpose. Their shadows fell across the door, and Parrish said, "Mr William Hoggin, sir."

"Come in, Hoggin," Harry said. "Take a seat. I'll stand, if you don't mind. Do enough sitting in London. Wear out the seat of my trousers."

"Ha, ha!" Hoggin laughed dutifully.

"Well, what can I do for you?" Harry asked. Hoggin was an important man in Hedlington now—the richest man in the town and its chief benefactor; but that didn't mean he had to like him, or put up with his company for longer than was necessary.

Hoggin sat forward on the edge of his chair . . . that's where Richard was sitting the day I told him I was not going to retire, at the beginning of war, Harry thought. Hoggin said, "We—myself and the other directors of H.U.S.L.—Hoggin's Universal Stores Limited— would like you to join us on the board, Mr Rowland."

Harry made to speak but Hoggin raised a thick, hairy-backed hand—"'Ear me out, Mr Rowland . . . We have twenty-four H.U.S.L. shops now in hoperation. By the end of next year our goal is one hundred . . . and we'll have them. Our business is in the millions now. Next year it'll be in the tens of millions—'undreds, perhaps. As soon as the war's over, it'll grow more, and quicker."

"What about competition?" Harry asked.

Hoggin said, "We're going to have it, Mr Rowland. We have some now. But we're going to beat it. If anyone's going to go under, it ain't going to be Bill Hoggin . . . nor his H.U.S.L. We pay directors well, Mr Rowland . . . not only with money but with options to buy common shares at par, when they're selling for three and four times par on the Stock Exchange."

Harry considered. He was not averse to earning some more money. Much of it would be taxed, in any case, to pay for the war. But how much time would he be able to spare for his duties as director? What did Hoggin want him for, anyway? Well, that was easy. An M.P. was always a good ally to have for a man like Hoggin. He wondered how Hoggin had managed, first, to get himself appointed as an expert adviser to a committee primarily looking into the operations of such as he; and then steered the committee into agreeing to dissolve itself, with self-congratulations all round. Swanwick had been in the Lords team on that committee . . . which might have had something to do with it, as he was now Chairman of H.U.S.L.

To Hoggin he said finally, "Your proposal flatters me, Mr Hoggin, and interests me, I confess . . . but I must refuse it. I do not have the time to serve on your board."

"That don't matter," Hoggin said eagerly. "Lord Swanwick hardly ever turns up. It's just 'is name we want, see."

"And that's all you want of me?" Harry said with a touch of acid.

"Oh now, Mr Rowland, his Lordship's not a business man, now, is

513

he? But you are . . . just your advice, whenever you want to give it. You'll be worth your keep, don't you fear."

Harry said, again, "I'm sorry, I must refuse. But I wish you all prosperity and further success. As a constituent of mine, your interests will always be my concern."

Hoggin stood up, and said, "One thing more, Mr Rowland. I made a considerable contribution to Mr Lloyd George early this year—a hundred thousand quid, it was . . ." Ah, Harry thought, here's the milk in the coconut. Hoggin continued, "I'm ready to give him some more. 'Ow could I get him to accept it . . . from my own hands, like?"

Harry considered. Lloyd George had a private fund, he knew, for which he was not accountable to anyone. It was large, it came from many sources and none of it went into the official coffers of the Liberal Party or of His Majesty's Government. He said, "May I ask how much you are considering donating this time—in strict confidence, of course."

"Three quarters of a million spondulicks," Hoggin said.

Harry whistled silently. Lloyd George would certainly see Hoggin personally for that. He looked at Hoggin, thinking—he doesn't do anything without getting something in return. Now, what on earth was his asking price for this huge sum? Suddenly he guessed, and knew his guess was correct. He said, "I'll speak to the Prime Minister myself, tomorrow. I expect you will receive a summons from him soon after."

"You're going back to London tomorrow?"

Harry nodded, and Hoggin said, "So I'll hear from Mr Lloyd George Tuesday or Wednesday. Good . . . Well, thanks, Mr Rowland. Sorry you won't join us. Any time you change your mind, just call me on the telephone."

*   *   *   *

Harry, Craddock and Mackenzie sat in the Savoy Grill, eating roast pheasant with Alfred Charles William Harmsworth, Viscount Northcliffe, owner of the *Times* and the *Daily Mail*. Northcliffe was laying down the law—"The man you must see is Charteris, Haig's Chief of Intelligence. He knows all the intrigues that are going on against Haig. He can warn you of specious arguments . . . whom to listen to, whom to take with a pinch of salt." He said suddenly—"Winston Churchill has been getting at you, has he?"

"He's spoken to me," said all three members of Parliament, simultaneously.

"Ah!" Northcliffe said, almost snarling. "He's an example, on this side of the Channel, of what I mean . . . always trying to find a way round, instead of facing the music and beating the Huns. He'd have that Jew Monash in if he had the power. Thank God he doesn't, not even now that he's back in the Cabinet. I gave Lloyd George a piece of my mind over that, I can assure you. I told him . . ."

Harry stifled a yawn in his glass of champagne. There might be suffering in the trenches, but not here. He saw several officers in uniform in the room, both Navy and Army, but mostly it was full of civilians—and mostly they were middle-aged, sleek, fat, gold watch chains stretched across the smoothly curving paunches. The air reeked with the savory odours of roast meats and game, the tang of wine. Glasses clinked, silver glittered, white damask napery shone.

". . . You must impress on Charteris that newspaper cor-respondents—even those of other papers—must be allowed to see Haig regularly. I intend making him a national hero, and it doesn't matter whether he wishes it or not—it has to be, so that the people here at home will trust him."

"He hates publicity," Mackenzie said.

Northcliffe said, "He's going to get it."

Harry said, "Are you not afraid, Lord Northcliffe, that if you make Haig too large a hero figure, that the Prime Minister will take instant measures to replace him?"

Northcliffe looked sharply at him—"So you've seen through our little Welshman's native character, have you? . . . Yes, it's possible. But I think I can make him understand that if he does, we'll raise such a row—my brother and I—that his own head will roll the day after . . . I . . . I . . . I . . ."

*   *   *   *

He awoke in the middle of the night to the insistent shrilling of the telephone in his son Tom's flat in Half Moon Street, where he was staying. He got up, pulled on his dressing gown and went to the in-strument.

"Hullo? Harry Rowland here."

"Harry, Leonard Kimball here . . . Sorry to wake you up. Stella had a girl, five pounds and an ounce, about four hours ago."

"Wonderful!" Harry exclaimed. "Is Stella all right?"

"Not as well as I would like, but nothing serious, as far as I can make out. But the baby's in a bad way . . . it's having quite severe shaking tremors and apnea—stoppages of breathing . . . that's fairly normal at this stage, but I must confess I don't like it. I'm having the baby taken to Hedlington Hospital at once. Stella will stay here . . . Sorry not to give you better news."

"It's all right, Leonard," Harry said. "Do all you can."

"Of course."

Harry hung up and went slowly back to bed. He'd known Leonard Kimball for, what—thirty-five years now. Perhaps Stella should have gone to a gynaecologist, as young women were beginning to do these days. But Rose never had, nor Margaret nor Fiona or Louise . . . Susan had, but she was American . . .

* * * *

Harry dressed slowly after his bath. General Charteris had allotted a soldier servant to each of the three M.P.s, and his clothes had been laid out on the bed. Their rooms were spacious, the beds comfortable, and though there was no central heating in the old château, coal fires blazed in the grate in each bedroom.

Eight o'clock . . . he had slept from five till seven, after coming back from the Front. It was his age that had made him dog tired . . . and what he had seen . . . and what he had not seen. They had brought Boy out of the line and he had been able to speak to him for ten minutes; but Boy was obviously anxious to get back, perhaps resentful that he had had to trudge and drive so far—for what? Harry had taken him aside and asked him point blank—"Do you have trust in Field Marshal Haig?"; and Boy had answered, "Yes, Grandfather." Then—"Do the men?"; and the same answer—"Yes, Grandfather." So what was wrong? Why were we suffering these huge casualties and making such small gains? "It's the damned staff," Boy had said. "They mess everything up." And, after a few more words, he'd saluted and started back . . . haggard, filthy, caked with mud, his groundsheet-cape glistening wet in the rain, water dripping off the rim of his steel helmet.

He'd seen Guy, briefly, at an airfield, between "shows." Guy's smile was frightening now, for only one side of his mouth curled up, the other staying down; and there was a long scar along the cheekbone, and a torn ear on that side. Guy thought Field Marshal Haig was doing the job as well as anyone could.

He had not seen Naomi. Nor Quentin, though the Corps commander had said he could easily be ordered back if Harry wanted to speak to him; but Boy had brought Quentin's message—"Uncle Quentin says he's sorry, Grandfather, but he can't leave the battalion now, even for half a day."

But he had seen a lieutenant colonel of the Coldstream Guards, who'd told him that in his opinion the offensive must be continued, to prevent the Germans from attacking the weakened French. Harry had heard that before; he had not heard something else the colonel told him—that Captain the Viscount Cantley was dead, killed in action at Poelcapelle two days before. Poor Swanwick, he thought, he'll take it hard, and so will Barbara and Helen and the Countess.

He himself was taking it hard—harder than over the death of Stella's baby, he acknowledged. He had, after all, known Cantley since he was a child, while he'd never even seen Stella's poor mite, died of natural causes—that beastly apnea, causing tremors and convulsions, and eventually suffocation after barely forty-eight hours of life. He could feel sad for Stella, but the baby . . . poor Cantley, gone, doing his duty.

He wrenched his mind back to the problem which had brought him to France: the military direction of Britain's war effort. He had not seen or spoken to any general, of any rank, who believed that Haig should be replaced; or that the main British effort on the Western Front should be defensive; or that the main British war effort should be elsewhere than on the Western Front. A lieutenant colonel of Charteris' staff had been with him all the time, and a major each with Craddock and Mackenzie. They had taken him as far forward as divisions' headquarters—he'd visited six divisions in the six days—and from there he had looked forward through binoculars. The binoculars were like a peephole on a different world—mud, ruins, cratered and destroyed earth, no human beings visible, for they were all underground or crawling through the slime. The incessant thunder of artillery had reminded him of his visit to the Somme battlefield the year before. There had been noise there, and obvious signs of slaughter in the streams of ambulances, the rows of wounded in the hospitals he had visited; but the land, though mangled and torn, was still earth, something that would bear your weight; and the skies were blue, with white clouds, and a summer sun. Here, before Ypres, there was no earth, only mud; no sun, only clouds; the dull diffused gloom of late autumn, sunless; and rain.

He finished dressing and was about to go downstairs when he heard a knock on the door. "Come in," he called.

It was Craddock, with Mackenzie at his heels, Harry's allotted soldier servant hovering anxiously in the background. Craddock said, "We thought we'd like to have a chat before we go down to dinner, Rowland . . . just the three of us."

Harry understood and said to the soldier, "See that we are not disturbed, Harrington. Thank you." The M.P.s entered and Harry closed and locked the door behind them.

Mackenzie produced a flat half-bottle of whisky from his coat pocket and planked it down on the dressing table. "D'ye have a glass, sir?"

Harry found glasses and Mackenzie poured, a stiff three fingers each. The others took a little water from the china jug, Mackenzie took his neat.

The other two sat down on the bed, and Harry in the chair by the dressing table. Craddock said, "We're going home tomorrow. We thought we'd better discuss our impressions . . . decide if there's anything more we ought to do . . . see . . . other questions we should ask."

"General Charteris is coming to dinner tonight," Harry said.

"Quite . . . Do you have the feeling that we have been led about by the nose?"

Harry said slowly, "To a certain extent. I suppose they are justified in refusing to let us go forward of divisional headquarters. They are responsible for us, after all."

Mackenzie fumed—"How can we tell what the condition of the battlefield really is, unless we see it?"

"I saw quite a lot, through binoculars," Harry said.

"So did I," Craddock added, "and it looked very bad. Which only confirms what everyone has told us. The generals have never denied that."

"They've been using the rain and mud as an excuse, or a reason—for their failure."

Mackenzie growled, "They never use the word failure. They say 'We're wearing the Germans down, and we have to go on doing it, because of the French.' Assuming that's true, the question is, is Haig using the right tactics, doing the job in the best possible way?"

All three were silent. Here were the horns of the dilemma. Where did the truth lie? The blinded young soldier appeared again before Harry's mind's eye, in his hospital blue, dark glasses hiding his seared eyes, his cane tap tap tapping: Do you know what you're doing? *Do you?*

And there was this universal feeling against the staff. That should not be—all soldiers should be working together, to win the war. But who was responsible, both for the efficiency of the staff, and for the way in which the staff and the fighting troops cooperated? Why, the commander-in-chief—Haig.

Craddock said, "I don't mind not being allowed up the line so much. But I think we've been steered . . . guided, as to what and whom we see, where we go. And with one or two hesitations . . . which were equivalent, in the circumstances, since the G.H.Q. major was standing right beside me, of an outright accusal of Haig . . . everybody backs him. They also hint that any attempt to replace him would be regarded as a loss of our will to win the war."

"That's what I found," Mackenzie said. "And yet . . . yet . . ."

Harry said, "I have an uneasy feeling . . . I can find no logical

518

basis for it . . . that the Prime Minister ought to make a change. Yet the consequences could be so serious, that I can not bring myself to recommend it, unless somewhere, somehow, I do find sound *reasons* to back it up."

There was a knock on the door, and Harry called, "Who is it?"

"Colonel Ray, sir . . . General Charteris has arrived."

"Thank you. We'll be down soon."

He waited till the sound of footsteps had receded down the château's stone floor and then said, "So we are agreed? That when we return, we must tell the Prime Minister that we can find no reason for removing Haig?"

After a minute the other two, saying nothing, nodded. Then Mackenzie said, "God help us, I hope we're right . . . and I suppose Charteris might reveal something new?"

"Not a chance," Craddock said emphatically. "He'll talk about the Americans . . . how great Pershing is . . . how they're adopting our—his—Intelligence methods . . . all will be well as soon as their main armies come . . . meanwhile, attack, attack, attack, to wear the Germans down."

"And after dinner he's going to take us to see Haig, Colonel Ray told me this afternoon. I suppose we might learn something from him . . . how he's taking the strain, at least."

Craddock said, "He's taking it very well. He won't crack before the last of his men has been killed, or drowned."

"And that's what we want?" Mackenzie said.

"Apparently, that's what we must have."

*   *   *   *

David Lloyd George was not in a good temper. Though Harry was twenty years older than the Prime Minister he felt as though he were a small boy facing the wrath of Dr Wickham, Master of Wellington . . . worse, for Dr Wickham's "anger" never amounted to more than a mild disappointment that anyone should have transgressed his gentle and proper Wykehamist code: while here Harry faced a bubbling Celtic explosion—"The three of you were in conspiracy with the damned generals," the Prime Minister snarled, banging the table in his office in the House.

"We reached our conclusion quite independently, Prime Minister," Harry said. "And, as I have just explained to you, it was not without serious misgivings." It is just that we can see no alternative to Field Marshal Haig."

Lloyd George growled. "So you swallowed all the flattery, took all the soft soap . . . gave me no help at all . . . and you still expect me to give a peerage to that butcher of yours, Hoggin?"

"Hoggin is in no way a protégé of mine," Harry said stiffly. "Whether he receives a peerage is entirely up to you, in consideration of whatever services he may have performed for you . . . or the country . . . if any."

Lloyd George looked up, suddenly smiling. He jumped to his feet, clapped Harry on the shoulder, and said, "He's a real hog, isn't he? But we need people like that . . . those H.U.S.L. shops are providing cheaper food, *and* making a lot of money. He did a very good job for us in America . . . it takes a cockney barrow boy to keep ahead of Yankee commodity traders. And there are some jobs that only people like him can do . . . dirty jobs, but necessary for the survival of the country . . . or at least, of politicians." He chuckled. "Thank you for going to France for me. I hope you saw some of your family out there . . . the grandson who's the flying ace? the one in the infantry . . . no, it's a son and two grandsons, isn't it? . . . Good, good . . . I didn't really expect you to bring back any different answer. If Churchill, Curzon, Wilson, and I can't find a handle to get rid of Haig, how can honest men like you hope to do so?"

The telephone rang and he picked it up with a curt, "Prime Minister."

He listened, expressions chasing each other across his face like sunshine and storm over his Welsh mountains. Finally he said, "All right. In fifteen minutes, at Number Ten." He put the instrument down and looked up—"That was Bonar Law. The Italians have broken near Caporetto. They're in full flight on a front of a hundred miles. The Austrians—with half a dozen German divisions as the spearhead—have taken 200,000 prisoners . . . or that number of Italian soldiers have deserted."

"Good heavens," Harry gasped. "What a terrible disaster!"

Lloyd George's eyes gleamed fiercely, as again he seized Harry's shoulder. "Disaster!" he hissed theatrically. "It's the best news of the war! Now we're going to *have* to send reinforcements there to keep Italy in the war. And they must come from the Western Front! Haig will have to stop his attacks at Passchendaele and Nollehoek!"

I wonder, Harry thought, remembering the determination and perfect confidence in his own rightness that he had felt emanating from the Field Marshal in the big room at G.H.Q. so few hours ago.

Daily Telegraph, Tuesday, November 6, 1917

TWO PREMIERS' JOURNEY

From Our Own Correspondent, *Paris*, Monday Night.
I am now allowed to announce that General Foch and Sir William

Robertson, the Chiefs of the French and British Staffs, went to the Italian front last week. I may add that General Foch two months ago was in Italy, and drew up complete military plans with General Cadorna. These were ready down to the smallest detail. Thus is explained the swiftness with which Anglo-French help has reached the Italians, and which has already been a surprise to the enemy.

The meeting of Mr Lloyd George, M. Painlevé, Signor Orlando, General Robertson, General Foch, and General Smuts in Rome, where the King of Italy will also see the representatives of France and England, has much political as well as military importance. Mr Lloyd George and M. Painlevé go to Italy to bring encouragement, sound advice, and, I may say, warning to the Italian Government. It is no secret now that the Second Italian Army on the Isonzo broke because it was undermined by the enemy propaganda, both Socialist and Catholic. It is no secret also that the Austro-Germans expected, and still expect, to clinch matters now after the Italian reverse by alternate threats and sops to Italian public opinion. Luckily the Italian people has pulled itself together completely. Its confidence will now be completely restored by the present visit of the political and military chiefs of Italy's Allies. That is the raison d'être of Mr Lloyd George's and M. Painlevé's mission to Rome.

Really, Cate thought, one's allies are sometimes more trouble than they seem to be worth. Now British and French troops would be, or were being, sent to prevent an Italian collapse. The Russians were in just as bad a state, but nothing could be done about them. One could only hope that the American power would develop before it was too late. The battle in Flanders was grinding relentlessly on, but now surely Haig would have to halt it, what with the winter upon them, and the loss of troops he'd have to send to Italy. It would be an anxious winter, and Christmas . . . better not think about it, until it was here. It might not be a bit merry.

He put down the paper. This morning he must go and tell Mayhew that he was going to sell his land, and that the new landlord would not renew his lease when the war was over—as he intended to build houses on it. He wished to God it could be avoided, if only on financial grounds: he'd get a much better price for those 124 acres after the war; but he could not wait: the tax collectors were at the door . . . to pay for the war. It was hard to imagine the swelling land of Upper Bohun, now covered with the marching ranks of hop poles, divided up into "gentlemen's estates" of two acres or so each, plus a large house, probably pseudo-Tudor in design, with stuccoed walls and false half timbering, standing up behind newly planted hedges . . . What would happen to the oast houses? Perhaps a way could be found to convert them into guest houses or garages . . . odd they'd look, but so would Walstone. What would happen to the village with such an influx? Mrs Warren would do a roaring trade at her shop; Miss Macaulay the postmistress would have much more exciting post-cards to read and gossip to dispense . . . people who'd buy houses like that would probably have two cars, and their children would go driv-ing round very fast and running over chickens and children . . . Mr Woodruff would do well, with more cars to mend, and sell petrol and oil for. The pub keepers wouldn't benefit much—that sort drank in their houses, or went to supper clubs in London. Old Mr Kirby would have opportunities for delivering some real blood-and-thunder ser-mons . . . but they wouldn't listen. They'd go to church on Sundays, because they'd know that that was part of being an English country gentleman. But their souls would be in London and they'd have no idea who was sitting in the pews opposite or behind or in front. The words "country gentleman" themselves would soon be meaningless: the country—turned into a dormitory for stockbrokers: and the gentlemen—taxed out of existence.

Oh well, must put the best face on it one can. Mayhew was the one to be comforted, now. And when he'd given Mayhew the bad news he must visit Stella. The poor girl didn't look well, and seemed to be withdrawing into herself. Losing the baby must have been a blow—it had been to him, so how much more for her?—but she must try to forget. She was young. Johnny would come home again to her one day, and . . . Dear God, Johnny might not come home again.

It was no use worrying about that. Every wife and son, every father and mother, all over Europe and America were facing that. If it came, it must be taken with courage, and self-respect. Meantime, there were closer, lesser wounds to be bound.

Belgian Flanders: Monday, November 5, 1917

32 Lieutenant Fred Stratton sat in the front seat of the ambulance, beside the driver, lurching and sliding toward the smoking wreck of Ypres. A khaki bandage round his left hand covered the scar, still raw, where a German bullet had grazed the back of the hand, severing a tendon. It hurt, sometimes with a dull ache, sometimes with sharp stabs; and he had no strength in the middle finger of that hand. The R.A.M.C. captain at the C.C.S. had been willing to send him farther to the rear, to a base hospital, for a few more days' rest, and to allow the wound to heal, but Fred asked to go back to his battalion, and, with a shrug, as much as to say, "Well, I tried to help you," the doctor had marked him "Fit for General Duty."

There was a big push coming, another in the series that had started on the last day of July. It would be bloody horrible, like the rest of them. He was a fucking idiot not to have let the doctor send him back. He'd catch a packet this time, for sure. The hand wound hadn't been enough for a Blighty; if it had been, nothing would have made him come back until he'd wrung every last minute he could out of the doctors. If he got any sort of a real wound he'd fake it worse than it really was . . . but that would depend on what sort of a packet he caught. There wasn't much leadswinging you could do if you'd really got six machine-gun bullets through the belly, or a shell splinter had taken one of your lungs out.

The guns were talking loudly now. Far away, they'd sounded, from the C.C.S., but now he was getting closer, and their voices, like hounds baying threateningly at intruders beyond the town, made him wish he could stop his ears with cotton wool. The sodden fields, glazed in the shade of the woods with frost, were becoming more and more marked with rutted roads leading to barbed wire enclosures . . . To the right, there was half a square mile of shells, mostly heavies; to the left, parked motor lorries of the Army Service Corps; beyond, rows and rows of wooden crates of rations, stacked high; more shells; deep dugouts, sentries at the entrance.

On to battle. They had skirted Ypres and were heading north-east, through Potijze. They were level with the guns now, seen near and far, in the woodland patches, at the edges of the copses, the barrels pointing skyward, jerking suddenly, the heavy wheels momentarily leaving the ground with the force of the recoil, thudding down again, the gunners trundling the next shell forward into the cradle. If the guns could reach the Boche from here, the Boche could . . .

A shell burst beside the road, a hundred yards off in a field. The ambulance driver said, "Only another quarter of a mile . . . We'd just as lief not have to do that bit . . . four times a day."

The convoy of ambulances, empty except for a few men in Fred's position, and some soldiers returning from leave who had cadged rides, turned off into a big farmyard, at the outskirts of the shattered village of Zonnebeke. Fred got out and began to walk.

The road that had so far been passable with difficulty, for mules and men, slowly seemed to sink into the ground, and become indistinguishable from the mud. All signs of normal human life as slowly, and as steadily, vanished—no one moved above ground, there were no houses, no trees, no woods, only the undulating cratered wasteland. The trench system began, and Fred sank into it, moving slowly, with painful steps through deep, clinging mud, his hand aching, among a trickling stream of humanity, toward the front.

November the fifth. Remember, remember the fifth of November, the Gunpowder Treason and Plot! Penny for the guy, mister, penny for the guy . . . Guy Bloody Fawkes' Day, that's what it was. Well, he'd see some fireworks before the day was out, he could bet his bloody life on that.

He became aware, with increasing horror, that the same process which had progressively destroyed the civilized habitations of man, from the rear forward, had now almost completed its work on its own body, the nervous and arterial systems of war. The trenches had been damaged at the rear, where he had dropped down into them: and at every yard became more so—punctured, ruptured, torn apart—just like the houses and, here, the human bodies all around; until, in the last four hundred yards, they had all but vanished. The war, having destroyed the works of man, and man himself, had here succeeded in destroying its own works: the trench system, the armour of barbed wire, no longer lived, there was now only a dead and decaying body of mud, covered with the festering pustules of shell holes, some loosely linked by veins of flowing mud, which might once themselves have been trenches.

God Almighty, Fred thought fearfully, this is the end.

*   *   *   *

Quentin Rowland waited in a forward shell hole, ten minutes before dawn, jammed in with scores of others ready for the attack. Shells howled and screamed overhead. The German artillery was deluging the whole area with counter-preparation fire. Like the men around him, and those huddled in the ditches just to the rear, Quentin waited, heads bowed uselessly against the storm, as though some giant steel umbrella was held over them by God, guarding them against the murderous thunder. It was raining lightly, but the drops stung cold on any exposed flesh, which was not much. The men were wearing greatcoats, and khaki scarves; the bulk of them, when full equipment, full ammunition pouches and gas mask cases had swollen them out, was enormous. Only their faces were bare, as there had been no gas alarm; and the tips of their fingers stuck out bare from the khaki mittens. The rain fell, the mud clung. Each soldier's clothing weighed 55 pounds, from the water and mud it had sucked up, or that was stuck to the boots and caked on the puttees. His arms, equipment and ammunition weighed another 35 pounds.

Quentin thought, this is a dream recurring. I have been here before, many times—standing in this trench, dim figures around, no one speaking, all waiting, in a hell of a noise. The faces would be different, if he could see them, but he couldn't, except now and then in the flaring descent of star shells.

He wrenched his mind away . . . Virginia wanted to marry a Battery Sergeant Major with only one arm. Fiona said the idea was ridiculous and of course they must not allow it. The girl was only eighteen, and would need their permission. The fellow had a D.C.M., she said . . . must have some guts, at least . . . but, a Battery Sergeant Major! He ought to see the man . . . Fiona should, but . . .

The dream returned, following its inescapable course. The whistles blew, the men climbed up as though held back by great weights, like those cinema shows where people's movements were slowed down . . . up the ladders, out of the mud below onto the mud above. The first light began to spread, revealing—the same dream, the same wire, rusty, thick, writhing, torn, whole, coiling and uncoiling . . . humps and bumps in the mud, some moving, the perpetual rattle and tearing

525

of canvas in the tattered darkness above, to the side, all round, ripping the night to shreds, viscous plops, at immense speed, as bullets whipped the mud into a brown froth.

"We ought to have a success signal from D and A by now," he shouted to his adjutant, Archie Campbell.

"Nothing yet, sir," Campbell replied. They were peering across No Man's Land, heads together on the parapet—"Can't see anything out there."

Quentin waited. Now in the dream he was scurrying across No Man's Land, falling from one shell hole to another, crawling, waiting for a machine gun to end its traverse and start swinging back.

He said, "I'll go forward and see what's happening . . . Don't want to launch B and C until we know . . . Kellaway, stay here, watch for the success signal . . . or a runner . . . Runners! Ready? Stay here with Captain Kellaway, Mr Dalley . . . Ready, Campbell?"

Up, slowly, out, trying to run, waddling, falling as a sniper got his sights on them, *crack* low overhead, and again—*crack* . . . slide down into a shell hole, wait a minute to catch his breath. Out again . . . near the German wire now. Two machine guns sweeping No Man's Land behind them, many single shots, the duller burst of grenades close ahead . . . through the German wire, his British warm ripped in long gashes, down into the trench.

The shattered German trench was full of men—his Wealds—huddled together, crouching, heads bowed, many without rifles. 2nd Lieutenant Walworth struggled toward him, stepping over dead Germans, treading on their faces. His face was white, his eyes starting out of his head, "Sir!" he shouted. "They've mutinied, sir . . . won't move!"

"Where's Captain Hatch?" Quentin snapped.

"Killed, sir . . . I believe Major Donkin of A is, too."

Quentin forced down the shallow, obstructed trench, Campbell and Walworth at his heels. This was the dream he had had a score of times, but in reality—if this was reality—it had never come to pass. In the dream he regularly faced them, their poor exhausted bodies, haggard, working, faces, bulging eyes, and knew they would not, could not do more; they had reached the limit. But in the dream he drove them on. *Was* this a dream, then? He gritted his teeth. It must be. He must treat it as such.

The men here now were mainly A Company. "Where's Major Donkin?" he shouted at a soldier cowering against the muddy wall.

"Dead, sir," the man said.

"Any officers alive?"

"Don't know, sir . . . don't know." He was shivering violently. His

526

hands were wringing together. He had no rifle. Another figure was crouched in the mud close by, and Quentin caught the glint of stars on his shoulder . . . a lieutenant. He peered down, shouting, "Are you wounded?" The man looked up and Quentin saw that it was Lieutenant Dale, of D Company . . . only been out three weeks. Dale croaked, "Can't go on . . . done enough . . . hopeless."

Quentin grabbed him by the collar and jerked him to his feet, "Get up, man. Get these men on their feet, now! Take rifles from the dead! We've only got half our objective. We've got to keep attacking!"

Dale stared at him dully, his mouth working, "Can't do more, sir. It's impossible."

Quentin grabbed up a German rifle from the trench floor and held the muzzle to the young officer's chest—"Get the men up, Dale! Call to them!"

The lieutenant mumbled, "Can't do any more, sir . . . done all we can."

Quentin pulled the trigger. The shot blasted the lieutenant against the back wall, where he slowly sagged to the ground, blood pouring from a ragged hole in the middle of his back. Quentin swung the rifle onto the other men, shouting, "Up . . . get up, you cowardly swine! Up!" The shot still seemed to echo along the trench, a sound of a quite different quality from any of the thousands of other shots being fired or bullets passing over or slapping into the mud. Madness gleamed in the soldiers' eyes, and they began to struggle to their feet, grabbing rifles from the mud. A few broke into wails and cries. A sergeant croaked, "Don't go! Don't go!" Quentin swung the rifle on him and fired again, aiming at his head. The rest were on their feet, together mouthing a meaningless scream of helpless fury at him, at fate, at death. Quentin shouted, "Campbell, get moving! . . . Come on, Wealds . . . Wealds! Follow me!" He scrambled and swung up out of the ditch. They followed, mouthing curses, weeping, stumbling, falling, but moving on.

Three minutes later and a hundred yards forward they fell into the second line of German trenches, almost destroyed, almost uninhabited. Grenades began to fly. German hands flew up. More Germans came out of the dugouts. Campbell appeared, shouting, "D's to your left, sir. They don't have any officers left except Walworth."

"Go back to them and take command."

Quentin turned to his runners, panting behind him with bloodstained bayonets—"Very pistol, quick!" One fumbled in his haversack and handed him the Very pistol. "Two reds!" Quentin barked.

A moment later he fired the first red Very light straight up into the low clouds, followed at once by the second. Leaning exhausted against the front wall, propped up in a German machine-gun post, he saw men scramble out of the old trench line . . . B and C were coming: they'd pass through, and they'd take the heaps of rubble that marked where Nollehoek had stood.

*   *   *   *

The ragged lines of men, square shaped, wearing wet steel basins as crowns, entered Nollehoek with Boy Rowland and his C Company to the right, and Charles Kellaway with B on the left. The German machine guns had left a third of each company crumpled in the mud of the last slope. Now the survivors scrambled painfully over the rubble and killed the machine gunners in their nests, or shot them running away through the ruins. Those that escaped here were caught by their own or British shells.

"Look in every cellar," Boy shouted. "Bomb first, then down!"

It was a long time since they had been fighting in the remains of a village and so many of the men were so recently out from the depots and base reinforcement camps that they did not know the drill. And they weren't the Weald Light Infantry, of Minden and Badajoz and Waterloo, except by name. They were men dredged from civilian life, of every age below fifty, men from a score of other regiments taken haphazard out of the reinforcement camps to keep the ranks of the battalions in the line as nearly up to strength as possible . . . which could not be done, as the myriad bodies rotting in the mud from Poelcapelle to Passchendaele, Broodseinde and Nollehoek, attested.

The bombs began to burst muffled and hollow sounding in the half-flooded cellars. Germans emerged. British soldiers began to escort them back.

"You!" Boy shouted. "What's your name? Come here!" He raised his revolver. They were sneaking to the rear under pretence of escorting prisoners, when they knew perfectly well that the C.S.M. would appoint men to do that any moment now . . . bloody fools, too, because the German artillery, not yet realizing that the British were actually into Nollehoek, were still sweeping the slope to the west. Soon, the information would get back to them, and then . . .

His uncle appeared, panting, and cried, "Well done, Boy . . . Many casualties?"

"I only have about forty men left as far as I can see, sir."

"A and D are coming up. The Boche will counter-attack, Boy . . . I'll stay here . . . try and get some artillery support."

Boy said, "Yes, sir." The shelling suddenly stopped, and he called, "Sarn't major, send the prisoners back now with the walking wounded—quick, before the Boche artillery opens up again!"

528

He hurried forward, followed by his batman. The village was rid-dled with cellars, broken down trenches, shattered machine-gun nests, hidden observation posts, and of course, rubble—a labyrinth. He struggled northward, shouting, "Captain Kellaway? Anyone know where Captain Kellaway is?"

A voice nearby mumbled, "He's at the end of the village." Boy turned to stare a moment at his cousin Laurence Cate. Laurence was sweating, clay-faced and hardly recognizable from the mud that cov-ered him from head to toe. He was swaying on his feet, his eyes glazed.

Boy shouted, "Thanks . . . You all right? Wounded?"

Laurence croaked, "No . . . all right." Boy hurried on, his mind instantly erasing what he had just seen and heard, thinking only of getting to Kellaway.

Laurence watched him go, then called, "Sergeant!"

His platoon sergeant, Fagioletti, rushed to his side, "Sir?"

"Hold the forward edge of the village . . . there . . . there . . . How many men left?"

"Thirteen, sir . . . two wounded, but they're staying."

"Follow me!" Laurence stumbled in the direction he had pointed. Fagioletti waved his rifle energetically at a soldier lying behind a pile of rubble and yelled, "Get up! Follow Mr Cate! You—up!" He pricked his bayonet into another soldier's buttocks. They all rose and trudged forward. Fagioletti followed, watching Laurence. The officer was shit-scared, he thought, as bad as I was the first time I was in a push—the time I shat my trousers. The poor bugger didn't know where he was, or what he was doing. He was scared himself, no good pretending any different, but . . . where could you go? What could you do? Except get angry . . . feel you wanted to stick your bayonet into a German the way you wanted to stick your prick into a wet hot cunt, a feeling that took hold of all of you and made you tremble and shake and think of nothing else until it was done.

The German artillery, already ranged to a yard on Nollehoek, and now sure that no German troops remained alive in it, opened a steady fire from a hundred guns, to pulverize the already powdered brick, bury the already buried dead, and wear down the already worn out British holding it.

*   *   *   *

Twenty-four hours later the German guns lifted their fire—as they had done six times during the afternoon, night and early morning. Six times the British crawled out of their dripping cellars and muddy holes to join the sentries on the makeshift parapets, facing out, rifles gripped, peering with smarting eyes into the dark for what might come. Six times, after three minutes, the German artillery had opened

529

up again, on the same targets, causing more casualties to the men now out in the open.

"I don't think the swine are going to counter-attack at all, sir," Archie Campbell said to Quentin, sitting beside him on the steps of a cellar in the middle of Nollehoek. The cellar was headquarters for both D Company and the battalion, so it was full of men—the R.S.M., the C.S.M. of D, Father Caffin, of course—half a dozen runners.

Archie lowered his voice as much as he could and still be heard above the shelling—"When are we going to be relieved, sir? Or reinforced?"

"No idea," Quentin said shortly. "I sent a runner back to Brigade in the night, to say we were on our final objectives, but were suffering heavy casualties from shelling. A message came from the Canadians—they've got Passchendaele. So we have the whole ridge now . . . but soon we won't have enough men left to hold our end."

"We don't have enough now," Campbell said; adding hastily, "But we'll do it, sir."

If it's humanly possible, he thought. Perhaps even if it isn't. Those wretched men in D and A had done the impossible yesterday morning, rousing themselves from their dreadful lethargy of despair. For a moment he'd thought they were going to go for the C.O. They'd had every right to do so, if you looked at it dispassionately. Which you couldn't . . . and somehow, driven by the C.O., they'd found enough anger to strike out once more against their fate. And now they were being systematically shelled to destruction. How much longer could flesh and blood, brain and emotion stand? How much more could . . . ?

Quentin Rowland spoke suddenly—"That was a German rifle I shot those two fellows with, wasn't it?"

"Yes, sir," Archie said.

The C.O. said, "Thank God!" He faced Archie—"Couldn't sleep again if I thought it was one of ours . . . not right for a man of the Wealds to die by a British bullet . . . Make sure those two are listed as 'killed in action.'"

"Of course, sir."

"Poor fellows . . . poor fellows . . . poor—"

Boy Rowland came through the smoking dawn rubble toward them, trying to run, falling, getting up. He fell again on the fourth step down. Campbell helped him up and he stood there, half in the open, half on the step, shouting, "Kellaway's got one through the eye . . . shell splinter!"

Quentin said, "Poor chap. Is he dead? Who's in command there now? I'd better go and see."

"What does it matter who's in command?" Boy yelled. His voice rose, "Kellaway's blinded if he's not dead! His company's going with him, one by one. So's mine . . . being torn to bits and used for manure!" He was screaming, and Archie rose slowly to his feet, not knowing what Boy might do . . . draw his revolver on the C.O.? . . . shoot himself? . . . run?

Quentin jumped to his feet, his face turning purple as he shouted into his nephew's face, "Do you think we like it here? Do you think I like watching my men being killed, in front of my eyes, all round me and not being able to do anything about it? Where are the reinforcements? I don't know! Where are the orders? I don't know! We're going to stay here till there's no one left . . . and they'll say the Wealds couldn't hold the position, got driven out by a counter-attack . . . but there won't be anyone here to stop them, and we'll be blamed. It'll be in the official history, we were driven out!"

Campbell listened, appalled. The C.O. was as near breaking as Boy was . . . as he himself was, come to that . . . and all of them in the cellar, from the R.S.M. down . . . and all the men out in the rubble, isolated by death from each other, each enduring a private purgatory, on his way to a private hell.

Quentin slowly, obstinately, with grated teeth, recovered himself. Mustn't let oneself go, got to keep a tight hold, the worse the conditions the more important that was. He'd been acting like a damned Frog, shouting and ranting and weeping . . .

Boy said tensely, "What shall we do, Uncle? Shall we charge? Oh God . . . Oh Christ!" He sat down suddenly, his face in his hands. They heard the stifled sobs through clasped hands and writhing fingers. Carefully Quentin lit his pipe. When he had it drawing well, he held it in his left hand and put his arm round his nephew's shoulders. He said, "We have to stick it out until reinforcements come, Boy. They can't be long. I'll come back to your company with you."

Boy mumbled, "Sorry, sir . . . made a fool of myself." He stood up. "There's no need to come with me, sir. The shelling's bad out there."

"I know," Quentin said. "But I have to come. I have to see that B's all right, without Kellaway. I hope Stratton's all right, to take over . . . Mr Dalley!"

The R.S.M. called up, "Sir?" from the cellar.

"Come with me, please. I'll want you to take over Mr Stratton's platoon in B Company, for the time being."

Father Caffin rose from the German ration box on which he had been sitting and made ready to accompany them.

Quentin went first to B Company, found that Lieutenant Fred

Stratton had taken over command, and that Captain Kellaway had been carried to the Regimental Aid Post, set up near his own head-quarters in another cellar. After leaving R.S.M. Dalley to take over Stratton's old platoon, he went to A and D Companies, at the near end of the village, to check over their defences; then up to C to steady Boy—here Father Caffin left him, to stay with Boy. All this done, Quentin returned to his headquarters. A little later the German shel-ling stopped suddenly, for the seventh time. For the seventh time the men struggled out, and to their posts. No German attack came. The German artillery opened fire again, all together, a 5.9-inch high ex-plosive shell bursting at Boy Rowland's feet and tearing his body into three bloody pieces.

*   *   *   *

Father Caffin came painfully to the mouth of the cellar, where a damaged German machine gun mounted on its tripod marked battal-ion headquarters. He walked slowly down the steps, and faced Quen-tin. After a time he said, "Sir, Captain Rowland's been killed."

Quentin took his pipe from his mouth and stared at the priest in the gloom. He felt cold, and for a moment thought he would cry, for his eyes ached and throbbed. He said, "Instantly?"

"Yes, Colonel."

"Sure?"

"I'm not lying, Colonel."

"Who's in command of the company now?"

"Lieutenant Wildeblood, sir. Captain Dickens was badly wounded a few minutes earlier . . . he's like to die, Wildeblood said to tell you . . . And I'm sorry, Colonel. Boy was a darlin' young man."

Quentin nodded absently—Dickens was a Weald—not a regular of course, but a Man of Kent, lived at Higham, by Rochester . . . but Wildeblood wasn't . . . a reinforcement sent up last month, really a Lancashire Fusilier . . . he wished it had been the other way round, with Dickens the one who survived. It was better to have Wealds' officers commanding Wealds' troops, in a situation like this.

He said, "I'll go and see them." He braced himself to face the steps and the staccato thunder of the livid day outside.

Father Caffin had his hand out—"These were Boy's."

Quentin glanced down: a gold wrist watch with a crocodile leather band: a wallet with a few francs in it: a cameo locket on a thin gold chain. He peered at the handsome oval face of a woman of about forty, fair hair piled on top of her head . . . It wasn't Boy's mother, Louise: too old to be any lady friend of his, surely. He turned the locket over and read "Werner von Rackow" and a rank, regiment, and serial number: very strange. One more thing—a letter, addressed to Lady Helen Durand-Beaulieu, High Staining, Walstone, Kent.

He put it all in his pocket. Must remember to give the letter to the post corporal as soon as he could; but not before he had had time to write a brief note to John and Louise, telling them of the death of their son. He started slowly up the steps. He heard footsteps following, turned sharply, banging his steel helmet against the side wall, and saw Archie Campbell—"What are you doing? Stay here to take messages."

Campbell said, "Sir . . . I'm commanding D now. I think I must go round again and see that they're all right."

Quentin hesitated. There ought to be an adjutant—someone to take messages . . . or the R.S.M. —but he had gone to B. There weren't enough officers . . . Enough to command the few men left. He'd be back soon. He said, "All right. Come back to here when you've been round. Make sure the machine guns in your sector are well protected . . . as well as they can be."

Then once more he started up the stairs, this time faster, and walked out into the storm.

*   *   *   *

Fletcher Whitman, poet, lay a few yards beyond the eastern outskirts of what had been Nollehoek, covered in brick dust and half buried in rubble. He had chosen the place himself when he arrived, moving with B Company, but his own master, for he was a Battalion Sniper. He was well protected from all sides except the direction he chose to shoot, which was to the south, across the front of C Company and part of B. A solid brick wall, its remains a foot high and now—with the piled bricks—its base three feet thick, protected him from directly in front, as he lay facing sideways. Some strewn sandbags which he had adjusted during the night protected his rear, and another heap of rubble protected his right, where the nearest sentry of B Company was twenty yards away. He had moved during the night—taken a shit, stretched, walked about a bit, talked with Mr Laurence and Dago, eaten some bully, taken a drink from his waterbottle, then—back, to lie motionless, watching, waiting. Two 5.9s had landed close, in quick succession, early in the morning, and a flying brick had hit him on the left shoulder blade. He thought the bone might be broken—it certainly hurt a fair sod; but he could shoot—and he had not moved . . . and the new bricks and flying mud piled on top of him had improved his camouflage so that now it would take a real expert, studying from close range with binoculars, to spot him . . . but, of course, the next

533

5.9 might be a direct hit. The body of the German officer who had tried to trick him into showing himself an hour ago lay hooked round an angle iron in the German reserve barbed wire, two hundred yards away, his binoculars blown into his eyes by Fletcher's shot.

He was glad his mother had got over her flu. She oughtn't to work so hard . . . she ought to take the jobs and the money Florinda kept trying to give her or get for her . . . but she wouldn't . . . He was glad his dad was a little simple, or he'd be out here, and this war was no place for him. That German officer would have got *him,* for sure. Dad trusted everyone. But Granddad would like it better than poaching, except for the orders and standing to attention, and the noise. Granddad didn't like noise.

He moved his head, bare—the steel helmet lay beside him, hidden: on his head its smooth round shape would betray him, even if he tried to camouflage it with leaves . . . for what leaves would be growing here naturally, in November? His eye moved up behind the telescopic sight . . . yes, he had seen right . . . something moving in the new No Man's Land . . . very close to the ground, crawling forward with great care . . . one, two, three, four figures . . field grey . . a German patrol. He knew the exact shape of the ground by heart, for he had been studying it for nearly twenty-four hours. The German patrol was entering a small depression now. They might come out of it in any direction. If they came straight ahead, they'd be in the open—not to C Company, but to him on the flank, for fifteen yards; if they then turned and came toward him and B, he wouldn't see them again until they appeared out of the ground barely twenty yards from him—near enough for a potato masher . . . In that case, they'd be after *him.* They couldn't know exactly where he was, but they'd know he must be somewhere outside this angle of Nollehoek.

He waited, the seconds ticking off in his mind. No sign of them . . . give them another minute . . . sixty seconds . . . They hadn't appeared, so they were coming for him. He shifted his position minutely. If he could tell Mr Laurence, so they'd bring a Lewis gun up on his flank, they'd get them all with a short burst. But he couldn't move. Snipers ought to have some sort of telephone that they could use without winding handles and shouting into the thing . . . bury the wire, of course . . . maybe one day there'd be a little wireless, very small, he could wear on his chest, the mouthpiece already strapped to his mouth, earphones to his head.

He waited, safety catch forward, a round in the breech, the magazine full. If he fired at once, as soon as the first Jerry appeared, he'd get that man, but the others would throw their bombs before he could hit them all. Also the shot would tell them just about exactly where he was. Best wait till they were all out . . . He lay, impassive, sentences drumming and swelling in his head.

They came up, one by one, very slowly, the helmets covered in cloth, and that caked with mud, faces muddied. They stared straight at him, twenty yards away, seeking him. A German shell, falling short, burst close behind them and they sank to the ground, waiting for the rest of the salvo. But the charge had been faulty in only one gun, and as they rose again, all their heads and shoulders showing, Fletcher worked his bolt and trigger four times. The feldwebel, the fourth to die, had time to hurl his bomb in a leaping arc, to land a few feet directly in front of Fletcher. The blast hurled mud and brick shards at his head, and a steel splinter grazed his forehead. Blood began to trickle down his face first on one side of his nose, then on the other. The four Germans lay still, each shot through the heart. Fletcher did not move a muscle until at last, through the blood, he saw what he had been looking for . . . the German with a rifle and a huge telescopic sight, about × 20, four hundred yards off, watching, waiting, for him to get out and run . . . to move. His left hand, already on the fore-stock slid slowly back, and moved the sights to 400. The German was clear in the circle of his own sight . . . wind, about ten miles an hour, from the south-west . . . He squeezed the trigger slowly, and, as the rifle jerked back into his shoulder, closed his eyes. When he opened them, the German was still on his belly, but his head, which had been raised a few inches, peering through the big sight, had dropped to the ground.

Five minutes later a fury of shelling burst round the angle of the village where Fletcher was. Trying to get me with the big guns, are they, he thought. Well, there's a chance, always is . . . and they know now just where I am, so I won't get many more of them from here. Time to move.

He started wriggling backward, on his belly, between the sandbags and the rubble, trailing rifle and steel helmet with him. Once out of the German view behind the low wall he put on his helmet, and ran, crouched, to the nearest ragged trench, and slid in with a whoop.

He found Mr Cate there, with the Dago, and the C.O., besides half a dozen men of B, the C.O.'s runner and Mr Laurence's batman.

"Who are you?" the C.O. asked, staring suspiciously at him.

"Private Whitman, Battalion Sniper, sir," he said.

"Oh, I didn't recognize you with all that mud on your face. And blood. You're wounded."

"A little, sir."

"Here, sergeant, help him clean up and put on his first field dressing."

Fletcher kept his face impassive as Sergeant Fagioletti washed his forehead with muddy water from the trench bottom, then dosed his wound with iodine, and applied the first field dressing. Now he'd have to wear his tin hat on the back of his head, if he was wearing it at all, Fletcher thought, for he surely couldn't get it down on his forehead over the dressing. While the bandaging was going on the C.O. said to him, "Any luck, Whitman?"

"I've got nine since first light this morning, sir. Six yesterday . . . I got four just now . . . thought they was p'raps making a reconnaissance for an attack, but it was a patrol sent out to get me. I got them."

"Good man!" The C.O. turned to Laurence Cate. "Everything all right here, Laurence?"

"Yes, sir. We're fine."

Fletcher looked at the young officer curiously. He knew him as well as he knew any of the gentry round Walstone, except perhaps his father, the squire; and he knew he wasn't fine, at all . . . but in just what way, it was hard to tell. The Dago had broken in, "We've just been to all the positions, sir, Mr Cate and me . . . both positions, sir, we only have eight men left in the platoon now . . . but we're all right."

Fletcher munched on an Army biscuit. The Dago was trying to show the C.O. that he was here, and would look after Mr Laurence and see that what ought to be done was done. Though what in the name of God that would be, now, sitting here under the bombardment, waiting to be blown to bits, he didn't know. His forehead burned and ached. How could anyone who hadn't been here understand this? By poetry, that's how. But it would have to be really good. Everyone ought to understand—especially Betty Merritt.

The C.O. said, "All right then . . . Stick it out, Laurence. Keep visiting the men, talking to them . . . We'll be reinforced soon . . . I'm going back to battalion headquarters. Come along, Cottrell."

"I'll come with you, sir," Fletcher said. "I'll have a look at D Company front now and find a new position there."

Fagioletti watched the three of them scurry across an open patch, struggle round the edge of a mud-filled shell crater, and disappear among the ruins and the smoking shell bursts.

"Have you ever seen any dead birds out here, sergeant?" his platoon commander asked him.

Fagioletti scanned the young officer's face anxiously; was this a joke? "No, sir," he said, "can't say I have."

Cate fished in the pocket of his tunic and drew out the corpse of a robin. He gently ruffled the red down on its breast and said, "I found this one out there—" he nodded toward the east— "just after dawn this morning."

Fagioletti said cautiously, "It's dead, sir."

"Yes," Cate said, "but—this village was full of birds, once—sparrows, starlings, robins . . . thrushes and blackbirds on the edges . . . Why did this one stay, when all the others left?"

"I'm sure I couldn't say," Fagioletti said. Poor Mr Cate wasn't here, that was a fact. He was somewhere else, where it wasn't raining shells and making a row fit to break your eardrums. He said, "We'd best go and see Corporal Leavey's lot, sir." Cate put the little corpse back in his pocket and said, "Oh yes . . . they're that way, aren't they?"

At the German machine gun the C.O. turned down the steps into the battalion headquarters cellar. Fletcher scurried on and a moment later passed a soldier running in the opposite direction. He turned to watch the man dive down into the cellar, then continued on his way.

In the cellar Quentin was taking off his tin hat and wiping his brow when the man appeared. Quentin said, "What is it?"

The soldier gasped, "Mr Campbell's hit, sir."

Quentin stopped, his big khaki silk handkerchief pressed to his forehead—"How badly?"

"Bad, sir. In the belly."

Quentin jammed his helmet back on his head and hurried up the steps, the runner and his batman Cottrell at his heels. Twenty yards away a deep cellar housed the Regimental Aid Post and Captain Sholto. The floor was covered with men with serious wounds, an arm missing here, a leg there, the stumps heavily bandaged, shots through the face, Kellaway with his bandaged head and eye, here another officer with teeth and jaw smashed, shoulder wounds, a man blinded, another coughing bloody froth. Someone was whimpering, less than half-conscious and unable to control himself; another was breathing fast and shallow with a rattle in his throat at each inhalation. The rest lay in the semi-darkness, staring at the ceiling, or at the doctor, water dripping on them, waiting, teeth and hands clenched.

Quentin said, "Campbell's got one through the belly, Sholto."

The doctor's chin was dark with stubble and dried blood, and there were black hollows under his eyes. He looked round the floor at the lying men. A few eyes met his. Quentin waited. He didn't want to give Sholto an order to come with him, but . . . he wanted him to.

Sholto said at last, "Nothing I can do for a moment . . . I'll be gone ten minutes, sergeant . . . fifteen."

He followed Quentin into the open. Five minutes later they hurried round the crumbling traverse of a destroyed trench and came upon Archie Campbell lying in the mud beyond, a private of the regiment on the firestep above him, looking out toward the enemy.

Sholto knelt and Campbell opened his eyes. He saw Quentin and muttered, "Sorry, sir." His tunic had been unbuttoned, his shirt and

537

vest lifted, and a first field dressing tied over the wound. It was soaked with blood, and blood was trickling slowly down the side of his bare belly into the mud. Sholto said, "If I could get him back to the R.A.P. . . ."

"Don't move him," Quentin said sharply.

The doctor said, "I must turn him over, sir . . . Here, easy does it." Campbell groaned involuntarily as they carefully turned him over. The exit wound had missed his spine by an inch. The doctor produced disinfectant and bandage from his satchel and dealt with the big ragged hole, seeping dark blood. Then together they turned Campbell back. His eyes had again closed and Sholto said, "I'll give him a shot of morphine now . . . that's all I can do, except make him a little more comfortable under cover in the R.A.P."

"Don't move him," Quentin said again, watching as the doctor injected the morphine into Archie's arm.

He moved a few paces up the trench and Sholto joined him. He said, "What chance does he have?"

The doctor said wearily, "Can't tell, sir. It's possible it went through without doing any serious damage. I can't operate to find out . . . All stomach wounds are dangerous . . ."

"All right," Quentin said. "You get back to the R.A.P. . . . and thanks."

The doctor disappeared round the traverse. Quentin stared anxiously at Archie. His face was pasty, sweaty, pale, his breathing fast and shallow . . . slowing a little as the morphine took effect. He'd got to pull through, or what would Fiona have to live for? And he himself? For, by God, Campbell had become as close a friend as he'd known in his life.

He turned to the private soldier on the firestep, who had not turned round through all this—"Where's Mr Walworth?"

"That way, sir."

Quentin ploughed along the trench in the direction indicated, struggled out into the open where the trench had been blown in and blocked, and a few minutes later found 2nd Lieutenant Walworth in a shell hole.

Walworth had somehow managed to shave. Good man, Quentin thought, he's one of ours, a Weald. He said, "Everything all right here?"

"Yes, sir, except that Campbell's been wounded. He wouldn't let me stay by him. I sent a runner to . . ."

"I know. I've seen him. Send another man to where he is, and make sure that he is not moved or given anything to eat or drink until he can be put on a stretcher and carried all the way back to an ambulance . . . which won't be until after we are relieved, of course. Do you understand?"

"Yes, sir . . . When will we be relieved, sir?"

"I don't know," Quentin said shortly. "Hang on until we are."

"Yes, sir."

Quentin struggled back to where Archie lay. He said to the soldier, "Any change?"

"No, sir."

Archie's eyes opened and he said, "That's grrrea' stuff, tha' morphine sirr."

"You just go back to sleep. Don't try to move. You'll be all right."

"Ah, mebbe, colonel dear, mebbe no' . . . Ah feel a mite drrunk, bu' Ah haven't had a drrap . . . Ah colonel dear, you ought to be getting a brigade, but they won't give it to you . . . 'cos of wha' ye said aboot the whusky at the Corps mess . . . Christ, I canna help laughing at tha' even now . . ." He was indeed laughing, a shaking silent chuckle. Then he gasped, and cried, "That hurts . . . !"

"Don't laugh," Quentin said sharply.

"Ah canna help it . . . An' colonel dear, don't be worrying about your dauchter marryin' the sergeant major. The times are changin', sirr, an' it's nae use to fart agin the thunder. Let the puir lassie find her man where she will . . . aah!" Again he grimaced in pain.

Quentin said, "I've got to go back. Get well soon. And when you reach a hospital in England, write . . . tell me where you are so that I can tell . . . her . . . And, Archie, do you hear me? I'm going to miss you. Archie? Archie? Do you hear?"

Archie was too exhausted and drowsy to respond, except to nod his head, and Quentin, after a moment more looking down at him, went on to his battalion headquarters.

$$*\qquad*\qquad*\qquad*$$

At ten o'clock that night a runner tumbled down the steps—"Sir, the Leinsters is here . . . Come into our area, A Company, ten minutes ago. Mr Wildeblood sent me to tell you. They're taking over from us. We're to go back right away, before it gets light."

"Who says?" Quentin said sharply. "Where's the order?"

"The Leinsters C.O. has it, sir, Mr Wildeblood said, he's bringing him here as soon as they've got their leading company into our trenches and dugouts."

Quentin said, "All right. Go back, give Mr Wildeblood my compliments and tell him the sooner he can bring the Leinsters' C.O. to me here, the better for all of us." He turned to his batman—"Cottrell, you go and warn the company commanders of B, C, and D to be ready to pull out, on my written order, when they have been relieved. Run now, man! Wait—tell Captain Sholto in the R.A.P. first."

Ten minutes later the commanding officer of the 9th Battalion, the Leinster Regiment, came down the steps, his hand to the brim of his steel helmet. He said, "Congratulations, Rowland! You got Nollehoek—and held it! You've been having a rough time, we could see from back there . . . Here are the orders."

Quentin read them quickly then pocketed the paper, and said, "It'll take us about half an hour to get ourselves clear, with what wounded we can move. I'll show you the company areas . . . I ought to stay to point everything out by daylight."

The other colonel said, "No need. We can look after ourselves. And I have a gunner O.P. with me."

Quentin was relieved. He wanted to get out of this hell as much as anyone; and if he stayed, who would see the battalion back?

He said, "There are the remains of an officer of mine in C Company area . . . where our C Company was, at least . . . He was rather badly mangled. I would be grateful if you could give him a decent burial, here in Nollehoek. He was my nephew."

"I'll see to it myself."

Daily Telegraph, Thursday, November 15, 1917

HEALTH AND SUNSHINE
BOURNEMOUTH

Visitors continue to arrive daily, and the autumn season is one of the busiest on record. Yesterday a special gathering was held in the King's Hall to celebrate the 70th birthday of Miss Wingfield Digby, president of the local Y.W.C.A., who has . . .

SOUTHEND-ON-SEA

The Mayoral procession was one of the most imposing in the history of the borough, and the accommodation at St. Mary's Church was inadequate. Upon the return to the Municipal Buildings the Mayor presented Mr F. Myall, late private, Royal Fusiliers, with the Military Medal . . . Mrs. H. W. J. Hobbs has been elected president of the Needlework Guild which . . .

TENBY

Weather is mild and genial, and visitors have been able to enjoy outdoor pastimes and walks under pleasant conditions. Captain

> **Hughes Morgan, who is serving his sixth term of office as Mayor, attended Divine Service at . . .**
> **Illustrated Guide, Town Clerk.**
> **Royal Lion Hotel, facing sea. Best position.**
> **Imperial—South. On cliffs. Cui. bourgeoise.**
>
> ### EASTBOURNE
>
> **From the number of visitors arriving the prospects of a brisk winter season are considered to be unusually good. It is intended to maintain a full supply of high-class concerts and popular amusements. Official reports point to the continued remarkable healthiness of the town. There is a very low death rate.**
> **Burlington for comfort and cuisine. Gordon Hotels.**

Cate sipped his coffee. It was nice to know that there was a low death rate somewhere on earth. The letter beside his plate was addressed in a crabbed, old hand . . . Blyth's. He began to open it, hoping to learn that the old man was enjoying a happy, and healthy retirement. Through the windows movement caught his eye, and he got up to investigate. It was John Rowland, looking like a ghost, his feet dragging, his shoulders sagging, his face grey and old, the hand of death on it. Cate dropped the letter and hurried round to the front door, reaching and opening it just as John was raising his hand to knock. The two men stared at each other, wordlessly. Then John began to cry, and Cate went forward and took him in his arms as John's head sank onto the rough Donegal tweed of his shoulder, sobs racking him.

After a while Cate heard the quiet voice of Garrod behind him— "Let me help you bring him in, sir."

America, England, France: November, 1917

33 The wind howling in from the north off the Wichita Mountains carried a hint of snow in its teeth. Leaden clouds hurried south low over Fort Sill, the thousand tents of Camp Doniphan, and, beyond, the compact little town of Lawton. The six officer candidates stood in a row behind the 75-mm field gun on the park at the west end of Camp Doniphan. Facing them was a Regular Army sergeant in breeches, leggings, and a short coat with sheepskin collar, his campaign hat pushed well forward over his forehead, the red cord and acorns dulled by age.

"Take post!" he shouted.

The six young men ran to the gun and took post beside it, some facing inward to the gun, some forward, one back.

The sergeant barked, "Call your duties! Gunner!"

The recruit officer at the Gunner's post bellowed, "Set the deflection—apply the deflection difference—give direction to the piece—set the site—give elevation to the piece—call READY—move my head out of the way before the piece is fired—measure a deflection—measure a site—measure an elevation—measure the minimum range—refer the piece!"

"Cannoneer Number 1."

This was Johnny Merritt's post, and he bellowed, "Set the range—open and close the breech—call set—fire the piece—use the rammer!"

"Cannoneer Number 2!"

The next man shouted, "Load the piece—throw the empty car-

tridge out of the way—in volley fire, call out the number of the round
. . ." His voice trailed away.

The sergeant screamed, "What have you forgotten, Anspach?
Think now! . . . Anyone?"

Cannoneer Number 4 shouted, "Handle the sight extension bar."

"Right! Cannoneer Number 3!"

"Set the corrector—set the range on the fuse setter—set the fuse
when the hand fuse setter is used—distribute the fuses for shell to
Numbers 4 and 5—receive the fused shell from Numbers 4 and 5 and
pass them to Number 2."

"Cannoneer Number 4!"

"In time fire, complete the setting of the fuse—in shrapnel fire,
pass the round to Number 2 . . . ."

Johnny's attention wandered. The telegram had been bad enough,
but the letter, from Father Christopher, even worse. He still found it
an effort to believe that his child, his first born, was dead. Poor Stella
. . . it was all very well for the doctors to say that apnea was a normal
condition of infants; that their lungs had not been functioning for
those nine months in the womb and often started very shakily . . .
"death from natural causes" sounded soothing, inevitable . . . but how
must Stella be feeling, having carried the child all that time, and then,
after suffering the pains of parturition, lost it?

"Change!"

He returned to reality with a start, and took the Gunners' post.
The recruit who had been acting as Gunner ran to Cannoneer Number 5's post, Number 5 went to Number 4, and so on. The sergeant
barked, "Prepare for action!"

Johnny removed the sight support cover, released the elevating
latch and operated the elevating and traversing mechanisms, leaving
the piece in the centre of its traverse on the axle. Cannoneer Number
1 handed him the sight; he seated it carefully, and checked that the
deflection setting was Plateau 1, Drum 100. Then he set the sight at
zero, levelled the bubble, opened the sight extension bar case, and
waited motionless at his post.

The sergeant barked, "Change!"

Johnny doubled back to the post of Cannoneer Number 5. His
hands were freezing in the cold wind, and his ears were blue and
numb with pain. The cords on his hat were that color—infantry blue
. . . one day, five or six weeks from now, they'd be the red of the Field
Artillery . . . no, they wouldn't, they'd be the gold and black of an
officer. . . .

"March order!"

I'm Number 5, Johnny thought to himself—so, replace or otherwise dispose of unused ammunition . . . but there isn't any . . . help Number 3 lower and secure the caisson door and raise and secure the caisson apron . . . secure aiming stakes on the right side of the piece's trail . . . take post . . .

Change . . . change . . . change . . . Prepare for action . . . March order . . . change . . .

The hours wore on.

*   *   *   *

The electric lights burned bright overhead in one of the hutted lecture rooms of the School of Fire. There was no heat, and all the students and instructors alike were wearing thick uniforms and heavy coats, either long greatcoats, or shorter coats lined and collared with wool. The instructor, a 1st Lieutenant of Field Artillery, stood by the blackboard, which was marked with a diagram of four field pieces labelled G1, G2, G3, and G4, and parallel dotted and solid lines labelled by other letters and figures. Under all was scrawled in the lieutenant's handwriting DEFLECTION DIFFERENCE.

Johnny listened, eyeing the lieutenant the while. His name was George Burress and he was a tall, scholarly man of about thirty, not unlike President Wilson in general appearance. He smelled of the classroom, not of the gun park or the stables . . . his wife Jean was a year or two younger and was very pretty—in Stella's roses and peaches sort of way . . . she liked entertaining the young officer candidates . . . so lonely and far from home, she chirped . . . Heaven knew there were enough of them here to keep her knee deep in admirers: that's what she seemed to want . . .

Lieutenant Burress was speaking, "The deflection difference is the difference in deflection which is applied to the several pieces so that each piece may be brought to bear on its own part of the target . . . What are the planes of fire of the various pieces, taken as a whole, called? Private Anspach?"

"The sheaf, sir."

"Right . . . the base piece—G1 on the diagram there—having been established on the base line, the other pieces may be laid parallel to it by the use of a common aiming point . . . establishing each of the other pieces individually parallel to the base line by using an aiming circle or some other angle measuring instrument, or . . . Corporal Merritt?"

"Reciprocal laying in the base piece, sir."

"Right . . . Now, let's form a parallel sheaf by using a common aiming point . . . The aiming point may be . . ."

Corrections for angle site . . . determination of the deflection dif-

544

ference . . . convergence difference . . . distribution difference . . .
For distributed fire the deflection difference is equal to the convergence difference increased algebraically by the distribution difference; or DD = p − t + F/N − 1 . . .

Johnny's head swam. At least, he realised, he wasn't thinking of
Stella and the lost baby . . .

Application of rules . . . formation of a parallel sheaf using a
director . . . First case—Orienting line materialized . . .

He jerked himself awake. He must learn, he must graduate, or
he'd never get back to France, or England . . .

* * * *

Lady Helen Durand-Beaulieu walked briskly down Walstone's winding street, a basket of tinned goods on her arm. Her boots crunched
satisfyingly into the frosty gravel of the road, a sharp wind made her
cheeks tingle and glow. It was three o'clock of a Sunday afternoon and
few people were about except some boys dribbling a soccer ball past
Mr Fulcher's cottage and police station. A train was chuffing out of the
station, headed for Ashford, its steam a dense cloud in the damp air,
the clanking of its coupling rods to be heard a mile away in the general
winter silence.

Lady Helen left the village proper behind her and a few minutes
later came to Probyn Gorse's cottage, made her way through the gap
in the hedge, and walked through the frost-starched grass to the front
door. No dog barked; so Probyn was out, with the Duke of Clarence,
she thought. That would make it easier, though he would know as
soon as he came in, for the Woman would tell him, as she should.

The Woman opened the door and Helen said, "May I come in?"

The Woman stood back, but said nothing. Helen walked in and
put the basket on the table. She said, "Mr and Mrs Rowland wanted
you to have these in good time before Christmas. They're not very
exciting, but we all hope you'll like them—baked beans, bully beef,
stew, some jam . . . and a bottle of rum."

"All from H.U.S.L.," the Woman said, glancing at the labels. "Mrs
Rowland wouldn't have gone there six months ago."

"We're having a hard time at High Staining," Helen said simply.
"Not compared with others, but we can't afford to be extravagant."
She began taking the tins out of the basket. She said, over her shoul-
der, "This is not what I really came about." She turned to face the
Woman squarely—"I'm going to have a baby."

"Captain Charles's." It was a statement, not a question, but she
nodded. "You want me to get rid of it, now that he's been killed?"

"Certainly not! Will you help me find a place where I can live, earn some money, do something useful, while I'm waiting for the baby? And will you come and help me have him when the time comes, wherever I am?"

The Woman's naturally harsh face softened. She said, "It will be a boy. You're sure, are you not?"

Helen nodded. "Yes."

The Woman said, "Sit down, milady. There." She put some slivers of wood into the stove and moved a simmering pot a few inches. Then—"You'll best go to London. There's work everywhere for women these days, but London has more . . . and it will be harder to find you."

"I'm not ashamed," Helen said. "I'm glad. But my father will be terribly upset . . . My mother, too, for a time, I suppose. And Mr and Mrs Rowland. I don't want to rub all their noses in it by staying."

The Woman said suddenly, "Do you know Ethel Stratton, that was? Mrs Fagioletti?"

Helen said, "Yes, vaguely . . . She married an Italian waiter and then he divorced her or something. Mr and Mrs Rowland have talked of her."

The Woman said, "They're back together—except that he's in the Army, in France. She has two rooms in London, and has been trying to find a boarder, to make a little money, till Fagioletti comes home. Fletcher wrote us about her . . ."

"Do you have her address?" Helen asked eagerly.

"No, but I know who will have it—her sister, Ruth Hoggin, or her mother, Mrs Stratton. Mrs Stratton's living with the Hoggins now."

"I'll go and . . ." Helen began.

The Woman raised a hand, "You'll go home and get yourself ready. Probyn will give you the address tomorrow."

"Then I'll leave at once."

"When will you have the baby?"

"About the end of March."

"Is it kicking?"

"Just started. Here, feel." She stood up, unbuttoned her overcoat and jacket, and laid the Woman's hand on her belly. Through the thick wool of her shirt she felt the baby kick once against the Woman's hand, then lie still, a minute, more . . . another. She found herself smiling with joy.

The Woman said, "I'd best take a look to make sure everything's all right. It's cold in here, but I won't be long. Take off your breeches, milady."

Helen began undressing, tears filling her eyes. The Woman said gently, "I'm sorry about the captain. But the boy will make it better for you."

546

"I know. But now . . . I remember, too much."

She lay down on the little table and the Woman began gently palpating, while tears ran down Helen's cheeks onto the bare wood.

* * * *

Fiona Rowland stared at the letter uncomprehending . . . token of esteem . . . happy to give the young couple goods to the value of one hundred pounds from the H.U.S.L. stores in Hedlington, or Aldershot . . . small compared with what Battery Sergeant Major Robinson has given for his country . . . modest start on married life . . . obedient servant, Bill Hoggin . . . What on earth was this about? She had been looking for a letter from Archie . . . or from Quentin about Archie . . . but this? Ah, it was to do with Virginia's engagement, which had now been announced in the papers: that dreadful man Hoggin was offering to give them a present.

She hurled the letter to the floor and began to pace the flat like a caged tigress. It was a week since Quentin's letter had reached her. But where was Archie? Quentin should have sent a telegram at once, then perhaps she might have been able to get out to France and intercept him on his way back through the Base Hospital . . . She was being silly. That would have been impossible. And Quentin had probably done right not even to write until he knew that Archie had survived at least through the first sort of hospital. Quentin had written, "You will be as sorry as I to learn that Archie Campbell was severely wounded on November 6, in Nollehoek. I know he reached the C.C.S. (that's Casualty Clearing Station) all right, but he had just been evacuated when I was able to visit it the day before yesterday. I spoke to a doctor who told me he was not out of danger, from complications, because the bullet had chipped a piece out of his liver and punctured the intestine. That is the last I have heard . . ."

Archie would write soon—as soon as he could. He knew she would do anything for him, and now he needed her . . . now he was free of Quentin and the awful magnetic pull of Quentin's sacred "regiment." He would come back to her now, for he had done what he had said he must—face the same dangers that Quentin did. He would live, he must, for her . . . but *where—was—he?*

Why didn't he get a doctor or another patient to write, just a few words to say he was alive and *where—he—was,* that was all she needed. Then she'd be out of her misery . . . why hadn't she read the casualty lists more closely? Once she knew he was wounded, she hadn't looked at the lists of the killed and died of wounds . . . suppose he'd died of wounds in some cold miserable tent in French mud . . .

Where —was—he?

She stopped her pacing, mesmerized by a new realization. The first person he'd write to, when he could, was Quentin. She'd have to beg Quentin to tell her where he was as soon as he learned. She found herself staring at a pen-and-ink drawing of Quentin, sitting in a dugout drinking cocoa, by candlelight, muffled in his British warm, wearing mittens, his steel helmet on. It was signed CAMPBELL . . . one of the best things Archie had ever done . . .

Did Quentin know? Surely not, or he would have had Archie transferred to another battalion, even another regiment.

Well, even if he did, she must write and beg. She must know where Archie was.

*　　*　　*　　*

I wish my mother could see me now with a grease-gun under my car,
Filling my differential, 'ere I start for the camp from afar,
Atop a sheet of frozen iron, in cold that'd make you cry.
"Why do we do it?" you ask, "Why? We're the F.A.N.Y."

> *I used to be in Society once;*
> *Danced, hunted, and flirted—once;*
> *Had white hands and complexion—once;*
> *Now I'm a F.A.N.Y.!*

The twenty women chanted exuberantly to a mournful psalm tune, conducted by Trooper Jelkes, the short fleece-lined greatcoat open at the neck, showing her khaki scarf, lace-up field boots on her slender legs, and a steel helmet on the back of her head, the chinstrap on her dimpled chin keeping it in place as she waved her arms imperiously, the right hand holding a long French loaf as a baton.

Naomi Rowland sang with the rest until the turn of another girl's head, a look in her eye, reminded her of Boy. She stopped singing. How could she be enjoying herself so much, with Boy gone? In another week or two she'd find herself praying that this awful war would go on for ever.

But she could not hold herself against the current in the room; and soon began to sing again with the rest:

> *That is what we are known as, that is what you must call.*
> *If you want "Officers' Luggage," "Sister," "Patients" an' all,*
> *Ring up the Ambulance Convoy, "Turn out the F.A.N.Y."*
> > *They used to say we were idling—once;*
> > *Joy-riding round the battlefield—once;*
> > *Wasting petrol and carbide—once;*
> > *Now we're the F.A.N.Y.*
> *That is what we are known as: we are the children to blame,*
> *For begging the loan of . . .*

From outside the shrill cry of "Barges! Barges!" cut through the massed trebles and contraltoes. Trooper Jelkes broke off in mid verse, shouting "Barges!" and jumped down from the bench on which she had been standing. With the others Naomi ran for her steel helmet, hanging on a peg on the wall by the door—she was already wearing her greatcoat, for the hut was not heated, except once in a blue moon when they could scrounge enough wood or coal for the derisory fireplace. Gauntlets on, she shoved through the door with the rest and out into the night.

It was blowing hard, driving snow horizontally into her face from the north-west. The snow lay only four inches deep as yet, she saw by the dim lights, but it would be slippery, especially on the slope down to the canal wharf where the barges unloaded the wounded. The Convoy would be lucky if another girl didn't follow Trooper Bainbridge's feat of last month, and go sliding into the canal. She reached her ambulance . . . the lieutenant was there, leaning in as she arranged the spark and mixture—"You'll have an orderly, Rowland. Wait for him . . . They'll be a minute."

"All right, madam," she shouted back into the wind, and climbed out with the starting handle in her gauntleted hand. Turn gently, turn again, and again, switched off . . . It wasn't cold enough for the Convoy to carry out what, they had told her, was the real cold weather drill, when drivers had to get out of bed every hour, start the lorries and ambulances, and run them for five minutes, so that they would start quickly in just such emergencies as this.

The R.A.M.C. private came stumbling to her, peering at the numbers on the canvas sides of the big Napier ambulances, and cried, "Evening, miss . . . lovely evening for a ride in the moonlight, I don't think."

She hurried back to the dashboard, switched on, and swung the starting handle. Two swings and the engine coughed and caught. She waited . . . blue headlights on. The lieutenant was by the gate, waving a torch slowly from side to side. The ambulances were moving out onto the pavé . . . turning right at the gate, groping cautiously through the blizzard to pick up the wounded soldiers at the wharf, men so seriously wounded that they could not have stood the long drive back from the rear areas of the battle zone to the base hospitals on the bumpy and shell-pocked roads. The canals were smooth—but now they'd have to suffer six miles of road travel as No. 12 Convoy of the First Aid Nursing Yeomanry took them to Abbeville Base Hospital No. 4.

Naomi peered through her goggles into the driving snow. Under the steel helmet her hair was jammed into a khaki woolen Balaclava, its chin piece down and only her mouth showing, breathing plumed steam into the night. "Do you have a handkerchief?" she shouted to the orderly, sitting beside her.

"Yes, miss." She felt him stirring, dredging in the pockets of his greatcoat.

"Keep wiping my goggles, please, when you see the snow caking on them . . . but don't let your hand block my view for long."

"All right, miss."

He edged closer, handkerchief at the ready. The headlights were no more than blue phosphorescence on the snow, and a dim reddish glow from under the tail of the ambulance in front. Naomi drove concentrated, all her being in her hands, her wrists, the touch of her booted feet on the pedals, her eyes, watching . . . the red light . . . slow now, she touched the brake in a series of light taps, daren't press hard, or suddenly, or she'd be in the ditch. The orderly's hand passed across her goggles . . . better . . . She took a deep breath. Was it this body, this person, who had fallen into Rodney Venable's arms in the Norfolk rain, barely a year ago? Unsure about her place in life, her identity as a person, above all as a woman? There was a letter from Rodney in her locker now—discreet, cautious, but reading between the lines he was still desperate. It was sad, but she would not see him again. She was Naomi Rowland, working now at the top of her capacity. She was doing her own job, by herself, responsible for the ambulance and the orderly and, soon, for six torn men . . . and no one could do it better. After this, she would never be afraid again, never doubt, just face, decide, and do . . .

The orderly's hand swept over her goggles again. "Well done, miss," he said softly. "Gawd, I'm glad it's you, not me, driving this thing tonight."

*   *   *   *

Wilfred Bentley walked at Rachel's side down the slushy street. Sleet had fallen during the day, but had soon melted under the wheels and the boots, and from the heat of the close-packed houses. It had not been a bad meeting, as meetings of the No-Conscription Fellowship went—the usual abuse, some hurled vegetables . . . but people were becoming chary of that; food cost money these days, if you could find it . . . a pair of policemen watching in bored silence, the usual drunken soldiers on leave. One of them swung a punch at Wilfred. The blow had bruised his cheek below the right eye, grazing the skin.

"How much money did we get?" Rachel asked.

He said, "Five and tuppence . . . the tuppence was from a man who told me to use it to take a tram up to the barracks and enlist." He laughed—"But there were several thoughtful faces. Almost as many as angry ones. The proportion changes every time."

She said, "The fighting at Ypres seems to have died down, at last . . . Haig ought to be shot, if you ask me. He's responsible for all that slaughter."

"It was pretty bad, by all accounts. I've heard every figure between a quarter of a million and four hundred thousand, for the casualties . . . but Haig will have his reasons. Everyone has his reasons, which seem incontrovertible to him."

She looked at him in the twilight—it was four o'clock in the afternoon, chinks of light showing from the curtained pubs. "That beastly drunken soldier broke the skin of your cheek."

Bentley said, "Yes . . . poor chap. He was 60th . . . my regiment. I said to him, 'What do you want to hit another Greenjacket for?' and he stared at me and said, 'You, a rifleman? Then what the hell are you doing up there with that woman?' and I said, 'Trying to save you, and the Regiment, from useless sacrifice.' "

"I don't know why you want to save that regiment, or any others," Rachel said peevishly. Wilfred had attitudes she could not share, and never would—"We're against *all* militarism, aren't we?"

He said gently, "There *are* causes worth fighting for, Rachel. Suppose a Napoleon were to arise in Germany twenty years hence . . . or suppose the Russians try to impose their revolution on the world by force . . . the Regiments would be needed then, but not for this . . ."

"Nor to keep the rich in possession of their money," she said, knowing that Wilfred had ample private means.

He said, "I'll gladly pay any taxes levied on me, my dear . . . and one day, if I am in a position to decide what taxes *should* be levied, and for what purposes, you'll see that my own money won't be a factor in my decisions."

Then they reached the house, and Wilfred stopped, handing over the little cloth bag in which he had collected the donations for the Fellowship. She said, "Come in for a minute."

He said in a low voice, "Bert has been so silent, when I'm there."

"He's thinking," she said. "And it's my house as well as his . . . Have a glass of beer, at least. And get warm. You've been coughing a lot."

Wilfred smiled and followed her into the little house. Bert looked up from the table, where he was reading a Trade Union pamphlet. He said, "How did it go?"

"Five and tuppence," Rachel said briefly. She went to the kitchen, found two bottles of beer, opened them, and gave one to Wilfred. Bert had returned to his pamphlet.

Wilfred said, "Chin chin," and drank from the neck of the bottle. A moment later he could not suppress a burp. Rachel laughed, Wilfred smiled, and Bert said, "Ah, so the gentry can actually belch."

Rachel opened her mouth in anger, but Wilfred said easily, "Of course . . . Yesterday I went to London and talked to Ben Tillett, Keir Hardie, and Ramsay Macdonald. I told them that I intend to stand as Socialist candidate for Mid Scarrow at the next election, whenever that is."

Bert lowered his book—"You, a Socialist?"

"Yes," Wilfred said. "Rachel's converted me."

"But you're not a working man, never will be . . . We don't want folks like you in the Labour movement. The committee will never pick you."

"Hold your tongue," Rachel said sharply.

Wilfred said patiently, "The Labour movement is not the same as Socialism, though they have many of the same aims. You're a trade unionist, really. What you want is practical things for working people—better wages, better housing, education, opportunities . . . You believe in the class struggle, so you're a sort of Marxist . . . But there's a theoretical side to social structure too . . . the Fabian Society way, what George Bernard Shaw and the Webbs believed in—not the class struggle, but the natural evolution of socialism as the best way for the whole of society to organize itself . . . That's what I'm for."

Bert said slowly, "A few months ago I was thinking of your sort as la-di-da arseholes . . . but I suppose we're going to need you as much as you're going to need us. We've got to work together, even if we don't really even like each other . . . and we don't . . . do we?" He looked challengingly at Wilfred.

Wilfred did not speak for a time then said, "I know you don't like me, but I have not been sure that it is because of ideological differences. I think it is because I have been falling in love with Rachel."

"Well!" Bert said. "You've come out and said it, at last."

Rachel was looking down at her shoes. Wilfred had said it to her, and now to Bert: at last it was in the open and must be dealt with. Wilfred said, "I don't dislike you, but we have little in common . . . except concern for social justice and decency in this country. That ought to be enough to enable us to work together."

Bert said, "P'raps you're right. I 'ope so . . . We've broken into Rowland's factories, at last . . . both J.M.C. and Hedlington Aircraft. We're getting new union members every week . . . secret members, so far, 'cos if Rowland knew, he'd sack them . . ."

"If you call a strike now, the men won't follow you," Wilfred said. "And if they did, the government would take over the factories."

Bert nodded—"Right! So we're going to go on organizing, go on signing up members, so that, when we're ready, soon's the war's over . . ." he snapped his fingers, "we'll close them down!"

"I hope to be in Parliament by then," Wilfred said. "I'm starting campaigning after Christmas, so that the voters will know me by sight, and know my name . . . If we ever get a Socialist government in this country, what will your attitude be—the unions'? Because, of course, a fundamental part of socialism is to nationalize the means of production and distribution."

Bert said, "Then you'll be the bosses. We'll strike against you, just the same as against Rowland, if you don't give us what we want—what we've earned."

"But who's to decide that, in a Socialist state?" Wilfred asked.

"We are—the working men and women . . ."

Wilfred finished his beer and stood up. He said, "I must go. But first—I'm going to ask Rachel to marry me." He turned to her—"Will you?"

Her face paled, then went red as she flushed. Tears came to her eyes. At last she found words—"I can't tell you now, Wilfred. I have to talk to Bert."

He said, "Of course. Good night, my dear. Good night, Bert"— and went out.

*   *   *   *

John Rowland leaned on the plough handle and cried, "Garrover, Duke, hup, hup!" He flicked the reins and the huge Shire leaned into the trace, the shining steel share slid forward, turning the earth in a long, curving dark wave, wet in the driving rain from the north-west, that carried in it a forewarning of more sleet or snow.

This field used to be pasture for the Friesians, or fallow for hay, but the government had decreed that more pasture should be turned to arable, and grain planted, to cut down the necessity of importing so much wheat from across the Atlantic, past the lurking U-boats; and they'd had to slaughter half the herd . . . selling cheap, to such as Hoggin, for the market became glutted when every dairy and beef herd in the islands was in the same boat—except the Scottish beef herds, for the land up there was mostly too poor to be put to wheat, or even rye. Now High Staining shared three Shires, bought by Christopher Cate, with Cate's tenants. Seagulls followed in John's footsteps down the furrow. They'd notice soon that he was not sowing, and fly away . . . not to sea, it must be rough in the estuary, worse in the Channel; they'd be back.

Boy wouldn't. His efforts to stop the war might help other fathers'

553

sons, but not his own. Boy had gone, leaving so little . . . a watch, a wallet with some French francs in it . . . there might have been a handkerchief, other little items which Quentin had not forwarded because they were soaked in blood. John had heard that in such cases the articles were quietly disposed of, to save the parents' feelings . . . And there was the locket, with Werner von Rackow's name and the cameo of a handsome older woman. Von Rackow was the famous German air ace, now second only to Richtofen in fame. What contact could Boy possibly have had with him? It would be easier to understand if it was Guy who had had the locket. The airmen on both sides seemed to behave to each other with almost mediaeval chivalry . . . but the infantry, in the hell of the trenches?

Duke reached the end of the field, at the top of the long gradual slope. This field was under hay last summer. It was here that he and Boy had scythed the sweet grass and charlock and clover, the bees humming in the dense summer air, the girls following, sweating, raking the hay out for drying. They had all worked together in England's greenness, at high summer, in inner peace and harmony.

He turned the Shire gelding, with much clumping of great hooves in the mud, splashing of thin water, shaking of the heavy feathers at the hocks, muscles bulging at rump and haunch. "Garrover . . . hup, I say, hup!"—again a flick of the reins, off again, this time down the slope.

He could not see the end of the field, for tears. He could not see beyond this moment, this work. He had thought to live here with Louise until they were too old to run the farm. By then Boy would have left the Army, perhaps a lieutenant colonel, to spend the rest of his days as an English gentleman—riding to hounds, attending the Sheep Fair, joining one of the old political parties, showing flowers or marrows at the Flower Show, accepting the magistracy. He'd have married long before that, of course, and High Staining would be filled with the sound of children's laughter when they were home for the holidays from prep school or public school; while Boy, until he retired, might be in Peshawar or Hong Kong, or Jamaica. By then he and Louise would have settled in a smaller house, perhaps in Walstone—or better, by the sea. If Boy was to be master of High Staining, it would be best if his father and mother were not sitting on top of him. Eastbourne wasn't far away . . . perhaps Rye or Winchelsea, very pretty little towns, Cinque Ports, too. And . . .

The tears dried, and he could see clearly enough—the high hedge at the end of the field; and the future—Boy was dead; Naomi would marry and go away; High Staining would die; there would be no children here. The future had passed, blown to bits at a shattered

Flemish village near Ypres. He, too, was broken, all passion, hope, and desire gone.

An hour later he unhitched the plough, led Duke up the lane to the barn, and handed him over to Joan Pitman, saying, "I'll be needing him again at two, Joan." Then up to the house, head bent, shoulders hunched, the coat flapping wet against his legs, the rain flicking his ears and dripping off his shapeless felt hat and down his collar.

As soon as he was inside the door he realized that something was wrong. There was an intense silence, quite unlike the murmurous quiet of a normal day. He took off his heavy boots, slipped his stockinged feet into slippers, went upstairs and washed, and came down again. Still the silence.

Louise was waiting for him in the drawing room, the rain beating on the window panes behind her. She said, "Shut the door, John." He did so, puzzled. Was she concerned that there might be a draught?

She said, "Helen's left, John."

He stared at her, not understanding—"Lady Helen . . . left? Left what?"

"She's left High Staining," Louise said with more than her usual patience. "As soon as you went off with Duke she came in and said she did not want to work here any more. She thought there was more important work she could do for the war."

John sat down in a chair. It was a shock, now that he understood what she was saying; but he was protected against shocks now. Since the telegram about Boy, there could be no pain, only numb acceptance. He said, "She's going back to the Park, I suppose."

"I'm sure she isn't," Louise said. "She told me she had told her parents, and of course I had to believe her . . . she left an hour later—must have packed last night . . . got Joan to drive her to the station."

John thought, Joan was looking rather strange when I handed Duke into her care.

"Joan says Helen didn't tell her where she was going, but it must have been the London train she was going to catch. Mr Miller can tell us. All we have to do is telephone the station and ask him."

John said, "We'd better tell the Swanwicks. We are responsible for her, even though she is twenty-five."

"I already have," Louise said. "Lady Swanwick didn't say much except, 'Thank you,' but I am sure she thinks the same that I do." She paused, waiting expectantly.

John said, "I suppose that Helen really couldn't stand farm life any more. It is hard work, and dull, after all, when she could be a V.A.D.

555

in a fashionable hospital in London, or . . . doing exciting things in France like Naomi with the F.A.N.Y.s."

Louise said, "The wretched girl is pregnant! I'm sure of it . . . and, as I said, I think Lady Swanwick is sure, too."

John said slowly, "Pregnant? How can you think that? Helen is so sweet natured, such a responsible person . . . and a lady through and through."

Louise said, "Ladies fall in love, like other young women—and older ones. Women feel in these times that they must seize happiness . . . passion . . . while they can, before it is destroyed, bombed, shelled, out of existence. They want to give the man they love what he might not otherwise survive to know."

John said, "Poor Helen. I thought you were unkind to use the word wretched about her, but I see now what you mean . . . Is there anything we can do to help her?"

Louise said, "I don't know . . . Not if she goes into hiding, has the baby, then gets rid of it, secretly, or has an abortion. And that baby's going to be our grandchild."

John sat up with a jerk—"Ours? You mean . . . good heavens, Louise, you mean that Boy is—was—the father?"

She nodded emphatically—"While he was home on his last leave. I told you she had fallen in love with him."

"All the girls did," John said.

"Not really. But Helen, yes. And he with her."

John said, "Our grandchild . . ." His eyes lit up. He felt a warmth coursing through veins and arteries that for weeks now had been filled with some cold, viscous fluid. He said, "If it's a boy he could inherit High Staining! We'd have to work here a few years longer than if Boy had been able to, but . . ."

"He—or she—will be illegitimate," Louise said.

John believed profoundly in the sacred nature of the marriage sacrament; but he could not at this moment find that he cared whether Lady Helen's child was going to be born legitimate or otherwise. It would be their grandchild. They ought to find Helen, and bring her home.

Louise said, "Helen will be in touch with us some time soon, I am sure of it. She is not going to leave us, or her parents, thinking that she might be dead, or has in some way deserted us all. I don't think we ought to make extraordinary efforts to find her. She doesn't want anyone deciding her and the child's fate for her. We must just offer our love and help as soon as she gets in touch . . . I'm coming to London with you tomorrow for the N.C.F. meeting."

John felt the heavy disinterest of the past weeks settle on him again. He said, "I'm not going. I'm resigning from the Fellowship . . . Boy's dead."

His wife said, "Well, I'm joining—because millions of other young men aren't . . . yet."

*   *   *   *

The Earl of Swanwick jabbed at a coal in the grate with the poker in a futile gesture of frustration. The coal settled down in a new formation, but no more flames burst to life. Swanwick remained standing, staring down into the nearly dead ashes, but seeing nothing, except their greyness. He said, "We ought to go to London next Thursday."

"What for?" the countess asked quietly.

"They're having a memorial service in the Guards Chapel at Wellington Barracks, for all officers of the Brigade killed this year . . . It'll be just the same as last year. But I don't think I can stand it."

"We must," she said, her fingers moving steadily at the knitting needles, knitting a khaki wool scarf. "The sad thing is that Cantley really hated it all. Arthur didn't, really."

Lord Swanwick grunted. Nothing. Both sons gone. Helen gone God knew where or why. This great barrack falling down about his ears. Servants leaving. The hounds . . .

He said, "I'm going to disband the hunt. Can't get enough meat for the hounds."

She said nothing. It was a pity, but she could see that it could not be helped. Roger seemed to have no idea of what might have driven Helen to running off like that. He thought she must have had a quarrel with John Rowland—or taken umbrage at some criticism from Louise; but obviously it was not that. Should she tell him what she thought—what, indeed, she was certain of? Better not. He had enough on his mind. Helen would write sooner or later, then he'd have to know. Then there would be a terrible scandal . . . and losing two sons for England would make no difference. There would be no charity—not for the Earl and Countess of Swanwick. It was Boy, of course . . . if only they had had time to get married before he went back to France. But would Roger have given his permission? Be honest . . . would she herself have been quite content? They needed money; they hoped for more. Helen should have fallen in love with someone like the Duke of Westminister, or Lord Derby's son . . . a great name, a great fortune. And, above all, she should have remembered who she was . . . making love in a field, they must have, like Fletcher Gorse and his doxies! Oh, this war, this war!

But one day even this war must end. Then what? They would never again be able to afford the number of servants they used to.

557

That meant—leave Walstone Park. Go where? A big flat in a not-too-fashionable part of London . . . say South Kensington? Roger must be urged to attend the Lords . . . more useful than a pack of foxhounds, when you came down to it; and it was his birthright. If people like him—the Backwoods Peers they were called—didn't attend, and vote, the country would be left in the hands of the radicals . . . Barbara could work in a livery stable and give riding lessons. There were plenty of such institutions round all sides of Hyde Park . . . Helen? Ah, who knew? That would have to wait. But Helen was the most sensible of them all (that's why the wild falling in love, the passionate surrender, so surprised her); she would steer her course in the current of the future. Herself? She was used to managing a large house, with many servants. She did it well—as well as the money had allowed. There must be a place for her somewhere. It would be in trade, of course, for she was much too old to learn a profession; well, so be it. Her father, an impoverished Welsh baron, had run sheep on his mountain land, and kept the family's head above water many years by his judicious buying and selling of the sheep, wool, and mutton. Perhaps she could become a buyer for a food shop, or chain of shops. She had some connections . . . come to think of it, that she certainly had.

The earl said suddenly, "I think Hoggin wants to buy this place."

She stopped her knitting, looking up, "How much?"

"One hundred and ninety thousand pounds . . . half down. We have not discussed how the rest would be paid. I haven't even said I would accept that."

She said, "You won't get any more. Take it, Roger. We don't have much time left for charades."

*   *   *   *

"Seen these?" Russell Wharton said, throwing the slim red bound book across the fireplace, from the armchair where he sat to Tom Rowland, sitting in another, its twin, on the other side. Tom was wearing uniform, Wharton in full evening dress. He was due at the theatre in an hour; but the part he was playing required that he wear evening dress for the first two acts, so he went to the theatre already dressed. Although evening dress was becoming rarer, as uniforms and dinner jackets became more common, the process had not gone far enough for him to cause any comment.

Tom glanced at the title *At the lip,* and subtitle *Poems from France, by Fletcher.*

Wharton said, "The title's from the first line of the first poem—'At the lip of the trench, a poppy grows from a man's eyeball' . . . It's strong stuff, sometimes rhymed, sometimes not. Some of the poems are bitter, others are lyric—even bucolic—about exactly the same subject. Some amazing insights . . . He's very good, whoever he is."

"Who is Fletcher?" Tom looked at the back of the dust jacket and read that Fletcher was a pseudonym for a young soldier, who wished to remain anonymous.

"He's not formally educated, I think," Wharton said. "It doesn't say so, but that's what I feel . . . he's like Isaac Rosenberg in that way, and also in the power of his imagery . . . Take it home with you."

"Thanks, I will," Tom said. "I find it very hard to imagine what it's like in the trenches. It must be so incredibly different from life in a cruiser . . . still more, from life at the Admiralty."

"How's that going, these days?"

"I was in Queenstown for a month, as you know. Went to sea a lot with the Americans. They have plenty of ideas . . . and they're all keen as mustard. It was great to be back at sea, even only as a passenger. It made the Admiralty seem pretty awful, especially with the feeling that nameless spies are watching me every moment, waiting for me to . . . fly my true colors—so that they can throw me out, court martial me, have me hanged, drawn, and quartered . . . The feeling against us is very strong, Russell, very bitter."

"Guilty conscience," Wharton said laconically. "Every man has something of sexual love for other men in him. If they ostracize us, or send us to gaol—they're doing it to the impulse in themselves at the same time . . . How much longer do you think the war is going to go on?"

"A year, at least," Tom said grimly. "When I got to the Admiralty in April, it looked as though it might end in a few months—with our defeat by the U-boats . . . but we have the measure of them now. This last campaign at Ypres doesn't seem to have got anywhere. The French are exhausted. The Germans are weakened but not enough for us to be sure of knocking them out quickly. They're stubborn, and courageous. They're not going to give in easily, just because the Americans are coming. We may well be fighting in 1919 still—even 1920, some say."

Wharton stood up, went to the sideboard, and poured himself a glass of sherry, which he brought over, with a couple of sweet biscuits in the other hand. This was what he normally took before a performance, or between a matinee and an evening show. He sat down again, and said, "Do you think you could get out of the Navy?"

Tom said slowly, "I suppose it would be possible. But I'm thirty-nine. I'd be conscripted at once . . . Why?"

"The time is ripe for you to apprentice yourself to Arthur Gavilan.

He told me last week that he badly needed a partner . . . and he said he'd like to give you the chance. Actually, he said you or Noel . . . incidentally, Noel's in this show at the Garrick with me. He's got tremendous talent—you really ought to come and see it . . . but he wants to stay in the theatre. Now's the time to get yourself established, before the war ends and a lot of others with the same idea come back out of the services."

Tom said, after a time, "It would be easy to get out of the Navy. I'd only have to come here a couple of times in plain clothes and they'd have me. They could court martial me for that, as I've been ordered to wear uniform, but they'd probably demand that I resign my commission. Then I'd be liable for conscription . . . and they'd see that I *was*, too . . . Anyway, I can't do it. It would be like desertion."

Wharton said, "Didn't you say your job was done? That you have the U-boats beaten . . . Well, then!"

Tom said, "I really do feel that I am a bit of a spare wheel now. I've given them my ideas, they've accepted them and they've worked. What I really want is to be given a destroyer flotilla in Western Approaches, and work out still better methods myself, at sea . . . but they're never going to send me back to sea—never!"

"So you'll never be promoted to captain?"

"I don't think so."

"Then you owe them nothing! And they're wasting you. Don't worry about being conscripted. There are some of us in quite high enough places to see that you are protected from conscription . . . no trouble at all. Get out, Tom, and start your new life, your new career, now!"

Tom stared a long time at Wharton. His lips tightened. At last he said, "All right. I've got a job to finish that'll take me a few weeks, then I'll see the 2nd Sea Lord and ask for a command at sea. If he doesn't give it to me, I'll ask permission to resign my commission."

"Good man!" Wharton said. "And I'll have to warn Tommy to find some suitable protected 'job' for you, while you're really working with Ronald. His confidential secretary, perhaps? Can't conscript an M.P.'s confidential secretary, can they?"

* * * *

Mary Gorse called, "I'm going out to the shops to get the late sweepings, Willum. Violet's coming with me, so listen for the baby . . ." Willum, sitting in the bedroom he shared with Mary and the two smallest children, did not answer—"Do you hear me?" she called again up the stairs.

"I hear," he said at last; and a moment later the front door banged, the latch dropped. The baby was quiet. The other kids were playing on the floor in the kitchen. Willum sat on the bed, staring at the oblong piece of newspaper in his hand. His stubby forefinger traced the words, which he spoke aloud under his breath as the finger moved, though he was often a word or two ahead, or behind the one the finger touched—for he could not read. A friend had shown him the piece a few days ago, and read it to him; and it had so horrified Willum that he had made the man read it again and again, until he knew it by heart.

The piece was cut out of the *Daily Telegraph* for Friday November 16, 1917. It read:

FAMOUS ENGLISH CRICKETER KILLED AT THE FRONT

Some six weeks ago Colin Blythe, the England and Kent bowler, left for France with a draft of the Royal Engineers. News has come that he has been killed by a shell. His death (writes a correspondent) will be regretted by all lovers of cricket. He was one of the world's greatest slow bowlers.

Willum's finger dropped. He couldn't remember any more. It hurt too much behind his eyes. Blythe dead! Four, five days now he'd been looking at this piece of paper, saying aloud what was written on it. They'd kill Frank Woolley next! How could anyone do it?

He had been grappling with the news all those days, nearly every hour, trying first to understand what had happened—no more Blythe, no more days in the sun at the County Ground, watching him bowl out Surrey, or Gloucestershire . . . seeing even Jack Hobbs tied in knots . . . what glee, what clapping and crowing where he stood on the boundary line! At last, yesterday morning, he had understood; the Germans had murdered Colin Blythe, a Man of Kent, Kent's greatest bowler, and with Woolley, its greatest cricketer. Next he had tried to know what to do. He had thought of asking people about it. He had asked the new manager at the shell factory, reopened a few weeks earlier, saying, "They killed Blythe, Mr Earl. What should we do?"

The foreman had looked at him as though he were mad, and said, "Do about it, Willum? Why, join the Army, of course, and go and kill the buggers that done it, eh!"

That was it. He'd be a soldier, go to the war, find the German who'd fired the shell at Colin Blythe and then . . . He stopped, puzzled. Then what?

Well, the other soldiers would know. They'd tell him.

He looked at himself in the mirror, combed his hair, and went downstairs and out of the house, heedless of the baby asleep in its makeshift crib, and the children playing round the kitchen table.

An hour later he had been enlisted, and become Private William Gorse, Weald Light Infantry, with a long regimental number. An hour after that he was lined up with others at the Quartermaster's Stores at Minden Barracks, being issued with his kit.

Daily Telegraph, Tuesday, November 29, 1917

RAILWAYMEN'S WAGES
NEGOTIATIONS BROKEN OFF

From Our Labour Correspondent.
A serious situation has arisen between the railway companies and their employees on the proposed wage advance. It was definitely announced yesterday that the negotiations which have been in progress for a fortnight respecting the men's application for a flat rate advance of 10s a week had been broken off.

In a statement to me at the adjournment of the men's delegate meeting, Mr J.H. Thomas, M.P., general secretary, said:

Negotiations are broken off owing to the action of the Liverpool men in their "slow gear" method, which is ruinous to the country, disastrous to negotiations, and instead of injuring the railway companies is merely aggravating the position of the poor in obtaining food.

A flat rate advance of ten shillings a week, Cate thought, why, a private in the infantry was now getting half a crown a day, or seventeen shillings and sixpence a week, so the Liverpool railwaymen were demanding an *increase* which would amount to over half a soldier's *total* pay. A railwayman was usually a skilled man, and some held in their hands considerable responsibility for the lives of the travelling public; but when you compared their sacrifice—even their essentialness—to those who were daily, hourly risking, and giving their lives . . . it was obvious that equality of sacrifice and universality of effort, were very far from being realities in England yet, in spite of the politicians' platitudes. Yet, what right did such as he, or Hoggin, or Lord Swanwick, or Richard, or the Governor, have to complain—though they all would? What had any of them suffered, when compared with the soldiers' sufferings?

He turned to another headline:

ACTING FOR THE GOVERNMENT

The Railway Executive Committee state: "In the Press comments on the negotiations now in progress with the railwaymen the statement has frequently occurred that the railway companies' representatives are meeting representatives of the National Union of Railwaymen. This is not correct: the Railway Executive Committee is acting strictly on behalf of the Government, and under their instructions, in the negotiations with the union, and the railway companies, as such, are not parties to the discussion."

Perhaps not, Cate thought, but it so happens that the interests of the railway companies, in this situation, coincide with the interests of the Government—and of the country, at war. He glanced down an adjoining column:

AIRCRAFT STRIKE

The strike at Coventry, which is so seriously retarding the output of aircraft and thereby interfering with the whole of the Government military programme, still continues, in spite of the fact that the employers have offered to meet the men's trade union representatives as soon as work is resumed . . .

A Coventry correspondent says that hundreds of men and girls were walking about the streets in idleness yesterday. The factories were picketed, and staffs were not allowed to enter, with the result that there will be no wages paid at the end of the week on account of the wages sheets not being made out.

Idiocy, Cate thought—worse, treason.

England, Palestine, Ireland, America:
December, 1917

34 The pub where Anne Stratton met Mr Chambers was the Lord Nelson, up the hill near the gaol. Mr Chambers chose it because he never went there with his wife or his male cronies. He was a portly man of medium height, with a tobacco-stained walrus mustache—a well-to-do plumber who wore a bowler hat almost as universally as Bob Stratton had, at least in part to hide his bald patch and the thin greying tonsure round it.

They were sitting in the saloon bar, with four other couples, each couple an island of its own, linked only by the men's trips to the little counter to refill their own or their women's glasses.

Anne was saying, "I had another letter from him yesterday. He says the big fighting's finished till spring now, because it's winter . . ."

"The war will be over by spring," Mr Chambers said confidently. "Then you'll have him back."

He had learned never to say anything derogatory about Frank Stratton. It didn't take much effort to get Anne into bed but she still loved her husband, and you had to watch your step—listen when she talked about Frank, and say the right things, to make it clear that you, too, thought he was a wonderful fellow. Well, that he was, really. Frank was no chicken, and there he was, badly wounded with the infantry and no sooner mended than gone back to France with the R.F.C. He was the sort of man that was protecting the rest of them, so they could have a pint in a pub, raise a family, eat decently, and get a little slap and tickle on the side now and then.

She was drinking port and lemon and she felt a pervasive anxiety, which for weeks now even alcohol could not assuage or remove. Making love to Mr Protheroe or Mr Chambers did, in a way, and for a time—just being under them, thrusting up, weeping, crying out—make her forget. Only to remember and know all the more strongly when they had gone. She was pregnant.

"Have another," Mr Chambers said softly.

"Oh, I couldn't, Mr Chambers . . . well, a little one, then." He got up and went to the bar.

She thought of Frank . . . the heavy fighting was over, he said. Well, the men in the R.F.C. who didn't fly—the mechanics and so on, like Frank—were never in much danger, except from German airmen dropping bombs or firing at them on the airfield sometimes. So Frank would come back. How could she think for a moment that it would be best if he didn't? She'd be having the baby in May. She had not seen Frank for months when she conceived . . . Mr Protheroe or Mr Chambers? Who knew? How could she tell him? Suppose she smothered the baby as soon as it was born, and dropped it in the Scarrow? Suppose . . . ?

Mr Chambers returned with her glass. "Here you are, my dear . . . You are looking pretty tonight, pretty as a picture."

"Thank you, Mr Chambers," she said. She drank deeply.

She couldn't kill a baby of hers! But what would Frank *do*? She began to sob silently and Mr Chambers put a protective arm round her. "There, there," he said, "he'll come back safe and sound, you'll see."

*   *   *   *

As he climbed into his car, Richard Rowland paused a moment to watch a Hedlington Lion start its take-off run. It was loaded to its full take-off weight, plus a thousand pounds, for it was powered by two American Jones & Gatewood A.4 radials of 500 h.p. each, giving it 250 h.p. more than it embodied with its normal Rolls Royce Eagle VIIIs. This was one of a series of tests the company was carrying out with the J & G radials before installing them in the new four-engined Buffalo. A crew of four were on board, comprising the chief test pilot, a second pilot, Betty Merritt, and the American mechanic from Jones & Gatewood who had come over with the first batch of engines.

The machine was going fast now, the engines roaring at full throttle. The tail gradually lifted. For a few seconds more the Lion ran on over the heavy turf, then, without changing the angle of the fuselage relative to the ground, it rose in the air, skimming, rising steadily.

Richard sighed with pleasure, climbed into his car, and said, "Home, please, Kathleen." He settled back in his seat . . . Things were going well. The United States Army had ordered two hundred and fifty J.M.C. lorries—they called them trucks—for delivery to them in France, with the possibility of increasing the order to a thousand before the end of January . . . The prototype Buffalo was almost ready for its first tests . . . But danger was lurking beneath the surface: Morgan, the works foreman at J.M.C., had warned him that a number of men there were secretly joining the union—the Union of Skilled Engineers—Bert Gorse's union. Morgan said he could not speak for Hedlington Aircraft but it was probably true there, too. Richard doubted it, but it would be wise to get Joe Mattingley, the Hedlington plant foreman since Frank Stratton left, to keep his eyes and ears open. Assuming he found it true—then what? Ignore it till they came out in the open and took some action? Even then, the proper response would depend on what action the union did take. As Overfeld had pointed out, a strong well-led union could be a great stabilizing influence—they'd drive a hard bargain, but they were in a position to enforce their side of it. That was all right in theory, but in practice . . . they were bolsheviks down there on Stalford Street. If he hired a private detective it would not be hard to find out who were in fact secret members of the U.S.E., in both plants, and simply sack them. The rest, who were not members, would not take any action, especially if the sackings were accompanied by some benefit—a small increase in wages, some improvement in working conditions . . . but Morgan was dead against it. He was an American, but at the same time Welsh through and through—he understood the men; and he said, "Don't do it, boss. It might work now, but they'll remember, and as soon as the war-time codes are ended they'll turn on you and have you down with a knife at your throat . . . Wait. We might be able to persuade the U.S.E. to send someone down here to take over the local branch. Someone we can deal with at J.M.C.—and at Hedlington Aircraft—would help us." Perhaps; but it wouldn't do any harm to hire the private detective as a first step. What use was made of the information obtained would have to be decided at the time. He'd go and see the Chief Constable tomorrow and get some advice on private detective agencies in the county . . . Must get that done before the weekend, when he had to look at those three prep schools that had been recommended to him for Tim. He would be nine next September, and should certainly start in the Michaelmas term. After that Tim was down for Wellington, in the Lent term of 1921, as it was going to cost less money than Eton, Richard's own school; and, though he was doing very well, now, the financial future looked black with a radical like Lloyd George at the helm . . . a great war leader of course, but not a friend of the capitalist, or the entrepreneur, and a dangerous demagogue . . . And Sally was to have a governess, but

Susan had insisted that she be an American. "You're taking Tim," she'd said, "and you'll take Dicky too, I know, and make them both English gentlemen, but I'm going to have Sally. She's going to know that she's half American . . . that she doesn't *have* to believe in *all* English shibboleths . . . just the good ones." Privately, Richard didn't believe that there was such a thing as an American governess; a sort of companion-teacher, perhaps, but there'd be no discipline . . . well, that was Susan's business.

She met him at the door, in the dark of late afternoon, and kissed him. "Dicky all right?" he asked.

"Quite all right," she said. She lowered her voice—"You must remember to ask after Sally and Tim, too. They can hear."

"Of course," he muttered; then, louder—"Sally and Tim?"

"They're fine," she said. "We're playing snap in the drawing room. They've had their supper."

He hung up his hat and coat and went into the drawing room. The children jumped to their feet and ran toward him—"Good evening, Daddy . . . good evening, Daddy." He stooped and kissed them in turn.

"Play snap with us," Tim wheedled.

Oh dear, he wanted a long whisky and a short soda . . . and a bath . . . but they'd be sent up to bed soon. He ought to read to them. His father had never read to him—nor had his mother—the one too preoccupied with the bicycle factory, and then the cars . . . and the other—remote, just remote; brave, and just, but remote, her thoughts perhaps lost in the mists of Ireland.

"All right," he said, sitting down, while they screamed, "Hooray!" and clapped their hands.

They began to play. The cards were flung down with great force, or crept out sneakily, giving the player time to see the face a fraction of a second before the others did . . . *Snap!* . . . *Snap!* . . . The hands of the clock crept round. The fire crackled in the grate.

"Snappool!" Tim screamed, grabbing the pool.

A smell of burning filled the room with acrid smoke. Sally leaped up, "Crikey! We were roasting chestnuts on the shovel . . . they've got burned."

"Never mind," Richard said. "Throw them in the fire and put some more on."

Susan came down, baby Dicky in her arms. He blinked in the light, not sure whether to cry or coo. "He was awake," she said, "and needed potting."

"Daddy," Dicky said.

Richard felt warm and loved, and fulfilled. Good heavens, he felt better even than when he was in the factory watching a lorry or an aeroplane take form before his eyes . . . Home now was more than its component parts of shelter, food, service, sex, affection, rest. It was more valuable to him than his work—it never had been before.

He shook his head, feeling guilty. How could he feel so happy, when his brother had lost his only son? And Quentin apparently lost a close friend, severely wounded . . . well, that must happen often enough in this war—except that Quentin had never had any close friends.

He could not feel guilty. The sun would rise tomorrow and his sons would grow up in a world at peace, English ladies and gentlemen.

"Start again," he said; and, soon—"Snap!"

*　　*　　*　　*

Captain David Toledano, Royal Horse Artillery, stood rigidly at the salute as General Sir Edmund Allenby, Commander-in-Chief of the British forces in Palestine and Egypt, strode past, his head high, gold braid gleaming on the peak of his cap, his demeanor somehow radiating a massive humility; for this ancient arch that he walked through, a conqueror, on foot, was the Jaffa Gate of Jerusalem.

Toledano thought he would cry, but contained himself, though a strange fierce joy was coursing through him. "Next year at Jerusalem," he had heard his father say a score of times, at Passover. The Sephardic rabbis at the synagogue in East London where his father used to take him, spoke passionately, in Ladino, of the Holy City, long lost; but he had never been there, and had never thought he would. Turf at Wellington, Big Side, Chapel (which he attended, with his father's permission, for there was no synagogue closer than Reading), the Iffley Road field of the Oxford Rugby Union, gay evenings at Claridge's with beautiful young women—very few of them Jewish—Colonel Billy Williams' "cabbage patch" at Twickenham and a hard game in the second row against the driving Harlequins; or out to Old Deer Park, to maul in the mud against Richmond . . . these had been the memories of his life, and the substance of his dreams. Now, as he watched the Commander-in-Chief march on, alone, unescorted, without pomp of lancers or hussars, or the tramp of marching infantry, the words of Balfour's recent declaration echoed in his mind and heart:

His Majesty's government views with favour the establishment in Palestine of a national home for the Jewish people, and will use their best efforts to facilitate the achievement of this object, it being clearly understood that nothing shall be done which may prejudice the civil

and religious rights of existing non-Jewish communities in Palestine
. . .

He and his father would take the forefront in that work, with money, advice, and planning for the oppressed Jews who'd come here from Russia and Germany, after Germany was beaten. The Toledanos—the English branch at least—would not themselves move here. England was their home and they were not oppressed. But they could help others.

Bugles blew, flags fluttered in the winter air. The watchers returned to their places, David Toledano to the tented camp of QQ Battery. He went quickly to his own tent, and, seeing that he had an hour before he was due to inspect the horse lines, sat down to write a letter:

Outside Jerusalem, December 11, 1917:

Father—An hour ago I watched General Allenby enter Jerusalem, on foot. It is ours, as Englishmen. Soon it will be ours, as Jews. I have never felt very strongly Jewish, and you have never tried to force it on me. But I felt it today, and will always do so now. Thank you for giving me this foundation for my life, without my even knowing it.

The details of the Battle of Cambrai at the end of last month are slowly filtering out here. It was a notable victory and apparently could have been much more decisive if there had been fresh troops available to exploit the initial success of the tanks. What a sight it must have been, 450 tanks crunching forward together! At last a way seems to have been found to escape from the wrestling match in the mud that the Western Front has been for so long. We could use massed tanks almost anywhere out here, of course—but of course we shall not get any. They'll be kept in France.

I have officially got my Jacket, and am now Battery Captain of an R.H.A. Battery in an Indian Cavalry Division. I am well, and fit. After all, I am home again!!

With affectionate best wishes, your respectful son,
David Toledano

P.S. To get your Jacket is to be accepted into the Royal Horse Artillery from the Field or Garrison artillery. No one is posted direct to the R.H.A. When on parade with our guns we march at the right of the line, ahead of any other troops. I'm looking forward to trotting the 13-pounders past a regiment of Dragoon Guards who had been thinking they would go before us!

*   *   *   *

The man in rough Irish peasant clothes sat on the right side of the jaunting cart, the whip in his hand; the woman, hands work hardened, shawl round her grey hair, head bowed to the winter wind, heavy skirt bedraggled with mud, boots holed and worn, sat on the left side, back to back with the man. The shaggy little brown pony trotted out manfully along the wet yellow road, bending its head a little away from the rain sweeping off the sea to the left, the east, two hundred feet below the end of swelling green fields.

The man threw over his shoulder—"There's three of them coming in now, Peg." Margaret Cate shielded her eyes against the rain and could just make out three low dark shapes, miles out to sea yet, steaming in line ahead for the narrow entrance to Cork Harbour, below them.

"American?" she asked.

"Aye . . . come in from a convoy. Another few hundred thousand tons of ammunition reached the British . . . or wheat . . . or airyplane engines."

Margaret eyed the distant vessels, streamers of black smoke trailing behind them across the ocean, with venomous hatred. America's entry into the war had obviously much reduced the chances of a German victory, and so of Ireland's early release from British bondage. But it had also cut away much support for the Sinn Fein movement in America, among ordinary Americans. The stream of dollars that used to arm the revolutionaries had become a trickle.

The jaunting cart approached two members of the Royal Irish Constabulary, leaning on their bicycles beside the road, looking out over the harbour toward Queenstown in the distance. Margaret burrowed deeper into her shawl. Doyle raised his whip in salute as he passed. One of the constables nodded in acknowledgement. The jaunting cart clipped on.

The driver said, "Wonder what they'd do if we told them 'twas Margaret Cate in the jaunty."

"Why don't we go back and kill them," Margaret said. "I have my pistol."

"Me, too, Peg . . . but I'm not here to kill the Royal Irish. Time enough for that when the war ends—if they don't let us free. I'm here to watch the ships, so's our friends can know where to find 'em."

Margaret said, "You're right, Doyle." Doyle, local crofter, and two other men living near Crosshaven and in Queenstown itself, kept tally of all comings and goings of ships into the great harbour—American, British, warships, merchantmen. The information was passed to German U-boat captains on lonely beaches in Kerry and Mayo, or from fishing boats rocking in the Atlantic swells off Aran. Increasingly, she knew, the submarines never appeared at the rendezvous—sunk by such as those destroyers sliding in now from the Atlantic, the Stars and Stripes streaming from their sterns.

Doyle had met her at Cork railway station, and was taking her back to his croft. Margaret, her hair dyed grey from its true dense shining black, bore the identity papers of Janet Doyle, his aunt, come to visit him from Limerick. Next week she would carry other papers, and she would be back at the movement's headquarters, in Dublin. The British might catch her at any moment—she was stopped on an average of once every month, and her papers inspected, as she went about her business—but there was no definite identification mark, that they knew about. The scar on her right breast, where the bullets had passed through when she and Dermot killed the policemen two years ago: the entry wound in her shoulder blade and the exit above her collarbone, when she was wounded in the Easter Rising—these were clear and inerasable, but they were all hidden by her clothing; and the British did not know about them in detail—only that she had been wounded.

Doyle said, "There's no hope now, is there really, Peg?"

She said fiercely, "There's always hope! The Germans will make a great assault in the spring . . . They may actually win the war. Even if they don't, the shock will be so great—they may sweep the British clean out of France—that there'll be a great outcry to make peace, at any price. And then . . ."

"We'll have to take what the British choose to give us. That's the truth of it," the man said gloomily, cracking his whip over the flagging little pony's back.

"Freedom—or the streets, the fields," Margaret said passionately. "This spying and sneaking around, without attacking, is a waste of time. We ought to be waging guerrilla war now. What's the point of waiting?"

"There'll be hard times, whenever it comes," Doyle said. "Whoa there!" The pony slowed, he turned it off into a narrow stone-walled lane, and headed it toward a sod and thatch cottage a quarter of a mile ahead, smoke curling from under the eaves—it had no chimney—and a woman leading a cow along a wall outside, on a rope.

Doyle said, "We heard you left a family in England for us, Peg."

"I did," she said shortly.

Damn him, why did he have to bring that up now, when she had been able to pass nearly a whole twenty-four hours without thinking of Laurence, her son? Christopher should have seen that he was not cut out for a soldier, but he wouldn't have. He was probably out in France by now. What chance was there that he'd come home alive out of that? And would Ireland ever be his "home?" But then, what chance was there that *she'd* come out alive? . . . She tried to think of Stella, but that was never easy. Stella was married, and she'd had a baby, and the baby had died—her first grandchild. The news did not move her when she'd seen it in the obituary columns of the *Irish Times,* any more than when, a few days later, she'd seen the announcement of Boy's death in action. Someone in the family was obviously putting those notices in the *Irish Times* for her benefit . . . She shook her head to make the thoughts fly away. She didn't want to think about Christopher feeding the robins by the window at the end of the hall, playing his violin on summer nights, the windows open, the sounds sweeping out across the velvet green, toward the yellow moon hanging over the Weald. She wondered briefly whether he had found another woman. He was a passionate man. What did it matter? That was all from another, meaningless world.

She said, "Make your full report as soon as we get in, and I'll give you your instructions for the next two months. And the cash you asked for."

"'Tis to pay Paddy," he said apologetically, "the night watchman at the docks. He sees goings and comings that we don't. But he's a mite greedy."

The cart stopped outside the croft. The woman came forward, wiping her hands on her apron. The rain hissed gently on the thatch, and Margaret stepped down into the mud, careful to move like a woman of seventy years of age.

*   *   *   *

The big room was jammed with them—the managers of the thirty-five H.U.S.L. shops now in operation, all seated on little folding chairs Hoggin had hired for the occasion; rather, that Miss Meiklejohn had hired on his behalf. Nineteen of the managers were women, sixteen men. Some of them had spent the previous night in London, and would do so again tonight, being unable to reach Hedlington and return to their bases in the single working day of the conference—which had started at 10 a.m. and was now, at 4.15 p.m., drawing to a close.

Hoggin rose to his feet. Miss Meiklejohn closed the door and click-clacked forward through the massed chairs, to sit beside his desk, her stenographic pad at the ready.

Hoggin said, "All right, you blokes—and ladies. You've heard from the banker. You've heard from the accountant . . . and don't think I ain't got my eye on you, every one of you . . ." He fixed a beady gaze on a man in the second row, held him for a moment, then moved to a woman, another, another—"Retail groceries is about the worst business there is for pilfering . . . until we get ways of keeping track of every tin of beans automatically, it don't pay to try. So managers, and assistants, and every little slut who gets a job . . . not to mention the customers . . . 'elps themselves to a bit here, a bit there, a tin here, a jar here . . . Well, I've got fellows—and women—watching, who you don't know is doing it. And first time they catches you with your hand in the till . . . out! And we'll prosecute. It'll be in the papers, your name and all . . . You've heard from me about buying in bulk, direct from the producers . . . and when this war's over that'll be easier . . . more goods, cheaper . . . You've heard from that New York Yankee, about getting people inside the shops, and when they're in, selling—*making* them buy. Specials, advertisements in the local paper . . . regular, same day every week. Keep the shops open late, one night a week . . . Don't pay any extra to the assistants who stay on late those nights, just sack 'em if they complain, or say they won't do it . . . Mark prices plain, clear . . . and about a quarter of the goods on the shelves oughter be marked 'Reduced from . . .' 'Course it hain't really reduced from anything, unless you mark it up first, then mark it down from that, see? But that only works well for 'igh priced items and we don't want many of them in H.U.S.L. shops . . . Keep the place clean. Everything easy to find. Everything in the same place all the time . . . and in the same place, as near as you can get it, in all the shops, according to the plan that bloke gave you this morning."

He eyed the managers benevolently. He'd got 'em where he wanted 'em . . . looking forward to making a lot of money, because they were all sharing in the profits of their own stores and of H.U.S.L. overall; afraid of him, because they knew he was a wide boy, wide enough to hire experts to catch 'em out if they cooked the books, or did a lot of pilfering on their own accounts. They were going to hire the best people they could find, and see they did their work, because they'd lose their own profits if they didn't . . . and, before you could say Jack Robinson, their jobs, too.

He stuck his thumbs into the waist band of his trousers, pushing up the waistcoat to do so. He said, "I'm going to America next year. They've got chains of stores what make little us look like children playing 'Shop.' I'm going over to take a look-see. When I come back, we'll do what they do, only better—before they get a chance to come over 'ere and take the bread out of our mouths, with bigger stores, more money, lower prices . . . Before I go I'm going to divide the shops into areas, and appoint Area Superintendents so soon you'll be reporting through them, and they'll be putting the ginger into you. It'll cost me a packet, but it'll be worth it . . . And we'll have a new headquarters. This is too small . . . 'cos though there'll be Area Superintendents, I'm going to get all the managers together once a year, at least, and that'll need a bigger place than this. Anyway, we're going to 'ave a bigger accounting department, with all sorts of ruddy electric machines . . . the buying department will be centralized in the new place . . . the inspection department, the secret service . . . my spies, see? . . . sales department, what decides on what we're going to sell in all the H.U.S.L.s and 'ow to do it, and then tells you . . . personal department, no, that ain't right, person*nel* . . . finding new people to put in *your* jobs when I give you the sack, 'cos you're not making enough spondulicks . . . Well, that's about all. Miss Meiklejohn, ring for taxis for these blokes—and ladies."

"They're here now, Mr Hoggin," the secretary said. "Eight of them, waiting in the drive. Everyone will have to squeeze into those. The London train leaves in half an hour."

The managers were all on their feet. One tall thin man near the back called out, "Mr Hoggin . . . sir . . . will this new headquarters be in London? It would be more, ah, convenient if it were, would it not?"

"It might," Hoggin growled, "but it ain't going to be. Rates there is too bloody high, by a long chalk. And they'll keep going up. No, it's going to be here . . . close to."

"Oh, that'll be good," the man who had spoken said with sycophantic enthusiasm.

The room slowly emptied, Hoggin standing by the desk, watching, thumbs in his trousers. Miss Meiklejohn went out, closing the door behind her. A moment later it opened with a bang and Hoggin's wife Ruth rushed in, followed slowly by the bent, creaking form of her mother, Jane Stratton. Ruth hurried up between the chairs to face him, then gasped breathlessly, "Bill! I have wonderful news! I'm going to have another baby!"

Bill took his thumbs out of his trousers and clapped his hands together, "Hey, Ruthie, that's good! Though why it didn't come sooner, I don't know, the number of times I bang you."

"Oh, Bill! . . . I'm three months gone, the doctor thinks, and that's what I say, too."

"You're sure, then?"

"Yes! Oh, Bill, isn't it wonderful?"

He took her in his arms then, and hugged her, and smacked a kiss in the middle of her forehead. He leaned back, holding her at arm's length. "All right, then, but this time I'm going to name the little bugger. No more Launcy Lotties."

"Oh, Bill." She sank forward, nestling her bosom against his bulk.

"I'm so happy for you both," Jane Stratton said.

The door opened and the frigid voice of Miss Meiklejohn cut icily through the room. "Swallowford's men have come to remove the chairs, Mr Hoggin."

574

"Well, tell them to fucking get on with it," Hoggin said, hugging his wife. Wait till New Year's Day and would he give *her* a surprise!

*   *   *   *

Alice Rowland stretched her wooden leg with an audible creak. It hurt sometimes—sometimes, a lot—but she loved it, loved the creaking of its knee joint, the harness that attached it to her thigh and waist. Leaning over the little table beside her she poured a cup of tea and, reaching across, handed it to her visitor—Mrs Dave Cowell.

Mrs Cowell was not weeping at the moment, but she had been, both before coming to the house, and for the first quarter of an hour of her visit. So far she had not said much, for the maid had been in and out with the tea, poking the fire, drawing the curtains against the winter dark . . . and she obviously had something private and personal to share with Alice.

Alice said gently, "Well . . . ?"

"He's gone and joined up, miss." The frumpy hat was askew, the skirt wrinkled and dragged up on one side, the face mournful and tear stained.

Alice said, "Dave has joined up?" Mrs Cowell nodded. "But he's over age."

"For being conscripted, miss . . . but he's volunteered."

Alice thought, Dave didn't believe in the war; he was anti-militarist; his family had no Service tradition; why had he done it?

As though answering her question, Mrs Cowell said, "It's nothing to do with the war, miss—*I* think . . . he's done it because he can't abide to live here without seeing you. He's hardly spoke to me since . . . since I told him you'd promised not to see him again. I don't think he wants to live at all."

"Had he got a job . . . employment? I saw that he had been dismissed from the school because he allowed the No-Conscription Fellowship people to use his classroom for a meeting."

"He did odd jobs, miss. Tutored boys—and girls—for exams. But he didn't make as much as he used to . . . and that wasn't much."

Alice sipped her tea. Mrs Cowell did the same, then took out a handkerchief, dabbed at her eyes, and began to cry again. Through the handkerchief she sobbed, "He says he'll be made an officer. They told him that at the barracks as soon as he joined up, so he is in a special course up there now, like an officer recruit."

"That's good," Alice said.

Mrs Cowell's weeping became louder, "Oh no, miss, officers get killed more than the soldiers . . . the lieutenants and 2nd lieutenants do, and that's what Dave'll be, isn't it?"

Alice thought, she's come for comfort; but what comfort can I give her? Dave's gone and may never come back—to either of us.

Again as though speaking to her unspoken thought, Mrs Cowell mumbled, "If I 'adn't come to you, an' said you shouldn't go with him, he'd still be home. We'd both have him . . . instead of neither."

Alice was about to reassure her but thought, that's just what I was thinking; why deny it? Would it have worked? Perhaps, perhaps not. But it couldn't be worse than this. She had kept to her promise, not to see Dave again. But that had not kept him out of her thoughts, her body. She loved him, wanted him, and needed him.

Mrs Cowell said, "I heard you were going to work for the Aircraft Company, miss."

Alice nodded, "I am, starting in the new year. I've passed my accountancy exams, and I'm very much looking forward to it. I don't mean I'm a Chartered Accountant—that will take years—but I've started toward it."

"How are you going to get up there and back, miss?"

"I am buying a motor tricycle."

"And live here, with Mr Harry?"

Alice said, "I suppose so . . . I don't have much to do with running the house nowadays. Mrs Stallings is housekeeper as well as cook . . . if she ever decides to retire, heaven knows what we'll do."

Mrs Cowell took a deep breath and her voice quavered as she spoke, "Miss . . . when . . . if Dave comes back . . . will you . . . I want you to see him, please see him . . . for my sake . . . he loves you, miss, I know it . . . An' you love him, don't you?"

Slowly Alice nodded, "I do . . . I shall never take him from you, though."

Again Mrs Cowell took a deep breath—"If . . . *when* . . . he comes back, we could live in one 'ouse, miss. It would be yours, and Dave and I would be like butler and housekeeper, to other people, or perhaps they'll take him on again at the school, but . . . we'd be together . . . and I could look after you proper, cook, clean, push you round to places you couldn't go by yourself . . . I'd like to . . ."

Alice found that tears were welling in her own eyes. She said, "Thank you . . . do you know, I've never heard your Christian name . . ."

"Daisy, miss."

"You are a saint, Daisy."

"You'll do it, when, if . . . ?"

Alice said, "We must wait until—"

"— he comes home!"

". . . and find out whether we, and he, really want it . . . can make it work."

*   *   *   *

Ethel Fagioletti sat in the tiny parlour of the little house in Soho, reading the letter, tears streaming down her face. Niccolo had never had a proper teacher, or school, what with his parents bringing him here from Italy, then having to learn English as well as history and geography at board school, all at the same time. So his letter was hard to read. But it was the first she had ever had from him that he had written in his own hand; the few earlier letters had been written for him by an educated soldier, Niccolo said. This was precious for that alone, and now that she had struggled through its misspellings and erasions and rewritings it was doubly clear. She read it again.

Dere Missus Fagioletti, I am saf I am platon sarjant to Mister Kate I lok after him he is a yung gent his cusn captin roland was kilt send me three ceks for crismus for men mi platon they ar god men mosli the CO ses I can sta on afte war if I wonto beta than wating eh im sori i send you away becas i luv you and we will have babi when war ove

She hugged the letter to her breast, crying happily. He had truly come back to her at last, his heart as well as his body, as she had always known he would—he must—because she loved him. Their brief time together in the Grosvenor Hotel on his last leave had been different from anything before. No baby had come from it, but after the war, there would, when there was time, time to love gently, not those furious, desperate attempts to forget the trenches. When he came home for good, then . . . why, he'd be Sergeant Fagioletti here in London, or Hedlington, not just in France! What a strange idea! What was the world coming to? But she must not leave matters to chance. They *must* have a baby. But who could she trust to help her? The gypsy women on the Heath always promised you'd have a baby, and gave you bad-tasting stuff to drink, and took your money—but mostly nothing happened. Why . . . Probyn Gorse's Woman! Everyone down there knew she'd get rid of babies, if she felt like it. But Ruth had heard it whispered that she could also ensure that a woman had one. She'd go and see her, as soon as . . .

There was a knock on the door, and she went to open it. A tall young woman with dark blue eyes and brown hair stood outside, a large leather suitcase resting on the pavement beside her. She said, "Mrs Fagioletti?"

"Yes, that's me," Ethel said. "But . . ." She peered more closely— "You're Lady Helen Durand-Beaulieu! I've seen you!"

Lady Helen nodded, smiling. "I am . . . I heard that you had a room to let."

577

"That's true, milady, but . . ." Ethel stopped, puzzled. How could her room concern Lady Helen?

Helen said, "I would like to take it . . . May I come inside?"

"Of course, milady." She hurried back in, fluffing up a cushion. "Sit down, milady. You look tired . . . Did you say you'd like to take my room?"

Helen said, "Yes, but first . . . I'm going to have a baby, Mrs Fagioletti. The father was killed before we could be married . . ."

"Oh dear!" Ethel wailed. "You poor lady . . . Oh, oh, oh, it was Mr . . . Captain Charles!"

Helen said, "It was. I want to find a quiet place to live . . . work that I can do in the house . . . I only have a few pounds now, but I expect I'll get some more soon. And I'll have to change my sugar card, of course . . . Probyn's Woman is coming up to help me have the baby. After that—I don't know."

"Oh, milady, of course you can have the room. It doesn't matter about money. I'll look after you, I'm a good cook . . . learned to cook some of those Italian things, too, for Niccolo . . . he's a sergeant now. We've been married again, by proxy."

Helen said, "Thank you . . . You're very kind. May I call you Ethel?"

"Oh, please, please."

"And will you call me Helen?"

"Oh, I couldn't, milady."

"Please! . . . Helen Rowland—Mrs Rowland, a woman whose husband has just been killed in action in France."

*　　*　　*　　*

Isabel Kramer faced Christopher Cate across the fireplace and said, "Christopher, this is my last visit here."

He stared at her, not comprehending. Then—"You mean you don't like the village people knowing, or guessing, that you are my mistress?"

She shook her head. "I'm beyond caring what the village people think, my dear. And I never did care what the people of Liverpool or London think . . . It's what *I* think that has made up my mind. I can no longer bear these separations. Our meetings and our times together are such heaven that the partings have become proportionately deeper hells. It is like having a piece carved out of my flesh each time . . . Virgil has obtained passage for me on the S.S. *Mystic,* due to sail for New York from Liverpool a few days before Christmas—probably the 21st."

Christopher said at last, "I can't blame you."

Tears began to form in the corners of her eyes, then, but her voice was still steady when she said, "I was going back to the States in any case, to see my son, Walter, before he is sent overseas. He's just been drafted into the infantry, as a private soldier. He refused a commission. I shall not return to England."

Christopher thought miserably, what can I say? How can I ask her to wait for me, when I don't know for how long? Margaret was likely to live at least as long as he did. Why did he not have it in him to throw up the Manor, and Walstone, and go with her? Get a divorce in America—there were several states that would grant it, in his circumstances, Virgil Kramer had assured him—marry her, and live over there? The only answer to that was—that he could not do it. He was Squire of Walstone.

She said, "Let's walk to the station, dearest. Holding hands. When they don't see me again, they'll understand."

*   *   *   *

The winter wind rattled the windows of the stone house on Officers' Row at Fort Sill, and blew the smoke from the chimney flat to the south, across the parade ground. It was near dusk, and Jean Burress was holding a little "cocktail" party—she was always in the front of fashion in these matters. A dozen young men from the course just completed at the School of Fire were attending, with only one other lady—a captain's very unfashionable and very plain wife: Jean did not like competition in these affairs. The young men were all, Johnny had noticed, from the upper crust of American society: none of the intelligent farmers' and artisans' sons on the course had been invited. Lieutenant Burress was at a conference in San Antonio, at Fort Sam Houston, to do with Fort Sill's part in the defence of the southern border against possible attack from Mexico, which was in its endemic state of political turmoil.

Johnny stood apart from the crowd in the front parlour, a drink in his hand. He did not know what was in it, but Jean had pressed it into his hands when he arrived, saying, "It's the latest thing, John dear, a Bronx—you must try it."

The telegram burned in his pocket—this one just come yesterday: *Stella broke left upper arm hunting yesterday is in hospital recovering well sends love Father Christopher.* First the baby, now this . . . the poor girl must be feeling terrible. He *must* get to see her, and comfort her. He had graduated well, and was now a 2nd Lieutenant of Field Artillery, the single bar heavy on each shoulder. In a few days, they'd all be posted. He had told the Adjutant that he wanted to return to

France—but so did everyone else on the course; and Field Artillery officers were desperately needed for the expanding National Army here at home . . . So, if he was sent to France, as soon as he got there, he'd apply for a few days leave—there wouldn't be any serious fighting until the spring; if he was retained in the States, he'd apply for leave at once.

He found the captain's wife beside him. She was forty, plump, and homely. She laid a hand on his arm, "I'm so sorry to hear about your wife's arm, Mr Merritt."

"Thanks," he said. Jean must have told her.

"And that on top of losing the baby. You must be longing to get back to her side."

"I am." He liked the lady; she was comforting in a genuine way; but . . . he was not in a mood to be sociable.

The woman said, "If you wouldn't mind, could you tell me what was the matter with your baby—why she died? It was a girl, wasn't it? . . . It's not just idle curiosity," she added quickly. "But I lost a baby, too, a long time ago . . . and I always wonder whether it was necessary, whether he need have died."

Jean, or one of the young men, put a very loud ragtime record on the phonograph; and Johnny raised his voice to be heard—"The baby had apnea—stoppages of breathing—shaking tremors—convulsions—and died of suffocation."

A cheerful voice at his elbow said, "Sounds like a heroin baby to me." Johnny swung round to find himself face to face with Lieutenant Aquila, one of the post's younger doctors. He was from New York, and had joined the Army's medical department as soon as war was declared. He was a loud spoken, curly black-haired man of about thirty-five, very proud of his conquests among the ladies. Johnny did not like him, but Jean Burress apparently did—though he was far from being in the Four Hundred.

Johnny said, "What do you mean?"

Aquila had a pale drink in his hands, which Johnny recognized as a Dry Martini; and he'd probably had a couple more earlier. His face was flushed and he said, "Overheard what you said . . . couldn't help it . . . I was an intern at Bellevue, then lived and practised in Hell's Kitchen . . . what you were describing are the symptoms of a baby whose mother was a drug addict—probably heroin—when the baby was born."

Johnny found his fists doubled and his chest constricting with fury. The captain's wife eased herself between the two men as Johnny said, "The death was given as 'natural causes.'"

Aquila said, "Twenty to fifty percent of all infant deaths are called 'natural causes' . . . but that's because the old medical fogies are too lazy to investigate. The baby's dead, so what does it matter? Don't rock the boat, don't cause a scandal."

Johnny said furiously, "This baby's mother was my wife, Lieutenant."

Aquila was drunk, but not very; he said appeasingly, "I'm sorry, I didn't know . . . apnea is very common in newborn children . . . even convulsions are not all that rare."

"Then why . . . ?" Johnny began.

The captain's wife cut in, "Now, Mr Merritt, I have to take Lieutenant Aquila to meet my husband . . ." She hustled the doctor away.

Johnny stood a long minute where he was, staring after them . . . heroin addict . . . which meant, drug fiend. Impossible!

Burress's striker, acting as bartender, poured him another drink. Time passed. The crowd in the room began to thin. He had another cocktail. Soon, it was time to go. He went to find his greatcoat, gloves, and cap. In the passage his hostess stopped him and whispered, "Don't go, John . . . I want to talk to you."

He hesitated; but she had gone, and slowly he returned to the parlour. The striker cleared the bar table and left. The last guest went. He was alone. Fifteen minutes later Jean Burress came in. She had changed, and was wearing now what looked almost like an evening robe, except that it left her shoulders bare, and Johnny had never seen a robe like that.

She sank onto a sofa, and patted it beside her. "Sit here, John . . . Do you want another drink? I'll make you one." She had always called him John, and he was beginning to think of himself as John rather than Johnny. Harvard, and careless youth seemed a long time ago.

He said, "I've had enough . . . thanks."

"I'm so sorry . . . but don't take it too hard. Broken arms heal quickly, and in a few days she'll be right as rain . . . except that she'll be wearing a cast for a bit. . . . And in a few days you'll be leaving Fort Sill. Where do you want to go?"

"France."

"Oh, I know you all have to *say* that, but do you *really?*"

"I do want to, Mrs . . ."

She put a finger to his lips, "Jean! How often have I told you? . . . Would you like to stay here?"

"Here, at the School of Fire?"

She nodded—"Or as a Field Artillery instructor at Camp Doniphan? George could arrange it. He says you could be a very good instructor. Of course, you're a Harvard man . . . and so handsome, too. It isn't fair."

Johnny said, "I really do want to go to France, Jean. Once I'm over there I can get leave and . . ."

She put her finger back to his lips and murmured, *"I want you to stay, John."* She looped her arms round his neck and gently pulled his face down onto hers. Her lips parted. They kissed. Johnny could not help himself; he was being kissed, and he responded. He felt an erection growing inside his trousers, and dropped one hand to her bosom, slipping it inside the robe to cup the naked swelling breast. She smelled marvellous, of perfume and women, her hair was a golden halo in the dim light, her body writhing against him, her breath coming fast. She was almost as pretty as Stella, and—

"Upstairs!" she whispered. "Upstairs, now!"

Stella! Oh God, Stella! His poor wife . . . He broke free, rushed out of the room, found his coat, cap, and gloves and ran out into the winter evening.

*   *   *   *

Stella Merritt pulled up her silk knickers, rose from the couch and brushed a hand through her hair. Charles Deerfield finished buttoning himself. The cast on her arm had not prevented him demanding his pound of flesh from her. She'd learned it was no good asking for the needle before he was ready.

He said, "Sit down, Stella. I have something to tell you."

"What?" she asked uneasily.

"I'm leaving Hedlington. An English alienist I met in Vienna—a Freudian, like myself—has built up a very successful practice in Wimpole Street, but unfortunately he is now dying—cancer. He has asked me to be his partner until he can no longer work, and then take over . . . of course I can not compel his patients to come to me, but he thinks most of them will, and so do I. There are not that many Freudian analysts even in London."

"But . . . but . . . what am I going to do?" she said.

He said seriously—the most seriously she remembered him speaking to her—"When I started giving you heroin—and sometimes sharing it with you—it was a game . . . something exciting, more exciting than drinking, you were drinking too much, trying to find adventure—that is your nature, my dear . . . I knew heroin caused addiction though I myself have never had that problem, but to tell the truth, I did not realize how deeply you would become addicted. When you became pregnant, I told you that you must cure yourself, and I tried to help you—with sedatives, hypnotics so that you could sleep, analgesics for the pain. But—you would not summon up the willpower to do it. Instead, you blackmailed me."

"I couldn't help it," she burst out. "I'm trembling now, sweating, because you haven't yet given me the injection. How can I ever cure myself?"

"You were taken to hospital to have your arm put in a cast, were you not?" She nodded. "Did the sister who bathed the arm comment on the needle marks?" Stella shook her head. "But she noticed them?" Stella nodded. "Then you may be sure that she also interpreted them correctly, even in a small country town like this . . . I suggest that you return to the hospital and tell them the truth—that you are a heroin addict. I suppose I can't stop you saying I gave it to you, but I shall deny it, and it won't help you, or your marriage, or anyone concerned—so please don't. If you submit to detoxification in a hospital, you could be clear in a week or two . . . I could certainly arrange for it in a London hospital, if you don't want to have it done here."

"For God's sake, Charles . . . !"

Shrugging, he got out the needle and the heroin, and injected her, saying, "I'll give you a week's supply. Within that week, you must get to a hospital. Or you're as good as lost."

Daily Telegraph, Friday, December 21, 1917

CIVIL WARFARE IN RUSSIA

The Bolshevik Petrograd News Agency now admits that Rostoff— an important city of over 200,000 inhabitants, about twenty-five miles from the mouth of the Don, which flows into the Gulf of Taganrog—has been captured by the Cossacks . . . The infantry has gone over to the Cossacks. The Red Guards laid down their arms and surrendered. General Kaledin has entered into communication with the Smolny Institute (the headquarters of the Bolsheviks) proposing a cessation of the civil war. He stipulates that the Maximalists shall not intervene in the affairs of the Don, and insists on the immediate formation of a National Government.

Meanwhile in Petrograd chaos, if not something worse, prevails. Martial law has been proclaimed by Lenin and his accomplices. Street fighting is of the commonest occurrence, and some idea of what is going on is afforded by Reuters' correspondent, who, in explaining some delay in the despatch of two telegrams on Wednesday, says that the firing in the street was too intense to permit of his reaching the telegraph office.

Drastic demands have been put forward by the Ukrainian Rada, involving complete freedom from interference by the Bol-

> shevik Government at Petrograd . . . There is no really authentic
> news regarding the peace negotiations at Brest-Litovsk. An Ex-
> change Company's message from Petrograd, dated Wednesday, as-
> serts that "the German delegates and the Austrian Minister, Count
> Czernin, agreed to the formula of no annexations and no contribu-
> tion (indemnity). They oppose the other formula as to the basis of
> self-government, considering that this is a question of internal pol-
> icy for settlement by individual States." This statement must be
> accepted with reserve. In any case, the enemy is merely bent on
> laying traps for the Russian Delegates.

So, for Russia, one war had ended, and another was beginning: war is
dead, long live war. It was impossible to guess whether the Bolshevik
regime would survive. It was almost impossible to realise that it had
come into existence at all, in what had been such a devout and
traditionalist country as Holy Russia. Now the Cossacks were rebel-
ling, and other peoples in the huge country would certainly do the
same. If Lenin succeeded in putting down the rebellions, and holding
Russia together, he would have worked a miracle. And if so, there
would be a new force in the world, a Bolshevik revolutionary Russia,
no longer a lurking, inward-looking sullen, only part-civilized bear,
but a hungry, angry, world-ranging bear. And the chief force to contain Russia, and counter-balance her enormous potential strength
was—as it had been for centuries—the Teutons . . . whom the rest of
the civilized world was intent on destroying. The future looked darker
every day.

Friday . . . in the old days he'd give young Hilda half an hour's
writing lesson on Fridays; but Hilda had long since left his service and
was working in Coventry, where no one cared whether she could write
well or speak well; but where she made more money. He'd ride Marquis over to Beighton and visit Stella. She wouldn't be out of the cast
yet, and perhaps he could do a few little things for her . . . then, back
here and round the village. That would help to restore his sense of
proportion. He'd lost Isabel, and nothing could heal that wound, but
he must go on living. Russia, Holy Russia was gone, but England lived,
and would live; Walstone lived, and would live; Cates and Gorses and
Rowlands and Durand-Beaulieus lived, and would live—changed, certainly, but still enjoying this air, this season, and sharing this land, this
time of history.

England and Flanders: Christmas, 1917

35 Christopher Cate read the paper with increasing despondency. Isabel was gone and the chances were strong that he would never see her again. In the night, lying awake, he had finally decided that he must sell Upper Bohun Farm to a land speculator from London; he needed the money. The Mayhews had been warned, and were understandably unhappy, even though Christopher had promised to stipulate that their lease could not be terminated until after the war ended. That suited the would-be buyer, who in any case would have to wait for peace until he could start his ambitious project—building medium-sized houses for fairly rich people to live in, and go to London by train every day for work. "The line will be electrified within ten years after the war ends," the man had said. "You'll see. The people who buy my houses will get the best of both worlds—town and country." Perhaps. Perhaps not . . . electrified trains were certainly cleaner and he supposed they were more convenient, but if they had a third rail, like the London tubes and the Metropolitan, there'd be terrible casualties among hounds if the fox ever crossed the line . . . but there wasn't going to be a pack after the first of the year. Swanwick was holding a New Year's Day meet as a farewell and then disbanding the hunt: another familiar sight and sound gone—the twang of the horn across the winter furrows, the music of the bitches on a screaming scent . . .

He returned to the newspaper:

> The master plan for 1918 is simplicity itself—hoard all our strength
> until the Americans can join in with full force, and with a reason-
> able amount of actual experience at the Front; then attack, and keep
> attacking to break the German Army in the West before winter
> comes. If that cannot be achieved, hold during the winter, and
> continue the attack as early as possible in the spring of 1919. On the
> seas—destroy the German U-boat fleet by all possible means, in-
> cluding bombing the vile artifacts in their ports and harbours, and
> where possible blocking their routes of access to the sea. In the
> air—destroy German air power, to clear the way for bombing of
> Germany itself, first, to destroy German munition plants, and sec-
> ond, to bring home to the German people some small part of the
> miseries they and their leaders, have inflicted on the rest of the
> world . . .

Simplicity itself . . . He thought of the old country problem about giving a horse a pill. You put it in a tube, insert the tube down the horse's throat, then blow . . . *but what if the horse blows first?*

And it was depressing to think of the generals cheerfully planning through Christmas, 1918, and on into 1919 . . . 1920? 1921?

He was about to turn the page when an item in the *Stop Press* caught his eye.

> **Liner torpedoed.**

His heart lurched and he felt sick. He read on fearfully:

> Naval authorities at Queenstown report intercepting an S.O.S. call
> from the White Star Liner S.S. Mystic. She wirelessed that she was
> torpedoed at 11.57 p.m. yesterday and was sinking in heavy seas.
> Her position was given as 350 miles west of the Old Head of Kin-
> sale.

The paper dropped from his hands, and he bowed his head, pray-ing.

*   *   *   *

The 2nd Sea Lord sat grim faced at his desk, his naval assistant stand-ing beside and a little behind his chair. Commander Tom Rowland R.N., stood in front of the desk, facing the admiral. He felt taut, as

586

though preparing for some severe physical test—jumping across a wide, deep chasm, perhaps—but not nervous. He said, "Sir, I have been in the Anti-Submarine Division here for eight months now. Lieutenant Commander Danby thoroughly understands the work, and has some sea experience. Also, he is physically unfit for further sea duty. I request that he should take over from me—releasing me for duty at sea."

The admiral said, "You are asking to go back to sea?"

"Yes, sir."

"Any particular appointment you would like?" The admiral's tone was harshly sarcastic.

"Yes, sir. Convoy work . . . or submarine hunting. Three weeks ago I submitted a paper to the Director, about forming hunter groups, of destroyers and mine layers, too . . ."

"I saw it," the admiral said. "It is a good idea. But you will not be given command of such a group, if we do decide to form some . . . You are living with a young man, an ex-rating. You are still associating with Russell Wharton, and now with Arthur Gavilan, Ivor Novello, Noel Coward, and other notorious homosexuals. You don't deny it?"

"No, sir. They are my friends."

"The rating, too," the admiral sneered.

"Yes, sir . . . Sir, as soon as the war is over, I intend to resign my commission. But while it is on, I ask to be allowed to do what I am trained for—command H.M. ships at sea. Plenty of R.N.V.R. officers beside Danby can do what I'm doing now, just as well, or better . . . but I am . . ."

The admiral snapped, "You are a bugger, Rowland. You will never get a sea appointment again . . . But wait a minute. Are you prepared to volunteer for a very dangerous job?"

"If it's at sea, yes, sir."

"It'll be at sea. The First Sea Lord will probably give it his final approval tomorrow or the day after. If he does, you will get a chance to wipe the slate clean . . . one way or another. If he does not, you will resign your commission—because we don't want you. I'm sure the Army won't, either—but they're going to have to have you . . . That's all."

Tom stiffened in salute, then turned about and left the big room, carefully closing the door behind him. There were all sorts of dangerous jobs going these days, but one very secret idea had been born in his own Anti-Submarine Division: a proposal to raid the German submarine bases on the Belgian coast in force, and sink blockships in the channels by which the U-boats had to get out to sea. It could be that. But after that, no more. He would have paid his debt, if he lived.

He had entered the Royal Navy as a cadet at the age of twelve. At sixteen he'd gone to sea as a midshipman in a battleship. In the intervening twenty-three years he had served in destroyers, cruisers, battle cruisers and other battleships in every sea and ocean of the world. The White Ensign had been to him as a crucifix is to the religious—a talisman and a symbol of love, service, and faith. No more.

*   *   *   *

For after this manner in the old time the holy women also, who trusted in God, adorned themselves, being in subjection unto their husbands; even as Sarah obeyed Abraham, calling him lord; whose daughters ye are as long as ye do well, and are not afraid with any amazement.

They streamed out of the little church into lightly falling snow, between two ranks of sergeants and bombardiers of Royal Field Artillery, the guard of honour, just as he had promised. Virginia clutched his good right arm with wild pride and love, her bouquet held to her breast with the other hand. Behind her walked her mother, in dark blue, the veil hiding her face, her head bent; then Stanley's father and mother, come down from Leeds, the mother crying happily, her round red face glowing with happiness, and wet with tears; then others—girls from the W.A.A.C.s, old Basin Tits, June Adkinson, a sergeant major, Uncle John and Aunt Louise, Granny McLeod from Skye, so many, so many . . .

The photographers were waiting, and Virginia huddled close to her husband, smiling into his face—"Look up, please," the photographer cried—"this way . . . Come forward, madam . . ." This to Virginia's mother, Fiona. "You, too, sir, and you . . ." They lined up, Rowlands and McLeods to one side, Robinsons the other. Mr Robinson was thin and perky, and had a waxed mustache; he was wearing a blue serge suit and a bowler hat, now held proudly in one hand against his chest. Fiona had raised her veil to look blankly at the camera. As soon as the photographs were taken she lowered it again.

Then they were in the big car, two other cars following. Fiona, squeezed between Mr and Mrs Robinson, stared at her daughter opposite. What sort of life had she chosen, deliberately, marrying this sergeant? When the war ended he'd have to leave the Army. Then what? Become a corporation dustman, like his father? Surely that was not possible, for Virginia's husband. He—Stanley—had said that there might be a place for him as Gate Porter at Wokingham School, in Berkshire, close to Wellington. It was a school Guy had played against at both cricket and rugby, two or three times. Stanley had been sounded out for the job on the strength of his Distinguished Conduct

Medal: but a Gate Porter was barely half a cut above a corporation dustman . . . and Virginia would have ten children, all of them with a Yorkshire accent you could make pudding out of, and not an H between the lot of them. Fiona's own mother obviously thought it was all due to Fiona's marrying an Englishman, and going south to live, instead of choosing a clan chief and settling on his domains.

Fiona was sorry Quentin couldn't be here. A girl ought to be given away by her father, not some dug-out old captain she'd never known before she came to this ghastly place. Thank God Quentin had never been stationed in Aldershot since their marriage. Perhaps, if he had, she would not have met Archie. The thought of Archie, suffering agonies in some unknown hospital, being tended by God knew what rich and beautiful society women, made her wince so that Virginia, sitting opposite, beaming with happiness, said anxiously, "Are you all right, Mummy?"

"Quite," she said.

She'd had no answer to her letter to Quentin yet. Perhaps Quentin hadn't heard from Archie. Or . . . he wasn't going to tell her. She writhed in inward pain.

Virginia watched her mother through brimming eyes. She was thinking of someone else, something else . . . she wasn't here. Daddy wasn't here—fighting in France. Guy wasn't here—somewhere over France in an aeroplane, perhaps dead. Granny wasn't here—wishing this was all happening in Skye. Only Stanley was here, her husband, where he would be the rest of her life, close, for her to feed and shelter and write letters for, to have children for, and be the best wife in the world for, because he deserved no less.

*   *   *   *

The brigadier general said, "I've spent a long time over this matter, a long time. I've been trying to think what is the best course for me to take—for the good of your regiment as well as of the brigade . . . and of the Army as a whole."

The new brigade major, this one of the Rifle Brigade, was standing to one side, looking pained but handsome: all brigade majors looked handsome, Quentin thought. The brigadier general wore the ribbons of the C.M.G. and the D.S.O. and a toothbrush mustache. He was quite young. He tapped the document in front of him on the makeshift desk and looked severe, but Quentin knew that his heart was not in it—not here at all, really; for yesterday the brigadier general had received news that he was to be promoted to major general and given a division in General Gough's Fifth Army. The document before him was Quentin's official report on the events of November 5 and 6, when parts of his battalion had for a while refused to obey orders. The report had gone all the way to Army Headquarters, and filtered back with the Army Commander's brief, pencilled instruction: "Brigade Commander to take necessary action."

The general said, "It is clear that for a period your battalion was in open mutiny, Rowland."

Quentin said, "Very few men, sir . . . They were overwrought . . . I don't think they knew what they were doing. They had been under great strain for a long . . ."

"Concerted refusal to obey orders is mutiny!" the general thundered.

"Yes, sir," Quentin said. If the general had been there in front of Nollehoek in that first captured German trench line, he might have understood, both how the men felt, and the necessity of shooting that wretched lieutenant and sergeant. But the general had not been seen in the front line for two days before and four days after the attack.

The general calmed again. He said, "The principal mitigating factor here is that your battalion did in the end advance and take Nollehoek, and hold it. You must be given due credit for that, just as you must be held responsible for the mutiny. You are the commanding officer."

"Yes, sir."

The general pushed the document aside and leaned on his elbow, regarding Quentin as man to man. "I was ready, before this incident, to recommend you for promotion. You have commanded your battalion, in the line, for some time now, have you not?"

"Since April 22, 1915, sir," Quentin said. How many brigadier generals had come and gone since then? Five, he thought.

The general whistled, "I didn't realize it was as long as that." He had only taken over the brigade in the spring, from a staff job at G.H.Q. He continued, "In view of this mutiny, I do not now consider you fit to command a brigade in the field—and, of course, as you have no staff training whatever, you can not be considered for a staff appointment. So I shall not recommend you for promotion."

"Oh, thank you, sir," Quentin said.

"Eh? What?" The general looked at him suspiciously. "You don't *want* promotion? Or don't you think you're fit for it? What?"

Quentin realized his exclamation would sound strange to some: personal promotion was the aim and object of the general's life, as everyone in the brigade had recognized since he took over. Quentin said, "I don't know about being fit for it, sir. Others must decide that. But I don't want to leave my battalion. The men have had a hard time the last five months. I would like to be with them until they have had a chance to rest and recuperate, be brought up to strength, and re-trained . . . do my best to make it a regular battalion again."

"I see," the general said. "Very well then. You do that, and I'll be checking on it. Or rather, the new brigade commander will." He nod-ded in dismissal, still looking puzzled, and a little contemptuous. Not want promotion, indeed! And Quentin a regular!

Quentin saluted, went out, and headed back for his battalion headquarters, in the same ruined schoolhouse in Wieltje where they had been when the German gas attack struck in April, 1915—a day before the C.O. had been killed and he had taken over. He sat down at the rickety table and his new adjutant came in. Lieutenant Woodruff's father ran a garage and taxi service in Walstone and Quentin had been hesitant about giving him the appointment. The adjutant was, after all, a C.O.'s personal staff officer and Woodruff wasn't a gentle-man, so there'd never be the closeness he'd had with Archie Campbell . . . but Campbell wasn't a gentleman, either. Quentin gave up: Woodruff was a steady man, in his thirties, married, with children, good at figures and paperwork. There wouldn't be anyone else like Archie.

Woodruff said, "Here's the list of fatigues ordered from us, sir . . . a hundred and eighty men, fifteen N.C.O.s."

Quentin growled angrily under his breath. The refrain of one of the battalion's favourite songs passed through his mind . . . *"The battalion commander had just a thousand men, but the brass hats buggered them all away."* This was supposed to be a rest period . . . in the war everything went round in circles, the same events and emotions, the same heights of exaltation and depths of depression, the same dreary plains between, all passing in ordered and repetitive sequence.

"Today we have to send home the name of the officer selected to go to the 8th Battalion in India, sir."

"I've been thinking about that," Quentin said. "I'm going to send Stratton. He's had a lot of experience in France and they'll probably give him a company out there. They certainly should . . . the rest of them must all be Territorials. When does he have to leave?"

"At once, sir. With luck, he might be able to spend Christmas in Hedlington—he has to report to the Depot first."

"All right, tell him as soon as you can. I want to see him on his way back."

"Yes, sir."

"I hope word of his M.C. will come through soon . . . Are those men the R.M.O. said have gonorrhea ready? They'll get docked pay, of course, but I want to find out which red light house they went to, and where. We've got to see that those places are properly inspected, so the men don't get these foul diseases, and go sick, when we need them . . . for fatigues."

The adjutant said, "Yes, sir," and marched out. Quentin waited. Poor devils. He composed his face sternly.

*   *   *   *

"The 12th Division broke and ran, that's why we never got what we hoped for out of Cambrai," 2nd Lieutenant Wylie said conspiratorially. "Our tanks broke clean through at first—then there was no one near enough to complete the job, and the Germans had time to pull themselves together . . . General Boy Bradford tried to get Corps to send a battalion up at once to hold Bourlon Wood, but the Corps commander had gone into dinner and wasn't to be disturbed . . . And when the Germans counter-attacked, our fellows broke."

Fred Stratton listened tolerantly. Wylie was the son of the battalion's 2nd in command. He had a small and expressive face and loved to gossip. He was barely twenty but had fought with the battalion through the whole Nollehoek-Passchendaele series of battles, and it showed in the downturn at the corners of his mouth, the crows' feet round his eyes, a haggardness belying the youthful down and roundness of his cheeks. He was now very animated, sitting in company headquarters with Lieutenant Fred Stratton, the acting company commander. He was just back from short leave, which he had spent in Paris, enjoying his first sex with a woman, courtesy of a young French war widow picked up at a boulevard café—by the lady, that is.

Fred helped himself to another spoonful of strawberry jam and spread it thickly on an Army biscuit. He'd just had dinner—but strawberry jam was not to be wasted, or allowed to grow mouldy or be eaten by rats—not even Hoggin's; strawberry jam was almost as wonderful as a Blighty. Wylie was talking fast now, gesticulating like a Frenchman. "I heard about something else, the worst railway accident in history. No one's supposed to talk about it, but this lady had heard, from . . ."

". . . another admirer," Fred said. He was becoming quite at ease with the upper class now. Wylie was an old Harrovian, and his grandfather was a viscount. Fred was aware of these things, and they mattered, but they didn't alter his manner now, as they would have a couple of years ago. He was neither truculent nor subservient. He had not quite lost his Man of Kent accent, but it was barely noticeable now.

The young man said, "Well, it might have been . . . she's awfully pretty . . . Anyway, there were seven or eight hundred French troops being sent home on Christmas leave. They'd been bolstering up the Eyeties after Caporetto . . ."

"We sent a lot, too. The battalion nearly went, I heard . . . Wish we had . . . would have missed that last show at Nollehoek, when old Kellaway lost his eye and Boy went napoo."

". . . and when they got to Modane, the frontier station, they had to change from Italian to French carriages, but there weren't enough engines, so the stationmaster said he could only send on so many of the troops and the rest would have to wait. Well, they were in no mood to wait and their officers knew it, so one of them stuck a pistol in the stationmaster's belly and said, 'Put on more carriages'—you know, the Hommes 40 Chevaux 8 wagons—and the stationmaster shrugged and ordered more wagons to be hooked on. And all the French soldiers piled in, far more than forty to a wagon, and off they went down the hill. And the engine driver soon had his brakes jammed on hard, but they wouldn't hold the train . . . it was too big, too heavy, just as the stationmaster had said . . . and the brakes got white hot and set fire to the wagons, which of course are wooden . . . and then the brakes failed altogether, burned out, so the train went faster and faster . . . and the faster it went the more it fanned the flames, and all the wagons were like flying torches—the whole train was a torch, with the soldiers in the wagons screaming, all on fire, some jumping off, at seventy, eighty miles an hour . . . until finally the train left the rails and burned to ashes—with the soldiers. Then they got hold of every survivor—there weren't many—and everyone else connected with the accident, and told them that if they said a word, they'd be shot . . . the dead soldiers' families were told the men had been killed in action, and lots of them are being given posthumous decorations and citations of all kinds . . ."

"'Fraid of another mutiny if the news gets out," Fred said laconically. "Or a revolution."

A battalion runner poked his head round the blanket covering the door of the cellar—"Signal from battalion for Mr Stratton, sir."

Fred put out his hand. Now what? Old Rowley telling him to keep the men's hair shorter? Another warning about clap in some of the red lamp houses? He read the message:

Lieutenant F. Stratton is posted to 8 W.L.I. with immediate effect. Lieutenant Stratton will report to W.L.I. Depot Hedlington as soon as possible. Report to Bn Orderly Room for transportation and documents immediately.

"Where in heaven is the 8th Battalion?" he asked the runner.

"Search me, sir," the man answered cheerfully. "Down by Arras, perhaps."

"It's in India, the principal jewel in the British Crown," Wylie said with equal cheerfulness. "But God knows where, exactly. Anyway, it's better than a blighty for you, Strat. All they do out there is lie on their beds and get natives to clean their equipment and bring them tea in the morning. *And* you'll be a *pukka sahib!*"

"India!" Fred said wonderingly. When he joined the regiment back in '14 there'd been a number of old regulars still serving, both officers and Other Ranks. They all used a great deal of Hindustani, and to him, then, service in India had been the hallmark of the old Army; and, concerning officers, proof that they were real officers— *sahibs,* as they said: not temporary gentlemen, such as himself. One of the most commonly used Hindustani words was *pukka,* and he'd soon learned that it meant "real" as against "false," "permanent" as against "temporary."And now, by God, he himself was going there, to be anointed as a *pukka sahib.*

*　　*　　*　　*

Betty Merritt opened her desk drawer, took out a slim red bound volume and turned to the title page where it read—*At the Lip. Poems from France, by Fletcher* . . . but on the facing page there was a printed dedication:

For my love

When he came home she would make him write those words out in his own hand, add a comma or dash, then the single word—"Betty"—and sign it.

She turned the pages slowly . . . *At the lip* . . . terrible but beautiful . . . as mystical as Blake . . . *Death passed,* tragic at first, then inexplicably lighter, almost happy . . . *My mate and I,* just the other way round, light at the beginning, with a powerful bite at the end . . . *Where are the guns that shout all night?*

The door handle turned and she quickly, guiltily stuffed the book back and closed the drawer. Ginger Keble-Palmer came in, stooped as usual, and said, "Richard says we have to find some less-complicated way to hold and release the bombs. This—" he tapped the drawing in his hand—"will work, he says, but it will be slow and expensive to produce."

She sighed, and took the drawing. The design had been hers in the first place, and now she would have to start all over again. Damn the bombs! The day would come when the Hedlington Buffalo would be flying to Berlin, but with passengers instead of bombs . . . and to Rome, Athens, Vienna. She sat back, while Ginger went to the tall draughtsman's desk and leaned over it, studying the diagrams pinned to it.

He spoke now, without turning round—"Someone told me you were the person to whom that new book of war poems by Fletcher is dedicated."

She looked across, at first upset—what business was it of his? Of anyone's? It was a secret between her and Fletcher, like the mysteries of each other's bodies, shared in Deal that winter night. Ginger had not looked round. She softened. Of course, he had always been fond of her, loved her even; but she had never been able to see him in that way. She said gently, "It's true, Ginger."

"Lucky man," he said in a low voice. "It's none of my business . . . one of the girls knew you'd been seeing Fletcher Gorse while he was at the Depot here . . . I hope you'll be happy."

"We will," she said confidently. "I love him."

"I love you," Keble-Palmer said gloomily, "but that doesn't mean we'd be happy. *I* would . . ."

She said, "You're sweet . . . but really, we'll be all right. We agreed that we mustn't get married until we have found out that we have more in common than . . ." she blushed, "well, being in love."

Ginger said, "He's a very good poet . . . awfully English, like his grandfather, that old poacher down at Walstone . . . wild . . . a sort of child of nature . . ."

"And I'm American, and tamed, and like everything hygienic and clean and artificial . . . Is that what you mean?"

Ginger swung round, "I'm jealous, Betty. I can't help it . . . but even if I wasn't, I would worry. There is such an incredible difference in your backgrounds. He can hardly write . . ."

"He can write this!" she snapped, banging the desk under which the poems lay hidden in the drawer. Again, she controlled herself, and continued, "You really are sweet, Ginger, to worry about me. But it'll be all right. I *know* it will! Everything will be all right when he comes home."

Ginger said nothing; and Betty thought, he's thinking, as I'm thinking, as everyone must think in these ghastly times—*if* he comes home.

She said, "Ginger, let's go up to London, to the Cat & Mouse . . . tonight."

He looked astonished, and she went over to the tall desk and put a hand over his, "Ginger, I don't love you, but I *like* you, very much. And I'm frightened—for him. And lonely . . . loneliness is like a cold heavy clammy blanket on me whenever I'm not here with you all, working. I understand now why women do such awful things when their men are in France . . . Until you get a girl of your own, will you help look after me? Help me look after myself?"

Ginger muttered, "Of course, Betty . . . And I won't bother you again. I'll try and think of you as my sister."

She squeezed his elbow—"Thanks, Ginger . . . I simply must find the right girl for you. You deserve the best."

"But I'm not going to get her," he said with a wan smile.

*   *   *   *

Bert Gorse trudged round the exercise yard at Hedlington Gaol, his boots slipping and sliding in the slushy and dirty snow. Visitors today. He wondered who would come to see him. Rachel had come once, two days after the beaks had slammed him in again—fourth time now, wasn't it? And all because he had punched up a big navvy who was heckling Rachel at one of her No-Conscription Fellowship meetings . . . that was a laugh, if you could see it that way, because he didn't belong to the Fellowship himself any more; and Rachel didn't belong to him! She hadn't actually gone off with Bentley—or perhaps she had, since he'd been put in gaol—but he was sure she would, sooner or later, probably sooner . . . Old John Rowland might come, but Christ, he'd changed since his son was killed . . . shrunk inside his clothes, turned twenty years older in a month. And he'd be busy at the farm . . . seemed like another world they lived in down there, in Walstone and Cantley and Taversham—village greens, cows plodding along the lanes dropping sploshy pats, men touching their forelock to such as John Rowland, Cate, Swanwick . . .

An elbow jabbed back into his stomach and the edge of a hard hand smashed against the side of his head. He reeled dizzily and two boots stamped down on his feet, the heels grinding in. He doubled over and another elbow jerked up under his nose, which spouted blood. The foot where he had shot himself always hurt, and was now shrieking in silent agony.

The prison warder shouted, "Keep moving, you there . . . number 9876!" He started forward, drawing his truncheon.

Bert reeled on. Bastards . . . the warder had seen the blokes set on him, although he pretended he hadn't. The man behind him muttered through closed lips, "'Ow d'you like your exercise, conchie?"

Bert muttered, "It's your lives they're trying to save . . ."

"Fucking conchie."

The warder shouted, "Stop talking, there, 9876!" then turned his back. Blows descended on Bert till he fell out, kneeling, retching.

"Get up!" the warder shouted, turning back. "You, 43 . . . 72 . . . pick 'im up. See that he gets 'is exercise."

*   *   *   *

Bert gazed at his two visitors through swollen eyelids. His lips and nose were puffed and his face bruised, but none of that hurt as much as his wounded foot.

Wilfred Bentley said, "It's a disgrace . . . bestial treatment. I'll see that this is brought to the attention of the House of Commons. I know two members well."

"It won't do no good," Bert said. "I'll just get banged up some more . . . What's the news?"

Rachel said, "Nothing really . . . but now that Russia's out of the war, and has become a real socialist republic, Mr Russell thinks the allies will realize that they must come to terms with Germany before they—the Germans—can attack in the West next spring. So now's the moment for us to redouble our efforts in the No-Conscription Fellowship."

Bert said briefly, "You're farting against thunder, Rachel."

No one spoke for a time, then Wilfred Bentley said, "I've asked Rachel to marry me. She has said yes."

"In a church and all?"

Rachel said, "Wilfred insisted, and, well, I don't mind."

Bentley said, "We must be friends, and work together."

After a while Bert said, "All right . . . can't shake hands here."

Wilfred said, "Thank you, Bert . . . We'll see that your house is in good order when you come out, all neat and clean and swept and ready for you. Rachel will still be in it, as we're not getting married till the new year."

*   *   *   *

John Merritt, wearing long greatcoat, and wool gloves and campaign hat with the red cords of the Field Artillery, stood at the upper deck rail of the liner, looking down on the massed soldiery on the foredeck below. A match flared from among the other officers standing behind and to each side of him. Officers and men were smoking on the crowded decks still, for the ship was gliding almost noiselessly down Upper New York Bay, past the Statue of Liberty, dim green under a quarter moon, out into the Upper Bay. The beat of the propellers quickened as the ship gathered speed, heading for the Narrows.

"On our way, at last," Rudy Anspach said. Rudy was a friend from Harvard days; by chance a fellow student at the School of Fire; their fates, now still more closely intertwined when they were both posted to Battery D of the 137th Regiment, Field Artillery. Five days after they had reported to the regiment, it entrained for Hoboken. On December 24, 1917, it sailed for France, with the rest of the division, in six ships.

"We're on our way," John repeated after his friend. For him, it would be a return. But this time he'd be seeing France, and the war, with other Americans, as part of his own country's effort, not a spectator, or a guest, of someone else's.

"Think we'll be thrown straight into action?" Rudy asked.

John said, "I doubt it . . . unless the Germans attack and we have to go in to help . . . but that's very unlikely in mid-winter."

"What'll we do then?"

"We'll be held in general reserve, training, until we can take over a sector of the line."

Anspach nodded. John had found that his short spell in France with the regulars of the U.S. 16th Infantry had endowed him, in the eyes of his classmates at Fort Sill, even of the instructors, with what amounted to universal knowledge of trench warfare. His opinion was always asked, and deferred to.

He had thought about advising Captain Hodder, the battery commander, about his need for leave to go and see his wife as soon as they reached Europe; but had decided to say nothing until they were actually there, and settled in. He wished he could be with Stella for Christmas, but here it was Christmas Eve, and he three thousand miles away, at sea, blacked out, wearing a life preserver.

Heroin . . . it was disloyal of him even to think of the word, let alone the idea that his wife might have been using it . . . but the word, at least, would not be dismissed for long from his mind, ever since Lieutenant Aquila had mentioned it at Jean Burress's cocktail party. Thank heavens he had never had to see *her* again . . . heroin: produced from the juice of unripe seed capsules of the opium poppy, *papaver somniferum*—C21 H23 N O5—an acetyl derivative of opium— legitimate medical uses for treatment of severe pain, diarrhoea, cough . . . used to achieve euphoria; as an escape; as a substitute for aggressive and sexual drives; for rebellion . . . high potential for psychological dependence, tolerance, and physical dependence . . . long-term effects: constipation, loss of appetite and weight, temporary impotence or sterility; painful and unpleasant withdrawal symptoms . . .

The ship entered the Narrows, the loom of Staten Island to the right, the low Brooklyn shore to the left, the Sandy Hook lightship flashing ahead. The ship's siren boomed tremendously, three times. On the foredeck the sergeants barked, "Out cigarettes, pipes, cigars! Take emergency stations . . . move your butts there!"

A destroyer appeared out of the night, a white bone in its teeth, no flag flying from its lean black silhouette. John and Anspach parted, each to his emergency station on the boat deck. The men shuffled silently to their places. All doors were closed, above and below decks.

The beat of the engines increased to full speed. Sandy Hook light sank into the sea astern, the half moon shone more brightly. John waited, his back to the lifeboat, facing the ranked Enlisted Men, all swaying in unison to the new roll of the ship.

Stella . . . He remembered the time he had come in late from work and found her drunk. Betty had warned him. Now he had left her for nine months, more lonely than ever . . . *as an escape* . . . When this war was over, he'd never leave her again. He'd find a little house. Where? Was he going back to Fairfax, Gottlieb as his father expected him to? It would be hard, after all that he had seen and done, the independence he had enjoyed since 1914—three years! A little house perhaps, say in Westchester, looking across the great river at his father's house . . . why, he could have a big mast put in the front lawn, and he and Dad could signal to each other, with naval flags—"Come over for dinner tomorrow" . . . "Cocktails being served . . ." Inside the house—just the two of them, husband and wife . . . well, a baby or two or three . . . *temporary sterility* . . .

He shivered. Captain Hodder came round—"Stand down from emergency stations. All ranks below decks by midnight."

The soldiers dispersed, mostly heading for the foredeck. Someone lit a cigarette, to be greeted by a furious bellow from First Sergeant Jesus Montoya, and a dull thud as of something hard being struck against a body. The cigarette went out.

A voice beside John said, "There sinks our innocence, with the Sandy Hook light."

John recognized the voice and shape of Lieutenant Walden, a strange lank man of about thirty from somewhere in the Middle West.

John said, "You think the French girls will corrupt our men?"

"That, of course," Walden said, "but much more . . . There's a deep, universal corruption over there that they won't recognize, because it looks like a mediaeval castle, or an '08 Clos Vougeot, or a beguiling countess . . . beautiful, subtle, full of hidden decay . . . and it will corrupt them—you and me, too, of course . . . When America comes back home after this war, it will never be the same again. Over there, it will eat of the fruit of the tree of the Knowledge of Good and Evil. Farewell, barefoot boy with cheek of tan!"

He wandered off along the deck. John thought, Walden's a little crazy. But not very: for he himself had already eaten some of that fruit.

The six ships turned in concert, four points to starboard, beginning the irregular zig zag course they would follow all the way to St. Nazaire. The destroyers on either bow leaned over to reach new positions farther on the flank. The destroyer astern hunted across the wakes, shuddering and heaving and shaking to the increasing thrust of the waves. Ice began to form on stanchions and bollards and railings, and on the decks. The fast troop convoy raced for France.

*   *   *   *

Guy Rowland pulled the stick gently back toward his stomach and the Sopwith began to climb, passing through six thousand feet over Ypres, heading east. The remaining aircraft of the flight followed their leader's course, in stepped-up echelon behind and above him. The desolate battlefields of Flanders slid back under the wing. He stole a glance down. During the long Ypres offensive God only knew how often he'd flown over here, when the weather permitted, and sometimes when it hadn't. The shattered ruins of Broodseinde, Passchendaele, Poelcapelle, Nollehoek, Zonnebeke and a dozen others had grown sickeningly familiar to him, like ulcers in the bloodsoaked mud-stained corpse of the land.

He looked up and round. His job was to search for enemy planes up here, not try to imagine how his father was surviving down there . . . and he couldn't imagine if he tried, even though he had several times visited the trenches. It was still impossible to imagine the reality.

He waggled his wings and heaved the Camel over in a gentle turn. But she could turn tight and sharp if she had to, and that was what made her a great scout . . . and a menace to the unwary. The Three Threes' pilots had complained long and loud when their S.E. 5As were taken away, and it became known that they were to be re-equipped with Sopwith Camels. They wanted Triplanes, instead—steady, maneuverable, predictable, easy to fly and a good sturdy fighter in battle. Guy had had his doubts, too, for the Camel came with an ominous reputation, of pilots killed, crashes for no apparent cause—especially on landing—spins when all seemed well—but a few days in the cockpit, and above all a dogfight with von Rackow's Jasta 16, when Guy had shot down two Fokker Dr. I Triplanes in his new Camel, and damaged a third—those had convinced him that the same qualities which made it a tricky plane to fly made it an almost ideal machine for battle—the light touch on the controls, the instant reaction or even over-reaction, its nervous, darting mannerisms in flight. These qualities had saved his life, when one of von Rackow's pilots had got on his tail while he was shooting down his second victim. He had only escaped by a climbing turn that stood the Camel on its tail, whence it slid down tail first two hundred feet, apparently out of control, before he eased it into a gentle spin, and a moment later, started climbing back to the fight . . .

A speck caught his eye . . . four, five specks . . . seven. "Tally ho!" he shouted, knowing that no one could hear him, and waggled his wings and pointed his gloved hand. The flight closed up tight and he pulled the stick back farther, forcing the Camel into a straining climb.

It wasn't von Rackow's Jasta this time . . . no Triplanes, though 16 had had them since October. These were Albatros D V As, biplanes.

The seven dots grew fast. Guy continued flying straight at them with his four Camels. Attack, attack, General Trenchard insisted; we are masters of the sky and must remain so, at all costs.

The leading German opened fire first, at very long range. Guy relaxed his lips in relief. He always liked to tackle pilots who opened fire when out of effective range. The Albatroses were painted in black and white checkerboard fashion, each with different colored wheels—red, yellow, blue, one with concentric circles. They were coming on in arrowhead, stepped-up. Guy picked the machine in the middle and flew straight at it. Two seconds later the German dived down to avoid collision. Guy did not dive after him, for that would have given the next German a beautiful target; but swung slightly and as he passed through the German formation, put a burst into the machine that had been next to the leader, on his right. It turned away, and Guy fired on another . . . clouds rolled up and they all disappeared into them . . . a minute, flying straight ahead, watching the instruments, thick wet wind, moisture pearling and running across the windshield . . . out into the winter air, cold, cold, his hands cold inside the big gloves . . . an Albatros, alone, dead ahead, going away. A sitting duck. He closed up, throttle wide and opened fire from a hundred feet. The biplane burst into an enormous orange ball of flame, momentarily singeing the skin of his face, and fell away, a few shreds and wires rattling against Guy's plane as they were hurled in all directions by the explosion.

He circled carefully . . . cloud enfolded him again . . . bump, heave, lurch . . . damp, rain . . . colder, ice forming . . . out . . . two of his Camels in sight, one vanished. No Albatroses. One of the other pilots pointed down and Guy saw, faint in the east, four black and white biplanes heading east, racing low above the ground . . . they must have got three. He looked at the numbers on the remaining aircraft of his flight . . . damn, Bunny Fuller was missing. He was a good pilot and a good sport. Perhaps he was all right . . . had had to go home or make a crash landing. He might have had to come down behind the German lines. The R.F.C. lost a lot of pilots that way because of Trenchard's insistence that the fight must be carried to the enemy. Trenchard had been posted to London, but his spirit still imbued the R.F.C. Have to wait and see. Twenty minutes' petrol left. He turned toward base, and the other two followed.

One of the Fokker pilots had been wearing something like a lady's silk stocking tied to his helmet. Florinda had given Guy one of her stockings after their night together, and he had thought of wearing it on his helmet, but decided against it. The fellows would want to know whose stocking it was, and there'd be nudges and good-natured jokes and innuendoes, not very subtle. He'd . . . By God, he'd end a flaming wreck if he allowed his mind to wander. Sulphuric Sugden's stern face came before him, and his harsh emphatic voice—"A Scout pilot's life depends on *continual* all-round look-out, even when on the way home, plus concentration."

He wiped his mind blank of everything except the sky above, below, to both sides—and what was in it.

The base came up. He picked out the huts in the foggy morning air down there and lined up by the windsock. If you were wise you landed a Camel with the same sort of intense concentration with which you attacked a Fokker Triplane.

He guided the machine to earth and taxied to his place in the squadron's line up. He switched off the engine and there was Frank Stratton, running, with the basin, climbing up on the lower wing as Guy's stomach heaved, he began to sweat and the vomit heaved up into his throat.

"There, there, sir . . . it's all right," Frank was saying, holding the basin close. "There . . . How many was it, sir?"

"One definite," Guy croaked, between his retches. "Two more, perhaps . . . don't know what happened . . . haven't asked the others yet . . . Any news of Mr Fuller?"

"No, sir . . . but, sir, the major's been promoted and is going home to command a wing of the new bombers . . . and you have another M.C., sir . . . and the gup is that you're going to command the squadron!"

Guy climbed groggily out of the cockpit. Command the Three Threes? He could do it, if Boom Trenchard or his successor had chosen him. He'd been out, good Lord, eighteen months. He'd survived—that was quite a feat in itself. He'd studied air tactics. He could do it.

"That makes your score fifty-four," Frank said reverently.

"Oh?" Guy said wearily. "I need some leave."

Frank's face fell—"I don't think they'll give you any, sir, not if you're just taking over the squadron."

Guy yawned, "What a bore . . . I'll go and make my report, then I'll lie down for a bit."

"Very good, sir. It'll take us two hours to get this fixed. They put a few bullets into you. Must have been at pretty close quarters, sir . . . like always."

602

Guy nodded. Good man, Frank Stratton. Needed leave as much as he did—more—he was a family man. Ought to talk to him more. He said, "How's Victoria coming on?"

Frank's face lit up—"Beautiful, sir! She'll do a hundred now, more when I can replace some of the parts with lighter steel, which Dad couldn't get . . . but where can I run her, out here?"

Guy shook his head, "God knows . . . when you get some leave you can take her away from the war zone, where the roads haven't been shelled and bombed and ruined by lorries and guns . . ."

"Oh, but sir, if I get leave I must go home," Frank said.

Guy shrugged and waved a hand as Frank saluted, then headed for the squadron offices. Old Sulphuric would send for him later, if he had anything to say to him. At this time of day he was usually absent at Wing, getting briefed for tomorrow.

Half an hour later he entered his hut, flung himself back on the bed and closed his eyes. Sulphuric wasn't there, but the adjutant had confirmed the bar to his M.C. and hinted mysteriously at more to celebrate later. So perhaps he was going to get the squadron . . . Sulphuric had been a good commander, but a bit old fashioned. The Three Threes were going to fight in concert from now on. The dogfight must be changed to a concerted attack, all aircraft mutually supporting each other. Shooting must be improved . . find out whether the experiments with explosive bullets had come to anything . . . work on a new sight that allowed better for targets crossing the front at different ranges . . . better aircraft recognition, and understanding exactly what each type of German aircraft could do best— and worst, where were its weak spots? And, as far as possible, the same for individual German pilots . . .

He yawned expansively and took out the large photo of Florinda he kept in a drawer. Lovely, smiling girl—woman. She wrote regularly, but did she feel the same about him? Girls changed their minds, everyone said. *La donna e mobile* . . . In his breast pocket he had a smaller photograph of her, dressed or rather almost undressed as she'd been in some revue. She had said she loved him . . . always had, she said . . . but what now? He knew that he loved her, that was certain. He had committed himself mentally to her on that last leave—God, a year ago! But was he fit to do that? He was a killer, and should be classified as a dangerous animal, rather than as a lover. Perhaps he should content himself with such as Poitrine. He would never get close enough to farmers' daughters and young widows to do them harm. To Florinda, he would—he was . . . But he didn't want any more Poitrines, or other women, only this one, smiling at him from out of the silver frame, her eyes wide, her breasts curving up out of the skimpy bodice.

603

Holding the picture in one hand, yearning for her, he began to masturbate.

*   *   *   *

Probyn Gorse, shuffling fast along Scarrow bank in the wintry dusk, a few snow flakes flying but not really meaning it, the bells of Walstone church ringing a muffled peal of Grandsire Doubles, saw a familiar figure walking slowly toward him on the same narrow footpath—the Right Honourable the Earl of Swanwick. Swanwick was wearing a deerstalker hat, like Probyn's, and not much more respectable; and a tweed raglan overcoat with overlapping capes on the shoulders, making him look more than ever like an eighteenth-century coachman. Probyn did not break step, or look right or left. The cock pheasant was still warm in the back pocket of his capacious and untidy coat, and the folding .410 was strapped to his left leg in its case, and he was on the earl's land; but there was no escape. What must be must be.

The earl peered at him in the gloom as they approached and stopped, "Oh, it's Gorse . . . Been up to your old tricks with my pheasants, I'll be bound."

"Oh, no, my lord," Probyn said. "Been visiting a sick friend in Taversham . . . I and my Woman was sorry to hear about Lord Cantley, my lord. Always treated us very nice, he did . . ."

"And you taught him how to handle ferrets . . . never did him much good, though. He preferred London and those artist johnnies. Couldn't make head nor tail of half the paintings he had in his flat. Never heard of the painters, either . . . names like Picasso, Matisse, I never could get my tongue round—a lot of damned Frogs and Dagoes . . . lucky to sell the lot last week for a thousand quid. Can't think why anyone would want to pay *that* for them."

"Yes, my lord," Probyn said respectfully. "Well, best wishes of the season to everyone at the Park, from my Woman and me . . . I'd best be getting along or she'll be thinking I've been shot by mistake by your keepers, ha ha."

"Those bloody old fools couldn't catch a poacher if he was deaf, dumb, and blind . . . and they couldn't hit a haystack at ten paces with a charge of buckshot." He stared at Probyn—"Tell you the truth, Gorse, I can't make head nor tail of half what's going on in England these days."

"No more can I, my lord," Probyn said heartily.

"No food for a perfectly good pack of foxhounds . . ."

"Terrible, my lord!"

". . . bloody profiteer from London buying up one of Mr Cate's farms to put houses on for bloody stockbrokers . . ."

"'Tain't right, my lord!"

". . . women working in the fields, the factories, on the buses, the trains, coal heaving, road mending . . ."

"It's against nature, my lord!"

Swanwick again looked closely at Probyn—"Lady Helen's working on a hush-hush project in London, y'know. She speaks French like a Frog, and that's what it's all about . . . can't tell us any more."

"'Course not, my lord. Military secret, like."

"Quite . . . You know, Gorse, when this war's over you and I'll be the only ones who haven't changed. If I'm still here . . . Everything else, everybody else, will have changed, for the worse."

"That's right, my lord."

The earl fumbled in the pocket of his jacket, through the slits in the side of the raglan. His hand came out with a coin. He pressed it into Probyn's hand—"Merry Christmas, Gorse. I'd say Happy New Year, too, but it won't be."

"Thank 'ee, my lord, thank 'ee." Probyn touched his forelock. The earl acknowledged it with a nod, and walked on, shoulders hunched in the falling snow. The bells were still ringing Grandsire Doubles. The coin was a golden guinea. He can't afford that, these days, Gorse thought, but he's got to; because he's the earl. He understands, and I understand, but no one else would, soon enough.

*　　*　　*　　*

Stella walked down High Street, hatless and coatless in the light snow. She had left her car in a side street near the South-Eastern. Heatherington's would be open, and the forged prescription in her purse would fool the old man. His eyesight was bad—and he would never think that Mrs Merritt, Stella Cate that was, would be using heroin unless a doctor had prescribed it. She was unaware of the snow, or her cold hands and ears, only of the pain in her head, the ache in her bones, the utter necessity of getting some more heroin, now.

This was the place, the chemist's shop was . . . closed! She stared at the door, rattled the door knob, kicked the wood panel below. In a frenzy she began to pound the door with her fists, screaming, "Open, open, for God's sake! Open!" Some people passed, bundled or stooped against the snow, but she was unaware of them, and they did not stop. After a few minutes she ceased her pounding and leaned on the door jamb, her head pressed against the cold, wet wood.

She'd find another chemist. It was nine o'clock on Christmas Eve, but someone had to be open, they must be! There was another chemist down near the river on Wilmot Street, half a mile north. She pushed away from Heatherington's door and hurried north on High Street, slipping and stumbling in her thin, high-heeled shoes in the wet snow. A clock struck in tones muffled by the snow . . . people passed . . . her bones throbbed in torture . . . she fell against someone, a man, who cried, "Hey, look where you're going, miss!" On . . . Luddon, Darby, Clarendon, Roberts, Wellington, Anglesey, Cardigan . . . here it was. She turned down, almost running into the dark street— narrow, leading down to the river, no lights.

The three men who had been following her for the past two hundred yards, giggling and slipping as much as she was—for they were drunk—broke into a run. In a moment the leader caught up with her, and grabbed her round the neck, pulling her to the ground and falling on top of her. They were soldiers, conscripts of the Weald Light Infantry, recently finished recruit training and under orders for France. The two on their feet were laughing and shouting, "Go on, Charlie . . . Poke it in!" The man on her was fumbling under her skirt, hiccuping, speaking thickly in her ear. "Lie still, ducks . . . I'm going to fuck you . . . not 'urt you . . ." She heaved her body up with all her strength and the man rolled off her onto his back. She could barely see him in the dark and the falling snow, but pounced where she thought his face was, and kneeling astride him, punched him time and again, her small hard fists banging his eye, his nose, his lips. She felt hands on her shoulders, tugging, and the others dragged her to her feet. She was being pressed close to one of their chests, and his beery breath was in her face as he crowed, "So you don't wan' Charlie, eh? Try me," and again a hand was pulling up her skirt, fumbling. She leaned suddenly forward and sank her teeth into the man's throat, at the Adam's apple, hanging on grimly as he gurgled, choked, gasped. The other two were tugging at her now, trying to free their comrade from the grip of her jaws. She kicked backward and caught one of them in the fork. He gasped, "Oh Christ, she's got me in the balls," and fell, kneeling, groaning in agony. The man Stella had by the throat was sagging against her and her mouth was full of blood. She suddenly let go, and turned on the third, the only one now on his feet, lashing out at his face with her fists. The one with the bleeding throat croaked, "Let the bitch go . . . the rozzers are coming!"

The three of them started back up the street toward High Street, Stella on their heels, screaming abuse, pummeling them on their backs and heads. Oh, if only she had a knife, a stick . . . anything! They had said the police were coming; but no one was coming. The men had vanished into the snow and the dark, and she was alone in the middle of Wilmot Street . . . outside the chemist's she had remembered, Parkley's . . . it was closed.

She walked slowly on down toward the river. Her arm hurt, for she had only recently taken it out of a sling. Perhaps she had broken it again. Johnny was on his way to France at this moment; and soon he would come home, to see her. What would he find? A hollow-eyed, gaunt, drug addict, and drunkard, a woman unfaithful to her marriage vows. The baby had been Charles's, of course. Perhaps it was better dead. And herself? The river was deep enough, and cold enough at this season. And surely no one would see her, to try to rescue her.

*   *   *   *

Christopher Cate sat in his usual chair in the drawing room of Walstone Manor, close by the fire, his mind a dully aching blank. Nothing more about the S.S. *Mystic* or her passengers. The waits were singing carols outside the front door, and the bells of the village church were ringing a peal of Grandsire Doubles. He heard both sounds, one close and clear, one distant and muffled, but they made no mark on his consciousness.

Across the fire from him his father-in-law, Harry Rowland, said, "There don't seem to be as many waits as there used to be . . . and not singing as well, either."

Alice sat on the sofa facing the fireplace, her artificial left leg stretched straight out, her right leg a little bent. She asked, "Who's singing, Christopher?"

Cate started, "Singing? Oh, it'll be the rector and some of the boys and girls of the village . . . no big boys now, though."

Alice said, "Could you open the curtains, Christopher, and let the waits see into the room, and the Christmas tree? And I can see them, without having to go to the front door."

Her father said doubtfully, "We've never done that before, Dormouse . . . I mean, it's rather like showing off."

Betty Merritt said, "We do it everywhere in America. Rather a nice idea, *I* think—sharing what you have, in a way inviting strangers to enjoy your tree with you."

Cate got up, found the heavy cords and pulled back the curtains. The light streamed out on a lawn thinly sheeted with snow, untrodden. The voices of the waits wavered, then they seemed to understand, and after a few moments came into view, blinking in the light, and lined up, staring in through the glass, beginning to wave as they recognized those inside. Alice smiled, and waved her hand.

There was old Mr Kirby, wearing a heavy black overcoat that must have been made for him in Savile Row about 1860, and his low John Bull topper, his hunting hat, a thick white wool scarf hiding his dog collar. There was Miss Hightower, always to be found as close to the rector as she could get on such occasions . . . old Commander Quigley, trying to look like a seadog facing down an arctic gale, but appearing as a dear old man with a rheumy drop on the end of his nose . . . Alice exclaimed—"There are John and Louise, at the back! I never thought they'd . . ."

Cate said, "I asked them to go carolling . . . told them how pleased Mr Kirby would be if they did . . . sort of proof that they'd forgiven the Germans for killing Boy . . . though I don't think the rector has, himself."

Harry said, "And Louise never will."

Betty said, "In time, perhaps . . . but Uncle John has. Boy killed a lot of their fathers' sons, too."

Harry said, "Nice of Richard and Susan to come, with the children. They're singing their heads off—I can see from here."

"They came into Hedlington yesterday, to wish us a Merry Christmas," Alice said.

". . . and give us Christmas presents," Harry added. He chuckled contentedly—"Do you know what those young scamps gave me? Sally gave me tweezers to pull the whiskers out of my nose, and Tim a mustache cup . . . must think I strain my soup through my mustache."

"Ha ha!" Alice laughed dutifully: her father did occasionally do exactly that. Her missing leg throbbed sometimes; but she no longer craved morphine or any other drug. The pain grew infinitesimally less every day; and her mobility with the artificial leg grew steadily more. Most of the time, when she was concentrating on the accounting manuals, she forgot it altogether—which proved that all she needed was something to do—especially for her mind, rather than her hands, or of course her legs. Once she actually started work at the Aircraft Company, she would soon forget even that she had an artificial leg. And then she'd have to make up her mind over Daisy Cowell's proposal . . . her amazing suggestion of a ménage à trois. Oh dear, why was the path of love always so complicated and . . . *messy*?

She glanced at Betty Merritt. The girl's young face was drawn and pale, and she sat very close to Christopher, looking at him from time to time. They shared the tension and pain of waiting for news of Mrs Kramer . . . Christopher had obviously become fond of her. You could see he was quite distraught.

The waits finished another carol and Christopher, through the window, made a ritual pantomime of lifting a glass to his lips, eyebrows raised interrogatively. Mr Kirby put up his hands in mock horror, and shook his head, smiling. Then the waits trooped away into the darkness and out of sight.

Harry Rowland cleared his throat—"What did the Governor of North Carolina say to the Governor of South Carolina?"

Alice looked at her father in shocked surprise—but of course he didn't know that Mrs Kramer had become a close friend—or more—of Christopher's.

Harry said, "It's a long time between drinks! . . . Heard that in the House last week."

Christopher got up, went to the corner cupboard and poured sherry, none for himself. "Not for me, thank you, Uncle," Betty said. Christopher handed full glasses to Harry and Alice.

Alice said gently, "We can drink to peace, Christopher . . ."

"And victory!" her father added.

"Let us pray to God that they're all safe and sound," Cate burst out—"All of them! . . . Laurence, Quentin, Isabel, Guy, Naomi, Virginia, Johnny—all those boys and girls, men and women, who have gone out from their homes, and not yet returned."

He remembered, two years ago, that his main worry at Christmas was a plan of Probyn Gorse's to poach a lot of pheasants from Lord Swanwick. He remembered the shock of hearing the guns from France, and feeling them shake the Kentish earth under his feet on Christmas dawn. The guns were shouting even louder now, over there, but now everyone in England heard them in their soul, even when they could not hear them in their actual rage.

The telephone rang in the hall, and Alice saw Christopher look quickly at Betty, his face falling and seeming suddenly collapsed and old. Betty was on her feet, going out of the room, closing the door behind her. The peal of bells continued from the tower of the Saxon church, the fire crackled in the grate.

They heard a cry from the passage and Christopher sank into a chair, his whole body trembling. Betty burst into the room, shrieking, "She's safe, Uncle . . . picked up by a ship . . . two days in a lifeboat . . . frostbitten toes . . . hospital in Liverpool . . ."

"Liverpool!" Christopher exclaimed.

"Yes, the ship was coming from Halifax with wheat . . . Uncle Virgil telephoned the Admiralty this morning for news . . . there wasn't any news, then . . . half an hour ago, it came in!"

Christopher was up, pouring himself a glass of sherry. He downed it in a single gulp, and poured another. "Oh my God," he cried. "Oh, my God!" and burst into tears.

*　　*　　*　　*

Lieutenant Billy Bidford, D.S.C., Royal Naval Volunteer Reserve, stretched out his hand to pour her champagne but the attentive waiter reached the ice bucket first and, carefully swathing the bottle with his white napkin, refilled Florinda's glass, then retired.

Florinda drank, put down the glass and said, "We ought to be washing those kids' feet with this, instead of drinking it."

"What kids? . . . Oh, the children begging in the Strand as we came in."

"Barefoot, in rags, on Christmas Eve!" she said. "Oh well, I've gone barefoot. It's not so bad."

Bidford eyed her cautiously. She was in one of her moods . . . not that he had ever had much opportunity to study them, being on duty with his Motor Torpedo Boat in the Dover Patrol; and that would become a good deal more exciting when Admiral Keyes replaced Admiral Bacon next week . . . patrols at all hours, trailing their coats miles up Channel, while fast cruisers lurked in the mists, ready to pounce if German destroyers tried to cut them off . . . practising with depth charge patterns . . . precious few U-boats made safe passage through the Straits even now, either going out or returning.

She was wearing her favorite long emerald-green gown of silk, plunging décolleté revealing much of the curve of her breasts, one ring, one bracelet, arms bare to the shoulder, an emerald and diamond tiara in her hair. She said, "I'm fed up. I think I'll join the F.A.N.Y. and go to France. Or do you think they wouldn't have me? I hear they're a proper lot of snobs, and they'd know who I am . . . was."

Billy said, "I don't think that would upset them . . . but they do want ladies with a knowledge of cars . . . how to drive and repair them."

"Which I don't know one bloody thing about," she said. "And I'm not going to scrub floors, or peel potatoes, or type letters for the W.A.A.C.s, even if I could get to France with them . . . no time to learn nursing . . . Hey, isn't there a women's service with the R.F.C.?"

"I really don't know," Bidford said.

Florinda drank moodily. She put down the glass—"I suppose I'll just have to go on taking concert parties wherever they'll let me . . . and get leered at by fat old generals who think they know who *I* am . . . and me hardly able to sing for looking at the poor men, watching me . . . They clap till their hands must hurt, and sometimes the shows are awful."

"They're grateful you've taken the trouble to come. They know you don't have to."

"I don't want gratitude. I want recognition," she snapped. "And that I won't get—because I don't deserve it."

The maitre d'hotel of the Grill passed, smiling. "Everything satisfactory, my lady, Mr Bidford?"

"Quite, thank you, Mr Schneider," Billy said, and Florinda flashed him a dazzling smile. Schneider passed on with a small bow of acknowledgment. Florinda said, "My mother thinks I'm a whore."

Billy held his tongue. Florinda needed to talk; he'd listen. She continued—"My dad's simple, but he's gone off and joined the Army, so Mum's not getting enough money in . . . there are other kids . . . She went to the barracks to get Dad out, but they said he'd got two legs and knew what he was doing, and they wouldn't let him go . . . I've been down to Hedlington, trying to give her money . . . bribing people to offer her jobs, that I'd pay for. She won't touch any of it."

"Why?" Billy asked gently.

"Because she thinks I earned my money with my cunt. Because my next sister—Violet, she's thirteen now—had a baby last year from a sixty-year-old man, for money—a bob a time . . . and now she doesn't look after the baby, and has gone back to whoring with anyone who'll pay her, Mum says. Mum doesn't come right out and say it's my fault, but . . . she loves me, but she isn't going to take any help from me, in case it sends the other girls the same way, I suppose. And that's final."

Billy waited a long time; and when she did not speak, but stared at the wall over his head, her face troubled, he said quietly, "Shall we go to bed, Florinda?"

She shook her head without speaking, her heavy auburn hair waving, settling, glowing.

He covered her hand with his—"If you think it more proper, shall we get married?"

She shook her head again, and he slid off his chair, and knelt beside her in his uniform, his hands clasped before his chest in supplication—"My dear Lady Jarrow, I humbly solicit the honour of your hand in matrimony. Messrs Coutts and Company of 440 Strand can vouch for my financial soundness. My heart is not so . . ."

She leaned down, suddenly laughing, caught his hands and pulled him to his feet. Everyone within earshot had stopped eating, forks halfway to their mouths, listening in awed silence, for Billy Bidford and Florinda, Marchioness of Jarrow, were as well known to the gossip and society columns as Lord Derby, Churchill and Lloyd George were to the political pages. Schneider, sensing the silence, and alert to every nuance of what was going on in his domain, stopped and glanced back; then, seeing what was afoot, turned back with a half smile and continued his majestic pacing.

"You meant that, Billy?" Florinda said.

"Yes. I've been thinking about it for six months. I wouldn't be much of a stay-at-home husband even in peace time . . . racing cars here, motor boats there, flying, polo, skiing in winter, but you'd be with me. We'd do it all together."

611

"Me, drive racing cars?" she said wryly.

"I meant, you'd come with me . . . watch, sort of."

She shook her head, "Might as well marry a bank clerk, really—watch, wait, clap hands . . ."

"Anyone else?" he asked cautiously.

"Sort of. But he doesn't own me . . . He frightens me, too. He kills people—very well. And likes it." She gazed into Bidford's anxious eyes. She said, "I won't marry you, Billy, but I'll be your official mistress."

"For ever?"

"For as long as I want to."

"My offer remains open."

"Thanks."

*   *   *   *

SOLDIER VISITORS
MERRY GATHERINGS

No member of the Forces need spend a lonely or a cheerless Christmas Day in London. Efforts are being put forth in every direction to provide welcome and good comfort, and a visit to a few of the principal huts revealed that decorations, music, and Christmas dinners will be offered everywhere. The special secretary of the Hospitality League of the Young Men's Christian Association has received large numbers of invitations from hostesses who are willing to entertain men from France. At the Aldwych theatre the Australians will serve dinner in three relays and any soldier who cares to walk in and seat himself will be made welcome. At the Young Men's Christian Association Shakespeare Hut celebrations will begin at 9.30 a.m., when groups of men, accompanied by guides, will start on a tour through London. Guides also will take strangers to the Christmas service at St Paul's.

At the Eagle Hut, Strand, there will be a dance on Christmas Eve. A tree will be lighted up and everybody present given a souvenir. At six o'clock the next morning the men in the hostel will be awakened by children singing carols.

At the Church Army, Buckingham Palace Hostel any man passing through London will be welcomed, given Christmas cheer and comfort, and a good send-off . . . At the Church Army Lord Kitchener Hut, Hyde Park, which is an immensely popular centre, wounded men are organizing a billiards' tournament, also a whist drive, with prizes, music and games which should keep everybody happy.

IN THE HOSPITALS
HAPPY SOLDIER PATIENTS

The spirit of Christmas prevails in the London hospitals, the wards of which have been made bright and cheerful. At St Thomas's soldiers and 450 civilian patients will each be provided with an excellent dinner of turkey and plum pudding. The King sent a cheque for 10 pounds toward the festivities there and his Majesty's thoughtfulness was much appreciated by the 600 patients. The usual Christmas fare was provided, strict regard being paid to the Food Controller. The members of the nursing staff sang carols to the patients . . .

Quentin Rowland sat in his dugout eating Christmas cake. His nephew, Laurence Cate, sat opposite, sharing the cake and the red wine which his uncle's batman had "won" when they were out of the line a week ago. Now they were back, and it was Christmas Day. The dugout was damp and battered. The trenches were barely more than linked shell holes.

"You've done all right, Laurence," Quentin said. "But sometimes you don't seem to be with us. You can't afford to be thinking about birds that are or aren't here, when the Germans are attacking."

"Yes, sir," Laurence said. He wished he could make his uncle and Sergeant Fagioletti understand that when the war came too close, in its actual terrible shape, he could not prevent his mind fleeing to shelter in what he loved—birds, trees, nature . . . of course there wasn't any here, or not much—no live trees, no grass anywhere near the front line, few birds . . . so he wasn't here at all in those bad times, but on Beighton Down, or walking Scarrow bank.

In some waterlogged mudholes close by the men of C Company, in battalion reserve, were singing:

> Send out the Army and the Navy,
> Send out the rank and file,
> Send out the brave Territorials,
> They'll face danger with a smile
>
> (I don't think!)
> Send out my mother, my sister and my brother,
> But for Gawd's sake don't send me!

Quentin got up. The cake was a present from his sister Alice, and it was very large. They'd only eaten a small piece of it.

Quentin said, "On Christmas Day the officers serve the men their dinner, but . . ."

"I know, sir," Laurence said eagerly. "I did it last Christmas, at the Depot."

"Well, we can't do it in the line, because the men cook their own rations. But we can share out this cake. Come along."

He went up the broken steps into the trench. The nearest men stopped singing, and Quentin said, "Here, have a piece of cake."

He cut off a slice and said, "Share it round . . . Merry Christmas."

"Merry Christmas, sir. Merry Christmas!"

Quentin passed on, sometimes in the open, sometimes below ground, splashing toward the front line. There he handed out more cake. Singing began again behind him:

> For he's a jolly good fellow,
> For he's a jolly good fellow,
> For he's a jolly good feeeellow . . .
> And so say all of us!

Laurence smiled with pleasure. Quentin's lips tightened, and he handed out another piece of cake—"Merry Christmas, Loader."

"Merry Christmas, sir."

> And so say all of us, and so say all of us,
> For he's a jolly good feeeeellow . . .
> And so say all of us!

The Germans began shelling a rear area, the shells whistling and sighing high overhead. To the south a British machine gun in Passchendaele fired a belt in four long bursts at some suspicious movement in No Man's Land.

Quentin struggled back to his dugout. Laurence saluted and returned to his company. Quentin began to write a letter:

Dear Fiona, I have at last had a letter from Archie Campbell. He has been in a coma off and on for weeks. It turned out that a tiny shell splinter had also entered his stomach close to the bullet's exit wound, and this was not discovered till much later. He is [—*he paused, pen held high. If he told Fiona where Archie was, she'd go to him, and Archie had said he didn't want to see her again. But he, Quentin, wanted her to be happy. He finished the sentence;*] in Charing Cross Hospital, London.

*   *   *   *

Not five miles away Lieutenant General Sir Launcelot Kiggell was inspecting the Ypres front . . . actually, the rear, as he was in a motor car, which could not get anywhere near the actual Front. Kiggell was Field Marshal Sir Douglas Haig's Chief of Staff, and thus held much responsibility for the planning of what was later to be officially called the Third Battle of Ypres, but which was already being generally referred to as "Passchendaele." This had begun on July 31 and ended on November 12, six days after the capture of Passchendaele itself. The advance had been of five miles, in three months, at a cost of some 244,000 casualties. A great many of those casualties had not been shot, but drowned—in the mud; and a man wounded in that mud was almost certain to drown within a short time. In fact, the landscape of the Ypres salient, which Kiggell was surveying, contained the pulverized corpses of 40,000 British soldiers, whose remains were never found. Not included in the total were hundreds of horses, mules, wagons, and guns that had also disappeared in the mud—sometimes shattered by shell fire, sometimes whole.

Now, as Sir Launcelot stood by his car, staring at the desolation, the shattered earth, splintered trees, abandoned artifacts, tears began to flood his eyes and he gasped, the words choked out of him, "Good God . . . did we really send . . . men . . . to fight . . . in that?"

* * * *

Fletcher Gorse lay thirty yards out in No Man's Land under the ruins of two German ammunition wagons, three dead horses, five dead men, and a scattered mountain of German whizz bang shell cases. This had been well behind the enemy reserve lines, in the field gun areas, before the long autumn offensive, when a salvo of British heavies had hit the battery with destructive effect—three months ago. The place didn't stink too bad, except when it got warm, and the maggots weren't too bad, for the same reason—it wasn't warm, it was bloody cold. The land sloped away gradually to the east, giving Fletcher a good view over the German trenches to a depth of six hundred yards. Lying under the litter of war, he was wearing a loose cloak of sandbags sewn together, and that plastered with mud and dotted with bits of green sprinkled with white paint, to match the thin snow on the ground. His rifle butt was rested an inch in front of his right shoulder, and his eyes ceaselessly scanned the terrain in front of him.

The wind was in the east and the smoke from Roulers, the big town down there, was being blown up toward him. With the smoke of the home fires came the sound of church bells, clanging and jangling against the pale sky, but muted and softened by distance. The ground was iron hard under his elbow, and under the corpse on whose body his rifle stock was propped. He wished he could be spending Christmas with Betty, but quickly dismissed the thought from his mind. Snipers couldn't afford to daydream.

From behind he heard the men of his battalion singing "For he's a jolly good fellow." Old Rowley must be going round, dishing out strawberry jam. None of the other officers had been in the battalion long enough for the men to sing that for them.

In the middle distance a movement caught his eye, and with an infinitesimal bend of his head he lowered his eye to the telescopic sight. There it was—a German lighting a cigar in the door of a dugout in their third line . . . a little over 400 yards . . . 440. Carefully he set the range. Behind him the men of the Wealds were chanting lugubriously:

> See him in the grand theayter
> Eating apples in the pit;
> While that poor girl what he ruined
> Wanders round through mud and shit.
> > It's the same the whole world over
> > It's the poor what gets the blyme,
> > While the rich gets all the pleasure—
> > Ain't it all a bleeding shyme!

There was a gap in the wall of the trench over there. The Jerries didn't realize that they were in full view down to just below the knees, as they stood in the entrance to that dugout.

The German's third tunic button rested on the cross hairs of the sight.

> Now she's living in a cottage
> But she very rarely smiles;
> For her only occupation's
> Crushing ice for father's piles.
> > She was poor but she was honest . . .

He was a long-faced fellow who hadn't shaved this morning, wearing the silly little round cap with the red button in front, sort of a fatigue cap, like our cunt caps . . . . he was just standing there, taking the air, not thinking of the war at all. Or of death. Was there poetry in death? There was poetry to be written about death, sure, but was there any in the thing itself? For a moment Fletcher thought of all his dead comrades, then of Betty Merritt, his love. The fellow would learn the truth about death one day, as he himself would. But not today.

Gently he lowered the sights until he had the German's right knee squarely in them. Then he squeezed the trigger. The rifle jerked in his shoulder, the German fell back into the dugout, disappearing suddenly as the gas blanket swung back into place behind him. Fletcher knew he had shot true.

"Merry Christmas," he said, but silently, making no sound, "and a Happy New Year."